LOOSE CANNON

The Tom Kelly Novels

DAVID DRAKE

LOOSE CANNON

This is a work of fiction. All the characters and events portrayed
in this book are fictional, and any resemblance to real people or
incidents is purely coincidental.

A Baen Book

Baen Publishing Enterprises
P.O. Box 1403
Riverdale, NY 10471
www.baen.com

ISBN: 978-1-4516-3794-6

Cover art by David Seeley

First Baen paperback printing, August 2012

Distributed by Simon & Schuster
1230 Avenue of the Americas
New York, NY 10020

Library of Congress Cataloging-in-Publication Data:
2011009556

Printed in the United States of America

10 9 8 7 6 5 4 3 2 1

THE RIGHT TOOL FOR THE JOB

When the door closed behind the civilian, the naval attaché coughed quietly for attention. General Pedler looked at him. "There's something in this man's restricted file that I think you ought to . . . note carefully, Wallie," Laidlaw said.

"Well?"

"It appears that when Kelly was in Vietnam he used to accompany troops on field operations as a matter of course," the captain said. "Kelly's duties, his assigned tasks at the time, did not require him to leave the base camps."

"So he did things he didn't have to do," the general said with a snort. "That's water over the dam—and besides, it's just that sort of thing that gave him the background he needs for Skyripper."

"No doubt, sir," said Laidlaw acidly. "I'm sure there must have been *some* reason to decide that Mr. Kelly was qualified. In this case, however, Staff Sergeant Kelly—as he then was, accompanied a ten-man ambush patrol under a Lieutenant Schaydin. They dug shallow trenches and set up Claymores—directional mines—"

"I know a Claymore just as well as you do, Captain."

Laidlaw looked up. "Yes. They set up Claymore mines about 25 yards in front of their position. During the night, a sound was heard to the front. Lieutenant Schaydin raised his head just over the lip of his trench and detonated a Claymore. The mine had been turned to face the friendly positions. It sprayed its charge of steel pellets straight back in Schaydin's face, killing him instantly."

Contents

Tom Kelly and Me 1

Skyripper 7

Fortress 411

Tom Kelly and Me

In the Spring of 1981 I was in my first year as a part-time bus driver for the Town of Chapel Hill, after having spent the eight previous years as Assistant Town Attorney for the Town of Chapel Hill. I wasn't an especially good bus driver, but I was an excellent employee: I showed up for work on time, I was courteous, and I came in on my off-days when the dispatchers needed somebody to cover a run.

I got a call at the bus garage—this was before cell phones—from Jim Baen. Jim had bought the first stories in the Hammer's Slammers series when he was editor of *Galaxy* magazine.

When Tom Doherty became Publisher of Ace Books, he had hired Jim to run the SF line; there they published my first book, *Hammer's Slammers*. Tom had left Ace to found Tor Books; Jim had joined him shortly thereafter. I had sold a linked series of stories to Tor, turning the material in on time and in accordance with

1

specifications. Though that book (*Time Safari*) hadn't come out yet, I'd convinced Tom and Jim that I could be trusted to behave in a professional fashion on a larger project.

Which is what Jim's phone call was about. Tom Clancy had begun to blow the socks off the marketplace with what came to be called techno thrillers. Tom and Jim wanted me to write a techno thriller for Tor and were offering me $8,000 to do so. (Parenthetically, I was earning about $4.25 cents an hour as a bus driver, up from a starting pay of $4.05; it was still better than being a lawyer.)

The offer should have been a no-brainer, but not for the last time I demonstrated a level of boneheaded stubbornness. I wasn't sure I could write the sort of book Jim was talking about, a reasonable concern. But also I wasn't sure I wanted to, because I was armpit deep in writing on spec a huge, plotless historical novel involving 17th century inheritance law, pirates, and the court of Aurangzeb (in the first hundred and some thousand words, that is). Looking back on it, worrying about the historical appears perverse to the verge of insanity, but I did.

Editors and publishers as experienced as Jim and Tom were used to dealing with screwy writers, though. They created a contract which promised heavy promotion for my unfinished historical but required that I write the thriller first. The only thing that has happened to the historical after that was that the stack of yellow pads on which I wrote with soft pencils moved with me to our new house.

I started plotting a thriller. I had read a fair number of

spy novels and intelligence memoirs over the years, but I got into the subject more deeply. I also got into the hardware side, the how-to of bugs, communications intercepts, and so on. *Skyripper*—which became the title of the novel—is one of the few books for which I did a great deal of book-specific research; usually I write about things that I already know in detail.

This led to one amusing story. I continued to drive a bus; when there was a layover of a few minutes, I read a book.

Or at any rate, I read books when the customers would permit me. Passengers don't see many bus drivers during a day, so we were new and interesting to them. Bus drivers see a *lot* of passengers, and they're not a bit interesting unless something goes wrong.

One early morning, before the start of my run, a middle-aged woman boarded my bus in an upscale neighborhood. I was reading, but she wanted to chat. I wasn't impolite, but I deeply didn't want to chat with her (or anybody).

She then asked what I was reading. I told her she didn't want to know. She insisted that she did, so I handed her the book: *How to Kill*, Volume III, by John Minnery. I don't know precisely how she felt about that, but it did shut her up.

I had spent a couple weeks in Algeria the year before, visiting a friend in the Foreign Service. That gave me a setting which would be unfamiliar to most readers, and it also gave me some insight into the parts of embassy life which don't ordinarily get into published accounts. (Laumer's Retief and Durrell's Antrobus stories, written by former low-ranking diplomats, are better guides to those realities than are any number of ambassadors' memoirs.)

Then I needed a viewpoint character. I did something unusual there. I was in the field in 1970 as an interrogator with the 11th ACR. Our tent was generally pitched adjacent to that of the Radio Research section: that is, the National Security Agency field unit. Their job was to intercept and record enemy communications and to transmit the data back to Fort Meade.

The Radio Research people were warrant officers and senior enlisted men, professional soldiers in all senses. They spoke multiple languages and demonstrated remarkable skills, but the job didn't require Ivy League degrees or Savile Row suits. (One had an ear collection.)

And they had stories. Some of them had been places most Americans had never heard of, doing things that Americans weren't supposed to be doing. They worked for what is reputedly the most secretive spy agency in the world, but they talked to other enlisted men who sat with them in the Cambodian night and waited for something to happen—knowing that anything which happened would be bad.

They talked to me.

I made my viewpoint character, Tom Kelly, a former NSA field man. I made my *hero* a former NSA field man; nothing about the job requires a saint, but the men I knew in 1970 were heroes in ways that Homer would have recognized.

I gave Kelly the skills and ruthlessness of the men I'd known. He drank, because men who do those things always drink.

And I gave Kelly the anger which also comes with certain lines of work. I didn't have to look far for that. I hadn't been all the places the RR people had been, but I'd been to enough of them to be furiously angry—at the world, at life, and at myself.

Writing *Skyripper* showed me that I was a lot angrier—still—than I had realized until then. That was useful to know, but that mindset wasn't one I wanted to revisit in this lifetime. *Skyripper* sold well, but I refused to do another Tom Kelly book when Tom Doherty asked me to.

Then Jim Baen left Tor to found Baen Books. Tom and Jim stayed reasonably friendly, but they were competing for very similar portions of the market. I remained close to both men, and I didn't want it to appear that I had chosen one of them over the other. I therefore told both immediately after the split that I wanted to write a new contract with each of them.

Jim wanted a Hammer novel for Baen Books. Fair enough, though I'd refused to write more in the series for him at Tor.

Tom wanted a sequel to *Skyripper*. Furthermore, he wanted me to show the (proposed) Strategic Defense Initiative (the Star Wars Defense) driving off an alien invasion. I argued against this for a number of reasons, but I'd given Tom my word that I would do what he asked—so I did it under the title *Fortress*.

Or at least I did as much of it as I could. I flat didn't believe in most of the proposed technology of SDI and just couldn't describe it working to spec. Further, even the optimists envisaged a twenty-year lead time, so rather than doing a true sequel to *Skyripper*, I started in 1963 in an alternate universe. (Despite my scruples, an article in the *SF Encyclopedia* claims that *Fortress* gives "quasi-fetishistic status" to the Star Wars program. Worse things happen in wartime, as we used to say.)

I set most of *Fortress* in Eastern Turkey, as the result of another visit to my friend in the Foreign Service. Part of the business involves the workings of a US Congressman's office, however. I owe that to time spent as rewrite man on Newt Gingrich's first book. Like Vietnam, editing *Window of Opportunity* taught me things which I could not have learned in any other way.

Skyripper and *Fortress* were written and are set in the '80s. The world has changed a great deal since then. Men like Tom Kelly still exist, though, as they have always existed. (Take a look at Homer.) Returning to these books reminds me more strongly than ever that I don't want to be one of them myself.

But it also reminds me that I could have been. There, but for the grace of God, went I.

Dave Drake
david-drake.com

Skyripper

DEDICATION

To Mr. August Derleth,
who spent more effort on helping young writers
than we were objectively worth at the time.

ACKNOWLEDGEMENTS

Friends are people who come through
when you need them.
Many of my friends came through for me
while I was writing this novel.
I regret that I cannot for their own sakes
acknowledge them by name;
but that does not mean that I have forgotten
or will ever forget their help.

Prologue

The sound of the weapon firing was as brief and vicious as the first crack of nearby lightning. There was nothing more, no thunder rolling, deafening. Banks of fluorescent lights staggered on all over the laboratory compound as the TVA grid took over again from the emergency generator. The yellow glow-lamps that had remained on during testing tripped out when the generator driving them did.

The Secretary of State frowned in a combination of surprise and mild irritation. He had seen laser weapons tested in the past. A pale beam would lick out of the ungainly apparatus. Relays might hammer, pulsing the available power into microsecond bullets of energy that were hot enough to do realistic damage down-range. The target was ordinarily a thin sheet of titanium whose thermal conductivity was so low that it concentrated every erg it received on the point of impact. Vaporized metal would curl away like smoke from a cigarette—incidentally and inevitably scattering the beam which still attacked the target surface. At last a hole would open in the sheet, expanding as the operator shifted the beam to nibble away at the edges.

In addition, if the laser were chemically fueled, there would be the roar and rush of fluorine and heavy hydrogen combining into an expensive form of hydrofluoric acid. The waste product cheerfully dissolved glass, platinum, and virtually everything else. Cleaning up after a test was similar to dealing with a spill of Cobalt 60, but presumably it would be all right to dump the crap straight into the upper atmosphere during service use.

All in all, a laser demonstration could be expected to be a spectacular show. It was that, even more than his frequent assertions that a strong defense was a necessary concomitant to a strong diplomacy, which had led the Secretary of State to accept the invitation to a Top Secret briefing by the Defense Intelligence Agency.

And this had not been spectacular in the least.

The Secretary turned away from the heavy lead-glass window of the observation room. He and his aide wore civilian clothes, but his aide would return to active duty as a lieutenant commander when he left the Secretary's personal service. The other three men were in dress uniforms, imposing with gold braid and medal ribbons. Still, there was no question as to where the power lay during *this* administration. "All right," said the Secretary of State, "what went wrong, Follett?"

The lieutenant general in Air Force blue was Director of the Defense Intelligence Agency. He understood his duties perfectly. His two top aides—a rear admiral and an army Brigadier general—were less experienced in testifying to hostile Congressional committees and like affairs. General Follett gave them a sweeping glance of reminder before he said, "Nothing at all went wrong, Mr. Secretary. That is"—he nodded to the observation window. Mechanical arms could be seen dollying toward the target—"This was a normal test. That's all that happens. Overtly."

He paused, coughing to clear his throat and to settle the wash of fear that had leapt up when he committed himself. Normally, high-ranking observers would have been in the control room with the scientists conducting the test. If anything had gone wrong under those circumstances, General Follett would have known before he had to make a fool of himself. This time the observers had to be rigidly separated from the scientists: top secret matters much more sensitive than the hardware were about to be discussed.

To calm himself by moving and to fill time before the opened target made him a hero or a buffoon, Follett rose from his chair. He fingered the duplicate target on its display stand. It was a missile nose cone, sectioned to split along the centerline and to display the dummy nuclear trigger within. Lead segments were individually pinned to the inner surface of a sphere the size of a soccer ball. In the original, mirror-polished wedges of plutonium would be held in place by the explosive lining itself. Follett and his aides had considered using a filling of flash powder or the like. In the end they had decided not to do anything that might have put their demonstration on a level with all those others which were intended only to maintain modest program funding. The DIA was going for the throat on this one. Nothing that would cheapen the effect could be permitted.

Metal squealed in the test chamber, audible even through the thick walls. It was the first sign that the weapon had functioned properly. The mechanical arms prizing apart the halves of the target had popped a fresh weld.

All five of the men in the observation room were staring intently through the window now. General Follett had remained standing; the others leaned forward in their chairs. The arms, controlled by the technicians invisible in the room next door, slowly rotated the dummy warhead. Floodlights especially rigged for this demonstration flashed on to illuminate the interior.

"I'll be damned," said the Secretary of State. The three uniformed men shifted stance minusculy. It had worked. At least—the hardware had worked.

The lead blocks which had been in the path of the momentary beam had slumped and twisted. Their surfaces were no longer dully metallic but rather a furry white where the lead had recrystallized after melting. Other segments only a finger's breadth away were unchanged from their original appearance.

"If this had been a live trigger and not a test unit," the general said, "the implosion charge would almost certainly have been set off by the beam. Even if it had not exploded, the elements of the fission trigger have obviously"—he waved toward the window—"been damaged to the extent that the device would melt down rather than detonate when the warhead reached its target. And if the particle beam had struck the booster stage of a missile rather than the nose cone proper, the fuel and oxidizer tanks—no matter how they were hardened and protected—would have been flash-heated to the point of catastrophic explosion."

"Particle beam," repeated the Secretary, staring at the damaged target. He turned slowly toward the military men. All of them now were standing. "All right, I'm not a bad person to impress . . . but I don't have a thing to do with the funding of this project, you know. And I don't have a thing to do with you or the DoD, either—not in any way that matters to you.

"So why did the Defense Intelligence Agency drag me out to Oak Ridge to see"—he waved—"this?"

Follett sucked in his gut. In round tones that masked his nervousness he said, "As you have seen, Mr. Secretary, particle beam technology has the potential of developing into the most important defensive tool in our nation's arsenal."

He paused. "In the arsenal of *any* nation. What concerns us—here in this room—is that evidence suggests that the Soviets have already developed the—principle— to a stage well beyond what you have seen here. If our information is correct, a Russian scientist has made a breakthrough as important as the one that gave the Soviets their initial lead in hydrogen bombs."

The Secretary's aide straightened in surprise. The Secretary himself was more direct. "What the hell do you mean by that?" he snapped, his heavy eyebrows closing together. "*We* had the H-bomb first. Have you forgotten Bikini?"

General Follett dipped his chin, knowing the

chance he was taking to make his point. "We—American scientists—detonated the first thermonuclear device on Bikini Atoll, that is correct," he said. "The device used tritium and deuterium to fuel the reaction. These isotopes were in such short supply that no significant—no military— use could have been made of the principle. Furthermore"—the Secretary of State's look was fading from irritation to puzzlement, but Follett avoided making eye contact—"the tritium had to be chilled. The entire apparatus would have filled two railroad boxcars. It could not have been *transported* by air, much less delivered in the military sense of the term. Unlike the bomb the Russians exploded nine months later, using lithium hydride instead of heavy hydrogen as the major fuel element."

"Fortunately," broke in Rear Admiral Haynes, "by analyzing fallout from the blast, we were able to duplicate the Soviets' research before their advantage became decisive. Our own personnel—scientists—had determined to their satisfaction that lithium hydride would not sustain a thermonuclear reaction. Fortunately, they were not wholly incapable of learning from their opponents. I assure you, the Soviets gained nothing from Klaus Fuchs and his like to equal what we learned from Soviet above-ground testing."

"All right, get to the point," said the Secretary, straightening again in his chair. The men in uniform had five minutes, a fact the politician made adequately clear by glancing at his thin, gold watch.

"The problem with particle beam weapons," said Follett, plunging toward the invisible deadline, "and with all energy weapons, is the energy source. It's all very well to tie into the commercial power grid when we're testing devices here in Tennessee or Nevada. For the weapons to be really effective, however, they need to be based in space, in orbit over the sites from which hostile missiles may be launched. For that . . . well, all manner of solutions have been suggested. But the simple solution, and a solution that might work for the microseconds which are all a particle beam"—he tapped the dummy nose cone—"requires, would be to detonate a thermonuclear device and focus portions of its energy output into, ah, beams."

"How are you going to focus something that's vaporizing everything around it the moment it gets there?" asked the Secretary. The demonstration he had just seen was real. If the reason behind it turned out to be nonsense, he was out the door and gone, though. "Look, Follett, we have a Science Committee at State, too. If you people want to go jaw them about this stuff, that's fine, but *I'm* on a tight schedule."

"Many of the best minds in the field agree, Mr. Secretary," the general said soothingly, "that such a proposal is impossible, even in theory. It would appear, however, that on the other side of the line there's a Professor Evgeny Vlasov, who has developed a—theoretical, at least—method of drawing several dozen simultaneous, magnetically focused, bursts from a single thermonuclear device."

"Oh, for Christ's sake, call it an H-bomb like a human being!" snapped the Secretary of State. He was not looking at the military men, though. His bushy stare was directed at some indefinite bank of instruments while his fingers drummed the side of the chair seat. His mind was neither place, turning over possibilities. He looked up at Follett.

"If that were true," he said carefully, "any missiles we attempted to send over the Pole would detonate a few yards out of their silos. That's what you're trying to tell me?"

Redstone, the Brigadier general, spoke for the first time since the demonstration. "Yeah, with normal allowance for error, of course. 95% of anything we launched, say. And we guess a bolt that can do that"—he thumbed toward the twisted warhead in the test chamber—"would pretty well scramble a B-52, too. Or the White House, if somebody wanted to get cute."

"All right," the civilian repeated. "Since I don't suppose you brought me here to propose we surrender now to the Sovs, what *do* you have in mind?"

"We would like," said General Follett, staring at his wedding band rather than the Secretary of State, "your support for a plan to secure Professor Vlasov's defection to the United States."

"Oh," said the Secretary. "Oh . . ." and he settled back in his chair, relaxing now that he had enough information at last to guess why he was being manipulated. A smile quirked the corners of his mouth. "Does the JCS know you've got something in mind?" he asked in amusement. "You people at the DIA, that is."

Follett's tongue touched his lips, but he managed to control his reflexive glance toward the Secretary's aide. He knew that Lieutenant Commander Platt was secretly reporting to the Joint Chiefs of Staff on all of the Secretary of State's activities. The DIA further suspected that Platt was also leaking information to the Office of Naval Intelligence. By charter, the ONI was supposed to be under the control of the Defense Intelligence Agency. In practice, it—and the other service intelligence staffs—were as parochial as the KGB and very nearly as hostile to one another. The presence of a known double agent at the secret meeting had complicated Follett's task enormously, but there had been no alternative. If the DIA had burned Platt, exposing him to the Secretary, his replacement might very well have been controlled by the CIA.

"I have briefed the Chairman, yes," Follett said, "on our intention to approach you, sir, and the necessity for it." With an appearance of steely candor, he added. "The Defense Intelligence Agency is only the information collection and assessment arm of the Department of Defense. My colleagues and I are as much controlled by the Joint Chiefs as are the lowliest recruits in training."

"Go on," said the Secretary in irritation. "I'm waiting for a concrete proposal." He could not know, of course, that Follett's bit of fluff was meant not for him but for his aide.

"Yes sir," said the general, nodding quickly and continuing to meet the civilian's eyes. "Well. One of our agents made contact with Professor Vlasov. This was fortuitous, rather than a major priority of the Agency"—perhaps he shouldn't have admitted that—"because the Professor appeared from all the information we had available to us to be at least as politically reliable as a member of the Politburo." Follett cleared his throat. "The Professor not only had all the perquisites available to a scientist of genius—which he is—within the Soviet Union, his love for his motherland is of exceptional and tested quality. He has only one arm, you see. He lost the other in

1943 during the Siege of Leningrad when the satchel charge he had been throwing into a German blockhouse exploded prematurely. He had refused several offers of evacuation previous to that occurrence, since it was evident even then to the Party leadership that Vlasov's endeavors would be more valuable to the State in the laboratory than on the front line."

"How did you get an agent into the Soviet Union, Follett?" demanded the Secretary as if he had not been listening to the remainder of the general's discourse.

Admiral Wayne coughed behind his hand. Follett warned him with a quick gesture. "Ah, Mr. Secretary," he said. "I'm afraid we can't go into sources and methods at this time. . . ."

"Look, General," the civilian went on, "either your agent is playing you for a fool—or the KGB is." He paused. "Or maybe everything you've just told me about Vlasov is a lie? Why would a man like that want to defect? Did somebody catch his son in Dzerzhinsky Square with a firebomb? Have we turned up photos of him with the Premier's wife? Because there's not a whole lot else that would make somebody like that decide to fly the coop, is there?"

One of Follett's subordinates cleared his throat nervously. There was an answer to that question, but it was an answer they had hoped to be able to finesse giving. They had even considered concocting a lie, but there were no lies they could think of which fit Vlasov's background and were significantly more reasonable than the story their agent had told them for true. "Well, Mr. Secretary," the general said, "it appears that Professor Vlasov has been experiencing difficulties of a, ah"—Follett locked his hands behind his back to stop himself from twiddling his fingers in front of the others—"problems of a psychiatric nature."

The Secretary of State blinked. Follett bulled onward, saying, "Ah, the Professor believes he is being persecuted by, well, aliens . . . And he appears to believe that we in the West will be better able to protect him from them."

The civilian hooted and slapped his thigh. "Say, that's *great!*" he roared. "And I suppose you want me to set up a Little Green Man Patrol in State? Jesus, that's great! Chuckie"—he prodded his embarrassed aide in the ribs— "how'd you like to head up the National Space Patrol?"

"I assure you, Mr. Secretary," the DIA chief said stiffly, "that we would not have developed this mission— even to the present extent—were we not. . . . Well, our agent assures us that Professor Vlasov was entirely lucid during lengthy discussions of nuclear physics. He may well have cracked under the strain of his work or of life within a police state—but he has not become stupid as a result; nor has he lost his expertise."

The uniformed men stiffened when the Secretary stood up, but the politician was walking toward the duplicate nose cone rather than the door. "All right," the civilian said, "I can see that. Does he speak English?"

"Ah—" Follett said.

Rear Admiral Wayne cleared his throat and replied, "No Sir, he does not, though we gather he may be able to parse his own way through technical material. His French is fluent—his mother was a Breton—and it was in French that our agent contacted the Professor."

That was more than Follett had wanted the Joint Chiefs—or the State Department, for that matter—to know about their agent, a Vietnamese physicist named Hoang Tanh. The Secretary, at least, ignored the slip. "Well, if he can't talk to them directly," the civilian said, "we can make sure the story we give the media is *our* story and not his own. All right." The Secretary's fingers traced the sharp edges of the blocks which simulated the plutonium core. His nails left a hint of a line across the lead oxide. With the unhurried certainty of a record changer cocking, he turned to the general again. "All right," he repeated, "what *do* you want from State, Follett?"

Brigadier General Redstone took over as planned. "Sir," he said, a mental heel click though his feet remained splayed on the concrete floor. "Mr. Secretary, you'll appreciate that however bad Professor, ah . . . the Professor may want to get out of Russia, it's flat out impossible for a scientist like that to do it. Some Jew doctor, sure, if he's willing to sweat for a couple years. But, ah, Vlasov, they *know* he's worth more to us than he is to them. They've *got* his math already. Any hint that he plans a bunk and *zip!* He gets it where the chicken got the axe."

General Redstone had the intense glare of a preacher warming to his subject. He cocked his upper body forward, bringing his face a few inches closer to that of the Secretary of State. The civilian edged backward reflexively. "Now, the Professor *will* be getting out from behind the Iron Curtain in a couple weeks," Redstone continued, "a conference in Algiers. That's his chance and our chance—and it's the only chance we're going to get. If Vlasov's as crazy as the reports say—" Follett and the admiral winced, but Redstone plowed on obliviously—"then the Sovs aren't going to leave him loose very long, even if they don't know we've contacted him."

"The conference on nuclear power?" said the Secretary's aide, speaking almost for the first time that evening. "The one in Algeria? We're boycotting it because it threatens still wider proliferation of nuclear weapons in the non-advanced world."

"That's right," agreed the soldier, "and there you've put your finger on the fucking rub. On both of them, I ought to say."

You ought to have said something else entirely, thought Follett; but the Secretary appeared to have been caught up in Redstone's enthusiasm, so the DIA chief did not interrupt. Not the sort of candor you ran into a lot in Foggy Bottom, he supposed. Or the Pentagon, come to think.

"Because the Algerians are just as red as the Chinks and the Russkies," the brigadier was continuing, "what with them and the Libyans carrying on a war against us in the Western Sahara—"

Here Follett had to interrupt. "Against our ally, the King of Morocco," he corrected.

"Right," Redstone went on. "That's the sort of people we'd be dealing with. They'll take our dollars for natural gas quick enough, but they're not about to help a top scientist escape from one of their Communist buddies. And the other thing is"—Redstone paused to take a deep breath, fixing the Secretary with his eyes during the pause—"we don't have a delegation to the goddam conference to plant a team in. The Canadians do, but they

won't play ball—all that new flap with *their* security force
scared them shitless."

"Ah, Red," Follett said, "I don't think the Secretary
is—"

"Oh, right, right," the brigadier said. "Well, if it
weren't for the agent who made the touch to begin with,
we still wouldn't have a snowball's chance of extracting
the Professor. But he's there in place. And if you can keep
the lid on at the UN—and the White House—if there's a
flap, we'll get Vlasov out."

The civilian gave Redstone a scowl of dawning
concern. "What sort of flap?" he demanded. "You don't
have some wild-hare notion about going in with a battalion of Marines, do you?"

"Huh?" said Redstone. "Oh, hell, no. Not Marines—"

"Let me take over here, General," Follett said loudly.
Brigadier General Redstone had wanted to use elements
of the 82nd Airborne Division for the snatch; Follett
was sure that he was about to blurt that fact. To anyone
outside the military community, that would have
appeared to be a distinction without a difference.

"Mr. Secretary," Follett continued, "we will—our
agents will be operating in what must for the purpose be
considered a hostile country. And Professor Vlasov,
despite his desire to flee to freedom, will be escorted by
KGB personnel who will stop at nothing to prevent
him from doing so. It may well be necessary to take"—the
general drew a deep breath; his Air Force background
permitted him to be queasy when discussing murder from
less than 40,000 feet up—"direct action to save the
Professor's life. Furthermore, while the operation will be

under the control of a DIA operative, the—heavy work— will be carried out by local agents. It is simply a fact of life that one cannot expect perfect . . . discretion from, ah, freedom fighters in a situation of this sort."

The Secretary of State turned away with a look of distaste. "You mean," he said, "that it's going to be World War III in downtown Algiers if you go ahead with this."

"No, Mr. Secretary," said Rear Admiral Wayne. "It's going to be World War III if we don't go ahead with this. And we're going to lose."

The civilian grimaced, but he did not respond at once. Finally he said, "General Follett, isn't the Central Intelligence Agency better suited to carry out this, ah, program with a minimum of, of publicity?"

Follett sucked in his gut again. "Sir," he said, "without a contact agent to keep Professor Vlasov informed of the plans, there would be absolutely no way of achieving his successful defection. Only we in the Defense Intelligence Agency have such an agent—or could have one in the time available."

"Well, you could tell the CIA about your prize agent, couldn't you?" the Secretary snapped. "Does he only talk Army jargon or something?"

"Sir," Follett said, standing as if he were about to salute the flag, "the Central Intelligence Agency is not responsible for the safety of our agent. *We* are. This is a man who has trusted us, who has provided valuable intelligence for many years out of his love of free society. I'm sorry, sir, I cannot permit him to be compromised by divulging his identity to parties who would throw away his life without hesitation if it suited their purposes."

"We can handle this, Mr. Secretary," added General Redstone. "Remember, it was us and not those state-department rejects at Langley who bribed the Russky to defect with his MiG-25."

"Jesus," said the Secretary of State. He was staring out the observation window at the melted target. "All right," he said, turning. "General Follett, you have my support for this project—"

"Project Skyripper," Redstone interrupted unhelpfully with a grin.

"My support for this project," the Secretary repeated, "let the chips fall where they may. And yes, I'll take care of the President. . . . But Genera"—he scowled at the trio of uniforms—"all of you! You'd better get him out. If you've made me a party to another Bay of Pigs, believe me—you won't have careers. You won't have heads."

The Secretary spun on his heel. "Come on, Chuckie," he snapped, "we're getting out of here. And I only pray I shouldn't have left an hour ago."

The door banged behind the two men from State.

"Well, that's settled," said Follett in relief.

"Whether it was or not, I think we had to go ahead with the operation," said Rear Admiral Wayne somberly. "You know how much I dislike the methods we have to use on this one, but the alternative is"—he shook his head—"just what the Secretary said it was. Surrender to the Russians now. I just hope that this man Kelly doesn't let us down."

General Redstone was rubbing his hands together. "Tom Kelly?" he said. "Oh, he'll come through. And what a punch in the eye for those bastards down in Langley!"

I

"Mr. Kelly?" called the lieutenant in dress greens. "Mr. Kelly? Over here—I'm here to pick you up."

Tom Kelly scowled across the security barrier at the green uniform, showing more distaste than he actually felt for the man inside the cloth. Of course, he didn't know the lieutenant from Adam; and he knew the uniform very well indeed. "In a second," he called back in English. Moving to the side so as not to block the flow of disembarking passengers, Kelly relaxed and watched the show that Orly Airport and the Russian Embassy were combining to stage.

Six men as soft and pasty-looking as maximum-security prisoners were being passed through the magnetic detector arch. None of them had hand luggage to be fluoroscoped. It was enough of a break in routine that the women and lone gendarme in charge of the barrier were more alert than usual. That was nothing compared to the attentiveness of the four bulky men escorting the others, however.

Two of the escorts had stepped around the barrier ahead of their charges. They had displayed diplomatic passports and a note to avoid the detector. Otherwise the alarm would have clanged at the pistols they wore holstered under dark suits. The suits were in themselves so ill-fitting as to be virtually a uniform for low-ranking Russians. The escorts watched the six pale men with angry determination. In general, the passengers bustling through the barrier in either direction ignored the scene, lost in their own meetings and farewells. If the crowd seemed to be edging someone too close to the men under escort, one of the guards would interpose with as little ceremony as a linebacker going for the ball. Squawks of protest from buffeted travelers were ignored with flat-eyed disdain.

The last of the six charges passed through the arch. The steel zipper in one's trouser fly had set off the alarm; there had been no other incident. The two escorts in the rear shouldered past the barrier in turn, waving passports without bothering to speak to or even look at the attendants.

The whole group tramped down the hallway toward the Aeroflot gates. Even a note from the Russian Ambassador would not have gotten armed men around the security check had they not been traveling on their own national airline. The charges shambled in a column of twos, with their escorts half a pace out at each corner. One of the latter gave Kelly a hard look as he passed. The American smiled back and nodded. Not a real bright thing to do, but he wasn't a surveillance agent. The Lord knew he wasn't that.

Tom Kelly was five-foot nine and stocky. In bad light he could have been any age; in the combination of sunlight and the fluorescents over the security barrier, he looked all of his 38 years. His face was broad and tan and deeply wrinkled. Black hair was beginning to thin over his pate. Though he was clean-shaven, an overnight growth of whiskers gave him a seedy look that his rumpled blazer did nothing to dispel. Sighing, he picked up his AWOL bag and his radio, then walked to the impatient lieutenant across the barrier.

"The general is, ah, anxious to see you, sir," the lieutenant said. "If you don't mind, we'll leave your luggage to be claimed later. There's need for haste."

"Here, carry my clothes, then," Kelly said, thrusting his AWOL bag at the officer. "Well, don't look so surprised. For Christ's sake, I was just over in Basel. Train would have made a lot more sense than buying me a ticket on Swissair."

"Er," said the lieutenant. "Well, we have a car and driver waiting at the front entrance." He began striding off through the concourse, glancing back over his shoulder at Kelly. The civilian paced him, moving with an ease surprising in a man so squat. He held his short-wave receiver out in front of him nonchalantly enough to belie its twelve-pound weight.

The car was there, all right, though the driver with Spec 5 chevrons on his greens was arguing with a pair of airport security men and a gendarme. "That's all right," the lieutenant called in English. He tossed Kelly's bag on the hood of the sedan and fumbled out—for Christ's sake!—his own black passport which he waved in the policeman's face. Must be great to work in an airport the dips use a lot, Kelly thought. He opened the door of the sedan and flipped the seat down.

The lieutenant swung back to the car, but he hesitated when he saw that Kelly was gesturing him into the back seat. "Go ahead," the civilian said. He peered at the lieutenant's name-plate. "Morley. I figure if I rate a chauffeured limousine"—it was an AMC Concord, olive drab, with motor pool registration numbers stenciled on the doors—"I can choose where I sit in it."

Lieutenant Morley ducked into the back. Kelly retrieved his AWOL bag from the hood and handed it ceremoniously in to the lieutenant. Only then did he set his radio on the seat beside the driver and get in himself. "The Embassy, as fast as you can make it," Morley muttered.

"Which is probably less fast than a local taxi would get us there," Kelly said, watching traffic as the driver eased into the stream of vehicles. "But then, it's still probably a lot faster than we really need to get there. Unless the Army has changed one hell of a lot in the past few years."

The lieutenant did not respond. The pink enamel of his Military Intelligence lapel insignia clashed with the green uniform. The insignia was a dagger, covered by a rose to "symbolize the *sub rosa* mission of the organization." Christ, if brains were dynamite, there still wouldn't be any need to tiptoe in the Military Heraldry Office.

Or in any MI unit Tom Kelly had ever been around. "Do you know what you were seeing in the airport?" he said aloud, leaning his back against the door to be able to watch Morley's expression. "The KGB types and all?"

"What?" the lieutenant said, sitting up abruptly enough to skew his saucer hat on the car's headliner.

Kelly rocked also as the sedan shifted to the right, around a wheezing stake-bed truck. For as long as it took to pass the truck, they were in a slot between a pair of buses who were moving as fast as traffic on the A6 permitted. Kelly could see no higher than the bumper of the second bus when he glanced into the rear-view mirror. "Right, KGB," he continued. "Four of them, big fellows guarding those other"—the car snapped left again, barely clearing the truck's radiator, but without danger since they were accelerating away—"Russians."

"Phillips, my God!" Morley said to the driver. Then he swallowed angrily and took off his hat. "I didn't . . ." he said to the civilian. "That is—I saw them, but I didn't know that's who they were. Good God, do you mean those hunched up little men were prisoners? What *was* that?"

Kelly smiled, leaning a trifle away from the door. The sedan was riding hard, transmitting the road shocks through the frame unpleasantly. "Oh, no," he said, "they were all free citizens of Mother Russia. Thing is, they were the embassy's code and communications staff, the folks who've been handling and encrypting all the message traffic for the past couple years."

The sedan braked heavily in the congestion of the approaching Boulevard Peripherique. Kelly braced his foot on the firewall and laid his left hand on the top of his radio to anchor it. "They come in the same way, under escort from the moment they leave the plane to the time the embassy gate shuts behind them. They spend the next two years in the embassy compound, working shift and shift—and generally stay in the same building that whole time besides. And when their tour's up, they're guarded back to the door of the plane. What they see of Paris is right out there—" he waved at the building fronts of the Citie Internationale they were passing. The sedan was accelerating at its sluggish best.

"You don't have to kill us, you know, Phillips," the lieutenant protested.

"No sir," agreed the driver. He crossed the Boulevard Brune on what the cross traffic thought was a green light for them. Brakes and horns protested.

Morley swallowed again but did not comment. The green shade of the Pare de Monsouris swept past the windows at speed. "You know," the lieutenant said at last, "that's really what sets the Free World off from the Reds. It's not economics, the way they like to pretend; it's the way each side treats human beings. What you've just described is quite simply inhuman."

Kelly shrugged. "Well, you do what you've got to do," he said. "They don't have many code clerks defect, for damn sure." He paused. The tires were drumming heavily over the pavement of the Boulevard Raspail. "Besides," he continued, "I saw a lot of Cambodia about the same way. Something short of a leisurely tour, you might say. And Laos, for that matter."

"You were in Laos?" Morley asked. He was keeping his eyes fixed on the civilian, apparently so that he would not have to be visually aware of what the sedan was doing.

"Off and on," Kelly agreed. "Hunting elephants, of all things."

"*Oh,*" the lieutenant said. "Oh." He laughed awkwardly.

"You see, I thought you meant while you were, ah, in service."

The civilian smiled back. "Right the first time," he said. "We were machine-gunning them from slicks—ah, from UH1 helicopters—"

"I know what a slick is," Morley objected stiffly.

"Good, good—shooting them from slicks at night, using starlight scopes. Somebody'd decided that the dinks were using the elephants to pack supplies down the Ho Chi Minh trail. We were supposed to be destroying hostile transport by blasting Dumbos."

The lieutenant's lips worked. "That's—that's. . . . I mean, elephants are an endangered species, and to just massacre them from the air. . . ."

"Don't expect *me* to argue with you," Kelly said with another shrug. "But we were getting some secondary explosions when we hit the beggars, too. So I suppose the folks in Washington were right, at least on the Intelligence side."

As they swung from the Quai Anatole France onto the approaches of the Pont de la Concorde, the sedan took the line in front of a Mercedes. Metal rang as the cars stopped. Traffic began to move again, and Phillips eased the sedan along with it. A plump man in a three-piece suit rolled down the passenger window of the Mercedes and began shouting curses in French. Kelly rolled down his own window and leaned out. He did not speak. The Mercedes window closed again. Its liveried chauffeur braked to permit a Fiat to slip between the two bigger cars.

Morley scowled into his clenched hands, but he said nothing aloud.

Kelly, on the outside of the sedan as it rounded the Place de la Concorde, could see only the base of the obelisk in the center. Perversely, he watched that nonetheless, rather than the Neoclassical magnificence of Louix XV's own time for which the obelisk was to be only the neutral hub. 220 tons of polished and incised granite, 75 feet high even without its 18th Century base, the obelisk was Kelly's own answer to Shelley's "Ozymandias." Indeed, look on that work and despair. Like its slightly smaller sister—Cleopatra's Needle—and the both of them well over a millennium old before Cleopatra was conceived—it had remained effectively unchanged as empire followed empire, as monarchs and nations fought and built and died. The stone remained, though no one knew the name of the men who had fashioned it, and few enough that of the Pharaoh—Thutmose III—who had commissioned its erection. Men, even men whom their age thought great, would pass utterly away. But with determination, a man might leave behind him an achievement that could be his personal—though anonymous— beacon to history.

In front of the American Embassy on the Rue Gabriel strolled a pair of French police carrying submachine guns. Kelly touched his tongue to his lips, a sign of momentary tension to anyone who knew him well enough. He had carried a gun like that, an MAT 49, in the field for several months, after he took it from an NVA officer killed by Claymore mines. In the field, in War Zone C . . . Khu Vuc C . . . and that gun had been rebarreled to chamber East Bloc 7.62-mm ammo, but the sight of the gendarmes took him back regardless.

And it seemed that the Pentagon wanted him back in those jungles of his mind. It was the only reason he could imagine for a terse summons five years after they had decided Tom Kelly was too erratic to keep on the government payroll.

At the embassy gate, the driver brought his sedan to a halt that did not squeal the tires but did rock both passengers forward from deceleration stresses. A uniformed Marine saluted from the guard post to the right. The gate slid back, allowing the sedan to accelerate through. Across the driveway, the statue of Franklin scowled. Kelly wondered whether his own expression mimicked the statue's—and the thought broke his heavy face into a genuine smile.

The car stopped in front of the entrance. "As ordered, sir," Phillips said. He opened his door.

Kelly got out without waiting for the driver to walk around the car. They met at the front fender while Lieutenant Morley straggled out of the back seat. The civilian kicked the tire and smiled. "Keep about forty pounds in there?" he asked.

The driver smiled back. "Thirty-six all round, sir," he said. "She's still a cow, but it helps a bit on the corners."

"Mr. Kelly, if you'll come with me," the lieutenant said at Kelly's elbow.

"Sure I will—if you'll get off my back for a minute," the civilian said. He pointed toward the building's steps. "There—go stand there for a minute, will you, Lieutenant?"

"But—" Morley began. He thought better of whatever he had planned to say. Nodding, he stepped a few paces away from the other men.

"Look," Kelly said quietly, "I apologize for what I said. I was wrong, and there wasn't any call to say it anyway." He consciously raised his eyes to meet the driver's.

The driver grinned. "No sweat, sir," he said. "Just remember there's a few of us around who still give a shit about the way our work gets done." The grin faded, then flashed back again full strength. "You know, he'll probably have my stripes for that—but I'd do it again."

Kelly stuck out his left hand—he held the radio in his right—and shook awkwardly with the enlisted man. "Maybe so, maybe not," he said. After ducking back into the sedan to get the AWOL bag which Morley had left on the seat, Kelly rejoined the lieutenant.

"Do you have any notion of what they want me for?" Kelly asked as they strode down a linoleum hallway. His crepe soles squelched in marked contrast to the clack of the soldier's low quarters.

"Not here!" the lieutenant muttered.

"I didn't ask *what*," Kelly said. "I asked *whether*."

"Here we are," Morley said, turning into the suite at the end of the hallway. "Oanh," he said to the Oriental secretary at the front desk, "General Pedler wants to see Mr. Kelly here as soon as possible."

The secretary nodded and touched an intercom button, speaking softly. In Vietnamese, Kelly said, "Good morning, Madame Oanh. Is it well with you?"

"Oh my God!" said the girl, jumping upright in her seat. Her accent was distinctly Northern. Though she was too young to have been part of the original resettlement in 1954, Oanh could of course have been born in a village of such refugees. They had tended to stay aloof from the original population of what became South Vietnam. At any rate, she was clutching at a crucifix. "Oh, I'm so sorry, you startled me," she rattled on. "It's so good to—I mean, my husband doesn't speak Vietnamese, and he—we're afraid of how it would look, with his job, you know, if I spent time with. . . ." Her voice trailed off. The intercom was answering her.

"I suppose there are a lot of members of the community here in Paris who aren't—exiles the way you are," Kelly sympathized. "Your husband is—"

The intercom crackled again. The woman stood up. "Oh, you must go in now, sir. Perhaps when you come back . . ." She scurried over to the inner door, clad in a prim white blouse and a navy skirt. How much more attractive she would have been in an *ao dai*, thought Tom Kelly; though as a well brought up Catholic girl, she might never have worn the flowing, paneled dress in her life.

An Air Force major general was standing behind a desk of massive teak. It clashed with the curves and delicacy, both real and reproduction, with which most of the embassy was furnished. On the other hand, the desk looked a great deal more comfortable under its mass of strewn papers than its Directoire equivalent would have been; and it matched Wallace Pedler's own bearlike solidity very well.

"Kelly?" the Defense Attaché demanded. "Come on in. Oanh, where the hell is Mark, I told you to buzz him, didn't I?" The secretary bobbed her head twice and disappeared back to her console. "And what in hell are those?" Pedler continued, staring at the bag and radio Kelly was carrying.

"My clothes," said the squat civilian, sitting down carefully on a cushioned chair, "and my radio. Want to listen to Radio Moscow? Take me a moment to rig the antenna. . . ." He took a coil of light wire, perhaps fifteen feet of it, from a coat pocket and began unwinding it as if oblivious of the general's burgeoning amazement.

There was a bustle at the door. A naval captain, no doubt the Naval Attaché and the second-ranking officer in a post this size, stepped past Lieutenant Morley. He was carrying a set of file folders, their contents attachéd to the manila covers by hole clips. "Glad you could make it, Mark," General Pedler said caustically. "Mr. Kelly, Captain Laidlaw. Morley, what the hell are you doing here? Close the door behind you."

Kelly had clipped one end of the antenna wire onto the receiver—length for length, a piece of supple copper worked just as well as a steel whip, and it was easier to transport without poking anything. Now the civilian took the six-foot power cord out of the other coat pocket and began looking for a wall socket.

"What is that?" asked Captain Laidlaw, poised over a chair at the corner of the general's desk. "Some sort of debugging device?"

"No, just a radio," said Kelly. "The general wanted to hear"— there was a socket directly behind his own chair—"Radio Moscow."

"Put that goddamned thing down!" the Defense Attaché snapped. "Mark, sit down." Pedler seated himself, breathing heavily and looking at his hands. The uncurtained window behind him looked along the Boissy d'Anglais. One of the roofs, a block or so away, might be that of the ETAP, one of the finest luxury hotels in Paris. Presumably Kelly would be put up in one of the block of rooms there which the embassy kept rented at all times for Temporary Duty personnel and high-ranking transients.

Kelly would be put up there if he decided to stay, at least.

"We—ah," General Pedler began. "Ah, Captain Laidlaw here will brief you on the situation."

Laidlaw smiled brightly over his crossed knees. "Well, Mr. Kelly," he said, "what have you been doing since you left the Army?"

The civilian took out a multi-blade jackknife and began cleaning his nails with the awl. Without looking up from his fingers he said, "That's my file there, isn't it?"

"Ah—"

"Isn't it current? Doesn't it say I've been selling office equipment for Olivetti?" Kelly glared at Laidlaw. The captain's eyes seemed focused on the glittering stainless steel of the knife.

"Well, it . . ." Laidlaw temporized.

"Look," said Kelly, "that's your quota of stupid questions for the day. You know about me or I wouldn't be here. I don't know a goddamned thing about what you want of me. You want to talk about that, I'll listen. Otherwise, I'll go back to Basel where at least I get paid to talk to turkeys."

"I think I'll take over after all, Mark," said General Pedler with surprising calm. He met Kelly's eyes. "How current are your Russian and Vietnamese languages?"

The civilian blinked and snapped the awl closed. "Not real current," he said carefully, "but I can still communicate well enough, I suppose." Wistfully he added, "I used to be Native Speaker level, 4-4, in both, you know . . . when we were monitoring the message traffic in. . . ." His voice trailed off.

"And your French?" Pedler continued.

"My French customers tell me I have a Corsican accent," Kelly said with a chuckle, "and I once had an Italian wonder if I didn't come from Eritrea the way he did. But nobody takes me for an American, if that's what you mean."

"You won't need Italian for this mission," the general said decisively. "Now, even though you were with a, ah, Radio Research Detachment in Vietnam rather than a combat unit—"

Kelly nodded calmly. "Right," he interrupted, "I was with the National Security Agency then, just like I was up to five years ago."

"But I gather you did have some combat experience," General Pedler said. "I believe there was even a Silver Star. I know what that means, especially for an enlisted man as you were."

Captain Laidlaw started to hand one of the folders to his superior. It was red-bordered and stamped Top Secret, unlike a standard 201 Personnel File. The Defense Attaché waved it off without taking his eyes away from Kelly.

"I'd admire to know what's in that file," the civilian said, but it wasn't a real request. He looked at the wall, at a framed photograph of General Pedler as a younger man, grinning beside the nose of an F-100. "That was at Fort Defiance," he said. "They named it that because they dug the Squadron in with a pair of 8-inch howitzers, right in the middle of War Zone C. They dared the dinks to come get us. They did, too; the Lord knows, they did that." He caught the general's eyes. "I didn't get that medal for fighting. I got it because somebody had to guide in the medevac birds with a pair of light wands, and it turned out to be me. I guess I'm about as proud of that as I am of anything I ever did in my life, if you want to know the truth . . . but I'm not looking for a chance to do anything like it again."

"We need," the general said, "someone to manage the defection of a Soviet Bloc citizen in a third country. That will require a certain facility with languages, which you have; but that could be supplied by a number of other persons with active security clearances—yes, yours still is, Mr. Kelly. The—mission, Project Skyripper—the mission, however, must be developed with speed rather than finesse. As I understand it, your name was suggested by General Redstone, who had served with you at one time."

Kelly broke into a smile. "That bastard made general? I'll be damned! I'd heard the Special Operations Group was pretty much a dead end for your career in the brass. Seemed like the folks who'd been running missions into Laos scared the crap out of the War College types back in the World when they got a few drinks in them and started telling stories." The smile broadened. "And Red has some stories to tell, *that's* God's truth."

"You accept the mission, then?" broke in the Naval Attaché, still smiling to hide his discomfort.

Kelly shrugged restively, looking at the picture again. "Five years ago, the NSA decided it didn't need a cowboy," he said. His hands, unnoticed, were still playing with the red and silver knife. "Right now, this cowboy doesn't need the NSA—or any other part"—he glared at Pedler—"of the fucking US Government. Oh, sure, you'll pay me—but last year I cleared, what, $37,000 it'd come to, cleared it honest without anybody trying to grease me or throw me under the jail." Kelly leaned forward in the chair, the words cracking out like shots. "If I want excitement—and I don't—I can get that walking the Genoa docks. Anything in the fucking world I want, I *want*, and I can get it or I know a guy who can get it for me. What do I need the USG for now, except another chance to get the shaft? Why do I need *you*?"

"You don't," General Pedler said, his voice a calm contrast to the civilian's spewing words and the anger growing on Laidlaw's face. "You didn't need a medevac bird in the jungle, either. *You* weren't wounded. You don't need your country at all; but she needs you. And that's enough, or you wouldn't have flown in from Basel when we contacted you. Would you?"

Kelly slapped the arm of his chair. "Don't *give* me that crap!" he said. "The country *needs* a few wogs blown away, so let's get Tom Kelly, he's good at it? No thanks. I had my share of that sort of diplomacy before, remember? Get somebody younger, General. This trooper's learned that the US doesn't need that shit—and the world sure as *hell* doesn't need it!"

The civilian thrust himself back in his chair, glaring angrily at both officers. To Kelly's surprise, the Naval Attaché was nodding morose agreement.

"As a matter of fact, Mr. Kelly," General Pedler said,

"I had a very similar reaction when the project was first broached to me. Like you, I've spent a great deal of my working life outside the US proper . . . and I learned very early that you don't work very well with foreigners if you think they're all wogs. What changed my mind about the mission is the information I'm about to give you."

"Ah, Wally," said the captain, "do you think it's a good idea to. . . ."

Pedler looked at the other officer. "Why yes, Mark," he said with a trace of mockery, "I *do* think it's a good idea to carry out this mission. That's why I'm going to give Mr. Kelly enough background to convince him of the same thing."

The Defense Attaché stood up and strolled to his window. "The counterintelligence boys check out everybody who rents a room over there that faces the embassy," Pedler said, waving an index finger toward the Boissy d'Anglais. "They still want me to put up opaque drapes, I say screw'em. Didn't join the Air Force to spend my life in a coffin. But a lot of things I say with my back to the glass." He turned toward the civilian.

"Very simply," Pedler continued, "a Russian scientist had found a way to destroy all US strategic weapons within seconds of launch. He had a particle beam device, you've probably heard mention of it before. The concept is simple, but a way to turn the concept into a weapon is something else again. It appears that the Russians have it. Fortunately, the hardware—the electronic nuts and bolts of the device—isn't simple either . . . and that, the Russians haven't got." He paused.

Kelly stroked his jaw. "Okay," he said. "They don't

have the gadget and we don't have the gadget. I haven't heard any reason to panic yet."

"The reason," said the general, and the intensity of his voice underscored his words more vividly than a mere increase in volume could have done, "is that the Russians will have the necessary manufacturing technology very shortly. If they can't develop it themselves, they'll get it from the West. Some nation, some private company or group of companies, will find it expedient to provide that technology. We live in a world, Mr. Kelly, in which nations as diverse as Libya and Israel find it expedient to send arms to the Iranians in their war with Iraq. The Russians will get their hardware. Within five years. There will be a nuclear exchange; and Mr. Kelly, only the Russian weapons will reach their targets."

Pedler took a deep breath. "That is what will happen," he concluded, "unless the Russian physicist who developed the weapon defects to the West, as he wants to do. As we want you to make possible."

Kelly eyed the two officers as if they were in a police line-up. "You could be lying through your teeth, General," he said flatly.

"No, Mr. Kelly," General Pedler replied, "I don't think I could—not to your face, not and expect to be believed. But if you want to think that somebody sold *me* a bill of goods . . . well, I can't stop you from thinking that. All I can say is that I *am* convinced, or I wouldn't be talking to you now."

"Jesus," Kelly said, rubbing his temples with his eyes closed. "Jesus." Then looking at Pedler with none of the hostility of a moment before, "Look then, do I have . . . have full control of handling the thing if I take it on?"

"Well, if you want *carte blanche*," said Captain Laidlaw, consciously trying to smooth the frown from his forehead, "that might depend on your definition of the term."

"You've got my fucking file, don't you?" Kelly snapped. "You *know* what I mean by *carte blanche*!" He looked back at the Defense Attaché and said, almost pleading, "Look, General, my skills—I'm not a diplomat. You say you need it quick and dirty, but . . . sir, it can get *real* dirty. And that's the only way *I* can be sure to get it done. There's people who wouldn't make waves, not like . . . not like me."

The Defense Attaché nodded. "That was considered," he agreed. "But—you see, there were two plans for getting the hostages out of the Tehran Embassy," he continued. "One of them was the CIA's. Everybody knows that one; it's the one they tried. Real slick. Minimum fuss and bother, minimum men and equipment committed so nobody'd make a big fuss in the UN afterward. That was one way."

The general sat down again. Captain Laidlaw licked his lips nervously. "Ah, sir, I don't know—" he began.

"If you don't know, then keep quiet!" Pedler retorted. His heavy voice continued, "The other plan came from the JCS, and as it chances, I worked on it. I'd been Air Attaché in Tehran a few years before, you see." The general's thumb riffled a stack of papers on his desktop. "What we wanted to do was use a ring of daisy-cutters to isolate the compound—" Laidlaw frowned in puzzlement rather than disapproval. "Not a piece of Navy ordnance, Mark?" Pedler asked with a smile. "Fourteen-thousand-pound high-capacity bombs, then. They take two pallets in the belly of a C-130 to carry them, and when they go off, they can clear a quarter-mile circle of jungle for a landing zone. They'd have done the same thing to the buildings in the center of Tehran. We were going to use Rangers, parachuting in on MC-1 chutes and coming back on a Fulton Recovery System with the hostages."

The general's grin was as cold as a woman's mercy. "That would have taken time, reeling in people who'd never used a snatch lift before. But it would have worked, which choppers couldn't, not flying that far. And there would've been plenty of time. It'd have taken the rag-heads three days to bulldoze through rubble and bodies the daisy-cutters would have left."

Kelly chuckled appreciatively, a sound that could have come from the throat of an attack dog. The hot glare of old emotions was making his palms sweat. "And when they got there," he said, "they'd have found every mothering 'student' with his balls in his mouth, wouldn't they?"

The general cocked his head. "That wasn't part of the written plan," he said.

"Sure it was," the civilian said. "You made that decision when you decided to send in Rangers. Sure you did. . . ."

Captain Laidlaw was beginning to look ill. Both his spit-shined low quarters were flat on the floor. Pedler continued, "This operation is being handled through Paris instead of Rome because my opposite number in Rome refused to have anything to do with it. Well, maybe he was right. But I've been told that *I've* got a free hand, so long as the job gets done. And that means you've got a free hand, too, Kelly. So long as you come back with the goods."

The civilian began rewinding his antenna wire to give his hands something to do while his brain worked. "You've got a full briefing set up, I suppose?" he said.

Pedler nodded. "Are you go or no-go?" he asked.

Kelly looked away and cleared his throat. "Oh, I'm go," he said toward a corner of the ceiling. "In a month or two I'll ask you if you still think you knew what you were doing. If I'm around to ask. But I'm go, provided you take care of one thing."

Pedler's face went as blank as a poker player's. "Let's hear it," he said.

"Somebody may try to run an Article 15 through on the guy who drove me in today," the civilian said. "Specialist 5 Phillips. I want the papers torn up—if there are any papers."

The Attaché's expression did not change. "What happened?" he asked. Captain Laidlaw was shifting uneasily in his chair.

"Nothing happened," Kelly said. "That's why I don't want to see the guy shafted." His smile flashed, as chill as a polar dawn.

"All right, Mr. Kelly," the general said as he stood, "I'll take care of it. And now that that's settled, I'm giving you the only order you'll hear for the duration: stay off the sauce. Period."

Kelly snapped his eyes back to the Attaché's. "I can handle it," he said.

Pedler leaned forward with his knuckles lost in the books and papers littering his desk. "Don't bullshit *me*, Sergeant," he said. "I've worked with juicers all my service life. Some of them aren't oiled all the time, and some of them work better than a lot of the rest of us even when they *are* oiled. But you're not selling typewriters now. If you drink the way you've been doing since the NSA fired your ass, you're going to get a lot of people killed and you're going to screw up the mission. Do I make myself understood?"

Kelly stood up, thrusting the radio cord back in his pocket. "I hear you talking, General," he said. "Now—I want a shower and a shave. Then we'll get down to details."

Pedler nodded toward the door. "Have Oanh look up Morley for you," he said. "He was supposed to take care of arrangements. Report back to Room 302 here at"—he checked a massive wrist chronometer—"1500 hours."

Kelly's hands were full of his own gear, helping him suppress an instinct to salute. Sergeant. Well, he'd been one, a platoon sergeant when they booted him out. He'd refused all offers of warrant rank. Just didn't want to be an officer, even a half-assed warrant officer. And now, by God, they needed him like they needed none of those brass-bound monkeys in the Pentagon. They needed Tom Kelly.

When the door closed behind the civilian, the Naval Attaché coughed quietly for attention. General Pedler looked at him. "There's something in this man's restricted file that I think you ought to . . . note carefully, Wallie," Laidlaw said.

"Well?"

"He, ah . . . it appears that when Kelly was in Vietnam he used to accompany troops on field operations as a matter of course," the captain said. He flipped pages up over the binder clasp until he found the correct one, though the report was too clear in his own mind for any real need for reference. "Kelly's duties, his assigned tasks at the time—this was 1968—did not require him to leave the base camps, of course."

"So he did things he didn't have to do," the general said with a snort. "Probably did a lot of things he wasn't supposed to do, too. That's water over the dam—and besides, it's just that sort of thing that gave him the background he needs for Skyripper."

"No doubt, sir," said Laidlaw acidly. "I'm sure there must have been *some* reason to decide that Mr. Kelly was qualified. In this case, however, Staff Sergeant Kelly—as he then was, accompanied a ten-man ambush patrol under a Lieutenant Schaydin. They dug shallow trenches and set up Claymores—directional mines—"

"I know a Claymore just as well as you do, Captain. We used them for perimeter defense ourselves."

Laidlaw looked up. "Yes. They set up Claymore mines about 25 yards in front of their position. During the night, a sound was heard to the front. Lieutenant Schaydin raised his head just over the lip of his trench and detonated a Claymore. The mine had been turned to face the friendly positions. It sprayed its charge of steel pellets straight back in Schaydin's face, killing him instantly."

Pedler shrugged. "All right," he said, "the dinks had

the ambush spotted and reversed the mines. Not the only time it happened."

"No doubt," the naval officer repeated. "But one of the men reported to a chaplain that before the patrol set out, Sergeant Kelly had warned each man individually to stay flat if there was any report of movement to the front. It had been on the man's conscience ever since."

"Give me that file," said General Pedler, reaching across the desk with a scowl. He scanned the report, a Xerox copy of a fussy carbon. "hell, this report wasn't filed till three years later," he said brusquely. "I wouldn't hang a dog on evidence like that."

"Nobody *did* hang Mr. Kelly," Laidlaw pointed out. "I just think you ought to know about it. Since there may still be time to . . . bring the matter to the attention of the Pentagon."

"Well, for God's sake, it's the Pentagon who sent us the file, isn't it?" the general snapped. He was continuing to read, however. His anger was the more real for being directed against a subordinate who was, after all, right. "For God's sake!" Pedler slapped the file closed. "It says Schaydin had gotten three men killed by a friendly mine when he took his platoon through an area before checking whether it'd been cleared." He thrust the folder back at Laidlaw. "Well?"

The captain stood up. "I'll return this material to the vault if you have no further need for it, then, General," he said. He walked toward the door.

"He wouldn't be much use on an operation like this if he weren't willing to kill! Would he, Laidlaw?" Pedler demanded.

The Naval Attaché turned. "Personally," he said, "I don't believe *anything* would be much use to an operation which depends on a known drunk and probable murderer," he said. "But I'll continue to carry out the orders of my superiors to the best of my ability. If you'll excuse me, sir."

He slammed the door behind him.

III

"Our contact agent is a Vietnamese national named Hoang Tanh," said the major with the toothbrush moustache. The patch on his right sleeve was the sword-and-lightnings insignia of the Special Forces. The silver and blue Combat Infantry badge glittered over the left breast pocket of his uniform. Kelly had disliked Major Nassif on sight. "He's a physicist, was involved with the Dalat Nuclear Facility before the Communist takeover. The Defense Attaché's Office recruited Tanh as a stay-behind agent."

"Hoang," the civilian said.

"What?" asked the major.

"His family name would be Hoang, the first name in the series, not the last," Kelly explained. "Same with most Oriental languages."

"To return to something significant," the soldier snapped, "this slopehead became of some importance during the past year when the Vietnamese government began to explore reactivation of the Dalat facility—it was disabled in 1975, of course—as a counterweight to Chinese pressure. Even if they couldn't build bombs, the option of sowing the border between the two countries with radioactive material might deter another incursion by the Chinks." The major fixed Kelly with what they probably said at West Point was a look of command. Maybe at West Point it *was* a look of command. "The Russians are always looking for chances to stab their former comrades in the back, of course. It's not surprising that they provided fuel and technical support to the gooks. And that's where our man made contact with"—he looked down at the briefing file— "this Professor Evgeny Vlasov. The target." Nassif paused. "Code named Mackerel."

"Christ on a crutch," said Kelly as he stood up. "What's my code name? Turkey?" He paced sullenly toward one of the spotless desks. Not everybody followed the Defense Attaché's own sloppy security practices. Though—having met General Pedler, Kelly was willing to believe that he dumped the clutter from his desk by armloads into his Mosler safe every day before he left for home. "What's the hold we've got on Hoang?" Kelly asked abruptly.

"Sergeant, if you'll sit your ass down where it belongs," said Major Nassif, "we'll get through this a lot quicker." He rapped the desk in front of Kelly's empty chair with his index finger.

Head-height, sound-deadening panels divided Room 302 into three alcoves. Everyone had been moved out for the briefing, but the walls and the hallway door were something short of code-vault secure. With that in mind, and the fact that he genuinely did not like to lose his temper openly, Kelly said in a normal voice, "Look, Major, if I'm going to trust my life to this bird, I've got to have *some* reason to hope I'm not being set up. There wasn't a whole lot in the way we left Nam in '75 to make somebody who stayed put want to risk his neck for us, was there? We lied to the Reds and we lied to Congress . . . but mostly we lied to the South Vietnamese themselves. And weren't they cute to keep right on believing we wouldn't *really* let 'em go down the tubes? Dr. Hoang sounds like the closest thing the new regime has to a homegrown nuclear physicist. That makes him valuable enough to coddle, even if he is from the South. Why should he work for us?"

The major glanced back at his folder, then up at the civilian again. "Sit down, Sergeant," he said. "You'll be told as much about the sources and methods involved in setting up this operation as you have a personal need to know. As for Mackerel's bonafides, they've been checked by the people whose job it is to check such things. That'll have to be sufficient, I'm afraid."

Kelly sat down, massaging his forehead with his fingertips. He was watching through his fingers, though. When Nassif opened his mouth to continue, the civilian said, "Shut up for a minute, Major. I've got a story to tell you, and then a suggestion."

"Serg—"

"And if you call me 'sergeant' once more, I'll feed you your teeth!" Kelly shouted. His voice was as raw as a shotgun blast, and for the moment as disconcerting.

Major Nassif started up, but he locked angry eyes with the squat man and subsided again.

"This is a Special Forces story, so you'll be able to appreciate it," Kelly continued quietly, hoarsely. He nodded toward the losing-unit patch on the major's right shoulder. "I was young, then, and I took orders better. . . ." Kelly coughed, trying to smooth the roughness from his voice. "I was with the Five-Oh-First Radio Research Detachment. We'd go out in the field with ground combat units and set up one hell of a beautiful communications intercept system. We'd pick up everything Charlie was saying on the air, whether it was out at the treeline with a handie-talkie or a divisional command near Hanoi. Everything was taped and flown back to NSA head-quarters at Fort Meade . . . but we were language-trained, too, you see. That way we knew to tag anything really hot for cable from Saigon."

Kelly sucked his lower lip under his teeth. He was hunched over as if the rain were driving at his back. "One afternoon we picked up calls from an NVA forward artillery observer. He was handing out targets to a mortar company getting ready to do a number on a Special Forces camp about thirty clicks away. The way we knew exactly what he was doing is he was using an Army Map Service sheet to give grid coordinates. A US map!

"So we sent a query to Theater HQ in Long Binh requesting permission to release the intercept to the camp. I mean, *they* didn't even know they were going to be hit. *We* knew exactly what targets, what order, how many rounds—and the exact time. We knew everything the dink battery commander did"—the civilian raised his voice and his angry eyes—"and our receivers were enough better than his that we got every coordinate the first time while the dink had to ask for repeats on a couple of them."

Kelly stood up and paced, his hands locked behind his back. The thick, blunt fingers wound together. "Long Binh wouldn't clear it. They shot it on to Maryland, though, in case somebody there would authorize release. We got word back three hours later, about an hour after the bombardment had ended. Fort Meade wouldn't clear it either." Kelly swallowed. "Compromise of NSA sources and methods was more important than the purposes to be served by such a compromise. Permission refused." The civilian slammed his right fist into the table. "I never did learn how many people got killed by that bullshit. They weren't any of them in NSA headquarters, though, and that was all that mattered to the top brass. But it wasn't all that mattered to me."

"Umm, well," said Major Nassif, as if he had understood the point of the story. They hadn't warned him that he would be briefing a psycho. . . . "Well, to continue," the major said.

"Sorry, Major, just one more thing," Kelly said tiredly. "I said I had a suggestion. I'm going back over to my room in the ETAP—" he thumbed toward the blank north wall of the office. "I suggest you check with whoever it takes, General Pedler, I suppose, and then drop the file off with me there."

Nassif started to rise in protest. "I said check, didn't I?" Kelly overrode him. "And the whole file, too—the file and every other scrap of data there is in this embassy, anything that *might* have something to do with it." The civilian opened the door and stepped out into the hall. Turning, he added, "If the ETAP isn't secure, you're *really* up a creek."

Major Nassif plucked at his moustache. Suddenly he glanced from the open door to the open file in his hand. He slapped the file shut, but it was another minute before he actually stood up.

IV

Tom Kelly heard the knock the second time and padded to the door. The fisheye lens in the panel distorted the figures of two men in shirt sleeves. Each wore his hair shorter than civilian standard. "A moment," Kelly called. He set down the short, double-edged knife and pulled on his slacks. When he opened the door, his right hand again held the knife out of sight along his thigh. Hadn't even started, Kelly thought, might *not* start, and already he was getting paranoid again. Bad as he'd been five years before in Venice, when he went to work wearing a uniform. . . .

"Mr. Kelly," said the visitor carrying the briefcase, "General Pedler directed us to bring some material to you. I'm Sergeant Wooley; this is Sergeant Coleman." His black companion, apparently bemused by Kelly's state of undress, blinked and nodded.

"Sure, come on in," the civilian said, stepping back out of the way. Already embarrassed, he slipped the knife hilt down into his side pocket as unobtrusively as possible. "Expected Major Nassif, you know," he said. He looked carefully at the two sergeants. "You fellows wouldn't have Crypto clearances, would you?" he asked.

Sergeant Wooley closed the hall door. Coleman had moved over to the writing desk on which the radio sat, crackling with the odd inflections of an Albanian news-reader. The younger men looked at each other. "Yes, sir," the first said slowly, "we're Communicators, if that's what you mean."

"I'm sorry, sit down," Kelly said, waving toward the upholstered chairs as he seated himself on the bed again. He flicked a hand across his own bare chest. "Just sitting here thinking," he said in what was meant for explanation. "When it wasn't that jackass Nassif, I figured they'd sent couriers. But I guess somebody over there"—he waved toward the embassy, beyond the heavy drapes and the other buildings —"got the notion that I might be prejudiced against officers." He smiled. "Might just be right, too. Want a drink? The refrigerator's stocked with one of everything, and I brought a bottle of my—"

"I think we'd better just turn these over, sir," Wooley said. He opened the case. It contained the briefing file which Kelly had already seen in Nassif's hands, plus two other, slimmer, folders and a clipboard with a receipt. The sergeant held out the clipboard and a pen to Kelly. "If you'll sign here, sir," he said.

"43 documents classified Top Secret," the civilian read aloud. "Well, that's enough to the point." He signed his name with a flourish and handed the receipt back to Wooley. "If the count's short, I know where to find you."

"What is this?" asked Sergeant Coleman, pointing to the short-wave receiver. "I mean—the station. Is it Voice of America?"

All three men paused to listen to the strident newsreader. He was attacking the Italian Communist Party with a passion that, combined with his accent, made the fact that he was speaking in English hard to ascertain. "Radio Albania," Kelly explained as Wooley's pen scratched his confirming signature. "The Sixth Fleet's about to hold exercises in the West Med, and the running-dog poltroons—don't think I'd ever heard the word spoken before—of the CPI did nothing to prevent this example of bourgeois imperialism. You'd think they'd be screaming about us"—he smiled again—"but with the Albanians, it doesn't seem to work that way."

"Thank you, sir," said Wooley, folding the receipt into his pocket. He left the rest of the material on the desk. "When you're ready to return this, or if you have to leave this room for any reason, will you please check with the Marine guards in the hallway. They'll escort you or call an authorized person from the embassy to watch the documents during your absence."

"I'll be damned," Kelly said. He strode to the door and opened it. A Marine E-5 in dress blues stood six feet to either side of the door. They carried bolstered .38s. The one on the left nodded to Kelly, but his companion kept his eyes trained toward the end of the hall. "I'll be damned," the civilian muttered again. "Well, if Pedler's willing to play by my rules, I can't complain if he plays by his at the same time."

The two Communicators shook hands with Kelly as

they left the room. Coleman paused a further moment in the doorway. "Why do you listen to that?" he asked, gesturing toward the radio with his chin.

The civilian shrugged. "I spent—a lot of time listening to signals that didn't mean a whole lot, piecing things together . . . listening. I think better now if there's somebody talking in the background, if there's a receiver or two live." He chuckled to hide his embarrassment. "Besides, I wind up knowing things that sort of seep in. . . . It helps, sometimes."

When the door closed, Kelly was alone again, just himself and Albania and a case of classified documents. Sighing, he took the knife carefully from his pocket. He had replaced the round, thin handle of the short-wave receiver with a sand-finished stainless steel strap over an inch wide. A hand-tooled leather wrapper cushioned the handle. Kelly unsnapped the two fasteners on the leather and set his knife into the cut-out machined into the steel strap. He had no idea of how many airport security checks he had passed through with this radio or one of its similarly-modified predecessors. He was simply not going to be at the mercy of whatever set of crazies happened to hijack a plane he was on.

Off to work. Kelly stripped to his shorts again and opened one of the supplementary folders. It contained only a four-page Current Policy Statement, issued by the US Department of State. It was the text of a speech delivered by the Under Secretary for Security Assistance, Science and Technology, to a—for Christ' sake!—to a national conference of editorial writers. The title, "Nuclear Power and the Third World," was about as clear as the discussion got. The speech was the typical Foggy Bottom bumf sent around to all missions. It was intended to give the official line on how to dodge awkward questions.

The question this time was why the US was opposing the International Conference on Nuclear Power Development. The Conference—though the US did not doubt the good faith of the Algerians who were hosting it—had been politicized in a manner not conducive to world peace and harmony. Israel and South Africa had been banned by a unanimous decision of the Conference Trustees—whoever the hell they were—though in fact neither republic had expressed an interest in attending. Further, if anything but political rhetoric *should* eventuate from the Conference, it would likely be a heightened interest in nuclear weapons among the nations of the Third World. The effect of this could not help but be unfortunate at a time when all nations must band together in the service of peace, with population control and greater agricultural productivity as primary goals.

Kelly snorted and went on to the file with the Top Secret cover sheet. The Department of State building had more floor space under one roof than the Pentagon; and there were probably more damned fools per square foot there, too. At least the Department of Defense would have managed to say *something* in four pages, though it would doubtless have been a lie.

The first classified document noted that arrangements could be made for the defection of a Professor Evgeny Vlasov during the—okay—International Conference on Nuclear Power Development in Algiers. The operation would, however, resemble an armed kidnapping or a paramilitary operation rather than an ordinary defection. A scientist of Professor Vlasov's stature would certainly be housed in the Soviet Embassy in El-Biar rather than in the Hotel Aurassi with most of the national delegations. Whenever Vlasov was outside the embassy, he would be escorted by armed KGB officers—intended to protect him, but certain to completely circumscribe his movements. Further, the KGB Residency in Algiers, already substantial, would be beefed up to take advantage of the concentration of Third World diplomats attending the conference. Even beyond that, there were an estimated 3,000 USSR military personnel operating in Algeria as advisors to the People's National Army and to the Polisario Front. These troops normally operated in uniform, though without rank insignia. At need, they would certainly be available to provide additional manpower.

In sum, the faceless DIA analyst concluded, Professor Vlasov's defection would require the neutralization of a minimum of four KGB/GRU officers. In addition, an indefinite number of local security personnel from the National Police and the Presidential Security Office would almost certainly become involved. The Conference would include ranking scientists and in some cases heads of state from countries which were mutually hostile: Brazil and Argentina, Iraq and Libya, Vietnam and China, among others. The Algerians would be expecting trouble and would be taking steps to minimize it through a show of overwhelming force.

The analyst had obviously determined to his own satisfaction that the proposed Operation Skyripper was impossible for both political and practical reasons. Kelly sighed. He was inclined to agree with the analyst, but it wasn't his job to care. If the USG were bound and determined that he was going to run the operation . . . well, there were plenty of slick types in the CIA, recruited from major universities and used to working through cut-outs, go-betweens. . . . Hiring local agents to hire more local agents, so that if the operation went sour—as it usually did—the President could blandly deny that the United States had been involved. Even the Bay of Pigs, an *invasion*, had been handled that way . . . and no wonder it came out a rat-fuck. But if they wanted deniability, they went Ivy League and Big Ten. If they really wanted results, maybe they went to a cowboy for a change. Maybe they went to Tom Kelly.

Kelly got up and ran the pitcher full of water. There was the usual pair of six-ounce water glasses beside it. He ignored the glasses, sipping from the pitcher itself as he walked back to the desk. He stared for a long time at the AWOL bag from which he had already unpacked his clothes. In the end he sat down without reaching into the bag again. He flipped the Kenwood receiver to 15 megahertz and then dialed up to the German Wave, thundering out of Wertachtal. With the selector set for wide band and the modulator damping the German pop music by 60 db, Kelly began looking at what he had in the way of assets for the job.

Besides himself.

The next document had a separate cover sheet, in some ways the most striking thing about it. It was marked "Top Secret—Dissemination ONLY by order of Director, Defense Intelligence Agency." On a separate line, typed in red caps, was the additional warning, "NO ACCESS BY CIA PERSONNEL!" Kelly grinned. Well, it was important to know your enemies. And it certainly answered the question of whether he could expect support from the CIA station in Algiers.

The Defense Attaché's Office in Algeria consisted of the Attaché, Commander William Posner, US Navy; and his staff, Sergeant E-6 Douglas Rowe, US Army. Rowe had an armor specialty. The two men and their predecessors had been trying to get a clerk-typist for their office, but they had been unable to justify one to the boys in budget. The only typist in the mission with a Top Secret clearance was the Ambassador's secretary—who was actually Third Secretary for Administration, in order to get her on the Diplomatic List with all the privileges that entailed. The Defense Attaché was rather low on his Excellency's list of priorities, so reports from Algiers were consistently late. That did not seem to bother anybody at headquarters enough to spring for a typist slot, though, probably because the reports were pretty dull reading even by the undemanding standards of the DIA. Posner spoke some French. Neither of the men on the ground had any Arabic, much less Kabyle.

And the Kabyles were the key to Skyripper, if there was a key at all.

At first Kelly thought that he had never heard of the Kabyles, but a quick reading of other background documents showed him his error: he had known them as "Berbers," that was all. "Berber" meant just what it sounded like, "barbarian." As with "Welsh," "German," and "Eskimo," it was a name affixed by foreigners and never used by the ethnics themselves when their ethnicity became important. The Kabyles were both the Barbary Pirates and the Moors who overran Spain in the name of Allah.

And they were not Arabs, any more than the Cherokees were English. The West had a tendency to equate Moslems and Arabs. That mistake was made by Arabs only when they were dreaming of Third World hegemony the same way the Russian Pan-Slavs of 1900 had dreamed of an ideal state dominated from Moscow. Every Moslem state had its Arabizers, just as British India had had its Babus. The Arabizers tended to be intellectuals with their values shaped at universities in Cairo and Beirut rather than in their native lands. In Algeria, they held virtually all the top posts in the government and army. They had done so since the French were driven out, though the bombed-out farms in the Kabyle Highlands still bore testimony to who had really done the fighting which led to that victory. There were already signs that the fighting was about to resume, and that this time the outside overlords would be Arabs and not Frenchmen.

Operational planning had started even before a courier from the DAO in Berne had caught Kelly making a sales presentation to a Volkswagen dealership in Basel. Another courier had been sent to Algiers, ordering Commander Posner to give full support to the agent or contract officer, as yet undetermined, who would be arriving soon. Further, the Attaché was ordered to alert his contacts within the Kabyle underground to a coming need for manpower and other support. The USG would pay for such support with up to one million dollars in gold or any desired currency and—Kelly whistled, clashing with the radio's rendition of "Danke"—full US support for establishment of a Kabyle Government in Exile in Rabat, Morocco.

Kelly got up and walked to the sink, partly to refill the pitcher. Mostly he needed to move as he thought. He wondered how the button-down types in the Fudge Factory at State had taken that news. Not real well, he suspected. It meant the probable end to diplomatic relations between Algeria and the USG, whatever came of the defection attempt itself. This thing was big, it was so big it scared him. Why in *God's* name they'd picked him to run the show. . . .

Kelly took the 750-milliliter bottle of Johnny Walker Red out of the bag. Scotch to Americans, malt to an Englishman; whiskey to the rest of the world. Kelly preferred Tennessee sour-mash whiskey, but you didn't find that outside the States except maybe as a dusty bottle on a high shelf in big liquor stores. Scotch you could find from Iceland to Japan . . . and besides, it didn't matter that much, Kelly had drunk peppermint schnapps when that was handiest; and if he preferred the taste of hog piss to peppermint schnapps, it had done the job just the same. He needed a drink now, needed it bad. But Kelly gulped water instead and sat down with the file. The dapper man in hunting pinks winked knowingly from the bottle's label at the American.

Outsiders could not be expected to reach Professor Vlasov, but Dr. Hoang would certainly be able to renew his acquaintance. No eyebrows would be raised by a private conference between physicists representing two communist states allied against the Chinese between them. That left the problem of contacting Hoang; but that, given modern electronics, shouldn't be insuperably difficult. As he continued to read through the assortment of documents, Kelly began arraying mentally the support and equipment he would request from General Pedler—and the back up he would arrange for himself. There were some things he did not intend to tell anyone in the Paris embassy. A passport, for instance. Nobody in the USG was going to know what documents Kelly was traveling under. In his years of knocking around Europe, Kelly had met people who could do the necessary job as well or better than anybody in a CIA smokeshop. Why use a false passport if you knew a Consul who would issue a real one for the right incentive?

And what if somebody talked to a girlfriend or a drinking buddy? A salesman who might be planning to run a load of hash under a squeaky-clean passport wouldn't interest anybody around the Russian Embassy. Government ID for Tom Kelly, a French-speaker who'd been on both ends of automatic rifles in his day—that was something else. And people do talk, no matter who they are, when their pricks are hard or they're half-seas over.

There was no way to be sure how well Commander Posner would be holding up his end, with his Level 2 French and a naval officer's rigid disapproval of something this unconventional. Time would tell, too goddamned little time, ten days. But at least a sailor could be expected to take orders, however much he might dislike them. Kelly sighed and ran his index finger over the embossed label of the whiskey bottle. And then he went back to the file.

V

Lieutenant Colonel Nguyen Van Minh dropped the report back on his desk. He shook his head toward the mountains out the window. If he read between the lines correctly, it was not simply a knifing he had to deal with. The fight between two of his staff, guards at the Dalat Nuclear Facility, had occurred during an argument over the prowess of their respective regiments during the War of Liberation.

Both men, might they rot in Kampuchea where he was transferring them, had been on the losing—Southern—side.

Colonel Nguyen sighed and loosened the collar of his uniform tunic. Bao, his predecessor as Chief of Facility Security, had been incompetent, no doubt about that. But how he had failed to do even basic background checks on these two . . . and how many other ex-Airborne and Marine personnel were *still* on the staff of this crucial part of the defense establishment? The situation no longer reflected on Bao's honor, it reflected on Nguyen's own.

The phone rang. Nguyen snatched it as if it were a rope out of his administrative morass. "Security," he snapped. The colonel was his own secretary. He spoke to anyone who called . . . and they had better have *very* good reasons to call him.

This caller did. Even before he spoke, the background wail identified a trunk line from the North. "Minh, good morning," squeaked the voice of the head of the Army Intelligence Bureau. "How would you like to take a little trip?"

Nguyen tensed. "General," he said, "I will be pleased to serve the State in whatever capacity she needs me, of course." For fifteen years, during the War of Liberation, Nguyen had spent more nights in the open than he had under a roof. After the victory, the Northerners had continued to load him with the dog work—including six months of shepherding gas rockets around Kampuchea. "Whatever capacity," the colonel repeated, "but matters here in Dalat are at a—critical stage. Surely there is some-one besides my own unworthy self who can deal with whatever problem you are having in Kampuchea?"

"No, no," interrupted General Ve. "You don't under-stand. This is a sort of vacation, a reward for you, Minh."

"That's what you said about this job," the colonel retorted more bitterly than was politic. "'Beautiful scenery, no danger—just a few administrative problems. . . .' Do you *know* who that idiot Bao hired for plant security?"

"If you'll listen for a moment, Colonel," the distant

voice said harshly, "you'll be better able to judge your orders, won't you?"

"Right, sorry, General," Nguyen said. He forced himself to relax. His service during the War of Liberation had been second to no one's; but Nguyen was a Southerner by birth, a member of the Viet Cong and the National Liberation Front—not the Hanoi establishment. Hanoi was in firm control since its armies had pushed home their invasion and achieved what twenty years of guerrilla warfare had failed to do. It behooved Nguyen to remember his place—or find himself commanding a garrison battalion in Kampuchea, an even worse job than that of the chemical warfare detachment to which he had already been assigned.

"You know this conference in Algiers that your Doctor Hoang will be attending?" said the general. The momentary asperity seemed forgotten.

"Yes, of course," Nguyen said. "I understand that he'll be escorted by a team from the central office." Of *course* a plum assignment like that would go to toadies from the Hanoi office. During the War, Nguyen had suffered in order to end injustice. Now—but if he thought too long about such things, the result would be a blast of homicidal fury which would serve no one, least of all the State.

"That was the original intention, yes," General Ve agreed. "It appears, however—despite my personal intervention—that the Treasury will not release enough hard currency to permit more than one person from this office to accompany the Doctor."

"Yes?" prompted Nguyen. He held his breath in a hope that he would not admit even to himself.

"And I have determined that you are the best suited member of the Bureau for the assignment as it has developed, Minh," the general went on. "To act as sole escort, that is."

The colonel was afraid to ask the obvious question, but it had to be asked if he were to know what he was getting into. "Ah, General," he said, "I'm flattered, very flattered . . . but why me?"

General Ve coughed, a bark of sound over the bad connection. "Well, you see, Colonel," he said, "I took another look at the list of attendees and . . . the size of the Chinese delegation concerns me. They have, I'm sure, a notion of our purpose in reactivating the Dalat Reactor. And they surely know of Doctor Hoang's importance to the program. Frankly, I tried to quash the whole trip, but Hoang seems to have convinced—certain officials—that his presence at the Conference will be valuable to his work. And also, the head of the Russian delegation has expressed a desire to see Hoang again. . . . Their Professor Vlasov, the one who visited last month. So Hoang is going, and well. . . ."

"General, I'm very flattered," Nguyen repeated. He was waving his free hand in the air in silent joy.

"Well, Colonel," Ve said. "I wouldn't want you to think that we in Hanoi were unaware of your . . . ability. Not that I really *think* the Chinese would try something at an international conference, but—" He paused.

"As well to be sure," Nguyen completed.

"Exactly," agreed the general, "exactly. We're working in liaison with our Russian friends. I'm sure you'll be able to share the duties with their contingent. You've worked with them before, I believe?"

"The technicians with the poison gas equipment," Nguyen agreed. "Yes, their manpower should be very helpful."

"Well, the written orders will be along in due course," General Ve said. "I just wanted to make sure you had time to take care of any arrangements in Dalat before you left. Good day, Colonel."

"Good day," Nguyen said to a dead line. He cradled the phone.

Arrangements. Well, somebody had to vette the entire guard staff, it appeared. Truong could handle that. Truong damned well *better* be able to handle that. As for trip preparations. . . .

Nguyen opened the top drawer of his desk. He took out the pistol, removing the magazine before he locked back the slide. The round in the chamber spun out onto the pile of paperwork. It was an old weapon, a Tokarev TT-33, thirty years obsolete in Soviet service.

Nguyen had killed sixty-two men with it when he headed an assassination team during the War. The Colonel worked the slide several times, studying its action with a critical eye. He had better get in some range time before he went to Algiers. Just in case.

VI

<hr>

"Can't say I'm in much of a hurry this time, Specialist Phillips," Tom Kelly remarked as he got in through the door the driver insisted on holding open for him.

Phillips was grinning as he walked back around the hood and settled himself behind the steering wheel. "I'm glad to hear that, sir," he said, putting the Concord in gear, "because I scared the crap out of myself the last time." He chuckled. "Not as bad as I scared the lieutenant, though."

The gate guard saluted as the sedan passed him sedately. Anybody picked up at the front of the embassy was worth a salute. It was a lot cheaper than explaining to the Gunny why you'd ignored the CinC Med, who happened to have been in civvies that afternoon. . . .

"Ah, look, sir," the driver went on, watching traffic and not his passenger, "I, ah, heard about what you did for me. And well, if there's ever something you need and I've got—well, look me up, huh?"

Kelly grinned back. "Hell," he said, "you just did what you were told to do. I only made sure that if anything happened because you followed a damned fool's orders, that the USG knew it could whistle for any help it was going to need from me." Kelly paused, watching the buildings past Phillips' face. Traffic in the left lane was sweeping around them, but the sedan's tires were riding the rough pavement with only a modicum of discomfort. "Where did you happen to hear about that, anyway?" Kelly added, as if the answer did not matter to him.

"Oh, a buddy of mine drives most nights for the Adjutant," Phillips said. "You know, when he's going off to a reception and doesn't want the flics to stop him driving home plotzed. He was talking to the Assistant Air Attaché. . . ." The driver shot a look over at his passenger. "We're machines, you know. Typewriters and telephones and drivers . . . but you know."

"Sure," said the civilian. "I know how it is." His skin was flashing hot and dry in pulses that came and went as his heart beat. "What do they say about my chances of getting the job done?" he asked, wondering if his voice sounded as odd to the driver as it seemed to his own ears.

"Look, sir," Phillips said in sudden concern. "I didn't mean they were talking about—whatever you and the general have on." The driver was frowning, dividing his attention between his passenger and the traffic. "General Pedler's been playing that one real close, I think. That is—I've heard a lot about you in the past couple days, Mr. Kelly, but it's all been about what a mean SOB you are. Not whatever you're doing."

Kelly laughed in a combination of relief and irony.

"Yeah, I've been acting ill as a denned bear," he agreed. "Could just be that's the way I am, too." Phillips had turned down the narrow Faubourg St. Jacques, between the massive and ancient hospital complexes of Port Royal and Cochin. Either the pedestrians had a somber look or Kelly's mind gave them one. He wouldn't have been alive himself without a damn good surgeon and all the help that science and centuries of other surgeons trying to improve on past practice could give. Even so, hospitals always reminded Kelly more of death than salvation. These, with their 17th Century stonework blackened and corroded by soot, gave him the creeps even worse than most such places did.

"But it could also be . . ." Kelly continued. He was looking out his window at the domes and colonnades of the Paris Observatory, not toward the man to whom he was speaking. "It could also be that I'm scared, and if I'm a big enough bastard, then nobody else may notice how scared I am. Could just be."

"Everybody gets scared," the driver said, relaxing a little over the wheel. "You aren't the sort to lock up when you get scared, are you? So what's it matter?"

"Sure," Kelly agreed, "sure. The matter is that they want me to do something I've never done before. I'm not sure *anybody* could handle the job, and I swear to God I don't see how I can. I'm over my head and I don't mean a little bit."

They were waiting to turn on the Boulevard St. Jacques, their view of the Place blocked by the closed deuce and a half van ahead of them. The driver turned and looked steadily at Kelly. "If you really thought that," he said, "you'd have told them to stuff the job, wouldn't you? You'll be all right, Mr. Kelly."

Traffic and the sedan began moving again. Kelly laughed, as pleased to be flattered as the next man. After a moment, though, he said with whimsey in only the overtones, "But you know why I didn't? Because they fired me five years ago, booted my ass out of the—well, it's no secret, the NSA. They couldn't give me a damned thing that mattered after that, not a damned thing . . . except a chance to ram that termination back down their throats. And that's what they offered me, that chance. Can't lose, after all. If I pull it off, they were dopes to fire me. And if I screw up, well, I don't have to worry about that or any other goddam thing ever again."

Phillips did not speak as he took the sedan around the fountain of the traffic circle and south at increasing speed down the Avenue d'Italia. He genuinely was not in a hurry. None the less, the mass of traffic jostling for position demanded the driver's skills and awoke the aggressiveness that honed those skills. "Were you," he said at last as he tucked behind the bumper of a Jaguar, "hitting the sauce a little heavier than they liked?"

Kelly glanced up at him sharply. "They do talk, don't they?" he said with something like a smile. Then, "No, then I—I wasn't very much of a drinker, to tell the truth. It was. . . . Well, I met a girl in Venice when I was back in port, pretty and she, she seemed to like me. I liked her, I—well." Kelly cleared his throat, his eyes on the Jag's British license plate again. "Smart as a whip, that's God's truth. Very sharp, she was."

They were in the congestion of the Boulevard

Peripherique, slowing with the car ahead, then slipping sideways as a motorcyclist accelerated up a ramp and opened a gap. The Boulevard was a gapped concrete roof overhead, tire noise echoing from its pillars in a deep-throated rumble. Phillips was taut at the wheel, his hands at ten o'clock and two, making the tiny motions necessary to keep the sedan tracking down what had become the Avenue de Fountainebleau. He seemed oblivious of his passenger as Kelly continued, "She was an American, Polish background but born in Chicago, I checked her passport. You get antsy, you know, when they keep telling you the Russkies are out to learn everything you've got to tell. So I checked her purse when she was asleep, but it wasn't like I was worried, not really. And the passport was fine. Only. . . ."

Kelly wished he could forget they were on the Avenue de Stalingrad now. He didn't need to think of Russians, and he assuredly didn't need to say what he was about to say. But the words were finding their own way out, directed not at the stolid driver but perhaps at the self-righteous man who had been Tom Kelly one day five years ago when. . . . "Languages are my business, though. They were then. And there was something about her English . . . So I put in a query through channels, insisted they get me a picture from the file at State, no big deal . . . and I still didn't *think* there was anything wrong, just a feeling. Funny. She knew something was up, but I didn't, almost till—" He cleared his throat again.

To the left was the Thinis Cemetery, green shade and an occasional flash of stone past the vehicles in the north-bound lanes. Hospitals and cemeteries, take them away and there would be a lot less of Paris. A lot less of the world, but you could have death and corpses without either, and all the canals of Venice flow to the sea. . . .

"The picture was wrong," Kelly said to no one present. "She was a girl, a college student who'd gone to visit grandparents in Poland, her parents had died in a car crash. And one of her friends got a postcard from Greece, but that was all, she never was seen again. And now somebody with her passport and a new picture was living with an NSA field man. Oh, the CI boys loved it, they'd play her like a fish and see who she reported to. Only—" Kelly's lips were very dry and the tendons on his neck were standing out "—some girl was gone, gone from the world so that they could play their games, all of their games. You kill enemies, sure, but some kid who just wanted to find her roots and didn't dream a government would have her greased to get a US passport. . . . I—it bothered me. And I let something drop.

"It hadn't been Janna's doing . . . the kid, I mean," the agent continued. "But she was wired, she'd been living with me long enough to—worry what might happen if I learned she'd set me up. So she made a bad move, went for a gun as if she could point it and I'd freeze. Me! And . . . well, some of the old reflexes were there. Reflexes don't care, Phillips. Reflexes don't love anybody."

They were within the airport precincts now. The airliner taking off on a parallel course was an Aeroflot 11-62, carrying civilized diplomats and vacationers to Warsaw and beyond. "When she disappeared," Kelly said softly, "my Janna who wasn't Janna, they figured at first she'd been tipped off. Only they learned that people in the

Russian Embassy—she was being handled from Rome, not the consulate in Venice—they were panicked too, thought she'd defected. And then they decided that they'd talk to me about it under pentathol . . . and I told them to go screw themselves . . . and they told me I'd just resigned for the good of the service." Kelly managed a smile. "There were four of them in the room with me at the last, and I swear to God they were wearing bulletproof vests. Four of them and they were afraid of me." He paused. "Well, I'm back," he said. "Tom Kelly is back."

Phillips pulled the sedan into the kiss and go lane in front of the south terminal. "Good luck, sir," he said. "It's nothing you can't handle."

"Hope to hell you're right," said Kelly. With his radio and his AWOL bag, the dour civilian began to walk toward his future.

VII

The pair of young customs officials peered into the packing crate with more bemusement than concern. The one with the pencil-line moustache turned to Kelly and said in French, "You understand, Mr. Ceriani, that this machine—" he tapped the case with his pen, over the stenciled "Rank Xerox—London"—"is cleared for demonstration purposes only? It must not be sold."

Kelly nodded in agreement. His lightweight suit had borne up well on the short flight from Frankfurt, but he was already wondering whether April in Algiers would not demand a warmer selection of clothing than what he had brought. The other customs man was poking desultorily through Kelly's suitcases, open on the inspection table beside the crated copying machine. "Yes," Kelly said in his Italian-accented French, "we understand fully. I may invite clients to my suite to inspect the product, but by law there may be no store-front display, and all orders must be shipped from out of country rather than a local warehouse. Ours—Rank Xerox" —Kelly fumbled from a leather case a card identical in format to the ones he really used as an Olivetti representative—"we will ship from our warehouse in Marseilles. We understand that Algeria is choosing the route it deems proper to national self-sufficiency. We will comply fully with all national regulations."

The moustached official riffled the spiral notebook prominently labeled SPESE. It was quite real, though from Kelly's past and not his present persona. Its slap-dash listing of business expenses was the final proof that he was the salesman he claimed to be. The official said something to the other in Arabic, apparently a joke because they both laughed. He gave Kelly a friendly wave of his hand. "Good day, Mr. Ceriani," he said. "Have a pleasant stay in Algeria."

Kelly smiled back and quickly loaded his gear onto a hand truck. The line he had given the customs men would have been no more than the simple truth had he been in Algiers as a real business rep. The big corporations did not cut legal corners to do day-to-day business in foreign countries. Only in the aerospace field did the bottom-line potential of a sale make it justifiable to bribe—a Dutch prince or a German defense minister, say. . . . Otherwise, the economic risk of being banned permanently outweighed the momentary advantage of selling your demonstrator to a customer who was hot to trot.

And Tom Kelly had learned as well that if you had a solid product to sell, you could work within any system. The Algerians restricted foreign corporations as a proof of their socialism and their rise from a colonial past. The

restrictions hurt no one as much as the Algerians themselves. It would be generations, at least, before there
would be any indigenous copier manufacture, judging
from the dismal result when the Algerians tried to make
their own televisions. But it was their own country, and
they had a right to go to hell in their own way.

It was only as a representative of a sovereign government that Kelly could imagine himself flouting laws in
order to do his job.

The first cab in the rank was a white Peugeot 201
with an enthusiastic driver named Hamid. He helped
Kelly manhandle the crate and suitcases into the trunk,
muttering instructions to himself under his breath.
Hamid was obviously impressed both by his passenger's
air of importance and the fact that Kelly gave the Hotel
Aurassi as his destination. The Aurassi was flagship of
the state-owned system and a world-class hotel by any
standards. "Ah," said Hamid as he drove out of the cyclone-
fenced parking area, "are you then a scientist come for the
Conference?"

Gravel brushed from the lot spewed from beneath the
tires as the taxi cut onto the highway. The rear wheels
twitched, then bit against the two-lane blacktop. The
roadway was unexceptional, practically identical to any
state secondary road in Kelly's one-time home of North
Carolina. In the French fashion the trunks of the palm trees
along the shoulders of the road had been whitewashed six
feet up to provide cheap warning reflectors. "Ah, no," the
American agent said, "I'm only a salesman trying to turn a
dinar in copy machines. Have you carried many
Conference attendees already, then?"

Traffic was steady and heavy enough in both directions to make passing a suicidal impossibility. Hamid was relaxed, giving more attention to his passenger in the rear view mirror than to the road ahead. "Not as yet, no," he said, "and no doubt they will travel in official cars with no thought of how a poor man like me should feed five children. But perhaps you are not aware, sir, that in three days the Aurassi will be cleared to accommodate guests of the Conference? Zut, out"—Hamid flicked his right hand in a gesture of full dismissal, turning directly to look at Kelly as he did so. The Peugeot quivered no more than the road surface would have demanded anyway—"460 rooms, all turned over to the Conference. There is still time, though—I can carry you to the St. George, very nice also and downtown?"

"Goodness, I didn't know that," Kelly lied with a realistic frown. "Still, the firm will have given the address to customers already. I'll have to check in at the Aurassi, if only for a few days."

Hamid kept up a flow of cheerful information throughout the long ride from Dar al-Beida to the hotel on the western heights of Algiers. There was nothing that could be called a circumferential road per se, but a long stretch of well-laid divided highway sped them more than they were slowed by its increased traffic. Cars were of typical European makes, but they appeared to Kelly to be unusually standardized. When he asked about that, the driver laughed.

"You see the license?" Hamid explained, pointing toward the sedan in front of them. It was a Renault 5 throughout the French-speaking world and 'Le Car' in the

United States alone. "One-six means Algiers. One means a car, not a bus, whatever. And the next two numbers—79—are the year Sonacome imported it. *All* cars are imported by Sonacome except those for foreigners and the very wealthy for their own use. And except for a few limousines for the Presidency and heads of departments, all the cars each year are the same model, whoever offered Sonacome the best price. Still, there are colors—and a car is a car, no doubt."

"Somebody goes first class," the American said, pointing toward the pair of leather-suited motorcyclists talking on a grassed median. Their parked bikes were BMWs, blue-painted and obviously official even without the fact that the riders wore holstered pistols.

"Oh, yes," agreed Hamid, "the National Police. They *are* first class, you must know, but yes, they do not buy their equipment on low bid. When Sonacome buys Volkswagens for you and me to ride in, the cars are built under license in Brazil. When the police buy Volkswagens, they come from Germany, yes."

The terrain on the outskirts of Algiers reminded Kelly of the two trips he had made between Oakland and Travis Air Force Base, on his way still farther west. The hills looked dry, hinting at the harshness of rock; but this was not desert. Considerable construction was going on, multiple complexes of high rises. The workmanship appeared good and the buildings were attractive in detail. Colored tiles picked out the stuccoed concrete, and each unit had a balcony shaded by a concrete screen in one of a number of patterns. The size of the buildings, however, hit Kelly as his background reading had not done. Each block contained a good 1600 apartment units, and during a twenty mile ride they had passed at least a half-dozen being built. The population of Algeria was exploding. Gas revenues might keep the lid on for a time, but there would be a reckoning in the foreseeable future unless diversification provided something for the new citizenry to do beyond sitting in a government room.

The taxi swept up the long, curving drive to the Aurassi, confirming in Kelly's mind the presumption he had already drawn from the briefing file: the operation would have to take place elsewhere. The Hotel Aurassi was as effectively separated from its immediate surroundings as if it had been on an island. Chopped into an expanse of rock which had been unbuildable until enough money became available—even the Moon is developable if enough money becomes available—the Aurassi could be reached by its drive, a ramped causeway. Even the most limited security precautions would make it impossible for a car to reach the highway if anyone thought it should be stopped before then; and security precautions were not the sort of thing the Algerians skimped.

The building itself, though obviously constructed according to expensive architectural advice, was less attractive than the massive apartment blocks which were being built for the citizenry. The architects were the problem, as a matter of fact. The mass units were built with an eye to efficiency. Because they were to be occupied by people, however, their lines were picked out with local touches, the tiles and moldings and vari-colored stucco Kelly had noticed on the way. By contrast, the Aurassi was classic Bauhaus: a box on a slab, with no more of taste or of beauty than an automobile's radiator has—and far less real functionality than the radiator. Judging from their own attractive blends of practical necessity and human desire, the Algerians had probably wondered at the ugly, expensive block which foreign architects had designed for foreign travelers; but there are men who choose to sleep on nails, and there is no accounting for taste. . . .

Hamid pulled up under the concrete beams of the skeletonized porte-cochere. "Sir," he said, sweeping Kelly's door open. His left hand gestured expansively toward the lobby. "There is a bank at the desk if you . . . ?"

"Thank you indeed," the American said, handing the driver a wad of sixty dinars he had bought from the Bank of Rome. There were ten Swiss francs folded into the midst of the local currency. A pair of liveried porters were approaching. One of them whistled for the boy with the hand truck when he saw the packing case. "If I am served as well during the remainder of my stay in Algeria, the business I do will delight my employers."

Though that was probably a lie, Kelly thought as he followed the porters across the red carpeting of the lobby. This one wasn't likely to delight anybody until, at best, years in the future. By then, most people would have forgotten the cost.

VIII

On the third ring from the embassy switchboard, somebody picked up the extension and said, "Attaché, Sergeant Rowe speaking."

Kelly's eyes were on the Bay of Algiers; he had never been enough of a TV viewer that he felt compelled to stare into a dial as he talked on the phone. "Hello," he said without trying to counterfeit an accent, "this is Angelo Ceriani with Rank Xerox. We are informed that you have been requesting a look at our desktop copying system." The cue was "desktop," the only information about his arrival which Kelly had permitted to be given through the DIA system.

"Huh?"

Jesus Christ. Many of the ships standing far enough off-shore to be tiny white slivers in the sun were in fact supertankers. With a good pair of binoculars—"Yes," Kelly said aloud, with a calm that he could not have managed without a moment to cool off, "my firm received the request through, I believe, a Mr. Pedler of your Paris branch. Perhaps if you would check with your superiors . . . ?"

"From a Mr.—oh. *Oh!*" Sergeant Rowe swallowed audibly. "Sure, that's right, Mr.—well, we didn't have the name is all. Are you at the airport? I'll bring a car right out."

"Oh, that won't be necessary," the agent said through a grimace. "The equipment isn't set up yet, of course. But I'd like to drop by with a brochure shortly, and then later you and your superior may come here to my room at the Aurassi for a demonstration."

"Right, of course," the sergeant agreed. "Ah, well, I'll inform Commander Posner. He's been very interested in the new equipment. It, ah, it should really speed up office routine."

Yes, friend, it surely will do that, Kelly thought. Aloud he said, "I'll get a taxi, then. Good day."

Of course, if he really wanted to look at ships, the Company doubtless had a Celestron telescope with a coupled 35 mm SLR taking pictures of everything in the roadstead. More and more it seemed to Kelly that he would be smarter to spend his time looking at boats rather than trying to make bricks out of locally available materials, not—it appeared—including straw.

What the hell. He showered and changed, removing the sheath for his knife from the suitcase lining. He clipped the weapon to his waistband at the small of his back. What the hell.

IX

One advantage enjoyed by embassies located in the Mediterranean Basin is that they need not raise eyebrows and insult the host government in order to make themselves secure. The cab pulled to the side in the middle of a curve and stopped abruptly. Kelly was staring at a whitewashed wall ten feet high. It was too close to permit his door to open. The driver reached back and unlatched the back door on his side, ignoring the scream of brakes as a passing Fiat missed them by inches.

"American Embassy, you wanted," the driver said. His passenger paid, then slipped out and around the taxi in a quick motion, hoping the next vehicle would not sheer him off at the knees. The taxi spurted away, leaving Kelly on a street filled with traffic and traffic noise which rebounded between the high walls on either side.

A patrolman in a blue uniform, not the black leather of the National Police, eyed Kelly from a hundred feet away. Presumably the man was an official recognition of the embassy. Kelly walked to the nearest gate. It was steel plating on a grill-work of the same metal, probably the only change in external appearance since the place had been built a century or more ago. When he knocked on the steel, a man-sized door opened in the larger panel and an Algerian in some sort of khaki uniform waved Kelly in.

"American Embassy?" the agent asked doubtfully in French.

"Ah, yes," asserted the guard. Kelly stepped through into the beautifully landscaped grounds. The building itself, set back a hundred feet from the wall, was white with the varied profusion of design which "Moorish" shares with other popular architectures. There were up to three stories—four, perhaps, because a domed turret or two were visible. Windows, even on the upper floors, were closed by gratings no less functional for being of attractively wrought iron. Glazed tiles set off the border of each flat roof. Against the wall to the right of the gate was a guest house. An archway over the curving drive was covered with wisteria. The vines were as thick at the base as a man's thigh. A red Mustang was parked beyond the arch, and past it along the drive approached a white Chrysler sedan. There was a passenger in the back of the Chrysler, dimly visible through the tinted glass.

The guard was already swinging the squealing gate open. Kelly moved aside, but the car stopped abreast of him anyway. The back window whined down. The passenger was a slender man of fifty or so with perfect features and a look of distaste as he viewed Kelly. He was tall enough to hunch a little in his seat to look comfortably at the agent. "Yes?" he asked without warmth.

"Ah, Angelo Ceriani, sir," Kelly responded. He held a sheaf of Xerox brochures in his right hand. "About the copy machine."

The passenger sneered with the disdain of a man who felt insulted at the suggestion a copy machine might interest him. He turned to the guard and snapped in excellent French, "Badis, you've been told to send trades-men to the Chancery at once instead of admitting them here. Do so now!" The power window was already rising, clipping the last syllable as the limousine slid out into traffic. The guard looked apologetic. "The next building," he said, pointing down the street toward the relaxed policeman.

"Guess I've met the Ambassador, hey?" said Kelly. He stepped onto the street again. "This is the Residence?"

The guard's head was nodding, perhaps in agreement, when the gate clanged shut behind Kelly.

X

The Chancery grounds had something less of a manicured look than those of the Residence, but the two main buildings themselves were equally impressive. Further, there was more of a feeling of life to the place. Half a dozen Algerians were lounging on the inner side of the wall, talking and laughing. One, a slim, neat fellow, was in khakis like those of the Residence guard. The other men wore dull-colored sport coats over ordinary work clothing. Only the guard seemed interested when Kelly stepped through the open doorway.

"I have an appointment with Sergeant Rowe," the agent said in French. "My name is Ceriani."

"Sure," the guard agreed, waving his hand toward the building which sprawled on the right of the drive. "Front door, ask the man at the desk."

Kelly blinked doubtfully, then walked on. A magnetic detector arch was set up a few feet within the compound, far enough from the gate that the steel plating would not affect it. Obviously, that was a relic of more troubled times. To the left of the drive and set closer to the front wall than the main buildings was a low outbuilding. He glanced through the open doorway; it was a restaurant of some sort, with what must surely have been one of the best-looking cashiers in Algeria. She was tall and her black hair, held up with combs, flashed highlights. Several men, apparently locals, walked out talking in a non-European language.

The agent felt increasingly uncomfortable about what he had gotten himself into. Algiers was one of only a handful of US Embassies which had no Marine guard contingent. The absence was not wholly a disadvantage. A dozen young men who do not speak any of the local languages and whose idea of a good time may be limited to booze and broads can provide problems for the diplomats running the mission. That was especially true in a Moslem country with strict notions of proper conduct and a government which was not on the take from Washington.

But the problems occurred when things were going smoothly. When the mob was coming over the walls, somebody had to carry the eighty-pound sacks of telegrams to the shredder and somebody had to stand out front laying down tear gas until the job inside was finished. Especially if Tom Kelly's name happened to be on some of those telegrams.

And even while things were quiet—tune in again next week—it would have been nice if somebody had at least checked the identification of the total stranger heading for the Defense Attaché's Office. Security improved inside the building. The front door opened onto a small anteroom with a high, groined ceiling. The inner door would require blasting to open it if the magnetic latch were not thrown. Above, a TV camera flanked by a four-inch outlet eyed the visitor. Kelly suspected that the outlet was ready to dump CS on intruders, the way a similar rig had done in Tripoli a few years before when Qadafi had sent his thugs to sack the US Embassy there.

Of course, like the magnetic detector, the tear gas system might have been disconnected by now. "I am Angelo Ceriani, to see Sergeant Rowe," Kelly said, carefully facing the camera.

"One moment, please," crackled a voice in accented English. About thirty seconds later, the latch buzzed and Kelly stepped into the Chancery proper. He was in a roofed court. To the immediate right was a middle-aged Algerian seated at a desk holding a TV monitor, a telephone, and a separate intercom. A young American in sport clothes but with very short hair leaned over the stone balustrade from the floor above. "Sir?" he called. "Glad you could get here so promptly. I'm Doug Rowe and—oh, come on up the stairs, the commander's waiting."

The steps were of the same polished granite as the balustrade and the railing around the second floor. Kelly trotted up them, then followed Sergeant Rowe down a hall. Someone stuck his head around the corner behind them and called, "Say, Doug—"

Rowe and the agent turned. The speaker was a balding man wearing a white shirt and a vest, a little older and a little heavier than Kelly himself. He folded over the cable copy he held when he realized the sergeant was not alone. He said, "Sorry, I'll catch you later," before disappearing back around the same corner.

"Sure, Harry," Rowe said, waving to the man's back. "Harry Warner," the sergeant remarked to Kelly in an undertone as he knocked on the last office door. "He's the Station Chief. Cover's in Econ Section."

"How big's the CIA station here?" Kelly asked.

There was a mumble from within the office. Rowe opened the door, continuing, "Four slots with the one in Oran. Plus the Communicators, of course, though the whole embassy uses them for the cable traffic. Gee, I wish we had the money to throw around that those boys do."

"You must be Kelly," said the Defense Attaché, remaining seated. He held a cigarette, and the ashtray on his desk was overflowing.

Kelly had never learned a good way of dealing with naval officers. Commander Posner extended a hand over his desk without rising. Kelly took it.

"Yes, sir," he said, "I'm Tom Kelly."

Posner gestured abruptly toward one of the basswood and naugahyde chairs with which his office was furnished. "I think the Ambassador would like to have the money Warner can throw around, Sergeant," he said. "But I gather that's just the sort of budget this office has suddenly been blessed with. *Is* that the case, Mr. Kelly?"

"Well, I understand this operation has a pretty high priority, that's right," the agent said. Posner's trick of staring at him through a stream of cigarette smoke made him uncomfortable. "I suppose if it all works out, there'll be promotions all round," Kelly added in an attempt to brighten the conversation.

Posner leaned forward. "From the little I have been told, Mr. Kelly," he said, enunciating precisely, "I would presume that if your scheme works out, the least undesirable result will be the immediate closing of this mission and the expulsion of all its personnel."

Kelly leaned back in his chair, crossing an ankle over a knee. Fine, if that was the way it was to be played. "Well," he said, "from what I've seen, all Third World countries'd be smarter to close all great-power embassies. It's the only way to keep their elections from being rigged and their politicians bought by outsiders. But since none of that has anything to do with our job—yours and mine and the sergeant's, here"—Kelly waved to Rowe, already seated in another of the American-made chairs—"I propose we move on. Have you got the contact we need in the Aurassi?"

Commander Posner held an icy silence for some seconds while the sergeant twitched on his seat. At last the Attaché said, "We have, yes, one of the desk clerks . . . the one who gave us the room numbers you requested. As we expected, none of the Russians attending the Conference will be billeted in the hotel."

"Sure," Kelly agreed, "but the number you sent me is the room that the contact agent, Hoang Tanh, will be using during the Conference, isn't it? That's the one I booked from London as Angelo Ceriani."

Sergeant Rowe fidgeted again. The commander said, "I'm afraid that wouldn't have been possible, Mr. Kelly. We gave you the number of the room across the hall from

Tanh's instead. The one in question is kept on a long-term rental for business purposes by the manager of a German cement firm. He'll be put out for the Conference itself, of course, but the clerk refused to take the chance of disturbing that arrangement for us. I made him a very sizeable offer." Posner's face worked, leaving no doubt of how he felt about raw bribery. "Fifty thousand dinars."

"Christ Jesus!" the agent snapped. "This German clown can screw his girlfriends next door for a couple days, can't he? He'll have to make other arrangements during the Conference, so he can make them a couple days early! How did you put it to this clerk, anyway?"

"Perhaps you'd like to try yourself, Mr. Kelly," Posner retorted. "The Pentagon seems to have the impression that you can walk on water, after all!" He stubbed out his cigarette and fumbled for the pack.

"Sir," said Sergeant Rowe. "There was his nephew, you know."

Commander Posner flicked his hand enough to drop the plastic lighter he held. "I checked that," he said. "I told you, it isn't possible."

"This whole damn thing may not be possible," Kelly said mildly. He rotated the chair seat so that he faced the sergeant's profile rather than the desk. "Tell me about this nephew, Sergeant."

"I said—" Posner began.

"If you will!" shouted the agent, snapping his head toward the Attaché like a gun turret. His right arm, cocked on the chair back, was tense. The tendons drew the skin of the thick wrist into pleats. In a quieter voice but one which would have been suitable for reading death sentences, Kelly continued, "Commander, I would not presume to tell you your business. This is my business, and I need to know absolutely everything about it." He turned back to the sergeant. "Ah—Doug?" he prompted.

The sergeant looked at Kelly rather than his own superior. Posner's hands were shaking too much to successfully light a fresh cigarette. "Well," Rowe said, "the clerk has a nephew, his sister's son, who wants to go to engineering school in the States. Got accepted at Utah, I think it is. Only"—he waved, caught Posner's eyes, and quickly focused back on Kelly—"the kid had goofed. A couple years ago he'd applied for a US visa while he was in Paris."

Kelly shrugged to move the story along. He had never heard that applying for a visa was a crime. The soldier bobbed his head and said, "It's a game the State Department plays with the Ministry of Foreign Affairs here, you see. The MFA only grants visas to US citizens who've applied at the Algerian consulate in DC. So we only grant visas to Algerians who apply here in Algiers. It's like asking why they dye pistachio nuts—doesn't make a damned bit of sense, it just happens."

"Rowe," said the commander, who had managed to light another cigarette at last, "keep to the facts and leave the insulting comments for our visitor, if you please."

"The nephew got turned down in Paris," the sergeant continued more quietly, "because of that. That wouldn't have mattered except that when he filled out the new application here, he said he'd never been turned down. Maybe he forgot, maybe he thought it'd hurt his chances the second time to have blown it before. Anyhow, they've got computers in Foggy Bottom, and they turned up the previous application right away. That's lying on a visa application, and that's the kiss of death for *ever* getting a US visa issued. They tell me."

Frowning, Kelly turned to the Defense Attaché. "OK," he said, "so we've got a kid who's eligible for a US student visa except for a technical screw-up. And we've got a clerk who'll give me the room I need if the kid gets that visa. Is that right?"

"We *don't* need Room 327, we can operate from 324," the commander said in a clipped voice. "And in any case, the rule can't be waived. I took the matter up with Ambassador Gordon himself."

Tom Kelly gave Posner a smile that no one in the room thought was friendly. "What's the word on commo here?" he asked, a cat testing the surface before leaping. "I know what I've been told in Paris, but that's not always how it looks on the ground."

Sour but uncertain, Posner said, "We received notice of this—operation—by courier. He also brought a set of program disks. We have been instructed to encode all operational materials ourselves on the embassy mini-computer, using the disks we received from the courier. We are then to pass the encrypted message to the Communicators. In other words"—the Commander's voice rose and he had to tent his fingers to keep them steady—"to completely divorce this office from the mission as a whole. I can tell you that the Station Chief regards all this as a serious breach of security—and that the Ambassador is considering filing a strong protest at the insult."

"Yeah, well," Kelly said. "Well, we don't want to add

to his Excellency's severe problems, do we? He might get peeved and slobber all over the finish of his limo. . . . So we'll hand in this cable in clear, Immediate—Night Action, addressed"—Commander Posner's mouth opened, but the agent did not let him speak—"DAO Paris. Arrange student visa issued—fill in the name and whatever else you need, Rowe—most urgent, reply copy Ambassador Algeria, signed Cuttlefish." Kelly's grin was real this time and a trifle rueful as he added, "That's me, Cuttlefish. We also serve who pacify budgies, I suppose."

Rowe was already out of his chair and swinging toward the door. "Sergeant, come back here!" gurgled the Defense Attaché. With his voice under a little better control, Posner turned to Kelly and added, "You can't send that. Are you insane?"

"It's got to be sent," the agent said. "Commander, it doesn't go out over your name, it's in mine. And if nothing comes back, I'm the idiot for getting mixed up with the USG again and trusting them to back me. Sergeant Rowe, I don't want to put you in the middle. If you'll guide me to the code room, I'll hand in the message myself."

Rowe looked at the Attaché. "Commander," he said, "the orders were specific. I'll take care of the cable." As he passed through the door, he added over his shoulder, "I still go by Doug, Mr. Kelly." The door closed. Behind Commander Posner, the great harbor glittered. It was closer than it had been from the Aurassi, but the film of cigarette smoke in the Attaché's office dulled the view. Coils stirred in the draft of the sergeant's departure. "Commander," said the agent, wishing there were a radio on in the room, "we've got to work together. I don't have the time to get you replaced, and you don't have the clout to get rid of me. It's just that simple." He hunched forward a little and added, "Would you like me better if I'd been to Annapolis and wore a yard of gold braid?"

"I wouldn't have liked this operation if the Joint Chiefs sat down in my office and briefed me on it, Mr. Kelly," the Attaché said. He hammered the palm of his right hand on the desk. Raising his eyes he added, "It stinks. It stinks like a *sewer*, and I don't appreciate being dragged into it."

Kelly nodded, holding the officer's eyes. "I understand that," he said as earnestly as any salesman ever spoke, "believe me, I do. But you and I have our orders. And behind those orders stands the nation we serve. There are decisions that are yours and mine to execute but not to make, just as good soldiers have been doing since the world began. If you can't accept that, Commander Posner, your argument isn't with me—it's with your uniform and the oath you swore when you put it on."

Christ, what bullshit, Kelly thought as he leaned back again. But not all of him thought it was bullshit, and he knew that too. . . .

A brick in the face could not have hit Posner any harder. The Defense Attaché swallowed. He started to draw on his cigarette, looked at it, and crushed it out in transferred anger. "Mr. Kelly," he said, "I"—he glared at his brass ashtray—"I apologize if I've seemed unhelpful. As you point out, we didn't choose this world, but we have our duties to carry out in it." He swallowed again before meeting the agent's eyes. "As for the Kabyles, I've arranged a meeting with what we believe is their leadership in the city tomorrow afternoon. At least, there is a group of some sort calling itself the Association of Kabyles. They have a rough idea of what you desire"—Posner managed a bleak smile—"which is all that I have, of course. I assume you'll conduct these negotiations yourself."

Kelly nodded. "Right, right," he said. "And we don't need an army, twenty people'll be plenty if they know what they're doing. God help us all if they don't . . ." He looked out at the Mediterranean, the dazzle from blue waves. He shook his head back into the present. He was a black-headed lion who knew the spearmen were close, knew the odds were with them . . . but also knew that there was nothing on the plain that he could not rend if he chose to. "No," the agent continued in a voice that barely reached the Attaché and was not really meant for him, "it doesn't matter if they speak for their people, whatever . . . so long as they can raise the muscle for one quick and dirty job."

Kelly blinked, fully present again, and added, "Where'd you get a contact, anyway? Not that it matters so long as you do have one."

Posner coughed and lit the last cigarette from his pack. He crumpled the foil and cellophane and skidded them off the end of his desk into a wastebasket. "I suppose you could call him a walk-in," the Attaché admitted. It was nothing to be ashamed of. The Algerians, while not positively hostile, kept the agents of imperialist powers on a pretty short leash. "One of the Chancery guards, actually, Mustapha bou Djema. He'd been working for a few weeks when he stopped me when I was going out one evening. I almost brushed him off, told him he could talk to the GSO if he had a problem. But it wasn't work, he wanted to talk about 'politics,' that's the normal formula"—Kelly nodded in understanding—"and he'd picked me instead of Warner because I was a military officer. He'd been in French service, it turned out, as well as fighting against them later during the Revolution. I really think that Mustapha's group may be . . ." the Attaché paused, "quite significant, but I suppose you'll be able to judge better. Mustapha's English isn't any better than my French, I'm afraid."

There was a knock at the door. Both men tensed instinctively. "Yes?" the commander called.

Sergeant Rowe opened the door. "Just me, sir," he said. "DeVoe says the cable's gone out."

"Then," remarked Kelly, rising from his chair with the awkwardness of a man just awakened, "I think we've covered all we need to for the moment. Is there some-place around here to get lunch? I don't eat much on planes, and"—he smiled at himself—"I left my packet of Lufthansa peanuts in my other jacket when I changed."

"Ah, why don't I run you down to the snack bar?" the sergeant suggested. "It's a damned good place to eat lunch—and besides, it's about the only place except for the hotels. Lunch isn't an Algerian meal. You want to come, sir?" he added to Commander Posner.

The Defense Attaché shook his head, managing a smile of his own. "If DeVoe's seen the message," he said, "then I can expect a visit from Harry Warner as soon as you leave the room. I may as well stay and take my medicine."

Kelly gestured toward the door. "Lead on, Doug," he said. "My stomach follows."

XI

Sergeant Rowe waited until they were outside the building to ask, "How do you like Commander Posner, then?" A haze was banked at high altitude along the line of the shore. The breeze across the grounds smelled of flowers, but it was brisk enough to make the agent's suit more comfortable than the sergeant's short sleeves.

"Well," Kelly said, "things'll work out. Only, people might remember when they're setting up a deal like this that you can't make much of a sow's ear from a bolt of silk, either."

It was almost two o'clock, local time, and the snack bar had generally cleared out. The stunning black-haired woman who had been at the cash register when Kelly first walked by had been replaced by a young Algerian male. The agent realized that he had not seen any local women—except the previous cashier—at work on the mission grounds. Welcome to Islam, where women have their place—and where they'd damned well better keep to it.

Rowe led the way to the counter at the back. A menu was chalked on a dusty blackboard. The room was packed with plastic chairs around small formica-topped tables. It looked much like a big-city lunchroom anywhere in the US. "Do you like veal parmigiana?" Rowe asked.

"Huh?" responded Kelly. He had been expecting a hamburger—with luck. "Oh. Sure. It's good here?"

"Two parmigianas and coffee, Achmed," Rowe called through the window. He began running coffee from the big pot into a pair of mugs. "Everything's good here, Anna sees to that," the sergeant explained. "Cream."

Kelly shook his head. "Hot and black," he said with a grin, taking one of the coffees and the chair to which Rowe gestured him. There were half a dozen men sitting in pairs at tables. Only two of them were North Americans, judging from their appearance. Beyond the partition in back came the hiss and clatter of kitchen equipment. "What is this, anyway?" the agent asked. "A private restaurant?"

"Well, it's operated as a service to embassy officers and employees," the sergeant explained as he sipped his coffee. "The prices are good, and anyway, there really isn't much place to get lunch in Algiers, like I said upstairs. For a while there, they were feeding all sorts of people off the street—which was great for the American School here, it gets the profits, but it was lousy security, of course. And even later, there was a problem with the maintenance people. The mission maintains all the off-post housing here, you see. The maintenance crews all decided they'd forgotten some part or tool and drove back to the compound here right around noon each day." Rowe glanced around at the local nationals talking over the remains of their own meals. "Still some of that, the GSO tells me. But except for here, you either carry your lunch or you buy a rotisseried chicken and eat it on the sidewalk. Somebody really ought to start a lunch counter, but the government isn't crazy about private enterprise even in traditional businesses. They'd probably have a cat-fit if even a local started something new."

Someone called from the service window and thrust a pair of heavy china plates out onto the counter. Rowe heard, even over the clashing of a boy hauling a tub of dirty dishes into the back.

Before Kelly could get up to help, the sergeant had fetched the plates and pocketed the check. "I always eat Italian here," Rowe said as he raised a forkful of veal, "but believe me, if Anna decides to fix Eskimo, that's going to be good too."

It was excellent, especially when Kelly had figured the price chalked on the board in dinars and found that it was less than three dollars. Naive travelers were often stunned to learn that a hotel room or a meal in Third World countries was generally more expensive than an equivalent would have been in New York City. Tom Kelly had not been called naive for a long time.

As Kelly and the sergeant finished their meals, the two North Americans carried their plates to the counter. "Say, Doug," said one of them, "did you check about the car?"

"Ah," said Rowe, "Syd Westram, Don Mayer, this is

Tom . . . that is, Angelo Ceriani. Syd and Don are in Econ Section."

"Actually, I'm in Consular," said Westram as he shook Kelly's hand.

Kelly grinned. "Right," he said. "I'm in business equipment." He continued eating without haste as the other three wrangled quietly over the car the two Company men wanted to borrow from the Attaché's Office for some trip or other. Rowe lost interest clearly enough to resume eating himself in the middle of the discussion. The others continued to push long after it was obvious that the sergeant had no authority to clear the loan. Still muttering to one another, the CIA officers finally walked off to pay. The kitchen door opened and out walked the woman Kelly had first seen at the cash register.

She wore white slacks and a red cotton blouse that was loose enough to be comfortable but left no doubt of her sex. She was as tall as Kelly but her weight was a good forty pounds beneath the agent's one-sixty. Kelly had never in his life dreamed of looking that good.

"Anna," called Sergeant Rowe, "we were just saying how good the veal is. Oh, Angelo Ceriani, meet Annamaria Gordon."

Kelly stood up carefully so as not to overset the center-balanced table. He made a half bow.

The woman laughed happily and extended her hand. "My, so gallant," she murmured in Italian.

"Lady," replied the agent in the same language, "so lovely a one as yourself deserves the gallantry of true gentlemen, not such as myself."

"Mother of God, he speaks like a Florentine!" Annamaria cried in delight. She clasped Kelly by both shoulders. "Oh, you don't know what it's like to—the Italian Ambassador is an old stick and deaf besides. And his *wife*—Dougie"—switching to English—"Where have you been hiding this one?"

"Well," said Sergeant Rowe, trapped in his chair by the table behind him and the woman reaching over his head, "he's—"

"Oh, of course!" Annamaria broke in, "he has to be the, the Thomas Kelly who has my husband so angry, that is so?"

Kelly's skin prickled again with fear and anger. This time the fear was not misplaced, though the last of the customers had left the room and it was unlikely that the fellow at the cash register could hear even if he did speak English. Anna was an embassy wife, that was clear, and her husband had done too goddamned much talking out of—

"I'm sorry if his Excellency is concerned," Sergeant Rowe was saying.

Jesus Christ, she was the Ambassador's wife.

Annamaria—Mrs. Ambassador Gordon—tugged Kelly out into the central aisle of the lunchroom. Releasing him and stepping back a pace, she eyed the agent up and down with the dispassion of a horse-buyer. Embarrassed but as much at a loss as was Rowe—who had finally struggled to his feet—Kelly found himself staring back at the lady.

Her chain necklace was of gold and heavy. It was the one thing besides her beauty that seemed to suit her status.

Reverting to Italian, the black-haired woman asked, "Have you seen the city yet? You won't have, will you, since you've just arrived."

"Well, I'm not here solely on pleasure . . ." Kelly temporized, distrusting the conversation though he could not believe it was headed where it seemed to be.

Belief be damned. "Come then, this afternoon. I'll be your guide instead of Doug here," said Annamaria. "It's been *so* long since I've heard Italian spoken by anyone in the least interesting. And if my husband is so angry without even having met you, you must be interesting."

"Ah, Mrs. Gordon," said the agent, switching back to English but trying not to show his horror, "I'd be delighted to see Algiers with you some other time. But we're going to be busy for the next couple days and—"

Annamaria smiled with a cheerful wickedness. Her eyes were set wide, their pupils very dark. She raised one finger and said, still in Italian, "You don't intend to see the city? Poof! And what are you going to do this afternoon, tell me?"

The sergeant blinked, aghast now that Kelly's words had shown him how things were tending. The agent himself met Annamaria's eyes. The humor of the whole business struck him and he started to laugh. The dish boy looked around in surprise, then ducked back within the kitchen. "All right," said Kelly, "to tell the truth, I was going to get a tour of the Casbah. Want to come along?" As a dip's wife, the woman had an automatic "Secret" clearance, barring the kind of negative evidence that would in all likelihood have prevented her husband from getting an ambassadorship. And by God, if there was a better way of giving the establishment a kick in the ass than this, Kelly couldn't imagine what it was.

"All right, give me fifteen minutes to shower and change," Annamaria said, her smile broader. "And remember, you have to talk to me."

"Sir," said Rowe.

"Tom, for Chrissake," Kelly remarked, his eyes still on the woman. "No, Mrs. Gordon, you two can pick me up in front of the Aurassi in an hour and a half. And one thing"—this in Italian, and the tone brought her around with her tweezer-shaped eyebrows rising—"what you do when you're alone is your own business . . . and slacks are fine with me, make a lot of sense. But if you're going to be with me in the Old City and I'm working, which you know I am—wear a skirt, please? With a skirt, we're tourists and nobody cares. In trousers, we're stupid tourists—and it's not our country to be stupid in."

Annamaria's expression was momentarily as black as her hair. "Do you take particular pleasure in ordering women around, Mr. Kelly?" she asked in a new tone.

"Sometimes I think I get the most pleasure from killing a bottle of Jack Black alone in my room," the agent said quietly. "But that won't get the job done this time. Mrs. Gordon, if you don't like something I say or do, just tell me to go piss up a rope." The phrase had a ring of unexpected obscenity in translation. "But if I'm working, don't assume that I do anything for fun."

After a moment, the beautiful wide smile flashed back across the lady's face. "In person, Rufus is going to like you even better than he does now, Mr. Kelly," she said. "Well—the Aurassi at four, then."

Annamaria strode off without self-consciousness. Her walk had the grace natural to a slim-hipped woman with perfect health and assurance.

"Let's go call me a cab from your office," said Kelly, pulling a wad of dinars from his pocket as he led the way to the cashier. "Just in case somebody's watching, I'd as soon not enter and leave the compound in official cars." Rowe had taken the check, but the prices were in plain sight on the menu board. Kelly didn't intend to bum even a cheap meal from somebody trying to make ends meet on a sergeant's pay. "You know," he added, "Mrs. Gordon isn't what you, ah, expect in an ambassador's wife."

"A human being, you mean?" Rowe replied with a smile as they stepped back onto the grounds. He sobered. "Yeah, well. I mean, Ambassador Gordon's a good choice in a lot of ways. He speaks French and he's traveled a lot, that's how he met Anna, I suppose. But he's old money, you see, his family's got a big ad agency in Houston . . . and a lot of the time, he seems to think the whole mission ought to be outfitted with servants' uniforms. There's a swimming pool on the Residence grounds. It's supposed to be for use of the whole mission and their families, but word got out as soon as the Gordons arrived in country that the hoi polloi had better keep to their own side of the wall, thank you."

Rowe opened the front door and paused in the Chancery anteroom. "Henri," he said into the voice plate, "would you call a cab to take Mr. Ceriani back to his hotel, please."

"I'll need to rent a car, I suppose," Kelly said as they

walked back toward the gate. "Right now, I need a guide, though."

The sergeant nodded. "Sure, they'll deliver one to the Aurassi, just check with the clerk." He said nothing for a moment, then resumed. "It's the usual thing, big frog in a small puddle. You see it in army posts, God knows. But maybe it's worse in an embassy because there's nobody this side of DC that ranks the Ambassador, even though he's got only twenty people under him."

"Few enough higher in DC, too," Kelly agreed.

"And I don't suppose it was political contributions to the Secretary of State that got him appointed."

"Sure, being able to call the President by his first name may—affect how you feel about a sergeant E-6," Rowe said. "Or a commander O-5, for that matter. But the thing is, I think a lot of the way the Ambassador acts toward everybody else is the way that Anna doesn't give a hoot in hell for all the crap and ceremony herself. She goes to receptions when she wants to—and she knocks 'em dead in a black dress, let me tell you—not that *I* get invited to many. But that's when she wants to. And instead of running the mission wives like happens at most posts, charities and garden parties and such, she runs the snack bar. And that's great for my wife, she'd be at the bottom of the pecking order same as I am with the mission . . . only I think life with his Excellency might be a little easier for the rest of us if Anna didn't rub it in quite so much."

Kelly chuckled. "When they come up with a perfect society," he said, "let me know about it. Not that they'd want my sort anywhere around."

The group loitering at the gate had changed slightly in composition but not in character. Someone had tuned a French transistor radio to a station that was playing Arabic music. Kelly had never learned the conventions of Eastern music, but tuned low—as this was—he found it soothing. It reminded him of CW traffic received through severe heterodyne, part and parcel of much of his life. "In Nam," he said aloud to the sergeant, "when I was in base camp on stand-down, the hooch maids used to listen to horse operas while they worked."

"Westerns?" Rowe said in surprise.

"That too," Kelly explained with a grin. "There'd be the sound of hoofs as the hero rode up to the ranch. He'd sing to the heroine, she'd sing back, and then the chorus of cow-hands sang to everybody. Eventually the hero would clop off, sing threats at the villain and vice-versa, and then they'd have a gunfight. 'Bang!' 'You scoundrel, you have wounded me, but my love gives me strength to overcome you yet.' 'Bang-bang-bang!' 'Haughty fool, I have slain your betters a thousand times—see the notches here on my gunbutts.' This'd go on through what I swear must've been a mini-can of ammo before the hero triumphed and married the girl."

"Jeez, that sounds awful," said Rowe.

Kelly grinned. "Well, maybe I'm not a good source for opera. I heard *Rigoletto* at La Scala and I didn't think a whole lot of that, either."

Voices loud enough to carry filtered in from the street. The North Americans looked at one another. Both stepped through the open doorway.

A Fiat sedan had pulled up near the Residence gate.

The driver, a tall black man in a dashiki and slacks, had gotten out and was arguing with the guard. Both men were gesturing and shouting—the guard in French, the black apparently in English disguised by distance and an accent. "That's part of the Ambassador's management style, what you see there," said the sergeant.

The black strode haughtily past the guard and into the Residence grounds. Still shrieking, the man in khaki followed with his fists clenched. "Jesus," muttered Kelly in amazement, "It's a damn good thing the guards aren't issued guns." Then, "What do you mean about the Ambassador being responsible?"

Rowe stepped out along the wall and motioned the agent to follow him, not that the Algerians within were showing any signs of interest in the conversation. Cars, braking and changing down as they rounded the curve, provided background noise. "The Ambassador's secretary," the sergeant said, "Buffy Tuttle. She lives in the guest house right by the Residence gate."

"I've seen it," Kelly agreed.

"Well," Rowe went on, "that's a good place because she has to be on call pretty much all the time. And she dates a lot—she's single and damned good looking. But his Excellency doesn't like it that the guys courting her park right in front of his door. He won't tell *her* that himself, maybe because she's black and he's afraid of being called a racist . . . so he tells the guards to make all Buffy's visitors park across the street in the Annex lot. And they pay about as much attention to the guard as you'd expect." Rowe nodded toward the Fiat.

Kelly shook his head. "His Excellency's going to have

blood all over his gravel if he doesn't watch out," he remarked.

"Sure," agreed Rowe. "And what's even worse is, well . . . there aren't a whole lot of blacks in Algiers, you know. Most of them calling on Buffy are from the Chaka Front office downtown."

"What!" the agent blurted. A great Magirus Deutz truck passed, its diesel blasting as it climbed the hill. During the interval, while both men squeezed their backs still closer to the wall, Kelly decided he must have misunderstood.

"Yeah, that's right," the sergeant said gloomily as the truck disappeared. "Goons from the South African liberation organization. They've got an information office here, may as well be an embassy. Which is fine, but . . ."

"But this is the secretary who's typing and filing most of the Top Secret material in the mission?" the agent said, not really asking it as a question. "Jesus."

"Neither Harry Warner nor the commander's real pleased about it," Rowe agreed. "In the country team meetings, the Ambassador says it may prove a useful channel of information from the Chaka Front. I don't know. Maybe he'd say the same thing if she was dating Mossad agents, maybe he wouldn't. . . . Anyway, he's the boss in this puddle, isn't he?"

A yellow Renault cab pulled up with a shriek of brakes. "Jesus," Kelly repeated. Then, as he got in, he called back, "We'll meet again soon, then, Sergeant, and get down to business!"

XII

It wasn't particularly a surprise to Kelly that Annamaria Gordon drove up in front of the Aurassi alone. It did surprise him that the Ambassador's wife was at the wheel of a Volkswagen, not the red Mustang which Kelly had seen parked in the Residence drive that morning.

Annamaria started to lean from her window to speak to the uniformed doorman. Kelly, striding from a bench near the lobby doors, caught that functionary's eye in time to avoid being paged. He got in on the passenger side, meeting the woman's bright smile as she thrust the car into gear. "I thought," she said, "that you might want to be driven around in something less conspicuous than an American car with diplomatic plates, so I rented this. If you want to drive it yourself, though, you have to be approved by the rental agency."

"Glad to know you're so scrupulous about legalities," the agent said with a smile. He adjusted the hang of his camera. "I'd figured we'd park at a distance and walk—"

Annamaria nodded. She was wearing a dress of gray silk, simple enough and rather high in the neck. While it showed little flesh, however, it did nothing to disguise the way her muscles worked beneath its opacity. Her hair was held up by combs of black wood instead of the plastic that had sufficed earlier. Annamaria might be unconventional, but she was not wholly unconcerned with the impression she gave, either. "We'll have to walk if you really want to see the Casbah," she said at Kelly's pause.

"Oh, fine," the agent said. "Anyway, it wasn't the end of the world if the car was conspicuous, but that was damned good thinking anyway. I appreciate it."

They were speaking in Italian. It provided a sort of time slip for both of them. For Kelly, the language returned him to his five most recent years as a civilian, where tension was the success or failure of a sales pitch. For the woman, Italian was a return to her early twenties, before the ten years of marriage that relegated the tongue of her birth to diplomatic gatherings—and that rarely.

Thinking about nothing that he should have been, the agent added, "Not that I don't think we'll attract more attention than Doug and I would have . . . but I doubt anybody's going to be looking at me long."

"A tourist couple," Annamaria said. She looked at her passenger and gestured. The habit made Kelly wince internally as they sped south. "And you with your camera for what? Protective coloration? Very clever."

"I told you I was working," the agent said, looking out his window at the two and three-story buildings stepping down the gradient of the street. "I might have needed to talk to Doug, you know."

"Not in front of me," the woman said. "Not business." She flooded Kelly with her smile again. "Besides, a couple blends in. Would you scandalize folk with the appearance of a menage?"

Kelly cleared his throat and turned his attention to the car itself on the assumption that he would be driving it soon. It was a standard VW Passat, basically what would have been a Dasher in the US. A decal on the back window announced in large, blue letters, "Made in Brasil"—surely as striking a monument to the omnipresence of English as one could have found. The engine seemed as peppy as the automatic transmission permitted it to be. None of the inevitable squeals and rattles seemed to signal any major mechanical difficulties.

"Unless you have a preference," Annamaria announced, "we'll park at the bottom. It's all a hillside, you know. The natives got the part of the city that the French didn't want to take over for themselves, and then just enough of them were permitted to stay to be servants for their betters. Not," she added with a rueful smile, "that we Italians can claim much better." Swinging right at a traffic light that had already gone red, she explained, "This is the Rue Bab el Oued, you know?"

"The Watergate," Kelly said, dredging up some fragments of Arabic gleaned during his years in the Med.

Annamaria turned to gesture behind her though there appeared to be nothing but office buildings and apartment blocks. She continued, "Back there in the Bab el Oued was the poor section of the city—but for whites, you see. That's where the Pieds Noirs lived, that's where the Secret Army terrorists hid and built bombs to kill Arabs with, to keep France from ever freeing Algeria. . . . But they weren't French, the Pieds Noirs, except in citizenship, the most of them. They were Italians, like me—or truly, they were Algerians or could have been, were they not so quick to slaughter innocents to prevent that result."

Annamaria pulled into a parking space. In the near distance sunlight glittered on a fountain which the agent supposed was in the Plaza of the Martyrs. "I guess it's natural that the people who're worst off fight the hardest to keep the little they think they have," Kelly said as he got out of the car. "And I guess it's natural that they do it in the most self-destructive ways possible, too, because the people with all the experts to advise them generally manage to do the same goddam thing themselves." He laughed and added abruptly, "They go out and hire people like me, for instance."

There were no vehicular streets in the Casbah save the Rue Amar Ali which bisected it on a diagonal opposite to the one Kelly and Mrs. Gordon were taking. Access was by pedestrian ways, sometimes covered and always lowered upon by jutting upper stories. Sometimes the passages were broad enough that a traveler could spread both arms and touch neither wall. More often, they were so narrow that two persons passed each other with difficulty.

As the couple worked north and steeply upward from the Ali Bitchin Mosque, Kelly took surreptitious photographs. His old Nikon F was fitted with a 24-mm semi-fisheye lens. The pictures would be severely distorted by the short lens, but nothing longer would have been of the least use in such close quarters. Further, the wide angle lens could be used without normal aiming. Kelly had brazed a stud to the camera's back. The other end was hooked in one of his belt holes. That kept the slung camera pointed forward and slightly upward as he walked. Whenever the agent was ready to take a photograph, he would turn his head and say something to Annamaria behind him. His right index finger stroked the release unnoticed. The heavy Nikon shutter made more noise than Kelly would have liked, but there was generally background sound chattering through the narrow passages. At any rate, the agent did not now have time to get used to new equipment.

The ground levels of the three-and four-story buildings were mostly shops, less frequently a hammam—a Turkish bath—or even the gorgeously-tiled anteroom of a neighborhood mosque. Store-front churches were not unique to American inner cities. In one open room, a man shaped chair seats with a draw-knife while two friends argued and smoked hand-rolled cigarettes. A shop sold horsemeat, dark and without the marbling of fat typical of even lean beef. That shop was flanked on one side by a display of wicker bird-cages, each unique; and on the other by kitchen equipment of plastic and aluminum, sold by a heavy-set woman in the white gown of a widow.

The passages twisted and forked. Rarely could Kelly see more than ten feet ahead or behind him. At intervals, a step or a flight of steps would mount the grade, making the tracks as impassible by donkeys as they were to motor vehicles. The thought of carrying out a military operation here, where the walls were stone and the twists and turnings left every attacker alone, was chilling. The Germans had found Stalingrad an icy hell. For the

French, the Battle of Algiers was a matter of entering a sarcophagus some moments before death. Kelly smiled and clicked his camera and occasionally consulted the French map he held folded in his left hand.

One could see shops only when on top of them. Some, however, announced their presence at a distance with odors as distinctive as display signs. A bread shop flooded one passage with the smell of baguettes, freshly baked on the premises; and the rich, chocolaty aroma of coffee pursued Kelly a hundred feet from where the beans were weighed and ground and blended from burlap bags. There was no stench of dung, of sewage. Once they passed a man urinating against a wall, but defecation was as private a matter as in any American suburb. Further, unlike many Western cities, the Casbah had no population of domestic animals spreading their daily burden of waste.

Near the top of the Old City, Kelly paused at a stone railing to rest and change film. Below them loomed the Safir Mosque. The ground rose so abruptly to them that the Mediterranean could be glimpsed over the roofs and clothing spread to dry. The agent found he was breathing hard. That irritated him. He made a reasonable effort to stay in shape, but age was creeping up on him with its claws out.

"How old are you?" he asked his companion. It was the first real conversation they had had since they left the car.

The woman laughed and tossed her head. "To think I called you gallant," she said. "But I'm 34, since you ask."

"It looks a lot younger on you than 38 feels on me,"

Kelly said, his eyes on the film leader he was cranking through the sprockets. Carefully, he set the camera back in place, then clicked the shutter twice to bring unexposed film from the cassette. "Well, no rest for the wicked," he said as he rose from where he knelt. "According to the map, the Fort de la Casbah should be just south."

"There's also a section of what Susette—Groener, the Political Officer's wife—says is a Turkish aqueduct," Annamaria remarked. She straightened from the rail against which she lounged. "But I'd swear myself that it's really Roman wall. None of the guidebooks help, even the Guide Bleu."

"That's fine," said the agent with a smile, "but I'll bet it hasn't been converted into a nuclear research facility—the way the fort has." A pace or two later he added, "Might be best if you didn't pay much attention to the place. I don't suppose the government thinks of it as a tourist attraction the way the Casbah itself is."

"*Oui, oui,*" said the woman, and the French made Kelly glance at her face in time to catch an impish smile.

The Fort de la Casbah—more recently the Caserne Ali Khodja and now the Institute for Nuclear Research—squatted on the Boulevard de la Victoire. It looked more like a brick-built 19th-Century prison than it did a military, much less scientific, installation. The walls were about ten feet high and topped with triple strands of barbed wire. The wire was electrified, from the look of the insulators between it and the supporting posts. There were low corner towers, the one nearest to Kelly manned by a soldier with an automatic rifle. Staring at the map with his head turned up the street, the agent began snapping pictures.

Annamaria leaned against Kelly's right arm as he was cocking the shutter. In loud French she said, "Darling, I'm *certain* the National Theater must be toward the harbor. Here, let me see the map."

The sun was low. She should have needed a coat to stay warm, Kelly thought. But the Lord knew her breast was as warm as it was soft where it pressed against his arm. The agent's breath caught—like a goddam little kid—before he said, "Well, if we follow this up to the corner and then left on the Ourida. . . ."

They walked south past the riveted steel gate of the Institute. The metal was painted a dusty gray, which made it look as solid as a vault. Not that Kelly was planning an assault. But it was obvious that they would have to play a lot of this one by ear, and the more the agent knew about the surroundings, the better. Annamaria continued to cling to his arm. Every few yards, she would tug him to a halt, facing the Institute and arguing volubly over the map. The map shaded the Nikon and Kelly's hand working the shutter. Anna-maria's perfume was floral and attractive in its suggestions.

"And now?" the woman murmured in Italian as they reached the Boulevard Ourida-Meddad and the south face of the Institute. She was very warm against his arm,

"Now, back though the Casbah a different way," replied the agent. "I think there's enough light left if we push-process the film. And anyway, there's plenty of light to see by."

"You think that you can memorize all the turnings of

the Old City in one afternoon?" the woman asked with a smile.

Kelly raised an eyebrow. "You doubt it? Tsk. I can do anything. Just ask the folks in the Pentagon."

Going downhill, the alleys of the Casbah resembled a bobsled run, steep and narrow. The footing was mostly asphalt, punctuated by low stone steps. In earlier times the Casbah had presumably been paved with cobblestones which would have been even slicker than ice during rain. Annamaria followed as before, but the memory of her was soft on Kelly's arm.

A soccer ball jury-rigged from a plastic bag with rag stuffing bounced toward the couple at an intersection. Kelly stopped. Three boys with bright eyes and hair cut as short as American boys of the '50s bounded after the ball. They caromed from the blank sidewalls of the passage, each blurting an apology to the couple as they darted past. Kelly waited. Annamaria rested a hand on his shoulder, but she did not speak.

A moment later, the boys were back, one of them holding the ball. The agent grinned and called after them in French. "Please, a photograph?" Giggling, the three children skidded to a halt. They arrayed themselves with linked arms across the passage in which they had been playing. As the boys mugged, Kelly raised the camera and checked the viewfinder for the first time that afternoon. He shot, turned the camera for a vertical, and shot again. Finally, he adjusted the shutter speed and f-stop before taking another photo. "Some day you may be famous," he called to the grinning boys as he lowered the camera again. "Many thanks."

"Don't tell me you aren't utterly devoted to work after all," said the black-haired woman as they resumed their descent. "An affection for young children, yet!"

"I'm not utterly devoted to work, no," Kelly said with a smile which the woman could hear in his voice, "but as for those pictures. . . . Did you notice the two back doorways facing each other across the alley?"

After a moment, Annamaria decided to laugh. She squeezed the agent's shoulder again. "Do you like couscous?" she asked unexpectedly.

"Damned if I know," the agent said. He photographed the Rue Amar Ali northward, then turned and pointed toward the Theatre National while he shot the southward length as well. "Do I eat it or—" He stopped himself.

"You eat it," Annamaria said, holding Kelly's arm again as they darted across the narrow street, "and you feed it to me. I think my guiding you has earned me dinner tonight, don't you? Not to mention the fact that I'm freezing myself for your duty."

"Tsk, did anybody make you come?" said Kelly, turning enough to let the tall woman see him grin. "And besides, you—" The agent stopped himself again.

"Doug Rowe couldn't have looked like anything but a soldier, even if you'd put him in a dress," Annamaria said. "And do you think *he* was going to make the guards ignore your camera by cuddling you?" She giggled. "Well, he might have at that. . . . Still. And as for my husband"— answering the question Kelly had not spoken—"he'll be right down there at El Mouggar where the Lovelace Jazz Quartet is playing on their ICA tour tonight." She waved in the general direction of the National Theatre. "I told

Rufus that I'd do my duty at the buffet with the quartet at the Residence Wednesday, but not then and tonight besides."

"That's not quite . . ." the agent began. His voice trailed off when he realized he did not care to say what he *had* exactly meant. Nor, he supposed, did he need to. "All right," he said, "I guess I'm old enough to learn about couscous."

Or whatever, he added to himself as he let a pair of veiled, heavy-set women step past. Or learn about whatever.

XIII

Kelly walked along the south side of the street where there was something of a sidewalk, albeit not a curb. He had followed Annamaria's Mustang back from the rental agency in El Biar where the Passat had been transferred to his name. The car was now parked in the GSO Annex, across from where the Mustang had pulled into the Residence gate.

The agent noticed that the Fiat was no longer in front of the Residence. That whole business could lead to bad trouble, international trouble, at the mission—which was about the last thing Skyripper needed. Kelly hoped that if somebody, a Zulu from the Chaka Front or an Algerian guard, were going to be knifed at the embassy, that it would happen after Professor Vlasov had defected—or the operation had failed of itself . . . in which case Kelly would be well and truly at peace with the universe, he assumed.

The agent darted across the street and rapped on the Chancery gate. A different guard opened the door. This one was a heavy-set man in his fifties, with a thick, black moustache and almost no hair above the eyebrows. The loungers seemed to have gone home. Perhaps they had been friends or family to the man on the day shift. "Is Commander Posner or Sergeant Rowe still here?" Kelly asked in French.

"Mr. Ceriani?" asked the local employee. "Commander Posner, no, but the sergeant is waiting for you." He waved toward the Chancery. As the agent strode down the walk he noticed the guard picking up the phone in his shack and dialing. He waved when he saw Kelly looking back at him.

Doug Rowe was coming out the front door of the building before the agent had reached it. The steel door within was open. The receptionist and another man were examining it.

"Anything wrong with the door?" Kelly asked with a nod toward the building.

"Oh, Henri says three men came asking for visas," the younger man explained. "He sent them over to the Consulate in the Villa Inshallah, but one of them leaned against the door or something—and it opened. The bolt must have stuck, I suppose. Seems OK now. Henri hit the siren, and I guess the poor guys are lucky they ran off before he dumped CS over them."

Rowe looked around. "Let's walk on the grounds," he said, waving a white cable copy to Kelly. In a lower voice he added, "All this stuff is making me a little nuts. I keep thinking maybe my office is bugged."

"Planted by a predecessor who was a KGB mole, no doubt," Kelly joked. The sun had set behind the mountains, but there was enough light to see by.

"KGB, hell," Rowe said. "I'm worried about Harry Warner. He went through the roof when this came in"— he handed Kelly the cable—"and so, I'll bet, did the Ambassador. You got a bull's-eye, Tom, a perfect bull."

Kelly read the flimsy brief. "They want the job done, they give me the tools to do it," he said quietly. Flowers, their colors turned to shadow, filled the air with their freshness as the men walked past. Kelly handed back the cable. "Run it through the shredder, then," he said. "Stapling it to the visa request would be adding insult to injury. Nobody's going to play silly games when there's an order from the Secretary of State in the mission files already."

"You'll handle it tonight, then?" the sergeant asked, darting a sidewise glance at his companion.

"Can you raise the commander if you have to?" Kelly replied obliquely, looking off toward the wall about the grounds.

"Well, he'll be at home. . . . Sure."

"Sorry," the agent said, noting the expected lack of enthusiasm in Rowe's voice, "but I want him to do it. And yeah, I want it done tonight. Posner's had the initial contact. He can follow it up without getting me involved. Let the clerk think I'm being set up, too. At least let him wonder."

Kelly paused. "And as for you, Doug," he said, lifting three film cassettes from his coat pocket, "you handle the darkroom work for the office?"

The sergeant nodded, his rueful smile hardly visible.

"Yeah, that's right," Kelly agreed, "a goddam all-nighter, and I'm sorry, but. . . . It's Tri-X and the cans are marked. Develop One standard, push Two and Three to ASA 1200. Then I need prints from every frame, numbered. Eight-by-tens. It's a bitch, I know, but we'll need the prints when we talk to the Kabyles tomorrow afternoon."

"I'll phone my wife after I get the commander," Rowe said. "After all"—his teeth glinted—"I wanted the job because of the excitement, didn't I?"

A car pulled in the gate behind them and made a U-turn. Before the headlights were shut off, their reflection from the wall brought out the car's red finish. The engine continued to purr at a fast idle.

Kelly gripped Rowe by the shoulder and squeezed. "Here, you best keep my camera for me too, if you would," he said. He unstrapped the Nikon. Then he added, "At least you know what the hell you're doing. I swear I don't. Though I suppose I had to eat somewhere tonight, didn't I?"

The two men began to walk back the way they had come—Rowe to a night in the darkroom . . . and Kelly to the Mustang that awaited him.

XIV

Kelly walked around the back of the car to get to Annamaria's door. She had started to unlatch it as soon as she had parked, but she waited when she realized what her passenger was doing. "Madame," the agent said, bowing low in self mockery after he had handed her out.

"You know," said the black-haired woman, "I rather thought you might be the sort of man who insists on doing all the driving himself." She arched an eyebrow. Annamaria wore the dress she had on when they toured the Casbah, but the effect was strikingly different now. Her shoes were straps with spike heels, comfortable for no more than the thirty yards they had yet to walk to the restaurant. Her hair was down in a black flood to her shoulders where it merged with the fur of her wrap—just as black, just as rich, just as clearly expensive. The perfume was the same, but it now was a part of the night.

"Is that what you wanted?" the agent asked, offering

his right arm with the stiffness of unfamiliarity. When her hand rested lightly on the crook of his elbow, Kelly began to pick a way for them toward the orange neon sign of Le Carthage. There was a street light at the foot of the Chemin de la Glycines, but parked cars bled shadows that could hide a pothole in the street beside them.

At first, Kelly thought that the woman had not heard his question; but when they had almost reached the doorway of the restaurant she said, "I would have cancelled the table I reserved for tonight if you had been that way. Men with their balls on display every day, every minute—" Kelly opened the door. Annamaria's grimace segued into a greeter's smile as she stepped down into the entryway. Within, the lights were low and the music just loud enough to meld the scores of separate conversations into an unintelligible murmur. The tune was Western, a blurred version of "The Tennessee Waltz."

"Gordon, please," the black-haired woman said to the maitre d'. The Algerian bowed without checking his book. He led them to a table in a front corner. Neon through the square-paned window brightened the table more than did the squat candle in the middle of it. The two diners themselves were in darkness.

"Did you know," Annamaria asked as a waiter took away the third place setting, "that young Foreign Service employees often have to grow beards if they're stationed in Arab countries?"

Kelly raised his eyebrow. He flipped his palm up in question on the tablecloth when he realized that his hands were the only parts of him that were visible until Annamaria's eyes adapted.

"Yes," she said, reaching for the wine list, "if they don't have any children. And especially if they aren't married. Arabs are likely to misunderstand about beardless men, you see, unless they have some other proof of their virility. Italy, I'm afraid, isn't a great deal better. I didn't need to see more of that."

Hanged if I know why you needed to see more of me, either, the agent thought. Aloud he said, "It was your car, not mine. You knew where we were going. For that matter, you're a good driver. It scares the crap out of me to ride with anybody else, just about, but that's not to say that you're bad."

"Since this is an experiment for you," Annamaria said, staring toward the agent's face, "I think we'll have the Cous-Cous Royal and a plate of charcuterie between us." She could see well enough now to tell that Kelly was grinning. She slapped the wine list shut between the fingers of one hand and said in a harder voice, "And for the wine, a bottle of Cuvee du Président. The Algerian reds are very good, strong but not raw."

"Water for me, thank you," Kelly said. "The meal sounds fine, though."

"You don't trust me to choose wine?" Annamaria demanded. *"That's* a man's job, then?"

"I remember killing a bottle of Juarez Straight American Bourbon one night," Kelly said in a reminiscent tone, his eyes directed out the window. "Haven't the faintest notion of how I got it. For flavor, I guess it was a toss-up between that and diesel fuel. But the stuff had enough kick to do what *I* was after." He looked at the woman across the table. "I'm easy to order wine for, you see, I'm a juicer. Only for the next couple days I'm going to try to dry out, that's all."

Annamaria looked away. "I'm sorry," she said.

"Your husband get on you that bad about climbing back onto your pedestal?" the agent asked.

The waiter appeared at Kelly's elbow. Kelly smiled and gestured to Annamaria. "Two Cous-Cous Royal and a plate of charcuterie," she said in a crisp French. "And a large bottle of Saida, please." The waiter nodded and sidled off. "The local mineral water comes from Saida," Annamaria explained.

"There used to be a training depot there for—" Kelly began. He paused with his mouth open. The restaurant's clientele seemed to be almost wholly foreign, and it was doubtful that even the nearest table could hear anything he said anyway. Still, it had been a long war. Kelly would not have discussed the SS in Tel Aviv, and he would not discuss the French Foreign Legion here. "For the troops headquartered at Sidi bel Abbes," Kelly concluded. "Never occurred to me anything else happened there. Shows where my head is, I guess."

"Rufus doesn't smother me by trying to do everything for me," said Annamaria, speaking toward her folded hands. The bead in her left earlobe, gold or silver, was washed orange by the neon. It winked as she moved her head. "Rufus likes to have other people do for him, you see. And that's not a problem, generally, because he has plenty of people around. . . . But there are some things that only the Ambassador's wife can do—not me, but my position. And then there's friction sometimes, yes." She raised her eyes to Kelly. He could now see the liquid gleam of her pupils catching the candle flame. "It makes me snappish when I think someone is reacting to what I am, not who I am. And so I'm sorry."

"Christ, I've been snapped at by experts," Kelly said with a laugh. "When everything gets straightened out, we'll go off on a toot together. And I promise to drink anything you order."

As they ate cauliflower and French bread, the couple talked about the Bay of Naples. It was a liberty port to Kelly and the site of a beach house owned by Annamaria's family. The locations about which they talked were both as near and as far from one another as Eden and the Wilderness. Annamaria had a quick, bubbling laugh. Kelly brayed like a donkey and knew it, so he kept a straight face throughout most of the things he thought really funny. His control broke several times, however, during Annamaria's description of the thirty-seven days she had spent as an infant-school aide at the American School in Algiers. Other diners glanced at them. Hell, when you were out with somebody as beautiful as Annamaria, you were going to get stares even if you sat on your hands all night.

The dark-haired woman combined the processes of eating and talking with more grace than the agent could remember complementing anyone of her verve. When Kelly blinked at his first forkful of cous-cous, asking if it were rice, he was treated to an expert cook's description of how the dish was prepared. As Annamaria chewed, her hands demonstrated how the millet flour was rolled into beads even smaller than rice grains, each one coated with cooking oil wiped from the cook's hands. Then the beads spent hours in a perforated steamer as the sauce simmered beneath it, cooking and imbibing the very essence of what other methods of preparation would have left as merely something to be poured over a completed dish. Finally the completed meal would be brought out to grace the low table of the husband and his honored guests—perhaps garnished, as here in the restaurant, with lamb chops; but first and foremost, the cous-cous itself.

"It's no accident," Annamaria concluded, "that the most stunning examples of Kabyle metalwork are the cous-cous sets. The great steamer, the serving bowls . . . the tray to carry it all in with, all chased and studded and sometimes inlaid. But that's only the male reflection of the art the wives perform daily in the kitchen."

"Craftsmanship's never a bad thing," Kelly said through a mouthful. The individual beads were crisp, not soggy as rice steamed without the coating of oil would have been. "Even for a bad reason, even in a bad cause." After a moment he added, "I've always told myself that, anyway."

They were getting up to leave when Kelly paused. His hand froze in the side pocket where he kept his paper money. His face wore a distant look. "Something's wrong?" the woman asked in concern.

Kelly brought out his hand with the fat sheaf of dinars folded around a bill clip. "No, no," he said with an odd smile. "Believe me, there are easier ways to make a living than to pick my pocket. Even when I'm bombed. . . . No, it's the tune on the muzak." He thumbed toward the ceiling, though the speakers there were not actually visible. "It just surprised me, that's all. It's an old ballad from the English side of the border. 'The Three Ravens.'"

"I don't think I know the words," said Annamaria. She was studying her companion more carefully than she seemed to be as he helped her on with her furs.

"Oh, three ravens are complaining," the agent said, leading the way to the door. "You learn the damnedest things from the BBC World Service. . . ." The maitre d' and the cashier greeted them cheerfully. Kelly smiled back as he paid, adding his compliments on the meal.

The cool air outside the restaurant was a shock. Annamaria held Kelly's arm more closely than she had when they walked toward Le Carthage. "There's a knight lying dead, you see," Kelly went on. "The ravens can't get at him, though, because his hawks and his hounds are guarding the body. And then his girlfriend, his leman, comes along and buries him before she dies of a broken heart."

In a strong and surprisingly melodious baritone, Kelly sang:

"God send every gentleman
"Such hawks, such hounds, and such a leman."

They paused beside the Mustang as Annamaria fished the keys from her tiny lamé reticule. "There's a Scots version, too," Kelly said, looking back toward the restaurant. "'The Twa Corbies.' Things don't come out so well for the poor bastard in the ditch in that version. But he was dead, so I don't guess it really mattered to him."

"Think you can find the way back if you drive?" Annamaria asked. She held the keychain out on the tip of her index finger. The chrome and her short, polished fingernail caught the street light.

"With a little help," said the agent, taking the keys carefully. "I guess I can do most things with a little help."

As Kelly pulled from the parking place into a tight, smooth U-turn, Annamaria said to him, "I suppose it's the Scottish version that you believe in?"

"Don't know that I do," said the agent, shifting without haste as they climbed the hill, then shifting again. "Sometimes seems that way, I guess. But there were a lot of guys I knew back in Nam who made pretty good hawks . . . not the sort of thing you can really tell till it happens. I made a pretty good hawk myself, when it had to be done."

Two Fiats were parked at the Residence entrance, close enough to narrow the gateway still further. Kelly blipped his horn for the guard. Nothing happened except that a car barreling down the hill locked all four wheels before coming to a stop behind them. Kelly laid on the button and the gate swung back at last. When he slid the Mustang into the grounds, the agent understood the problem. The guest house to the right of the entrance was lighted up. The windows were open and through the curtains bellowed reggae music. It was no wonder that the first beep had been lost in the background.

"I was going to have a discussion about keeping awake on the job with your guard," Kelly said as he pulled up beside the main building where he had first seen the Mustang parked, "but I guess he's got enough problems right now." There was no sign of the Chrysler. It was still a few minutes till ten, however.

"It's easier to be an individual with somebody who's— an individual himself," Annamaria said as she let the agent

hand her out of the car. "It's been a delightful evening"—
her teeth winked in a wide grin, lighted by the lamp at the
side door—"Angelo. I hope there'll be—wait a minute!
Do you like jazz?"

"Well enough, I guess," Kelly said, eyes narrowing a
fraction at the woman's change of subject.

"Wait here," she called, already darting to the
unlocked door. "It'll just be a moment." The latch clicked
behind her.

Kelly grimaced, but he realized that he was still
holding the car keys. There was no practical way he could
leave even if he wanted to . . . and a good deal of him did
not want to, anyway. In the event, Annamaria was back in
little more than the moment she had promised, holding
what seemed at a glance to be a note card. "Here," she
said, handing the card to Kelly.

Christ, it was an invitation with a US Seal embossed
at the top.

The Ambassador of the United States of America
and Mrs. Rufus J. Gordon
Request the pleasure of the company of
Mr. Angelo Ceriani
at a *buffet with American Jazz*
on *April 19*
from *8 pm to 10 pm*
R.S.V.P.

"Mr. Angelo Ceriani" was hand written; the other
blanks in the printed form had been filled in on a type-
writer.

"Anna," Kelly said. He touched his lips with his tongue. "I've got—I don't know what I'll be doing day after tomorrow. It, it's apt to be pretty fluid." He felt that he was stuttering, though he knew he was not.

"Come if you can," the woman said simply. "And— wait." She stepped back and reopened the door. Kelly strode forward with the car keys. Instead of entering the house, Annamaria only reached inside. The light clicked off. She took the keys in the sudden darkness. Kelly heard them clink in her purse. Then she was in his arms, her waist softer than her furs, her lips softer yet on his.

"Jesus God," Kelly whispered as Annamaria stepped back from him.

"Come if you can," she repeated. "It's more pleasure than I can tell you to—speak Italian again."

Kelly still stood with a bewildered look on his face when the door closed behind her. "Jesus *God*, Mrs. Gordon," he whispered to the panel.

He began to be conscious of the reggae music again. Time to check in with Doug at the Chancery, set up things for the next day. A lot to do the next couple days.

He slipped the invitation carefully into the breast pocket of his coat. A lot of things to do the next couple days.

XV

The voice that responded, "Yes?" to the Chancery bell was American.

"Angelo Ceriani," Kelly said, "to see Sergeant Rowe." The guard had said Doug was still in the compound—where indeed, the photo processing was sure to keep him considerably longer.

The lock buzzed open and Kelly pushed the door back. At the reception desk with the phones and monitor was a blondish man in his late twenties. His suit coat lay folded on the edge of the desk, but he still wore a tie and a white shirt. "Ah, hello," he said, rising to take the agent's hand. He was looking at Kelly as he might have looked at a Doberman pinscher that had wandered through the door. "I'm Steve Tancredi—I've got the duty tonight."

Kelly laughed and shook hands. "Join the club, I guess," he said. "I need to talk some things over with Doug. Any notion where I'd find him?"

"Down in the darkroom, Mr. K—ah—"

"I figure it'll confuse the other side as bad as it does everybody around here," the agent said, forcing a smile. "The KGB can run around gossiping and trying to straighten out its files, instead of worrying about anything that matters a damn. But can you tell me where the darkroom is?"

"I'd better call Sergeant Rowe up here," the duty officer said apologetically. "I shouldn't leave the lobby, and you'd get lost, the place was built in 1620. Say! Charlie!"

A big, soft-looking man of about fifty was shuffling up the stairs to the right of the lobby. He wore jeans, a gray sweatshirt, and a thoroughly disgusted expression. At Tancredi's hail, he looked up without brightening in the least.

"Charlie," the duty man continued, "I know you're P.O.-ed, but look—could you take Mr. Ceriani here to the darkroom? Or, say, if you'll just watch things up here for a minute, I'll run him down. It's just that I'm sort of expecting a, ah, follow-up on that earlier cable. You know?"

"Say, that's a joke!" said the older man. There was nothing in his face to suggest he saw anything funny about that or any other facet of his recent life. He studied Kelly. The agent met his eyes steadily. "Sure, why not," Charlie said. "He's screwed up the evening so far, why not another ten minutes? Come on, buddy." He turned back down the stairs, beckoning disinterestedly.

Kelly followed. "Sorry about your evening," he said to the man's back.

"Not your fault," the other grunted. "Besides, this gives me a chance to have another slug before I drive home. As a matter of fact"—he halted on the stairs and turned, extending his hand to Kelly—"as a matter of fact, Mr. Kelly, I'm going to give *you* a slug too. I'm Charlie DeVoe, I'm a Communicator as you probably guessed. And you know why I'm giving you a drink?" Kelly's facial shrug was unnecessary, but he offered it anyway. "Because whatever you did, you pissed off the Ambassador royally. And anybody who's in that bastard's bad book is a man I want to drink with. Come on, I'll find you the darkroom and then I'll find us all some Scotch. Doug deserves a shot too—Posner's as big a shit as Gordon, if he just had the rank."

Kelly could have located the darkroom with proper instructions, but the basement corridors of the old building were as complex as the duty officer had suggested. "Code Room's the other way," said DeVoe at a T intersection. "So's the bottle." He laughed. "I keep one in the code safe," he explained. "Nobody but me and the other guys are authorized in it. Not that it matters, I've got my papers in already. Should've stayed in the fucking Navy."

At the end of the plastered corridor was a door with a hand-lettered sign reading "KNOCK DAMMIT!" Kelly knocked, shave-and-a-haircut.

"Who the hell is it?" demanded the sergeant in a muffled voice.

"Simon Legree," the agent called back. "Here to lend a hand."

"Oh—oh, just a second, Tom. Let me get these in the hypo." There were sounds of movement within. The

Communicator gave Kelly a thumbs-up signal and began striding back down the hall.

An inner door opened, then the hall door itself. Sergeant Rowe, looking tired but smiling, stood in the room which was being used as a light trap. "Come take a look," he invited. "Some of them aren't bad, but the angles. . . ."

"Look," the agent said in a low voice, shutting the corridor panel behind him, "DeVoe, the Communicator, he'll be back in a minute. He just sent out a cable about me. If you're in a good place to take a break, maybe it wouldn't be a bad time to shoot the breeze and see what we could learn."

Rowe shrugged and gestured toward the darkroom proper. Kelly could hear water circulating in the print washer and the buzz of the dryer's heating element. "Be ten minutes before I can put anything else in the dryer," the sergeant said. "And it turns out there was a pouch for you. . . . It's up in the commander's office now. I don't mind getting out of this hole for a while." He grinned, "Oh—the commander took care of your room. Went out to the Aurassi tonight and just called in a few minutes ago. He's about as happy as you'd figure, but he soldiers on like the rest of us."

Kelly opened the door almost before DeVoe's knuckles could strike it the second time. The Communicator held up what was left of a liter of Glenfiddich in its odd, triangular-cross-section bottle. "Come on upstairs, Charlie," the agent said, "and we'll take a look at what the pouch bringeth."

That was a calculated risk. All Communicators were

CIA employees. While they were officially forbidden to discuss cables with anyone, their promotion and merit raises depended on the Efficiency Reports they received from the CIA Station Chiefs at the post where they served. Smart Communicators learned early to run everything of interest past the Company rep—and from what had been said, Harry Warner would have given his left arm to learn what was being pouched to the DIA man.

On the other hand, DeVoe was obviously disaffected; and if he had really put in his retirement papers, he had little to gain from spying on embassy operations in the usual manner. Letting him in on a bit of Kelly's operation was a hell of a good way to get details of the equally-secret cable the Communicator had just sent.

The ploy worked like a charm. "It better be something you can take care of somewhere else than Algiers," DeVoe said as their steps echoed up a back staircase. "Because you're not going to be here any longer than the next flight out if his asshole Excellency has anything to say about it. Took him nearly a thousand groups to say it, but that's what it boiled down to, pure and simple."

"I'll be damned," said Kelly in genuine surprise. "Hell, it doesn't matter to him about one visa request or another, not really. Does he think his prestige is on the line because I've got a channel to State myself?"

"Wasn't that," said the Communicator. He looked back down the corridor. There was no one, of course, but he still waited for Doug Rowe to unlock the Attaché's office and usher them in. "No, he got that one before he left the Chancery this evening," DeVoe continued behind the closed door. "Before *I* left, too. I get home and bam!

there's a rush call to come back and shoot off an Immediate. Don't eat, don't help your wife move the Bird of Paradise plant in the back yard—she's screaming she's had it, she's going home, and goddam if I don't wish she would sometimes. . . ." Gloomily, the Communicator unscrewed the cap of the Scotch. "Rustle up some glasses, Dougie," he said. "Or hell. . . ." He raised the bottle and drank deeply from it.

"Let's see what we got," Kelly said, squatting on the floor beside the steel-banded packing crate, the "pouch." The exterior was stenciled CORRESPONDENCE DIPLOMATIQUE several times, and in all likelihood the Arabic markings said the same thing. Rowe handed a pair of pliers to the agent. Kelly cut the bands with them one after the other. The twang of the tensioned steel was the only sound in the office for some moments.

Under the wood was a layer of lead foil to block X-rays. Kelly drew his pocket knife, the Swiss Army folder and not the double-edged sheath knife clipped to his waistband. The small blade sheared the lead neatly against the top of the case within. This one was stenciled POUDRERIES REUNIES DE BELGIQUE, SA. "Right," the agent murmured as if his mind were not almost wholly occupied with what DeVoe had said about the cable. He lifted the inner lid. The top layer of the twenty-four cylindrical grenades, fused and ready, squatted in the styrofoam packing. "Right . . ." Kelly repeated. "Here's the smoke. I hope the tear gas shows up tomorrow, but we still got a little time."

"Jeez," said the Communicator, in sudden awe of the grenades.

"The Ambassador say anything about his wife?" asked Kelly without looking up from the crate.

Rowe started. DeVoe smirked in surmise and clapped Kelly on the shoulder. "Well, you bastard!" the Communicator said with delight, "no *wonder* he was so pissed. Say, that's a goddam fast job, boy. You should've been a sailor." He pummeled the agent again and quoted, "'Personal activities benefiting neither accomplishment of the task in hand nor the reputation of the American community in Algiers.' Pretty *goddam* quick!"

"He's exaggerating," Kelly said with a false, knowing smile, "but my tour's not up yet either—whatever his Excellency may think." DeVoe handed over the bottle. Very deliberately, Kelly drank. "Well," he said after he had taken a breath, "have we got a place to store these, or do we just leave them here with the radio equipment?"

"We'll put them in the armory, I guess," Sergeant Rowe said after a moment. "The commander'd have kittens if he found them in his office in the morning. Come on, it's right down the hall." He lifted one end of the heavy crate. Kelly took the other after handing the Scotch back to DeVoe. "Oh," the sergeant added diffidently, "why are these French? Are they better?"

"Belgian," the agent corrected as DeVoe opened the door for them. The crate would surprise anybody checking the mission stocks, but presumably that didn't happen very often at a quiet post. "And I think the word is 'deniability.' Wouldn't be terribly surprised if the fellow who bought these let out that he was from the PLO . . . or Mossad, for that matter. It may not really fool anybody, but the folks in the Fudge Factory like to be able to lie gracefully. Anyhow, the chemistry's pretty much the same in anybody's product."

"You know, I used to get around some when I was younger," said the Communicator, taking another pull from his bottle as he followed the others down the corridor. "Jesus, I'll never forget the day I DEROSed—or maybe I ought to say I'll never remember most of it. But what I *do* remember—" He chortled.

The armory was a walk-in closet in the Deputy Chief of Mission's office. Rowe had keys to both the office and the recent steel door of the armory itself. Within, under the light of the bare bulb in the ceiling, were racked a dozen 12-gauge pump shotguns and a single M16 rifle. Revolver holsters were suspended from pegs across from the long-arms; the handguns themselves were presumably in the metal filing cabinet beneath them. Against the walls were stacked cases of gas masks, ammunition, and a crate of spherical gray grenades. Rowe and the agent set their own load down on the other grenades. "Hope to God those are gas and not the old Willie Pete," the agent remarked, "White phosphorus scares the crap out of me."

"Scaredest I've ever been in my life," said DeVoe, "was getting up the morning after, like I said. See, I'd told my wife I was getting out the next day, so I could stop off in DC. Picked up a black whore on Dupont Circle—" he drank and offered the bottle to Rowe.

"Thanks, but I've still got pictures to print," the sergeant said. "Can't know myself on my ass like I'd like to."

"Anyhow, next morning I felt like all kinds of shit," DeVoe continued, passing the bottle to Kelly. The rest of the story was obscene even for a sailor. DeVoe told it with a knowing smirk, man to man. At the end, his laughter boomed in the narrow room.

Doug Rowe managed an uneasy smile, but Kelly laughed too, laughed and wiped his sweaty palms on his trousers and slid open a drawer of the filing cabinet. From its box within the agent took a revolver, a snub-nosed S&W Military and Police. "Used to be pretty good with one of these," he remarked as he unlatched the cylinder, showed the others the six empty chambers, and closed the gate again with the pressure of his thumb. "Quick draw, even."

"Go ahead, show us," said the sergeant, relaxing a little now that the talk was of weaponry.

Kelly shrugged and took off his coat. If the others noticed the sheath knife, neither remarked on it. The agent belted on one of the holsters, standard police pattern with a strap to secure the weapon for carrying. Kelly bolstered the revolver and rotated the strap out of the way. "Now we need some room," he said, stepping out in the office proper, "and a quarter."

"A dinar piece do?" asked DeVoe, fishing one out of his pocket.

"Perfect," said Kelly. "Oh—and some lubricant."

"I've got a can of WD-40 in my office," said the sergeant. "Shall I get it?"

"Naw, not for the gun," said the agent, grinning, "for *me*!" He took the Scotch from the Communicator again and drank, his throat bobbling. After three swallows he handed back the bottle, nearly empty, and burped.

"Now . . ." Kelly said, facing the hall door. He held his right hand above the holster with its fingers extended. The dinar piece lay on top of the webbing between thumb and forefinger. His arm moved, the wrist pivoting, down and up. The revolver was pointed at the center of the doorway and the office echoed with the dry *clack*! of the hammer falling on an empty chamber.

"Say, that *was* quick," said Rowe uncertainly.

With his left hand, Kelly gripped the bottom of the holster and lifted it, leaning his body forward to help. The coin, on his hand before he drew the weapon, rolled out of the holster into which it had dropped. The aluminum disk pinged and spun on the tile floor.

"Yeah," said the agent, unbuckling the rig, "quick enough." He handed the revolver and holster to Rowe, keeping the muzzle of the weapon pointed safely toward the ceiling. "Haven't forgotten everything I used to do. . . ."

Grinning like a death's-head, Kelly took the bottle from DeVoe again.

XVI

The car whose lights had been behind Kelly most of the way back to the Aurassi continued up the driveway when the agent turned right into the hotel parking lot. The other vehicle was of no immediately recognizable make, dark and gleaming and rather large by Algerian standards. It was not a tail, at least not a professional tail. Only tension and the whiskey had made Kelly notice it at all.

The lobby of the Aurassi was spacious, but its furnishings showed the same extreme of Western tastelessness as the building's design did. Swivel chairs of molded purple plastic shared the orange carpet with bright yellow sofas and glass-topped coffee tables. Three swarthy men in dark suits sat together at the far left, where the lobby formed an L with the hotel bar. Apart from those three and a desk clerk, the big room was deserted.

"Room 324," Kelly said to the clerk. "Any messages?"

"Let me see, sir," said the Algerian, turning to the

151

mail slots and taking a yellow form from that of 324. He frowned and murmured to himself before raising his eyes to the agent's. "Sir," he continued, in French again, "I'm very sorry but your room has been changed. You're directly across the hall in 327 now."

"Tonight?" said Kelly. He had just enough of a buzz to resent the move he had rung bells in Washington to achieve. "Christ on a crutch!"

The clerk shrugged helplessly and handed over the key to 327. "Very sorry," he repeated.

Kelly had not bothered to unpack the copy machine or his suitcases, so the move was quick and simple. The packing case skidded acceptably over the carpet when he lifted the front end; the suitcases and radio made only one further load. Kelly plugged the receiver in and draped its wire antenna from the top of the closet door to stretch it out. A commentator on the BBC Italian service was considering and discounting the possibility of a clash as the US Sixth Fleet and the Soviet Mediterranean Squadron prepared to hold simultaneous exercises in the Western Mediterranean. Kelly wondered if he could buy a bottle in the hotel. He didn't like drinking in bars, it made him feel too much like a zoo specimen.

Someone knocked in the hallway.

Kelly had been taking off his shirt. He froze and the knock was repeated, not on his door but on one nearby. He stole across the carpet and put his eye to the wide-angle lens set in the door panel.

Three men stood with their backs to him in a semicircle around the door of 324. From behind and through the fisheye lens he could not be sure, but the trio was certainly dressed like the men who had been waiting in the lobby when he came in. There had been a number of people in the sedan that followed him, too, but—

The man in the center held a wallet open in his hand, obviously official identification. After the second knock went unanswered, another of the waiting trio opened the door. All three slipped into 324 without wasted motion. The door closed behind them.

Kelly blinked at his distorted view of the empty hall. 324 had a spring lock as well as a deadbolt to be engaged with the key. Kelly had not bothered to throw the deadbolt when he left the room; but the visitors had not seemed to fumble with a passkey to open the spring lock either.

A moment later, the door opened again. The three men left as quickly as they had entered. One was replacing something in a breast pocket—or a shoulder holster. The strangers were down the hall and out of view in a moment. They moved with quick, short steps, all three sets of legs in unison. None of them glanced at 327 as they passed.

The agent relaxed slowly. Using both hands to keep from jabbing himself, he put his double-edged knife back in its sheath. Police of some sort, clearly. Presidential Security Office?

But what had he done so far to concern the Algerians? Kelly himself had had no contact with the underground as yet . . . and why had they gone to the wrong room—if it *had* been a mistake.

After a moment's further consideration, Kelly slid one of the chairs over to his door and tilted it under the knob. The chain bolt was a joke, scarcely even a delay for a pro who knew how to use his boot. Not that it really mattered.

If the authorities wanted in, they were going to get in. But why?

The Italian Service had closed out its broadcasting for the day. The Kenwood hissed with static. Kelly started to play with the tuning, then changed his mind. He stripped and lay down on the bed with the lights out. The radio dials shone as cats' eyes, but he had dimmed them also.

Kelly wanted a drink very badly, but he had no intention of opening his door again that night. After a time, he slept.

XVII

"Seven-zero," Kelly whispered to the mirror front of the bathroom medicine chest.

After a moment, the speaker of his short-wave receiver rasped, "Go ahead," in French.

"Up five," the agent said in the same language. He was still speaking toward the shaving mirror. He reached down and adjusted the receiver so that its digital read-out said 10.430 in megahertz instead of 10.425. He cut the power. From the mirror came the faint, tinny sound of someone counting to ten in French.

At 'dix' Kelly whispered back, "Got it. Four-one out." He turned. Sergeant Rowe was standing in the bathroom doorway. "There it is, Doug," the agent said. "Now, if the rig'll just keep working for the next couple days, we've got our link to Doctor Hoang." He frowned. "Not that that puts us out of the woods either, but it's a start."

The sergeant stepped past Kelly and slid open the left

door of the medicine cabinet. "Pretty slick, even if I do say so myself," he remarked.

A transmitter and a separate receiver, neither of them much larger than a standard hearing aid, had been glued to the inner surface of the mirror. Hair-fine wires spliced them into the circuit serving the shaving lamp built into the cabinet. Spray enamel had melded the wires into the metal surface; it reeked at the moment, but the odor would have dissipated by the time Kelly surrendered the room the next day.

The transmitter had, as a matter of fact, been an off-the-shelf bugging device, powered by and broadcasting on the building's own electrical circuitry. It was sound-activated with an interlock to keep it from re-broadcasting noises from the receiver. Ideally the transmitter would have been monitored within the Aurassi, but Conference security measures would make that impossible. Instead, Kelly and the sergeant had been forced to position a separate and far more powerful transponder in the outside wall of the bedroom. It broadcast on an integral antenna, easily capable of driving a signal to the American Embassy.

The transponder installation was behind a sculptured divan. All the fragments of drywall had been swept into a bag which Sergeant Rowe would carry away with him. The hole had been covered with an aluminum plate 150 mm square, anodized to a close match for the beige wall paint. With luck, even someone who took the time to cut loose the plate—it was sealed to the wall with quick-setting epoxy—would still assume that the featureless gray box of the transponder had something to do with the power line to which it was connected.

The receiver had been more of a problem.

"Damn thing was a good 25 kilocycles off," Kelly grumbled to the sergeant. "I don't see how a sealed unit like that could slip off frequency, even being flown to Algiers in the guts of a Xerox machine. Either it works or it doesn't work—it doesn't just decide to work on a different frequency."

Rowe slid the cabinet door closed again. In order to see the paired devices, one had to actually stick one's head into the cabinet. That would require more than a mild suspicion that there was a bug in the room. Anyone who searched the medicine chest would already have dismantled all the light fixtures and wall receptacles in the living quarters. "They'd have tested it, wouldn't they?" Rowe asked. "Whoever made it, I mean?"

The agent cracked a smile. "I wonder who Pedler and the boys did get this one from?" he mused aloud. "It's not quite the NSA's cup of tea, is it? And if it came from the Company's Tech Services Division,"—he laughed aloud—"I wouldn't be surprised to learn it had a tracer built into it someplace."

More soberly, Kelly shook his head as if lulling his fantasies to rest. "No," he said, "they probably tested it, but not under field conditions."

"Like the commander wanted to do?" the sergeant suggested.

"Right, right," agreed the older man, nodding vigorously. "If we'd tried this next to the transmitter the way Posner suggested, it'd have worked fine because the signal was so strong. Hell, you can make a light bulb talk if you drive a signal at it hard enough. But a few miles away with some walls in between, well . . . that little matter of 25 kcs"—Kelly had been in radio before "hertz" replaced "cycles per second"—"isn't so little any more."

"Lucky thing we had your shortwave so that we could be sure it wasn't the base unit that was messed up," the sergeant said, kneeling for a closer look at the Kenwood.

The agent raised an eyebrow. "Luck?" he said. "Luck isn't planning Skyripper, Doug my boy, Tom Kelly is." He paused, then went on, "God knows we're going to need more luck than I expect us to have. . . . But that doesn't mean I haven't crossed as many Ts as I could."

The two men looked at one another for a moment. "Well," Rowe said, rising, "it's time to get ready for the meeting. It took longer than I expected, setting up this commo."

"Yeah," Kelly agreed. He unplugged the Kenwood and lifted it carefully. "It'd have been quicker if I'd run it up first, instead of going down fifty kcs before working up from what it was supposed to be."

"If you'd done that," said Sergeant Rowe, following the agent out of the bathroom, "they'd have been off on the low end instead."

The communications set-up, including the transponder, was live only when the bathroom light was on. There were ways to control units from a distance, switching them on and off as the person monitoring desired; but that added a level of complexity and potential failure. If a switch failed in a satellite, tens of millions of dollars might be pissed down the drain. If one failed *here* it would very likely mean Kelly's ass . . . and that was not something the stocky agent trusted to high-tech solutions when there was any other way.

There was a fair likelihood that Hoang—or rather, the security people sure to accompany the physicist—would sweep the hotel room for bugs as a matter of course. The usual technique involved a sensitive receiver that lighted in the presence of a signal. The searcher walked around the subject area, talking in a normal voice and seeing if the indicator lighted up as a bug broadcast his speech. Unless the bathroom fixture were on, the bug would not be live; and it was very unlikely that the searcher would turn on the light and risk masking the weak glow of his own indicator.

Kelly took from his closet a brown corduroy blazer and stuffed a blue knit cap in the side pocket. He folded the jacket over his forearm, lining outward. "Let's go, then," he said. He glanced sidelong at Rowe as they walked to the door. "Ah, Doug," he added, "you'll be at the meeting too?"

The sergeant shook his head sharply. He did not look up from the carpet as they strode down the hall. In a low voice he said, "No, I . . . the commander won't let me get into something like . . . illegal. I've got a red passport, you see. The commander'll drive you. Anyway, he's had all the contact with the group himself."

Kelly had said nothing about the three visitors across the hall. Rowe was too subdued by his own circumstances to notice that his companion kept darting glances to the rear as they walked toward the elevators. Someone could run up behind them, his or their footfalls swallowed by the soft green carpeting. "What about your passport?" Kelly responded in vague irritation, wholly alert but only partially listening to what was being said.

"Oh—red," Rowe explained. "Official, not black like a dip's. The Attaché has a black passport—and diplomatic immunity. Staff travels on red and takes its own chances when something blows up." He pressed the elevator button, staring morosely at the bag of wall fragments in his hand. "He's doing it for me, really; but it's the way the book says, and that's the way the commander was going to do it anyway. Well, it's a direct order."

The elevator signal pinged. "Look," said Kelly in sudden decision, "meet me at your car. I'm going to walk."

Before the elevator doors slid open, the agent had rounded the corner to the stairs. Rowe heard his shoes echo briefly within the smoke tower before the door swung shut behind him. Frowning at last in perplexity, the sergeant waited for the passengers within the car to exit before he could ride it down.

XVIII

Kelly got into Posner's rented Peugeot 204 before the vehicle had come to a full stop. Cigarette smoke twirled into phantom hands at the suction of the door.

The commander pulled away from the curb with only a glance of irritation at his passenger. Wearing the brown jacket and knit cap, the dark-complexioned Kelly was scarcely distinguishable from the local men lounging back at the Chancery gate.

"I don't know what you're playing at," said Commander Posner in a tight voice. "There's nothing suspicious about two foreigners visiting an antique shop. Perhaps it's as wise not to use a car with diplomatic plates, I'll agree. But that doesn't mean you have to dress up like a thug. . . . And it *certainly* doesn't mean I have to pick you up on a street corner, instead of at the Chancery as we'd arranged previously."

The agent rubbed his temples tiredly. "Tell me,

Commander," he said, "how many salesmen do you take on shopping trips?"

Posner cleared his throat. He glanced sideways in more of an apology than Kelly had expected to receive.

It didn't make the agent feel more comfortable, however. The excuse was fine for silencing the Defense Attaché, but Kelly himself knew that he had begun acting irrationally. There *could* be reasons for his sudden paranoia; but if there were, he was not consciously aware of them.

He wasn't sure which was worse—having premonitions or going nuts. Kelly had wondered the same thing toward the end, there, with the girl in Venice whose name was not Janna. He had not reached a solid conclusion that time either.

"No problems with the radio gear at your end, then?" Kelly asked to break his own train of thought.

Posner stubbed his cigarette out into the ashtray and tried to get another one-handed from the pack in his pocket. "No, no, it appears to be quite in order, once we found that fuse this morning," he said. He looked at the agent more fully. "Once you found the fuse, I should say."

"Sometimes they're blown right out of the box," Kelly agreed mildly. "There's people pretty much that way too, so I guess we ought to figure it for fuses." The Attaché was trying to pull a disposable lighter from between the cellophane and the liner of his cigarette pack. The Peugeot did not have a resistance lighter. "Here," said Kelly, taking the pack. "I'll do it."

Commander Posner was not a natural driver; he

constantly overcorrected with jerky movements of the wheel, brakes, and gas. Still, he relaxed a trifle with the fresh cigarette between his lips and said, "I'm surprised there's no scrambler in the system. Of course, it's possible that no one will be monitoring the frequencies—but quite frankly, I can't conceive of Washington authorizing you to give operational directives this sensitive in clear."

"Yeah, there's people who'd have conniptions if they knew," agreed the agent with a wry smile. He cranked his window down an inch but found as he expected that it simply drew more smoke past him instead of clearing the air. "Thing is, there's no way to fit a scrambler/unscrambler to hardware as small as what we've got to use in the Aurassi. Our contact'll almost certainly be sharing the room with a security man. We can't just stick a PRC-77 in the closet for him to use . . . or phone him."

"I should have thought that a risk of the sort you intend to . . . put us all through would have had to be cleared at very high level," Posner said distantly. The car wheels thumped on the right curb and rubbed for several yards. The commander continued on, apparently unaware of the scraping.

Kelly wiped his chin with the back of his hand. His whiskers bit at the skin. "Look," he said, "we do what we can. Nobody'll be talking on the system but me and the contact—and we'll be using Vietnamese. Sure, it can be recorded; but unless we're completely SOL, it'll be days before anybody here'll have time to figure out what the language was, much less translate it. There are risks; but that's a fact of life."

The Defense Attaché snorted in what turned out to

be an unexpected outburst of humor. He looked at Kelly despite the fact that a boxy, green bus was stopping in their lane. "There *was* a Vietnamese community in Algiers during the last years of the French, you know," he said. He looked up just in time to jam on the brakes. Algerian passengers, loaded like cattle in a truck, peered down from the back window.

"Yes, secret police—refugees after Dien Bien Phu," Posner continued. "The French brought them here to deal with the FLN. Torturers, of course. . . . The FLN blew up a barracks full of them, killed over fifty. And after Independence, well—I don't think we need worry about local Vietnamese speakers, you're correct."

The two-stroke Fiat diesel of the bus whined. After a moment, the commander realized that the lane was no longer blocked and drove off himself. "I think it's— Yes, we turn here."

They were far to the south of the Casbah, in one of the small connecting streets near the Boulevard Victor Hugo. The buildings lining the street were two-story. They had flat roots with iron railings around the upper-floor balconies. At street level, most of the buildings were shops. Plaster, originally painted white or light gray, flaked in patches from the masonry beneath. Save for the ironwork, the block could have passed for an aging downtown anywhere in the United States.

Posner pulled up behind a panel truck. The shop directly beside them had no sign, but the metalwork displayed on faded velvet in the windows was an adequate description. Kelly got out quickly, scanning the street in both directions as unobtrusively as haste permitted. There was nothing untoward. The parked cars were the usual mixture of small European makes, with light colors predominating. The Defense Attaché was slow locking his door. Kelly waited for him, needs must, but he felt a helpless fury at the delay that kept them in the open. It was like the moment your chopper hovers, just before dropping to insert you in somebody else's jungle.

Brusquely, concerned only about political and not physical danger, Commander Posner strode past Kelly and into the shop. A string of bells rang. Within, the unassisted light through the display windows was barely adequate. It would have given the advantage—should the need arise— to the teenager seated in the corner to the left of the door. "Ah—good afternoon," the Attaché said in his stilted French. "My American friend here is looking for brass of exceptional quality."

Instead of answering, the boy gestured toward the back with his left thumb. His right hand was in his lap, under a copy of *El Moudjahid*, the French-language official newspaper. Not lazy or disinterested, Kelly realized. The kid was so hyper that he was afraid to attempt anything as complex as speaking.

The center of the shop was a large, cloth-covered table which supplemented the broad shelves around all four sides of the room. The wares were a medley of work, ranging from obvious antiques to the glisteningly recent. A copper cous-cous steamer, decorated with curves of hand-applied stippling, lay beneath a 20-inch bayonet. The weapon itself was French, of the narrow-bladed Gras pattern of the 1870s. The scabbard, however, was of brass lacework, almost a filigree—weeks or months of work for some craftsman in a Kabyle village. Elsewhere, the eye met lamps and trays and an incredible variety of bowls; brass and copper predominantly, but with an admixture of silver, gold, and even aluminum. Even at this juncture, their craftsmanship impressed Kelly. If Kabyles could execute Skyripper with the same meticulous ability, things were going to be fine.

The two Americans walked past the guard, feeling his eyes on their backs and hearing the paper in his lap rustle. In the shop's rear wall were a curtained stairwell and a door. Posner hesitated at the door. Kelly wondered whether or not the Attaché had ever been through it before. With only the brief delay, however, the commander pulled the panel open. The agent followed him in to join the five men and two women already there.

This time the gun—one of them, at least—was quite openly displayed. A Mauser 98 was aimed squarely at the center of Kelly's breastbone. The agent smiled, wondering what that implied about his status relative to that of Posner. "God be with you," he said in French as he pushed the door closed.

The waiting group was varied. One man wore a suit as good as any of those Kelly owned, while another was the man the agent remembered as the late-shift guard at the Chancery. He was still in his khakis. Most of the Kabyles, including the women, were smoking. The odor of their tobacco was harsh and thick in the small office. The middle-aged man with the rifle bore a strong facial resemblance to the youth in the shop proper. He sat on the only chair in the room and supported the Mauser along the slanted top of an old writing desk. Even if he were the shop owner, however, his eyes glanced deference to the patriarch wearing a flowing white djellaba.

The old man nodded severely to Kelly. His moustache was huge and as white as his outer garment. Looking at the agent, he spoke briefly in a non-European language. His eyes were fierce.

Kelly glared back. He could make an educated guess as to what the Kabyle demanded. There was nothing to lose by trying—and perhaps a great deal to gain. Standing at a rigid parade rest, the agent retorted in French, "No sir, I cannot speak your own language—nor can I speak the Arabic of those who would demean you. I come to you as a man needing help—but as a strong man ready as well to help you and help your nation. If we can speak together as men in a tongue foreign to all of us"—he nodded around the circle—"so be it. If not, we each will fight our enemies alone."

"I am Ali ben Boulaid," said the old man in French. His face broke into an enveloping smile. The Mauser clicked on the desk as the hand of the man holding it relaxed minusculy. "Ramdan, coffee for your guests!"

The shop owner stuck his head back into the shop and shouted instructions. His Mauser disappeared behind a section of wall paneling and he brought out a rug for the office floor. There was no room for more chairs, even if they might have been available. Kelly joined the Kabyles, sitting with crossed ankles and no particular discomfort. Posner attempted to squat with his back against the shop door. He had to move when a woman bustled in with a beaten silver coffee set carried from the living quarters above the shop. The Attaché slid his balancing act into the corner by the desk. The unfamiliar posture cut off his circulation. At intervals during the discussion he had to hop up embarrassingly and massage his calves. A few years before, the Kabyle movement had been little more than demonstrations—often spontaneous—against the tendencies of the government. Every such attempt at public protest had been put down with riot sticks backed with machine guns. Arrests were ineffective against a movement without leaders. Mass beatings by the police were seen as more likely to get results.

The results they got were the creation of Kabyle leaders all over the country.

The old networks still existed among the survivors of the War of Independence. After the victory, leadership of the Front of National Liberation and of the new state had been taken by those who had spent the war in French prisons, planning their memoirs. Those who had done the fighting, though, were still in the rural areas and the Casbah. If a new need to fight arose, well . . . it mattered little, after all, if the enemies of freedom spoke French or Arabic.

As generally happens, the government itself had been the dissidents'—now rebels'—strongest recruiting agent. Now there were nodes around which could coalesce those dissatisfied with any aspect of autocracy, any aspect of rule: tribal chauvinists, goat-herds disgruntled by reforestation projects intended to block the advance of the Sahara; squatters evicted from public housing so that the proper applicants could move in. . . . The sufficiency of the reasons for which people will fight is determined by the individual fighters alone.

The coffee was thick and sweet, cloying on Kelly's empty stomach. He continued to drink it anyway as he argued quietly and listened to the others wrangling among themselves. The agent had expected to meet a single leader. What he got instead was democracy with a vengeance. It was possible that Ali ben Boulaid could have made and enforced the decision himself, but the old man showed no sign of wishing to do so. There had been no decision on whether the group—they did not use any formal name in Kelly's hearing—would go through with the operation.

Finally the agent opened his attaché case of 8x10 glossies of the Casbah. That killed theoretical discussions about whether an office in Rabat outweighed the risks of a gunfight in the center of Algiers. The arguments slid at once into the practical questions of who and where, how many and by which route. Kelly sipped his coffee. He made small comments when he had something useful to add . . . and he kept his smile inside, knowing that he had just begged a question that was likely to get a number of people killed.

After the initial discussion had burned out, Kelly took charge. He used both the map and the corresponding photographs. "Here," he said, pointing with a blunt fore-finger, then stirring the glossies to find the same location, "a truck blocks the complex of streets from the south by sliding across the intersections just west of the Institute. On the other end, the motorcade will be coming and we won't be able to insert a blocking vehicle into it. We need to cut the intersection of the Boulevard de la Victoire and the, whatever, Boulevard Abderrazak. Can you handle that?" He looked challengingly around the circle of Kabyles.

A young man with sideburns and a black turtleneck sweater glanced at his companions. When no one else spoke, he shrugged and said, "There must be a drain there from the Institute . . . the main sewer's on the east side of the boulevard. Twenty pounds of *plastique* in that and—" he gestured with his hands and lips. "Sure, we can cut the street."

Kelly felt Posner beside him shiver. "Right," the agent said, "and that'll make the perfect signal for our boy to run. He'll have plenty of company when pieces of the pavement start raining down—it won't get him shot by his own people." Kelly cleared his throat, hoarse and dizzy from the layering smoke. "Next," he said, "we need to cut off visibility on the ground. We can fill the truck with oily rags and set them afire, that may help, but the wind's going to be straight uphill from the sea unless we're lucky. I've got a case of smoke grenades. If you've got a few people to volley them from upper floors at that end of the street, they'll do the job for as long as we need it done."

"The roof will be best," said the man in the three-piece. He had a nervous trick of inserting a finger under his collar-facing, but to Kelly's surprise he had been one of the hawks of the earlier discussion.

Now the agent shook his head in violent disagreement. "There'll be troops on the wall and towers of the Institute," he said. "Will be or should be. And look, this is dangerous, maybe the most dangerous part of the whole deal. Those smoke grenades'll leave a track back to where they come from as broad as a highway. The guards across the street won't shoot down maybe because they won't know what's going on down there with so many of their own people. But they'll damn well open up on the windows things're being thrown from. We'll tie the grenades in bundles of six. There'll be plenty of range from a third floor window."

"They won't shoot if we've shot them first," said the younger of the two women. "They made their choice when they put on the uniforms of the oppressors." She mimed a throat-cutting with her index finger.

"Look," said Kelly, "the less shooting, the better off we all are. Bullets'll ricochet like a bitch between those walls and the pavement. Even if you know what you're doing with a gun you don't have any notion where the slug's going to wind up. I've got some gas grenades which we can use as soon as the, ah, the target's clear—"

"Tear gas?" interrupted the older woman. Her hair was black save for a thin white zig-zag that marked old scarring as surely as an X-ray could have.

Kelly met her fierce eyes. "CS," he said with a nod of agreement. "The kind of 'tear gas' that makes people puke their guts up if they get a good whiff of it. Toss that into the smoke and you don't have to worry about anybody on the ground chasing you."

"Toss satchel charges into the cars," said the woman, "and nobody chases you either."

Posner was swearing or praying under his breath. Kelly shrugged and turned his palms up. "Look, what you do *after* my man clears the area is your business. But you might keep in mind that it's not just troops and cops and security people going to be down there. There'll be scientists from maybe fifty countries. I don't know and you won't know just who it is in the line of fire. Start throwing bombs and you'll be able to read the body count in just about every paper in the world, right on the front pages. That won't bother me a bit . . . but I'm not about to start a government in exile."

"We will consider that among ourselves," said ben Boulaid, his cracked voice sweeping through the others' miscellaneous chatter like a horseman through wheat. "There is still the matter of price. Qadafi paid *ten* million dollars to have the Jewish athletes killed in Munich."

"Did Qadafi stand with his gunmen or did he send them off alone to die?" the American agent snapped back. "*I* offer a million dollars and recognition that you would not be able to buy at any price, not even from the enemies of the government you oppose. *And* I stand with you, a warrior among warriors."

"Good God, man!" blurted Commander Posner in English. "You *know* that's against your orders. It *must* be!"

"If I must stand alone," Kelly continued, ignoring the Attaché, "so be it. I do not need the help of those who can be bought for cash alone." He was light-headed, had been for what seemed like hours. He almost burst out laughing at the image of himself charging the motorcade alone, hurling CS grenades with both hands. Might be better than going home and trying to explain to folks how he'd blown the deal before it even got off the ground, though. . . .

"I did not say that *we* were merely terrorists seeking dollars," the old man said stiffly. "We will consider the offer among ourselves."

"How are we to know the person you want?" asked the man who knew about the street drains. "You say 'when he's clear'—but who?"

Kelly took a thick 9x12 envelope from the lid of his case. Commander Posner was already saying, "Obviously, that has to wait until you have decided if you are going to—"

The agent opened the envelope and began handing fuzzy enlargements around the circle of Kabyles. "We are warriors," he repeated. "Will we betray each other, even if we cannot agree? This one is Vlasov, a professor, a scientist. He wishes to escape to freedom. We wish to help him because that is our way."

Ben Boulaid stared at the photograph and nodded solemnly. "We will reach you soon—through bou Djema, as usual." The Chancery guard bobbed his head enthusiastically. The old man rose, his compatriots to either side braced to help him. They were unneeded.

Kelly quickly swept the photographs of the Casbah back into his case. The locals could study the site on their own, he could not. "Peace be on you," he said, bowing first to Ben Boulaid and then to each of the other Kabyles in turn.

"The peace of God be on you," replied the patriarch, bowing back to Kelly. "If it pleases God, we will speak again soon." The agent tugged the weak-kneed Attaché erect and opened the door. The still, cool air of the shop washed his face like a shower.

The Americans had barely closed the door when they heard the voices behind them resume. The words were indistinguishable, but the tones were not those of peace and moderation. "Hooked them," whispered Kelly in English as they passed the guard again. "Hooked them, by God, as sure as I got hooked myself!"

Posner turned the car in the street, heading back toward the embassy complex. As they cornered onto the Boulevard Victor Hugo again, Kelly caught a glimpse of something in the rearview mirror. He spun to look over the back of his seat, but the Attaché had already pulled through the intersection. If there had been a black sedan turning toward the shop from the direction of the Rue Boukhalfa, it did not follow them to the embassy. Kelly was quite certain of that, because he kept looking back the whole way.

XIX

Commander Posner had not spoken on the trip back, even to ask what his passenger expected to see out the window. Any hopes the Defense Attaché may have had that the operation would be bloodless—or better, would not even be attempted—had evaporated during the meeting with the Kabyles. There would be blood in the streets, and the leader on the ground would be an American working for the DIA, just as Posner himself did. . . .

The car stopped in the lane between the Chancery and the Villa Inshallah, the building in which Admiral Darlan had been assassinated in 1942. Posner set the emergency brake. He looked at Kelly and said with a deliberate absence of inflection, "I—am told that his Excellency received a cable regarding you this morning."

The agent regarded the naval officer levelly. "I presume," he said, "I would have been notified if I'd been booted out. So I presume further it wasn't that. Shall we play 'Twenty Questions,' or are you going to tell me what it really was?"

Posner scowled. "I could only speculate about the contents, and I have no doubt that you can do that with at least equivalent accuracy yourself, Mr. Kelly, The—the DCM is a friend of mine. He was, I think, warning me. . . . Ambassador Gordon is very angry about what he sees as the situation. And while you will no doubt be going home, the rest of us may have an unpleasant aftermath to deal with."

The commander paused. Kelly put his hand on the Peugeot's door handle, but before he opened it the Attaché went on, "Mr. Kelly, I have no reason to doubt your abilities, since obviously they are held in high regard by my superiors . . . and of course, what you said earlier about a soldier following orders is quite correct. But I think there may come a time soon when I will take the second option you suggested and resign my commission. I only hope that if I do make that choice, I will make it soon enough."

Posner got out and began walking rather quickly toward the Chancery. Quickly enough that the agent would have had to run to keep up with him. Kelly did not do that. The sea was already dark with the shadow of the mountains. After waiting long enough to permit the commander to get inside, Kelly strolled toward the Chancery himself. He needed to run a cable out to Paris. It was better to hold one of the Communicators over than to call one back as the Ambassador had done the night before.

Kelly still needed to clear out of the Aurassi and pick

up his VW from the hotel lot. The place would be tight as a tick from midnight on; and Kelly had seen and heard enough about Algerian thoroughness to know that they would damn well clear things out themselves if he did not do it in time. When the Pan-African Games had been held in Algiers, the government had decided as an aesthetic measure to clear the balconies of the high-rise apartments fronting the parade route. Clearance had been effected by squads of troops who marched from room to room. Everything found on a balcony was pitched over the rail. Not infrequently that meant the sheep which recently-rural families stabled on the balconies in anticipation of the Feast of Muharram. The pictures of sheep flung twelve stories onto concrete looked like nothing Kelly had seen since the days VC prisoners were transported by helicopter.

The Algerian employee at the reception desk admitted the agent before he had time to ask through the speaker. Kelly gave the local a V-sign and trotted up the stairs to Rowe's windowless office next to the Attaché's. There was no light on in the latter—Posner must have been with one of his friends elsewhere in the building. Sergeant Rowe was just setting down the intercom, however. His door was open and he gestured to Kelly happily when he saw him. "Say, that was for you," he said. "Anna. Do you want me to buzz her back?"

"Business first," the agent said, trying to manage a smile. He had not thought about drinking since he got up and started to install the communications rig in his room. Mention of Anna reminded him that he had meant to pick up a bottle in the Aurassi that morning. "I need a desk to draft a cable on," he said. "Then you or I are going to have to encrypt it on the computer." He smiled ruefully. "And we're going to have to hold somebody to shoot it off, it won't wait till morning. See if you can get DeVoe—I've got some other stuff to talk to him about. . . . Oh—and I want to sweeten the pot a little on that one, too. How do I get a bottle of booze around here?"

"Well, from the top," Rowe said, smiling back, "you can have my desk while I go see that the computer'll be free." He frowned. "You know, the Code Room's down in the basement with a lead lining on all sides and cushioned floors. There's no way anybody could eavesdrop while they're encrypting. The computer, that's in one corner of a hallway with movable partitions around it—that was the only place there was room. It's not exactly the most secure spot in the mission, you know."

Kelly waved a hand. "Sure, the Company boys may record the click of the keys and fire them off to Langley— or Meade, for all I know—and they can read them out in clear. But by the time they get that back"—his grin was a wolf's grin—"I'll be long gone and they'll have a better notion of what we were up to than the cable could give them anyway. That's the name of the game on this one, you see—the main enemy's the guy in the next office."

The sergeant shrugged. "Ours not to reason why," he said. He picked up the intercom and punched 121 on its pad. "Say, Pete," he said after a moment, "we've got a TDY officer"—he winked at Kelly —"here who needs a bottle of. . . ." He paused.

"Johnny Walker Red, I guess," the agent supplied. "Say—there wouldn't be some Jack Daniels around, would there?"

"Walker Red and Jack Daniels," Rowe relayed. "Yeah, the Black, I suppose." Kelly nodded vigorously. "And 750s—" Another nod. "Sure, Pete, I'll be over in a minute or two—I know *you* want to close up and get home. . . . Yeah, don't feel like the Lone Ranger."

The sergeant hung up. "I'm going to get over to the Annex and pick that up right now," he said. "The GSO's a friend of mine, but you don't stay friends if you keep people around this place after hours." He smiled broadly. "Meaning nothing personal, you know. . . . Oh—I'll get Charlie on the way. Better see him than ringing down to the Code Room, I suppose."

Kelly sat at the sergeant's vacated desk and began composing, using a single sheet of typing paper and a soft pencil. He had deliberately left the office door open, so that he could hear any movement in the corridor. The footsteps a moment later were not precisely surreptitious, but neither did they call unnecessary attention to themselves.

Kelly folded the draft with three quick motions and thrust it in the breast pocket of his coat. Then he stepped to the door. Harry Warner, the CIA Chief, was coming down the hall very slowly. The agent grinned at him. "Good evening," he said.

Warner nodded abruptly. "Wanted to see Bill," he said.

Kelly stepped sideways and rapped on the door of the Attaché's dark office. "Sorry," he said to Warner. "I'll tell him you're looking if he comes by."

"Funny as hell, isn't it?" the Station Chief snapped. He turned on his heel, repeating, "Just funny as hell!"

"Want to buy a copy machine?" Kelly called to the man's back.

He had scarcely begun writing again when another set of heels began slapping down the hall—wooden-soled sandals and a long leggy stride. Kelly sighed and refolded the draft. Perhaps he should have done the work at his hotel, where the door locked and CW traffic on the Kenwood would blur even the sound of knocking. But that would also mean driving back to the Chancery with the draft cable in his pocket. Most security precautions were silly on a realistic level, but carrying that cable in clear would have been a violation of common sense as well as tradecraft.

"Anna," the agent said as he stepped to the door. "Look, I'm sorry but I'm busy like you wouldn't believe right now. If you really need something, I'll give you a ring when I'm clear—whenever that is."

Annamaria smiled. She was back to Western Informal, blue slacks and a red and blue pull-over which read "Sun Walley"—local manufacture, obviously. "You still have to move and pick up your car, don't you?" she asked.

That was no secret, but it made Kelly uneasy all the same—for reasons that had nothing to do with business. "Yeah," he said nodding, "that's part of it. Look, Mrs. Gord—"

"Doug and I can take care of that, then—I caught him as he was going past the snack bar," the woman said. "You don't have to do that in person, and the car will take two to get it anyway. Give me the keys and we'll leave you to your work."

Kelly brought out the Passat's keys. He was unable to argue with the logic and unwilling to argue with the rest. As he held out the chain, however, he hesitated and instinctively closed his fingers back over the keys again. "Oh, look, Anna," he said, his eyes frowning at the chain and his mind somewhere else. "Have Doug give my car a quick once-over before he drives it back, will you? I mean, just so there's no extra wires from the distributor, that sort of thing. I'm getting screwier as I get older, that's all. But"—he raised his eyes—"carry him over in your car, OK? And he drives back in mine."

The woman's fingers touched Kelly's as she took the keys. "We'll see you soon," she said, "so work hard."

The basic preparations for the extraction had been made before Kelly left France. The MARS boat had preceded him by diplomatic pouch in the same shipment that brought the base unit transmitter and receiver to be used for Skyripper. The timing had to be adjusted to circumstances as Kelly found them on the ground, however; and the method put enough other people at risk that the agent had directed that it not be executed until he had given a specific go-ahead himself.

The cable he was drafting was the go-ahead. He combined it with a Situation Report with enough detail to see whether anybody had gotten fainthearted in Paris or DC. It was no worse than they must have expected, though. Presumably the Powers That Be had decided they wanted the omelet before they contacted Kelly in the first place.

The agent left Sergeant Rowe's door unlocked behind him because he did not have a key to readmit himself if he needed to. His trouser cuffs swished and echoed at every step. They sounded much like a blade on a whetstone.

Ideally, the mini-computer would have been located with the General Services Officer in the Annex across the road. The system's main day-to-day use was for inventory control. Other officers, with more clout, if less need, had lists of their own which they wanted on disk too, however. There was also some reasonable concern, Doug had said, that the local employees who swarmed about the Annex would find the new Western toy irresistible—and fragile—if it were where they could get their hands on it. That meant that Kelly had only to walk up to the third floor of the Chancery instead of hiking up the Chemin Cheikh Bachir Brahimi and back.

The computer sat on its cabinet, partially obstructing the entrance to the tower from which the harbor was monitored. The agent cut on the power, then checked the tower room more or less for the hell of it . . . though it wouldn't have been wholly beyond possibility for one of the Company men to have been inside, "checking the cameras." When the CRT screen announced the machine was PRET—Christ, it was a Thomson-CSF unit with all its commands and controls in French—Kelly took a program disk from his inside coat pocket and inserted it.

There was a set of similar—though not, of course, identical—code programs locked in the safe in the Defense Attaché's office for emergencies. For the purpose of Skyripper, however, Kelly was assuming that the disks issued to Commander Posner had already been compromised; that is, that CIA officers had made a surreptitious entry to the office, burgled the safe, and copied the programs therein.

In all likelihood, that had in fact occurred.

Kelly began typing from his draft. He turned off the CRT since the letters that would be appearing on it were garbage anyway. The program simply coupled the keystrokes into a series of random numbers generated, Kelly had once been told, by cosmic ray impacts. It was the electronic equivalent of a one-pad code, totally indecipherable without an identical program. Because the patterns were random, even possession of the clear text of one message would not have permitted the deciphering of the next.

With the report complete and stored in the working memory of the computer, Kelly checked to see that the paper was straight in the sprocket feed of the printer. It was. Sighing, he punched COM and watched with his usual fascination as the daisy wheel raced back and forth across the paper. Even after five years of selling and servicing the damned things, Kelly still got a wrenching feeling every time he saw a machine working happily away without the necessary attention of any human being. It made the agent think of missile silos in North Dakota and Siberia, controlled by computers just as conscienceless as this one.

Of course, somebody still had to punch START.

The printer was a fast one. It had completed its task before Kelly's mind had proceeded from the air bursts at 10,000 feet to the firestorms sucking houses and men into the heart of hell. Somebody else's worry, that. Kelly pulled the sheet from the printer and checked it.

Satisfied, he removed the program disk, put it back in its envelope, and cut the computer's power—dumping the internal memory. With the encrypted sheet folded in his hand, he walked down the empty stairs to the basement and the Code Room.

There was no response when Kelly knocked on the heavy steel door. The agent's frown began to smooth into the blankness his face took on when he was really angry. Then Charlie DeVoe called, "Hey, Cap'n," from behind in the corridor. "Let me take that." The Communicator was grinning. "Sorry I wasn't here, but it hasn't come to the point we can't take a leak while we're on duty, you know."

"Just got here myself," the agent said, handing over the encrypted report. At the top he had printed in block capitals the cable address and priority. No one had thought to tell Kelly where the normal word-processing program was kept. The address, if typed on the code program, would have been just as indecipherable as the text. "Sorry as hell to keep you on again," Kelly said, "but maybe Doug told you—I hope a fifth of Scotch'll make things a little smoother for you."

The Communicator raised his eyebrows at the statement, then glanced down at the coded document. "Oh, didn't have to worry about that. . . ." he said, meaning one fact or the other. Then, "Yeah, that sure as hell does smooth things. You know what a fifth of Johnny Walker runs me?"

Kelly was taken aback by the question. The liquor was, after all, a gesture rather than payment *per se* for work within the Communicator's normal duties. "Well, about three bucks, I suppose," he said mildly, "but I've always found it's a good way to spend three bucks."

"Three bucks to somebody on the dip list," DeVoe corrected. "Somebody who can order duty-free from Justesen, sure. To Foreign Service *Staff*, like yours truly"—he thumped himself on the chest— "It's the full duty. That's about eighty bucks in Algiers, that's what it is."

"Christ," said Kelly in amazement, "I knew it was that way on paper . . . but I thought missions generally pooled their duty-free allowances and everybody got some. I mean, they keep telling us America's a democracy, don't they?"

DeVoe sneered. "Not the Algiers mission," he said. "And that's not a policy that'll be changed by his Excellency Rufus Jackass Gordon, either." The Communicator's face brightened. "Say, you know that bastard's looking for you, don't you?"

"Heard there was a cable on the subject," admitted the agent. The situation reminded him of the business deals he had made in men's rooms across Western Europe. DeVoe could not take him into the Code Room, and a suggestion that they move anywhere else would have broken the rapport.

"Sure was, short and sweet," the Communicator said. The problem with making people violate their oaths in order to keep their jobs was that once the initial sanctity was gone, the oath itself meant very little. DeVoe had lost his cherry a long time back. "'Request denied,' it said, and I'd have given a month's pay to see Gordon's face when Buffy carried it over to him. God *damn* I would!" He sobered, even as his hand raised to slap his thigh. "Say, though, that's not what I meant. The duty officer's been calling all around the building looking for you. He had Gordon on the line, wanted you ASAP." DeVoe waved the sheet of gate-fold paper and grinned. "Guess he didn't try the computer, did he?"

"Hell, I was busy," said the agent. "I wouldn't have answered if somebody did ring. Though come to think, I didn't see an intercom up there anyway." He sighed. "Well," he went on, "I guess I better go put in an appearance or you'll be here til morning with the Ambassador's cable traffic. . . ."

XX

Kelly could hear the angry voices as he mounted the stairs to the lobby. Even so, he was surprised when he stepped through the doorway and saw that one of the three men wrangling in the reception area was Ambassador Rufus Gordon himself.

"Ah—" said the youngest of the three men, presumably the duty officer. He pointed toward the stairs and Kelly.

Ambassador Gordon and the plump, suited man of about forty turned at the gesture. "What in *God's* name do you think you're doing?" Gordon demanded in a voice on the high edge of control.

"Ah, Mr. Ambassador—" the plump man beside him said anxiously.

"Reeves," quavered the Ambassador, "when I need the warnings of my DCM as to what I should say in my own embassy, then I'll ask for them!"

The Deputy Chief of Mission bit down on his lower lip. Kelly said very carefully, "Sir, I'm doing my job, just like anybody else. I'll be leaving—"

"Who told you you could waltz around the Chancery unescorted?" Gordon shouted. He wheeled on the duty officer like the cutting head of a turret lathe. "You—Byrne! *You* let him loose this way?" In his silver-gray suit and agitation, the Ambassador looked like a man who had witnessed a murder on the way to a dinner party.

Kelly did not know the junior officer, but he knew his own duty as a human being. Raising his voice in a verbal lightning rod to draw the anger back on himself, the agent said, "My permission to use embassy facilities freely came to me through Major General Wallace Pedler, the DA in Paris. If you feel the confirmation of those orders which you've already received is not enough, then I suggest that's a matter for General Pedler's superiors and yours. *Sir.*"

Ambassador Gordon's face was pale enough under ordinary circumstances. Now its pallor was less that of a corpse than of the bone beneath the flesh. He took a step toward the agent. Kelly, with the chill certainty of the knife he would not need to draw, spread his feet a half step and waited.

"Good God!" cried the DCM, leaping between the two men. Kelly had not advanced, and the Ambassador had paused when he met the agent's eyes. Reeves bobbed between them, suddenly ridiculous—separating two motionless men already ten feet apart.

"Kelly, I swear one thing," the Ambassador said, breathing hard. "*I'm* the President's representative here, and *I* decide the use of embassy premises. And if you don't leave my wife alone, you'll rue the day you were *born*!"

It wasn't the parting shot Kelly had expected. Gordon turned and strode out of the Chancery. The entryway door was too heavy to fling open as the Ambassador would have liked, but it made a satisfying slam behind him.

The three men in the lobby looked at one another for a moment of silence. Then the agent said quietly, "Look, I don't suppose either of you like me worth a damn . . . and I don't blame you. But I'm sorry, for what's gone down and what's coming."

Reeves rubbed his fleshy cheeks with his hands. Instinctively, he glanced at the TV monitor as if to be sure that the Ambassador was not in the anteroom with his ear glued to the door. "This is officially a hardship post, Mr. Ceriani," he said. "A 15% differential over base salary is paid to personnel stationed here. The weather is splendid, the government is stable—the people are quite friendly, really, if you go out and meet them, none of this 'US go home' stuff or jacking up the price for an American. . . . But there are times, you know, that I don't think 15% is nearly enough."

He drew himself up. "Well," he concluded, "I will go back to my wife and cold dinner and *not* explain to her why his Excellency saw fit to call me away." Shaking his head, he left the Chancery.

Kelly waited for the door to close. Without looking at the duty officer, he said, "Look, it doesn't matter to me . . . but I'd suggest you not tell anybody about this either. If it gets beyond the, well, four people who were here, somebody's going to get real embarrassed. That wouldn't be good for anybody who needs a fitness report to get promoted . . . however much fun the embassy wives might find the story." He looked up at Byrne at last. The duty officer nodded agreement.

"Well, I'm gone then," said the agent, striding to the door. He closed it gently behind him, then waved to the TV camera before stepping out of the antechamber. He had forgotten to check on Sergeant Rowe, who should have returned by now. And on the liquor.

The first question resolved itself, while the need for a drink became more acute: Annamaria sat on one of the benches beneath the cantilevered roof covering the entryway.

The tall woman was dressed as Kelly had seen her earlier that evening, but with the addition of a dark jacket, suede or wool so far as the agent could judge in the entrance light. She was smoking a cigarette as well, something Kelly had not seen her do previously. She ground it out against the side of the stone bench before she rose. "Your things are in the St. George, the room your 'firm' had booked," said the woman. "Your car is parked at the Annex, all very proper—Doug insisted. Now, if *I'd* been driving, you'd be right down there where I am." She pointed toward the lane between the Chancery and the Villa Inshallah.

"That's fine, sure," Kelly said. "Look, Doug—"

"Doug has gone home, I told him to," Annamaria said. She raised a finger to forestall any comment by the agent. "Of course, you can call him there if you really need to destroy his little girl's birthday supper, which was supposed to have been last night."

"Oh, hell, he didn't say a thing about that," Kelly mumbled. "Not that there would've been a choice—we needed those enlargements."

"Well, tonight there was a choice," Annamaria said primly. "I can't imagine any errands Doug could run that I can't . . . or any keys that he has and I don't, either, though I suppose I shouldn't admit that. Oh"—she reached down behind the bench and straightened with a topless Haig and Haig box—"Doug says these are for you."

Kelly took the box. The metal foil seals of the two bottles winked above the cardboard cells. "Yeah," he said, wetting his lips and pretending he had not heard the question in the woman's voice. "Look," he went on, facing the ground, "I need to get these inside. . . ."

"I'll wait out here." Annamaria spoke brightly, but as Kelly buzzed the Chancery door he noticed the flame of a cigarette lighter behind him.

Byrne turned out to be one of the vice consuls. If he was surprised at the agent's request that he give the Scotch to DeVoe when he left, it did not show. Kelly had no intention of disturbing the Communicator while he was in the middle of sending Kelly's own urgent cable. As for the sour mash waiting for the agent's return—it was more than a temptation to open it and take a quick slug before walking back into the night. Kelly did not do so; but he was not sure he would not until he had closed the outer door behind him.

"Look, Anna," he said as the woman stood again and the second cigarette joined the first, "maybe we need to talk, but I don't think—this—is the place. . . ."

"I brought my car," she said smiling. She held out her arm, insisting on linking it with Kelly's despite his hesitation.

"Your husband—" the agent began as they walked to the Mustang.

"Hush, you said you didn't want to talk here," Annamaria retorted, patting the inner angle of Kelly's elbow. "We'll find a place that's quiet. Here, I'll drive."

They pulled past the Residence gate, accelerating. Two Fiats were parked there again. For an instant a reggae beat puffed over the wall before Kelly rolled the side window firmly closed. Annamaria showed no sign of wanting to talk as she whipped the little car north. Kelly said nothing either. The woman was driving over her head at the moment, and the agent did not want to distract her. Besides, he didn't really know what he was going to say. He very much wished he had brought the whiskey along.

They climbed west toward Village Celeste, around switchbacks so sharp that the tires squealed at little more than a walking pace. The gradient was well over 12%. Unexpectedly, Annamaria pulled hard right and braked. The headlights glared back from the pressed steel guard rail; then the black-haired woman cut the lights and the engine together.

Both of them sighed. Annamaria took out a cigarette but did not move to light it. "That's Notre Dame de Afrique," she said, gesturing through the windshield. Below, the dome of the 19th Century cathedral shone in the moonlight, barred by the shadows of its own towers. Beyond the black slither of National Highway 11, the main coastal road, the Mediterranean was itself a metallic shimmer. Mercury vapor lights were blue-white pinholes in the fabric of the dark city.

"You must have been there when your husband came out of the Chancery," Kelly said finally as he studied the ghost of his own reflection in the windshield. "What did he say?"

"Nothing," Annamaria said quietly from her side of the car. "Which is what I expected." Her lips quirked. "Chuck Reeves said, 'Goodnight, Anna.' But Rufus didn't say anything at all. When he gets very angry, he's like that—he pretends I don't exist." She was looking at her fingernails, flared on the steering wheel in the moonlight.

She flicked the cigarette, still unlighted, up onto the dashboard as she continued, "The last time he did this was when I told him I was taking over the snack bar. Chuck had been complaining about the problems—they'd fired the local manager, he was robbing the place blind and couldn't do even *that* well. I said I'd take over—I'd heard that an ambassador's wife had run the place a few tours before, and I figured it was something I could do as well as anybody else. I told Rufus, and he said I wouldn't, and . . . it was two weeks or so before he spoke to me again. I think he'd ruin Chuck's career completely if he even suspected the notion had anything to do with him."

Annamaria reached over and took Kelly's hand with her own. "It bothered me, it bothered me a lot when we were first married. But not now, not for years. It's only when I really *do* exist, when I'm doing something that isn't being his shadow, that Rufus pretends I'm not there."

Kelly leaned toward her. They kissed. His arm bumped the steering wheel as he reached around her shoulders, his fingers caressing the black suede and feeling the coat slide over the light shirt beneath.

Annamaria fumbled with the steering wheel latch. She swung the column as nearly vertical as it would go. She reached back for Kelly, her knee now pressing against the gearshift.

"Anna, wait," the agent said. He caught her hands in his, bending to kiss the backs of them. Their bones and tendons were tense beneath his lips. "Listen," he said, speaking to her hands as she had done moments before, "I want this a lot, more than—" he paused, swallowed and dropped her right hand into his lap. Her fingers gripped his erect penis through the trousers, stroking greedily, but he lifted her away again.

"A lot," he continued huskily. "And I don't give a God damn about what your husband can do to me, because he can't do a thing. Wouldn't matter anyway. And you"—he looked up, met her eyes —"you're an adult, you know what kind of trouble you're going to get in or not, that . . . that's your business, not mine. My business is to finish a job, though . . . a job I've been sent to do."

Annamaria squirmed, her left hand slipping under Kelly's jacket and trying to tug him closer. His ribcage was as hard as an oak tree—and as immobile.

"Anna, listen," the agent repeated desperately, "I can't handle this, not without blowing the other—I just *can't*. And I don't want to screw it up because my mind's on you. *Please*, Anna, for God's sake, understand."

"God?" Annamaria said. She straightened. "Oh, God, yes, God *indeed*," she repeated and slammed the heels of her hands against the steering wheel. She bent forward, her face against the hub, her arms straining on the wood-grained plastic. At last she took a deep breath and faced Kelly again. In the lights of a passing car, her face looked calm except for the strand of hair twisting across it like an unnoticed serpent. "Yes, you're really going to leave me this way," the woman continued in a savage voice. "I really have a talent for bringing out the cold fish in men, don't I? Rufus freezes up when he's angry enough to chew nails, and now you—with a sense of duty that makes you impotent!"

The agent said nothing. He bent his head down but did not turn away. He had in fact lost his erection, but it was not a subject he would have debated in any case. "Anna," he said into the waiting silence, "until Professor Vlasov's in somebody else's hands, you're right. I'm no kind of man at all. Afterwards, if you really care, I'll come to wherever you are, but . . . I'm sorry. My God but I'm sorry."

Annamaria sighed. "Oh, lover," she said under her breath, "you're sorry and I'm sorry and we're all a lot of sorry fools, aren't we?"

She started the car, glanced over her shoulder and backed onto the road again. Before Kelly could speak, she had cursed and pulled the headlights on. "I'll drop you by your car, then," she said as they lurched forward and down the hill.

"Oh, Chancery gate if you would," the agent said. "I've got. . . ." his voice trailed off. "I'm sorry."

"It's not your fault I'm a fool," the woman responded coolly. After a moment she added the last words that were spoken between them until she let Kelly out of the car: "Or mine if you are, I suppose."

XXI

The liquor in Kelly's gut was sending little tendrils through his whole body like mold spreading across a bread loaf. He had not drunk much, well aware of how long it had been since he ate. Still, his step was jaunty and the bottle now had enough air in it to slosh. Byrne had found him a paper bag to carry it. Kelly shouldn't have broken the seal—Lord knew what Algerian liquor laws were like. All he needed was to be jailed after a fender-bender because he had an open bottle in the car . . . and no trunk to lock it in, either.

As Kelly slanted across the street to the Annex, he saw in the corner of his eye the glow of a car's courtesy light winking on as the door opened. A tall man was getting out of one of the parked Fiats. The distant street lamp turned the black of his aristocratic face to something near purple.

The agent stepped up on the far curb. He wondered if the Chaka Front could possibly do a more brutal job of governing South Africa than the present government did. Possibly, yes; it was barely possible. Look at Idi Amin, Macias Nguema . . . Bokassa the First—and, thank God, only—who gave diamonds to a European President and tortured young girls to death by the hundreds. Look, for that matter, at King Chaka himself . . . though in comparison to some of *his* European contemporaries, the great Zulu leader did not seem so bad. God knew that he hadn't done as much bloody evil as Napoleon.

But that was State Department business at the national level. And here in Algiers, it was the business of his Excellency the Ambassador. No business of Tom Kelly, who had more than enough on his plate right—

Two men stepped from the shadowed trees between the street and the sidewalk. They were blocking the dirt pathway some twenty feet from the Annex gate. The men wore dark slacks and dashikis decorated with incongruous floral prints. They were smiling as they faced Kelly; at least, the agent caught the flash of their teeth. There was nothing at all cheerful in that.

"Hello, hello," Kelly murmured and jumped back for the street. The third Zulu, the man Kelly had seen getting out of the Fiat, caught him about the arms and waist. He held the American with the ease of a father with a six-year old throwing a tantrum. The Zulu was not wearing shoes. The whisper of his long strides across the pavement had been lost in the buzz in Kelly's skull.

A hundred yards up the street, the headlights of a parked car went on and froze the struggle in their glare. The car began to move with only the hiss of its tires on the pavement.

"Help!" Kelly shouted.

The car passed, still accelerating. It was large and black. The faces of the three men in the front seat were dim, silent blurs.

The absence of the headlights deepened the earlier darkness.

The man holding the agent wrestled him back onto the pathway, away from even the dim blue security of the distant streetlight. One of the two waiting Zulus joined him, seizing the American by the left wrist and elbow. Kelly kicked at the man's groin, missed, and tried to stamp on the bare instep of the one holding him from behind. His crepe heel connected, but it did not affect the Zulu's diaphragm-level bear hug. Kelly had no illusions about his ability to match three bigger, younger men in hand to hand combat.

The third attacker stepped forward; light danced over his right hand for the first time. He chuckled.

The weapon strapped to the Zulu's hand and wrist was known the world over, but it was most common in societies existing in proximity to big cats. Four tines had been opened from a section of ductile iron waterpipe. The metal had been twisted and sharpened with a file into ragged edges that winked like diamonds where they caught the light. They could kill, of course, as even a rolled newspaper can kill; but the real purpose of the claws was more dramatic than mere death. . . .

The man with the claws laughed and feinted with his weapon. Kelly screamed and kicked harmlessly. There was no one on the street. The courtyard walls were as blank as those of a Roman amphitheatre. The three Zulus snickered together. The one to Kelly's left grabbed a handful of the agent's trouser front. He pulled. The belt held, but the fly and the cotton briefs beneath ripped away. The sagging fabric hobbled Kelly's knees. The man behind the agent shifted his grip, now holding Kelly by both elbows. The claw-wielder said something abrupt and strode forward.

Kelly screamed again and slammed the liquor bottle down with all the strength of his freed right hand. The thick glass held, but bones smashed in the knee of the man behind him. The Zulu's grunt of pain mingled with Kelly's own outcry. The claws missed because the injured Zulu could not prevent the agent's backward lunge.

One man still gripped Kelly by the left wrist. The American, supported in a half-squat by that grip, brought his paper-clad bottle around like a flyswatter. The Zulu threw up his free hand to protect his face. The side of the bottle caught the point of the man's raised elbow. This time glass and bag burst together in a spray of sour-mash whiskey. The Zulu cried out and loosed Kelly to hold his own damaged limb. Kelly jabbed him twice in the face with the ragged neck of the bottle.

Like a sap glove, the iron claws were heavy enough to impede the user's coordination. By the time the third Zulu had recovered from his vertical swipe at Kelly's groin, his two companions were down. The Zulu's face was in full shadow. Light washed between two tree boles and lapped about the American. Behind Kelly on the pavement, the man with the crushed knee was retching. The agent reached out with his left hand and peeled the remnants of the bag from the neck of the bottle. He held it advanced. The glass winked in a tight circlet. There were no long blades like those of resin dummies used in films. The stubby edges were smeared with blood and humours from the eyes they had just destroyed.

The Zulu raised his claws. Kelly lunged forward with a guttural cry. He stumbled on his torn trousers. The Zulu dodged around a tree and into the street. As he ran, he was calling to his companions and fumbling with the strap that bound his weapon to him. He had learned a lesson that his ancestors had taught the British at Isandhlwana: if your opponent is willing to die to get to you, you had best be willing to die yourself.

Kelly picked himself up from the dirt. He shuffled a step forward, then regained enough composure to tug his pants up with his left hand. He staggered to the Annex gate, walking with an adrenalin tremor. He banged on the steel with the heel of his right hand. Nothing happened. "This is Ambassador Gordon, you wog bastard!" Kelly shouted in English. "Open up or you're out of a job!"

The gate swung open abruptly. Kelly stumbled within and closed the portal behind him with his shoulders. Then he doubled up in front of the nervous guard to vomit bile and whiskey onto the drive.

At last the agent managed to raise himself into a kneeling position. He mumbled in French, "Do you have something to eat?"

The guard gave him a terrified smile but did not speak. "Food!" Kelly shouted. He got control of himself again. He found the pocket of his torn trousers with some difficulty and drew out the money clip, "Food," he repeated more calmly, peeling off a pair of hundred-dinar notes, enough to buy a meal in the best restaurant in Algiers. "I'm drunk, maybe you heard me shouting in the street . . . ? I just need to get something in my belly before I drive home."

This time the guard nodded. He slipped back into his shelter. In the street a small car roared to life and squealed into a turn. The shouting was muffled by the wall and gate. But the time the guard returned with two navel oranges and a baguette of bread, the car had started again and was screaming north at too high a speed for the gear.

Kelly wolfed a bite of the crisp bread, choked, and swallowed it anyway. His fingers shook too badly to permit him to peel the oranges. After a moment's hesitation, he took out his jackknife and cut each orange across the axis. He squeezed the halves into his mouth. The tartness of the juice masked and almost smothered the bite of stomach acids high in his throat. Then, methodically, the agent finished the bread.

The guard stared as Kelly stood. The American looked down at himself, torn and bloodied and reeking of his own vomit and urine. "Tsk," he said, "I'll certainly have to change before I go to his Excellency's musicale tonight, won't I?"

Kelly watched cross streets and his mirrors as he drove downtown to his new hotel. He was not followed so far as he could tell.

XXII

The window in the Defense Attaché's office looked north, toward the sea and directly away from the Aurassi. Kelly, no less than Posner and Rowe, found himself staring anxiously through the glass anyway as they all waited for the radio to speak.

"I don't know why I'm worried about this," said the Attaché, turning sharply in his chair and standing up. He paced toward the closed door. "Best thing that could happen would be this whole house of cards coming down before anyone gets hurt. Either the equipment doesn't work or your contact wasn't told how to use it after all. I had *nothing* to do with that."

And nobody said you goddam did, the agent thought. Aloud he said, "Well, if they didn't make contact en route like they were supposed to, then we'll have to arrange something here. Phone from the desk, ring off if the security man answers instead of Hoang. . . . I dunno, whatever. Right now, all that I'm afraid of is that our boy isn't in 327 after all. Then we *have* got a problem."

"For Christ's sake, man!" the commander snapped, "you heard Tarek on the phone yourself. They've checked in, they're in 327—and Hoang isn't contacting us, for whatever reason!"

"Or Tarek," Kelly said, standing to stretch his legs more than to look at the scintillating water again, "was afraid to tell us something went wrong for fear we'd jerk the kid's visa again. Which we by God *will* if this falls through. I don't care why!"

The intercom buzzed. The three men froze; then Sergeant Rowe, who would normally have screened incoming calls from his own office, reached over his superior's glass-topped desk and took the instrument. "Rowe," he said. He listened intently for a moment. Cupping the receiver with his palms, he whispered to the others, "There's a crate like yesterday's in the pouch for you, Tom."

"Can they—" Kelly began. He pursed his lips. "No, I want to check it before we dump it in the armory after all. Doug, can you have somebody haul it up to your office until things are straight here?"

Rowe gave him the high sign. "Henri," he said, "I'll be down for that in a—"

The radio blatted, "Hello, are you there?" in loud, distorted Vietnamese.

Kelly motioned a fast, unnecessary "cut" to the sergeant as he twisted back the gain with his other hand. He keyed the mike. "We're here, Doctor," he said in the same language. "Can you hear me all right?"

"Not so loud, please!" the other voice hissed desperately through the receiver. "I have the bath running, but my guard is very close."

The agent dialed back on the transmitter's output. "Can you hear now, Doctor?" he asked.

"Yes, yes . . ." said the receiver, tinny but no longer a painful roar. "But go quickly, I am very nervous with this."

Kelly paused a moment to make sure the Vietnamese had finished speaking. "All right, Doctor," the agent said, "listen and don't speak until I say so. You must deliver this message to—" he paused. Did Hoang know Vlasov by the code name Kelly had been given? Hell, better discovery than misunderstanding.

"You must deliver this message to Professor Vlasov tonight at the banquet. Tomorrow morning you are scheduled for a tour of the Institute for Nuclear Research near the Casbah. The signal will be either an explosion or a nearby traffic accident. This will be as soon as the Professor gets out of his car. A bomb or a crash, either one." The timing on the truck shouldn't be that close, but Kelly was afraid that the driver might get overanxious.

He cleared his throat and continued, "At the signal, Vlasov is to run across the road, the Boulevard de la Victoire. People will probably be running or ducking under cover. There will be one man standing up across the street with a white coat over his arm. Vlasov is to make for that man as fast as possible. If he can look like he's in a panic, so much the better.

"Is that clear? You can speak now."

Briefly the only sound from the radio was the popping and hiss of the electrical sea which surrounds the planet, the archetype of the theoretical ether. Sergeant Rowe had slipped away, his leaving unnoticed in Kelly's total concentration on the microphone in his hand. Then the speaker said, "I understand that, I will tell him. But what about me?"

The agent blinked. "You'll, ah—" he began. Kelly had not been interested in the arrangements already made with the Vietnamese physicist. Setting up a one-time net in Algiers had been plenty to occupy his imagination. Hoang Tanh was like the US Navy: necessary to the ultimate success of the mission, but out of Kelly's own hands and therefore not to be worried over. Otherwise, you worked yourself into a complete and completely useless dither.

Maybe, however, Kelly should have learned more about Hoang.

"You'll be handled by your regular control," the agent said, adding with what he hoped was assurance, "The arrangements will be carried out to the letter. In fact, there'll be a bonus for you."

That much Kelly could guarantee, even if it had to come out of his own pocket. Why the *hell* didn't somebody warned him that Hoang would need his hand held?

Because any control officer knows that, just like you don't have to tell a radioman to key the mike before speaking, the back of Kelly's brain told him. He hadn't known it, because he didn't have any goddam business—

"No," the radio was saying in southern-dialect Vietnamese. "I must come too this time. This is very big, yes? You must now give me a position in one of your universities—that is fair payment, is it not?"

Christ on a crutch.

Well, it probably *was* a fair deal; and yes, assuming Doctor Hoang had halfway reasonable credentials, the USG probably could find him a slot somewhere. . . . The Pentagon laid out a lot of grant money in the course of a year, enough to convince more credentials committees than not. But why in *God's* name was Hoang springing it now?

Or was it the first time the matter had been raised? "Ah, Doctor," Kelly asked carefully, "what have you been told so far about provisions for you to defect?"

"Told? Told nothing!" the voice spluttered through the atmospherics. "In good time, yes, they tell me, but stay a little longer. I have stayed long enough, I say! I have earned my reward!"

"Yes, of course, and we've anticipated your request," Kelly lied. "You will be taken out in Frankfurt, while you change planes. The German Federal Police will separate you from your, ah, bodyguard at Passport Control. You'll be rushed straight to the American Consulate. You need do nothing—by telling me you want to come over, you've done everything necessary. Do you understand?"

The agent's grip on the microphone was tight with anger rather than tension. He forced his fingers to relax. You don't get mad at guns that jam or cars that won't start. It doesn't change things, they're just the way they are. And you don't get mad at people who act like fools either, not unless it's going to change things. What the hell, the plan as described might work—if Pedler and the boys back in Europe got on the stick. At least, it ought to keep Hoang happy until the snatch had been executed. Or at least attempted.

The Vietnamese did not sound particularly happy,

though, when he said, "I hear you. All right, I understand. And I will carry out *my* part.

"Now I must go."

White noise from the speaker replaced the contact agent's voice. Kelly shook his head wearily and cut the transmitter power. "We need to keep the tape recorder hooked to the receiver until all this is over," he said, speaking indiscriminately toward Posner and Rowe—who must have returned. Presumably one or the other of the men could handle it. If they didn't, the hell with it. . . .

"No," the agent said, aloud but to himself. Then, "Doug, got the recorder? I'll hook it up myself."

The heavy reel to reel recorder fit comfortably beside the receiver on top of Posner's desk. A length of coaxial cable bound them into a neat unit. Whenever a signal was received, the recorder would tape it and shut down again. Generally, since the pick-up was automatic, that meant that they would get a tape of the toilet flushing and perhaps the security man singing in the shower. There was an off-chance that the rig would function as a true bug and hear an important conversation; and a rather less improbable chance that Hoang would try to contact them again. The recorder made sense.

Kelly had a splitting headache, compounded of the dry air and the smoke-filled meeting with the Kabyles the day before. Well, if it weren't his sinuses, it might have been his prostate. . . . He turned from the recorder to the Defense Attaché. Posner's smoking wasn't helping a whole lot either, but it *was* the man's own office. "Commander," the agent said, "there's a glitch with our contact—he wants to defect too."

Both the other men grunted in surprise. Kelly nodded. "Yeah, I about danced for joy myself when he dropped that one. I told him sure, it was already set up. The Germans'd take him away from his guard in Frankfurt, then *zip*, off to the States and Ivy League tenure. Or whatever the hell. Thing is—and it's not that I'll shoot myself if it doesn't work out . . . but I did tell him that."

The agent looked from one of the military men to the other. He was embarrassed that it mattered to him that he had made what amounted to a promise. "Anyway, we need to get a cable out to Pedler to see if he can pull the deal off on pretty goddamned short notice. I'm not going to be able to handle it and check out the drop site during daylight. Can you, Commander?"

Posner jetted smoke from both nostrils. "Yes," he said, "yes, that's reasonable enough." He managed a smile at Kelly. "It's even the sort of thing I imagined I might be doing when I transferred to the DIA. Which, God knows, very little else that's going on is."

Kelly handed Posner the program disk. "Fine, sir. Here's the code. And—ah, if you'd keep this on your person at all times, I'd appreciate it. Orders, of course."

As they closed the Attaché's door behind them, the agent said, "Let's take a look at that pouch before I forget it, Doug. Then we can haul it to the armory too."

The grenades in the second case were similar in size and shape to the previous load of smoke bombs. The tops of these were painted white, however, in line with US practice for marking CS.

Kelly drew out one of the heavy bombs and looked at

it for a moment. "Got some Kleenex or a roll of toilet paper handy, Doug?" he asked.

The sergeant shrugged and tossed over a box of tissues from his lower desk drawer.

Carefully, the agent matted three tissues together. Then he unscrewed the fuse assembly from the grenade canister itself. The assembly was a slender tube that fit the length of the grenade's axis. It contained the striker, fuse, and the black powder booster charge that actually ignited the filler and caused it to spew tear gas. Kelly stuffed the tissues down into the well to keep the filler where it belonged. Then, with another wad of tissue, he wiped the tube clean before dropping it into his side pocket.

"We'll bury this under a rose bush after dark," he said with a grin, thumbing toward the defused canister. "Till then, let's hope nobody knocks the thing over, or else you don't use your office for a while. A *long* while. And now"—he bent over to take one end of the packing case—"let's get this to the armory and ourselves to lovely Tipasa, resort of the best defecting physicists."

XXIII

"I want you to take a look from up here," said Sergeant Rowe, panting a little with the climb from the parking area. "Otherwise when you see the harbor itself, you'll bitch. This isn't much of a coast for fooling around with rubber boats, Tom."

"Hell, you can say that again," Kelly muttered. "You mean this is a *good* area?"

"Typical," corrected the sergeant. "The harbor's good, but you can't really tell from this angle."

The cliff on which the Americans stood dropped eighty jagged feet to the Mediterranean. Tipasa's Roman wall, four feet of rough stone in a concrete matrix, had ended just short of the edge from which they watched. Only the foundations remained, their massive construction belied by their state of total ruin. Over a kilometer to the west, another promontory completed the bay into which harbors had been cut ever since the Carthaginians settled here. Knowing that, and seeing the chop of the Mediterranean, Kelly appreciated how rare decent harbors were in North Africa.

There was nothing like a beach at any point the agent could see, although the ground fell away along the southern edge of the bay and gave him a good view. Low cliffs, the corniche, alternated with jumbles of rock which stretched far out into the water. There the waves bubbled away from the ruddy stones like foam from blood-smeared teeth.

"Now, I think this is going to work," Rowe said. He was pleased at the impression the view had made on his companion. "But you've got to recognize that if you're being extracted by boat, you're pretty limited. Closer in there's the beach at Chenona, but the buildings all around it are housing for government employees. And on the other side of the mountain, at Cherchell—" He pointed. A cone at least three thousand feet high stabbed abruptly from the coast just west of Tipasa. Clouds blurred its peak. "—there's an even better beach. But there's also an armor school, and *no* foreigner wants to get too close to that. So Tipasa's pretty much the choice."

Kelly shook his head. "Damn," he said, "you look at charts; and sure, there's enough water to get a sub in close enough for a pick-up. Looking at those rocks down there, I—well, I sure hope they don't scrape the bottom at any speed, because I'll bet it doesn't look any softer half a mile out than it does here."

"Well," Rowe suggested cautiously, "the first thing is to get the rubber boat out half a mile, isn't it? Let's take a look at the harbor."

The modern city of Tipasa stretched somewhat farther south than had the ancient one, but its total occupied area appeared to be much smaller. Much of the area enclosed by the fallen walls was now meadow. Sergeant Rowe drove carefully back to the highway from the parking area east of the city.

They were paralleling the foundations of the Roman wall. Kelly noticed that the grassy slope was littered with hollowed stone blocks. Each was more than five feet long and a foot in width and height. A few of the blocks still had their stone lids in place. "What the hell are they?" the agent asked. "They look like coffins."

"Right, sarcophagi," the sergeant agreed as he turned onto the highway. "Nothing fancy, just the local stone squared and hollowed. Once in a while you'll find a Chi-Rho cut on one end, but usually not even that. And they weren't buried, just placed on the hillside outside the walls."

Kelly licked his lips. He did not reply. It would have made no difference to his plans if he *had* known the extraction point would be in the center of an arc of ancient graves.

It did not make him like the situation any better, however.

Just inside the ancient walls, the marked highway branched left and away from the bay. Rowe continued straight, toward the row of buildings that looked like a business district. The hundred yards of ground between the street and the sea was broken and overgrown. "Shall I drive all the way to the harbor?" the sergeant asked. "Or do you want me to park on the street for now? It's not far to walk."

"No point in calling attention to ourselves," Kelly decided. "Let's walk."

Two blocks away, near the entrance to the excavated portion of ancient Tipasa, was a group of boys. One of them broke away and began running toward the two men. Rowe locked up the car and the men walked seaward. The breeze was mild.

There was no chop to speak of here to mark the brilliant, ultramarine water. Nonetheless, frequent tongues of foam reminded Kelly that there were rocks near enough to surface to gnaw the bottom out of his boat. He leaned forward. "Christ," he said. There was a beach of sorts after all. It was narrow and of pebbles rather than sand, but it would do . . . except that it was a good ten feet below the sharp lip of the corniche.

The boy came running up to the Americans. "Watch your car," he panted in English. American cars were identifiable and virtually unique to the national community here, it seemed.

"No," said the sergeant harshly.

"A dinar," said Kelly. He flipped the aluminum coin high in the air, then repocketed it with a smile.

"*Two* dinars," said the boy in pleased surprise.

Kelly pointed to the car. "Watch it well," he said. After only a moment's hesitation, the boy began to saunter back to the Volare.

Looking out over the crystalline sea, the agent said, "First, we can't afford even the *tiny* chance that he'd let the air out of our tires. Second, it gets him away from us quicker than trying to ignore him. And third"—he looked at Rowe and grinned—"I sort of like kids. But don't let word of that get out or I'll lose my all-star bastard rating."

Rowe cleared his throat. "Well," he said, "well. Where we want to go is back to the east. We'll drive it when we put the boat in the water, but for now. . . ."

The ground just beyond the corniche was driveable, though it was not in any sense a proper road. Absinthe bushes—wormwood—must have been planted ornamentally at some time, perhaps millennia in the past. The bushes grew profusely, their white-dusted leaves shading the rust-red native stone. Ahead, foam and rocks shared a deep cavity which the sea washed but did not hold. Closer yet, there was a trench cut in the—

"Well, I'll be damned," Kelly said. "It's a staircase cut down to the beach!"

"As requested," the sergeant agreed. "One beach, with access. And as open as all this is"—he waved his arm in a southerly arc, taking in the blocks of stone and scrub to the nearest buildings—"nobody can see you launch the boat. The cliff hides you to anyone on the road until you're out beyond the breakwater. Okay?"

Kelly clapped the younger man on the shoulder. "You're the best damn travel agent *I've* ever met," he said. "You know, I was worried that the local support I'd get would . . . leave a lot to be desired. But I was wrong, at least about you. . . . I'll tell the world!"

The sergeant blushed and looked away. "Well," he said, "glad it's okay. We'd better take a quick look at the safe house now and stash the gear. Hope it does as well as the sea did for you."

Their car was visible around the edge of the nearest

building. It would have been half a block shorter to cut straight to the vehicle, but the waste area was a tangle of uncertain footing. They retraced their steps along the sea front instead.

Kelly noticed a simple shaft monument. He had ignored it before when his mind was on other things. "Just a second," he said. There was a small bronze plaque set in the concrete face of the shaft. Translating its French inscription aloud for the sergeant's benefit, the agent read, "'Sacred to the memory of six sailors, their names and nationalities unknown, who washed ashore here on March 6, 1942. Rest in peace.'"

There was a small cross incised beneath the inscription. Someone had made repeated efforts to gouge away the relic of Christianity. The message had been scarred as well.

They walked on. "Interesting," Kelly said in a neutral voice. "There's a political statement made with a chisel. Made by somebody who was probably illiterate, at least in French; but he knew that defacing crosses was a patriotic thing to do. . . . It doesn't give me a lot of hope for world peace and understanding."

After a moment he added, "A guy in Paris convinced me I wasn't going to be doing the same goddam thing myself. He'd better have been right."

The house Commander Posner had managed to rent on short notice was several blocks south of the harbor, near the present edge of town. It had a courtyard wall and a wooden gate which Kelly unlocked to pass the station wagon.

The building was not prepossessing. The plaster had

cracked from much of the facade and lay scattered in the courtyard. Patches of discoloration beneath the windows, and the areas of bare concrete elsewhere, combined to give the house the look of something in wartime camouflage. It would serve though.

"The phone's connected and the electricity," Rowe said as the two men wrestled the boat out of the back of the wagon. "Other than that, it's pretty much what you see. Concrete and dirt." He kicked at the baked ground. It was as bare and as refractory as the walls of the building.

Kelly shrugged. "That's fine," he said, staggering a little with the weight of the collapsed MARS boat. "Just so long as we can stash the boat and radio here, and we can lay up until dark tomorrow ourselves." He laughed. "I have simple tastes," he added. "I want to get this whole thing over so bad I can simply taste it."

The men grunted simultaneously as they set the package down in the hall. "We should have brought the other five men this damned thing's built to hold," Kelly grumbled. "Though I swear, it'll look small enough tomorrow when I get to take it out to sea. Well, one more load."

"Ah," the sergeant said. "We thought—my wife and me, Tom. Maybe you'd like to have dinner tonight with us?"

The agent stopped in the doorway. "Doug, that's— well, I really appreciate it. I—I've got something else that I"—and his tongue stumbled, but he got the next word out anyway—"need to do tonight. But I really appreciate it."

"Well, let's shift the other stuff," Rowe said. He smiled cheerfully. "And good luck tonight."

XXIV

The upper lot by the DCM's house was already crowded when Kelly arrived. Mercedes predominated, but there were a fair number of top-quality Citröens and Renaults as well as more exotic makes. At least one of the Citröens bore cream-colored Presidency license plates with a damned low prefix: either the Minister of Foreign Affairs himself or someone high-ranking from his shop. The agent smiled and shook his head as he eased past. His VW was going to feel lonely.

Loneliness was the wrong subject for a joke, even to himself . . . especially to himself. Kelly's stomach knotted around the liquor he had drunk in his hotel room to nerve him for the evening. Scowling, the agent pulled into a space between the GSO Annex and the line of brown-painted Conexes. The building was a metal temporary, and the Conexes were shed-sized shipping containers that doubled here—as in Nam—as lockable storage for the

General Services Officer. In sum, the scene was as romantic and Eastern as downtown Milwaukee.

Kelly got out of his car, locked it, and checked his pockets. The invitation was in the breast pocket; and the grenade fuse made an unsightly bulge on the right side. Kelly removed the fuse to check it. He had put thirty wraps of plastic electrician's tape around the charge tube and the arming spoon. Henri, the Chancery receptionist, had found him the tape without asking questions. Doug could have gotten it, but Kelly did not want to involve the sergeant.

Working by the light outside the GSO building, the stocky American pulled the cotter pin that locked the spoon in place. The tape wrappings still kept the spoon from flying up to hit the striker and ignite the fuse. The plastic tape was amply strong to hold for the foreseeable future.

With the doctored fuse concealed in his hand, the agent began to stroll up the long drive toward the gate to the Annex grounds. Under his breath he was mouthing a phrase from the folk song "Sam Hall":

> ". . . you're a bunch a' bastards all,
>   Goddamn your eyes."

There were cars parked solidly for a block either way from the Residence on both sides of the street. Most of the vehicles had green Diplomatic plates. Those which did not were of a luxury which conferred equal immunity. Pairs of Civil Police stood at the limits of sight in either direction, directing traffic with yellow light-wands on the ends of flashlights. Another pair of blue-suited patrolmen lounged against the wall outside the open Residence gate. They were laughing and talking to one another unconcernedly, but their pistols were real and they each carried a walkie-talkie—unusual for the regular police. It was not a gate that anyone smart would try to crash.

The Fiat was right where Kelly had spotted it when he drove in, fifty yards from the DCM's entrance and on the same side of the street. A little farther than the Zulus normally had to park from their lady friend's front door, but not much. Kelly had not expected the car to be there, not tonight, maybe never again . . . but he had been prepared just in case. The agent's lips were dry, his right palm sweating on the fuse assembly. He sauntered toward the car, his mind tumbling over the last stanza of the song though his mouth was too stiff to pass even the shadow of the words:

"Now up the rope I go, now up I go. . . ."

Kelly's suit was of a wool-silk blend, well-cut as befitted a man who sold big-ticket items to conservative businessmen. It was also charcoal gray. Even if any of the policemen had made the effort, they would have seen only one more shadow gliding between the parked cars and the courtyard walls. The Fiat's gas cap was not of the locking type, though Kelly would scarcely have been delayed if it had been. He twisted it open, using only the tips of his left fingers on the knurled rim. He dropped in the taped fuse, then replaced the cap when the splash assured him that the fuse had slid into the tank proper. He gave an extra twist after the gas cap had seated, smearing his prints illegibly instead of wiping the metal with a rag. Whistling under his breath, Kelly walked back to the Annex gate before stepping into the street and the view of the policemen at the entrance. The blue-suited men straightened slightly as they saw Kelly approach through a gap in the traffic. Cars were being fed in alternate directions by the police with wands. There was not room for them to pass both ways at once with the parking as it was. The agent tipped his invitation toward the men in a mock salute, smiling. They smiled back and relaxed again, young men in long, boring duty. They were not westernized enough to appreciate the jazz from beyond the wall as music, and they were not affected enough to succumb to its snob appeal.

At the Residence entrance proper, a tuxedoed servant checked Kelly's invitation with no more than the usual care. He gestured ceremoniously within, saying, "Refreshments are being served to the right, by the pool, sir."

The Residence grounds were lighted by yellow paper lanterns spiked to the lawn on iron bases. Couples and small groups—mostly men—strolled on the grass among the cedars, in separate, low-voiced conversations. A sidewalk curved to the entrance and across the front of the house. At the right end of the rambling building was a blaze of electric light. The guest house was lighted also. Kelly noted with amusement that there was no reggae tonight from behind the closed, curtained windows. He walked along the sidewalk without haste, his eyes open for anyone he knew—and for anything he needed to learn.

The social area proper was a flood-lit patio to the right rear of the building. It was a full story lower than the front entrance. The swimming pool was near the courtyard wall, a lighted jewel dazzlingly brighter than the moonlit Mediterranean visible over the wall coping. A temporary stage had been constructed against one wing of the Residence, but it held only instruments and a pair of large speakers at the moment. Either Kelly had arrived between sets, or the entertainment was over for the evening.

Commander Posner was resplendent in dress whites for the occasion, talking with animation to the Station Chief near a tiled wall fountain. Kelly started toward them, hesitated, and walked to the bar instead. Three tuxedoed Algerians were decanting wine, mineral water, and a variety of fruit juices. There was no hard liquor in evidence, perhaps in deference to the fact that more than half the guests were locals. Kelly snagged one of the glasses of red wine and sipped. After a quick glance around, he slugged down the rest of the glass. Reaching around a portly, bearded man in a fez, the agent traded his empty glass for a full one. Annamaria had been right: the local vintages did have a bite.

Harry Warner saw Kelly approaching. He waved to silence the Attaché. Commander Posner turned, his face registering multiple levels of surprise.

Kelly smiled easily, the portion of his mind that was tuned to business slipping to the fore. Everything was stable, was crystalline, when he concentrated on the job. Though that was only by contrast, of course. "I won't intrude now, sir," the agent said, "but if you have a moment later, I'd like to check on our business."

Warner waved dismissal. "Sure," he said, "I was going

to get another drink anyway." The CIA officer smiled coldly at Kelly as he walked to the bar.

"For God's sake!" Posner whispered, "what are you doing here? This is a Section Heads Only affair!" He looked around hastily. "You know I can't pass you your code disk here."

"No problem," the agent said, swallowing more wine without really tasting it, "you can hold it. I just wanted to make sure the cable got off okay."

"Well, I said it would, didn't I?" snapped the commander. "You're an *idiot* to come here tonight, you know. How did you ever get past the gate?"

The fountain was dry, but the alcove itself was tiled in a running-water pattern. Blue and yellow slip glazes rippled over a white background. More than a hundred individually different tiles had been arranged in a unitary design which had been planned at a factory . . . perhaps four centuries before. Kelly let his eyes rest on the soothing, hand-painted curves as he said, "Oh, I had something to attend to . . . and I felt like coming, I guess that's the reason I do most things. Thank you, Commander."

Both men were shaking their heads when they parted.

Annamaria was nowhere to be seen; neither was her husband. For all his bravado in attending the affair, Kelly rather hoped that he would not meet the Ambassador again. He was not sure what either of them would say.

The general language of the gathering was English, though there were varieties of it that had more to be translated than understood by a native speaker. At the hors d'oeuvres table was an obvious member of the jazz group, a gangling blond man in slacks, a long-sleeved shirt, and a red vest. He towered like a derrick over an Algerian girl who was perhaps older than the fifteen she looked. The American was offering the girl stuffed olives and very earnest conversation. To the musician's other side was another, shorter, American in a light sport coat. He was equally earnest and far less relaxed.

The musician finally turned to the shorter man and said, "Say, Cal, can you speak to her? Don't think she knows any American at all."

"Gerry, when is the *set* going to start?" the other man demanded.

"When Dee gets out of the shitter, I suppose, Cal," the musician said. He turned back to the girl. "Go tour-direct somebody else, man," he added over his shoulder.

The girl was very nice indeed. She was wearing clothes from Paris with a style that belied her youth. Kelly grinned and started to join the couple as an interpreter. The girl was obviously flattered at the attention—and obviously, as even Gerry had surmised, completely innocent of English. Before the agent could speak, however, the musician made one last thrust at international understanding. He bent down so that his face was on a level with the girl's. Then he asked with the exaggeratedly slow delivery of a Voice of America language lesson, "Would . . . you . . . like . . . to . . . fuck?"

Kelly turned, choking to keep from spraying out the mouthful of wine he had just taken. Annamaria stood three steps behind him, wearing a black silk dress and a look of delighted amazement.

"Angelo!" she cried, "you *did* come! What a surprise." She touched Kelly's hand in friendly greeting.

The agent checked his watch. "Well, I . . ." he said. "Things happen and things, ah . . . things change." He wished to God his glass was not empty. "Look, Anna, I need"—he looked at his watch again, this time to take his eyes off the woman—"I'd like to borrow a phone for just a moment. But I"—he faced her but lowered his voice—"I don't want to fall over your—his Excellency. I'll go next door if I need to."

"Not at all," Annamaria said, using her fingertips on the back of Kelly's hand to draw him after her. "We'll use the extension in the front hall, if that's all right. Rufus has been upstairs with—" her own voice fell "—someone from the MFA since the reception line closed. If he *does* come down, he'll go out by the back door anyway."

The wisteria overhanging the entrance was a rich purple fragrance that penetrated the flagged court within. It even touched the hall beyond. The ceiling light was small, but it glanced in more than adequately from the blank, white walls. A phone sat on a circular table, beside a coat rack of age-darkened wood. "I'll wait around the corner," Annamaria said, gesturing toward the instrument and walking on. "Call when you're through."

The agent opened his mouth to say that was not necessary; but then again, the less known. . . . God, she was lovely. Kelly's mouth was dry again as he dialed the six-digit number he had memorized from the register on Sergeant Rowe's desk. Dryness was good. It would change the timbre of his voice, and a trace of nervous anticipation was just what the doctor ordered on this one.

"Yes?" said a woman on the other end of the line. Kelly had never met the Ambassador's secretary, but it was her home phone he had dialed.

"Buffy," the agent whispered urgently, "this is Chuck Reeves. You've got to get him out *fast*. The Ambassador's going to cover up for last night by getting them all thrown in Lambese Prison on open charges. The Minister's just agreed and the arrest team's on the way. If he's still there in five minutes, he'll only leave the prison when they put him on the roads!"

Kelly slammed down the phone on the yelp of alarm from the other end. He was smiling, and it was not a nice smile to see. Then he looked down the hall and saw Annamaria looking back at him, alerted by the clash of plastic. Christ, he was trembling again. "Let's get out of here," he said in an attempt at a normal voice, "and—but, hell, I'm sorry, you'll have things to do."

Annamaria's heels clicked even through the thick carpeting as she strode back to the agent. "If his Excellency the Ambassador can disappear," she said, linking arms as she had before, "surely her Excellency the Ambassador's wife can do the same. My car?"

"No, I . . ." Kelly said. "I don't really need to go anywhere. Let's walk over to the Annex grounds, that's—" The stocky man met her eyes, finally. He smiled without the murderous delight of a moment before. "Just want to talk, that's all."

They were another indistinguishable couple on the lawn as soon as they stepped beyond the lighted sidewalk. It was warmer than it had been for the past few evenings. Annamaria had not bothered to wear a wrap. Her dress was slashed off the right shoulder, leaving her skin to glow in the ambient light. Worth a glance, even in the darkness, but the attention of all those nearby seemed to be focused on the scene taking place at the guest house.

The front door was open, a harsh rectangle in contrast to the light diffusing through the window curtains. A slim woman with a splendid Afro stood in silhouette in the doorway, shrieking back into the house.

Annamaria missed a half step in wonder. Kelly continued walking, his gentle momentum drawing the woman on. "What on earth is Buffy doing?" Annamaria marveled in an undertone. "Goodness, if word gets back to Rufus that she's had a public scene with her boyfriend tonight, with everyone here, she'll be shipped back to America by the next plane. Of course," she added thoughtfully, "he'll have someone else sign the orders."

A tall black man stamped angrily out of the house, snarling something to the woman. His shoes were in his hand. "God damn you!" she screamed in reply. "Go on! I won't have them taking me too!" Her gesture was imperious. She looked like a back-lighted statue of Queen Ti.

The man bent to don his shoes, then changed his mind and loped for the gate. The house door slammed. He looked back over his shoulder and light from a window fell on his face. As Kelly had assumed, he was the man who had held the claws the night before. The American agent kept his right hand unobtrusively under his coat tails, thumb and forefinger resting on the steel hilt of his utility knife. There was no cause for concern. The Zulu was not looking at him, was not really looking at anything at all tangible. His sculptured face bore an expression

melded of fear, anger . . . and the indescribable tension of
something that knows it is hunted.

"Lovely sky," Kelly remarked conversationally as they
walked through the gate a moment later. He nodded past
Annamaria toward the two policemen on duty there. One
nodded back, but they were more interested in the Fiat.
Its headlights dimmed with the starter whirr, then flared
as the engine caught. Police the world over suspect the
unusual, and a Zulu running from a diplomatic function
with his shoes in his hand was nothing if not unusual.
"Electric lights every few yards may make the streets
safer," the agent continued, "but it's a shame the way they
hide the stars over most cities."

Annamaria looked at the American strangely. Her
mouth quivered with the questions that she did not
express. The Fiat pulled away hard enough to make its
tires and engine howl. Kelly paused on the curb. The black-
haired woman clung to him with a shade of nervousness.
The policemen tracked the car with narrowed eyes as it
accelerated past them. One man fingered his walkie-
talkie.

Gasoline had been dissolving the plastic tape ever
since Kelly had dropped it in the tank. Thirty wraps, thirty
minutes, as a rule of thumb. The tape must have finally
parted under the spoon's tension a moment after the Zulu
had started his engine. The timing could not have been
closer if Kelly had been waiting to put a rocket-propelled
grenade into the Fiat as it slid past.

The first result was a mild thump, as if the car—twenty
feet down the street—had rolled over an empty box. The
booster had gone off in the sealed gas tank. The explosion

itself was almost lost in the engine noise. It was quite sufficient, however, to rupture every seam in the tank and spray gasoline over the road and the car's undercarriage.

A fraction of a second later, five or so gallons of gasoline ignited. Because the fuel-air mixture was unconfined, the result could not technically be termed an explosion. The *whump*! and the fireball from the finely-divided mist made a damned close equivalent.

Kelly swung Annamaria to his right side as the tank burst, interposing his own squat body between her and what was about to follow. The blast flicked across his neck between collar and hairline, heat in momentarily palpable form. The Fiat twisted, out of control but running on the gas still trapped in its fuel lines. It side-swiped a parked Mercedes and swapped ends in a spin. The street behind and beneath it was a gush of flames. A moment later the back tires exploded from the heat, one and then the other. They sounded like the double barrels of a shotgun, louder by far than the fuse detonation that had started the process.

The side-swipe had torqued the car body enough to wedge the doors shut. The driver was trying to get out. One of the Algerian policemen who had been directing traffic threw down his flashlight. He took two steps toward the car before the flames beat him back. The screams from inside could not be heard over the roaring fire, not really.

The patrolmen at the upper side of the embassy complex were gaping, forgetting the traffic they were there to control. The huge flaming barricade brought cars to a halt in front of the Chancery gate and back up the street in screeching sequence.

"Let's cross quick," the agent said. He still gripped Annamaria by both shoulders. People were jumping out of their stopped cars, babbling in polyglot amazement. Kelly and the woman darted between the bumpers of a Peugeot and a Dacia pick-up as quickly as Annamaria's spike heels would permit her to follow the guiding hand. The flames, fed now by the asphalt roadway itself, threw their capering shadows down the street in demonic majesty.

XXV

The gate of the GSO Annex had been left open during the affair at the Residence. The guard was the man who fed Kelly the night before. He stood open-mouthed beside one of the gateposts, his eyes filled with the nearby inferno. He gave no sign of noticing Kelly and Annamaria.

The agent started down the drive, primarily from inertia. Annamaria halted him with a gentle tug on his arm. "People will be getting cars," she said. "They won't be able to leave, but they'll be coming over here anyway. There's a place we can talk, though. . . ."

Kelly let the woman direct him to the right, along the inner face of the compound wall. They passed the playground and buildings of the American School. Kelly had not realized the Annex area was so extensive. The path narrowed between the wall on one side and the steep hill down to the Conexes on the other. The shrubbery was rough, obviously untended. Suddenly there was a small, square building in the midst of the trees and brush. It was barely touched by the streetlight reaching over the wall and through the foliage.

The white exterior plaster had flaked somewhat at the corners and around the jamb of the round-topped door. It gave the squat building the look of a soldier who has gone through a battle in his parade uniform. A double band of ceramic tiles encircled it just below the roof line. The flat roof humped in the center into a dome.

Annamaria reached up and fingered one of the smooth tiles, the care of its decoration obvious though the dim light washed its varied colors into shades of gray. "The tiles are mostly Dutch, you know . . . here, the Residence, most of the really old buildings in Algiers. 16th Century Delft tiles here. . . . It was a saint's tomb, a sidi was buried here. The body is long gone, of course."

The door was a thin plywood panel, clearly not original to the building. It was held shut with a twist of wire, perhaps part of a coat hanger. "Why the mania for Dutch tiles?" the agent asked as he unwound the wire. "Not that they aren't very pretty. . . ."

"The price was right," Annamaria said. She was so close to Kelly that her breast touched his left arm. "Charitable societies in Holland used them for centuries to ransom Christian seamen from the pirates. The Barbary Pirates, the Berbers. . . . Do you suppose he slept better, the saint, knowing that his tomb was covered with the ransom of infidels?"

Kelly swung the door open. It scratched on the stone flooring. There was nothing within but hollow echoes and a few leaves. He turned deliberately to Annamaria and kissed her as her arms slipped under his jacket. When the pressure of her fingers on his back relaxed, Kelly also relaxed slightly to allow their mouths to part. He murmured something that even he did not understand, his eyes screwed shut in hope and pain.

"Darling," said Annamaria quietly, her fingertips ten moth-wing touches above the line of his belt, "what happened to you last night after you left me? Or was it this morning?"

The agent's eyes were open, now, and as still as pools of quicksilver. "Oh," he said with a smooth, false nonchalance, "did your husband say something was going to happen?"

"It was Rufus who did something, then," the woman said. She stood with the perfect calm of a gymnast the moment before she executes a particularly difficult series. "No, darling, Rufus said nothing. . . . I told you, Rufus doesn't talk when he's angry, not to me. But you—" She raised one hand and traced the index finger from Kelly's ear-lobe down his jaw line, then back and down his chest. He shivered. "You made a decision, and you stood by it last night when I think it might have been easy not to." Her finger tapped Kelly's belt buckle and skipped lower, briefly, enticingly. She giggled.

Kelly mumbled and tried to draw the dark-haired woman close again. Annamaria leaned back, away from the fulcrum of his hands. "No, darling," she said seriously. "I have to know."

"I—" Kelly began. Then, his eyes on hers, he went on. "Last night I got reminded that people don't live forever. I won't live forever. You know, the plane you were supposed to be on crashes, or a roof tile nips your ear before it busts to hell on the sidewalk. I'd decided, maybe I couldn't handle two things at once. But I decided, yeah: and maybe I can't handle either one alone. But even if I live in a cave and have people slip food through a slot, something can still go wrong. That's not a reason to be afraid to try. . . ." He swallowed. "Afraid to do things that are important to do."

Annamaria's left hand still held Kelly gently where his rib cage tucked under. She spread her right hand on his shirt, over the nipple, and looked at her own fingers rather than the agent's eyes. She said, "Darling, if you were very angry with—my husband, with Rufus—" she looked up. "How would you get back at him? You *would* get back at him."

Kelly took his hands away so abruptly that the woman stumbled back a step. He did not notice because he had turned and smashed the heel of his palm against the tomb as hard as he could. He slowly raised his left hand to the arch of the door, feeling his way along the plaster. His face was bent toward the empty floor within.

After almost a minute poised against the tomb, the stocky man faced about. In a hoarse, tired voice he said, "I've done things, Anna, you're right. . . . Not, not just to get even, but why should you believe that? And anyway, it doesn't matter." He wet his lips and paused. Annamaria stood with her arms crossed, her long fingers touching her own shoulders. Kelly said, "Anna, I'm not subtle. I— I might kill, sure, because there're some things, some people that—I'm not going to have go on. But—not your husband, because he *is* your husband. And I. . . . Nothing

I"—he looked away—"nothing I wanted from you had anything to do with your husband."

Annamaria's face warmed by stages in a broad, slow smile. "Wanted?" she said, extending her right arm with the delicacy of a plant sprouting. "Want-ted? Darling, don't try to tell *me* that you don't want it still." She continued to caress his groin until she moved her hand to permit their bodies to press closer together while they kissed.

Kelly slid his hand up and cupped a breast through the silk dress and nothing more, Jesus, nothing more. The nipple hardened beneath his palm. Annamaria leaned away, raising her hand to Kelly's. Their lips parted. An apology rose in his throat but caught there as the black-haired woman slid the silk off her left shoulder and let the dress fall free of her torso. It was caught momentarily by Kelly's hand on her breast, then held at her waist as they embraced again. The aureolae were small and very dark against Annamaria's white skin, black in the diffused light of the street lamp.

Kelly bent. She touched her own left breast, lifting the erect nipple to meet his lips. When his tongue began to quiver over the surface of the nipple, Annamaria moaned and sagged a little against the hand with which Kelly supported the curve of her right hip.

Annamaria reached down and touched her groin, through the dress at first, sliding a finger up and down over the slick fabric as she arched herself to meet her hand. Then she gave a tiny gasp, a catch of her breath, and hiked her skirt up with a convulsive movement that threatened the material. Kelly knelt in front of her, feeling but ignoring the bite of pebbles on his knees. When his

mouth left her breast, Annamaria touched the wall of the
building with her left hand and leaned sideways until her
shoulder braced her. Her face was slightly lifted, her eyes
closed. From her throat came a purr that may have been
intended for words.

Annamaria's panties were simple and very brief. They
were white and more noticeable against her skin for their
reflectance than for any difference of shade. Kelly hooked
his thumbs under both sides of the garment, then gently
tugged it down. The fabric clung at mid-thigh, then
dropped around her ankles.

She tossed her head sideways, looking down past the
dress she held bunched at her waist. She lifted her left
foot carefully clear of the panties, then kicked out sharply
with her right leg. The slight garment flew off into the
darkness from the tip of her open-toed shoe. Annamaria
giggled and ran the fingers of one hand through Kelly's
hair.

Bending forward, Kelly divided the lips of the
woman's vulva with an index finger. They were already
moist. Her pubic hair was a small black wedge with a stem
up her midline toward the navel. He touched, then kissed,
her exposed clitoris, slipping his finger back and deeper as
she thrust her pelvis toward him.

Annamaria began breathing with short, rasping
intakes. The fingers of both her hands danced over Kelly's
scalp, guiding his rhythm with their pressure but never
attempting to force what they already controlled. After a
moment, she began to caress his earlobes between her
thumbs and index fingers. The skirt had tumbled across
Kelly's face in a spidery flood. He lifted it away with his

right hand while his left hand and tongue continued to probe gently and rhythmically.

Annamaria's gasps stilled, her hands froze in brushing contact with the man. Only her hips continued to move, once, twice, and as she thrust the third time she screamed in a perfect counterfeit of pain. Kelly continued to hold her, continued to stroke, until her body relaxed and she bent over him. Annamaria murmured endearments as she drew him upright, kissing him and clinging with a supple muscularity.

After a moment, the woman stepped back. *"This,"* she said with an angry intensity, looking down at her dress. *"This!"* She found the concealed zipper in the side, then pulled the garment off over her head instead of stepping out of it.

Kelly, grinning, took the delicate dress from Annamaria's hand as she turned to fling it into the dark after her panties. "Now, always treat your equipment kindly," the agent said. "Never know when you'll need it again." He leaned into the tomb and hung the dress carefully from the upper edge of the door. He tossed his own suit coat over the panel as well.

Annamaria giggled again and bent to test the ground. "I think," she said as she straightened, "that cracked stone has it over cedar twigs." Wearing only high-heeled shoes and the dappling shadows, her beauty was startling. Kelly had tossed his shirt over his coat. He was leaning against the door jamb, struggling with a shoelace and wondering if there were not somehow a more sensual way to undress. The dark-haired woman stepped close and kissed him. "Well," she said, eyeing the tomb floor speculatively, "not the most romantic setting I could have found, is it? But I doubt somehow that I'll notice that the stones are cold."

"Romance is something you bring with you," Kelly said, "not something that's there." He lifted his right foot out of his shorts and trousers together. Without being fully conscious of the fact, he was using his torso to keep the small sheath knife out of the woman's sight. Her eyes were not on his clothing. Her hand reached out again to stroke his genitals. "And as for the floor," he added in a huskier voice, shifting his weight to clear his left leg in turn, "I know a trick worth two of that. . . ."

Kelly spread a hand under each of Annamaria's buttocks. Their groins pressed together. He was a strong man, proud of his strength, and never more of his mettle than now. Their lips met, damping to a murmur the question in Annamaria's throat. Kelly lifted her easily, her calves wrapping instinctively around his thighs and taking much of the weight off his arms. The lips of her vulva, spread naturally by the motion, slipped easily as he entered her for the first time. Her cry was a muted echo of her previous climax. They rocked together, Kelly's knees flexing and straightening. Annamaria's head was turned to the side, her fingers splayed on her lover's shoulders. She gasped and gasped, and at last cried out in pleasure that wracked a spasm from her vagina and brought Kelly to climax as well.

For him, the experience was a unique combination of delight and a bludgeoning. His blood pressure went momentarily off scale, a vise over his skull and the veins of his throat. Then his whole body relaxed, the muscles of his legs trembling. His arms felt as if they were no longer parts of the body he controlled.

Annamaria felt his sudden weakness. She uncoiled her legs, setting her feet on the ground again. The two of them leaned against the plastered wall, still joined, their arms tightly around one another. The woman's high heels had been pressing against the muscles of Kelly's thighs without either of them being consciously aware of it. Both of them were flushed, able to ignore the increasing cool of the night, but the noises of the outside world began to reenter their awareness. The sirens had stopped. Cars were moving in the street and the lot by the DCM's house. Headlights swept within the compound wall. Horns and curses, mostly in French, marked the labored departures.

"I suppose I've got a handkerchief in my pants pocket," Kelly said after a time.

Annamaria ran a hand over his left hip, feeling the play of muscle beneath the skin. "What do you do tomorrow?" she asked, her head turned aside and her eyes half closed.

"Work," the agent replied. He was interested to note that he had not tensed at the question. "All day. I'll—I'll see you again, if you . . . if you want that. Not tomorrow, and maybe not in Algeria. But again, I hope."

Annamaria turned and nibbled at his left earlobe. "Well, we shouldn't waste what we have, then, should we?" she whispered. She felt him stir within her. "Now, if we're careful, I think we can lie down without—oops!" She giggled again as Kelly slipped out of her. "Well. . . ." She sat back, first on her heels and then on the stone floor of the tomb. She stretched her hands toward Kelly from the darkness. "Come here, darling. I told you the stone wouldn't feel too cold."

Later, the walls were an echo chamber for her happy cries.

XXVI

"Oh, by the way, Kelly," said Commander Posner, "we got a reply from Paris on your cable. The general will look into it."

Kelly straightened from the recorder more abruptly than he should have. The shock of motion was as severe as if he had brought his head up under a cabinet door. It drew a wince and a muffled groan from the agent, "Which cable was that?" he asked, fashioning his pain into a frown of question. Drinks in the bar of the Hotel St. George were just as expensive as Charlie DeVoe had suggested, but Kelly had pretty well decided that he had enough money to last the rest of his life.

Sergeant Rowe rapped on the office door. He unlatched it before either of the others had time to grunt him an invitation. Rowe was keyed up in a cheerful, anticipatory way quite at variance with the other men. The Defense Attaché's face was a map charting the alternate disasters of success and failure. As for Kelly—Kelly would have been grim and tense had he not been hung over. To the extent his pain distracted him, he became less grim—and more dangerous. "Say," said the sergeant happily, "what's the Company doing here so early on a weekend? I saw all three of their cars when I parked. Harry got something on too, do you suppose?"

"Maybe they've got a tap into the MFA sewer and they're raking shit," Kelly snapped, more sharply than he had intended to speak to Doug. "Christ," he added more plaintively, "we've got enough here to hold us, don't we?"

"The cable is the one you requested me to send, you might remember," Commander Posner said with a hint of his own frustration. "The duty officer brought the reply over to me at the Residence last night. I looked around for you, but you seemed already to have disappeared"—Kelly was tense but he did not jerk his eyes toward the Attaché—"and I eventually decrypted it myself. There was a traffic accident on the street that took hours to clear up. I decided I might as well use the time by reading the cable, since I couldn't get home and you had left me with the program." Perhaps misinterpreting the agent's stiffness, Posner added, "If that was a mistake, no doubt you can put enough in my next Fitness Report to quite destroy my career, if you so desire."

Kelly shook his head, then winced again. "Oh, hell, that's fine," he said. "Like you say, you had the program disk. I. . . . Pedler's going to get Hoang out through Frankfurt, then?"

"Apparently there's some problem with that," the Attaché said, speaking somewhat more mildly himself.

"The Vietnamese—Hoang and his escort—are flying in and out through Paris . . . and of course our relations with the French aren't quite what they are with the Germans, especially on a matter that could be seen as impinging on the Arab world. The Conference being in Algiers, that is. But the General will make an attempt."

Kelly managed to grin, then forgot it and let it fade. "Well, I said I wasn't going to worry about what I couldn't change." He glanced at his watch. It was a good half hour before he wanted to leave. They would be using one of the mission's Plymouth Volare station wagons. It was as conspicuous as an ox in a sheepfold, but it was so obviously the property of a foreign diplomatic mission that the Algerian police were unlikely to try to stop it. If worst came to worst. . . . "Doug, you still have your key to the armory?" Kelly asked in sudden decision. "I need to get in for a moment."

"I—" the sergeant began.

"Sergeant Rowe has already delivered the grenades," said the Defense Attaché sharply.

"Yeah, I put them in the trunk of Mustapha's car," Rowe said with a glance between the other two men. "He parks on the grounds when he's on duty. That way there wasn't anything happening except on"—his smile was wry—"diplomatic premises. Just like I can't come and help today."

"Tell the truth," the agent said, facing toward the window but not seeing any of the things toward which his eyes were trained, "I thought I'd borrow one of those Smiths for the morning. Just to have in my trouser pocket." He slapped his pants, shapeless corduroys of a blue as drab as the brown of his jacket. "Not one chance in a thousand it'd make any difference, but . . . but then, it doesn't do any harm sitting there if it's not needed, does it?"

"No," said Commander Posner. "You can't have a pistol."

Kelly turned to the taller man. The first touch of conflict was clearing pathways in his brain that the night before had clogged. "I can be trusted with a revolver, Commander," he said in a voice with a rasp in it. "I've never shot anybody who didn't need shooting."

"You can't be trusted with an *embassy* gun," the Defense Attaché said on a rising inflection. He shook his right index and middle fingers in Kelly's direction. The cigarette he held jerked its trail of smoke in nervous angles. "*I* can't tell you you can't go armed," the officer continued. "It's an act of war, you know, an act of war— but I can't help that. What I can stop is the notion that you'll be found with a weapon straight out of embassy stores. And if you think you can ruin me for that, then you go ahead and do it. I swear, I'll make the whole business public!"

"For Christ's sake!" the agent shouted, "How the hell many Smith and Wessons do you think've been made, anyway? A couple million? Unless the damned USG *gives* the Algerians a list of serial numbers, how do you think it's going to be traced anywhere?"

"I said no and I meant no," the officer repeated flatly. "You're responsible for planning the operation, I'm well aware of that. If your plans require that you be armed from the embassy arsenal, then you should have said so in time to have it cleared by the competent authorities. What you're suggesting is contrary to all the regulations under which those weapons are stored, 'Defensive Purposes Only' does *not* include using them for kidnapping and murder on the streets of a friendly power."

The veins in Kelly's head were pounding him hard enough to make him nauseous. Sergeant Rowe put a hand on the agent's arm and said, "Ah, Tom . . . ? I've still got the packing cases from those grenades in my personal car. You've got a minute—come down and give me a hand getting them up the incinerator, will you?"

Kelly blinked. The sergeant's thumb squeezed his biceps. "Yeah, I guess I can handle that," the agent said, surprised at the apparent calm of his own words.

Rowe gestured toward the dingy trench coat Kelly would be carrying to mark him for Professor Vlasov to home on. "Might bring that too, sir; it's still cool."

The commander's face registered only relief when the other men left.

In an undertone as the door latched shut behind them, Kelly asked, "You want to tell me what this is all about now?"

"When we get to the car, sir," the sergeant whispered back.

"Look, you weren't just afraid I was going to deck the sanctimonious son of a bitch, were you?" the agent pressed. "I wouldn't dirty my hands."

"At the car," Rowe repeated.

The sergeant owned a Plymouth sedan. At an appropriate charge, embassy mechanics and stores could be used to repair the personal vehicles of mission members;

but that was a benefit only if the personal vehicles were similar to those of the mission fleet. Rowe unlocked his passenger door and the glove compartment while the agent waited with a frown. The white walls of the Chancery and the Villa Inshallah were glowing with the coming dawn. Details were still indistinguishable.

"Here," said the sergeant. He handed Kelly a box about two inches square and an inch deep.

"Jesus," whispered the agent, his hand accepting the unexpected density of what it had received. Across the top of the green paper tape sealing the box was the legend:

25 CARTOUCHES DE 11,43 MM
POUR PISTOLETS

"Didn't want to carry it loaded in the car," Rowe explained as he walked around to the trunk. "And that's all the ammo I've got, I'm afraid."

"Not that I'll really need a gun . . ." the agent said in a low voice, his eyes scanning the barred, black windows of the flanking buildings. "I don't know, I've been antsy, real antsy the past couple days. It's not—"

The trunk lid swung up. The sergeant tugged aside a folded blanket—"Jesus," Kelly repeated. "Doug, I don't want to get you in trouble. Does Posner know you've got this?" The agent ran the fingers of his right hand over the square, gray receiver of the silenced sub-machine gun the soldier had just displayed.

"Oh, no," Rowe said, "but in my last post—Qatar, when they were having the trouble, you know—I told my CO that I was worried about my wife having to be alone in the house. . . ." He smiled reminiscently. "The Colonel was a Marine. It was a different world from working with Commander Posner . . . but I told him what I wanted and he signed the paperwork, 'Required by serviceman on active duty,' you know the drill."

Kelly turned the weapon over with one hand. He was careful not to raise it above level of the trunk well or into a position that could be seen from any of the windows of the flanking buildings. It was as square and functional as a traffic sign; and like the sign, it was stamped in the main out of sheet steel. The bolt enclosed most of the barrel, so that the whole gun was only 10 1/2 inches long when its wire stock was telescoped back against the receiver.

The silencer almost doubled the length.

"Who made the can?" Kelly asked, touching the inch and five-eighths tube that had been Parkerized the same shade of grays as the weapon itself. "It isn't a Sionics."

"Better," said the sergeant, grinning with pride.

The agent turned to look at Rowe directly. "If it's better than Sionics," he said, "it's pretty damn good. Whose product?"

"LARAND," explained the sergeant through his smile. "Instead of baffles, it's filled with thick washers woven from stainless steel wire. Mitch WerBell did a fantastic job with the Sionics, but I don't think there'll ever be a machine that's perfect." His face sobered. "You know, the gun's one of the lot the government tried to confiscate when WerBell left MAC. I couldn't believe the way they've been persecuting somebody who's served this country as long as he has."

The agent tossed his coat into the trunk, then

removed it with the weapon hidden securely in its folds. "It's like Kennedy's ghost-writer said, Doug," Kelly remarked. "'Ask not what your country can do for you.' Absolutely right. The *real* question is what your country can do *to* you if somebody sitting on his ass in DC decides it's a good idea. Somebody figured WerBell had spent long enough in clandestine ops that they wanted to be real sure he was under control . . . and framing him into a three-year fall in Atlanta seemed about as good a way as the next to take him out of circulation." Kelly patted the sergeant's shoulder with his free hand. "See why I've spent the past five years in Europe? Maybe I'm crazy, but—it still seems like it was a pretty good idea."

Sergeant Rowe thumped the trunk lid down. "Well," he said toward the car, "I just don't like to think the USG treats its people that way, I suppose."

"And your boss doesn't like to think the USG treats friendly countries the way I'm about to treat this one," Kelly agreed. "The world might be a better place if either one of you were right, I suppose." He turned back toward the Chancery door, his arm guiding the sergeant; but before the agent actually stepped forward, he paused and said, "Seriously, Doug—this could be trouble like you wouldn't believe. Maybe—"

"Tom, listen," the sergeant said. He looked older and more certain of himself than Kelly had seen him look before. "The commander says I don't have a black passport so I can't get involved in anything illegal on Algerian soil. Like you say, he's my boss, it's an order. OK. But this is something you think you need and I happen to have. Don't *you* come all chickenshit over me and talk about regs and trouble. It's my decision, I'm an adult, and by God I'm a soldier in the US Army!" The corners of Rowe's eyes crinkled again with humor. "Beside, if anybody but you and me learn about this gun today, you're in a lot worse trouble than I am."

Kelly clapped the younger man on the shoulder again. His headache was almost gone. "That's nothing to the trouble the folks on the muzzle end are in," he said as they walked toward the door. "Now look, you tell the commander my tummy's acting up and I'm going to be in the john for a while. And that's God's truth, because there isn't any fast way to load twenty-five rounds without stripper clips that I don't have."

XXVII

With the stall door bolted and his trousers around his ankles for verisimilitude, Kelly began to load the borrowed weapon. The French ammunition had an abnormal appearance. The bullets and cartridge cases were of the same, unusually pale shade of brass. The agent wondered briefly whether the bullets might not be solid gilding metal as some French rifle loadings had been, instead of having a jacket of the harder metal over a lead core.

Better his mind should wander that way than that it should fill with images of the Ambassador's wife, her nipples shrunken to black spikes, beckoning toward him. . . .

Like the Uzi's, the Ingram's magazine slipped into the hand-grip as if it were an ordinary autoloading pistol. That put the weight of the ammo in the best location and permitted the off-hand to find the shooting hand easily in the dark to reload. That wouldn't matter now, the Lord knew, since Kelly had less than the full 30-round capacity of *one* magazine. . . . And anyway, this was just a security blanket. An eight-pound, .45 caliber, security blanket. . . .

By the time Kelly had finished loading the magazine, the ball of his thumb hurt from pressing each round down against the follower spring. The magazine lips had rubbed into the skin in parallel grooves. Part of the cost of doing business, like crazy fears and a tendency to duck when a car backfired. . . .

Kelly slipped the magazine into the butt well and rapped it home with the heel of his hand. Only then did he unlock the bolt by twisting the knurled knob on top of the receiver. He did not draw the knob back to cock the weapon. No safety in the world could keep a sub-machine gun's bolt from jouncing forward if the weapon dropped the wrong way. The Ingram had no firing pin, only a raised tit on the bolt face that fired the weapon as soon as the breech slammed closed.

Besides, Kelly was not going to *need* the gun, not really . . . any more than he needed Annamaria Gordon, so supple that her heels could stroke his buttocks in time with his thrusts within her. . . .

His headache was back. Kelly methodically cut the ammunition box into quarter-inch strips, then flushed the cardboard down the toilet. Don't make mistakes just because you feel like death warmed over, no. . . . Adjusting the coat over his right arm to conceal the weapon, Kelly stepped out of the stall just in time to catch the restroom door as someone opened it from the outside.

Sergeant Rowe looked in. His worried expression

smoothed as soon as he saw the agent had the gun covered. "Ah, the commander—" he began.

Posner himself looked around the door jamb. "It's getting later, Mr. Kelly," he said, "and I thought I'd see if you were about ready to go." He seemed inclined to be pleasant rather than gloating as a result of what he had been told was the human weakness of Kelly's bowels.

"Ready as I'll ever be, Commander," the agent said hoarsely. "And I hope to God that's ready enough."

XXVIII

"Beep," went the receiver as its loop antenna rotated slowly. "Beep beep beepbeep-beep-bee-beebee—"

Harry Warner turned the volume down. "Well," he said to his two subordinates, "it works when it's attachéd, too. I'd breathe a lot easier if we could be sure they'd be using the wagon and not one of their personal cars, though."

Syd Westram had a scholarly forehead which he knew was as prelude to his father's baldness by age 40. His expression was always gloomy, and it fit the present circumstances perfectly. "They should have sent us more tracers," he said. He glared at the receiver's directional antenna. "We could have put one on each of their cars."

"*You* could have put one on each of their cars," retorted Don Mayer. "Look, I can understand why we had to wait to the last minute to save the battery life. That *doesn't* mean I wanted to get caught by that Kelly, planting a tracer under the bumper of his car."

"All right, it's an embarrassment," Westram said, "but the worst thing that could come of it is we lost our tracer. After all, what can Kelly do? Complain to the Ambassador?"

The Station Chief glanced down at the red-bordered file on his desk. He had not shown its full contents to either of his subordinates. "Weil," he said, "maybe Don's right. This Kelly. . . ."

As Warner's voice trailed off, the muted tone of the tracer slowed also. Westram strode quickly to the window and peered through the gap in the blinds. "It's the station wagon," he reported tensely. "Kelly's in it with Posner driving. I don't see Rowe, but they're the main ones."

"All right, boys, you'd better get moving yourselves," said Harry Warner. "I'll give you directions, and the second channel of these ought to buzz when you get within fifty feet or so of the tracer." He slid the two walkie-talkies an inch closer to the edge of his desk to call attention to them. "Remember, keep these plugged into the chargers except when you're using them—and for God's sake, don't walk off and leave them in your cars. They're fifteen hundred bucks apiece. It'll come out of your next check if you lose one, I swear."

The two operatives picked up the hand units with the care which the threat demanded. "Right," Mayer said slowly. "Well, I hope you can vector us onto them with the direction finder. I never trained to follow people in a car."

The Station Chief nodded. "This will work," he said, "Your own receivers are just for searching an area if they park. Call me when you've got their car in sight."

As the others started to walk out to their vehicles,

Warner added, "Oh, boys?" Mayer and Westram turned. "This one *is* going to work," their superior said. "The first word to Langley about what those uniformed twits are up to *is* going to come from this station. Understood?"

Both men nodded. As they walked through the door, Mayer began to whistle under his breath. The tune was the first few bars of the "Dead March" from "Saul."

XXIX

"It is very good of you to permit us," the little Vietnamese colonel was saying in his accented English.

"We are always ready to join our socialist brothers," said Colonel Korchenko with only a perfunctory smile. "Professor Vlasov wished to spend some more time with your Doctor Tanh." And besides, Korchenko had come with instructions from Moscow to help with security arrangements for the Vietnamese physicist. It was desirable to keep up the fiction that the nuclear devices to be emplaced on the Chinese-Vietnamese border were of indigenous Vietnamese manufacture. A Vietnam without a single known nuclear physicist would embarrass the plan.

The tall KGB colonel glanced toward the door of the Ambassador's residence. The physicists should already have come out by now. The circular drive was crowded with waiting men and cars. One sedan would be filled with

KGB personnel. Two more would transport a mix of lower-ranking scientists and more security men. The fourth car was the Ambassador's own armored limousine. In it would ride Professor Vlasov, under the care of Korchenko and the colonel's personal aide and driver.

And with them, at Vlasov's insistence and Moscow's prodding, would be Hoang Tanh and this absurd little colonel who stank of fish sauce.

Even Nguyen had to bend to see into the low-slung Citröen. Schwartz and Babroi were seated in the front bucket seats. They stared back without interest. "A very beautiful car," Nguyen said appreciatively. "Our Ambassador tells me he is trying to get a new car for the mission here, but Hanoi will not approve it."

Korchenko smiled patronizingly. "Yes, well," he said. "Foreign missions always pretend they need more glitter to impress their opposite numbers." Which, of course, explained the limousine, even though Ambassador Miuseck was not the head of the Russian mission to Algeria. In normal fashion, the chief of the KGB Residency—in this case Kalugin, the Consul—had such real authority as Moscow chose to delegate. The Ambassador was still permitted to glitter, however; and the car was useful for functions like this one, squiring around dignitaries from home.

And what the *fuck* were the scientists still doing inside? Having a circle jerk?

"You have two radios?" asked Nguyen, still bent to study the interior of the Citröen. The big pistol made the tail of the Vietnamese officer's coat jut out absurdly.

Colonel Korchenko glanced down. "Oh, the large

one's for communication with the other cars and the base unit here," he said. "That other thing's a toy of Babroi's own—he picked it up in Tokyo last year. It's a"— Korchenko paused to get the technical term correct—"a programmable synthesized scanner. Babroi likes to listen in on local radio traffic wherever we go. He says it keeps him alert, so that he never goes on the air himself unless the signal will be scrambled."

Nguyen nodded in what the KGB man thought was a counterfeit of understanding. The Vietnamese did not say what he was thinking. His eyes compared the flat, off-the-shelf Japanese scanner with the bulky tube-driven transceiver which was presumably the height of indigenous Russian manufacture. "Yes, very interesting," Nguyen said as he straightened up.

The door of the building opened. First voices, then the clot of scientists themselves spilled out. Vlasov and Hoang walked in the middle of the group. They were talking in French. All the security personnel, even Colonel Korchenko, struck a brace.

Damned well about time, the KGB officer thought. The sooner this was over, the sooner he could get back and explore just what the First Secretary's wife had meant by her invitation. With any kind of luck, this was going to be an interesting day.

XXX

The sun over the Church of the Holy Cross was in Kelly's eyes every time he glanced across the boulevard. It bothered him that he did look around, toward the Institute and the ambush site. It was a sign to himself of his own nervousness.

It was not, at least, out of his assumed character. Kelly was portraying a friend of the owner of a small epicerie. He lounged against the glass case of crackers and Camembert, sunglasses and the rack of fly-specked postcards. The real owner was at a wedding in Oran. He was sympathetic to the cause, but his shop would still be there after the security forces had time to catch their breath and examine what had happened. The human participants in the operation, with luck, would all be gone. The owner's cover story would simply be that he and all his household had closed the shop to attend a family wedding 400 kilometers away. The owner would have no idea of who might have broken in during his absence.

Taking the owner's place behind the counter was Ramdan, the heavy-set proprietor of the brassware shop. Though middle-aged, the Algerian was as wired as Kelly had ever seen an 18-year old rifleman on his first insertion. And, speaking of rifles, the agent had cringed to see Ramdan stuffing his Mauser into the cabinet below the display case. Although—if the police were going to search the place, that was not the only gun there were likely to find in the Casbah.

Kelly glanced at his own trench coat, lying folded atop the case. No, not the only gun.

A woman in a veil and black wrapper stepped in to buy a handful of hard candies for the three children she had in tow. The agent tried to talk to the eldest child, a boy of eight or so. His French pleasantries got first a blank stare, then a quick and meaningless rattle of Arabic or Kabyle. The mother herself watched for a moment as Ramdan tried to find, then weigh out, "his" wares. Suddenly the mother snapped an order and hustled out of the shop gripping the two younger children by their hands. The eldest continued for a moment to stare at Kelly. The woman turned and shouted at him with a touch of hysteria in her voice. All four of them disappeared down the mouth of a nearby alley into the heart of the Casbah.

Christ on a crutch. . . . But it was already very close to time.

Two BMW motorcycles led the motorcade up the Boulevard Abderrazak. They had their sirens wound out and their blue turn signals flashing alternately. The black Citröen DS 23 that followed mounted a blue light on the dashboard. Its headlights pulsed nervously, like the heart rhythm of a man on the point of death.

Below the counter, Ramdan's handie-talkie babbled in excited Kabyle.

"For *Christ's* sake!" Kelly snarled at the older man. 'Turn that thing off till I tell you to transmit!" He should have disabled the sending keys of the other units before he turned them over to the Kabyles, the agent thought angrily. Their only proper purpose on this operation was to permit Kelly to order the other personnel into action. No one but Ramdan should have been talking, and Ramdan only at Kelly's direct order.

The two bikes swung expertly at the guidance of their leather-clad National Police drivers. They halted on either side of the Institute's main entrance, facing back toward the street with their engines throttled to a fast idle. The pair of military guards at the door braced to attention. They wore dress uniforms finished off by pistols in white-leather holsters. The soldiers in the tower above wore their dress uniforms also. Kelly had little doubt, however, that their AKM rifles would function just as well as if they were used by men in battle dress. The Algerians held their rifles slung from their right shoulders with the muzzles forward and their right hands resting on the handgrips.

"Get down behind the counter where nobody can see you with the radio," the agent ordered Ramdan. Without waiting to see if he had been obeyed, Kelly draped his white coat carefully over his right arm and strolled back to the edge of the sidewalk in front of the shop. He resisted the impulse to grip the Ingram so tightly that his hand would cramp.

The entrance of the Institute was at one point of an extremely complex intersection. Five vehicular streets from the south met there, while the whole warren of the Casbah lay to the north. With the truck jamming the intersection proper, though, and the fork of the Victoire and the Avenue Taleb Mohammed blasted where they met the Boulevard Abderrazak—almost on top of National Police Headquarters—nothing would be driving through any time soon. For now, though. . . .

The leading Citröen swung halfway across the boulevard, just beyond the entrance. Its ready position would aid the Kabyles immeasurably when the burning truck careened down the hill and into the intersection. Three men, then a fourth, got out of the sedan, leaving the driver behind the wheel. The three doors were open. The security men were not carrying long-arms, but Kelly did not need X-ray vision to guess what was racked within the car.

The Algerians wore dark suits which tweaked an uncomfortable memory . . . but the car that had been—following him?—had not been a Citröen, whatever it was. None of these men looked anything like the three who had entered the room at the Aurassi.

The second car was a Mercedes limo. It had green diplomatic plates, though Kelly had not been in country long enough to recognize the particular mission. Three men in London-tailored suits and Arab burnooses got out of the back. As they walked toward the door of the Institute, the steel leaves opened inward. A pair of suited Algerians stepped out to bow in greeting. The Mercedes pulled carefully around the security car and turned up the Ramp des Zoaves, past the south front of the building.

The next car was not an old Fiat but rather a Volga, Russian-made and almost certainly Russian-occupied at the moment. The American tensed. He spread a meaningless smile across his whisker-stubbled face. His peripheral vision showed him that there were a number of other bystanders watching events. The escort had cut its sirens, but the procession of expensive cars was still more interesting than most of Algiers' drab scenery. Despite the company, however, Kelly felt as obtrusive as a prisoner facing the sentencing judge.

Three men got out of the Volga. All of them were obviously low-ranking security men from their bulk and East-Bloc clothing. Rank hath the privilege of a decent tailor. . . . But that meant the next car, another Citröen limo, this one with AMB—Ambassador—on the plate was—

"Roll the truck!" Kelly shouted back over his shoulder. "*Just* the truck!"

The Volga sedan showed an inclination to hold its position at the intersection. One of the Algerian security men walked over to it and began talking and gesturing to the driver. The Russian car moved off slowly in the wake of the Mercedes.

The Citröen behind it pulled up under the watchful eyes of the Algerians and the three Russians who had dismounted from the Volga. The long back doors opened. From the right-side jump seat a—for God's sake, a *Vietnamese* got out. Another tall European got out a moment later, also from the right side, toward the Institute. He wore an excellent suit but he was too young to be Vlasov. And from the left door, staring at Kelly even before he was out of the car, climbed another Vietnamese. Their eyes met at twenty yards distance. Kelly remembered in a series of flashes strobing between visions of Anna displaying her body that he had told Hoang that his defection would take place in Frankfurt. Since the physicist knew that his flight was through Paris, he had known that he was being lied to.

The last man out of the car was Professor Vlasov. The cuff of his right sleeve was pinned against his shoulder. He followed Hoang through the left door, putting the car between himself and his escort.

"Hit it!" Kelly snapped, and the truck, howling down the Rue Debbih Cherif, unexpectedly exploded just as it came in view.

The cab of the big flat-bed dissolved in a white flash so bright that the sunlight a millisecond later seemed dim. The explosion was oddly muffled. It sounded more as if a safe had fallen onto concrete than the crackling propagation wave of high explosive in open air. Perhaps because the light was so intense, the relative silence did not seem out of place. Sensory cross-over was telling the brain that the ears as well as the eyes had been numbed. Somebody had put an anti-tank rocket into the truck, Kelly's instincts told him. The hood and even the engine block were gone, blasted away, and the shredded front tires were letting the vehicle slow to a halt well short of where it was supposed to stop.

Because the noise was that of metal shrieking and sparking over concrete, the security personnel reacted a hair less quickly than they might have done for a true explosion. Hoang darted toward Kelly and the epicerie behind him. His escort's smile was only beginning to slip as the Vietnamese glanced across the car to the physicist. Then both Vietnamese, like Kelly and everyone else within a block, were dumped to the ground by the explosion beneath the intersection to the north.

Part of what went flying skyward was a car, but it was omelette time and too bad about the other poor bastards who found themselves eggs. Kelly got to his feet. His left palm was bleeding from its scrape along the sidewalk as he fell. He racked back the bolt of the Ingram without noticing the pain.

Instead of a twenty-pound charge, the Kabyles must have filled the sewer pipe with explosives. Hoang Tanh was on his feet and running again. Vlasov himself still lay groggy on the pavement. A pair of the Russians from the Volga were up and staggering toward their charge. The Vietnamese security man vaulted the hood of the Citröen. He was shouting something inaudible in the aftermath of the huge explosion. A ragged disk of asphaltic concrete, six inches thick and the size of a man-hole cover, spun out of the sky. It hopped once on the roadway and took the Viet's legs from under him as neatly as ever a bowler made a spare.

Kabyles were hurling smoke grenades as directed, the streamers gushing into parti-colored floods as the compound burned. It was a scene not of Carnival but of hell. Against specific orders, somebody opened up from the Casbah with an automatic rifle. The muzzle blasts could scarcely be heard through the ringing of the agent's ears, but plaster and powdered stone spurted from the upper facade of the tower. The guards there went down, one of them spinning under the impact of a bullet.

Kelly was standing as upright as a reviewing officer. Both of his hands were now hidden by the folded coat he held as a beacon. Vlasov stood up. The two Russians grabbed him and threw him back for safety. They knelt above the physicist, each with one hand on their charge's back to keep him down. Their other hands held pistols muzzle-high as they looked for targets through the wisps of smoke already swirling. Kelly cursed and killed both security men with short bursts from the Ingram.

Compactness is fine for something you have to carry, but for use it would have been nice to have a proper stock . . . or at least to have had time to extend the latch-and-wire contraption with which the sub-machine gun was fitted. Christ, it would have been nice to have a rifle and an explosives expert who would not have leveled a square block when his task was to cut a street. But you use what you got. Sights at eye level, bloody left hand gripping the suppressor tube, Kelly aimed to the left of one Russian and let recoil walk the second and third rounds into the man's chest.

As his partner collapsed, the remaining security man screamed and fired into the rooftops from which he thought the shots were coming. This one was trickier, because the target lay squarely over the physicist's body. The agent held higher than he should have, but one of the gleaming bullets caught the Russian at the hairline and dropped him dead as Trotsky. The two rounds that missed spalled plate-sized flakes of paint from the doors of the ambassadorial limo. They did not penetrate the armor beneath.

Hoang Tanh snatched at Kelly's left arm, shouting for

help. He was tall for a Vietnamese, scarcely less than Kelly's own 5'9". The physicist was a rotund man whose pleasant face was now distorted by tension and the need to be heard over gunfire.

"Get in the goddam shop!" Kelly shouted, turning the Vietnamese and shoving him toward the epicerie with the full strength of his left arm. Hoang staggered forward and almost collided with Ramdan. The Kabyle was shuffling out onto the sidewalk with his rifle at high port. "Put that away!" the American shrieked at him, but the Kabyle leveled his weapon and slammed a shot at something across the street.

By now the smoke was as thick as pond water, translucent or less beyond arm's-length. The lighter grit and dust drifting down from the explosion site added its own camouflage and the tang of burning tar. Kelly ran forward, waving the coat like a flag in his left hand. Blended red and purple smoke roiled about the sweeping fabric. A bullet whanged off the pavement near his feet. Momentarily it was a spark, incandescent with the energy released on impact. The American had no notion of whether it was a stray round or one deliberately aimed at him.

He tripped over Vlasov. The Russian scientist had crawled free of the pair of bodies that had pinioned him and was closer than Kelly had expected. The agent sprawled. A burst of automatic fire laced across the boulevard close to where Kelly's torso had been a moment before. The shock waves of the bullets spun curls of smoke as they cracked past.

Kelly could be sure the man he now held was Vlasov

because of the pinned-up sleeve. "Come on, Professor," he shouted in Russian, "we have to run!" He waved the raincoat, his identity signal, then tossed it onto the street to free his hand.

Vlasov did not get up. He seemed to be staring through the smoke at the suppressed Ingram. Kelly remembered too late that the defector was nuts—and what he was nuts about. The Lord knew, the gun and can did look more like something whipped up for a sci-fi film than the piece of functional, real-world ordnance that they were. Screw that, there was no time. "Go!" Kelly shouted. "I'm your contact!" He tried to tug the Professor upright by a handful of shirt front.

The black snout of a car thrust toward them through the man-made fog. Kelly dropped the scientist and hosed a burst through the windshield, just above the hood line. The car accelerated as the driver's muscles spasmed. The vehicle missed Vlasov by inches, missed Kelly only because he leaped sideways. It was the security vehicle that had led the procession. It must have doubled back into the chaos for reasons the driver, at least, would never be able to explain.

Even in normal surroundings the suppressed weapon would have made less noise than a bottle being kicked along a hallway. Under the present circumstances, it was effectively silent. The bolt, a tool-steel clapper ringing back and forth against the breech, was overwhelmed by the ringing of the explosion in everyone's ears. But the empty cartridge cases dancing from the ejection port were the same as those of a more standard submachine gun. Unexpectedly reassured, the Russian defector jumped to his feet as the car rolled past. "Quickly, then," he said, his lips close to Kelly's ear to be heard. "For they are here, I have seen them."

There is no good way to cross a flat area raked from all sides and elevations. Running upright made as much sense as anything else. While Vlasov was evidently crazy, Kelly found no reason to question the Russian's courage. The older man sprinted beside the agent toward what Kelly hoped was the doorway of the epicerie. The smoke swirled. Ramdan faced them over the sights of his old Mauser. Kelly struck the weapon away and screamed in useless Italian, "Back, for God's sake, play your war out later!"

Flames were beginning to envelope the security car wrecked to the north. The draft caused a freak of the breeze to tug clear a lane in the smoke boiling across the boulevard. "There!" cried the Kabyle. He made a quarter-turn and fired without seating the rifle against his shoulder. He spun again as return fire gouged his thigh.

Two uniformed soldiers stood twenty feet away with pistols and a clear field of fire. Standard service handguns are man-killingly accurate at fifty yards or more, but accuracy in combat is something more than an exercise in paper-punching. Kelly had time to turn and sweep a burst across both Algerians. One of them was still trying to fire with his slide locked back on an empty magazine. They were brave men, but soldiering was a bad business for people who make mistakes . . . and they were not the first to make the mistake of shooting at Tom Kelly and missing.

"Now go!" the agent shouted again at his charges. He planted his left hand in Vlasov's back and the Ingram's receiver in Ramdan's—the *idiot*! The Kabyle had dropped his rifle and was clutching his right thigh with both hands, but he staggered forward at Kelly's push. Vlasov followed him into the epicerie.

"Take him out the back," the American shouted as he tossed the sub-machine gun to the counter-top and turned. An accordion-pleated metal screen could close the front of the shop when it was unoccupied. Kelly unlatched the screen and slammed it down. He shouted curses in several languages when one side caught momentarily in its track. The only light within was the back door opening on another unlighted room. That was a gray blur to the agent's day-adapted eyes. The Ingram met his groping hand—and so did the CS grenade which he had snuggled into a corner behind the counter.

Kelly pulled the pin with his right thumb and stumbled through the back door. He tossed the grenade into the shop as he closed the door behind him. It was a piss-poor thing to do to a supporter's property, but there were other people out there catching bullets. It had to be done. The Casbah was a maze. Closing the entrance to the track the fugitives were taking would, with luck, delay pursuit until there was no longer a trail to follow.

With luck.

XXXI

The back room was furnished as living quarters. Vlasov waited uncertainly at the door in the far end. Ramdan was doubled up on the rug, moaning and clutching again at his wounded thigh. "Come on, Professor," Kelly said in Russian, opening the second door for the defector.

Beyond was an alley less than a meter wide—Alexandria Street, if you wanted to believe a French map-maker to whom there was no such thing as *terra incognita*, even if the cognition were in the map-maker's office alone. A Kabyle with a Kalashnikov half-hidden in the folds of his robe beckoned them urgently from the top of a pole-supported staircase a few meters away. Kelly gestured Vlasov toward the stairs, then called over his shoulder in French, "If you don't roust, you'll be there when they come looking—that'll hurt worse'n now, believe me."

No one ran toward them down the alley from the

killing ground on the Boulevard de la Victoire. Vlasov mounted the steep, unrailed stairs with as much agility as could be expected of a scientist in his mid-60s.

Kelly risked a glance down at the Ingram. His left palm was throbbing and beginning to swell. Long bursts had heated the suppressor tube enough to make the air above it dance. It had seared the abraded flesh of the hand that gripped it. Like the gas-filled epicerie, that came with the turf. Kelly tried to extend the sub-machine gun's stock, but he found that he could not figure how to lock the folding butt-plate into position in the instants he was willing to spare. It was more important to spot the people coming down the alley whom he might have to kill.

Vlasov squeezed by the guard at the narrow landing. The American pounded up the stairs himself. The guard ducked inside behind Kelly and slammed the blue-painted door panel.

An entire family waited inside the room. There was a grandfather, parents, and four wide-eyed children spaced from six to the infant in the woman's arms. The rugs that provided bedding were rolled up against the wall. A table holding a plastic bucket of water completed the furnishings. The family might be related to someone taking an active part in the operation . . . or it might not. No matter. In all likelihood, the father had been a babe in arms when similar scenes were played out in the struggle against the French; and his father had not talked, either.

At the end of the room, where a hanging blanket filled the place of a door, stood Hoang Tanh. "You did not tell us about him," said the rifleman accusingly to Kelly.

The agent nodded curtly. "Let's go," he said. No point

in trying to explain. The Kabyle, after all, did not have the real problem of trying to get the stupid son of a bitch out of the country.

It would have been faster to run to the Rue Amar Ali down the Rue Porte Neuve. The latter was one of the few pedestrian ways in the Casbah that deserved the name of street. It would be faster for the security forces too, if they blew their way past the gunmen who were supposed to lie in ambush at its head. To the Kabyles, a room to room, central courtyard to stairs route had the advantage of involving large numbers of people who therefore had excellent reason to fear the police and army. In for a penny, in for a pound. . . . Kelly himself had spent enough time in another kind of jungle to have learned that you did not follow established trails if you wanted to go back to the World under your own power. It did not occur to him to question the technique as the Kabyles applied it.

They reached the Amar Ali through a hammam, a Turkish bath, which they had entered by a trap door from the cellar where the oven was. In the cellar, dampness was a thing you could touch. Kelly had shrugged his jacket off. He carried it slung over the Ingram as he had the trench coat when the morning began. With his dark complexion and his cheap, styleless clothing, the American agent was not worth a second glance from the bath attendants and their early customers.

The two defectors were another matter. Hoang had generalized Oriental features. There must have been Chinese or even Korean in the physicist's ancestry. Conceivably, he might have gone unremarked in the dim light. Professor Vlasov, on the other hand, stood out like a pregnant bride. He was six-foot-three, and his forebears had certainly included many a blond "Rus," as the natives called the Viking "rowers" who had founded Novgorod and the Grand Duchy of Kiev before the Mongols swept across the Siberian plains. But no one looked at Vlasov, either, proof that the would-be rebels had done their homework—even if their aggressiveness had put Kelly and the operation in jeopardy.

At the entrance of the hammam, the plain, cream tile of the hallway gave way to a mosaic of intricate knots on a golden background. Kelly blinked at the sunlight of the open street beyond. Their original guide had been replaced by an older man whose right hand never left the side pocket of his coat. "Quickly, get out," he hissed to Kelly. The agent still hesitated. 'This was all our arrangement."

The Volare wagon waited across the street. Commander Posner was drumming on the steering wheel, his eyes trying to look in all directions. The Attaché's nerves were screwed as tight as the breech of a cannon. Ordinary traffic noises had given way to sirens from all directions. In the open air again, the thump of gunfire could be heard.

The car parked three spaces behind the Volare was a Volkswagen Beetle. Presumably the Defense Attaché had not noticed it pulling in. The driver was Mayer, one of the CIA personnel Kelly had met in the snack bar.

"I'll go first," Kelly said in French. His right arm crawled with a sweaty desire to put a burst through the Beetle's door. If those bastards thought they were going to get in his way, they'd better be ready to die. . . .

He started across the street with the quick, nervous

stride of a man dodging traffic on any busy artery. Kelly's eyes darted around him at street level and above, trying to anticipate the shot that would pay him back for the many mistakes of others on which he had capitalized. There was no shot, though a van missed him by less than the small part of his mind devoted to traffic had calculated. The Company man saw Kelly before Commander Posner did. His eyes widened and he raised a walkie-talkie enough for Kelly to see it.

"Start the goddam engine!" Kelly shouted to Posner through the open window. His anger was flashing out at the closest victim, not the cause. Face black as thunder, the agent waved curtly across to the hammam entrance.

It said something about the sparseness of CIA assets in Algiers that Warner had to use Amcit officers for a surveillance operation. It said something about how badly Langley wanted to know what the DIA was up to that they had gone ahead with the surveillance regardless.

Vlasov, his white hair flashing like a marker pennant, stepped into the street. He was more cautious than even Kelly had been. The American agent still stood on the traffic side. His thigh was trembling as the door transmitted the vibration of the engine's initial fast idle. Posner was saying something, but the words made no impression on the mirror surface of Kelly's mind. Something was about—

Hoang ran past the tall Russian scientist. His body, ten feet or less from Kelly, disintegrated in a white flash like the one that had vaporized most of the truck cab.

The vehicle from which the rocket-propelled grenade must have come was a black sedan a hundred yards away.

It was just turning left out of the Boulevard Ourida-Meddad, the shortest way from the Institute by car. That was goddam good shooting, even with the scope sights fitted to the RPG-7, Kelly thought as he blew out the sedan's side windows with the last four rounds in the Ingram.

"Get over!" the agent screamed to Posner. He tossed the empty gun through the window with little concern for where the Attaché's head might be at the moment. With his freed right hand, Kelly jerked open the driver's door. A weary Simca screeched to a stop in the traffic lane. Its driver looked as horrified as Mayer. The CIA officer was gaping through his windshield at a scene right out of *The Battle of Algiers.*

The Russian had been thrown sideways by the blast. He lurched upright under the tug of Kelly's left hand. On the pavement beneath Vlasov lay a shoe, sock, and probably a foot from the ankle down. The American had seen its like before, when a dink had been almost on top of a Claymore mine as it went off. Hoang had made his own choice, and it appeared to have been a very goddam bad one for him. The chance of his location, however, had saved Professor Vlasov from taking the grenade himself.

The Defense Attaché had not yet grasped that Kelly was taking over the driving. When the operation had been planned, they had decided that Posner, who knew the city, would drive. Too much had hit the fan in the past few minutes for Kelly now to trust the naval man's reflexes to get them out of what might be coming next. The agent threw the Attaché aside with as little ceremony as he bundled the Russian in after him. That put the defector between the two Americans with no chance of changing his mind and leaping out of the car again.

The driver of the Simca had gotten out of the car. She was staring at the disembodied foot on the pavement. The knuckles of both her hands were pressed against her mouth. Welcome to the world of international diplomacy, Kelly thought as he jerked the wheel left. He took the Volare into the street with as much verve as its slant-six engine could muster.

"We'll go straight up along the coast road," Kelly said, remembering to speak in French so that both his companions could understand. He cut right at the first intersection, feeling his guts tense as he waited for a trio of white-robed widows to cross in front of him. Things were not quite bad enough that Kelly was going to kill old ladies to save a few seconds. Not quite.

"They have decided to kill me," said Professor Vlasov in a voice that belied the apparent calm of his face. "I thought they would, if I tried to reach the West."

"Why did you turn, then?" Commander Posner demanded in peevish English. He had just stuffed the sub-machine gun gingerly under the seat. "We could have gone straight and turned at the Abdel Kader Lyceum."

The agent heard brakes and felt metal jolt as he pulled left across traffic onto the Rue Bougrina. A Peugeot's driver had not been alert enough when the relatively huge American car took his place in what was already a solid line of traffic. The Peugeot's bumper dragged off with a clang on the Volare's right rear fender. The Defense Attaché stared open-mouthed at Kelly. His cigarette, still unlighted, stuttered like a telegraph key between his fingers.

Kelly ignored the sounds. He said, "Because traffic on the Abderrazak'd be blocked by that procession even without that goddam bomb cratering the road four blocks south. God willing, we can get through by the Lycee if we're on the north side of the square."

"My hope was," the Russian said in the same taut voice as before, "that they would be taken off guard. Before, they spared me because I was harmless with no one to build my devices. Killing me would prove that I was right."

He raised his head. "Now that I have started," he said, "I must succeed. If they catch us, we have no hope and the world has no hope."

XXXII

The nearby shooting had stopped. Most of the smoke particles had settled to paint the street like the wing of a giant butterfly. The screaming still continued.

Someone was plucking at Korchenko with maddening persistence. The colonel rushed back to awareness with a flush that made his whole skin prickle inside. Babroi had an arm under Korchenko's shoulders and was trying to feed him a swig of vodka. The colonel did not need either the help or the liquor. He needed full consciousness—that was returning—and better luck than seemed probable.

"Get away, dammit," Korchenko muttered to his aide. He rolled to all fours and stood. Babroi hovered beside his chief. He had dropped his flask uncapped into his pocket to free both hands in case the colonel fell. Only Schwartz' own door was still closed on the limousine. The driver was hunched over the wheel, as rigid as a gargoyle. Schwartz was the best driver Korchenko had ever met, skillful and utterly fearless while performing his functions. When he was faced with any other sort of danger, however, he froze—until someone ordered him to drive.

The back compartment of the Citröen was empty. Through its open doors Korchenko could see bodies sprawled on the pavement. The Professor's body was not among them.

The other shoe dropped. "The bastard is defecting!" Korchenko shouted. He slammed his hand down on the limousine's roof.

The Vietnamese security man raised himself by his grip on the car's bumper. His face was as blank as a pelt stretched to dry. The pain within illuminated the skin. "If you please, sir," he said in a calm voice, "where is Doctor Hoang?"

"Shut the hell up, I'm busy!" Korchenko snapped. He forgot to use English, but the tone translated well enough. The KGB colonel ducked to use the microphone. The motion made him dizzy for a moment. Angrily, Korchenko blipped the mike button three times for attention. The nervous babble on the control channel ceased.

Car One was the Citröen, Car Two the Volga which had dropped off the KGB team in front of them. Three and Four were the Volgas further back in the procession. "This is Korchenko," the colonel snarled into his microphone. "Everybody shut their fucking mouth. Car Two, report your location."

Nothing. "Car Two, come in or I'll—" Korchenko shouted.

Beside him, Babroi clucked in the back of his throat and said, "Colonel, their radio wasn't working in the compound when we tested it."

Korchenko licked the edges of his front teeth. The sole survivor of the team from Car Two was wandering dazedly down the street with his pistol in his hand. The man's eyes appeared fixed on the bodies of the men who had accompanied him moments before. "Right," said the colonel. Then he keyed the mike and went on, "Car Three, report your location."

"We're not up to the National Police barracks yet and everything's stopped," the radio responded. The speaker's calm was surprising until Korchenko remembered the situation. No one more than a block from the explosion and firefight knew more than that *something* had happened. "What's going on?" Car Three continued. "The police are all running out and it sounded like there were shots?"

"Shut up," the colonel said. The Vietnamese officer had groped his way around the hood of the car. He stood, listening intently as if he understood the Russian being spoken. "Can you turn—" Korchenko began to the microphone.

Babroi's scanner blurted unexpectedly in English, "Harry! Good God! He's got a machine gun! They're *killing* people here!"

Korchenko stopped speaking with his mouth open. The two-way set asked, "Say again?" in Russian. "I didn't copy that."

"Shut up," the colonel screamed into his microphone.

The scanner picked up a different voice saying, "Don, cool *down*. Who's shooting? Are you safe?"

"It's Kelly," responded the first voice in a less shrill tone. "He's got somebody with him in the station wagon besides Posner. I'm all right, I'm . . . they're driving off east on the Rue Amar Ali and I'm staying here. He's shooting a machine gun. Harry, there was a bomb and somebody. . . ."

"Tell the other cars to turn around. One of them goes up the Arbadji Abderrahman, the other Rue Bab el Oued," said Nguyen. Because he spoke in English like the voices on the scanner, Korchenko listened instead of shouting him to silence reflexively. "Look for an American car, there can't be any other here."

The scanner was moaning in the first voice, "They blew somebody *apart*, Harry. There's a *foot* here in the street."

Korchenko relayed Nguyen's suggestions—orders, from the tone!—in quick Russian. The KGB officer had not memorized the street layout of Algiers, and for all he knew there was no map of the city in the car—even if he had time to check it out. But if this fish-eating nigger was wrong, the colonel would personally see to it that he never saw home again.

The trunk lid closed solidly. Babroi strode around to the door again. He was holding out to his superior one of the automatic rifles he had gotten from the trunk. At the head of the street, an armored personnel carrier nosed around the truck still burning in the intersection. There had been no shooting for several minutes. Now some unseen marksman down the Rue Porte Neuve spanged a round off the APC's glacis plate. The vehicle halted with its front wheels up on the curb. The heavy machine gun in the turret blasted a response to the rifle fire. The whole steel-clad mass of the APC rocked with the recoil of the automatic weapon.

Korchenko cursed. "We've got to get past them," he said. He waved forward as he slid into the seat beside the driver. His rifle was impossibly awkward in the space cramped by the floor shift and the tube-driven radio. The colonel dropped the weapon over the seat as Babroi got into the back.

The rear doors slammed, one and then the other. Korchenko drew the pistol from his shoulder holster. "Sir, we'll try," Schwartz said. He put the Citröen in gear.

A second APC from the Mobile Guard barracks south on the Avenue Mohamed pulled up beside the first. Both began ripping long bursts down the pedestrian way. White smoke from their guns drifted to mix with black curls from the burning truck.

Instead of trying to force his way through the firefight, Schwartz cramped the wheel hard and took the limousine up the narrow alley between, the Institute and the Church of the Holy Cross. A squad of Algerian troops was coming the other way. The KGB driver went through them. He slowed just enough that the car's glass leading edge did not shatter as it brushed a pair of soldiers out of the way.

"Call your base," directed an unexpected voice. "Have them alert all other available cars."

Colonel Korchenko jerked his head around. His throat was caught between a curse and inarticulate rage. The Vietnamese officer was poised behind him in the back seat, holding the rifle Korchenko had tossed there.

But before the colonel's anger could find words, the speaker of the two-way radio bleated, "We see them! We've got them for sure!"

XXXIII

Islam's day ends at sundown Friday. The downtown traffic was therefore roughly what was to be expected in an American city on Saturday morning. Many of the cars were filled with shoppers and families headed out of town for the weekend. The paved square surrounding the tawny, Romanesque pile of the Ketchouan Mosque was thick with pedestrians, many of them foreigners. Kelly was momentarily more concerned with the pedestrians than with vehicles, so only the squeal of tires warned him that a Volga sedan on an intercepting course from the Rue Bab el Oued was trying to ram them.

With one hand, Kelly slammed the gear selector into low, cursing the car for having a slush box instead of a standard transmission. His left hand was spinning the wheel to the right. The agent did not brake. His tires had limited traction. At this point, he needed cornering force a lot worse than he did braking. Broadsiding around an acute corner scrubbed off enough speed anyway.

They might not have made it, but the lighter Russian vehicle brushed the rear of the Volare. It hit with enough force to crumple sheet metal and keep the back end of the station wagon from breaking away as it had started to do. Vlasov jolted forward. Posner's head rapped against the side window. The man in the back seat of the Volga was jolted badly enough that only Kelly realized that the Plymouth was being fired at.

The agent kept his foot in it, winding the sluggish engine to five grand in low before he let it shift. They were barreling up the center of the Rue Aboulker, past the only Protestant church in downtown Algiers. Twice Kelly used the Volare's bulk to muscle a lighter car into the curb. As they blasted through the Place Touri, between the National Theatre and the Square Port Said, a city bus took their right headlight out in a glancing blow.

Kelly was pretty sure that the Volga just behind them now was not the car they had bumped. It would have taken longer than that to get the first car backed off the sidewalk into which it had spun with the impact. But that meant that there were at least two cars in immediate pursuit, the reasons did not matter now, and Kelly had to shake them goddam fast or it was a question only of who tortured him to death. The KGB might hand him over to the National Police, or they might keep him and do the job themselves.

"Posner," the agent said, "you've got *some* weapons here, right?" He did not look away from the road.

The Defense Attaché's forehead was swelling under the pressure cut it had taken when he bounced against the window. "Of course I don't, you idiot," he said, squinting as he tried to squeeze the pain away with his palm. "What in God's name is going on?"

"The aliens are going to kill me," Professor Vlasov muttered. It must have been coincidence, because he could not have understood the question in English.

The Volare's mill was no hemi, but they still had a better power to weight ratio than Volgas loaded with three or four big men. What was keeping the Russians in the race, and indeed on their bumper, was the fact that the American car cleared a path through obstacles like a Rome Plow in brush.

Something had to change suddenly or it was going to change for the worse.

"Hang on!" Kelly shouted. Instead of speeding through the Place Emir Abdel Kader, he slewed to the right, then counter-steered to bring the Volare out at right angles to its original course. They were squealing down the Rue Morris, using all of the sidewalk on the left side of the street to do it without exceeding a 15° turn—all the soft tires would allow.

The four corners of the square between the central and circumferential vehicle ways were grassed and set off from the pavement by curbs and slack chains. The driver of the leading Volga tried to follow Kelly. He had less time to react and an even lower threshold of control. The Russian exceeded that threshold, trying to hurl his over-loaded car into a corner that it could not have negotiated empty at the speed it was traveling. In panic, the driver touched his brakes. Their limits exceeded, traction and cornering force dropped instantly to zero.

The Volga slid off the pavement. It maintained exactly

the angle and attitude it had when the brakes were applied. When the left-side wheels hit the curb around the green space, the tires stripped off and the car over-turned sideways. It rolled three times before coming to rest on its side, against a utility pole. Gas, oil, and radiator fluid pooled in the street. There was no fire until one of the Russians tried to kick open his door with a steel-shod boot.

Two more black Volgas skidded across the far end of the Rue Morris, four hundred feet away and no cross streets between.

They had probably come from the Palais du Gouvernement, less than a block away. That mattered, because it meant they would not be stuffed with armed security men. Kelly kicked down the emergency brake with his left foot, locking the rear wheels. He cramped the power steering hard left. The back end broke away and the station wagon swapped ends with a suddenness that cracked Posner against the window a second time. Vlasov's considerable weight slid against the Attaché's hips.

The Volare had been at less than 30 mph when the Russian cars appeared in front of them. Now Kelly was braking to a dead stop, using a steady pressure that laid rubber on the street but kept the tires rotating enough to preserve traction. The air in the Volare stank with their own burning tires and brake pads.

The driver of one of the blocking cars reacted with an initiative that would have been commendable had it turned out better. When the Russian saw the Volare had turned in its own traffic lane and was about to speed off in the direction from which it had come, he turned his own wheel to follow. The Volga accelerated out of the cross-wise blocking position.

The bootlegger turn had slammed all three men in the American car against their seat back. When the car momentarily stopped, Kelly reached away from the steering wheel with both hands. His right slid the selector back into low range while his left popped the emergency brake release. The agent tweaked the wheel just enough to keep the tires off the streaks of slick, fresh rubber they had laid on the pavement in stopping.

A Volga with a crumpled fender, the car that had made the initial pass at them near the Ketchouan Mosque, turned onto the Rue Morris. The gouting pyre of the leading Russian vehicle marked the intersection for its consort. A man with eyebrows that met in a black bar was leaning out of the passenger side. He fired a pistol at the Volare. Kelly cursed and steered directly toward the Russian car.

There was nothing of the kamikaze in the agent's action, nothing of patriotic sacrifice and noble self-immolation. It was berserk bloodlust, pure and simple, the rage that had sent the Kellys of a thousand years before across the beach at Clontarf, as naked as the axes in their hands. As the armored Vikings broke that day in bloody ruin, so the KGB driver, neither coward nor incompetent, violated training and orders. He snapped his car to the right, out of the path of the great square grill. The Russian tires squealed but the driver had not lost control, not really, until his car slammed head-on into the Volga that had begun to pursue from its blocking position.

At the moment, Kelly did not particularly care what might be going on behind him. The latest brush with a Russian car had stripped chrome from the Volare's left side and replaced it with smudged black paint. None of the tires were rubbing and there were no other immediate mechanical problems.

Ammunition was exploding within the first wrecked Volga. It was harmless enough without a gun barrel to channel the energy, just bits of metal spitting and whining like bees and no more dangerous.

The smoke rending the clear sky in whorls from the flame tips was as black as what spewed from the ovens at Dachau.

"What's the fastest route to Tipasa from here?" Kelly asked. He turned onto the Rue Larbi again. He swung as widely around the balefire as the street's width allowed.

XXXIV

When the Citröen's windows were rolled down, the wail of sirens made it difficult to speak in a normal voice and still be heard. Babroi had locked the scanner onto the channel the Americans were using. Otherwise the car would have been flooded by the sudden torrent of emergency traffic in Arabic which none of the four occupants understood.

A squad of troops in red berets diverted the limousine a block west of the Place Emir Abdel Kader. The pall of smoke beyond was the visual counterpart of the sirens. Before the radio in Car Four went permanently silent, it had transmitted the sound of rending metal.

Schwartz turned left in obedience to the directions waved by the muzzle of an automatic rifle. Korchenko cursed under his breath but said nothing. "Pull up here," suggested Babroi. "I'll run over on foot and see what happened."

The driver glanced uncertainly at his superior. "Yes,

that's a good idea," the colonel said abruptly. His face became fractionally less grim. "Who knows—maybe they collided with the American car and *all* of them are dead."

"Syd," said the scanner. "I'm getting a clear direction." The occupants of the limousine held their breath. "They're heading south and pretty fast, from the way I'm having to turn the antenna to keep it on them. What's your location?"

Colonel Korchenko put a hand over the back of his seat needlessly to keep his aide from getting out of the car. All of them, even Schwartz who did not speak English, waited like snipers.

"Look, I'm down by the train station, Harry," said the American with the mobile unit. "But what do you mean by south? There's a whole desert out there."

"Dammit, Syd, you know I can't give you more than a direction from here," said the voice of "Harry," "Turn south and we'll trust to luck."

"Harry, this isn't going to work," Syd's voice responded. "Look, I think I'd better go find Don. He may be in real trouble."

"God dammit, Westram, this is a direct order! The car we want is going south and you're as far north as you can get without falling into the harbor! Now, get off your duff and head south!"

"Acknowledged." The voice from the scanner was cold and formal. "Proceeding south to the Malika and then south on it until ordered otherwise. Mobile One, out."

"From here they must be intending to take National One," said a voice. Again it was an instant before

Korchenko realized the Vietnamese behind him was speaking. Again also, the colonel's flash of anger was quenched by the reasonableness of Nguyen's plan and the fact that he at least had *some* plan. Like the puzzled CIA operative, Korchenko could only think that the Sahara was a big place.

"We'll follow," Nguyen continued. "Tell your driver to turn right, then right again at the Rue Mellan Ali, that seems as good a way as any. If we do not catch up with them before they reach National 38, we'll turn right anyway. They were trying to go west originally, before we headed them off. Likely they will try to go west again when they are out of the city." He paused. "It is some chance; and if you will just bring in the Algerian authorities, a very good chance."

Korchenko gave his orders in crisp, commanding Russian. Schwartz slid the Citröen back into traffic like a shark joining a school of mackerel. The colonel picked up the two-way radio again. He had no intention of bringing in the locals. In the end, that would require explanations at the ministerial level. The colonel's superiors were not going to be pleased with events in Algiers. They would be even less pleased if the matter were not somehow kept in the family.

But at Blida, there was a training cadre of three hundred Soviet troops. They had both ground vehicles and helicopters available from stores being supplied to the Polisarios. Those troops could be fanned across possible escape routes, looking for an American station wagon. With luck, they would be able to strike a more direct blow for the safety of Mother Russia than anyone had expected.

Korchenko began giving instructions to the operator on the base unit in the embassy. The troops would find Vlasov again, that was almost certain. The Americans with the Professor clearly did not know their own personnel had put a tracer on them.

But the colonel very much hoped all those involved would be captured without injury. He wanted to conduct their interrogations himself, and he wanted them to be in good physical condition.

When he began.

XXXV

On the outskirts of Birkhadem, ten kilometers from the center of Algiers, construction vehicles had blocked one lane of a bridge. Traffic on National Highway 1 stopped abruptly, then resumed in fits and starts. A flagman using a T-shirt on a pole directed clumps of cars in alternating directions like beads on an asphalt wire. Two National Policemen leaned against a house wall close enough to the road that Commander Posner could have touched them as the Volare halted for the third time. Posner was unlikely to do so. He sat so rigidly in his seat that his front-facing eyes seemed not to blink.

Kelly put the transmission in neutral so that the radiator fan would run. The water temperature was already higher than he liked to see it at idle. He leaned past his companions for a glimpse of the Algerian policemen. The roof of the car still hid their faces. The black leather suits must have been warm, but only one of the men had even bothered to unzip his tunic as far as the belt that slashed across it. The cross-belt supported his pistol holster and mounted his star-burst badge. The agent could hear only enough of the Algerians' conversation to be sure that they were not speaking a language he knew. From their gestures and cheerful volubility, though, Kelly was pretty sure that they were laughing at the condition of the American car.

The flagman waved, a circular gesture in time with the beat of the transistor radio in his left hand. Kelly put the car in gear and followed the vehicles ahead of him around the back of a truck loaded with sections of concrete culvert. "You know," he said in French, "I'd really like to know how the KGB had us spotted but the Algerians themselves could care less."

"This is all insane," the Defense Attaché muttered with his eyes closed. "To die for my country, well, I swore my oath. But to die only to harm and humiliate the United States"—he faced Kelly to glare at him past the disinterested Russian—"I should never have come, I should have resigned."

"We're not dead yet," the agent remarked mildly.

"Those aren't KGB," Professor Vlasov said. "They're the aliens who want to kill me." He sounded more impersonal than was to be expected from a man contemplating his imminent murder.

"Professor," Kelly snapped, sick to death of the counterpoint of disaster from his passengers, "I can't swear what language the people after us were talking, but the cars they drove were made in Smolensk, not Mars. And I'll need a hell of a good reason before I believe this"—he fumbled between his seat and the side panel—"was done by a ray gun and not a Makarov." Kelly found what he was after, the left wing mirror which he had wrenched off as they sped south from the Place Emir Abdel Kader. Angrily, he dropped the mirror in Vlasov's lap.

All the bullet had left was the chromed shield, and even that with a puckered hole in it. The glass and the thin metal that backed it lay in shards somewhere on the Rue Morris. From the direction of the impact, the shot had been fired in the instants that Kelly and the Russian sedan were headed straight toward one another.

Less emotionally, his eyes still on his driving, the agent said, "I'm not worried about dents in the sheet metal, not the way traffic is in Algiers. . . . But I sure hope we didn't pick up any more bullet holes besides this one. I'd hate to have had to explain *that* to the police."

The Russian turned the mirror shell in his hand, closing the bullet hole momentarily with the tip of one finger. As Kelly had said, it was about the right size for a jacketed 9-mm bullet to have made in light metal; though there was no real way to deduce a brand of weapon from a bullet hole. "Ah, well," Vlasov said tiredly, "you think I am mad also, do you? Well, I have gotten used to that from my colleagues, from the officials I have tried to talk to. I say, 'My conversations are being listened to, I'm being followed.' And of course they think me mad, because the KGB follows everyone, listens to everyone, doesn't it?" He waved his hand parenthetically, adding, "Everyone like me, who knows things that our enemies would wish to learn."

Commander Posner looked at Vlasov with more interest than approval. "You mean ex-enemies," he said.

Kelly could not see Vlasov's eyes when the Russian turned to stare at the Attaché. No one, however, could mistake the chill in Vlasov's voice as he repeated, "Enemies!" More gently, the older man went on, "But human enemies, you see. We have known many of these, we Russians, from East and West. We will deal with you as we dealt with Hitler, with Napoleon, with the Khans. Time and courage . . . we will deal with you. But these others, who can say?"

Kelly knew he had to defuse the conversation fast. Though he had no desire to hear a nut expound on the subject of his nuttiness, he said, "Ah, why do you think these aliens are after you, Professor Vlasov?"

The Russian turned around. "Oh," he said, "for the same reason everyone else is after me—you, the Kommission, yes. . . ." He juggled the mirror in his palm so that light danced on the chrome. "Unscientific, was I not? To assign causes without inspecting the data . . . but still, I am sure that they must have informed the KGB, they like to work through humans, I believe, it keeps their true role hidden. . . ."

"Go on, what purpose, then?" Posner interrupted needlessly. At least he wasn't trying to rake the scientist over the coals for inadequate US patriotism. They had too many miles yet to go to spend them wrangling.

"Why, the beam device," Vlasov said in genuine surprise. "The focusing lens, really, the principle. They did not tell you, your people?"

"We know a little, but we're not scientists. Professor," Kelly said with a smile that had time now to be sad. There was no time to reflect when your life depended on keeping the muzzle down and killing the other bastard first.

Vlasov studied the agent with more interest and a touch of respect. "Yes," he said after a moment. "I have seen that. I too was not always a scientist, you know, Mr. American."

Kelly looked the defector in the face. "All I know about your present work," he said, "is that I'm told you're respected by the front rank of scientists. Well and good . . . but Professor, I can see your empty sleeve myself, and I need no briefing book to tell me why you are to be respected for that."

The Russian smiled broadly. "Come," he said, "I have already defected. You do not need to stroke me any more." He looked out the windshield again. The landscape was undistinguished. Even plants in the gardens near the road looked dusty. They had driven through the initial ridge of the Atlas Range which pinned Algiers against its gulf. The reverse slopes now rose abruptly to the right as they followed the highway west.

"You want to know why they pursue me, these aliens that you do not believe in, eh?" continued the Professor. "I think because they will be coming to Earth in great numbers soon, they plan. And if Earth is protected by weapons that kill fifty targets with a single shot, then their fleet, their Armada"—he smiled at the Spanish word — "will come no closer to Earth than we, its inhabitants, choose." Vlasov's smile slumped like wax in a fire. "No closer than you, the inhabitants of Earth who are Americans, choose . . . but I had no choice, my own, my fellow children of my Russian soil, can not turn my formulae into weapons. Not quickly enough." The defector swallowed. He looked at neither of the men flanking him.

"I pray that we are in enough time now. There is very little grace remaining, I am afraid."

The notion intrigued Kelly enough to cause him to treat it seriously. He asked, "Aren't these, ah, weapons pretty vulnerable themselves, Professor? I mean, as I understand it, you're just hanging a bomb up in orbit with a lot of electronics around it. Or do you plan to armor them or whatever?"

Vlasov seemed to have forgotten that he was on the verge of certain death. "Vulnerable, you say?" he responded. "Yes, in the sense that any object in space would be equally vulnerable to another. These beams, these particle beams have no limiting range, you see, not if the focus is tight enough—as it can be. They command the Solar System; and beyond, even, if targets could be found for them. So our satellites could be destroyed by the fleets that are coming, to be sure. But the risk is equal, attacker and satellite. And here, not light-years away from our bases, we can replace *our* pawns indefinitely. The aliens must spend the very heart of their invasion at every attempt. If they were not threatened by my research, they would not have bothered about me . . . as they have. And they are concerned as well to keep their dealings on Earth secret, for what I could do, another might equal."

"So we're fine so long as we can keep building rockets, hey?" Kelly joked. He immediately regretted his flippancy. This was not a bull session with everybody half looped, this was a very bright boy who happened also to be nuts in one area—and who had better stay happy until he was delivered to the submarine. Then he became somebody else's problem.

Vlasov chose to respond to the agent's question as if it were real. He raised an eyebrow and said, "Rockets? Why bother? These are small packages, I tell you. *Shoot* them into orbit. Twenty years ago, you and the Canadians were doing this, two battleship cannon end to end. . . . How could the aliens invade when the Earth is ready to fire scores of new defensive satellites into orbit in a few hours?"

The road signs did not help since they were in Arabic alone. Kelly had been watching the odometer, however. A cluster of one-story houses had been a crossroads village. It would soon be dwarfed by the apartment block under construction on the near outskirts. "Commander," the agent said in English, his foot off the gas, "is this where the Vilayat road goes straight and the National bends more to the south?"

The Attaché bent over a Michelin map, unprepared for the question. "Yes, yes; I guess it does," he said after longer than Kelly's temper cared to wait. "It seems to be called Four Roads—the village. But I'm sure Route 1 would be faster."

"That may not be all we have to worry about," the agent said grimly. He pulled through the controlled inter-section at speed, avoiding a southbound Mercedes tour bus by less than its driver or his own passengers could believe. Kelly had his foot to the floor again. He had been looking in the rear-view mirror as he spoke to Posner.

"You—" the commander cried, but as his eyes turned to the agent, they took in the blank rigidity of Kelly's face. Posner had seen that look before, when the agent was hauling them through Algiers with death on their bumper.

Posner and Vlasov both turned to stare out the back window.

"You thought me mad," said the defector with flat certainty. "They could not get the Kommission to kill me, so they are coming to do it themselves."

The square back end of the station wagon had sucked a layer of road dust over the window like frosting. Vlasov turned around after only a glance, satisfied that any and all possible threats were his aliens. Commander Posner continued to lean over the seat back, squinting. The local road was narrower and significantly less smooth that the National route had been. All that the dust and hammering left certain was that there was a car approaching.

It was approaching very fast, despite anything Kelly could coax out of the Plymouth. This was not an underpowered Volga. . . .

Ten feet from the American car's rear bumper, the pursuing vehicle slowed to match speeds as perfectly as the road surface would allow. "AMB-51," Commander Posner was saying. "Why—I believe that's the Russian Ambassador's car! Surely—"

"Get your head down, Professor," Kelly interrupted, his thick wrists trembling as they fought to hold the wheel steady. The Volare was rapidly overtaking a truck which filled more than half the roadway.

"It doesn't matter," the defector replied gloomily. He was staring at the approaching car. "You saw what their weapons did to Hoang at the—"

"*Get your fucking head outa the mirror!*"

"Kelly!" cried the Attaché. His voice was as sharp and

sudden as the bullet that snapped between the passengers and out through the windshield.

Kelly braked, half in hope that the pursing vehicle would overrun them. Its driver, however, was very possibly as good as Kelly himself was. The limousine's four-wheel disk brakes scrubbed off speed in a straight line while the Volare wallowed across the road. A long crack staggered the width of the windshield from the starred, milky area around the bullet hole. There, only the interior layer of gum held the two shattered layers of safety glass together.

Kelly let up on the brake and steered right in the same instant. He threw the Volare into a sweeping turn that took the near corner and the far edge of the dirt track he had seen as the truck rolled on.

Vlasov was hunched over, deferring to Kelly's wishes if not his beliefs. In the rear view mirror, the agent saw the pursuing vehicle spin on the asphalt as it overran the turn-off. It was not, Kelly realized, out of control. Rather, the driver had used a controlled drift as the fastest way of reversing, much as Kelly himself had done on the Rue Morris. The bastard was good, all right.

Kelly recognized the car now that he had caught a broadside glimpse of it. It was the limo that had brought Vlasov and Hoang to the Institute, a Citröen SM Sedan. With four doors, jump seats, and the armor that stray shots had displayed that morning, the sedan version was slower off the line than the 1,500 kilogram coupe with which it shared an engine and drive train. That did not mean that its 260 kph speedometer was for show. Powered by a Maserati V-6 with six Weber carbs and a 6,500-rpm red-line, the Citröen was definitely the class of *this* race.

Kelly had turned into a track meant for 4x4s—or perhaps for camels alone. The Plymouth jounced. Its oil pan rang on something solid. All three occupants bounced in their seats. "That bastard'll just dial up the air suspension and clear these ruts!" Kelly shouted pointlessly. Vlasov was as tense as a martyr at the stake. Commander Posner had the wide-eyed disbelief of a skydiver whose reserve chute had just streamed.

Unlike the others, Kelly had something to do. That fact kept him out of the utter despair which circumstances made reasonable. He could hear the shots being fired as the limousine closed again. The guns were less of a threat now than they had been on the highway, however. The Citröen was being hammered despite its high clearance. The KGB men within could not lean out of the windows for fear of being cut in half by the coaming on a particularly bad bounce. They were thrusting their weapons in the general direction of their quarry, a pistol from the right front and an automatic rifle from behind the driver. None of a dozen shots had been close enough to ring from the Volare's sheet metal. Still, if the Russians fired long enough, they were going to get lucky . . . and if Kelly ever bogged his car in a sand-swept hollow. . . .

The Citröen had moved up within a few meters again. Its driver began to ease it into a line to the right of the one Kelly was taking. Either the Russian planned to pass or he was giving the rifleman a clearer field of fire. The cars were climbing a slight rise, the road straight within reasonable parameters of the term. "Hang on!" Kelly cried. He took his foot off the gas and dropped the gear selector into second, tramping the throttle simultaneously.

The wagon trembled in an incipient fish-tail. The skittering induced by the road surface masked the change. 45 mph was as fast as the agent could hold the car to. The feedback to the wheel even through the power steering mechanism was brutal on his flayed left hand. The Citröen moved up another two feet. Its glazed front slope grinned above its bumper like a demon's smile. Two of five bullets ripped the Volare right to left, entering through the side window a few inches from Commander Posner's face.

Kelly stamped on the emergency brake as his right foot came off the gas.

The Russian driver was good, but the Volare's mechanical brake was not connected to the stop light. The first warning any of those in the Citröen had was sight of the blunt wedge of the Volare's left rear fender swinging toward them as the tires broke away. The collision anchored the station wagon's rear end and kept it from continuing around in an uncontrollable spin on the loose road surface. Glass from the Citröen's leading edge exploded back toward the windshield like a charge of langridge. Kelly flipped the brake release and tried to accelerate smoothly away.

The closing impact had been less than 15 miles per hour. With tons of metal on either side of the equation, however, the kinetic energy involved was awesome. The Volare's frame was buckled, but there was none of the steel-on-rubber howl which Kelly had dreaded would announce the incipient blow-out of their left rear tire.

The Citröen had gone into a wild skid, but the Russian driver recovered with the skill which Kelly had learned to fear and respect. Without losing the car into the shallow ditches to either side, the Russian straightened out and came on again. The Citröen's notched leading edge snarled like a boxer with his bridgework out. The AK's muzzle was already beginning to poke out of the back window again.

The Volare cleared the top of the rise and hung with all four wheels momentarily airborne. The shock when the car hit would have tested the suspension of a Baja Unlimited. The station wagon rang like an ingot dropped on stone.

"P-professor—" Kelly tried to say.

The Citröen topped the hill behind them. It spun in a huge explosion of dust and gravel as the engine locked up. All fourteen quarts of coolant lay in a black splash at the crash site where the Volare's fender had ripped the core out of the horizontal radiator. The alloy block of the Maserati conducted heat splendidly, but it had nothing like the latent heat capacity of a cast iron unit. When the coolant went under stress, the engine welded itself into a 6-cylinder brake in less than a quarter mile.

"Jesus!" Kelly cried in delight as figures spilled out of their hopelessly wrecked pursuer. "If this road just goes somewhere and we don't have to turn around and go past them a—"

Steel bullets on sheet metal slapped like traps closing on the Volare. Two, three more. Posner grunted and the windshield starred to either side of the hole already there. More impacts, a thump as something hit a back tire and then the *whang*! and explosive decompression of a round through the wheel itself. Unlike punctured tires, the track drilled through the steel would not pucker closed and let the car run on a slow leak.

The Volare spun, trading ends twice. That may have been a blessing, because during the seconds that Kelly was fighting for control nothing else hit them. There was nowhere to go but forward, away from the gunner. When the bullets had started sleeting in on them, Kelly had already assumed they were a safe distance from the fellow bracing an AKM against the roof of the Citröen. Bad guess, real bad guess.

One of the last rounds smashed the rearview mirror out through the windshield. Kelly struck at the crazed, opaque glass in front of him with the palm of his right hand. He tore loose a hole through which he could again see enough of the road to drive whatever the gunfire had left him. At last the road dipped, cutting the two shattered vehicles off from one another.

XXXVI

Colonel Nguyen raised the muzzle of the AKM as he pushed himself upright again. The rifle's wooden foregrip was already hot with the thirty rounds he had fired.

Babroi had staggered out of the wrecked Citröen just in time to see the distant American car spin as well. "You hit it!" the Russian shouted. The station wagon was under control again, pulling out of sight. "You hit it!"

"While our car was moving, I could not shoot," said the Vietnamese. "When we stopped—well, a target going straight away from you is not difficult, surely? Have you never used a rifle yourself?"

The aide jerked back, but after a moment he decided that the comment had been only naive. Korchenko, glancing up from the microphone, was not so sure. The Vietnamese was the member of an inferior race, the representative of a nation which would not exist at all without aid from the USSR. Nonetheless, the KGB colonel had the impression that Nguyen's bland face and bland words cloaked raw scorn for his Russian counterparts.

The Vietnamese knelt. He massaged his left thigh where the block of pavement had spun him down. As the radio answered Korchenko, Nguyen asked the aide quietly, "Is there more ammunition for the rifles? I emptied my magazine."

Korchenko cursed, but there was an undercurrent of satisfaction in his voice as he said, "Well, we know where *your* charge is, Nguyen. The Algerians have found part of his body in the Casbah. Witnesses say the Americans—the people in the big car—blew him up before they drove off."

The Russian began to speak into his radio again. Nguyen frowned and pulled himself erect. He used the edge of the back door as a handhold and the automatic rifle as a crutch in order to manage unassisted. Babroi and Schwartz were struggling to pry open the hood. It was obvious that the Citröen was beyond any repairs they could make in the field.

Korchenko flung down the microphone with a curse. "Junk!" he shouted, "junk! Now they're saying that they can't hear me!"

The Vietnamese officer did not speak Russian, but he had enough experience with the language and with problems in the field to add them up this time. "With the engine dead," he said in English, "the battery does not have the power to transmit from here to Algiers very long. Especially a tube radio, so much is lost in heat."

The look Korchenko gave him would have killed if the KGB man could have arranged it. "Very fine!" the Russian spat. "An explanation for every failure. No doubt you will explain to your superiors why there is so little of Doctor Tanh to ship home?" The colonel's venom was punctuated by squealing metal. Babroi and Schwartz had finally wrenched apart the warped hood and fenders.

"I do not understand that," Nguyen responded, as if to a question and not a gibe. "Why should they kidnap Hoang first and then kill him at once? Perhaps it was an accident. There was too much shooting, too much smoke. . . ." He smiled, and Korchenko wondered that he had ever thought the little man was bland. "It reminded me of Hue in '68," Nguyen concluded. "Yes."

Colonel Korchenko opened his door and got out. He towered over the Vietnamese officer. That gave back some of his confidence. "There's a group of military vehicles being diverted to us," he said. "We'll go back to Algiers in one of them while the rest track down the—Americans." He had almost blurted, "defector," a word that must not be used outside KGB circles if Korchenko were to have even a prayer of a career remaining.

Nguyen stripped the empty magazine from the AKM, wincing as the motion put weight on his right leg again. "Is there more ammunition?" he repeated. "I will accompany the troops. I want to—catch—the men who killed Doctor Hoang."

"Little fool!" Korchenko shouted. "Shall I leave you here, is that what you want? *I* shall be in charge of the operation from my base in the embassy. But the capture shall be the responsibility of the army alone, the *Red* Army! Do you understand?"

"Yes, I understand perfectly," said the Vietnamese

officer in a soft voice. His nod could have been mistaken for obsequiousness. "I hope we will be informed of your success," he added. "From government to government, if you think it would be improper to exchange such information between ourselves."

Behind his still face, Nguyen was balancing possibilities. The Algerian government had a stake in the day's events which the Russians seemed willing to overlook. Nguyen had made only a courtesy call on the Algerian responsible for Conference security, a Captain Malek; but that should be sufficient entree under the circumstances. With the manpower and records of the local authorities, and the skills that had sometimes made Nguyen's own superiors look askance at him, it should be possible to get a quick break in the affair. The Vietnamese officer was quite sure that Korchenko was not the man to defeat the one the radio had called "Kelly." The man orchestrating things from the American—was it really American?—side was very good.

"It shouldn't be too difficult," the KGB colonel was remarking. "Their vehicle is unmistakable—and very likely damaged as well." He gave Nguyen a patronizing nod. "And most important, the fact they didn't answer our fire . . . well, it's obvious that they don't have guns or shells any more. Didn't want to compromise a diplomatic vehicle, I'll bet—the fools!"

Korchenko chuckled. "No," he repeated, "it really shouldn't be too difficult."

XXXVII

"Professor, are you all right?" Kelly asked. He dared not stop yet. A quick glance to the side showed him only that his two passengers were sprawled across the seat.

Vlasov straightened up slowly. He had been pressing his ear against the Defense Attaché's chest. "Yes," he said quietly in Russian, "but your friend, I am afraid, is dead. I am very sorry."

Kelly slammed his hand against the padded dash as he had hit the wall of the tomb the night before. "Shit," he whispered. He had not cared for Posner, an officious turkey who let his illusions get in the way of doing the job . . . but he had lived by those illusions, and now he seemed to have died by them. "The world," muttered the agent, "just might be a better place if everybody was a Posner and there weren't any Tom Kellys to fuck things up."

"Eh?"

"I'm going to pull over and change tires," Kelly said aloud. "This wasn't autostrada even with four tires."

They were three quarters of a mile beyond the Citröen, and there were a number of twists and turns besides. In theory, that was a matter of only some minutes' run for a trained man. It was still an adequate safety margin with this surface, this sun, and with the probable burden of fifteen pounds of automatic rifle if somebody really was determined to run after them.

Vlasov had tried to straighten the commander's body against the seat back. The bullet that ripped through the top of Posner's chest had already been tumbling. Death might have taken a few minutes, but consciousness must have spilled out instantly with the hemorrhage through the fist-sized exit hole.

"Shit," Kelly repeated as he swung open his door.

The smell of raw gasoline warned him. Besides the *ping* of hot metal finding new tolerances, there was a muted gurgle at the back of the car. Kelly swore and flopped on the ground. One hole was round and neat and could have been plugged; but it was already above the level of the gas remaining. The other hole was the work of a ricochet, skipping up from the road metal and doing a job that could not have been bettered with a cold chisel. The bullet had spun through the bottom of the gas tank in a long line.

The left rear tire was dead flat and the right rear was noticeably slumping, but there was no time now to worry about them. By the time Kelly had changed a tire, there would be no fuel left to drive away on. The agent jumped back into the car and put it in gear.

"Where are we going now?" Professor Vlasov asked. In the interval, the Russian had struggled one-handed to lay the Attaché's body out in the back seat.

"As far as we can this way," Kelly said dourly, "which won't be very goddam far, I'm afraid." He paused. "Somebody back there is good with a rifle. He managed to hit us ten, maybe fifteen times out of a thirty-round box— if it was even full when he got the gun. I'd like to meet him again sometime, when I've got more than a steering wheel to hold myself."

"There is something up on the next hill," Vlasov noted. He pointed forward. The best speed they could manage with the road and tires as they were was under 20 mph. It was slow enough that the lack of windshield was not a handicap.

"Given what the gas tank looks like," Kelly said, "I wouldn't bet the farm that we were going to make it that far. It's a mile and a half, and it's uphill, which is worse." But at least it was a better goal than anything else on the immediate, dingy landscape.

The object was a square, flat-roofed tower on a hilltop overlooking the road and many miles of countryside. At its base, the tower was surrounded by a low wall. "It's a granary," Kelly explained aloud. "Kabyles've been building them like that to store grain for a couple thousand years, my background stuff said."

Vlasov frowned, then looked at the American. He smiled. "You are joking of course. That is a fort."

Kelly flashed a grin back at the defector. "You could make a case for that, couldn't you, Professor? Well, all I know is what I read . . . but it just might be that it wasn't only long droughts that families built places to protect their grain from."

The top of the tower was notched with embrasures.

Below them, on what was presumably the second floor, there was a single slit window per side. The slits flared outward to give a rifleman within the broadest possible field of fire while only his gun muzzle was exposed to the shots of his opponents. The tower itself was plastered, but the core was almost certainly stone like the fabric of the wall around the tower's base. If the stones were as thick as their length and breadth suggested, more than light artillery would be required to blast them aside.

"Professor," the agent said, "if we've got a chance to stay clear for the next couple hours, it's up there. I . . . if I hadn't screwed up, you wouldn't be in this mess. It's not much consolation, I know . . . but I'm as sorry as I can be."

Vlasov smiled at the American sadly. "It is not you," he said. "Perhaps there is nothing that human beings could have done against—these others."

Kelly's face worked in disgust. He did not like being whipped by the KGB. Coming in second to non-existent aliens turned the thought of defeat into insult.

The slant-six engine continued to chug away happily until they crested the hump in the road beneath the granary. The Volare rode like a sled in the summer, but that was as much as could have been hoped under the circumstances. Kelly grinned. Perhaps he should have been thankful that the ricochet had only ripped the tank and had not ignited it. And then again, maybe he ought to wish he was dead in the back seat instead of Posner. Kelly had been in the business long enough to know that there are worse things than death, especially if the other side has questions they need answers to.

When the nose of the Volare pointed down at a

noticeable angle, Kelly shut off the engine. None of the remaining gasoline would drain out, at least, though he was sure that the car would not carry them much further. "Professor," he said, "we're going to walk up there and I'll try to talk to the people. Hope to God they speak French. . . . If we're lucky, they'll give us a drink of water before they shoo us out the door. And if we're real lucky"—he fumbled beneath the passenger seat and came out with the empty sub-machine gun —"if we're real lucky, they just might have some .45 ammo. Who knows?"

XXXVIII

There was no path from the road to the granary. The soil was friable, a mixture of baked dirt and soft stone. It was spattered with close-cropped plants that seemed each to defend a barren territory a foot or more in diameter. Vlasov and Kelly proceeded slowly. The ascent was over 30°, and the soil rolled and crumbled from beneath their shoes. Both men dabbed a hand down repeatedly, the touch of the grit taking just enough weight to give them traction again.

At first, Kelly could see only the surrounding wall and the tower when he paused and looked up from the ground before him. As the agent drew nearer, however, the design became more clear. It was as much a dwelling as a place of refuge. The wall around the base of the tower proper was of ashlar-cut stones laid in courses and mortared into place. This wall had been extended forty feet to one side by a wall of much cruder construction in which stones of varied shapes and sizes were fitted to one another dry. Within the courtyard thus created could be seen the roof of either a house or a stable.

There was a wooden gate in the newer wall. Standing ten feet from the gate and in plain view of whoever was moving behind the gun slit in the second floor of the tower, Kelly called, "Friends, we are travelers in need. For your souls' sake, aid us!" He held the Ingram in his right hand, muzzle down and with the stock extended. In his left hand, Kelly waved the empty magazine.

After a long time, the gate creaked back. An old man walked out and dragged the gate panel to behind him. He wore a dun-colored robe and a burnoose. The old man did not hold a weapon, but someone still watched from above.

"Father," the agent said, "we have run far, but our enemies still pursue. Grant us water before we go on."

The old man's face rumpled in disdain. He gestured toward the sub-machine gun and said in cracked French, "Do peaceful travelers come calling with guns in their hands, then? Go on about your business."

Kelly swallowed on a dry throat, "Father, our business was with the Association of Kabyles. In Algiers this day we have struck down some of the tyrants who would forbid the Kabyle language, who would prevent grandfathers from speaking to their children's children who have gone to the city. We do not ask for shelter; that would be your death. But God will reward those who offer water to the thirsty."

"Come in, then," the old man said abruptly. "Mind the hens." Stepping back, he called to someone inside in what must have been Kabyle.

The chickens running loose in the courtyard were white and scrawny and berserk at the sight of strangers. There was the usual farm odor of dung, though no animals larger than the chickens were evident at the moment, such as the sheep and perhaps goats would be penned here during the night. Now they were presumably at pasture, doing whatever further damage they could to the already barren hillsides nearby.

There were four humans besides the old man lined up in front of the low, beige-plastered house. Three were children, none of them more than six years old. The last was a black-robed woman as old as the man. She had not bothered to veil for strangers: these were Kabyles, not Arabs. There were no men of—military age, that covered it. They would be off with the flocks.

And there was no woman young enough to be mother to the children. Kelly did not need the crawling between his shoulder blades to guess where the mother was or what she held in her hands.

Still, what the *old* woman offered was a copper cup and a ewer of water. She filled the cup first for Vlasov as the elder of the guests. The Russian drank and passed the cup to Kelly, for whom the woman refilled it in turn. The agent nodded and passed the cup back to Vlasov. He took the empty magazine from the waist-band of his trousers where he had thrust it to free his hand. "Father," he said to the old man again, "men cannot reward men for the gift of water which is the gift of life; but God will reward you and your house. There is a thing, now, that I would ask without offending you—though it involves laws that are strict and would be enforced with rigor."

The Kabyle chewed the inside of his lip. "Ask," he said. "This is not the City, that every man must beg permission to shit."

Kelly nodded in solemn agreement. "While it is well known that the government of the City"—he had not been five years in sales without learning to pick up a cue—"forbids men to own guns today—though it was those same men and guns that drove out the French—if it could be that you knew someone with 11.43-mm pistol ammunition . . . ? Or it may be called .45 ACP, as for the Colt pistol and the tommy gun . . . that would serve a great need of ours. We are men, we fight our own battles; but without ammunition for our gun, we are unarmed."

The old Kabyle took the magazine Kelly handed him. He studied it at length while the American drank another cup of water. The others in the courtyard were spectators as silent as the woman in the tower. At last the old man fumbled in a pocket somewhere beneath his robe and brought out a loaded pistol cartridge. It winked as he compared it with the magazine lips. It was patently too small, either a .380 or the short 9-mm Makarov round on which the Russians had decided to standardize their sidearms.

The Kabyle shook his head sadly. Kelly nodded glum agreement. "Father," he said in decision, handing the Ingram to the old man, "to us, this would be only a burden. Take it and use it in the cause of freedom as a man should." He tapped the LARAND suppressor. "With this attachéd, the gun will make less noise than you would believe possible. Out here"—he waved toward the miles of empty sky—"that is a little thing. But the day will come that you and your sons may have to go to the City to make your will known. . . . This will serve you well, there."

The old man took the sub-machine gun and turned it over in his hands. Kelly touched Vlasov on the shoulder. "Come on, Professor," he said wearily, "we'll drive as far as we can and then hoof it. Until they catch up again." He turned.

"Wait," the Kabyle said. Carrying the Ingram, the old man strode through the door at the base of the tower. Voices echoed from the building. They were muffled by the thick walls but still loud enough to be intelligible had they been in French. The old woman gave the strangers another hard look, then darted through the doorway herself.

"Do you suppose he is going to give us the ammunition after all?" asked Professor Vlasov. He spoke in Russian. He might be crazy, but Kelly had no reason to think the defector was stupid.

"What I'm hoping," said the agent, "is that they've got an old pistol in there that they'll part with. Even a .380's better than nothing." He shook his head. "Didn't like giving away Doug's gun that way, but it made a hell of an impressive gift. If I get back, I can get him another one."

First the old woman, then the man, and finally a woman in her twenties spilled back into the courtyard from the tower. The younger woman carried a Garand rifle at the balance. She held the weapon easily despite its size and her slight frame. There were a lot of Garands knocking about the world, and you could still make a case for it being the finest weapon ever issued to American troops.

What the old man had brought out with him was considerably more interesting, however.

The magazine well was in the top of the receiver, and for a moment Kelly thought he was being handed a Bren gun. The double trigger—front for single shots, rear for full auto—corrected him even before he took the weapon from the Kabyle. It was a Chatellerault, the French copy of the BAR, and an excellent automatic rifle for all its weight and complexity. The bipod had been stripped from this one some time in the past, but even so the rifle had an empty weight of at least 18 pounds.

Weight made a gun difficult to carry, but it also meant that you could control bursts of the powerful cartridge for which it was chambered. At this point, that looked like a good trade-off.

The old man gave Kelly a long, straight magazine. Apologetically, he said, "We do not have much ammunition for it—only seventeen shots. But—if Allah wills, it may help you."

Kelly locked the magazine home. That freed his hand to take the Kabyle's. The old man's palm was dry and rough and as solid as a tree root. "If Allah loves warriors," the agent said sincerely, "we two shall meet again in Paradise. Go with God."

In brusquer Russian he added to Vlasov, "Well, Professor, let's see if we've got any gas left."

Kabyle voices resumed their argument behind the two men as they skidded down the hill to their car.

XXXIX

The Volare started and bumped off along the road. The right rear tire was by now as flat as the left. Kelly was no longer interested in getting somewhere. Rather, he was hoping to put at least a mile between himself and the Kabyles. It was the least he could do for people who had helped strangers at such obvious risk to themselves. Folks with guns in their homes were often willing to make their own decisions. That was a fact that had not escaped many governments.

The car made it about the hoped-for mile before the road began to struggle upward again. The engine sputtered only once before quitting for good.

"Well, Professor . . ." Kelly said. He took a last look at the road map before he stuffed it into his hip pocket. "If we're where we seem to be, Douera's that way a few miles." He gestured up the road. "Farther than I'd like, and I figure word'll have traveled there faster than we could anyway. But I don't know a better way."

"There is a helicopter," Vlasov said.

In the stillness after the Volare died, the chop and even the turbine whine of the bird should have been obvious to the agent before it was called to his attention. Kelly cursed and stuck his head out the window. Nothing was visible. The aircraft must be flying very low and slow. The sound of its passage was echoing off the rocks ahead of it. "Quick, Professor," the agent said, "out your side and under cover fast. They may strafe the car."

Even as he spoke, the American was rolling out his own door and darting toward a bush twenty yards away up the low hill. Its foliage was sparse, but the shadow itself would go a long way toward hiding the outline of a man and an automatic rifle.

The station wagon was beige. Kelly had planned to shove it to the side of the road. With a little luck and the long shadows that would be on the hills in half an hour, the car might have been hidden from observation from above. No hope of that now. The helicopter was searching the length of the road from a hundred feet in the air. It was no chance overflight but a searcher summoned by either the KGB or the Algerian authorities themselves. Or by the little green men, of course, but this was not the time to mock Professor Vlasov. He had proven as cool as a paramedic in circumstances that would have reduced most civilians to mewling incapacity.

If there was one good thing about the helicopter, it was the fact that it was not a gunship as Kelly had initially feared. The agent squinted at the aircraft through the warped branches of the stunted fig that hid him. As soon as the pilot saw his presumed quarry, the bird lifted. The maneuver would have given Kelly a criminally easy shot had he wished to advertise the fact that he was armed again. He did not dare do that until he was sure of his opposition.

The twin-turbine helicopter was much the same size and shape as a Bell Iroquois, though the two designs could be quickly told apart by the fact that this one had tricycle landing gear in place of skids. This was an Mi-2. Though its fuselage and rudder bore the Algerian star and crescent on a green and white field, Kelly knew the crew was likely to be as Russian as the aircraft's designer. At any rate, all the pursuit to this point had been Russian.

The helicopter rose vertically to a thousand feet. It began circling slowly. The pilot had either been told to take no chances after he located the car, or he had made that decision himself. "Professor," Kelly called, "can you hear me?"

"Yes, of course," Vlasov's voice responded, slightly attentuated by the wind. "What shall we do now?"

Kelly could not see the Professor, though they were probably level with one another on opposite sides of the Volare. "Without transport, we're screwed," the agent said. "That bird's bringing somebody, sure as hell. Could be that there's more coming than we can handle, but right now I'm looking to hijack a Russian car as the best ticket out of these rocks. Thing is, Professor, it'll work a lot better if you're willing to draw their attention. Can you run up the hill when I say to?"

"Of course," responded Professor Vlasov. "We are all soldiers now against the coming invasion. We all must do our part."

"Well, for Christ's sake, hit the dirt if they start shooting," Kelly called. He would not have minded having Vlasov guard his back in Cambodia, the agent thought. Except that Vlasov would have been on the other side there. . . .

The sound of two vehicles long preceded the machines themselves. The road kinked a hundred yards short of where the Volare lay. Kelly could hear engines roaring beyond it as the vehicles backed and filled in the narrow road. Then the blunt steel prow of an eight-wheeled armored personnel carrier lurched around the corner.

All the APC's hatches were buttoned up. Gun barrels projected from the three rifle slits on the side of the troop compartment which Kelly could see. There was a small turret forward. It seemed to hold an automatic grenade launcher in place of the more usual 14.5 mm machine gun. The vehicle paused while its turret scanned the rocky slopes to either side of the road. The grenade launcher twitched as if it were the whiskery muzzle of a mouse. Neither Vlasov nor Kelly moved. They were practically invisible at this time of evening, especially to men who were handicapped by searching through prisms of armored glass.

The armored vehicle began to roll forward again. Its separately-sprung wheels lifted and fell in individual rhythm as it presented its left side to Kelly. The APC stopped again. The American heard a hatch open on the other side. A moment later, a soldier in mustardy-green fatigues swung around the vehicle. He ran to the Volare in a crouch. The soldier carried a folding-stock AK ready for action, and his eyes flashed around in all directions. He moved too abruptly, too nervously, to notice the waiting fugitives. Though the man wore no rank or unit insignia, his uniform marked him as Russian as surely as if he had been covered with red stars.

The soldier peered into the car, then snatched open the back door. With his rifle advanced in his right, the Russian reached in with his left hand and touched the Attaché's body for reassurance. After a quick look around the car's riddled interior, the soldier ran back to the APC and banged on the bow slope.

The turret hatch opened. Another Russian with steel-gray hair and an aura of command raised himself far enough out to see the trooper. The scout and the vehicle commander talked, neither's voice fully audible to Kelly. At last the commander dropped back out of sight. The soldier scurried to the side hatch.

An open-topped Land Rover drove around the corner a moment later. It carried two more men in unmarked Russian uniforms. The plump passenger still held a radio handset. The vehicles had apparently switched position when they neared potential trouble. The officer had proceeded only after the scout had signaled that the Volare was abandoned to the dead. Overhead, the chopper dropped again to about two hundred feet. The officer in the 4x4 glanced upward at it as he continued talking on the radio.

"Now, Professor!" Kelly shouted in French.

The noise of the helicopter and the engines of the two ground vehicles pulsed within the shallow bowl. Professor Vlasov heard the command, however, and he responded like a veteran paratrooper getting the green light. The defector scrambled from the base of an artemisium bush and began bounding uphill with an agility that belied his age. The Land Rover's driver saw Vlasov before anyone else did. He pointed, shouting. Kelly's signal had either been ignored in the ambient noise or forgotten in the new excitement.

The Russian officer shouted into his handset. The Mi-2 dipped and rotated 30° while the APC commander popped out of his turret for a clear view. With everyone's attention on the running defector, Kelly began killing people.

Off-set to the left of the Chatellerault's magazine was a tangent rear sight. It was screwed all the way down for point-blank fire. Using the front trigger, Kelly put single shots through the chests of both the men seated in the Land Rover. Echoes from the sharp reports rang among the rocks like a long burst from a machine gun. The officer flung the handset in the air as he died. The body of his driver flopped over him.

The armored vehicle was within thirty-five yards of Kelly's muzzle. The driver had already started to cramp his wheels right to follow Vlasov up the hill. Kelly put a five-shot burst into the wheel well, which he knew was not armored. The tracks of his bullets crossed the seats of both driver and co-driver. Sparks flew from the shadowed well as the bullets spat back chips of steel ignited by the friction of their passage. The APC's diesel roared, then died, as the drivers fell over their controls.

Vlasov had thrown himself down at the first shot. The vehicle commander had disappeared into his turret as quickly. Now the grenade launcher began to rake the slope around the Professor. Echoes had hidden the source of Kelly's shots. The Russian was aiming for the only target he had. The muzzle blasts of the grenade launcher were hollow *chunks*, but its projectiles burst on the rocks with a cracking as sharp as the white flashes that accompanied them. Pebbles and fragments of casing zinged through the air. Kelly ignored the shrapnel because there was nothing he could do about it for the moment. He cocked his left elbow under him at a sharper angle as he raised his rifle toward the helicopter.

The helicopter crew was insulated from events on the ground by the racket of their turbines and rotor. The bird was still hovering, turned away from Kelly and within a linear hundred yards. Nobody could call himself a marksman and miss a target the size of a bus at that range. The agent used his front trigger again, holding the foresight just above the rear notch to adjust for range.

A helicopter is nothing but a frame of thin aluminum on which are hung engines, fuel tanks, and seats for the occupants. Anyone who had ever been inserted into a hot landing zone knew exactly how vulnerable a chopper is. It was with feelings that went beyond revenge that Kelly turned the tables. He fired, the heavy weight of his weapon muting its recoil against his shoulder.

There was nothing in the helicopter that would keep the powerful 7.5 mm MAS round from drilling a path straight through it the long way—through fuel lines, hydraulic lines, power cables, and the pilot himself if he happened to be in the way. As Kelly's brass clinked on the rocks beside him, he squeezed off a second, then a third

shot. The Mi-2 yawed until its rotor was cutting an arc like
a table saw. Then the whole aircraft spun down with the
suddenness of an EKG going flat. It struck on the rocky
hilltop beyond where Vlasov was hiding. The fuel tank went
off like a napalm bomb. One of the broken rotor blades
whirled into the air. It reflected sunlight and the ruddy
gasoline flames from angles like the facets of a jewel.

The soldiers within the APC's troop compartment
were firing in aimless abandon to either side. The tracers
interspersed in their magazines were green sparks howling
off the rocks with the other, invisible ricochets. Many of
the bullets bounced back against the vehicle itself. They
sang off the sloping steel sides. The raving blasts of the
grenade launcher had paused on the far slope, perhaps
while the commander fitted another belt of ammunition.

Kelly rolled twice to the side, using an almost non-
existent swale as cover. He had expected at least one of
the Russians to notice his muzzle flashes and answer them
with aimed fire, but apparently none of them had. Panic
and the restricted view from within the troop compartment
were as much shield as the agent could have hoped for. The
wild bursts of rifle fire were all high. Ricochets were the
only danger—and hell, you could get run over crossing the
street.

Kelly aimed at the side of the vehicle. At this short
range, the Chatellerault had a fair chance of penetrating
the armor. This was not a tank, after all, but a truck with
a steel shell. Then, even as the agent's finger started to
take up the slack in the trigger, a side hatch swung open.

Almost by reflex, Kelly shot the soldier poised in the
opening. The hatch was an empty black rectangle two feet

square, framed in his sights. A bullet which entered that opening would have no other way out of the angled steel box. It would clang and howl within the troop compartment until it had spent all its momentum on the occupants and their equipment. Kelly slipped his fingertip back to the auto trigger. The hatch was beginning to swing closed. Before it could shut, the agent poured every remaining round into the APC.

The first result was silence. All the firing from the troop compartment stopped as abruptly as if a switch had been thrown. The shattering muzzle blasts of moments before had been so loud that Kelly was too deaf to hear the sounds that remained to the landscape: the sucking breath of the blazing helicopter, and the moans from within the APC.

The gasoline burning on the hilltop lighted the road which the sun had by now practically abandoned. The armored vehicle's shadow pulsed in counterpoint to the fire above. The firing slits on the side toward Kelly were glowing. Tiny flames had smoldered into life within the troop compartment.

Kelly stood up. He left the empty Chaterllerault on the ground. "Professor," he called as he stumbled toward the road. He stepped between the Volare and the armored vehicle, each of them at present a steel coffin. The APC was not quite silent. Flames were crackling within the armored box—paper and fabric and insulation had all been sewn with flecks of blazing metal as the bullets passed and repassed inside. "Professor!" Kelly shouted again more nervously. He began to scramble up the slope with the pyre of the helicopter's crew in his eyes.

Vlasov rose to a kneeling position, a sharply-defined silhouette against the red background. "I am sorry," he said in carefully enunciated Russian, "but I do not seem to be able to hear anymore. Perhaps that will change. The shells. . . ."

Professor Vlasov had been at the white center of a storm as the vehicle commander poured a 30-round belt of grenades in his direction. His clothes were ripped in a score of places. Sometimes the torn edges were stained with blood as well. But Vlasov had known to stay low, the only real defense during shelling and a better one than most people realized. The shrapnel that had grazed him must have been uncomfortable. Indeed, he probably felt as if he had been rolling on barbed wire. But from the way the Professor moved, and from what Kelly could see in the firelight, there were no dangerous or even incapacitating wounds.

"Professor," the agent said, bending close to the other and raising his voice, "we'll take the jeep and get the hell out of here before somebody else—"

Vlasov tugged urgently at the American's arm. He pointed back downslope. "Quickly," he cried, "run! I've seen that before!"

Kelly scowled and glanced over his shoulder at the vehicles. As soon as he saw the armored personnel carrier, he understood why the Russian was trying to pull him away from it. Though that would mean leaving the 4x4 as well. . . . The steel hull of the APC had been as black as the death within it only a minute before. Now the armor was glowing dull red like an overstoked furnace.

The two men stumbled forward, hindered by the

slope on which they stood and the darkness. The billowing gasoline above them was little help. It washed the ground with shadows that waved like momentary trenches in the rocks. Vlasov tripped in a runnel notched down the hard soil by the last heavy rain. He risked a look back. The red glow was now a lambent white. Heat waves dancing from the armor made the outline seem to quiver. "Down here!" the Russian shouted, suiting his motion to his words. He dragged Kelly with him.

For several seconds, defector and agent tried to wriggle into a wash-out only inches deep at the most. Then the shock wave turned the ground itself momentarily fluid. Both men bounced into the air.

The interior of the APC had been brewing up in a near absence of oxygen. When the grenades cooked off, the compartment ruptured and the whole superheated mixture within detonated. The closest equivalent would have been a 500-pound bomb.

The roof of the troop compartment was a steel plate weighing half a ton. It spun skyward like a flipped quarter. Diesel fuel, atomized by the first explosion, equaled it with a bubble of orange flame which swelled to a diameter of thirty yards before it collapsed in sudden blackness.

The ground pounded Kelly and Vlasov even as it protected them from shrieking metal. They jounced under full-length blows that bloodied cheeks and left Kelly feeling as if a horse had repeatedly kicked him from groin to shoulder. The airborne shock wave stunned both men for long enough that the knife-edges of pain were blunted by the time they became aware of them.

When Kelly returned to full consciousness, the night

had taken on a campground hominess. Scores of tiny fires had been scattered by the explosion. Bits of rubber and cloth, some of it still dressing body parts, had been fountained across the rocks. The fragments glowed where they had fallen. Higher on the hill, the helicopter was more a bed of coals than a bonfire. Its fuel had roared up with a savage intensity that had quickly consumed itself and everything else inflammable. Even the aluminum fuselage was gone.

One gasoline fire still burned. The Land Rover had been hurled twice its own length when the APC exploded beside it. It was ablaze, and with it vaporized Kelly's hopes of driving quickly into Douera.

Professor Vlasov was already moving. He appeared to be uncoordinated rather than seriously injured. Kelly tried to sit up and felt a rush of nausea. "Your timing was great, Professor," he said. His voice sounded thin even in his own ears. "But I'm damned if I don't think walking into town isn't going to finish what the explosion didn't."

Vlasov patted the agent's shoulder. He pointed north, in the direction they needed to go. At first Kelly thought the Russian was urging him on with more enthusiasm than the agent could have managed at the moment. Then he realized that there was a powerful headlight bouncing and thrusting down the road as a vehicle from Douera negotiated the ruts.

The light was a halogen unit. On high beam it was so intense that it completely hid the vehicle which mounted it. The nervous pitching and rolling of the lamp indicated an ultra-short wheel base, however. Even before it had driven slowly past the hidden fugitives, Kelly had identified the newcomer as a BMW motorcycle—ridden by a National Policeman.

The Citröen had been summoned by God knew what, the chopper and the APC by the Citröen. This bike, the first Algerian involvement in the chase, had come from Douera in response to the fires and explosions.

The BMW pulled up alongside the wreckage of the armored personnel carrier. All four tires on the left side had been deflated, and the wheels themselves had been blown off into the dark on the right. The policeman stood, balancing the motorcycle between his thighs as he surveyed the carnage.

Kelly stared down at the bike. It was an old machine with drum brakes front and rear instead of discs. Its two opposed cylinders pumped away with the ease which made BMWs the standard of motorcycle reliability.

Finally the Algerian kicked down his sidestand and dismounted. After a pause, he switched off the engine and headlight. The night was left to the hellfire illumination of the burning vehicles. The policeman's leather suit was no more stark than the shadows. Still wearing his helmet, he approached the overturned Land Rover as closely as the flames would let him.

"Professor," said Kelly in a whisper he hoped was audible, "could you make it to that bike if you had to?"

Vlasov frowned. "To divert the rider, you mean?" he said. "I suppose so. If the shells did not kill me, perhaps the pistol will not kill me either."

Kelly shook his head and winced at the pain. "No," he said, "I'm in no shape to jump a healthy cop, even if you've got him looking the other way. But if he'll just move a little farther, I'm going to try to steal that Beemer."

The Algerian was alone with a catastrophe. His radio could not raise help through the intervening rocks, and it was obviously necessary to learn as much as possible about the occurrence before he left the scene to phone in a report. After poking at the crumpled Volare, the policeman began to scramble up the slope toward the helicopter, a hundred yards from the road.

"Easy now," the agent murmured as the Algerian scuffed his way further up-slope. He had continued to wear his white crash helmet. It obstructed the policeman's peripheral vision, though it also kept Kelly from trying to club him with a rock. When the Algerian was well above them, Kelly led the defector down toward the silent bike at something more than a crawl.

The fugitives paused in the pooling shadow of the APC. The agent motioned Vlasov to stay where he was. The policeman's helmet was bobbing, halfway up to the smoldering red of the helicopter. Kelly darted from the shadow to the motorcycle. He used the massive tank and air box to shield him in case the policeman should glance back. The agent reached upward, feeling rather than exposing his head to check the ignition lock in the headlight nacelle.

The key was not there.

His face as calm as that of the Sphinx, Kelly reached into a trouser pocket and came out with his Swiss Army knife. He clicked open the awl blade. It was not what the knife was meant for, but beggars can't be choosers. . . . Rising to his feet, the agent rammed the thin wedge of the awl down into the ignition.

Older BMWs did not have true keys. Rather, they had plungers with a transverse groove cut for spring detents to hold them depressed. The edges of the awl cut into the brass keyway, holding the blade down as securely as the detent could have. Three tiny indicators lighted on the speedometer face—neutral, alternator, and oil pressure. Kelly swung his leg over the seat, cracked the throttle, and mashed the starter button with his right thumb. The hot engine wheezed angrily as it spun; then it fired and Kelly kicked the bike into gear.

The agent turned the motorcycle, slipping the clutch and feeling every rut on his bruised groin. "Get aboard and hang the hell on, Professor," he shouted as he pulled abreast of the APC. Vlasov mounted awkwardly, his legs dangling against the pipes before he locked down the rear foot pegs. Kelly gassed it, ignoring the jolts as best he could. As the bike spat gravel backward, Kelly twisted the knife to turn the headlight on.

Anything the Algerian policeman cried was lost in the whine and clatter of the bike's long push-rods. As they twisted around the first bend on to Douera, Kelly could hear the pop-pop-pop of pistol fire. Ed McGivern would not have been a threat at that range.

Operation Skyripper was go again.

XL

The Renault Dauphine had not been a particularly well-built vehicle at the time of its introduction. The example Kelly had stolen had been deteriorating for the past twenty-five years besides. Even so, the car had been a better choice than the police motorcycle for reasons beyond the latter's conspicuousness. BMW has an international reputation for building reliable, comfortable motorcycles. On rough roads, however, no motorcycle is comfortable—or, for that matter, particularly reliable. That was especially true in the dark, when potholes sprang out like missiles and the forks had not recovered from one jolt when the next compressed them.

This Renault had been parked behind the closed Sonatrach gas station in Douera. It had half a tank of gasoline and it had started when Kelly shorted its ignition. For the hot wire, the agent had used a piece clipped from the car's own instrument panel; not pretty, but it worked.

The Renault wallowed on the wilayet road, and when they reached National 11 it developed an alarming steering hammer at 70 kph. For all that, it was a Mercedes-class ride compared to that of the motorcycle pitching along ruts.

Professor Vlasov was still daubing at his wounds. They had both gotten through surprisingly well, the agent thought. It would be several days before he knew for certain whether his ribs had cracked or not when the ground rose up and slammed them. In a couple days, that would not matter—one way or the other. The other injuries the pair of them had received were extensive enough, Lord knew; but they were also superficial. They were the sorts of scrapes and cuts and bruises you got from high-siding a dirt bike, if you were lucky.

The pair of them. Not Commander Posner. Well, Posner had gone west with an escort. However this one ended, the Russians were not going to feel it had been cheap.

The highway bent sharply to the left, then back, to avoid the buildings of a pair of farms. The Renault's one, dim headlight flashed red from the retinas of a goat which was peering over a stone wall. Then the road dipped toward the lights of the town below.

Kelly began squinting through the dusty windshield, trying to imagine the look of the intersection he had seen only once—and that by daylight.

"This is the Tipasa we are going to?" asked the defector. "What do we do here?"

"Hell," Kelly said, "I never told you how we were going to get you back to the Land of the Big PX, did I?

Hell, I'm sorry, I always get hacked off when people keep me in the dark. I didn't mean to pull that on you."

"Pardon?" said Vlasov, patiently hiding his confusion.

The agent was feeling more than a little dizzy. His ribs and his left palm were both afire. Too close now to lose it. . . . Aloud he said, "There's a submarine waiting for us offshore. We've got an emergency radio beacon; they'll be monitoring that frequency. We blip the beacon, then they blip back at ten point four one, shortwave so I can pick it up on my Kenwood and low power so that nobody else pays much attention. We inflate a rubber boat and head on out. When we're a quarter mile or so offshore, we kick the beacon on again and leave it on till they locate us. Then it's somebody else's problem."

"We must reach international waters in a rubber boat, then?" said the Russian. "Or—oh. That was very foolish, I see."

Kelly smiled and wished he had not. Torn patches in the skin of his face had dried. The smile cracked them open again. "Yeah," he said, "there's been a lot of things worse than a violation of Algerian territorial waters lately, hasn't there? But I tell you—there's the goddam turn!"

Kelly swung the wheel left and his chest felt as though it were being broken on a rack. "*Jesus!*" the agent gasped. Then, in a tight voice that underscored the pain it tried to conceal, he said, "I tell you, Professor, the sub is the dicy part so far as the USG's concerned, though. If they catch me, the President can stand up and swear I'm an Italian national and never got within a thousand miles of the US. Hell, he tells bigger lies than that every day, he's a politician. . . . But if something goes wrong and the

Algerians catch a State-class submarine in their back
yard—well, that's a lot bigger than the U-2 was. And it'd
be bad even without a Russian defector and twenty-
thirty bodies scattered all over the Algerian countryside.
Hell!"

The iron-sheeted gate registered in Kelly's mind as
the Renault rolled past it. The car's brakes were in no
better shape than its lights—or Kelly's body, for that
matter. Cursing, the agent twisted to look over his shoulder.
He gasped and froze on the wheel. After a moment, he
backed up with his eyes on the rearview mirror.
"Professor," he said, almost too quietly to be heard over
the car's rasping idle, "do you think you could unlock the
gate and open it?" Kelly took the paper-tagged keys from
his pants pocket, rising a little in his seat so that his torso
could remain straight. "I'd do it, but. . . ."

Professor Vlasov took the keys solemnly and ducked
out of the car. He looked like death in the side-scatter of
the headlight, Kelly thought, but compared to Kelly, the
Russian was in good shape. Posner might yet turn out to
be the lucky one of the three.

The agent used his left arm to turn the car into the
opened courtyard. Even so, the pain almost made him
black out. There was no choice. They were going to have
to call for help.

Vlasov had locked the gate behind them before Kelly
could hoist himself out of the Dauphine. The Russian
hovered solicitously, willing to help but well aware that
any outside torsion could make a bad situation worse.
"Just unlock the door, Professor," the agent wheezed. He
held himself braced between the roof and the door of the

car. "I'll be fine. Just get the door open and see if you can hunt up a phone."

The safe house was as cold as it was empty. Kelly stared at the collapsed boat and his radio receiver. Both sat on the bare tiles of the entrance hall. The MARS boat with its motor weighed over two hundred pounds. Hell, Kelly could not have managed half the receiver's weight in his present condition, much less that of the boat. And launching it into surf was going to be interesting at best.

"Here is the telephone," Professor Vlasov called from further inside.

The agent found Vlasov in a living room as empty as the hall had been. No one had told Posner to waste money on furnishings. The phone sat on a window ledge, more than ample for the purpose because the concrete walls were a foot thick. Kelly had been in bunkers less solidly constructed than an ordinary Algerian house. That was part of the reason that this one *rented* for the equivalent of $45,000 a year, of course. Cheap if it got Vlasov to the folks who were footing the bill.

The long-distance operator answered in Arabic, but he handled without comment Kelly's request in French for "60-14-26 in Algiers, please." As the phone clicked and buzzed in proof that something was going on, the agent lowered himself gingerly to the floor. The cold tiles might have felt good on his ribs. After a moment, Kelly did lay his left palm on them.

The ringing on the other end of the line shocked Kelly out of a reverie. He was momentarily uncertain of where he was or what he was doing. He had recovered a moment later, however, when a voice answered in

English, "Embassy of the United States. Can I help you, please?"

"This is Angelo Ceriani," Kelly said in the same language. "It is absolutely critical that I speak at once with Sergeant Rowe. I need his home phone or the number of whatever other phone you think he might be near. I know this may be irregular, but I swear it's as important as you can imagine."

"Ah, one moment," said the duty officer. There was a click and Rowe's attentuated voice called, "Tom, is that you? Jesus, we've been sitting by the phone ever since the reports started coming in. Are you all right? Is Vlasov?"

"Ah, Doug, do we have a secure line?" the agent said. Though anybody with a tap on the embassy phone was about to get an earful, even without proper nouns. "Things could be worse," Kelly went on, "though not for your boss. Or the car. We're where we're supposed to be, but I don't think we can move the goods without help. Doug, I need you to get here as quick as you can. I'm sorry. These are my orders and they take precedence to any other orders you may have received. There's nobody else I can trust."

"You can trust me," the sergeant said simply. "That's why we're waiting here. See you—I hope before midnight."

"Oh, Doug," Kelly added, "try to get a van or another wagon. The stuff's pretty bulky, you remember."

"We'll be there," Rowe said. He broke the connection before the agent could.

Kelly cradled the phone and looked up at Vlasov. The Russian was standing beside the curtained window, as erect as a hatrack. "Well, Professor," the agent said wryly, "I suppose I ought to be doing a lot of things . . . but what I'm going to try to do is get some sleep. We ought to have some help here in a couple hours. I suppose that means you can change your mind about defecting. Wouldn't blame you after the way I've bitched things up so far."

"On the contrary," said Vlasov, his face and tones as serious as those of a priest at a memorial service. "Everything I suspected earlier has been proven to be true. I *must* escape the aliens and the humans they use as tools. I must, because they strive so hard to prevent me."

Kelly took off his coat by himself. He rolled it up as a pillow. The chill of the tile on which he carefully stretched himself seeped into his bones. The numbness it brought was a sort of relief.

After Kelly closed his eyes, the thought of Vlasov kept him some minutes awake. Vlasov, brave and brilliant and quite surely as cracked as a coot. But if Tom Kelly were damned to hell for exploiting a madman's obsession, then he was damned for a thousand better reasons besides.

Sleep came not as a relief but as a hiatus.

XLI

"Someone is here," a voice in Russian whispered harshly. Something was gnawing Kelly's earlobe. He flashed awake and caught himself before a sudden lunge reknotted muscles which had relaxed somewhat while he slept. Professor Vlasov knelt beside the agent. He was pinching Kelly's right earlobe between thumb and forefinger instead of shaking the battered body awake.

A large engine was idling nearby. Its exhaust note echoed within the courtyard walls. Doug must have kept a key to the place. "Tom," called a low voice through the bolted door.

Kelly stood, slinging his jacket over his right forearm and the knife which had been bare in his hand all the time he slept. He walked to the door. His smile was as stiff as one painted on the face of a golliwog. Kelly unlocked the door, then drew the panel open. He hoped to see Doug Rowe, but he was perfectly willing to meet the muzzle of an AKM.

Rowe was there, a step behind Annamaria Gordon.

"My God," Kelly whispered.

Annamaria's face when she saw Kelly went whiter than her breasts had been in the starlight by the tomb. Then she stepped forward deliberately and kissed the agent's bruised lips. She guided Kelly, drawing him back into the house and making room for the sergeant to enter.

In the courtyard beside the Renault stood a Chevrolet Blazer. It loomed as huge as a tank over the stolen car. The Blazer would be perfect for running the boat down to the harbor, better even than the station wagon would have been.

"I was waiting with Doug," Annamaria said. "If you need help, then we're here to help."

Kelly licked his lips. "Professor Evgeny Vlasov," he said nodding. "Annamaria Gordon, Doug Rowe." Kelly's left arm was around the black-haired woman's waist. He clung as if she were a spar and he a shipwrecked sailor. "That's bad tradecraft, I suppose, but if we're any of us caught, we're beyond tradecraft for help."

The tall Russian bowed, offering his hand first to the woman and then to Sergeant Rowe. He looked at Kelly. "I know it makes no difference, sir," he said, "but—what is *your* name?"

The agent blinked. "Christ on a crutch," he said. "I'm Tom Kelly. And Professor, if we get out of this, I want to sit down with you and a case of beer some evening and swap stories. I—you aren't what I expected. And you're a lot of the reason we're still golden."

Sergeant Rowe had not followed the last of the discussion, since it was in French. After fiddling for a moment with the massive 10x70 binoculars on his neck strap, he said, "Ah, Tom—what do you need us to do?"

"Right, right," Kelly agreed. He sheathed his knife with care before he donned his coat again. "First, we load the gear into your car and carry it down to the waterfront. We unload there and you take the car back up to the street—it's too conspicuous right on the water. We get clear with the"—he looked from Rowe to Annamaria, then back; she had not been specifically told about the submarine—"with the sub and go out to meet it. You make sure we've gotten fairly away and you—both of you—you get the hell outa Dodge. Clear?"

The boat and motor were a job to maneuver over the high tailgate of the Blazer, even with the newcomers doing most of the lifting. Kelly found he was in better shape than he had expected, but that still left him far from being the dark-haired woman's equal at the moment. Annamaria should not have come, but thank God she had.

The agent smiled as he thought of her. When they all stepped back from the car, breathing hard with the successful effort, he leaned over and kissed her lightly on the cheek. Professor Vlasov looked bemused. Sergeant Rowe stared at his hands and said nothing, though he cleared his throat.

"All right," Kelly said, "let's roll. It's going to be a while before we get out far enough to meet the sub, and I want to be underwater before daybreak. It'd be nice to be out of the shallows, too, but we'll do what we can."

The agent sat on the passenger-side bucket seat while Rowe drove. The MARS boat was a four-and-a-half by two-foot package. It took up all the floor in back between the two facing bench seats. Annamaria rode leaning back against Kelly's seat with her legs stretched out to the rear. Her hand reached back to clasp the agent's between seat and door. The four-block ride to the harbor was as soothing to Kelly as his hour of comatose sleep had been.

The brief calm ended when the sergeant pulled up beside the sunken staircase. The ancient harbor was empty but not still. The wind over the rocks had a constant static hiss. Its amplitude went unremarked until one noticed that the rumbling idle of the V-8 engine was completely masked except when one stood in the lee of the vehicle itself. The waves could be heard though, a vicious, unmastered sound like zippers rasping to open the fabric of the world. Kelly checked the tuning of his short-wave receiver. He was running it now from its separate battery pack. The blue digits were correct. He faced seaward and tripped his beacon for a five-second count.

The submarine's crew was as tight as Kelly was. Their response began to beep from the Kenwood within fifteen seconds of the moment the agent shut off his beacon.

Kelly cut the receiver power to save the batteries. "Let's move," he said. "One more stop and we're shut of this deal."

Unloading the Blazer was fast and comparatively easy, but it seemed like a lifetime's task to all four of those involved. Professor Vlasov was becoming increasingly nervous. Kelly could not be sure whether this was a return of the defector's old fear of aliens or if it had a more rational cause. The sand-colored Chevy looked square and huge on the corniche. Anyone strolling about at night was apt to wander over out of curiosity. Any policeman who was out would almost certainly do so.

As soon as the gear was on the ground, Kelly said, "OK, Doug—run the car up the street and park it, then get back as quick as you can to help launch. Up there it won't call attention to us."

"I'll go," said Annamaria. "You'll need Doug to get the boat down the steps without wrecking it." She slipped around to the driver's side of the Blazer without waiting for a response.

The agent glanced at her, a slim figure in a dark wind-breaker. The breeze molded the nylon to her breasts like a silken sheath. The car door closed. "Right," he said as the Blazer pulled away.

Annamaria had been correct. The stairs were perfect for concealment, but they were barely wide enough to pass two men abreast. Without Sergeant Rowe's strength up front, the boat would have brushed the stone walls and stone steps repeatedly on its way to the beach below. The nylon was tough, but there was a lot of water out there. The stone as building material was no less able to scrape holes in the rubberized fabric than it was in its natural state in the surf beyond.

The tide had been going out for an hour or so. At the foot of the low cliff was a beach of coarse shingle. Panting and thankful, Kelly grounded his end of the boat on it. Sergeant Rowe began unfastening restraints, preparing to inflate the vessel.

The agent scrambled back up the stairs for his Kenwood. He was feeling a dreamy lightness after his exertion. It did not keep him from being aware of the pain in his torso, but it allowed him to perceive the pain as something happening to another person. Kelly stumbled on the last step as he returned with the radio, but neither of the other men seemed to notice.

The defector was rigid, but his eyes moved with the quick jerks of a mouse looking for a bolthole. He was as patently fearful as he had been when the shooting first started in front of the Institute. At that time, Kelly had taken the panic as a normal enough reaction to a firefight. Now that he had witnessed the Professor's calm under shellfire and worse, Kelly realized that there was something else going on.

Time enough to worry about that later, he decided. Doug Rowe was ready to inflate the MARS boat. "Just a second," the agent said. "Let's make sure I'm still on frequency." He pushed the receiver's power switch.

The noise blasting from the speaker was as unexpected as a bomb. It seemed for an instant to be as loud. Kelly twisted the attentuator dial by reflex. Even damping at 60 dB—each decibel a log-3 diminution in intensity—made no discernible difference in the beeps. The agent punched the power button again. He stared at Rowe in amazement.

"What the hell are they thinking of?" Kelly said. "They're putting out enough signal to rattle china. That's *bound* to bring somebody down on them—on us!"

Rowe had been shaken as well by the unexpected blast of noise. He shook his head. "Maybe it's not the sub," he said. Raising his glasses toward the horizon, he added, "Something's up there now, a plane. Maybe it's broadcasting."

Lights were coursing over the waves at low altitude,

only a half mile out. Kelly was sure they had not been there when the Blazer was being unloaded. Now, when he listened carefully, he could hear the breeze-pulsed whine of a jet engine. "Doug," he said, "you don't understand." He was squinting toward the intruder, wishing he had the glasses. "That signal's like tuning to Die Deutsche Welle when you're in Wertachtal. It's nothing you could transmit from a plane, a signal like that. Christ, I'm surprised they've got that kind of power in the sub!"

"They have come for me again," said Vlasov in Russian. "They are broadcasting to thwart us."

A white spotlight glittered at sea. It disappeared as the aircraft banked abruptly. The plane's new course brought it shoreward. It was no more than twenty meters over the water. "What is it, a helicopter?" Kelly said, though even he could clearly see that the red and green lights were outboard on wing tips.

"No," said the sergeant in an odd voice, "but it can hover like one. It's a Yak-36. Tom, we're in trouble."

"Great," said Kelly, "those idiots have called the Algerian Air Force down on us now. These Yaks are armed, I suppose? If they're not, maybe we can run for it in the boat after all."

"It's not Algerian," Rowe said. His voice was barely loud enough to be heard. "The Russians have kept all of these for themselves. The Mediterranean Squadron's holding maneuvers off the coast, you know. This one must have flown off the *Novorossik*. It might have some under-wing stores of its own, but I'd say she was dragging a MAD package at the moment. I guess there'll be a couple frigates along soon for the heavy work."

There was a scuffing of shoes down the passage behind them. Both Americans turned. Kelly had palmed his knife again. "Is everything all right?" Annamaria asked as she rejoined them.

Rowe lowered the glasses. "The sub can't go deep," he said, "not anywhere near this coast. Maybe they can run for it—it depends on just where the Russian ships are. But if the Algerians give them the go-ahead to use their anti-sub missiles—well, they don't have to be very close to drop an SSN-14 in, not with that Yak overhead to guide them."

"I don't understand." the black-haired woman said. She put a hand on Kelly's forearm, feeling the concern but without knowledge of the cause.

"Okay," said Kelly, "we pack up and run. The boat and motor are US Marine issue and I don't want to leave them if there's a choice. We'll—"

"Tom, there's a hundred and fifty men out there going to surrender or be killed!" shouted the sergeant.

"*I* didn't tell them to signal that strong!" the agent shouted back. "Come on, let's move!" He tried to reconnect the ends of a turnbuckle that would hold the boat in a tight package. The metal slipped in his hands. "Besides," he added in a voice as weak as a child's, "I told them I'd only consider using a sub in these waters if they'd promise to give it air cover. I can't make them—not have lied to me. But when I get back, I'm going to—"

The sky flashed dazzlingly red. The four of them on the beach looked up.

"Well," said Kelly in a changed voice. "I don't have to kill anybody in Paris after all. But we do need to move."

Where the Yak had been quartering the sea with its

magnetic anomaly detector, there was an expanding cloud that rained fragments of burning metal. Before the explosion itself rocked houses, the crack of a sonic boom reached the shore at the tangent of a line of flattened waves. Spewed jet fuel began to dance and burn on the water.

"But what happened?" Annamaria said. "Did it just blow up? I don't see another airplane."

Sergeant Rowe connected the strap Kelly was struggling with, then a second one. The MARS boat was tacked into a manageable package again. "They credit Phoenix missiles with a 60-mile range," the soldier said as he worked. "I hear it's about twice that. And I think you just watched the first field test of a Phoenix."

"The first was off the coast of Libya in '79," Kelly said. He was smiling with relief. The extraction had been blown, he wasn't sure how; but they were alive and he'd find another way out. "I couldn't have found a better time for an encore, Lord *knows* I couldn't!"

Several lights had gone on in houses along the street, Kelly noted as they staggered back up the stairs. The Yak was a dying glow out at sea. Doug Rowe supported the upper end of the boat again. He set it down beyond the last step. "I'll bring the car around," he called to Kelly and Annamaria across the burden. He began striding across the broken terrain toward the Blazer parked a block away.

"Come on up, Professor," Kelly called over his shoulder. "We'll get out of this one yet." It felt good to have Annamaria's arm around him and her scent in his nostrils. He gave her a peck on the cheek, but when she turned to respond, he patted her away. He sat carefully down on the boat, watching activity in the town.

Doug Rowe was just getting into the Blazer. The courtesy light winked on, then off as the door thumped closed. Spies were not supposed to have cars with dome lights, Kelly thought. Well, maybe none of the batch of them were much in the way of spies. Stick to selling typewriters in the—

The flash that ate the Blazer was as bright as that of the exploding Yak.

The forty-gallon fuel tank spread orange flames the width of the street. The initial flash had been blindingly white. It left imprinted on Kelly's retinas the image of the hood and tailgate of the car collapsing inward because the steel body between them was gone.

"Professor, come on!" Kelly shouted down the black pit of the stairs. Behind him, the fire leapt and roared. "*Come* on!"

"Where's Doug?" Annamaria cried.

Kelly swung his legs over the boat, ignoring the woman's question as he struggled to get to the defector. Annamaria began running toward the flames.

"They are here to kill me," said the Professor, standing at the foot of the passage. His voice rasped.

"Then we'll have to kill them first, won't we?" the agent snarled. "Move! This beach is suicide if they come looking for us!" He clenched his left fist around the fabric of the taller man's lapels, guiding and dragging him up the steps. The knife in Kelly's hand was pure silver in the moonlight, but the blazing gasoline touched it with hellfire as they dodged through the jumbled rocks.

"Where are we going?" panted Vlasov when they had scrambled to the road a block from the fire. The uncertainty that had momentarily frozen him was gone. "Where are the others?"

No one had menaced them as they stumbled away from the corniche. With every step Kelly had expected a shot. He was moving on his nerves now, his nerves and a killing fury. It would drive him until he found an outlet for it or found his death first. "The KGB didn't have us," he said as he led Vlasov across the road at a clumsy trot. First south, then east to the safe house and the stolen car. "They didn't have us, then they did again. Maybe you're doubling, maybe the embassy's tapped or bugged. . . . Nothing I can do about that."

They were walking now, leaning forward as if to speed progress that their weary legs could not maintain. A mercury-vapor lamp on a street corner distorted their shadows into blotches on a pale blue field. "Nobody connected with the embassy's going to hear a goddam word about this from here on out."

"You still think it's humans, don't you?" remarked the Russian wearily. "Well, in the long run I don't suppose it matters."

"You're right," said Kelly harshly. "It doesn't matter at all!" But his waist was cold for lack of the arm that had encircled it.

The safe house was quiet, the gate locked as they had left it an hour before. Kelly pulled the gate open and then unlatched the Renault's engine compartment. "Stand back, Professor," he said.

"What are you doing?" the defector asked as he watched Kelly probe at the shadowed engine block.

"Wasting my time in the dark," the agent responded.

He lay down on the gravel, wincing as he tried to see the underside of the engine. "Don't have a light, though, and we don't have time to get one. So. . . ." Kelly stood up again and slammed the engine cover. He wished that he had found something, a bomb, *something*. . . . If he had disarmed a bomb, he could have felt that much more confident that he was going to survive the next few seconds.

He got in on the driver's side. Vlasov started to open the other door. The agent snapped, "Get clear, goddammit!" He began fumbling with the hot wire.

If there had been a key to turn instead of a pair of bare leads to twist together, Kelly would not have noticed it. Now his fingers brushed against something beneath the ignition lock which had not been there when he stole the car.

The agent bent over. He could see nothing because of the darkness and the sudden rush of dizzying pain. The object was no bigger than a button. From the way it slipped as he applied pressure it was magnetized. Holding his breath unconsciously, Kelly pried the thing loose from the lock. A twitch of resistance suggested that a hair-fine wire had parted after the magnet released. Even trying to silhouette the object against the streetlight showed nothing but a thin disk.

Without speaking, Kelly got out of the car. He hurled the button over the wall to the street. The tiny tick of metal on cold asphalt could not be heard above the breeze. There was no other response.

"Come on, Professor," the agent said as he got into the car again.

"But what was that?" Vlasov asked.

"A bug, I guess," said Kelly as the motor fired raggedly. "And I hope it was the only thing somebody decided to leave this car with."

As they turned east toward Algiers again, the mirror showed that the sky over the center of Tipasa was aglow. If Kelly lived, that fire would not be the only monument to Staff Sergeant Douglas Rowe, 23, husband and father . . . and a better man, perhaps, then some of those he had just died for.

XLII

The door had a spring latch and a draw bolt in the center of the panel. There seemed to be a second draw bolt just above the threshold. Kelly kicked the keyplate squarely with the heel of his boot. The blow tore the bolt from its seat in the jamb and left the lock sagging on half-stripped screws. The panel was only half-inch plywood.

"Brace me," the agent muttered to Professor Vlasov. He kicked again, angling his heel toward the lower bolt. It gave and the spring latch fell off as well.

"I never figured," Kelly said as he pushed the panel out of the way, "how anybody managed to knock a door down with his shoulder. Or why anybody'd want to try."

Moonlight through the doorway let the agent find the cord to the desk lamp. He tugged it on, reaching past Vlasov to push the door closed now that they were inside. The office of the brass shop looked larger than it had with nine people filling it during the meeting. "Ramdan!" Kelly shouted. "Ramdan! Come down, we're friends!"

"This is a friend's house but you smash in the door?" questioned the defector.

"This isn't the time to be standing in the street shouting," Kelly said grimly. "Besides, I don't think he'd have opened up for us."

The alcove behind the paneling where the Mauser had been hidden was now empty. The agent had seen the rifle abandoned during the fire-fight outside the Institute, but it would have been nice if there were something remaining there now. A gun might change their negotiating posture somewhat for the better. Or again—perhaps this was just as well.

There were muted sounds from the living quarters above. They changed abruptly to footsteps on the stairs. Heavy steps, shuffling; and a lighter pair behind them as nervous as a mosquito readying to land.

Vlasov seated himself on the swivel chair and fiddled with the dark tie he still wore. As the steps neared, the Russian stood and took a half step toward the door. The agent stopped him with a shake of his head. "No," he said, in French lest the Kabyles think something was being hidden from them. "We'll wait here real quiet and not take a chance that anyone gets startled." Kelly's own hands were empty and in plain sight in front of him. They itched to at least palm his sheath knife.

Ramdan jerked open the door from the shop. He had lost weight, and the flesh of his face seemed to have been replaced by sagging gray wax. It was less than eighteen hours since the gunfight, but fear and his leg wound had aged the Kabyle a decade in that time. "What are you doing here?" Ramdan demanded in a voice as haunted as his eyes.

Behind the shop owner was the boy who had been in the front of the place during the meeting. His eyelids flickered but the pupils did not move a micron. They did not even tremble, as did the hand holding the Enfield revolver. The muzzle of the old gun wavered in an arc that covered Kelly and Ramdan's kidneys about equally. The elder Kabyle was nuts, thought the agent, to allow the boy behind him with a gun. The kid was wired like a carnival wheel.

"We need a little help, Ramdan," Kelly said aloud. His hands were still, his voice reasonable. "Everything's fine. Just a little help, and that we'll pay for."

"*Help*," Ramdan repeated. His tongue hissed on the French syllables. The shop owner took a further step into the office itself. He supported his weight on the right side with a crutch-headed cane. His slippered feet glided over the floor, rasping in the grit. "Three of us already have died—perhaps more! *My* leg, it could have been my *head*! They say 'Flee!,' but my leg . . . and who would look after my wares? And you want help!"

The boy behind the shop owner had not moved. His eyes glittered above the older man's shoulder.

Kelly shrugged. "You wanted to make a battle out of it," he said. "Me, I'd already seen as much shooting as I thought I needed to. . . ." He held Ramdan's eyes, the cold certainty of his gaze quenching the Kabyle's anger. "You've got channels across the border, Morocco or Tunisia, right? I want you to smuggle us out."

"Madman!" Ramdan shouted. "Get out of here!" The Kabyle raised his stick to gesture or threaten. Weight shifting onto his right thigh seared him like a fresh wound.

His mouth gaped soundlessly. The cane wavered, its ferrule flicking back to the floor and skidding. The heavy man started to fall.

Kelly did not move. The boy, startled back into reality, tried to catch the older man. The angle was wrong. The Enfield clubbed at Ramdan's back as the boy grabbed reflexively. The agent stepped forward then and took the shop owner's weight on his own shoulder and flexed knees.

Professor Vlasov stood and pulled out the chair. Kelly guided the older Kabyle into the seat as gently as if he held an equal weight of electronic gear. When the agent straightened, he plucked the revolver from the boy's hand without looking around to give warning.

"We want you to smuggle us out," Kelly repeated in a voice from which his control kept the need to pant with exertion. He thumbed the Enfield's latch and dumped the six fat cartridges into his left palm. He laid the empty revolver on the desk top; the ammunition tumbled into the pocket of the agent's shirt.

The boy snatched up the weapon again.

"How do you know we could get you out if we wanted to?" Ramdan asked in a sick, weary voice. His words were an affirmation of what had been no more than an assumption in Kelly's mind until then.

"Hell, are we little children?" the agent sneered. He deliberately turned his back on the others and sauntered toward the alley door. His thumbs were hooked in his belt. "You need to raise money, to talk to journalists . . . to buy guns and ammo, for Christ's sake! Don't you?"

Kelly spun more abruptly than he would have done if

the .38 S&W cartridges were not a shifting weight in his pocket. "And I don't suppose your couriers get their visas stamped every week at the border, do they?" he continued, hectoring the injured man. "We need a quick trip out and we'll pay for it, like I said. And I don't mean some Swiss cloud-cuckoo land, either—green dollars, five thousand of them, cash in hand when you've earned it."

Both of the Kabyles were watching Kelly with a different sort of interest. The boy had cradled the Enfield to his chest as if it were a kitten. Now, the fingers of his left hand paused in stroking the empty cylinder.

The agent unbuckled his heavy belt. His face wore a sneer as professional as a rock star's. He slid the belt through the pants' loops, stepping past Ramdan to use the desk front as a support. The belt was thin leather, folded lengthwise in three overlapping layers. Kelly raised the top layer.

The chair squealed as the shop owner swiveled to watch. Kelly reached into the pocket formed by the middle and bottom layers. He plucked out part of the stuffing and dropped it into Ramdan's lap. "Forty-nine more where that came from," the agent said. "Just get me and my friend across one border or the other."

The Kabyle's hands quivered as he opened what had been tossed to him. It is one thing to talk of a million dollars in the abstract. A US hundred-dollar bill, folded into sixteenths, is money in human terms.

"Just get us out," Kelly said very softly.

Ramdan smoothed the bill with the edge of his right hand. "It is . . ." he said, staring at Benjamin Franklin's face. "Just perhaps. . . ."

The telephone was in a lower drawer of the desk. The Kabyle took it out and dialed quickly. The instrument was balanced on one knee, the crinkled bill on the other. The phone rang repeatedly. Ramdan looked up in nervous embarrassment. Kelly was buckling his money belt on again.

"I'm afraid—" the shop owner began. All four men could hear the click of someone finally answering on the other end of the line.

Ramdan's eyes immediately flashed down to his lap again, the telephone and the money. He began talking, low-voiced but very quickly. The burr of response was not to his liking. The shop owner began to speak louder and even faster. His voice gained back the timbre and animation it had had the previous day, before a bullet had tempered his spirits in his own blood. He picked up the hundred with his free hand and began to snap it back and forth in the air, as if the person on the other end of the line could see it.

The exchange in Kabyle was long and heated enough that by the end, the other voice was audible also. Ramdan lowered the handpiece but did not cradle it. He was breathing hard. "All right," he said, "Tunis. But only one of you. That is all that will be possible for three weeks, perhaps a month. And the money in advance."

For the moment, Kelly ignored the demand about the money. He slotted home the tongue of his belt and said, "Why only one? What's the deal?"

Ramdan looked at the phone, then the agent. Vlasov was silent in a corner of the room. Only his eyes moved. The older Kabyle said at last, "It is a plane, a very small plane. We must land and take off outside the regular airfields, even in Tunisia. The ground is rough, we must not overload the plane." He paused, then concluded with a note of anger, "It is only because there is room available that Sa'ad would agree. Not the money. And because he said you fought like a tiger yesterday."

Kelly's smile was as stark as a gun muzzle. "Does he say that?" the agent asked with a mildness that deceived no one. Then, "Well, I don't try to fight the laws of physics, though. Okay. It's a deal." Everyone else in the room tensed. "You land near Tunis, I suppose?"

Ramdan nodded. The telephone blipped an interrogative. The shop owner snapped back at it in Kabyle without taking his eyes from Kelly's face.

"Okay," the agent repeated. "You'll take my friend here. We aren't going to use names, you understand, because I don't like some of the things that happen when names are used. . . ." He looked at Vlasov. A tiny smile lifted the corner of the Professor's mouth. "Sure, you hang out with crazy people and you start to get funny yourself," Kelly added. He rubbed his face with the knuckles of his left hand.

"My friend will have the money in his pocket," the agent continued in a stronger, certain voice. "He'll hand it over as soon as somebody delivers him to Carthage-Tunis airport on"—Kelly looked at his watch—"Monday morning. He'll also turn over that revolver"—he pointed to the Enfield—"which he'll be carrying until then."

The boy sprang back. "No!" he gasped. He pointed the weapon in what would have been a threatening gesture had it been loaded.

Ramdan looked up at Kelly and sighed. "In the base of

the lamp," he said, gesturing behind him. "I understand."

Kelly nodded and unlocked the porcelain fixture from the wall. As the American slid the fiberboard cover off the bottom, Ramdan went on curiously, "But why at that time? That means we must feed him, hide him two days?"

There was a tiny Beretta .25 pistol in the lamp base. "Because," Kelly said as he checked the magazine—it was full—"it's going to take me that long to get there myself if you won't take me." He handed the autoloader to Vlasov. "Tell you the truth, Professor," he went on in French, "I don't doubt their honesty or I wouldn't be doing this at all. But if I can't be with you myself"—he smiled—"the next best thing is a gun."

No one laughed.

Kelly sobered. "One more thing," he said. "I've got a car of sorts, but I'll need plates for it. 58 through 60 series'll do, or out of country—I don't care which. They just can't be reported stolen until Tuesday, that's all."

Ramdan still held the telephone. He raised the handpiece and began talking into it in muted tones, looking up at the agent repeatedly.

"You are going to drive?" asked the boy. Both Kelly and Vlasov stared at him. That was the first connected sentence either of them had heard him speak. "They will stop you at the border if your license and registration do not match."

"Yeah, I'll have to think about that one, won't I?" the agent said. The kid might have a future after all. Not for field operations, though. He was the sort who threw the igniter and crouched down holding the fused satchel charge until it went off.

Ramdan lowered the phone again. "No more demands, then?" he pressed. "The deal as you leave it now?"

"Well, clothes—a jacket, hell, that'll do," Kelly said. His smile was back and there was at last some humor in it. "And one more thing—a bed for a couple hours. Or a floor where people won't mind stepping over me." He stretched. His yawn camouflaged the stabs and ripples of pain that avalanched through his body.

Ramdan began speaking into the phone.

Aloud but to no one in particular, Kelly said, "Got a long way yet to go." His mind chorused from "Sam Hall"—"Now up the rope I go, now up I go. . . ."

XLIII

The Temple of Minerva in Tebessa was almost four hundred years older than the city's Byzantine walls. As one of the best-preserved Roman temples in the world, it was an obvious magnet for tourists passing through the border city. Kelly was pretending to study the Roman funerary monuments in the fenced temple yard when the Renault 18 pulled up across the street beneath the massive wall. The car had Tunisian plates. Even better, they bore a CD prefix—Corps Diplomatique.

The American agent continued to face the stele as he watched the two couples. They locked up the car, laughing. They were all on the young side, the women in particular. One of them had black hair and a bouncing giggle that cramped Kelly's groin despite his nervousness. It was the men he needed to concentrate on, however, and one of them would do well, do very well. . . .

The couples were talking in French as they entered

the gate. They passed Kelly with a murmured "Bonjour," all around:" The temple had become a museum while Algeria was still a French colony, and the Algerians had kept it up to the extent of having a caretaker present.

The leader of the visiting couples was a half-step ahead of his companions. He was speaking volubly as he waved toward the carven transoms of the pillared but roofless entryway. He was in his mid-thirties with a dark complexion; he was Kelly's height and weight besides, though he carried more of the latter in a chair-bottom spread. The Frenchman was contrasting the temple with the one they had seen in Djemila, and that was especially good. It meant that they were returning home after a stay of at least several days in Algeria. It would have been more awkward if they had just crossed the border, though you could finesse a lot with a diplomatic passport. . . .

Kelly strolled out of the temple yard. His hands were in the pockets of the jacket Ramdan had been cajoled into giving him. In the borrowed clothing, Kelly was not a prepossessing figure, but at least he was no longer dressed in blood-stained rags.

"Well, I hit him on the head," the agent sang under his breath, "and I left him there for dead. . . ."

The hilt of his knife was blood-warm in his hand.

XLIV

It was chill and dark in the hour before dawn. Lieutenant Colonel Nguyen Van Minh felt as weary and gray as the sky. They had to wait for the other team to get in position in back of the shop, and they seemed to be a long time doing so.

This was the sixth arrest—or arrest attempt—the Vietnamese officer had participated in during the night. Two of the suspected Kabyle terrorists had been missing. The squad, three civil police under Captain Majlid of the Presidential Security Office, had ransacked the houses and arrested all family members present. That might in time help the local security forces with their Kabyle problem, but it was of small use to Nguyen.

He had not found the three successful pickups to be a great deal more helpful to him. Nguyen was quite certain from their reactions that two of the Kabyles arrested had known nothing about the plot. The third man had owned the shop through which the kidnapped—or defecting, that was obvious—scientists had been spirited away. The Kabyle was anything *but* innocent . . . but his claim to have been attending a wedding in Oran would probably hold up. It meant that he had isolated himself from the operation. Whatever the prisoner might divulge in the interrogation rooms next to the Civil Prison, it would not include detailed information about the American operatives and their plans.

"Allah, four more of these," muttered the Algerian captain. "And then they'll add more to the list if I know them." He took out a French cigarette and looked at it before dropping it back in the packet. The policeman with him at the front door said something in Arabic. Majlid laughed and took the cigarette out again.

Faintly through the air came the whistle that meant the other two men had found the correct back door. Radios were less common than was needed for them this night in Algiers.

The captain cursed and threw the cigarette toward the squad's blue and white Mikrobus. He hammered on the door and shouted in French, "Open up in there! At once!"

Nguyen stepped instinctively to the hinge side of the shop door. The front wall was mostly display window and no protection, though. The police seemed only tired. The uniformed man clicked off the safety of his sub-machine gun without any apparent concern. Out of deference to his hosts, Nguyen kept his hand away from his own pistol. He was taut, ready to move in whatever direction was required.

Majlid cursed again. He nodded to the man with the sub-machine gun. The uniformed man stabbed the butt of his weapon through the glazed door panel. He jerked the tube stock up, then sideways, spilling more glass on the floor within the shop. Nguyen thought that he could hear movement inside.

The Algerian captain reached carefully through the opening to avoid the rippling edges above the putty. He worked the paired locks without haste. When he had turned the knob to actually unlatch the door, Majlid withdrew his hand. He kicked the panel open, shouting, "Come out, Ramdan!"

There was a crash within the shop as someone met the pair at the back door and tried to retreat. Majlid frowned and took a step into the darkness. He tugged at the pistol in his shoulder holster.

"*Don't!*" Nguyen shouted. His Tokarev was already in his hand. "The light's behind you!"

A red cordite flash hit the interior of the shop. The captain's head snapped up. He toppled against the policeman behind him.

The Vietnamese officer shot twice, aiming for the muzzle flash. Through the echoing shots cut the howl of a ricochet. That did not mean Nguyen had missed. The high-velocity bullets of his pistol would not have been stopped by anything as slight as a man's chest.

Within, something hard dropped. The uniformed Algerian was trying to clear his own weapon. "Not now!" Nguyen screamed. He dived into the shop just as somebody in back found the switch for the overhead fixture.

A stepped display platform filled the center of the

shop. A boy gripped it to hold himself upright. The revolver with which he had shot Majlid lay on the floor at his feet. The boy's face was as white as a flag of surrender—except for his lips. His lips were brightened by bubbles of orange pulmonary blood. There were two holes a finger's breadth apart in the center of the boy's shirt. In his back would be matching holes.

The team from the back door was pushing a third, heavy-set Algerian ahead of them. There was blood on the prisoner's trouser leg. Since there had been no shooting from the rear, it was probably a reopened wound. As the older man was frog-marched in, the boy slumped to the floor of the shop. He covered the revolver with his corpse. The older prisoner wailed and tried to catch him. The policeman holding his arms jerked him back.

"Are you all right?" cried one of the men from the back. "Look what this one had—good thing he didn't pull the pin!" He raised a fragmentation grenade with a block of plastic explosive molded around it. The combination would lift the roof of a bunker or spread pieces of an automobile over a square block.

"Hey, where's the captain?" asked the man holding the prisoner.

"Him? Oh, dead," Nguyen said absently. He threw the safety of his pistol and holstered it without unloading the chamber. Majlid had taken the bullet through the bridge of his nose. His eyes bulged in ultimate surprise.

The Vietnamese took the bomb from the Algerian who was holding it. The prisoner inches away stank of fear and urine.

"Yes," Nguyen said as he examined the explosive, "this

is very good. It will save us going back to headquarters to question this one."

"Wait a minute," objected the man with the sub-machine gun. "You can't—"

The Vietnamese colonel turned and looked at him. Words choked in the policeman's throat.

After a moment's silence, Nguyen began to give his instructions.

XLV

When the French couples came out of the museum, Kelly was standing on the broad firing step of the city wall. He was gazing out through one of the crenellations. The firing step was a good five feet above street level, so that even though the agent was standing beside the Renault, the grade separation kept him from being a part of the scene. The couples ignored him as he seemed to ignore them.

The tourist who looked most like Kelly began to unlock the driver's door. Kelly dropped into the street in front of the Renault. "Excuse me, please," the agent said with a smile. His hands lay atop one another, waist high.

The would-be driver scowled at the American. "We don't need a guide, thank you," he said, holding the door ajar with his hand. Behind him on the street side stood the black-haired woman. She looked more interested than anxious at the moment. There were other cars, other people, nearby, but no one else was within fifty feet.

"Oh, not a guide, no," Kelly said with a chuckle. He stepped around so that the man and woman were to either side of him. Their bodies masked the knife which the agent suddenly displayed. Only they and the other couple, staring across the car's low roof, could see the steel shimmer in the bright daylight.

"I am an agent of the Second Bureau," Kelly continued in soft, persuasive French, "but there is neither the time nor the opportunity for me to make this request through channels. I am so sorry, but three of you"—his smile and the splayed fingers of his left hand indicated the woman beside him and the other couple—"must accompany me back to Tunis."

"You're mad!" blurted the nearest man. "We have done nothing!" The woman beside him had drawn in her breath, but she was staring at Kelly's battered face and not at his knife. The other couple was straining, wide-eyed, trying to hear what the agent was saying in his deceptively mild voice.

"Of course you have done no wrong," the American agreed. "You have by chance the opportunity to serve France at only a slight inconvenience to yourselves. Here, give me the keys—" Kelly did not force the key ring from the other man's hand, nor was the way his knife rotated actually a threat. Between firm pressure and the winking edge, however, the Frenchman released what he at first had intended to hold.

"Madame," Kelly went on with a nod to the black-haired woman, "if you will enter and admit your friends?" He swung the door open, keeping his body in the opening so that he could not be closed out. Puzzled and hesitant, the three tourists got in the car. The knife was hidden again, but it was more real to the others than was the smile which never slipped from Kelly's face.

"And you as well, sir, for the moment," the agent said to the last Frenchman. The man obeyed awkwardly, because he kept his eyes on Kelly instead of watching what he was doing himself.

With all four of the tourists inside, Kelly knelt. He braced his left hand on the top of the steering wheel. A small rubber band was wrapped several times around the last joint of his little finger. Blocked circulation darkened and distended the fingertip, "Now, it really doesn't matter whether you believe that what I am doing is necessary to the survival of France," the agent continued reasonably. "You can believe I'm a Mossad assassin, if you like, it's all one with me. But—you must believe that I am serious when I say that none of you will be harmed if you cooperate, yes?"

The others nodded, mesmerized by the gentle words and the mirror-finished steel.

"But you are not, I judge," Kelly continued, "persons used to violence. It is necessary that you believe me utterly when I say that I will kill you all without compassion if there is the least trouble from you."

The blonde woman in back nodded again, but the meaning of Kelly's words had not penetrated the gloss of fear upon her.

Kelly reached up with his knife. He slashed off the last joint of his own left little finger. The fingertip spun into the lap of the man behind the wheel. The Frenchman sagged as if his spinal cord had been cut. There were tiny droplets of blood spattering the inner slope of the window.

Kelly felt as if he were being bathed in hot sand. There was a notch and a streak of blood on the steering wheel where the blade had cut through his finger. In a voice that rushed through fire, the agent said, "I am very serious. Now, madame, please remove your husband's passport and identity papers. He will stay here. You will drive, I will sit beside you . . . and you will all be released unharmed near Tunis as soon as we can get there."

Kelly carefully wiped both flats of his knife on the coat of the man who had fainted. The wet streak soaked away instantly in the dark fabric. There was very little blood. The rubber band tourniquet prevented that. The bandage Kelly would apply when they got moving would handle infection for as long as it would have to.

The blonde woman managed to stick her head out the window before she vomited.

"Sorry," the agent repeated, "but it can't be helped."

There would be no trouble from this crew on the long drive. Of that, Kelly was sure.

XLVI

Fear had drawn all the blood from Ramdan's skin. The pigment remained to turn the prisoner's naked body into a construct of yellow wax. Only his eyeballs and the occasional tremors that shook his whole plump frame proved the shopkeeper was still alive.

The two policemen still on the lower floor were silent and increasingly uncomfortable. Nguyen himself kept up a constant flow of conversation as he completed his preparations. "Did they ever talk of Doctor Hoang Tanh?" he asked with a glance at Ramdan. "You see, I'm not in the least interested in your friends, only in the foreigners who were involved in all this."

One of the policemen stirred uneasily. He said nothing. Nguyen turned to him sharply. "Here," the Vietnamese said. He held out a shallow silver bowl. "Take this upstairs and fill it with water. When you've brought it back, you can go up again and help your colleague guard the women."

The Algerian hesitated only a moment before he clumped up the stairs on his errand.

"Or perhaps," said Nguyen, again in a mild voice, "they talked of Professor Evgeny Vlasov?"

That brought a tremor from the prisoner, but he still did not speak.

The police had cleared the central display platform. They had bound the shop owner to it in a sitting position after stripping him naked. The swivel chair in the office would have been too easy to tip over. That would have given the subject something to think about other than what Nguyen intended. Ramdan's limbs were tied to the platform supports. A final loop locked his waist to a pillar behind him so that he could not throw himself forward. The edge of the platform's second step caught the prisoner in the small of the back. That provided just the slight measure of discomfort which the Vietnamese officer wanted for the moment.

"I don't suppose you know the real name of the American in charge," Nguyen said, "but perhaps you'll tell me what name he used? Kelly, perhaps? Ah, well."

He found what he wanted for the demonstration in the tangle of objects which they had brushed off the platform. It was a glass plate on a stand of bronze filigree. Nguyen held the plate up to the light fixture and rotated it. The heavy glass threw a lens across the floor. It wavered briefly across the head of the teenage boy who still lay where he had fallen. The blood which had gushed from his mouth was dry now. It was as black as his hair. Ramdan's eyes followed the light across the floor. He began to tremble again.

The policeman who had been sent for the water returned. He carried not only the bowl but a full plastic bucket as well. "In case you need more," he muttered, keeping his eyes turned away from both Nguyen and the interrogation subject.

"Very thoughtful," said the Vietnamese, "but I would not have called you back anyway." Torture requires a particular mind set, the capacity to think of the subject as a thing to be manipulated rather than a human being.

Effective interrogation, which is not necessarily the same thing, requires the same mind set.

Nguyen set his paraphernalia on the ledge of the display window where it was directly in front of Ramdan. Most of the objects were not threatening. There was the bowl of water, the plate . . . a roll of adhesive tape from the office and a pad made by folding a strip of the velvet which had covered the platform. The incongruousness of the objects was itself disconcerting.

"You know," said Nguyen, working a bit of plastic explosive off the block, "I could understand if you were doing this to save your friends. But I'm not interested in your friends, you see, only in the foreigners. Who they are, what their plans are . . . where I might find them, yes. . . . That's all."

The explosive was white, with the consistency of grainy modeling clay. The piece Nguyen's thumbnails had cut from the block was no bigger than the last joint of a man's little finger. The Vietnamese officer rolled it into a ball, set it on the glass plate, and began to repeat the process. "Yes, I'm really sorry that you're doing this to yourself, Ramdan," the Vietnamese went on. "The only people who deserve to be punished are the foreigners who used you and your friends as pawns in their own games. But if you insist. . . ."

Nguyen set down the second bead of explosive—on the ledge rather than the plate. Both Ramdan and the remaining policeman were watching him with a similar mixture of curiosity and repulsion. "Did you know," the Vietnamese said cheerfully, "that *plastique* will burn without exploding? You mustn't step on it then, but otherwise it just burns. Very, very, hot."

Nguyen took a disposable lighter from his pocket. Smiling once more at his subject, he thumbed the flame to life and began to play it over the explosive on the glass dish. The bead of *plastique* quivered. A thread of black smoke wobbled up, and the point at which the lighter touched looked momentarily green. Then the explosive ignited.

The flame was sword-thin and a foot high. It twisted like the blade of a kris. Nguyen dropped his lighter and picked up the bowl of water. He gripped the metal through the velvet pad as he held the bowl over the flame.

"Isn't it an interesting color?" the Vietnamese remarked. "The way it seems to be pure white, but its light makes other things show a green tinge?" He did not raise his voice. The hiss of the fire and the hiss of air being driven out of the water overlay his words.

"How hot, do you wonder?" Nguyen asked. The last of the explosive was burning from the puddle it had made on the dish. The heavy glass exploded at the direct touch of a 1200° flame.

"*How hot?*" the Vietnamese repeated in a shout, and

he flung the water boiling in the bowl across Ramdan's chest.

The Kabyle's screams took almost a minute to die away. He strained at the ropes holding him. The heavy platform rocked and thumped on the floor. The skin of the prisoner's chest blushed a bright scarlet and began to puff up.

"Now you see what I mean," Nguyen said reasonably when he could be heard again. He was using a shard of glass from the shattered plate to cut a length of tape from the roll. "*You* don't deserve to be punished. It's the foreigners, Vlasov and the American. . . . They're the ones who are at fault. Where are they now, do you suppose?"

Ramdan was blubbering now, but he still would not speak. Fresh blood was again leaking from the bullet wound in his thigh.

"Well, if we must, we must," murmured the interrogator. He spoke barely loud enough to be heard. He set the second bead of plastic explosive on the edge of the strip of tape. "Perhaps you think," he continued, "that I plan only to scald you with water? No, no . . . that was only a demonstration. I thought it only fair that you learn how hot the *plastique* burns. Learn indirectly, that is, before you learn. . . ." Nguyen stepped forward with a sad smile.

Ramdan began to scream again before the Vietnamese officer had even touched him. His body thrashed to the narrow limits of the ropes. They threw him back against the wood of the platform each time. Nguyen waited for the moment of exhaustion. The policeman was staring in horrified fascination.

Ramdan paused, gasping for breath. Nguyen's hands

darted for the Kabyle's groin. He wrapped the ends of the tape around Ramdan's genitals before the subject could even scream. The bead of *plastique* poked out from beneath the tape. It was clearly visible against the dark skin of Ramdan's penis beneath it.

"What a monster that American is to put you through this," said Nguyen sympathetically. He clicked his lighter. The flame was turned high, wavering.

"No," begged Ramdan. "No! *No*—" He tried to jerk back and the jet of butane singed hair from his scrotum. *"No-no-no*—Allah *I'lltellyouI'lltellI'lltellI'lltellI'lltell. . . ."*

Nguyen stepped back. The subject's voice had sunk into bubbling sobs. "Ramdan, my friend?" the Vietnamese said quietly.

The room stank with the feces that the shop owner had evacuated. He tried to raise a hand to wipe his eyes. The bonds stopped him. "I'll talk," he said dully. "Only before Allah, take the tape away. . . ."

"As soon as you have told us what you know," the interrogator promised. "As soon as you've helped us punish the foreigners who did this to you."

The remaining Algerian policeman suddenly bolted for the stairs, retching. Effective interrogation requires a particular mind set.

XLVII

"American Embassy," said the bored voice through the crackling of the Tunisian phone system.

"Don Marshal, please," replied Kelly in English. There was no pay phone in the restaurant, but the proprietor had no objections to Kelly making an important business call with the phone beside the cash register. No objections when he had assured himself that the American hundred dollar-bill was real, at any rate.

The agent could have used the phone in the office, as a matter of fact, but this way he could keep an eye on his three companions. The French tourists were at a booth in back of the Western-style restaurant. The waiter had already arrived. Lucie, the black-haired woman, was ordering for Kelly as well as herself. The American smiled. Lucie waved a reply. The other couple, the Clochimonts, looked askance at her.

The Clochimonts had slept all night in the hotel's

small bathroom. A string tied from the knob to Kelly's wrist would have awakened him if the door had been opened. Lucie, though, had spent much of the night talking to the agent. Whatever she might believe about Kelly's real mission, she and the agent were no longer on terms of mutual mistrust.

"Two-one-two," said the phone.

"'Working,' you mean, don't you, snake?" Kelly replied, dropping into the past with the tremble of an anchor through deep waters.

"Who the hell?" said the voice on the other end of the line. "This is extension two-one—"

"Think way back," the agent continued. "Nineteen and sixty-eight. A buck sergeant with black hair, one-sixty . . . I wore a bandanna for a sweatband back then—"

"*God almighty!* Carried a Swedish K? Sergeant Tom Kelly! God almighty, man, I thought I'd never see you again!"

Bingo. "Tell the truth, snake," Kelly continued, "I wasn't just sure I'd ever see you again either, the way you looked when they started slapping IVs in your arms."

"Hell, yes," agreed Marshal more soberly. "I was conscious there for a while, you know, before the morphine got to me. I wouldn't have had a snowball's chance in hell if you hadn't packed me back to the bird, man. And I know it." The speaker paused. "Ah, what brings you to Tunis, Tom? Or are you even here?"

"Well, a friend and me'll be getting in tomorrow morning," Kelly said. The cashier met his eyes occasionally, but there was no harm done even if the Tunisian did understand English. "That's sort of what I needed to talk to you about. You see, I've been selling office machines for a few years, but right now I'm back with the old firm again."

"Oh?" said the other man carefully.

"And I hear you never left the, ah, company you were with back in '68. In Cambodia. I need help, snake, and you're the only one I know who can give it."

Marshal's voice was more distant than the breadth of Tunisia accounted for. "I'm not sure what kind of a mistake—" he began.

"Listen, man," Kelly cut in harshly. "I didn't call to embarrass you, I didn't call to put you in a bind. I'm telling you, I *need* you and our Uncle needs you bad, worse'n you'll ever know. If I go through channels, I'm dead and everybody's dead, just as dead as you'd have been if there hadn't been somebody to carry you back to the slick under fire. Now, you can turn your back on that and on me—or you can take my word for it that there's no other way that'll work for Uncle. And snake? This doesn't go in my report. I've got other stories I don't tell besides this one."

After a long pause, the other man said, "What do you need, then?"

"Well, my friend and I thought you might meet us for a drink at the airport tomorrow before we fly out. Got a pencil?" Marshal grunted.

"Six-three, one-eighty, age 61 . . . white hair, blue eyes. And five-nine, one-sixty, age 38, black and brown. Europeans, I think . . . or hell, US is okay, this is a one-shot anyhow."

There was another brief pause. Then the other man

asked, "How good are you expecting these to be, then?"

"Man," Kelly explained, "if they're looking for us, we're shit outa luck anyway. But it'd be a real pisser to have the deal blow up because somebody forgot there should've been an entry stamp for Tunisia, hey?"

"All right," Marshal said. "Noon in the airport lobby. I'll see what I can do. I don't know why I'm doing this."

"Because it's your job," the agent said softly. "Oh—and snake? One more thing."

"What the hell now?" But Marshal's voice too was soft.

"Could be I need that Swedish K again, but it wouldn't do me much good what with metal detectors and all," Kelly said. His eyes were on the booth and the French tourists. The food had come. Lucie beckoned him with an impish smile. "I hear you boys got involved in some of the off-shoots of the Sky Marshal program. If anything like that was lying around—it'd come in handy. I'm not going to beg you, man . . . but I need it worse than anybody who's ever carried one so far."

"Tomorrow at noon," Marshal said. The phone clicked dead.

In 1968, Don Marshal had been CIA liaison to the Special Operations Group. Most of Marshal's peers had left the heavy work to Special Forces and indig— Hmoung—troops. Marshal, however, had gone on an operation into Cambodia. That had earned him a line of bullets across the abdomen and a ride on Kelly's back to the extraction chopper.

At the time, Kelly had thought the Company man had been in the wrong place at the wrong time. But after getting out of the hospital, Marshal had been reassigned to the Middle Eastern section. He had risen there—and he had missed the post-Nam RIF that had caught hundreds of his former colleagues. Kelly had heard in a bar in Rome about Marshal's later history. The information had not been of any importance when he first heard it, but it got filed in Kelly's brain for future need.

The future had arrived when the agent began developing his private contingency plans, to get out in a hurry and without using channels that anyone knew he had open to him.

"Excellent, excellent," Kelly said as he walked back to the booth and the chicken dish which awaited him. "Madame—"

"Lucie." She pouted, patting the seat beside her.

"Lucie, your taste is excellent," Kelly continued. His left hand felt as if a truck had run over it, but he forced himself to use it to unfold his napkin. He smiled at the woman, then the Clochimonts. "You have all been very kind in the hour of your country's need. It will be with regret that I leave you tomorrow. But I will leave you with hope that your vacation has not been too badly disarranged."

Lucie snickered. "Poor Jacques," she said. "Back in Tebessa worrying himself silly. We'll have to phone him at once." She looked at Kelly in concern. "As soon as you say we may, Angelo."

"I am a luckier man than your friend," the agent said after a mouthful, "for having had the pleasure of your company for a day."

And *that* was a goddam lie, thought the agent as he ate: but at least Tom Kelly was a damned sight luckier than he might have been. The morning would tell.

XLVIII

A Boeing 737 was landing with a whine and a roar as Kelly walked to the terminal building. The plane bore the blue and yellow livery of Cub Scouts and Lufthansa . . . and Christ Jesus! he'd better not start free-associating at passport control or he'd blow this one yet.

Jacques Blondin's suit fit Kelly rather well, though the agent doubted that he looked much like a Second Secretary of the French mission to Tunisia. He was not going to use Blondin's passport anyway, not unless it became absolutely necessary.

He wished he could have treated the tourists a little better at the end. He had dumped them afoot on the outskirts of Tunis and doubled back to reach the airport without their knowing his destination. Their car was now abandoned in the airport lot. With luck it would be days or a week before it was located there. And of course they had all been more or less terrorized, while Blondin himself

had been left across the border with no passport and no
way of knowing what was happening to his friends and
mistress.

Lucie had not been all that terrorized, come to think.

They had been civilians, and that was a damned
shame . . . but it did not seem so very long ago that Kelly
had been wrapping a poncho around what was left of a 14
year old boy. The kid had been driving his water buffalo
down a trail before dawn. The Claymores of the automatic
ambush had put between fifty and a hundred steel pellets
through his body. This was a war, baby; and if you doubted
it, ask the ghost of that Yak-36 pilot.

Carthage-Tunis was a tourist airport; but it was also
the port through which hundreds of Tunisians came and
went to jobs in France. The locals and their families stood
in voluble clots within the terminal. They were more
colorful than the modern pastel mosaics on the walls of
the lobby. Kelly walked among coherent groups, watching
carefully for Professor Vlasov. A man nine inches taller
than the average of the crowd should not be able to—

"I am glad to see you," said a voice speaking French.
Kelly whirled, just as the Professor touched him on the
shoulder. The tall Russian looked the agent over carefully.
"You are at least no worse," he said, sounding a little
surprised. "Except—your finger?"

"Cost of doing business," the agent said, glad for the
momentary pressure of the other's hand. He switched to
Russian and added, "I'm expecting our papers to arrive
in"—he checked—"half an hour. The papers or God
knows what. I'm counting a lot on somebody I only knew
six hours. No trouble on your end?"

Vlasov shook his head. He was guiding Kelly back to the corner from which he had spotted the agent. "Your friends were honorable," he said. "The gun would not have been of much use many times, of course."

"Yeah, well," Kelly said. He was staring at his hands, unconsciously curling the maimed, bandaged finger out of sight. He looked up at Vlasov. "Professor, do you know how we—how everybody—intercepts microwave communications? I don't mean the signal, that's just a matter of sticking up an antenna in the right place. But how you get one phone call that you want out of a million that're just garbage so far as intelligence value goes?"

Vlasov frowned. "No . . ." he said. Then, "This is important?"

"Professor, I—" Kelly said. "I don't know what's important." He shook his head, then continued. "Anyway, the trick is you run everything through a computer. The computer's programmed to kick out transmissions that have key words in them. 'Qadafi,' for example. Then a human being checks the few transmissions with the key word in them—and we get a tape of Qadafi telling a buddy in Ethiopia how he's going to go about killing the President of the United States."

"It still seems very burdensome," the Professor commented.

"Sure," Kelly agreed, "sure; there's still mostly garbage, and that's why the business costs the USG five, ten *billion* dollars a year. That's a fact. But it works, and my friend"—the agent gestured with his index finger—"I think your buddies on Dzerzhinsky Square have come up with a way to do the same thing with ordinary speech. I think they've been keying on your name since before you set foot in Algiers, trying to scope out the opposition."

Professor Vlasov was too much of a scientist to speak before he had done the math in his head. After he had done the math, he was also too much of a scientist not to blurt, "Why, that's absurd, *absurd*. Even if the KGB could *collect* conversations the way antennas do radio signals, the magnitude is—my name is not uncommon, surely you know?"

The agent nodded glumly. "Sure," he said, "in the right places it's like yelling 'Levy' in Brooklyn. But I'm telling you, Professor, they've been on top of us or just a step behind all along the way. The one place your technical people have had the jump on ours—our spooks—is in bugging devices." He spread his palms, flipped them an instant later to hide the bandage again. "As for impossible . . . if I read the background data right, there's about a hundred people on our side of the line who say what you claim to be able to do is impossible. *I've* met you, and I don't doubt you at all . . . but I've been picked up by the KGB too often on this run to doubt that something's up. And it's been okay since we've stopped using—that word."

Vlasov smiled sadly. "You believe that of human science," he said, "and still you refuse to believe that I might be correct—"

"I believe in AKs and BTR-60s and Mi-2 helicopters," the American said in a rising voice. "*That's* what I've been seeing on this run. And if any of the bodies were green, I guess I missed them." His face and tone went neutral again. He added, "And I believe that's Don Marshal. Wait here a minute, Professor, while a friend and I make a little trip to the men's room."

The intervening years had been harder in some ways on the CIA operative than they had on Tom Kelly. Marhsal had been soft; now he was fat. The walk from the parking lot had beaded his face even in the dry Tunisian air. On the other hand, Marshal's suit fit him and he had not been prevented from shaving—as the agent had—by his scraped face.

The CIA man saw Kelly approaching and shifted the attaché case to permit him to shake hands. His glance at the agent was an appraising one. If not warm, then it was at least less hostile than Kelly felt he deserved for clamping down on Marshal's guilt glands the way he had.

"This shouldn't take very long," Marshal muttered as he followed Kelly to the rest rooms.

"No problems, then?" the agent pressed.

"Only with my conscience," the other man said glumly, "And I suppose that was going to be a problem either way."

The CIA man took the first stall that came open. He locked the door behind him. Kelly waited for one of the adjacent stalls. He tapped on the partition as he seated himself in one of them. "Okay," he said.

Marshal passed a manila envelope under the partition. There were two worn-looking passports in the envelope—Austrian, which was a nice touch since Austria had business and refugee communities from all across Europe. The fuzzy photograph of "Jean Gastineau" looked surprisingly like Professor Vlasov. That of "Axel Brandt" did not look anything like Kelly, but neither did the photograph in Kelly's own real US passport.

"Fuckin' A," the agent murmured. "Snake, your people did a job to be proud of. I owe you one."

"Just don't saw off the branch behind me, you bastard," Marshal whispered back. "Here. And if anybody hears where you got this, I'll cut your balls off if I have to break into Lubyanka to find you."

The CIA man was passing another envelope under the partition. This envelope contained a gun.

General Electric had run off a batch of them under contract to the Department of Agriculture—a subterfuge which fooled only Congressional staff members who were trying to track down the billions of dollars spent annually on the intelligence establishment. The weapon was made entirely of a form of Lexan plastic. It was light amber to human eyes, and it was absolutely transparent to fluoroscopes and magnetic detectors.

That transparency extended to the ammunition. The gun had four barrels, stacked in pairs. Each barrel was sealed at the factory with a .60 caliber plastic bullet and a charge of black powder which was clearly visible through the wall of the tube. The lockwork was piezoelectrical, and the only part of the system that would show up on an X-ray was the tiny pellet of lead azide that primed each load.

It wasn't a cannon. The plastic bullets shed velocity like a suicide hitting the sidewalk, making it a weapon for across the room at the farthest. But as Kelly had said, he could not have taken a Karl Gustaf sub-machine gun aboard the plane, even if one were available. This would serve his need—if it had to.

"Like I say, man," Kelly said, "I owe you and Unk owes you—though he'll never know it. Hang on a minute." The agent slipped the pistol into his pocket. It was bulkier than a Chief's Special, but its light weight kept it from significantly bulging the coat. Kelly unclipped his little sheath knife and passed it under the partition to Marshal.

"What the hell is this for?" the operative demanded tensely.

"It's been a friend for a good long while," Kelly explained quietly. "I ought to ash-can it right here, since I can't take it on the plane this time, but . . . look, snake, hold it a month for me. Open letters with it or something. If you don't hear anything by then, do what you please with it."

Across the thin panel, the CIA man muttered in irritation. The knife was not merely fifty bucks worth of double-edged steel to Kelly, however. For five years, the agent had sunk himself in a world without a human being to cherish. The human emotions had spilled out onto objects. Understanding the phenomenon did not make it any the less real to Kelly.

"Well," said the agent, "I'll be seeing you later."

"Hope to hell you don't," Marshal snapped back. But as Kelly started to open the door of his stall, the operative added softly, "Keep your head down, snake. And you don't owe me—we're even."

No one looked at Kelly with unusual interest as he left the restroom. Professor Vlasov followed the agent around to the Lufthansa ticket counter. Kelly did not bother to watch for Marshal, knowing that the CIA officer would wait a minute or two before he exited. Kelly had never taken an action simply because it would put someone else in his debt. Certainly he had never risked his life on the slim chance of a survivor's future gratitude. But favors were like the clap: what goes around, comes around. This one had come around at a very good time.

Kelly paid for the round-trip tickets in American dollars, took his change in Tunisian dinars. The Tunisian dinars had been originally pegged to the New Franc rather than the Old, so that it was even now worth about ten times as much as an Algerian dinar . . . and all the currency he had in either form was so much waste paper to Kelly now. He had no intention of ever seeing the wrong side of a North African border again, just in case somebody figured out his responsibility for the previous day's carnage in Algiers.

While the blonde female clerk made out the tickets, Vlasov kept up his end of a conversation in French about the one-day conference the two would be attending in Frankfurt. There was nothing illegal about traveling without luggage, but it made the fugitives memorable. A bad story was perhaps better than none at all, in case somebody checked passenger lists with the clerk.

It was nice to see a woman working again. Beyond everything else, the Arab world would forever be imprinted in Kelly's mind the same way SouthEast Asia was. Blood, bodies, and a paranoia that was not psychotic only because it was necessary.

"How are your instincts doing, Professor?" the agent asked as they walked slowly toward the exit control stations. They were clutching their Austrian passports and the forged currency and customs-control cards which Marshal had supplied as a necessary part of the package.

"Instincts?" repeated the defector uncertainly. He had been glancing about the crowd with animation.

Kelly grinned. "When you figure things are about to go through the floor, you're jumpy as a frog on a hot plate. I figure things must be okay by you if you can stand and talk like a tourist, huh?"

Vlasov smiled back. "Yes," he said, "but you must also remember that I am insane and therefore untrustworthy, yes?"

Kelly began to laugh. But not immediately.

The short man watching the fugitives in the window's reflection had brown skin and wore a djellaba. Even a glance at the man's face would have displayed his Oriental features, the flat nose and the epicanthal folds at the corners of his eyes . . . but the watcher was a careful man. In any case, Kelly's perceptions had been whip-sawed to nothing by exhaustion and elation combined. The American had not noticed the watcher as a local, much less as the Cultural Attaché of the Vietnamese Mission to Tunis.

As Kelly and the defector moved off to have their papers stamped, the Vietnamese turned to look at them directly for the first time. Then he strode briskly for the bank of pay phones in the lobby. His call was brief and simple.

It was the staff at the embassy proper, after all, who had the problem of relaying the information through an international operator.

XLIX

"Colonel," the voice whispered. "Colonel. . . ."

Nguyen rolled upright. His right hand snaked under his pillow in a motion the embassy clerk did not recognize. The pistol was not needed here, of course. But Nguyen Van Minh had been back in the jungle while he slept, not in an office of the Paris Embassy of the Democratic Republic of Vietnam.

The clerk was holding out a phone. Beyond the blinds, rain was spattering the windows of the dark office. "It is Tunis," the functionary said. "You asked to be awakened. . . ."

Nguyen took the phone. He waved the other man away. "Yes," he said, "Nguyen here."

"Colonel," said the thin voice on the other end of the line, "we have spotted them in Tunis-Carthage Airport. Their flight is Lufthansa 505, arriving Frankfurt at 18:32 local time. Today, that is."

Nguyen cursed under his breath. He had gambled that the fugitives would head directly to Paris. Well, Frankfurt was workable, the trains were fast and direct. . . .

Anything was workable. Nguyen had a man to kill, and nothing would prevent him from doing so. Honor demanded it. He would describe the act to his superiors as a duty to the State when he finally made report; but the reality went much deeper. Headlines and the colonel's identification card had carried him through some obstacles. It was Nguyen's own personality, however, that had enabled him to run rough-shod over bureaucratic delays even before Hanoi cabled assent.

"You're sure of your identification?" the colonel asked. There had been no photographs available, and only Nguyen himself of the personnel in the West had seen either Vlasov or the American who had killed Hoang.

"There can be no question," the voice from Tunis insisted. "The Russian, Vlasov—tall, pale . . . his right arm missing? And he was in company with another European, not certain, of course, but he *could* be the man you described."

"Right," Nguyen said. "Well done." He hung up abruptly, staring for some minutes at the dial of the telephone.

"Is there anything else you need, sir?" asked the clerk who still stood near the door.

Nguyen looked up as sharply as a firing pin releasing. "Yes," he said, "a line to the Frankfurt Consulate. They should be expecting the call."

He would need someone to follow the fugitives from

the airport, someone else to meet him at the train station and pass on the information. Simple enough, even for a three-man consulate which included only one intelligence officer.

The last of the work might be tricky, but that would be the colonel's pleasure to handle himself. It was work he did as well as any man alive.

Nguyen checked the magazine of his Tokarev by habit before he replaced the weapon in his holster.

L

"Come on, Professor," Kelly panted as he swung open the front door of the hotel, "you people are supposed to be used to *real* cold where you come from." The agent was tired, but he now had a loose sense of victory. Besides, he felt as if he were returning home after a long trip. Kelly always stayed at the Excelsior when he had an overnight in Frankfurt. Coming back to the hotel was a return to more than a building.

"Where I come from, we dress for the cold," Vlasov grumbled without bitterness. The agent's good humor was infectious, and the Russian, too, seemed to feel that they were at least in reach of safety. Like Kelly, he was damp from the drizzle. They had started to run the block from the train station to the hotel, but the events of previous days had simply not left either man enough strength or energy.

The desk clerk brightened as he saw the men. "Ah, Mr. Kelly," he said, "I had almost given up hope of you. Welcome."

"Emil," the agent said, "I almost gave up hope a time or two myself. Can you find a double room for my friend and me? Sorry I didn't phone ahead, but things got rushed. Oh—and our luggage is back in the airport somewhere. Do you suppose you could find a place to deliver a couple suits after hours? We'll pay what it takes to be able to change into something dry."

"Why yes, I can arrange that," said the clerk. He handed Kelly a registration card and a key with a long brass tag. "But I believe the lady said she had brought some luggage of yours along with her."

"The . . . lady?" repeated Kelly. He turned smoothly, his eyes wide open so that he had the full arc of peripheral vision that he might need. In front of him, the stairs; to the left, the front door and the rain-slicked dark beyond; to the right, the passage to the dining room and the tiny lobby beneath the stairwell. Kelly's lips smiled, and his right hand was firm on the butt of the gun in his pocket.

"What?" said the clerk. "Oh—"

"Good evening, Tom," said Annamaria Gordon. She walked from the lobby toward the reception desk. "I suppose I can call you that here." Her smile was nervous, but when she stopped a pace from Kelly she stood with lady-like dignity.

Vlasov was puzzled but not concerned. He looked from the woman to Kelly and said, "I had not understood you would be meeting us here, madame."

"How?" Kelly mouthed. His hand was still in his pocket. His eyes were staring, trying to scan everything that might be a threat, a target.

Annamaria reached into her purse with a thumb

and forefinger. She brought out Kelly's account book. "You left this in your luggage," she said. Her smile was suddenly brighter. "All I knew was that you were making up your route as you went along. You didn't have to come to Frankfurt, but it was logical, you know the city and you had to go somewhere you knew—" She riffled the pages of the spiral notebook. "You always stayed at the Excelsior when you came here. And Tom—I had to go somewhere."

"Mr. Kelly?" said the puzzled clerk.

The agent turned abruptly and completed the registration card. Over his shoulder he muttered, "I'd have come back." He looked up at the clerk. "Emil," he said, "we'll wait on the suits, thank you, until we sort things out." He started to take the room key in his right hand but stopped.

Holding the key in his left, Kelly led his companions to the stairs. His free hand hovered near the pocket of his coat.

Annamaria said in a low voice to the agent's back, "No, I had to leave. Buffy came and told me what . . . what Rufus had done. She had to talk to someone, poor thing. I . . . it was me by default, I suppose."

Kelly unlocked the door nearest the stairhead on the second floor. "If she told you that, I suppose you got a notion of what I did, too." He gestured the others past him with his left arm.

"You acted by the rules you lived by, Tom," the woman said as she entered the room. "Rufus acted by no rules at all, his or yours or anyone's. That makes him not a man but a bomb, ready to go off at random." She turned and smiled, at Vlasov and past him to Kelly. "If you get random, I'll leave you too, dear Angelo. But until then, I'll stay if you'll have me."

The agent shot the deadbolt lock. Then he reached for Annamaria. Professor Vlasov smiled and edged aside, but Kelly stopped himself anyway.

"Oh, don't worry about me," the defector said. He looked around the room. It was plainly furnished with a desk, a pair of chairs, and two single beds with feather ticks. "I can—or there is another room, the one you have, madam?"

"No!" Kelly snapped. He took a deep breath and forced a smile. "First things first, Professor," he said. "You don't leave my sight until I put you in the hands of General Pedler or somebody I've met on his staff. We're not going anywhere near the Consulate-General here, either. There isn't anybody there at night who'd be able to figure out what I was talking about. And even in the morning—well, I trust Pedler, I don't trust a Consul General I've never met. Not to make decisions that might be your life and mine if they're wrong."

"I thought you might go straight to Paris instead of—dodging again," Annamaria said. "Or Rome, or—but there aren't too many direct flights from North Africa. A friend in the Paris embassy would tell me if you were heard from there, and I—I thought I'd wait here for a few days, and then make plans if I had to."

"I've got visions of being tracked down by a world-wide network of embassy receptionists," Kelly said with a grin. He squeezed Annamaria's hand. "Anyhow, I'm glad that this time when I left clues, it was somebody I wanted to see who picked them up." He stepped over to the phone, taking off his damp jacket as he did so.

"Actually," the woman remarked with some asperity, "it wasn't a receptionist. In Paris, the Marines do that anyway. It was the Deputy Chief of Mission."

For the first time, Annamaria appeared to notice how wet both men's clothing was. "But here," she said in a cheerful voice again, "I really do have your suitcases in my room." She glanced at Vlasov. The Russian had seated himself on a corner of one of the beds. "At least you can sit in something dry, Professor," she added, "though I don't suppose it'll fit you any better than an outfit of mine would."

"Ah, take the key," the agent said. Looking at his own outstretched hand, he added, "That was a pretty dumb thing for me to say. I'll work on doing better."

Annamaria's touch and her smile were electric. Then the door clicked shut behind her.

Kelly dialed the desk. "Need to start the ball rolling," he remarked to Vlasov. As he waited with the phone to his ear, the agent noticed his coat on the bed where he had tossed it. He reached into the side pocket and brought out the pistol. "Suppose I'll have to deep-six this when you're clear," he said. "Tempted to keep it for a souvenir, but that wouldn't be fair to—"

"Yes?" said the phone.

"Emil," the agent said, "see if you can get the US Embassy in Paris for me—I don't have the number either. I need the Defense Attaché's Office, General Pedler himself if he's around. I'll wait as long as it takes."

As the phone hissed, Kelly tucked the pistol back into

the coat. He began to massage his scalp. "Never occurred to me I'd need to phone Pedler," he said to the Russian, filling the empty seconds, minutes. "Figure there'll be somebody there in the office who can raise him in an emergency. And he must have got enough word from Algiers already to know this is an emergency."

The defector was edging backward on the bed. His eyes flicked from the window to the door.

"What the hell's the matter?" Kelly demanded tensely. "Professor?"

There was a sound in the hall. Kelly looked from Vlasov to the door, his scowl smoothing to greet Annamaria. The panel swung inward without a click from the latch. There were three men in black, filling the doorway. One held an open badge case. The other two pointed objects that looked less like guns as they stepped forward. The door swung shut behind them.

The phone in Kelly's hand made a sizzling sound. Then it went dead.

"Professor Evgeny Vlasov?" said the one with the badge. He spoke in Russian with neither accent nor tone. "We are from Section T of the Bundespolizei."

"What is Section T?" Kelly asked, putting the handset down very carefully without cradling it. He watched the intruders. The distance to his coat, to his pistol, he measured in his mind rather than with his eyes or his poised right hand.

It was too far.

The intruders did not respond to Kelly, though one of them kept his—gun—trained on the agent. "You must come with us, now, Professor Evgeny Vlasov," the middle one said.

Without changing expression, the third man in black turned. He was already raising his weapon when the hall door burst inward.

If the self-styled "Federal Policeman" thought his gun was a magic wand, he reckoned without Nguyen Van Tanh. The Vietnamese colonel knew he had to kill everyone in the room; he started even as the door swung. The first five shots were so fast they could have come from an automatic weapon. Two through the torso of the man facing him, two through the spine of the man who had spoken to Vlasov. The 87-grain steel bullets howled through their initial targets; one of them shattering a window pane as it exited the room. All five shots ripped out in less than a quarter second. The last of them was kidney level through the intruder covering Kelly.

As it tore out of the body, the Tokarev bullet hit the man in black's gun. The narrow entryway dissolved in a white flash.

The muzzle blasts had been deafening in the confined space anyway, but even later the survivors were sure that the flash had been almost soundless. It was as dazzling as a magnesium flare, however, and it was by blind memory alone that Kelly dived for the coat and his pistol within it. He scrabbled to find the pocket.

Nguyen, blind as his opponent, caught the blur of motion and aimed for it by instinct. His trigger finger was as much a part of his pistol's lockwork as the firing pin itself. As it started to squeeze, Annamaria threw a jacket over Nguyen's head and jerked him backwards.

The Colonel's sixth shot cracked above Kelly's head. Kelly fired twice through the fabric of his coat. The plastic bullets smacked audibly as they hit. Nguyen thrust behind him with his left hand, weighted with a spare magazine. Annamaria caromed back into the hallway, tearing the blindfold from the Vietnamese even as Kelly shot him twice more—once in the center of mass, once behind the ear—and the Tokarev slipped from fingers which had already swung it on target one final time.

The pistol skidded on the carpet. Its owner did not. He sprawled instead like rice pouring from a fifty-kilo sack.

Kelly raised himself. His coat was smoldering, adding its fumes to those curling from the muzzle of his pistol. White sulphur smoke mixed in layers with the sweeter odor of nitro powder. The American stared at the fallen Tokarev. The pistol looked as worn and as deadly as a Marine sniper.

Annamaria was getting up. Kelly stepped to her, over Nguyen's body. "Are you all right?" the woman asked before the agent himself could speak.

"Bastard was better than me," said Kelly, tossing his own empty weapon to the nearer bed. Professor Vlasov had stood up also. There was an expression of hope dawning slowly over his face.

"Good thing I wasn't alone this time," the agent said. He drew Annamaria up with a controlled grace that belied the adrenalin tremors shaking all his muscles. "Best thing in the world that I'm not alone any more," he said.

"They can be defeated," the Professor said. "By guns, by my devices. By thousands of my devices above Earth."

Kelly released Annamaria. "It was the KGB," he said

loudly. "It was the KGB, and one of them dropped a grenade!"

Doors were opening, spilling bursts of pop music and questions in a variety of languages. Wet air through the broken window swirled the powder smoke.

Professor Vlasov bent. The body of only one of the intruders remained after the blast, eyes staring upward. Vlasov ran the fingers of one hand over the floor. In the center of the area, the carpeting was gone and the hardwood surface beneath was charred through to the concrete base.

Inches further from the heart of the blast, the nylon nap had melted and been drawn up in long spikes toward a momentary vortex. Annamaria knelt beside the defector.

There was a loud gasp from the hall. Emil stood there, gaping into the room. Kelly could not be sure whether the clerk was more horrified by the dead bodies or the blast-eroded walls and floor. "Mr. Kelly!" Emil said. "Mr. Kelly!"

Kelly nodded. "It'll be taken care of, Emil," he said. "You know me. It'll be taken care of."

The clerk opened his mouth, but further words would not come. He turned briskly and clattered down several steps before he paused. "Oh, Mr. Kelly," he said, a good servant even in the midst of disaster, "there was a fault with the line, somewhere; but your call has been put through now." He bounded down the rest of the steps to his desk.

The phone muttered. Kelly looked from Vlasov to Annamaria. The woman was running her fingers over the face of the man in black. Kelly picked up the fallen handpiece. "Hello?" he said.

"Hello!" the phone repeated. "I said, this is Major August Nassif. You'll have to state your business to get through to the general, I don't care *who* you are, and I'm not going to hold this line much longer!"

"This is Tom Kelly," the agent replied. "I'm about to be waist deep in Frankfurt cops." He looked from the living humans to the body on the floor. "I think General Pedler's looking for me. Tell him my business is Skyripper."

Annamaria's hand gripped and tugged. The face of the thing on the floor was the color of raw cinnabar. The nose was a single slit, the mouth a round hole with teeth like a lamprey's around the inner margin. Fragments of the mask Annamaria had removed still clung to the skin like tendrils of white gauze.

"Tell him," Annamaria said in a clear voice, "that the business of the world is Skyripper."

Fortress

DEDICATION

To Tom Doherty,
who published my first book also,
and most of those in between.

ACKNOWLEDGEMENTS

Among the people who helped with bits of
unclassified background on this one are Glenn
and Helen Knight; Bernadette Bosky
and Arthur Hlavaty; and Congressman
Newt Gingrich and his personal assistant,
Laurie James. Many thanks to all of them.

Prologue

Another 1965

Sergeant Tom Kelly listened to John F. Kennedy's fifth
State of the Union Address—his so-called "Buck Rogers
Speech"—at a firebase in the Shuf Mountains, watching
Druse 122-mm rockets arc toward Beirut across the night
sky.

The broadcast, carried live over the Armed Forces
Levantine Network, hissed and sputtered in the plug
earphone of Kelly's cheap portable radio. Inside the high-
sided command track against which he leaned, the young
sergeant could have gotten a much clearer signal through
some of the half million dollars worth of communications-
intercept equipment which the Radio Research vehicle
carried. This was good enough, though, for a soldier who
was off duty and waiting for the attack Druse message
traffic made almost certain.

Shooooo . . . hissed the green ball of a bombardment
rocket.

"Our enemies, the enemies of freedom," said the President, more distant from Kelly's reality than seven time zones could imply, "have proven in Hungary, in Cuba, and in Lebanon that they respect nothing in their international dealings except strength. Their armies are poised on the boundaries of Eastern Europe, ready to hurl themselves across the remainder of the continent at the least sign of weakness among the Western democracies."

By daylight, the berm which bulldozers had turned up around the firebase for protection was scarcely less sterile in appearance than the crumbling rock of the hills from which it was carved. Now, in the soft darkness, the landscape breathed, Kelly's left hand caressed the heavy wooden stock of his M14, knowing that beyond the berm other soldiers were nervously gripping their own weapons: Mausers abandoned by the Turks in 1917; Polish-made Kalashnikovs slipped across the Syrian border in donkey panniers; rocket-propelled grenades stamped in Russian or Chinese . . .

"In Europe and the Middle East," continued the President in a nasal voice further attenuated by the transmission and the radio's tinny speaker, "in Africa and Latin America—wherever the totalitarians and their surrogates choose to test us, the free world must stand firm. Furthermore, ladies and gentlemen of Congress, we in the United States must undertake an initiative on behalf of the free world which will convince our enemies that we have the strength to withstand them no matter how great the forces they gather on Earth itself."

The five tubes of howitzer battery—the sixth hog was

deadlined for repair—cut loose in a ragged salvo. The white powderflashes were a lightninglike dazzle across the firebase while the side-flung shock waves from the muzzle brakes hammered tent roofs and raised dust from the parched ground. The short-barreled one-five-fives were firing at high angles and with full charges. Nothing to do with the turbaned riflemen crouching to attack, perhaps nothing to do with even the Druse rockets sailing down toward the airport in the flat curves of basketballs shot from thirty feet out.

"We must have an impregnable line of defense and an arsenal of overwhelming magnitude in the Heavens themselves," continued Kennedy through the squeal of hydraulic rammers seating the shells of the next salvo. Clicks of static from command transmissions cut across the broadcast band, but Kelly was used to building sense from messages far more shattered and in a variety of languages beyond English. He was good at that—at languages—and his fingertips again tried to wiggle the magazine of his rifle, making sure it was locked firmly into the receiver.

"Space is both a challenge—" said the President as Kelly's hearing returned after the muzzle blasts of the howitzers which were more akin to physical punishment than to noise. "—Now also the unbreachable shield of freedom and the spear of retribution which cannot be blunted by treacherous attack as our land-based weapons might be."

The breechblock of a fifty-caliber machine gun clanged from the far side of the firebase as the weapon was charged, freezing time and Tom Kelly's soul. Only the sounds of the howitzers reloading and traversing their turrets slightly followed, however. Nothing Kelly had seen in ninety-seven days in the field suggested the hogs were going to hit anything useful, but their thunderous discharges made waiting for an attack easier than it would have been with only the stars for company.

"My detailed proposals . . ." said the radio before the words disintegrated into a hiss like frying bacon—louder than the voice levels had been, so it couldn't be the French dry cells giving out. . . .

"Fuckin' A!" snarled Chief Warrant Officer Platt as he ducked out the rear hatch of the command vehicle. He, the intercept team's commander, was a corpulent man who wore two fighting knives on his barracks belt and carried the ear of a Druse guerrilla tissue-wrapped in a watch case. "We're getting jammed across all bands! What the fuck *is* this?"

Something with a fluctuating glow deep in the violet and presumably ultraviolet was crossing the sky very high up and very swiftly. A word or two,—"dominance"—crept through a momentary pause in the static before the howitzers, linked by wire to the Tactical Operations Center, fired again.

"Commie recon satellite," Platt muttered, his eyes following Kelly's to the bead shimmering so far above the surface of dust, buffeted by hot, gray strokes of howitzer propellant. "You know those bastards're targeting us down to the last square meter!"

Tom Kelly reached for the tuning dial of the radio with the hand which was not sweating on the grip of his rifle. Anybody who could come within a hundred yards of a point target, using a bombardment rocket aimed by adjusting a homemade bipod under the front of the launching tube, ought to be running the US space program instead of a Druse artillery company. The hell with the satellite—assuming that's what it was. If the rag-heads could jam the whole electromagnetic spectrum like that, there were worse problems than Radio Research teams becoming as useless as tits on a boar. . . .

"—domestic front," said the radio just as Kelly's fingers touched it, "the curse of racial injustice calls for—"

Tom Kelly never did hear the rest of that speech because just as normal reception resumed, a one-twenty-two howled over the berm and exploded near a tank-recovery vehicle. It was the first of the thirty-seven rockets preceding the attack of a reinforced Druse battalion.

The only physical scar Kelly took home from that one was on his hand, burned by the red-hot receiver of his rifle as he worked to clear a jam.

Another 1985

The three helicopters were orbiting slowly, as if tethered to the monocle ferry on the launchpad five hundred meters below. When the other birds rotated so that the West Texas sun caught the cameras aimed from their bays, the long lenses blazed as if they were lasers themselves rather than merely tools with which to record a test of laser propulsion.

The sheathing which would normally have roofed the passenger compartments of the helicopters had been removed, leaving the multi-triangulated frame tubing and a view straight upward for the cameras and the men waiting for what was about to happen on the launchpad.

Sharing the bay of the bird carrying Tom Kelly were a cameraman, a project scientist named Desmond, and a pair of colonels in Class A uniforms, Army green and Air Force blue, rather than the flight suits that Kelly thought would have been more reasonable. The military officers seemed to be a good deal more nervous than the scientist was; and unless Kelly was misreading them, their concern was less about the test itself than about him—the staff investigator for Representative Carlo Bianci, chairman of the House Subcommittee on Space Defense. Sometimes it seemed to Kelly that he'd spent all his life surrounded by people who were worried as hell about what he was going to do next. Occasionally, of course, people would have been smart to worry more than they did. . . .

The communications helmet Kelly had been issued for the test had a three-position switch beneath the left earpiece, but only one channel on it was live. He could not hear either the chatter of the Army pilots in the cockpit or the muttered discussions of the two officers in the passenger bay with him, though the latter could speak to him when they chose to throw their own helmet switches forward. The clop of the blades overhead was more a fact than an impediment to normal speech, but the intake rush of the twin-turbine power plant created an ambiance through which Kelly could hear nothing but what the officers chose to direct to him through the intercom circuitry.

"Someday," Kelly said aloud, "people are going to learn that the less they try to hide, the less problem they have explaining things. But I don't expect the notion to take hold in the military any time soon."

"Pardon?" asked Desmond, the first syllable minutely clipped by his voice-activated microphone. The scientist was Kelly's age or a few years younger, a short-bearded man who slung a pen-caddy from one side of his belt and a worn-looking calculator from the other. It was probably his normal working garb—as were the dress uniforms of the public-affairs colonels, flacks of the type which Kelly would have found his natural enemy even if they hadn't been military.

"I'd been meaning to ask you, Dr. Desmond," said Kelly, rubbing from his eyes the prickliness of staring into the desert of the huge Fort Bliss reservation, "just why you think the initial field test failed?"

"Ah, I think it's important to recall, Mr. Kelly," interjected one of the colonels—it was uncertain which through the headphones— "that the test was by no means a failure. The test vehicle performed perfectly throughout eighty-three percent of the spectrum planned—"

"Well good *God*, Boardman," snapped the project scientist, "it blew *up*, didn't it? That's what you mean, isn't it?" Desmond continued, snapping his head around from the officers across the bay to Kelly seated on the portion of the bench closest to the fully-opened starboard hatch. "I certainly don't consider that, that *fireworks* display a success."

Kelly smiled, the expression only incidentally directed toward the colonels. "Though I gather many of the systems *did* work as planned, Doctor?" he said, playing the scientist now that he had enough of a personality sample from which to work. Even among the project's civilians, there were familiar—and not wholly exclusive—categories of scientists and scientific politicians. Desmond had seemed to be in the former category, but Kelly had found no opportunity to speak to him alone.

The public affairs officers were probably intended to smother honest discussion within the spotting helicopter the same way the administrators had done on the ground. That plan was being frustrated by what was more than a personality quirk: Desmond could not imagine that anything the military officers said or wished was of any concern to him. It was not a matter of their rank or anyone's position in a formal organizational chart: Colonels Boardman and Johnson were simply of another species.

"Yes, absolutely," agreed the project scientist as he shook his head in quick chops. "Nothing went wrong during air-breathing mode, nothing we could see in the telemetry, of course—it'd have been nice to get the *hardware* back for a hands-on."

"I think you'd better get your goggles in place now, Mr. Kelly," said the Air Force officer, sliding his own protective eye wear into place. The functional thermoplastic communications helmets looked even sillier atop dress uniforms than they did over the civilian clothes Desmond, and Kelly himself, wore. "For safety's sake, you know."

Kelly was anchored to a roof strap with his left hand by habit that freed his right for the rifle he did not carry here, not on this mission or in this world where "cut-throat" meant somebody might lose a job or a contract. . . . He looked at the PR flacks, missing part of what Desmond was saying because his mind was on things that were not the job of the Special Assistant to Representative Bianci.

The colonels straightened, one of them with a grimace of repulsion, and neither of them tried again to break in as the project scientist continued, "—plating by the aluminum oxide particles we inject with the on-board hydrogen to provide detonation nuclei during that portion of the pulsejet phase. Chui-lin insists the plasma itself scavenges the chambers and that the fault must be the multilayer mirrors themselves despite the sapphire coating."

"But there's just as much likelihood of blast damage when you're expelling atmosphere as when you're running on internal fuel, isn't there?" said Kelly, who had done his homework on this one as he did on any task set him by Representative Bianci; and as he had done in the past, when others tasked him.

"Exactly, *exactly*," Desmond agreed, chopping his head. "Just a time factor, says Chui-lin, but there's *no* sign of overheating until we switch modes, and I don't think dropping the grain size as we've done will be—"

"Fifteen seconds," boomed a voice from the control center on the ground, and this time Kelly and the scientist did slide the goggles down over their eyes. The cameraman hunched behind the long shroud of his viewing screen. A guidance mechanism as sophisticated as anything in the latest generation of air-to-air missiles should center the lens on the test vehicle, despite any maneuvers the target or the helicopter itself carried out. Machinery could fail, however, and the backup cameraman was determined that he would not fail—because he was *good*, not because he was worried about his next efficiency report.

The monocle ferry was a disk only eighteen feet in diameter, and at its present slant distance of almost half a mile from the helicopters it would have been easy to ignore were it not so nearly alone on a barren yellow landscape. With Vandenburg and Cape Canaveral irrevocably surrendered to the US Space Command when it was formed in 1971, the Army and Air Force had chosen Fort

Bliss as the site for their joint attempt to circumvent their new rival's control of space weaponry.

Not only was the huge military reservation empty enough to make a catastrophic failure harmless, but its historical background as the center of Army Air Defense Training lent a slight color to the services' claim that they were not trying to develop a "space weapon" of their own in competition with the Space Command.

Not that that would help them if Carlo Bianci decided the program should be axed. The congressman from the Sixth District of Georgia had made a career—a religion, some critics claimed—of space defense, and it wasn't the sort of thing he permitted interservice squabbling to screw up.

"Now, there *may* be a critical limit to grain size," Dr. Desmond was saying, "below which none of the aluminum will form hot-spots on the mirror surface, but at these energy levels it won't take more than a few *molecules* to—"

"Go," said the control center, and the landscape changed in intensity.

The beams from the six chemical laser lift stations in orbit above the launch site were in the near infrared at a wavelength of 1.8 microns. Not only was light of that frequency invisible to the human eye, it was absorbed by the cornea instead of being focused by the lens to the potential injury of the retina. The wavelength was a relatively inefficient one for transmitting power, especially through an atmosphere which would have passed a much higher percentage of the ultraviolet. The five megajoules of energy involved in the test, however, meant that even the least amount of reflection raised an unacceptable risk of blindness and worse if the operation were in the visible spectrum or shorter.

"Go-o-o . . ." whispered Desmond, probably unaware that he had spoken aloud. Tom Kelly leaned outward, bringing his shoulder and helmet into the dry, twenty-knot airstream.

The six-ton saucer quivered as it drank laser energy through the dozen windows of segmented corundum which ringed its upper surface like the eyes of a monstrous insect. The central hub of the ferry contained the one-man cockpit, empty now except for instrumentation, which did not rotate as the blast chambers around the saucer's rim began to expel air flash-heated within them by laser pulses.

Dust, as much a part of West Texas as it was of the hills above Beirut, rippled in a huge, expanding doughnut from the concrete pad. It formed a translucent bed for the ferry, a mirage landscape on which the saucer seemed to rest instead of lifting as planned. Then the dust was gone, a yellow-gray curtain across distant clumps of Spanish bayonet, and the ferry itself was a lens rather than a disk as it shot past the helicopters circling at five hundred meters.

"All *right*!" blurted Kelly, jerking his eyes upward to track the monocle through the frame members and shimmering helicopter rotors against a sky made amber by his goggles.

"Twenty-two g's!" babbled the project scientist happily. "Almost from the point of liftoff! There's no way Space Command's ground-lift barges can match that—or *any* chemically-fueled launcher."

The chopper rocked between paired sonic booms, a severe one followed by an impact of lesser intensity. The monocle ferry had gone supersonic even before it reached the altitude of the helicopters, buffeting them with a shock wave reflected from the ground as well as the pulse streaming directly from the vehicle's surface. The roar of the ferry's exhaust followed a moment later, attenuating rapidly like that of an aircraft making a low-level pass.

"All *right*," Kelly repeated, disregarding the colonels, who he knew would be beaming at his enthusiasm. There was a hell of a lot more to this "air defense" program than the mere question of how well the hardware worked; but hardware that *did* work gave Kelly a glow of satisfaction with the human race, and he didn't give a hoot in hell about who knew it. It was their lookout if they thought he was dumb enough to base his recommendations on that alone.

Their helicopter and the other two essed out of their slow starboard orbits, banking a little to port to make it easier for the cameras and observers to follow an object high enough above them to be effectively vertical. There were supposed to be chase planes, T-38 trainers with more cameras, but Kelly could see no sign of them at the moment. The ferry itself was no more than a sunstruck bead of amber.

"Normally," Dr. Desmond explained, "we'd continue in air-breathing mode to thirty kilometers before switching to internal fuel. For the purpose of his test, however, we'll convert to hydrogen very shortly in order to—"

"God almighty!" cried Boardman, the Air Force flack, so far forgetting himself that he started to lurch to his feet against the motion of the helicopter. "For the *demonstration* you do this?"

"We're modifying the test sequence in response to earlier results, of course," the scientist said, glancing over at the military man.

Kelly continued to look upward, squinting by habit, though the goggles made that unnecessary. Boardman didn't matter. He was typical of people, not necessarily stupid ones, who cling to a view of reality against available evidence and their own presumable benefit. In this case, the public affairs officer was obviously so certain that the ferry would blow up that he preferred the test do nothing to advance the project rather than have Bianci's man watch a catastrophic failure.

The bead of light which had almost disappeared detonated into a fireball whose color the goggles shifted into the green.

The cameraman had been only a nervous spectator while his unit's servos tracked the ferry with inhuman skill. Now he squeezed the override trigger in the right grip and began to manually follow the shower of fragments picked out by the sun as they tumbled and danced. His left hand made minute adjustments to the focal length of his lens, shortening it to keep as nearly as possible the whole drifting mass within his field of view.

"God damn it to hell," said Dr. Desmond very distinctly before he lowered his head, took off his commo helmet, and slammed the helmet as hard as he could against the aluminum deck of the helicopter. It bounced, but the length of communications cord kept it from flying out the open hatch as it tried to do. The two officers straightened their backs against the bulkhead with expressions of disapproval and concern.

Kelly slid his goggles back up on the brow of his helmet, sneezing at the shock of direct sunlight again. He put a hand on the scientist's nearer shoulder, squeezing hard enough to be noticed but without trying to raise Desmond's head from where it was buried in his hands. " 'Sokay," the ex-soldier muttered, part of him aware that the scientist couldn't possibly hear him and another part equally sure that it *wasn't* okay, that even future success would not expunge this memory of something which mattered very much vaporizing itself in the Texas sky.

"It's okay," Kelly said, repeating words he'd had to use too often before, the words a lieutenant had spoken to him the fire-shot evening when Kelly held the torso of a friend who no longer had a head.

"Maybe switching to straight calcium carbonate'll do the trick," Kelly's lips whispered while the PR men grimaced at the undirected fury in the veteran's eyes.

"Oh, good evening, Mr. Kelly," said the young woman at the front desk—a second-year student out of Emory, if Kelly remembered correctly. She looked flustered as usual when she spoke to the veteran. She wasn't the receptionist, just an intern with a political science major getting some hands-on experience; but the hour was late, and service to the public—to possible constituents—was absolutely the first staff priority in all of Representative Bianci's offices.

"Marcelle, Marcelle," said Tom Kelly, stretching so that his overcoat gaped widely and the attaché case in his left hand lifted toward the ceiling. His blazer veed to either side of the button still fastening it, baring most of the shirt and tie beneath but continuing to hide the back of Kelly's waistband.

He'd been on planes that anybody with a bottle of gasoline could hijack to God knew where; he'd been walking on Capitol Hill at night, a place as dangerous as parts of Beirut that he'd patrolled in past years with flak jacket and automatic rifle; and anyway, he was a little paranoid, a little crazy, he'd never denied that. . . . It was no problem him going armed unless others learned about it . . . and with care, that would happen only when Tom Kelly was still standing and somebody else wasn't.

Kelly grinned at the little intern, broadly, as he had learned to do because the scar tissue above the left corner of his mouth turned a lesser smile into a snarling grimace. "It you don't start calling me Tom, m'dear, I'm going to have to get formal with you. I won't be mistered by a first name, I've seen too much of that . . . and I don't *like* 'mister.' Okay?"

All true; and besides, he was terrible on names, fucking terrible, and remembering them had been for the past three years the hardest part of doing a good job for an elected official. But Marcelle, heaven knew what her last name was, colored and said, "I'm sorry, Tom, I'll really remember the next time."

Filing cabinets and free-standing mahogany bookshelves split the rear of the large room into a number of desk alcoves, many of them now equipped with terminals to the mainframe computer in the side office to the right. Another of the staff members, a pale man named Duerning, with a mind as sharp as Kelly's own—and as

different from the veteran's as Brooklyn is from Beirut—
was leaning over a desk, supporting himself with a palm
on the paper-strewn wood. It was not until Carlo Bianci
stood up beside Duerning, however, that Kelly realized
that his boss was here rather than in the private office to
the left where the closed door had seemed to advertise his
presence. Never assume. . . .

"That's all for tonight, Murray," said Representative
Bianci, clapping his aide on the shoulder in a gesture of
camaraderie as natural as it was useful to a politician. He
stepped toward Kelly as Duerning, nodding his head,
shifted papers into a briefcase.

Carlo Bianci was Kelly's height and of the same squat
build, though the representative was further from an ideal
training weight than his aide and the difference was more
than the decade's gap between their ages. Nonetheless,
Bianci's thick gray hair was the only sign that the man
might be fifty, and he was in damned good shape for anyone in an office job. Kelly suspected that Bianci's paunch
was really a reservoir like a camel's hump, enabling the
man to survive under the strain of constant eighteen-hour
days for the decade he had been in Congress.

At the moment Bianci was wearing a blue jogging
suit, which meant it was not expectation of a roll-call vote
which kept him in his office at ten PM, and something was
sticking worry lines around the smile of greeting which
accompanied his handshake for Kelly. "Wasn't sure you'd
be in tonight, Tom," he said, and there was an undercurrent
below those ordinary words. "Thought you'd maybe want
to get some rest."

"Well, don't count on me opening the office tomorrow

morning," Kelly said, expecting to be led toward the door of the congressman's private office. Instead, Bianci guided him with a finger of his left hand into what was basically the workroom of the suite in the Old House Office Building, a bull pen where the mainframe, the coffeepot, and a crowd of desks and files would not normally be seen by constituents. "I'm on El Paso time and anyway, I always need to wind down awhile after I get off a plane. Figured I'd key in my report if you weren't around for a verbal debrief tonight."

"Well, how was the demonstration?" Bianci asked. He leaned back against a desk whose legs squealed slightly on the hardwood as they accepted the thrust.

"It really *was* a test," Kelly said, frowning as he made the final decisions about what to present to his employer, "and I guess the short answer is that there's bits of graphite composite and synthetic sapphire scattered all over West Texas and New Mexico."

"Sounds like I was right six months ago," said the congressman, with a nod. "Overripe for the ax, *exactly* the sort of boondoggle that weakens the country in the name of defending it."

"That's the hell of it, sir," Kelly said with a deeper frown, the honorific given by habitual courtesy to a man he felt deserved it. "Like you say, typical interservice wrangling. And you bet, the ferry went off like a bomb, she did that. But—" He shrugged out of his overcoat, his eyes concentrating on that for a moment while his mind raced with the real problem. When he looked up again, it was to say, "Damned if I don't think they've got something useful there. Maybe useful, at any rate."

"'Hard-nosed Investigator Suckered by Military'?" said Bianci, quotes in his voice and enough smile on his lips to make the words a joke rather than a serious question.

"Yeah," said Kelly, sitting straddled on a chair across the narrow aisle from his employer, the wooden chair back a pattern of bars before him, "it bothers the *hell* outa me to believe anything I hear from the Air Force. I remember—"

He looked up grinning, because it hadn't happened to him and this long after the fact it wouldn't have mattered anyway. "I remember," he said, rubbing his scalp with a broad hand whose back was itself covered with curling black hair, "the Skybolt missile that was gonna make Russki air defense obsolete. Hang 'em under the wings of B-52s and launch from maybe a thousand miles out beyond the interceptors and the surface to air missiles. . . ."

He was tired and wired and there were too many memories whispering through his brain. "B-52" had called up transparent images, unwanted as all of that breed were unwanted except in the very blackest moods. The Anti-Lebanon Mountains were lighting up thirty clicks to the east with a quivering brilliance, white to almost blue and hard as an assassin's eyes: seven-hundred-and-fifty-pound bombs, over a thousand of them, dropping out of the stratosphere in a pattern a kilometer wide and as long as the highway from Kelly's family home to the nearest town. The flashes could be seen for half a minute before the shock waves began to be heard at Kelly's firebase; but even at that distance, the blasts were too loud to speak over.

"Damn, that was a *long* time back," Kelly muttered

aloud, shaking his head to clear it, and Representative Bianci nodded in agreement with what he thought he had heard, part of a story about a failed missile. "Early sixties, yes?" he said aloud, again giving Kelly the impression that he was being softened up for something on an agenda the congressman had not yet broached.

"Oh, right," the younger man said with an engaging smile to cover an embarrassment known only to him. He couldn't lose it with Carlo, couldn't have his mind ricocheting off on its own paths in front of his boss. Kelly and Representative Bianci were as close to being friends as either's temperament allowed, and his support—what he told Kelly he had done, and what the aide knew from the result he *must* have done—had saved the veteran from the very bad time he'd earned by the method of his separation from the National Security Agency. But Carlo couldn't afford to associate with a psycho, a four-plus crazy like some people already said Tom Kelly was.

"Right, they tested Skybolt and they tested it, the Air Force did," the aide continued. "Kept reporting successes and partial successes—to the Brits, too, mind, the British government was basing its whole defense policy on Skybolt—right down to the time the Air Force canceled the program because they never once had gotten the thing to work right."

Kelly leaned back, flexing his big arms against the wood of the chair they gripped. "Turned out on one of those 'partial successes,' they'd detached the missile from the bomber carrying it, and it hadn't ignited, hadn't done *anything* but drop a couple miles and put a new crater in the desert. S'far as anybody could tell, the only thing the flyboys had tested successfully was the law of gravity, and that continued to perform up to specs."

"Which is why you're on my staff, Tom," said Bianci after an easy chuckle. "But you don't think the monocle ferry's another Skybolt?"

Kelly sighed and knuckled his eyes, relaxed again now that he was back in the present. "Well, Hughes isn't prime contractor," he said, "that's one thing to the good."

He opened his eyes and looked up to meet the congressman's. Kelly was calm, now, and his subconscious had organized his data into a personal version of truth, the most he ever tried to achieve. "Look, sir," he said, "they've got a glitch in the hydrogen pulsejet mode they need from a hundred thousand feet to, say, thirty miles, Probably soluble, but on this sort of thing you won't get guarantees from anybody you'd trust to tell the truth about the weather outside."

The aide spread his hands, palms down to either side of the chair, forming a base layer for the next edifice of facts. Bianci's eyes blinked unwilled from Kelly's face to the pinkish burn scars on both wrists. The man himself had when asked muttered, "Just a kerosene fire, price of bein' young and dumb," but the file Bianci had read carefully before he'd hired Tom Kelly spoke also of the helicopter and the three men dragged from the wreckage by Sergeant E-5 Kelly, who had ignored the facts that one of the men was dead already and that the ruptured fuel tank was likely to blow at any instant.

"If they *do* get that one cured," Kelly continued, absorbed in what he was saying, "then sure, there's a thousand other things that can go unfixably wrong, all along the line—but that's technology, not this project alone, and the one guy out there in El Paso willing to *talk* gave me a good feeling. Don't think he'd be workin' on a boondoggle. And okay, that's *my* gut and I'm not in the insurance business either."

He looked at the print on the wall before him, then added, "But I think it might work. And I think it might be nice to have an alternative to Fortress."

"Which works very well," said the congressman. The only sign that his own emotional temperature had risen was the way his fingers , playing with the modem beside him on the desk, stilled. Belief in space-based defense, as embodied in Fortress, had more than any other single factor brought Carlo Bianci into politics.

The framed print on the wall behind Bianci was from the original design studies on Fortress. The artist had chosen to make the doughnut of shielding material look smooth and metallic. In fact the visible outer surface was lumpy and irregular, chunks of slag spit into Earth orbit by the mass driver at the American lunar base and fused there into armor for Fortress.

The space station itself was a dumbbell spinning within the doughnut. Living quarters for the crews were in the lobes, where centrifugal force counterfeited gravity, but the real work of Fortress was done in the motionless spherical hub. A great-winged ferry, launched like an aircraft from a Space Command base in Florida or California, was shown docking at the "north" pole—the axis from which the station's direction of rotation was counterclockwise.

The array of nuclear weapons depending from the

south pole had been left out of the painting. Three thousand H-bombs, each with its separate reentry vehicle, would have been too nightmarish for even the most hawkish of voters. That was often the case with the truth.

Mounted on the shielding were multi-tube rocket batteries intended to smash any warhead that came close enough to Fortress to do harm. The primary defenses were out of the scale of the picture, however: the constellation of X-ray lasers which orbited with the space station. Each was a small nuclear weapon which, when triggered, sent in the moment of its dissolution up to a hundred and forty-four simultaneous pulses, each capable of destroying any missile or warhead which had risen above the blanket of the atmosphere.

"It's everything that President Kennedy dreamed of," Kelly agreed, aware of what he was saying and too tired to more than wonder why he was now voicing an opinion that could cost him a job he needed. "An orbital arsenal defended by X-ray lasers and armored with lunar slag that can stop the beam weapons, which the lasers can't."

Bianci nodded, both because he agreed and because he *wanted* to be able to agree with his aide on a matter of such emotional importance to him. "A point in vacuum," he said in a voice that carried a touch of courtliness with no sign of accent from his Italian grandparents, "that can be defended as regions smothered in an atmosphere can't be. No matter how many missiles the Russians build, no matter *how* accurate they become, they can't pierce the defenses of Fortress and knock out our retaliatory capability—as they could with missile silos on Earth."

"And could with submarine launchers," Kelly said,

nodding in the same rhythm as his employer, "if they can find the subs—which we can't prove they won't be able to do tomorrow with hardware no more unlikely than radar would've seemed fifty years ago."

"Then what's the problem with Fortress?" said Bianci, relaxing.

"Fortress is the ultimate offensive weapon," Kelly said softly, straightening his fingers and looking at the backs of his hands. Philosophy wasn't something he really got upset about, and that's all they were discussing here. If space weaponry ever became more than a matter of philosophy, *all* the survivors were going to get real upset. . . . "Well, nothing's ultimate, say the 'here-and-now maximum' offensive weapon."

"Defensive weapon in our hands, of course," the representative said, more in correction than as part of an expected argument. His buttocks shifted enough that the desk scraped beneath him.

"Boss," said Tom Kelly, standing and swinging the solid chair to the side rather than stepping around it, "it's defensive because the Reds—or whoever the hell—know that if they attack us, Fortress'll blast 'em back to the Neolithic—with bone cancer. You think *nobody'd* do that, not a risk but a guarantee. . . ."

The squat aide had taken two absentminded steps deeper into the bull pen. Now he turned and smiled as he faced his employer. "And I 'spect you're right, Carlo, for the politicians. But I've met folks who weren't going to back off whatever happened to them or behind 'em." He sighed, then added, "Hell, boss. On bad days I've been that sorta folks."

Congressman Bianci looked at his subordinate and, as if he had no inkling of what had just been admitted, said, "Then we can agree that we're safe so long as the politicians control the Kremlin—as they have at least since Rasputin died"—Kelly chuckled—"and that was true even under Stalin."

"Oh, hell, yes, Carlo," agreed Kelly easily and honestly. "Fortress is the most practical road to peace—bottom line peace—that anybody's come up with yet." He grinned in a way that would have been boyish except for the lines in and on his face. "There's just a certain beauty to a fleet of mirrors up there"—he gestured toward the ceiling and beyond with his trigger finger—"reflecting laser beams into however many warheads're coming over."

"We'll think about it," said Bianci, straightening onto his feet again. "Specifically, you'll have me a report in sixty days on the probable result of moving the project to Space Command. If we *do* decide to save it, there's no point in making a 'logical' change that results in a balls-up."

Well, he was still on the payroll, thought Tom Kelly as he nodded and said, "Yeah, like transferring ground-support aviation from the Army that needs it to the Air Force that isn't interested in anything yucky like mud and Russian tanks."

The veteran stretched, figuring that tomorrow was time aplenty for him to write up the report since he'd given Carlo the core of it verbally. "Well, boss," he said—

—And Representative Bianci said, toward a far corner of the room, "There are two people who said they'd like to talk to you today, Tom."

"My goodness, two of 'em?" Kelly straightened deliberately from his back-arched posture and swept the room with his eyes: nobody but the two of them. He'd have heard breathing or motion if a team were hidden behind filing cabinets and privacy panels. . . . "What'd they want to talk about, Carlo?"

Bianci was not deceived by his aide's voice, though it was as smooth as the lockwork of a fine revolver slipping to full cock. For all that, nothing in the congressman's own background permitted him to translate data from Kelly's file into the shock and flame of reality. "Not Fortress, I believe, Tom," said Bianci. "Not—" He looked up with the appearance of candor, a politician's look, but possibly real this time. "This appears to be a new development of some sort on which they think you can be of some help." Everything Tom Kelly saw or heard stood out from its background for the length of time he focused on it. Representative Bianci was a figure with only a blur behind him—unless something should have moved in the periphery of Kelly's vision—as he licked his lips and continued, "This isn't in the purview of your employment with me, Tom. But it would be a personal favor to me if you agreed to talk to them."

"Sure, boss, I understand," said Kelly, and he *did* understand. Bianci had been too smart to give him an order regarding a subject on which Kelly took orders from no one; and the kind of pressure that could be exerted on an elected official, even a powerful one, even an honorable man like Carlo Bianci, whose eyes had been pretty well open when he hired a man who'd been training Kurdish guerrillas for the National Security Agency before he separated on very bad terms indeed. . . . "Where do they want to see me? Langley? Meade?"

"I told them," said the congressman with the stumbling enunciation of a man thinking of the result of what he was saying rather than the specific words his tongue tried to form, "that I'd relay their message, and that they were welcome to wait in my private office, though I had no reason to expect you in tonight." Bianci smiled. "I gather they had a better notion of your schedule than I did."

"Better'n both of us, I guess," Kelly said, unbuttoning his sportcoat and stretching again, bending forward at the waist and raising his hands locked behind his back. It was the position of a man being lifted to the ceiling in the cheap medieval substitute for the rack. The position loosened the great muscles of his shoulders—tension had locked them as tight as the cables winching in a whale for flensing.

If you watch a man carefully over a period of time, you *do* know him better than he knows himself, because the habitual activities that never reach his conscious mind stand out as statistical peaks in the summary of his behavior. Of *course* Tom Kelly would check in at Bianci's office, because he always did after a tour—though there was no necessity to do so, and though Kelly himself thought he was flipping a mental coin in the airport to determine whether he went to his Arlington apartment or the office in the Longworth Building.

"Well," said Kelly, massaging first his left hand with his right, then reversing the activity, "if they've been waiting this long, I guess it's only polite to look in on 'em."

"You don't have to, you know." The congressman

stood up faster than he had intended, his muscles reacting sharply to the charged atmosphere. "Believe me, Tom, that wasn't an order."

The veteran clapped Bianci on the shoulder with his left hand while the right clenched and unclenched in its own set of unconscious loosening exercises. "No sweat, boss," Kelly said. "You're a good enough friend to ask me a bigger favor'n that." He grinned; and though he saw his employer cringe away from the expression, Kelly didn't broaden the grin into something that might have been socially acceptable.

The two men walked into the front office, moving with tight, precise steps and resolutely looking at desks instead of each other. The door to the private office was covered in dark blue leather tacked down by brass studs corroded to a dull similarity. The chemicals used to tan leather were hard on brass, so you should never keep cartridges in leather belt loops for any length of time. . . .

Wrong thing to think about.

"Carlo," said Tom Kelly as they stepped around the receptionist's desk. Everyone was gone from the office but the pair of them and whoever was beyond the blue door, "I can lock up. Probably just as well if you went home and got some sleep yourself."

"I can go in with you, you know," Bianci said, pausing and touching Kelly to bring the younger man's eyes to meet his.

There was sound of a sort, maybe voices, coming from the inner office. Kelly laughed, a barking sound because of the circumstances, but a gesture of real amusement nonetheless. "With all due respect, boss," he said, "I doubt you're cleared for whatever it is. Of course"—the feral grin came back and all humor fled—"the last time I checked, *I* had a negative security clearance, so it's hard to tell. . . ."

He gripped the congressman by both shoulders, continuing to hold their eyes locked. "Go on home, Carlo; it can't be too heavy if they only came with two of 'em," Kelly said. A part of him hated the operative portion of his mind for the care with which it examined Bianci's face, looking for a reaction to "only two of them" that would imply there was a full team behind the leather door.

Nothing of the sort. "Right, Tom," said Representative Bianci as he strode out of his office. He added over his shoulder, "And thanks. You know I appreciate it."

Everybody's got a handle, thought Kelly as he closed and locked the outer door behind his employer. Carlo had fewer than most; but everybody's got things they don't want to lose if somebody thinks it's worthwhile to dig and to push.

Kelly shrugged again to loosen the cling of his jacket. Then he opened the door to the private office, using his left hand.

The sound within the office came from the television monitor facing Kelly above the desk, rather than the man and woman kitty-corner to it at the far end of the room. Gunfire, flattened and compressed by the signal, rasped from the set for a moment before the waiting man touched the remote control of the videocassette recorder. Sound and picture faded almost instantly, but Tom Kelly's mind was bright with echoes and afterimages.

The man strode forward with his hand out and a

professional smile on his face. He was a good-looking
fellow in his early thirties, too young for his beefiness to
become real fat. The dark blond hair was nicely styled,
and the cotton shirt beneath his pinstriped three-piece
suit had probably cost as much as Kelly had spent on his
own sportcoat. The fellow stood six feet three inches, with
shoulders to match—which made them as broad as
Kelly's. "Glad to see you at last, Mr. Kelly," he said. "I'm
Doug Blakeley, and this is Elaine Tuttle."

"Right," said Kelly as he accepted the other's hand,
"and I'm John Patrick Monaghan." That was the cover
name he'd been issued when he trained Kurdish guerrillas
outside Diyarbakir in another life. He was very ready for
what would come next, might as well get it over with, he'd
warned them. . . .

"*Doug!*" said the woman very sharply. Her companion
relaxed the hand he had been tensing to crush that of Tom
Kelly, to prove that he was tougher than this aging cowboy
whose file he had read. Doug's handshake became just
that, perfunctory and as professional as his smile or the
names he had given.

Kelly grinned at the woman as he released Doug's hand.
He knew the type well enough, because a reputation like
Kelly's had made him a frequent target for boys of various
ages who needed to prove their manhood. Usually there
had been constraints on Kelly's own response: discipline,
the mission, or a sheer desire for self-preservation.

This time he'd been pretty sure he had nothing to
lose. He had no doubt that the grip in his own right hand,
his pistol hand, could have matched any stress Doug put
on it. It wouldn't have stopped there, however, within the

civilized norms of the tennis club and the smoking room. It would have stopped when Kelly grabbed a left handful of Doug's crotch and used the double grip to swing the bigger man face-first against the mahogany door.

Elaine smiled back at Kelly tightly, with the irritation of a woman who knew that boys would be boys but who didn't in the least like the way such antics screwed up business. She was five four and somewhat fuller in the face than in the trim body beneath it. Her hair was short and as black as Kelly's own, surprisingly black unless she dyed it or was much younger than the forty suggested by the crow's-feet at the corners of her eyes. It was hard to tell with women's clothing, but Kelly suspected she could buy a pretty solid used car for what she had in her linen blouse, skirt, and sequined jacket.

Not that she'd even have considered buying a used car.

And the lady was smart, smart enough to defuse a situation her companion didn't recognize and Kelly had been willing to play out just to end the waiting.

"We aren't here because of a problem with you, Mr. Kelly," she said in a clear contralto. There was a ring on the third finger of her right hand, a gold wedding band or something with the setting revolved toward her palm.

"Say, I'm really glad to hear that," said Kelly in a voice louder than he had first intended. There was a catch in his throat that he had to clear with volume inappropriate save as an indicator of how wired he was. Elaine already knew that, *that* was obvious, and Doug's concern seemed to be focused solely on striking a properly macho pose now that the woman had startled him out of testing the veteran.

Kelly took the VCR's controller as the bigger man stepped back. Doug looked surprised, but he did not object as Kelly switched the unit on again and began to rewind the tape.

There was an ordinary television in the lounge area, with the refrigerator and coffeepot, but the set here in Bianci's office had been unhooked from the building's cable system after Kelly had come on board. Kelly'd explained how easily the set could be used to monitor conversations within the room; and, when nobody believed him, had hooked an in-line bug to the cable lead outside the office and used the TV speaker itself to pick up sounds in place of a planted microphone. The television had immediately been replaced by a VCR and screen without antenna connections. Nobody in the office questioned Kelly's judgment about security again.

The videotape clicked to a stop and the screen's neutral pattern coalesced to a picture as Kelly pushed the Play switch. "You've got the ABC version," he said in a voice so distant in his own mind that he could not be sure he was speaking aloud. "I always thought that was the best one, too, what with the computer enhancement."

The tape had the stutter and low resolution to be expected from an original made with a hand-held minicam from the deck of a sixty-ton torpedo boat. The ship filling the frame looked to be an ordinary cargo vessel of moderate size, unusual only in lacking the swatches of rust that stain vessels if even inches of their steel sides are flaked open to salt water. The antenna arrays were there if you knew what to look for; but even to an expert, they tended to be disguised by the multiple booms and gantries dating from the period before the USS *White Plains* had been converted from an attack cargo ship into a technical research ship.

The water boiled just forward of the squared super-structure amidships. Kelly had turned down the audio track, but network engineers had laid a flashing violet arrow onto the picture as they magnified and outlined in complementary yellow the gap blown in the *White Plains'* hull by the torpedo launched from two hundred yards away. The man with the camera had not started filming until moments after the explosion, even as the shock waves pounded his own vessel.

The engineers isolated on another portion of what was originally a panorama shot with a short-focal-length lens. The bow, with its designator TR4, expanded grainily on the screen, flecks of random phosphor blurring the sharpness somewhat as raster lines were added in processing between those swept on the videotape original. The amidships three-inch gun installations had been stripped from the *White Plains* to make room for additional antennas when she was converted to her new mission, but one twin turret on the foredeck had remained.

The guns pointed skyward, their outlines slightly jagged from the computer enhancement. Somebody had told Kelly that three-inch seventy-caliber guns should always be mounted in pairs so that there might be one in operating condition when the need arose. In the case of the *White Plains*, both tubes had jammed at the first shots at the fighters diving to strafe the vessel. The crew had continued to traverse the weapons in a desperate attempt to bluff the attackers, however. Now a helicopter, a big

Super Frelon, made a leisurely pass at mast level to fire rockets point-blank into the gun turret. Flashes of white, then orange as ammunition detonated in a secondary explosion, threw bits of men and plating skyward.

The engineers expanded the helicopter again in freeze-frame. This time the arrow and highlight were on the national insignia above the flotation and landing-gear sponson of the Super Frelon: the six-pointed star of the Israeli Air Force.

"Hard to tell," said Tom Kelly in a voice that did not tremble the way his hands did, forcing him to hold the VCR controller against his left leg while his right palm dried itself fiercely on his slacks, "whether it was that scene that bothered people most, or . . ."

The screen flashed back to a full shot of the *White Plains*, listing so that the hole ripped by the torpedo was already beneath the angry surface of the water. A lifeboat, white against the smooth gray hull, was being lowered from the davits amidships. There were about a dozen sailors in it, far fewer than its capacity, but somebody had decided to launch it before the ship's distress made that impossible.

Tom Kelly aimed the controller with a hand which no longer shook, and thumbed up the sound. The picture jumped, the cameraman flinching at the muzzle blasts of the 20-mm cannon near where he was standing. Shells from the automatic cannon burst against the flank of the *White Plains*, then traced from stern to amidships across the swaying lifeboat. The lifeboat's bow plunged as the sailor there on the winch lowered abruptly in a vain attempt to avoid the gunfire. His companion on the stern winch had leaped into the sea an instant before the shells chewed his position into flying splinters and the black smoke of bursting charges.

The gunfire paused and the video camera picked up the sound of men shouting on the deck of the torpedo boat, though the words were indistinct. Then the automatic cannon opened up again, its rate of fire deliberate enough that the crack of shells bursting could be heard as counterpoint to the louder, deeper, muzzle blasts. The bow of the lifeboat exploded just as it touched the water foaming into the torpedo wound. Even without enhancement, one could see the sailor's bare arms fling themselves wide as a white flash hid his torso.

The picture paused a moment later in a crackle of colored static: the Israeli cameraman had either run out of tape or stopped recording of his own volition. The ABC engineers had not ended there, however. As Kelly dialed off the audio again, the final picture flashed back onto the screen. A glowing outline expanded and drew with it the image of the man in the bow of the tilting lifeboat, his hands bracing him upright on the lowering tackle.

In jerky slow motion, his chest exploded and his body, hurled backward, rebounded from the steel hull. At the final degree of processed magnification, nothing could be seen of the American's face but a white blur and the blotch that was his open mouth. The hull behind him was red with the spray of all the blood in his chest cavity.

". . . or maybe," said Tom Kelly as he switched off the picture, "it was that one that caused most of the flap after it was shown on the evening news."

"Which one bothered you, Mr. Kelly?" said Elaine,

one of the figures in his peripheral vision, ignored by the part of Kelly's mind that was now in control. . . . Ignored unless they moved suddenly, in which case he would kill them—in this moment he would kill them, and the release would be worth any regrets he had afterward.

"On principle," said Kelly in a voice like a pond of melt water, still and deep and very cold, "it all bothered me. If Israel had a problem with the way we pulled out of Lebanon so sudden, that's fine—I understand that, getting mad about being left in the lurch. But you don't shoot up an American spy ship off your coast just because you're pissed at people in Washington. None of the poor bastards on the *White Plains* were behind the bugout from Lebanon."

Kelly tried to set the controller on top of Congressman Bianci's desk, but his fingers slipped and the unit thumped instead to the blue-carpeted floor. The veteran's whole body shuddered and the room sprang into focus again.

"Shouldn't do that to me," said Kelly as he kneaded his cheeks and forehead with both hands. "Really shouldn't."

His voice had changed back to its usual lilting tenor as he went on, "If you mean personally, Danny Pacheco was in the SIGINT Tank in the midships hold, right where the torpedo hit. Guess he was one of the fifty or so who drowned there before they knew what was going on. And yeah, he was a good enough friend that it bothered me. But that's already in the file, I guess."

"You had good reason to hate the Israelis, Mr. Kelly," said the woman, giving a hitch to her skirt as she leaned her hips against the ceiling-height bookcase behind her. There was a tiny purse in her left hand, the gold-plated clasps an inch open. If she was smart enough to have *that* good a grasp of the situation, then she was smart enough to know that she had no real chance to clear the gun in her purse in a crisis—unless she planned to preempt Kelly.

The veteran laughed, briefly euphoric with the catharsis of having watched the attack on the *White Plains* for the first time since the slaughter came to its true climax in a military court in Jerusalem. "I don't hate anybody," he said. "Nobody in the world."

"You hated them enough," retorted Doug, "that you left your post in Turkey and spent two months tracking down that tape or something like it."

Kelly looked at the other man, whose present splay-footed stance suggested karate training. Elaine was playing with her subject, a tense game because of Kelly's emotional charge, but all the better thereby to flesh skeletal file data into a man. Doug, on the other hand, was genuinely belligerent instead of professionally playing the bad cop in an interrogation routine. That was fine. . . . "When I brought my boys back to Diyarbakir," Tom Kelly said in a soft voice and with a smile that gouged, "that was the third time I'd been over the line in Iraq, officially—"

Doug said nothing, though the pause dared him to speak. The Tasking Order had specifically forbidden American citizens to accompany into Iraq the guerrillas they trained at Turkish bases.

"When I came back, I had maybe a year of leave I'd never got around to taking. If I needed some time off, then I had it coming. And—"

"That doesn't—" started Doug.

"And *don't* give me any crap about leaving my post, the way NSA pulled the plug on the Kurds as soon as Iraq kicked out its Soviet techs," snarled Kelly in a voice like machineguns firing.

"It's the Kurds we're here to discuss with you, Mr. Kelly," said Elaine, reaching out with her right hand to stroke Doug's biceps and remind him of who and where he was. "Nobody cares that you released copies of that tape to the media three years ago."

"The Ford Commission came to no decision as to how that tape got into the hands of the press," Kelly corrected, rubbing his eyes and forehead again but with only his left hand, his eyes winking at the others through the gaps between his fingers.

"We're *not* here to trick you into an admission," said the woman in a sharper tone than any she had used earlier this night. "I've told you, it doesn't *matter*."

"Bullshit," said the veteran, the word soft and savage. He was as wired as he had been the moment he walked into the room.

They were lying to him the way they had lied so often in the past, and through the flashes and roar of that past in his memory Tom Kelly shouted, "I told 'em I'd leave 'em alone if they'd do the same! I wasn't gonna talk to anybody, I wasn't gonna claim a fucking pension, and if they thought the answer was a chemical debriefing, then the team they sent to take me better be ready to play for keeps. Are you ready? *Are you ready, sonny?*"

"The material at the head of that tape," said the other man in confusion and bureaucratic concern, a turnabout so unexpected that it penetrated Kelly's fury as the woman's voice could not have done at this moment, "was simply to explain to third parties why we were bringing it to you, Mr. Kelly. If something happened on the way, that is. The real information's further back on the tape."

"Jesus," said Tom Kelly, the rage draining from him like blood from a ruptured spleen and leaving him flaccid. "Jesus."

"We understand that your fuse is short, Mr. Kelly," said Elaine. "We have no intention of lighting it, none whatever." She snapped her purse closed and set it deliberately on a bookshelf before she stepped over to the VCR.

"Nobody cares about the—incident, do they?" said Kelly, slumping back against the door and almost wishing there were a chair in arm's reach for him to sit on. "Well, that's a relief."

He looked around the office, taking stock as the VCR whirred to eject the tape into Elaine's hand. The only thing that didn't belong was the attaché case lying on Bianci's otherwise orderly desk. Dull black and unremarkable at first glance, the case was in fact a Halliburton—forged from T-6061 aluminum like the plating of an armored personnel carrier. The three-rotor combination lock hidden under the carrying handle was not impossible to defeat, and the sides could be opened with a cutting torch or the right saw—but anything of that sort would take time, and you could park a car on the case without even disturbing the watertight seal.

"It's old news," Doug was saying. "Do you care that somebody blew away the secretary of defense in Dallas in '63? It's like that."

"Like I say, glad to hear it," the veteran said. It wasn't that he believed Doug in any absolute sense. Public release of the *White Plains* footage had squeezed the US government to take action against the State of Israel in ways that the highest levels had no wish to do once immediate tempers had cooled. A matter that had subsided into legal wrangling and the bland lies of politicians on both sides exploded into popular anger, spearheaded by members of Congress and the Senate to whom the massacre of American servicemen was not to be ignored as a matter of Middle Eastern policy.

There had been an immediate cutoff of aid to Israel—the munitions which fed the war in Lebanon to which US policy had abandoned Israeli troops, and the hard currency which alone kept afloat an economy which could not support its own welfare state, much less a protracted war. The aid had been resumed only after the Israeli minister of defense had resigned and thirty-seven serving members of the armed forces were given prison sentences ranging from two years to life after a public trial humiliating to the State which tried them.

"They buried Danny at Arlington," said the veteran inconsequently. "Seemed to make his widow happy enough. Me, I always figured that I'd want something besides a stone if it happened to me. . . ."

There were a lot of folks in both governments and, less formally, in Shin Bet—the Israeli department of security—who weren't in the least pleased with Tom Kelly since copies of the tape showed up in newsrooms across the US and Western Europe. There'd been one in the hands of TASS besides, just in case somebody got the idea of trying a really grandiose coverup. For sure, nothing Doug Blakeley had to say was official policy above a certain level—but the big blond wasn't a good enough actor to be lying about *his* mission, his and Elaine's.

The woman took from the Halliburton what looked like a small alien wrench and stuck it into a curved slot on the underside of the tape she had just ejected. The narrow slot didn't, when Kelly thought about it, look like anything he'd seen on a tape cassette before. Neither did it look particularly remarkable, however, even when Elaine clicked something clearly nonstandard into a detent at the farther end of the arc, then removed the wrench.

"Now it explodes?" the veteran asked, making it a joke instead of a flat question so that the pair of them wouldn't gain points if they chose to ignore him.

"There's a magnet inside the cassette," Elaine said as she reinserted the tape in the VCR. "The tape pauses at the end of the news segment. If anybody tried to play it beyond that point without locking the magnet out of the way, they'd get hash." She poked Play, picked up the remote control which still lay on the carpet, and stepped back close to Kelly as the tape advanced with a hiss and diagonals of white static across the screen.

"Look, you ought to understand," said Kelly with his eyes on the television, "the people in Israeli service who—got that tape to the guy who released it. It wasn't just personal payoffs, and it wasn't in-house politics alone, either. There were some people who thought shooting allies in lifeboats was a bad idea . . . and thought getting away with it once was an even worse one."

"That really doesn't concern us, Mr. Kelly," Elaine

said flatly, and the murmur of empty tape gave way to a segment recorded without an audio track.

"Sonofabitch," muttered Kelly, for the location was unmistakable to him despite the poor quality of the picture. The segment had been shot with a hand-held minicam, like the footage of the *White Plains* before, but the earlier portion had at least been exposed in the bright sunlight of a Mediterranean afternoon. This scene had been recorded at night in the angle of massive walls illuminated by car headlights, while drizzle flicked the beams and wobbled across the lens itself.

But there was no other stretch of fortification comparable to that on the screen save for the Great Wall of China. Kelly had trained Kurds for two years at Diyarbakir. He could recognize the walls of the great Roman fortress even at a glance.

"Corner by where the Turistik meets Gazi Street," the veteran said aloud, a guess rather than an identification— the sort of thing he did to keep people off-balance about what he knew or might know; the sort of thing he did when he was nervous and off-balance himself.

The walls of black basalt were gleaming and light-struck where their wet lower surfaces were illuminated; the twenty feet above the quivering headlights was only a dark mass indistinguishable from the rain-sodden sky as the cameraman walked forward and jiggled the point of view.

Close to the wall was a clump of figures in dark overcoats, who shifted away abruptly, backs turned to the approaching camera.

"Who filmed this?" asked Kelly, looking up at the

woman who watched him while her companion seemed mesmerized by the television itself. "And when?"

"It was taken three days ago," Elaine said, nodding toward the screen to return the subject's attention to where it belonged. "And officially, everyone at the site is a member of Turkish Military Intelligence."

There were two bodies on the ground near where the men in overcoats had been standing. The wall sloped upward at a noticeable angle, providing a broad base of support for the eight-foot thick battlements at the top.

"Didn't think relations between us and MIT had been so close since Ecevit was elected Prime Minister," the veteran said, pumping them because it had always been his job to gather information.

"Watch the screen, please," the woman said as Doug snorted and said, "No problem. Third Army Command, old buddy. No problem at all."

Elaine paused the tape and gave her companion a hard look. Kelly faced the television and grinned, amused at the two others and amused at himself—for gathering data on a situation that didn't concern him and which he wouldn't *allow* to concern him, no matter what.

The tape resumed. One of the cars must have been driven forward as the cameraman walked up to the bodies, because his shadow and those of some others who had scurried out of the scene were thrown crazily across the basalt wall. The point of view moved even closer, shifting out of focus, then sharpening again as the cameraman adjusted.

The screen steadied on a head-and-torso view of a man facedown in a puddle with one arm flung forward.

He wore a dark blue coat and a leather cap which had skewed when he hit the ground. A gloved hand on an arm in a black trenchcoat reached from out of frame, removing the cap and lifting the dripping, bearded face into full view of the camera.

"Son of a bitch," Kelly repeated, softly but very distinctly this time. "Mohammed Ayyubi. He was one of my section leaders back, back when I was workin' there and points south. . . . He was from the district himself."

"Ayyubi has been living in Istanbul for the past three years," Elaine said coolly, watching the screen to keep Kelly's attention on it. "Recently he began to travel extensively in Central Europe."

The hand holding the Kurd to the camera dropped him, letting his face splash back onto the puddled stone. It didn't matter to Mohammed, whose eyes would never blink again until somebody thumbed the lids down over the glazed pupils; but Kelly's own body grew very still for an instant.

"He had a brother in Istanbul," the veteran said softly. "Think I met him there once. . . ." When the brother came to see Mohammed in a base hospital so expertly staffed that all but one of the Kurd's fingers had been saved despite the ten days since they were mangled.

"Ahmed, yes," said the woman as the cameraman walked his point of view over to the other body. The same hand and arm reached into the frame to angle the victim's face toward the headlights.

Kelly glanced from the arm's wristwatch, a momentary black smear on the screen before the cuff of the overcoat hid it again, to the Omega which Doug wore. The quality of the data proved nothing but possibility, and the possibilities were endless. . . . "I don't know that one," said Kelly to the television.

"No, you sure don't," said Doug, and there was more in his voice than mere agreement.

The cameraman had panned the second body only incidentally in maneuvering for a head shot. The figure appeared to be of average height, perhaps a little shorter if American rather than Anatolian males were the standard of comparison. Its clothing was ordinary, trousers of a shade darker than the coat—both of them brown or taupe—and a cloth cap that lay beside the head. The features were regular and unusual only in having no facial hair. In Turkey, where a moustache was as much a part of a man's accoutrements as a pack of cigarettes, that was mildly remarkable.

There was a silvery chain and a medallion of some sort high up on the figure's neck. The hand and overcoat sleeve entered the field of view to touch the bauble.

The camera jumped a moment later, the lens panning a crazy arc of the walls and night sky as the cameraman's heels slipped on the pavement. Doug's right hand gripped his left as fiercely as if it belonged to someone else and was holding a weapon. Elaine was taut, watching Kelly until the veteran glanced at her.

Kelly was affected only at a conscious level, touched by wonderment at the emotional reaction of the others to what was, after all, a fraud. TV trickery, makeup, and muddy camerawork to make the gimmickry less instantly patent. But it couldn't frighten an adult, not somebody like Tom Kelly who knew that the real face of horror was human. . . .

The camera steadied again, though it was six feet farther from the subject than before, and it was some moments before the cameraman thought to adjust his focus. Not makeup at all, thought Kelly, squinting. The "head" above the necklace was smaller than that of any human beyond the age of six, so whoever was responsible had used a dummy. . . . "Roll back and freeze it where he touches the necklace," Kelly said.

He expected the woman either to make excuses or ignore him. To his surprise, she reached over with the remote-control unit and said, "Go ahead, Mr. Kelly. Freeze any part of the film you choose to."

The veteran cued the tape back in three jerky stages, angry that he had not been paying enough attention to get to the point he wanted in two tries at worst. Neither Elaine's stillness nor Doug's outthrust chin disguised the fact that the pair was nervous; and this time the cause was not the very real one of Tom Kelly's anger.

The bland, human face, only partly hidden by the gloved hand reaching for the medallion. Then the hand jerked back and, in the instant before the startled cameraman jumped away also, Kelly was able to pause the VCR into as close an equivalent of freeze-frame as a television's raster scanning could achieve.

Somebody was pretty good. Kelly couldn't see any sign of the transition, but what filled the screen now was nothing close to human.

Not only was the head the size of a grapefruit, it had no apparent eyes. There was a mouth, though, a blue-lipped circular pit lined with teeth hooked like blackberry thorns. The nose was a gash like that of a man Kelly had met in a village near Erzerum, his limbs and appendages eaten away by the final stages of leprosy. Either water droplets were creating an odd effect, or the surface of the dummy was scaly, and the scales divided at the midline of the face in a row of bony scutes.

Kelly thumbed the Pause button and let the tape roll forward. When the camera achieved focus and steadiness again there was a somewhat clearer view of the alien visage, but nothing beyond what Kelly had already seen. "All right," he said, "what happens next? The mothership comes down and vaporizes Diyarbakir? You know, I'd miss the place."

"There's nothing more on the tape," Elaine said shortly. The screen dissolved into diagonal static again as if it were ruled by her voice.

Kelly tried to switch off the VCR. When his thumb touched the Eject button on the controller as well, the tape whirred and cycled itself halfway out of the feed slot. The veteran's anger flared, though no one in the world but he knew the act was nervous clumsiness instead of deliberation. He was allowing himself to be spooked!

"We need a Kurdish speaker," Doug said with a toss of his head that seemed to clear a dark aura from his soul, "and we may need someone who was involved with Operation Birdlike—assuming Ayyubi wasn't the only member of that group who's gotten involved in this new business."

"Go home." Kelly spoke flatly as he shook himself and set the remote unit back on Bianci's desk. "Go home so I can lock up behind you and go home myself." He rubbed his eyes with his left forearm. "Been a long day, been a long three years. I'm just not in a mood for government-issue bullshit any more."

"It's not bullshit, Mr. Kelly," the woman said as she watched him with the inscrutable eyes of a cat viewing a bird too big to be prey. "Earth has been visited by aliens— *is being* visited, we think. Men who you know have been in contact with them."

"Don't you think," Doug Blakeley interjected, "that it's time the USG got involved instead of leaving things to barbs whose only link to the twentieth century is a machine gun?"

Kelly turned toward the other man, prey indeed if he chose—as he did not. Doug was trash, the discussion was trash, and Elaine—

Elaine stepped between the two men, close enough to Kelly that she had to tilt her face to meet his eyes. "He doesn't matter, Mr. Kelly," the black-haired woman said as if she had read the veteran's mind. "This matters very much, if it's true. You know it does."

"And *you* know a videotape doesn't prove jack shit!" Kelly shouted, as if to drive her back by the violence of his reaction.

"Then come look at the body itself, Kelly," Elaine said with an acid precision. "If you're man enough."

She would not back away from him and he would not face her glare, so Kelly spun on his heel to stare out at the reception area. "Figured you'd tell me that, 'Gee, the Turkish police had it'—or maybe the plane bringing it back to the World had flown into a mountain." Even five years after the last tour in the Lebanon, Kelly had the veterans' trick of referring to the continental United States as "the World."

"The evidence—the body—is at Fort Meade," said

the woman behind him. "We have a car. We can have you there in forty minutes to examine it yourself."

"Are you doing a job on me, honey?" Kelly said as he turned again to face her. "Is this all a way to get me behind walls with no fuss 'r bother?"

"Oh, come now, Kelly," said the blond man standing behind Elaine, arms akimbo. "Don't you think you're being overly dramatic?"

There were only two things in the office which were not Congressman Bianci's—or alive. Kelly stepped toward the VCR. Elaine, who thought he was trying to close with her companion, sidestepped quickly to block the veteran. She was wearing sequined flats rather than the high heels to be expected with the formality of her suit. The sensible footgear saved her from falling when Kelly's shoulder slammed her back as remorselessly as a hundred and eighty pounds of brick in motion.

Doug shouted something that began as a warning and ended in a squawk as his hands by reflex clasped the stumbling woman. Kelly bent, his back to the couple momentarily as he took the videotape from the VCR. The cassette was cool, its upper edge rough beneath his fingers. As Elaine's hands touched Doug's, in part for balance's sake but also to restrain her companion as both stared at Kelly, the veteran pivoted and smashed the tape down on the aluminum attaché case.

The impact did not scar the anodized surface of the Halliburton, but the polystyrene videocassette shattered with a sound like the spiral fracture of a shin bone.

"Hey!" Doug shouted. Elaine's hands clamped in earnest on those of the man behind her.

Kelly slammed the cassette down again. The lower half of it disintegrated like a window breaking, spilling coils of half-inch tape along with the take-up sprocket. The veteran raised his right hand and opened it, letting the remainder of the cassette fall to the floor. Bits of black plastic clung to the sweat of his palm, and an inch-long shard had dug a bloody gouge into his flesh.

Kelly grinned at the others with his hand still lifted like a caricature of a wooden Indian. "You know," he said in a voice so light that only his eyes suggested what he was saying was the baldest truth, "I figured when I walked in here it was fair odds I'd kill you both. Guess I'll go back to Meade with you instead—but no more jokes about me acting crazy, okay?"

"You can call Representative Bianci and tell him where you're going," the woman said, twisting sinuously out of Doug's arms and stepping to the side, her fingertips smoothing the lines of her skirt.

"*I'm* doing this to me," Kelly replied, dusting his palms together like a cymbals player to clear them. Sweat stung the open gash, and he felt like a damned fool; overdramatic just like the blond meathead had said. "I don't want Carlo getting involved if it's me being too dumb to keep my head down."

Doug massaged each wrist with the opposite hand, then knelt and began gathering up the tape and the larger bits of the cassette as well. Elaine said, "It might reassure him, you know."

"He'll be happy enough if he doesn't get a call from Housekeeping about the blood on 'is upholstery," the veteran said with a savage laugh. "Look, let's get this over, okay? I said I was going, didn't I?"

◆ ◆ ◆

The attaché case contained no files or papers of any sort, not even a manila envelope into which Doug could pour the remnants of the tape cassette, so they had to lie loose on the nylon-covered polyurethane foam instead. There was, however, a compact two-way radio in a fitted niche. The radio had no nameplate or manufacturer's information on it, but neither was the unit a piece of government-issue hardware that Kelly recognized. Well, he'd been out—way out—for three years, and equipment was the least of what might change.

The stub of the coiled whip antenna hobbled as Doug spoke into the radio, glaring unconsciously at Kelly as he did so. All data was useful somewhere, in some intelligence paradise—you couldn't spend a big chunk of your life in Collection and not think so. But it was only reflex that made Kelly's mind focus on the chance of hearing a one-time-only code word, and that no more than the means of summoning a car. Doug's bridling was an empty reflex as well—and both reactions were complicated by the fact that each of the men had been top dog for a long time, in ways that had nothing to do with chains of command.

Kelly was just loose enough at the moment to both recognize the situation and find it amusing. "Hey, junior," he said to Doug as the radio crackled a muted, unintelligible reply, "I think you lost your place in the pecking order."

"Let's go," said Elaine in a neutral voice, waving Doug out the door ahead of her and falling in behind him—separating the men since she knew that Bianci's aide must be last out of the office to lock up.

The guard tonight at the side entrance of the

Longworth Building was a heavy black woman. Kelly had seen and smiled at her a hundred times over the years as she rummaged harmlessly through whatever briefcase he happened to be carrying. It wasn't an effective way to defeat a serious attempt to blow up the building, but it didn't hurt Kelly—who, even when he was on active duty, had not traveled with documents he minded other people inspecting. Today the guard drew back as she saw the trio approaching her post from down the corridor. "Good night, Ethel," Kelly called, never too tired—or wired—to be pleasant to anybody with a dismal job like guard, refuse collector, or code clerk. This time Ethel only nodded back, her concentration preoccupied by Doug and the Halliburton he had carefully locked. There was no reason in the world not to have opened the case like a citizen when he entered the building. Instead, Doug had obviously flashed credentials that had piqued the curiosity of even a guard who saw the stream of visitors to members of the House of Representatives. It was the same sort of bass-ackwardness that caused CIA officers operating under embassy cover in foreign venues to be issued non-American cars. They could therefore be separated with eighty percent certainty from the real State Department personnel by anyone who bothered to check traffic through the embassy gates.

"By the way," Kelly goaded in a voice that echoed on the marble, "who do you work for? SAVE? Or are you Joint Chiefs Support Activity?"

"You *stupid* bastard," Doug snarled, twisting in mid-motion to glare at the other man, his palm thumping on the door's glass panel instead of the push bar.

"Mr. Kelly," said Elaine as she reached past her companion to thrust the door open, "you might consider whether in a worst-case scenario you wish to have involved a number of outsiders in this matter." Her voice was clear but not loud, losing itself in the rush of outside air chilled by the shower that had been threatening all day.

Two cars pulled up at the curb outside just as the trio exited the Longworth Building. The follow-car was a gray Buick with a black vinyl roof, but the vehicle its lights illuminated was a bright green Volvo sedan. The Volvo's driver got out quickly, leaving his door open, and trotted around to the curb side.

Elaine muttered a curse at the weather and hunched herself in her linen jacket, Doug strode forward as if there were no rain, the attaché case in his left hand swinging as if it weighed no more than a normal leather satchel.

"Sorry 'bout that," Kelly said as he and the woman hesitated under the roof overhang. "Shouldn't let my temper go when I'm around innocent bystanders. Not for silly shit, especially."

"Let's go," the woman said, darting across the wide sidewalk as a gust of wind lashed raindrops curving like a snake track across the pools already on the concrete.

The driver had opened both curbside doors for them. The veteran paused deliberately to see whether or not Elaine would get in before he did. She slid quickly into the back seat, showing a length of thigh that amused Kelly because it really did affect him. There were people who thought that sex was something physical. Damn fools.

"You can sit anywhere you please, Mr. Kelly," the

woman called from the car with a trace of exasperation. "All the doors work normally."

The front seats were buckets, so they really hadn't planned to sandwich him between the two of them—or more likely, between the former driver and Doug, who was now behind the wheel of the Volvo adjusting the angle of the backrest. "Right," said Kelly, feeling a little foolish as he got into the front for the sake of the legroom. The man who had brought the Volvo to them closed both doors and scurried back to the follow-car.

Doug did not wait for the former driver to be picked up before goosing the Volvo's throttle hard enough to spin the drive wheels on the wet pavement. The right rear tire scraped the edge of the curb before the sedan angled abruptly into the traffic lane and off through the night.

"If these're the radials I'd guess they were," said Kelly, angling sideways in the pocket of the seat, "then that's a pretty good way to spend twenty minutes in the rain, changing the tire with a ripped sidewall."

Doug glanced at his passenger, but then merely grunted and switched the headlights to bright. Raindrops appeared to curve toward them as the car accelerated.

Doug's face had a greenish cast from the instrument lights. Kelly glimpsed the woman between the hollow headrests, her features illuminated in long pulses by the oncoming cars. The black frame of Elaine's hair made her face a distinct oval even during intervals of darkness.

You couldn't really see into a head like that, thought Kelly as the hammer of tires on bad pavement buzzed him into a sort of drifting reverie. Not in good light, not under stress. Sometimes you could predict the words the mind within would offer its audience; but you'd never know for sure the process by which the words were chosen, the switches and reconsiderations at levels of perceived side-effects which a man like Kelly never *wanted* to reach.

The veteran straightened so that his shoulder blade was no longer against the window ledge. He was physically tired, and the meeting in Bianci's office had been as stressful and disorienting as a firefight. If he didn't watch it, he'd put himself into a state more suggestible than anything an interrogation team could achieve with hypnotic drugs. Even the thought of that made Kelly's skin crawl in a hot, prickling wave which spread downward from the peak of his skull.

"Which of you's in charge?" he asked. The hostility implicit in the question was another goad to keep him alert.

"You'll meet some of the people in charge tonight, if you care to," the woman said, her face as expressionless in the lights of an oncoming truck as it was a moment later when backlit by the follow-car.

"No," Kelly said. "I mean which of *you* two has the rank. When it comes down to cases, who says 'jump' and who says 'how high?' "

Doug turned with a fierceness which their speed and the turnpike traffic made unwise, snapping, "For somebody who claims he doesn't intend to talk to anybody, you show a *real* inability to know when to shut the fuck up!"

Kelly grinned. The woman in the back seat said to his profile, "Would you take a direct order from either one of us, Mr. Kelly?"

The veteran looked at her directly and laughed. "No," he said. "No, I don't guess I would."

"Then our ranks don't matter," she said coolly, and Kelly decided that wasn't much of a lie in comparison to other things he'd heard tonight. And would hear later.

"Oh, Christ on a crutch," Kelly muttered, locking his fingers behind his neck and arching his shoulders back as fiercely as he could in the cramped confines. "You know," he said while he held the position, headlights flicking red patterns of blood to his retinas behind closed eyelids, "This's going to be a first for me. I worked eighteen years for NSA, more'r less, and I never set foot in the building." He opened his eyes, relaxed, and as he stared through the windshield toward the future added, "Can't say I much wanted to."

Kelly hadn't intended to draw a reaction from Doug, but the driver half-turned—realized that the woman was sitting directly behind him, out of his sight no matter how sharply he craned his neck—and then tried to catch her eye in the rearview mirror.

"Mr. Kelly," Elaine said, and Kelly surmised that she was speaking with greater circumspection than usual, "I don't want you to be startled by something you misunderstood. We won't be going to NSA headquarters or any portion of Fort Meade dedicated to the National Security Agency. Some disused barracks within the reservation were—taken over for present purposes. You shouldn't be concerned that we enter at a gate different from the one you may have expected."

Kelly laughed. "Well, that explains the *big* question I still had."

Doug glanced at him, but the veteran had been pausing for breath, not a response, "Couldn't figure," he

went on, "how you'd gotten NSA to cooperate with *any*
damn body else—which you are, even though I don't
much care who, not really."

Headlights picked out a tiny smile at the corners of
Elaine's lips as she said, "We're government employees,
Mr. Kelly. As you were, and as you are now—through
Congressman Bianci."

The Volvo and the Buick behind it had cloverleafed
from the Baltimore-Washington Turnpike onto the cracked
pavement of Highway 1. Dingy motels and businesses
lined both sides of its four undivided lanes. There was
very little traffic in comparison to the turnpike, and Doug
made only rolling stops at the signal lights, presumably
counting on his ID to get him past a late-cruising
Maryland cop.

"If you've got it, flaunt it" had always been the motto
of the intelligence community. It wasn't a great way to do
business, but it attracted to the profession bright, aggressive
people who might otherwise have done something socially
useful with their lives.

Christ, Kelly thought, he was too tired for this crap.
Too tired in every way.

The gates in the chain link fence encircling Fort
Meade were open, but there was a guard post and a red
and white crossbar, which a GI lifted after a glance at
Doug's identification. As the car accelerated again, Kelly
got a glimpse of the unit patch on the left shoulder of the
trooper's fatigues: a horse and bend dexter worked in gold
embroidery on a shield-shaped blue field.

"Goddam," the veteran muttered as the car swept by,
"Twelfth Cav, wasn't it?"

"You were assigned to them, weren't you?" said the woman, finding in a mis-memory of Kelly's file a safe topic for an interval of increasing tension. "During operations in the Anti-Lebanon?"

Kelly laughed, glad himself of the release. He got antsy nowadays around uniforms, even when he was just mixing with brass at a Washington cocktail party or visiting a research installation far too sensitive to be compromised by an attempt to hold Thomas James Kelly for questioning. The only sensible explanation for tonight's affair was that it was an operation intended for just that end: to close the doors around Tom Kelly unless and until folks in DC and Jerusalem decided they should be opened again. But he was going along with it, he'd said he would, and he was in favor of anything that took his mind off the barracks they drove past and their insulation from what civilians thought was the real world.

"That was a different armored cavalry regiment," Kelly said, lifting himself by his left shoulder and feet so that he could hitch up his trousers. The Volvo had leather upholstery, and he was sweating enough to stick slightly to the seat cushion. "Close, but no cigar. These guys—" They were coming to another checkpoint, and this time the gates were shut. The fencing gleamed in the headlights as the car paused for a soldier with a small flashlight to check Doug's ID. The earth raked smooth around the postholes had a raw, unweathered look.

"These guys are a public relations unit," Kelly said, trying to control his voice the way he would clean a bad signal on tape—trimming out everything but what communicated data, as if there were no such things as static, bleed-over, or fear. "The President needs troops for a parade, visiting brass wants to review something—you know the drill—the Twelfth takes care of it. Nicely painted tanks and APCs, troops in strack uniforms—you know. They even paint the roadwheels of the tanks. Rots the rubber, but it sho' do look black from the reviewing stands."

"You may pass, sir," said the guard, and as the gate opened he saluted.

There was a second chain link barrier twelve feet within the first, with its gate inset further to permit a car to stand between the checkpoints while both gates were closed. The inner fencing was covered with taupe fiber-glass panels, translucent and sufficient protection against anyone trying to observe the compound from ground level. The soldiers manning the inner guard post wore fatigues and carried automatic rifles with a degree of assurance very different from that of the Twelfth Cav guards with pistols in patent leather holsters.

The man who examined the credentials this time stooped to look at all three occupants of the car. He wore neither a unit patch nor rank insignia, but there were chevrons and rockers in his eyes when he met Kelly's.

There but for the grace of God, the veteran thought, if his gift for languages was really a manifestation of grace rather than a curse. Being able .to process intercept data in real time had put Tom Kelly farther up the sharp end than he ever would have gone if he knew *only* how to sight a cal fifty and handle twenty-ounce blocks of *plastique*. He'd spent a lot of years in places where discipline was something you had yourself because there was nobody around to impose it on you.

When the people who thought in hierarchies realized that Platoon Sergeant Thomas J. Kelly was both willing and able to make a major policy decision for the United States government, it made him very frightening.

"*Christ,* I'm scared," Kelly said with a lilt and a bright smile to make a joke of it as the guard stepped away.

The woman in the back seat smiled with the precision of a gunlock. "I've read your file, Mr. Kelly," she said as the gate squealed open. "If I had any doubt about the purpose of this exercise, I promise I wouldn't be the person nearest by when you learned the truth."

Doug glanced up at the rearview mirror again as he drove forward, his expression unreadable.

Within the second enclosure were four frame buildings, a number of cars—Continentals and a Mercedes, all with opera windows—and more armed men in unmarked fatigues. Incandescent area lights were placed within the fencing on temporary poles, throwing hard shadows and displaying every flaw in the peeling, mustard-colored paint on the buildings. They had probably been constructed during the Second World War as temporary barracks, and had survived simply because military bureaucracy misfiled a great deal more than it discarded.

Well, Kelly had once been very glad for a case of Sten guns hidden against need, decades before, in a warehouse in Homs. It wasn't the sort of waste that bothered him.

Three of the buildings were two-story, but the fourth was one floor with a crawl space, like the shotgun houses built in rural areas at about the same period. It would have been a company headquarters and orderly room; now it was the prize which the troops billeted in the other three buildings were guarding.

Drivers stood by their limousines, one of them polishing a fender with his chamois, as they watched the newcomers. Instead of parking along the fenceline with the other cars, Doug pulled up to an entrance at one end of the low building and shut off the engine. Kelly reached across his own body to open his door left-handed. The latch snicked normally, permitting Kelly to step out of the car while he tried both to observe everything around him and to look relaxed.

Neither attempt was possible under the circumstances. When Kelly met Elaine's eyes across the roof of the Volvo he laughed as he would have done at sight of his own face in a mirror.

"Hell," he said to the woman, "when I was a kid there was a lotta people thought I'd be hanged before I was old enough to vote. I beat that by just about twenty years, didn't I?" He followed them inside.

There were no guards within the building, no women besides Elaine, and only one uniform—Major Redstone when Kelly served under him in the Shuf, and now, from the star on each shoulder, a brigadier general. He was one of the six men waiting in what had been the orderly room, the east half of the structure. The others wore not uniforms but suits, and suits—in this sort of setting— tended to blur together in Kelly's mind. Fight-or-flight reflexes pumped hormones into his bloodstream. It wasn't the sort of situation he handled very well.

"Hey, Red," the veteran said with a nod. "Hadn't heard you were gonna be here."

"Hi, Kelly," said the general. "Glad you could make it." Even as he spoke, Redstone's eyes were checking the faces of the men to either side of him. Any intention he might have had to say more was lost in whatever he saw in those faces.

They had prepared for this business by moving into the orderly room a massive wooden table, scarred and as old as the building, and a complement of armchairs whose varnish was ribbed and blackened by long storage. No one was seated when Kelly entered the room, and if they expected *him* to lock himself between a heavy chair and a heavy table, they were out of their collective mind.

The men, the Suits, ranged in age from one in his late twenties—younger than Doug—to another who could have been anywhere from sixty to eighty and with eyes much older than that. That one's motions were smooth enough to put him on the lower end of the age range, but the liver spots on his gnarled hands were almost the same color as the fabric of his three-piece suit. "Tuttle?" he said with a glance at the woman.

"Mr. Kelly has agreed to look at the physical evidence, Mr. Pierrard," Elaine said in her most careful voice. "He has his own life to live, and he certainly won't become involved in the present matter unless he's convinced it is of the—highest order of significance."

"Well, does he think *we'd* be here?" Pierrard snapped. He stared up and down Kelly with a look not of contempt but superiority—the look a breeder gives to someone else's thoroughbred. "*Do* you, Kelly?"

The veteran had instinctively frozen into a formal "at ease" posture: feet spread to shoulder width and angled

45° from midline; shoulders back, spine straight, hands clasped behind his back—and the hard feel of the weapon there was no comfort now. He was furious with himself and with everyone around him because the simple answer hadn't been right: they hadn't brought him here to arrest him.

Reflex wanted to say, "No sir." Very distinctly, Tom Kelly said, "Why don't you get to fucking business and show me this thing?"

"Take him in," Pierrard said curtly, with an upward lift of the chin which Doug and Elaine took as a direction to them.

"This way, Mr. Kelly," Elaine said without looking back at him. She walked toward the room to the side, which had been an office for either the company commander or the first sergeant. She took a deep breath, and Doug echoed the sound hissingly as he followed the others. Perhaps it was the smell in the smaller room, but Kelly did not think so.

There was a white-enameled cooling case in the office, purring with a normality belied only by its present location. Condensate on the slanted glass-and-chrome top hid the contents until Doug threw a switch. Floodlights mounted on the ceiling illuminated the case starkly, and the odor which had been present even through the tobacco smoke in the orderly room became so overpowering now that its source could not be denied.

The creature under glass was the same as whatever Kelly had seen on tape, and it stank like the aftermath of an electrical fire in a spice warehouse. Neither the chemical nor the organic components of the odor were particularly

unpleasant, and even the combination could have been
accepted in another context. Somebody in the other room
swore.

"Didn't look this big," said Kelly as he walked over to
the case and the flaccid gray thing within. "This tall."

Without clothes, the creature—or construct—but the
men in the other room wouldn't be playing games with a
little scut like Tom Kelly—looked very frail; but the
height should have been more than six feet. When the
veteran bent over the case his shadow cut the direct
reflection from the glass and gave him an even clearer
vision of the creature. The arrangement of torso and
appendages was that of a human being, but the limbs had
the appearance of flat-wire antenna lead rather than the
more nearly circular cross section of a man's.

Of the limbs of an animal that belonged on Earth.

Elaine lifted the center section of glass; the cooler
really was an ordinary grocery case. "It's a refrigerator, not a
freezer," she said while Doug muttered something unintelligible in the background. "Freezing would have broken
down the cell walls. Of course, it can't be kept this way
forever. When they've completed the autopsy, they'll . . ."

The torso had been laid open in a long curving incision,
but the flap of fine-scaled integument had been pinned
back in place when the pathologists paused in their
examination. Doctors tended to be self-ruled men in
whom arrogance was a certain concomitant of ability if not
proof of that ability. Kelly wondered who was handling the
autopsy, whether the men in the other room had chosen to
go with the best pathologists available or rather to use
doctors whom they knew they could control.

They were trying to deal Tom Kelly in on this business. That gave him a notion of where their heads were.

Christ on a crutch. It really was what it seemed to be.

Kelly's left hand reached into the case, his fingers tracing but not touching the surface of one of the arms. The hand had four fingers and no thumb, but it looked as though the two halves could be folded over one another along the central axis.

"There're surgical gloves, if you want," the woman said. She was looking at Kelly while she held the lid open. Only the flare of her nostrils implied that her eyes were on him to excuse them from having to view the alien. "It doesn't have knee and elbow joints the way we do. Each arm is a double column of bones like paired spinal columns, and they're connected only by muscle."

"You can close it," the veteran said, jerking his hand out of the cooler and flexing it repeatedly to work off the damp miasma that clung to the skin. The lid thumped behind him as he turned, and he thought he heard a grateful sigh. "How did it die?" he asked, facing Doug. "Did Mohammed kill it?"

Men waiting in the other room either glanced away when Kelly caught their eyes or matched his with stares of their own. Pierrard nodded coolly as he tamped a tiny meerschaum with a pipe tool shaped like a pistol cartridge. Doug shrugged, his expression less nonchalant when it remained fixed even though the rest of his body moved.

"They were both killed by nine-millimeter bullets," Elaine said as she walked into the veteran's field of view again. "Turkish service ammunition lots, though of course that indicates nothing. We'd had reports that bullets didn't—affect them, fired at very close range. Those reports appear to be in error."

The palm of Kelly's right hand stung where he had gouged it, partly from his sweat and partly from the aura of burned pepper and phenolic resin which emanated from the thing in the cooler. "You can't be too close to miss what you're aiming at," Kelly said. "Take my word for it, honey."

He walked back into the larger room, again facing the men whom he'd never wanted to see and who didn't see him even now that he stood in front of them. Except for maybe Redstone, Kelly was no more human to the eyes sliding over him like water over a statue than was the dead thing in the cooler behind him. Not officer material, that was God *damned* sure, and both sides would feel thankful for that. . . .

"Where's his clothes?" Kelly asked Pierrard in a harsh, hectoring tone. "And the necklace he had on? Was that all?"

Pierrard took a deep pull on his pipe. Its bowl was discolored almost to the shade and patterning of briar.

The youngest Suit said, "The clothes were probably of Turkish manufacture—handwork, no labels, but local manufacture. The shoes were Turkish, made in Ankara, The legs must have *twisted* to form an ankle joint, the sockets in the leg and arm columns are offset enough to do that."

Kelly stepped closer to Pierrard, so that he was wrapped in coils of pipe smoke whose bitterness underlay the cloying surface odor. "Where's the hardware,

Pierrard?" he demanded. "If this isn't all phony, then that damned thing had a gadget to make him look like a man, not a lamprey. Where *is* it?"

Pierrard's lips quirked as he lowered his pipestem. He blew a careful smoke ring toward the low ceiling.

"There were six items of equipment which couldn't be identified," said the young Suit, who was too beefy to be really aristocratic and whose forehead now glistened with sweat. Redstone knuckled his jaw and grimaced, but nobody else Kelly could see appeared to be breathing.

"None of them were larger than a cigarette case, and none of them did anything noticeable when they were tested. We think that when—" The young Suit glanced up and beyond Kelly. "—We think that when the medallion was first touched, all of the equipment shut down. The units we've sectioned after testing appear to have melted internally, but we can't be sure what they looked like before they came into our hands."

"*Shit!*" Kelly said and turned abruptly. He slapped the doorjamb, shaking the partition wall and making the overhead light jounce. Doug jumped aside, though this time the veteran's anger was directed against the situation rather than any human.

Any human except himself and the fact that he didn't seem able to walk away—that he had buttons that cynical bastards in suits could still push.

"Kelly," said General Redstone from the far side of the room, "we need you on this one. It's no time to fuck around."

"Yessir," said Kelly, slowly facing around and taking a breath that lifted his eyes back into contact with those of the others in the room. "What did you think you could get me to do? Give you names?"

"Because members or at least a member of the Kurdish separatist community had contact with the aliens," said Pierrard, "we need a knowledgeable person in place in that community at the earliest possible moment." His lengthened vowels had probably been natural for him before they were popularized by the Kennedy and Culver presidencies.

"You've got other Kurdish speakers." Kelly walked over to a window and stared out at the lighted fence with his hands on the sash. "Hell, you've got agents, CIA's got agents, every damn body in the *world's* got Kurdish agents."

"We've had no reports regarding—alien presences," said a voice Kelly hadn't heard before, a Suit of his own age with more gut and less hair. "It may be that depending on foreign nationals in this venue cannot guarantee satisfactory results."

"We aren't looking for a translator, Kelly," said General Redstone as the veteran turned to face them again. "We don't need somebody to man an intercept receiver. To get on this as fast as we've got to, there's got to be somebody the sources'll trust—and somebody who can go to them. There's some other training officers— paramilitary types—but they *don't* speak Kurdish, not really. You were the only real NSA staffer in Birdlike, the only one with a real language specialty. Otherwise the operation was slotted there just to keep clear of the Freedom of Information Act."

"Got a problem with Kurds not trusting the USG all

of a sudden, hey?" Kelly said, his voice struggling against the leash his conscious mind was trying to keep on it. Pierrard's face was the only thing in the room which was not receding from focus. "Couldn't be because of the way Operation Birdlike was wrapped up with all the finesse of a hand grenade, d'ye suppose?"

"Yes, of course that had something to do with it," the old man agreed unemotionally as he lifted his pipe again.

"There were people in fucking *Iraq* waiting for the C-130 to duck in with the pallet of *supplies*, you bastard!" Kelly shouted. "And instead folks are shaking hands in some air-conditioned hotel and there's not a problem anymore. There was a fucking *big* problem for the men on the ground, believe me! And the secretary of state tells the Senate, 'You must remember, international diplomacy isn't Boy Scouting,' and gee *whiz*, how foolish those Kurds were to have believed the word of the United States government. It was all right, though, because they weren't 'pro-Western freedom fighters' anymore—they were just an Iraqi internal problem."

"They never were pro-Western freedom fighters," said the middle-aged Suit who had spoken before.

Kelly stared at him. "They were men," he said in a voice that quivered like the blade of a hacksaw. "That's more'n I see in *this* room."

"Are you always this offensive, Mr. Kelly?" said Elaine, as clear and hard as diamond.

The world collapsed back to normalcy, a room too warm and far too smoky, filled with men who didn't like Tom Kelly any better than he liked them. Nothing to get worked up about, just the way the world generally was.

"Only when I'm drunk or scared shitless, Miz Tuttle," Kelly said as he heaved himself away from the sash against which he had been braced. "And I could really use a drink right about now."

He walked past Doug and Elaine, flanking the side door to the office. One of the Suits muttered, "Where's he going?" but only the woman fell in behind Kelly as he approached the grocery cooler for the second time.

The handle was cool and smooth, vibrating with the purr of the refrigerator motor in the base of the cabinet. Kelly raised the lid and reached toward the alien's face. The floodlights had been switched off, but the analytical part of Kelly's mind doubted that he would be able to see much anyway in his present emotional state.

"There are gloves," Elaine said sharply.

"You can't not do things because you're afraid," Kelly said in a crooning, gentle voice, more to himself than to the woman beside him. "I can't not go back in because I'm scared of international flights and dark alleys . . . and because this thing scares me, scares the livin' crap outa me. . . ."

He placed his stinging right palm on the head of the creature, the portion that would have been the forehead if the thing were instead human. The tips of the scales were lifted enough to give the surface the feel of something covered with hairs too fine to be seen. With firmer pressure there were differences in the way the alien flesh and bone resisted the weight of Kelly's hand, but the texture of the covering was the same over hand and head. He lifted his hand away and let the lid thump closed.

"You're not afraid of it anymore?" said Doug, standing hipshot in the doorway like a gunslinger ready to go into action.

The veteran dusted his palms together. The electric tingle in his right hand had spread to his throat and chest. It was probably psychological rather than a physical reaction to the alien's chemistry; and either way to be ignored.

"Sure I'm scared," Kelly said, looking at the big man and thinking how young the fellow was—and biological age had little to do with that. "That's nothing to do with the price of eggs, is all."

Pierrard stepped into the doorway. He touched Doug on the shoulder with an index finger, removing the younger man from his path abruptly. "Have you reached a decision, then, Kelly?" Pierrard asked. His mouth trembled with wisps of pipe smoke.

"I'll make a deal with you," Kelly said to Elaine. "You call me Tom from here on out, I call you Elaine."

"With a proviso." The dark-haired woman met his eyes with enough of a smile to indicate her amusement at the operational necessity of ignoring Pierrard for the moment. "If you ever 'honey' me again, you can expect to be 'Sergeant Kelly' for the duration. I think I'd prefer the honesty of being called 'you dumb twat' if you can't remember my name."

"We'll work on it," Kelly muttered with an embarrassment he had not thought he was still capable of feeling. To the old man in the doorway, he said, "Can she brief me?"

Pierrard rotated his pipestem in a short arc. "If you wish." Kelly could see others in the orderly room staring at the old man rather than the couple in the office beyond.

"Okay, that'll work," the veteran said, half his mind already considering the people to whom he was going to have to excuse himself if this went the way it looked to. Meetings to cancel, phone messages to be taken and ranked for action. . . . "Some place that isn't here to sit down at—"

Pierrard gestured. "Of course," he murmured.

"—and Dougie goes home or to his kennel'r whatever. I don't need the aggravation, I really don't."

"All right," said Pierrard with no more expression than before, and Elaine looked down at her fingers, which had begun to fold a pleat in her skirt.

"Sir, I don't think—" came Doug's voice from behind the partition wall, out of Kelly's sight. Pierrard turned his head just enough that Blakeley would have been in the corner of his vision. Doug's words stopped.

"Let's roll." Kelly took a shudderingly deep breath before stepping toward the doorway. "Elaine?"

Nobody came out of the building after them. Kelly reached for the driver's side door to open it for the dark-haired woman. The door was locked, and Elaine brushed Kelly's hand away from the latch before she inserted the key into a slot in the doorpost, then unlocked the door itself.

"Very gallant, M—Tom," she said with a smile to dull the sting of the words and the situation. "But on this car, the alarm is set automatically when it's locked, and the last thing we need right now is for everybody in three blocks to lock and load before they come looking for the problem." She smiled brightly at the nearest of the uniformed gunmen. Dazzled, the soldier smiled back.

Kelly walked around to his side of the car. The lock button had risen when the key was turned on the driver's side. Well, the world had never had much real use for chivalry.

He sat down again, finding the seat a great deal more comfortable now than it had been before. Heading toward the meeting, his body had been a collection of bits and pieces as rigid as the parts of a marionette. He could bend at all the normal joints, but tension had kept the muscles taut as guy wires except when they were being consciously relaxed. "Bad as an insertion," Kelly muttered to himself, knowing that the back deck of a tank would have given him as good a ride as the leather upholstery had on the way to Meade.

Elaine was still struggling with her seat, repositioning it from where the long-legged Doug had left it. "It adjusts on four axes," she snapped, knowing that Kelly was smiling, "which gives you the theoretical possibility of finding the perfect solution, and the high likelihood that *every* acceptable solution'll be lost in the maze of other alternatives."

She sat back, grimaced, and started the car anyway. "It's a lot like the information business, isn't it?" she added, and her wry smile mirrored Kelly's.

It had stopped raining, and the overcast had broken patchily to let a few stars glitter down. The air was so clear that lights reflected like jewels from all the wet surfaces around them. "The Buick going to be tagging along again?" Kelly asked, nodding at the follow-car as the inner gate opened. The bigger vehicle's engine was running and its park lights were on while it waited outside the enclosure.

Elaine pulled through the second gate and clutched,

looking over at the veteran. "Unless you don't want it to," she said in a voice whose surface brightness Kelly had already learned to associate with a mind nervously in overdrive.

"No problem." He chopped his left hand down the road as if the woman were a squad he was sending forward. "Dougie-boy got on my nerves, that was all. But I really don't bite, I promise."

"Sure, Kelly." Elaine gassed the car and shifted directly from first to third after revving smoothly to the top of the powerband. "And one of these days I'll get a job instead of living off my daddy's money." After a moment she added, "But I know what you mean. Thanks."

There was no bar for traffic outbound from the fort, but the woman slowed and waved toward the guard post. This time she accelerated away fast, keeping the back tires just beneath the limit of traction throughout the radius of the turn and beyond as she straightened onto the highway.

"You didn't get the keys from Doug before you came out," Kelly said while they waited at what he remembered as the last of the traffic lights, if they were headed back into the District as they seemed to be.

"I'd given him my spare set," the woman said, coming off the light as if she were dropping the hammer at a drag strip. "I'll pick them up tomorrow."

Eyes on the entrance ramp and the possible traffic on the turnpike into which they were merging, she added, "Blakeley doesn't get *only* on your nerves, Tom. But let me keep my mind on what I'm doing right now, okay?"

They were heading south for the skyglow above the

capital much faster than Doug had brought them to Meade, though there was no similarity between the styles of the two drivers. Doug had a heavy foot for brake and accelerator, and a muffled curse for other vehicles which did not behave in the manner he wished them to.

Elaine dabbed, sliding diagonally through interstices in traffic with a verve which Kelly had thought only a motorcycle could achieve. She was anticipating not only the cars nearest in front and beside them, but the next tier of vehicles as well, so that the drive had the feel of a chess game. Most of the time she kept the Volvo's engine snarling in third gear or fourth. Only on the rare stretches of really empty pavement did she shift up into the over-drive fifth, trading acceleration for the car's absolute top end.

"Motor's to European specs," she called in satisfaction over the engine note at one of the fifth-gear upshifts. "And the suspension's had a little work."

The team in the follow-car must be royally pissed, thought Kelly as he relaxed against the seat cushions, but they had a destination and might even be used to this sort of run if they were assigned regularly to Elaine. She wasn't in a hurry, particularly, and she wasn't trying to prove her competence—or manhood, though it was a joke to think about it that way—to Kelly.

Driving on the edge of control—and control was what was important, not speed—was a hell of a good way to burn away hormones and emotions which had to be bottled up in social situations. If you understood what was going on, you could achieve catharsis without acting as if you were furious with everyone else on the road at the same time. Elaine knew that very well, and she drove with a razorlike acuity not muffled by the need for false emotions to justify it.

"You know," said the veteran as they halted at the first traffic light in downtown Washington, "you could fool me into thinking that you don't like the people you work for a whole lot better than I do."

"You had an escape valve in that meeting." Elaine proceeded through the intersection sedately. The sodium-vapor street lights emphasized the color raised on her cheeks by the high-intensity drive. "You could always decide you were going to try to kill everybody else in the room. I didn't have that luxury."

Kelly turned sharply to stare at her profile. Her hair had fluffed during the drive, shading her cheeks, but she cocked her head enough toward the veteran to let him see her grin.

He smiled as well, releasing the catch of his seatbelt in order to shift the weapon in the hollow of his back. "I wouldn't have, no sweat," he said. "But yeah, sometimes it's nice to know that endgame's *your* choice, not some other bastard's."

Kelly was wondering idly at the facades of Central Washington buildings, lower and more interestingly variegated than those of most comparable cities, when the Volvo cut smoothly toward the curb. The veteran glanced from Elaine, thumbing the trunk-latch button on the console, and back with new interest to the hotel at which they had stopped. The ground level expanse was of curtained glass and glass doors printed with "The Madison" as tastefully as gold leaf can ever be. Despite the hour, a uniformed attendant was coming out almost simultaneously with the muffled pop of the trunk.

Elaine had her door open and was stepping into the street before Kelly could even start around the car to hand her out. "They're gonna confiscate my shining armor, lady," he called plaintively over the green roof.

"Get the case, Tom," she replied as she pointed out the keys still in the ignition to the attendant, who slid behind the wheel.

The sound from above was unmistakable, but it was so unexpected in the present context that Kelly could not fully believe what he was hearing even after he paused to stare up into the darkness. "What the hell?" he said as Elaine walked back to him and glanced upward as well. "There's a helicopter orbiting up there."

The clop of rotor blades was syncopated by echoes from building fronts and the broad streets, but the whine of the turbine waxed and waned purely as a result of the attitude of the aircraft to the listeners below.

"Get the case," Elaine repeated calmly. "It's not us— not that they told me." She shrugged and pursed her lips in a moue. "The President of Venezuela's in town. He's probably staying here."

Kelly hefted out the black Halliburton in the trunk. The attaché case was not so much heavy in the abstract as it was disconcertingly heavier than the norm for things that looked like it. "I congratulate you on the excellence of your expense accounts, ah—" he said as he slammed the trunk, "Elaine."

He followed the woman at a half step and to the side as they strode through the lobby, heeling really, as if he were a well-trained dog. Which was true enough, very true indeed, though he wasn't sure just whose dog he was right at the moment. Not NSA's, certainly not that of the bastards he'd just met at Meade, whatever their acronym turned out to be for the moment.

The hell of it was, the *hell* of it was, Tom Kelly probably still belonged to an abstraction called America which existed only in his mind. It didn't bear much similarity to the US government; but he guessed that was as close as you came in the real world.

Fuckin' A.

Elaine had fished a key from her purse as they walked between a quietly-comfortable lobby and the reception desk. She ignored the clerk as she strode toward the elevators, but Kelly noticed the man turned and spun his hand idly in the box that would have held messages for room 618. Kelly winked, and the clerk waved back with a broad grin.

The graveyard shift was boring as hell, even if you were pretty sure the other side had you targeted for a night assault.

Kelly entered the brass-doored elevator at the woman's side and pushed the button for the sixth floor before she lifted her hand. "This isn't the briefcase you had earlier?" he said, staring at his poker-faced reflection in the polished metal.

"No, it's the one that stayed under guard in the car until we knew we'd want it," Elaine said, eyeing the veteran sidelong with an expression resembling that of a squirrel in hunting season.

Keep 'em off balance, Kelly thought as his expression

of wide-eyed innocence looked back at him. Especially when you don't know which end is up yourself.

Room 618 had a king-sized bed, a window that would show a fair swath of the city by daylight, and a Persian carpet which didn't look like anything near the money Kelly knew its equivalent would cost in the shop in the lobby.

There was also a small refrigerator in one corner.

Kelly set the attaché case down on the writing desk and knelt beside the refrigerator. "Gimme the key," he said, holding out his left hand behind him. When nothing slapped his palm, he turned and seated himself on one buttock on the edge of the desk.

Elaine stood with the thumb and index finger of either hand on the keys, the larger one for the door and the small one that unlocked the refrigerator which formed the room's private bar. Her face was as blank as it would have been if construction workers had whistled at her from across a street.

"You've got no right to judge me, woman," Kelly said. His right leg was flexed, and his hand gripped the raised knee in a pattern of tendons and veins. "No fucking *right!*" he shouted as if volume could release the pressure inside him or crack the marble calm of the woman who met his eyes.

"I have the job of judging you, Tom," she said with no emphasis as she bent and handed the paired keys to him. "Shall I get a bucket of ice?"

"Naw, I'm not warm," the veteran said, his throat clogged with residues of the emotion he hated himself for having let out. "Thanks." He fitted the key into the lock and opened the little door. "I'm not warm, just thirsty. Anything for you?"

"Orange juice," Elaine said as she rotated the three-dial combination of the attaché case. "Grapefruit, something citrus."

At least, and for a wonder, it wasn't Perrier—which Kelly had always found to taste like water from a well contaminated with acetylene. And at least she did not stare at what Kelly brought out for himself, a minibottle of Jack Daniel's and a can of Lowenbrau.

"There's a really good Pilsner beer in Turkey," he said as he twisted a chair so that he could see both the woman and the files that she was beginning to place on the desk. "I got to like it." He twisted the cap off the bottle of whiskey, took a sip, and washed the liquor down with a swallow of beer.

When Elaine still said nothing, the veteran prodded, "You've got a dead Kurd and a dead alien. And you've got me, until I drink myself into a stupor, hey? So why don't we get to it?"

"I don't like self-destructive people," the woman said as she set the emptied case to the floor and sat at the other chair by the desk. "I like it even less when an exceptionally able person I have to work with seems bent on destroying himself. But I don't like it when an airline manages to lose my luggage, either, and I've learned to live with that."

Kelly finished the whiskey, his eyes meeting the woman's. "My work gets done," he said, wishing that his tone did not sound so defensive.

"And it'll continue to get done," Elaine responded coolly, "until one day it doesn't. Which may mean that people get dead, or worse. But since it's like the weather, something that can't be helped, then we don't need to talk about it any more,"

She wasn't particularly tall, Kelly thought, but she looked just as frail as her black linen jacket, through which light showed every time the fabric fluffed away from her body. He felt like a pit bull facing a chihuahua which was smart enough to be afraid, but wasn't for all that about to back down.

He got up, carrying the can of beer, and walked toward the bathroom. "What is it you think I can do for you?" he called over his shoulder, the phrasing carefully ambiguous. He poured the rest of his beer down the sink and ran water into the aluminum can.

Elaine, still seated, twisted to face him when he returned from the bathroom. "Your personal contacts with the Kurds are more likely to get you information about what's going on than the formal information nets are. The fact that we've heard so little about something so major proves that there's a problem."

"What *do* you have?" Kelly asked, stretching himself out on his back on the carpet between the bed and the window. He set the can of water down beside him and cupped his hands beneath his skull as a pillow.

"Reports of men going off for military training," the woman said. "Many of them men we'd had on the payroll ourselves during Birdlike."

"Mohammed Ayyubi one of them?" Kelly asked from the floor. Rather than relaxing, he was bearing his weight on shoulders and heels with his belly muscles tensed in a flat arch. Elaine could not tell whether his eyes were closed or just slitted, watching her, and the effect was similar to that of being stalked in the darkness.

"No," she said, "but he'd been closely associated with some of the people who disappeared. He was living in Istanbul, living well and without a job, you know? He'd make trips east and we think probably to Europe, though we were never able to trace him out of Turkey. Or even far in-country, except after the fact. Somebody would tell us that somebody's wife had a lot of money, now, and her husband had gone off with Mohammed Ayyubi, in a new struggle for Free Kurdistan. That sort of thing."

Kelly rolled onto his side, facing Elaine, and took a deep draft of water from his can. "Haven't found much use for hotel glasses but to stick your toothbrush in," he said with a disarming grin. "The .22 Shorts of the container world." Without changing expression, he went on, "What do they say when they come back, Elaine? Who's training them?"

"Russia, we thought," the woman said. She shifted on her chair, crossing her right thigh over the left and angrily aware that there was no normal etiquette for discussions with a man who lay at one's feet. "Now, of course, we're not sure. And none of the—recruits we've targeted seem to have come back, on leave or whatever, though their families get sizable remittances in hard currency, not lire."

"You've tried to get people close to Mohammed before now," Kelly said, his flat tone begging the question. "I don't think money'd do much to turn his head if he's— he was—convinced somebody was offering a real chance for Kurdish independence . . . but you people'd think money was the ticket, wouldn't you? What'd he say?"

There was nothing lithe about the man sprawled on the carpet, Elaine thought. He was as close-coupled as a brick, built like a male lion—and with all the arrogance of the male lion's strength and willingness to kill his own kind.

"We don't know," she said carefully. "There was a car bomb explosion—in Diyarbakir—the day before the shooting. Three people were killed, two of them as they came out of the hotel in which they were to have met Ayyubi. We don't know whether they did or not, or what was said."

"Hardball, aren't we?" said the veteran in a very soft voice to the beer can. He held it between thumb and middle finger, at the top where the braced crimp in the cylinder would have made it impossible for even Godzilla to crush the can with two fingers. The mottled skin and the way the tendons stood out proved that Kelly was trying, though, or at least spending in isometrics an emotional charge that would otherwise have broken something. "Amcits, I suppose?"

"Our personnel were American citizens, yes," Elaine said. "They were assigned TDY to the missile tracking station at Pirinclik, just out of town."

"NSA's being cooperative after all." Kelly put the can down again. His eyes, as calm as they ever had been, were back on hers. Elaine had read enough between the lines of the psych profiles in the veteran's file to know that he really didn't have as short a fuse as he projected under stress. The anger was there, but there was a level of control that could handle almost anything.

The flip side of that, and the thing that made him so

much more dangerous than a man who simply lost his temper, was that Kelly did not go out of control when he chose to act.

People were entering the room next door, jostling and cursing as more than one husky man tried to get through a narrow hotel doorway at the same time. Kelly grinned and thumbed toward the common wall. "The cavalry's arrived," he said. "You can breathe normally again."

Elaine scowled, realizing that she was just as tense as the words implied—not that the arrival of the team from the follow-car would change anything to her benefit if the shit really hit the fan. She stretched in her chair, twining her fingers behind her neck and, elbows flared, arching her chest forward.

Nothing in the file indicated whether Kelly was a leg man or a breast man.

"You know," he was saying, "you're a hell of a driver."

She relaxed her body and said, "For a girl."

"Goddam," said Kelly as he twisted to his feet and walked toward the bathroom with the can emptied now of water. "You know, I hadn't noticed that."

His delivery was so deadpan that the woman's mouth opened in shocked amazement—replaced by a flush by the time he returned with more water and a broad smile at how effectively he had gotten through her professional facade.

"They're not going to talk to me either, you know?" the stocky man said as he seated himself normally on the chair beside Elaine's. "Some folks I worked with might remember me, sure. But I was US, just as sure as the boys who got blown away the other day. Free Kurdistan is a lot more important to—to somebody like Mohammed—than any personal chips I could call in."

"Word of how you terminated from the service got around very quickly when you didn't return from leave," Elaine said. Her voice had never lost its even tenor, and her mind was fully back to business as well. "Around the personnel of Operation Birdlike. Even though there was an attempt to stop it or at least replace the"—she smiled—"truth with rumors less embarrassing to the USG.

"Since the indigs—the Kurds—were Muslims and strongly religious, the fact that you'd dynamited the government of Israel did you no harm with the men you'd been training. And they're quite convinced that you aren't—won't ever be again—an agent of the United States."

Elaine paused. Then she added, "Besides, I think you underestimate the level of personal loyalty that some of your troops felt toward you. It was a matter of some concern during the interval between the time you— terminated and Birdlike was wrapped up."

"You wouldn't believe," said Kelly to his hands flat on the desk, "how many people'd follow you to hell if you're willing to lead 'em there. We got thirty-seven MiGs in their revetments at Tekret the one night."

He looked up and his voice trembled with remembered emotion. "The whole sky was orange from ten klicks away. Just like fuckin' sunrise. . . ."

Kelly stood abruptly and turned away. "Shit," he snarled. "Don't fuckin' _do_ this to me, okay?"

"The only reason," Elaine said softly, "that we'd ask

you to use the people you know is that it might take too long to reopen normal channels. We don't know how long we have before the—apparent hostiles—execute whatever plan they have in progress."

"Don't *bull*shit me, Elaine," he said as his hands clenched and the muscles of his shoulders hunched up like a weight lifter's. He faced her again and went on deliberately, "You wouldn't be where you are if you had a problem with asking your grandma to penetrate massage parlors. You sure as *hell* don't have a problem with askin' me to burn people who trust me."

"I've got a problem with wasting my time," she said calmly, leaning back to look up at the angry man. She uncrossed her legs. "I wouldn't waste time asking you to do something you wouldn't do with a gun to your head. This one's necessary, you know it is—and you know that whatever your friends may think, nobody's coming to Earth from another *planet* to set up an independent Kurdistan! Don't you?"

"Well, there's that," Kelly agreed with a sigh. He sat down again on a corner of the bed. "How many recruits are we talking about? Kurds, I mean." He was studying the backs of his hands with a frowning interest that would have been justified for a fat envelope with a Dublin postmark.

"About twenty that we're pretty sure of," Elaine said, genuinely relaxing again. She gestured toward the files with red-bordered cover sheets, which she had spread on the desk. "It's here, what we have. Certainly we've got only the tip of the iceberg—but at worst we're not talking about—" She smiled; it made a different person of her, emphasizing the pleasant fullness of her cheeks and adding a touch of naughtiness to features which otherwise suggested wickedness of a thoroughly professional kind.

"—a land war in Asia," she concluded.

"I'm not subtle, you know," Kelly said. "If I go in, I'll make a lotta waves. If I think it's the best way to learn what's going on, I'll tell people every goddam thing *I* know. And if it gets rough, it's likely to get *real* rough."

"Slash and burn data collection," the woman said with a grimace, though not a particularly angry one. She shrugged. "The more waves you make," she went on, "the more likely it is that the wheels come off before you—or we—learn anything useful. But there isn't a lot of time, and the people who picked you for this operation had seen your profiles too."

"Goddam, goddam, goddam," the veteran said without heat as he lay back on the white bedspread and began to knuckle his eyes. His feet were still flat on the floor. "It's going to take me a while to get my own stuff on track. Maybe a week. Couple—three days at least."

"You won't need a cover identity," Elaine said. Because Kelly's eyes were closed, it was only in his mind that he saw her face blank into an expression of professional neutrality. "Your job with Congressman Bianci has taken you out of the country in the past, and—"

"No," Kelly said. He neither snapped nor raised his voice, but there was nothing in the way he spoke that admitted of argument. "Carlo doesn't get involved in this."

"The congressman will agree without question, Tom," Elaine said in a reasonable tone. "I don't mean we'd put pressure on him—you can clear it with him yourself. He's a, well, a patriot, and if you tell him you're convinced yourself that it's a matter of national security then—"

"Stop," said Kelly. He had taken his hands away from his eyes, but he continued to look at the ceiling, and it was toward the ceiling that he spoke in a voice as cold and flat as the work-face of a broadax: "Carlo hired me to keep him *out* of shit. He doesn't get into this bucket if he swears on a stack a' Bibles he wants to."

Kelly paused, for breath rather than for rhetorical effect. "I'll go in as a civilian tech advisor, Boeing or RCA, that sorta thing. There must be a couple thousand Amcits like that. Pick one with the right build who's rotating home and make me up a passport. God knows you can square it with Boeing. I may be carrying some electronics, so make that reasonable enough for Customs."

Elaine did not even consider arguing the Bianci matter again. "Check," she said. "Though there's no need for you to carry things in country yourself."

"There's no need for me to carry a lucky charm," said Kelly, shifting his weight a little, though the mattress was too soft to make more than a mild discomfort of the weapon in the hollow of his spine, "but if it ain't broke, you don't fix it.

"Besides . . ." As he spoke the planes of his face changed, tiny muscles reacting to mental tension. "I want to keep clear of whatever you've got on the ground already. I for *damn* sure don't want to be showing up at the US Mission to collect my mail."

"If you need something in a hurry and it isn't pre-positioned," the woman warned, "the chances are it'll have to come in by pouch."

"If I *ask* you for something, it's my lookout," the veteran said as he sat up and met Elaine's eyes. "But don't hold your breath, because, because I'd rather call in favors of my own than trust"—The woman smiled, and perhaps for that reason Kelly softened the remainder of his sentence to—"people who don't owe me."

He stood up again, stretched his arms behind him as the woman watched in silence, and went on. "What I *want* from you people is to be tasked and left the fuck alone. Don't ask me for sitreps, don't try to help, and for *God's* sake, don't get in my way."

"You expect too much," Elaine said calmly.

"I *expect* to be fucked around to the point I can't work," Kelly answered in a harsh whisper, "and *then* I expect to pack up and go home. That's what I *expect*."

"You'll have a case officer," Elaine replied as if there had been no threat. "Me, unless you prefer otherwise. And there'll be support available in country. If you don't need it, that's fine, but throwing a tantrum doesn't give you the right to flout common sense. Mine. But nobody's going to hamper your activities, Tom."

Kelly smiled broadly and rubbed the heavy black stubble on his chin. "Well, that's something for the relationship," he said mildly. "You tell the lies you gotta, but it seems you stop there. Hell, maybe this thing's going to work."

He stepped over to the desk and riffled one of the files there. "Look," he said, "go off to your friends or wherever"—he gestured toward the partition wall behind him—"for however long it takes me to read in. It'll go quicker if I'm alone in the room." He didn't bother to add that he wasn't going to try to leave.

Elaine nodded, stood up, and walked toward the door. She paused just short of it and said, with her back toward Kelly and the well-stocked refrigerator, "Would you like some coffee from room service before you start?"

"Don't press your luck, Elaine," the veteran said in the glass-edged whisper again.

She turned, wearing her professional smile again. "And don't press yours, Tom," she said. "Don't pretend, even to yourself, that you can walk out on this now that you're in."

Kelly laughed. "Hey," he said with a cheerful lilt, "who greased Mohammed?"

"We presume," Elaine replied in a neutral voice from a neutral face, "that the car bomb and the shootings were the work of the same parties. Either the aliens or their agents made an error, or there are third parties already involved in the matter.

"Good night, Tom."

The brass bolt and wards clacked with finality as Kelly's case officer drew the door shut behind her.

It had been a long night. Around the edges of the rubber-backed outer drapes, saffron dawn was heralding what would probably be a long day. The veteran sighed, set the chain bolt behind Elaine Tuttle, and got to work.

There was a telephone on the bedside table and another extension, weatherized like a pay phone, on the wall of the bathroom. Kelly unplugged the modular jack from the base unit of each phone. He was too tired to trust his judgment, though his intellect floated in something approaching a dream state, functioning with effortless precision in collating information. By allowing habit to take over, Kelly could for the time avoid the errors of judgment he was sure to make if he tried to think things out.

There were a lot of ways to bug a room. Some of the simplest involved modifying the telephone to act at need as a listening device. A fix for the problem was a small, battery-powered fluorescent light. When it was turned on and set near the phone, the radio-frequency hash which its oscillators made in raising the voltage to necessary levels completely flooded the circuitry of most bugs. Unplugging the phone was even more effective, though no one could call in or out while the unit was disconnected, Kelly didn't need the phone, so that didn't matter.

Of course, no sound he was going to make in room 618 mattered either—but it was habit, and it wasn't going to hurt either.

Kelly unplugged the television set next to the refrigerator and then wiggled loose the bayonet connector of the coax to the hotel's common antenna. Lord! how people worried about bugging—some of them with more reason than others—and how rarely any of them hesitated to have cable TV installed. There is a perfect reciprocity in many aspects of electricity and magnetism: if you reverse cause and effect, the system still works. As a practical matter here, that meant that the television speaker also acted as a microphone monitoring every sound in the hotel room—and that the data was available for pick-off through the antenna connection or, with more difficulty, through the hotel's power circuitry.

"If they want to know what I'm doing, they can damn well ask me," the veteran said as he straightened.

The key ring clinked against the face of the refrigerator as his knee bumped it. Kelly looked down. For a moment, the unobtrusive appliance was the only thing in his mind—or in the universe. It had been a long time since the whiskey, a *bloody* long time.

"You're too goddam smart for your own good, woman," Kelly muttered; his palms were sweating. "Too smart for mine for sure."

The hell of it was, she didn't think he *couldn't* stop drinking, she thought he could. She was right, of course; Tom Kelly could do any goddam thing he set his mind to . . . but why he cared about disappointing some bitch he'd just met, some hard-edged pro who'd spend him like a bullet, that part of his mind was beyond his own understanding.

Coffee'd do for now.

Kelly tossed his jacket on the bed, then went over to his own zippered, limp-leather briefcase to remove the small jar of instant coffee and the immersion heater. He looked at the beer can and grimaced. He could cut the top off to insert the heater, but that would leave a jagged edge, and a thin aluminum can wasn't a sensible man's choice for drinking hot liquids.

A few ounces of coffee at a time was better than none. He needed fluids to sip while he worked, and if coffee was the choice this time—there were four glasses in the bathroom; he filled them all, brought them to the writing desk where he dusted them with instant coffee, and inserted the immersion heater in the first.

Next, from his briefcase, Kelly took a radio rather smaller than a hardcover book. It was an off-the-shelf

Sony 2002, and for less than $300 it would pick up AM, FM, and short wave signals with an efficiency NSA would have spent $15,000 a copy to duplicate a few years before.

Hell, governments being what they are, NSA was probably still paying fifteen grand for similar packages.

The little world-band radio ran either from batteries or from an AC/DC converter; but the latter caused a hum on shortwave, and batteries—unlike public power grids—were the same voltage worldwide. Sound in the background, even if it was no more than the hiss of static, was as necessary to Kelly's study habits as something beside him to drink. He used the scanner to pick up an FM station, classical music, something he had last heard on Radio Sophia when he was a long fucking way from the United States.

Funny. Music cared less about time and nationalities than just about anything except stones. Of course, politicians were pretty similar worldwide, too. As were spies.

Tom Kelly unplugged the immersion heater. There was one final preliminary to getting comfortable. He drew the snub-nosed revolver nestled at the small of his back and set it on the desk beside the bubbling glass of coffee.

The exposed metal of the weapon had been sand-blasted and anodized an unattractive dull gray about the color of phosphate-protected steel. There was a line of wear around the cylinder where the registration lug rubbed, but the weapon had actually been fired only a handful of times in the thirty-five years since its manufacture.

A patch of Velcro—hook-side—had been epoxied to the right side of the barrel just ahead of the five-shot cylinder, and there was a corresponding patch of Velcro fuzz sewn at the back of the waistband of every pair of pants Kelly owned. There were a lot of circumstances in which a holster was slower to ditch than the gun itself. The Velcro was unobtrusive, added neither bulk nor weight, and was actually more secure than the usual belt-clip holster.

Apart from its finish and the nylon hooks, the revolver looked like a standard Smith and Wesson Chiefs Special, the choice of tens of thousands of people who wanted the punch of a .38 Special cartridge in a small, reliable package. Kelly's gun was something more than that. Though it was dimensionally identical to the ordinary version, the only steel in the weapon was the slight amount in the lockwork: frame, cylinder, and barrel had all been forged from aluminum in response to an Air Force request for the lightest possible revolver to equip pilots who came down behind enemy lines. Almost the entire run had been melted down shortly thereafter, when the decision was countermanded; but not quite all.

Tom Kelly didn't care that the gun weighed ten ounces empty instead of the steel version's nineteen. He cared very much that its magnetic signature was so low that it would not show up on airport magnetometers unless they were set low enough to trip on three or four dimes in a pocket as well.

The ammunition Kelly had handloaded for the revolver was also nonstandard, though the components were off-the-shelf items. He'd used commercial 148-grain wadcutter bullets, swaged from pure lead instead of being cast with an alloy to harden them, ahead of three grains of Bullseye, a powder fast enough to burn almost completely within the snubbie's short barrel. The bullets were formed with a hollow base, a deep cavity meant to be upset against the rifling grooves by the powder gases in the manner of a Civil War minié ball. Kelly had loaded them back to front, and the deep cup had expanded the soft metal very efficiently in a gelatine target despite the relatively low velocity of the bullet on impact.

Keeping pressures within levels that a cartridge-company engineer would have found acceptable in 1920 had been the bottom line for the load. The all-aluminum revolvers had been tested by the Air Force with ordinary ammunition and with blue pills—proof loads developing forty percent greater pressure than normal. There was no reason to believe that in the ensuing thirty-five years the metal would have work-hardened into a state that made it more likely to rupture.

Still, better safe than sorry. . . . Kelly wasn't particularly worried about being hurt if the revolver blew up— the person holding a handgun at arm's length is the one least likely to be harmed if the chamber bursts. He was very much concerned that in a crisis so severe that he had to use the weapon, it would fail and give him one shot when he desperately counted on having five.

The master sergeant who'd sold him the gun at Wheelus had said that no government was going to put an unsafe weapon in the hands of its troops. That would have been more confidence-building if Kelly hadn't seen the USG issue a tactical nuke, the Davy Crockett, with a fall-out radius greater than the range of the launcher. Not that anybody'd explained that at the time to the Marines who were expected to fry themselves with the thing.

For the remainder of the morning, the veteran read files and made plans. He had two bars of Bendicks chocolate, the Military and Sportsmen's blend, in his briefcase. They did little to quell the roiling of coffee and fatigue in his stomach, but the caffeine in the dose of fifty-seven percent pure chocolate did its own share of good.

The files were a maze, reports pared to the bone and beyond, filled with agent designators which could be collated with real names only through separate documents. There had been no evident attempt to censor what Kelly was being given: his own name appeared in one report as the source of a case of M14 rifles said to have been received by another Kurd who had disappeared shortly thereafter. Kelly remembered the agent from Operation Birdlike and was amused to note that the man's present reporting officer classed him as "generally reliable." Kelly wouldn't have taken the fellow's word for whether the sun rose in the east.

And that was the problem with most of the information: the three agents among the Kurdish community whom Kelly did know were venal, cowardly, and thoroughly untrustworthy. Results suggested that the remainder of the reports were from similar trash, men and women who had, at best, secondhand information on whatever Mohammed Ayyubi was involved in. Had been involved in, until somebody shot him and a monster dead on a rain-sodden street.

The files covered approximately the past year. There was nothing in them regarding aliens, and for all but the past two months they were concerned solely with the normal collection from a nationalist movement: money and arms; smuggling and training camps; foreign contacts in general and the dark suggestions of Russian involvement certain to show up in reports approved by American station chiefs.

Not that the KGB and other Russians paid to meddle in Third World problems were any less likely to be doing so than their US counterparts.

There was a change in March which was so abrupt that it must have resulted from a change in emphasis at client level—the members of the US government who received the information—rather than a watershed in what the agents themselves chose to send in. Suddenly Kurds were making UFO reports which would have been right at home in small-town papers throughout America.

There were no, thank God, conversations with little green men, although one case officer had sent a number of reports of angelic revelations before somebody further up the line had rapped his knuckles. There were airplanes that flew straight up, huge cylinders with lighted windows along their sides, and a score of other shapes and styles. Some reports referred to incidents as much as thirty years in the past, proving to a certainty that the sudden spate of reports was only a result of tasking.

In general, the only similarities between objects sighted occurred when two or more reports were made by the same agent. There was a single exception: disks twenty meters in diameter which lifted silently, wrapped in auroral splendor—from locations separated by a hundred miles, and with no duplication in the chain of data. That could mean something; and certainly there *was* something to be learned; the dead alien proved that. But even if one or all of the reports were true, they were garbage which did absolutely nothing to indicate what was really going on.

And that was all there was. No wonder Pierrard and his crew were willing to try a card as wild as Tom Kelly.

A thing with a mouth like a lamprey, and a couple dozen—maybe a few hundred—Kurds whose families thought they were going off to be armed and trained in the cause of Kurdish nationalism. Well, the connection would be obvious just as soon as Kelly learned what it was.

When the files were stacked neatly again on the top of the desk, the veteran walked to the bathroom. The toothbrush and toothpaste from his briefcase, and the hot shower that he let play over him helped but could not wholly remove the foulness throughout his system. Fear and anger and fatigue, but most especially fear, leave their hormonal spoor on a man.

Kelly looked at himself in the fogged mirror when he stepped out of the shower, but that was another mistake. His outline was intact, but the condensate on the glass turned his hundred and eighty pounds, tank-solid and scarred with experience, into a wistful ghost. He was crazy to get back into this; aliens or no, none of it would matter when he was dead.

But death would come regardless.

He lay down on the bed, his skin warm with the harsh toweling he had just given it. He'd have them book him into the Sheraton in a room facing the Golden Horn. He'd treat it as a perk—they understood perks, these folk in suits they never saw the bills for, and no eyebrows would lift because Kelly wanted a room in the most expensive hotel in Istanbul. They would understand the implied test, also, the precise instructions which they could either carry out or not—and the implications if they did not or even chose to argue.

And because they understood both those things, they would not foresee their agent's—"their agent's"—real reason for wanting a room just there.

He needed to talk to people after he shook free from the box Elaine would try to put around him no matter what she said. There were folks who owed him, though the good ones didn't keep score any more than Kelly did himself. Individuals, unlike nations, were capable of keeping faith.

For now, however, what he needed most of all was sleep. He closed his eyes, and sleep came with the fireshot dreams Kelly had expected. But the dreams changed, and by the time he awakened at twilight he could remember nothing but moving figures and black walls that reached toward heaven.

Airport terminals have certain worldwide similarities, but Istanbul's had more in common with the military portion of Beirut Airport than with any civilian structure Kelly'd walked through. Luggage from the Pan Am flight that had just landed was arrayed on a single long, low table in the center of a hangar converted for baggage examination.

Each individual claimed his or her own suitcases under the eyes of armed guards, and carried them to the examination booths—porters took the weight for some passengers, mostly foreigners, but no one else could accept the responsibility.

Beyond hand luggage Kelly had only one suitcase and that—a solid, vinyl case of Turkish manufacture—held clothing. He had no need, himself, to bring unusual hardware into Turkey, as it had turned out, because his overseas phone calls had been more successful than he had dared hope. Funny. It always surprised him when other people came through the way he would have done for them—120 percent and no questions asked that didn't bear on the fulfillment of the request.

It would have been easy for Kelly to snatch his bag and stride ahead of the remaining passengers, and reaching an empty examination booth would have saved half an hour of waiting for civilians—nervous, belligerent, or both—to be processed through ahead of him.

But even though the stocky veteran had nothing to fear from Customs, he let his training override his instinct to go full bore and finish whatever he was doing by the most direct route possible. He kept a low profile, deliberately followed a middle-aged man with a bag in either hand and a brown Yugoslav passport held with his entry documents between two fingertips and the side of the smaller case.

The Customs agent for whom Kelly opened his bag wore khaki pants with a tie and white shirt. The uniform of the National Policeman watching him was of gray-green wool and included a Browning Hi-Power in a holster of white patent leather. Beyond the line of booths was a squad of soldiers in fatigues, smoking and occasionally adjusting the slings of the Thompson submachine guns they carried.

Prime Minister Ecevit had taken the Defense portfolio for himself, but that was cosmetic. He was also making a real attempt to control the radical violence from both sides before a military junta ousted him to cure the problem more directly. The open display of armed force seemed to concern most of the foreign passengers. Kelly himself had enough other things to worry about.

"I love Istanbul," Kelly joked in Turkish with the Customs agent, "but do they let me stay here? Surely there must be runway sweepers to be maintained in a more lovely part of Turkey than Incidik!"

"You are a Turk?" asked the National Policeman, running a knowledgeable hand along the hinges of the suitcase instead of prodding through the shirts as he had done with the Yugoslav minutes before.

"No," said the Customs agent, flipping from the front to the back of the artistically-worn passport, but sizing Kelly up sidelong as he stamped the entry data. The American was a hair taller than the Anatolian norm, but his stocky build was right as were the dark complexion and straight black hair. With a moustache and a few days polish on his Turkish, he could pass as a native—of the country, though not of any specific district.

He might have to do just that.

"Not, but should be," Kelly agreed with a smile. "It's good to be back. Even headed for Incirlik."

"Go with God, Mr. Bradsheer," the Customs agent said, closing the suitcase with one hand and returning Kelly's false passport in the other. The currency declaration form went into a file beneath the examination table.

Kelly smiled, snapped the latches of the case—no time to buckle the safety straps as well—and said, "Go with God, brother," as he walked out the rear of the canvas booth.

Elaine Tuttle was standing at the back of the building, beyond the low barrier that separated incoming passengers from those waiting to greet them.

She wore a long-sleeved blue dress today, with ruffles at wrists and throat and a belt of light gilded chain. It had been three days since Kelly last saw her, and his recognition now was not instantaneous. Partly it was the beret that covered the rich curls of her black hair, partly that Tuttle carried a large purse on a shoulder strap for the first time since he had met her. In large measure, Kelly did not recognize Elaine because the physical reality of her was so different—so much less threatening—than memory suffused with the woman's personality.

He did not dream about her, but he had begun to dream—and if the strange landscapes he remembered on awakening were not nightmares, they would do till worse came along.

Kelly stopped at the barrier and rested his suitcase on it while he buckled the straps over the latches. None of the soldiers paid him any particular attention. There were enthusiastic greetings in half a dozen languages, chiefly Turkish and German—a Turkish Airways flight from Frankfurt had just disgorged its load of "guest workers" from West Germany. Kelly had to wait for a large family reunion at the nearest opening in the barrier, but he wasn't in such a hurry that he would attract attention by scissoring his legs over it instead.

Elaine, who had not moved while Kelly meandered through the entry building, stepped to his side as he began to walk out the door. "It's a long way to the car," she said, nodding toward the parking lot set off from the terminal area by barbed wire and cyclone fencing. There were more troops outside, and an armored car painted blue to match the berets of the paramilitary police. "Do you want to wait for me to bring the car around?"

"No sweat," said Kelly, swinging the suitcase at arm's length in front of him to prove that he could handle the weight. He continued to saunter toward the pedestrian gate at which Elaine had gestured. "You know, I was afraid you people were going to walk me through Customs and make a fuss. I should've said something before. Glad you had better sense than I—gave you credit for."

"Given the present political climate," Elaine said with her eyes on where they were going, "with Ecevit using America as a whipping boy for all the troubles of his administration, I don't know that we could have done much. Not in the Istanbul District, at any rate."

She looked up sharply at the man beside her. "Not that you seemed to need help very badly."

"You wanted somebody who was comfortable in Turkey," Kelly said. "That much you got."

He shifted the case from one hand to the other as she led him through a row of parked cars and, on the other side, wrapped his arm around her shoulders in a hug. "Hey, Elaine," he said, releasing her almost before her light frame began to stiffen beneath the dress, "I'm pumped, but right for the moment I'm feelin' good."

He grinned across at her as they continued to stride along, switching the suitcase back to his right hand to prove that the hug had been no more than a friendly gesture. "Look," he explained, "going—back to work's— my equivalent of riding the roller coaster, I guess. It'll be a rush while it lasts, and you don't have to worry about how I'll get along *with you* so long as we're on the same side, okay? And you handle your end the way I'd want to be able to handle it if it was my job."

"Rather than handle it like you, you mean?" Elaine asked with the beginning of a smile.

"Right," agreed Kelly with a broader one, dodging a little Ford Anadol that was being backed from its parking space with more verve than discretion. "Rather than by getting the admin types so mad that they insist on fucking with the operation, which is exactly what I'd do if anybody were silly enough to put me in that slot. I never had a lotta tact, and when things get tense for one reason'r the other—"

He laughed, and stopped. They passed, one to either side, a dejected-looking palm tree in an island protected from cars by empty oil drums. When they rejoined on the other side, Kelly chuckled in embarrassment and said, "After all, there aren't a lot of times it's helpful to point a gun at your colonel's eye and tell him he's history if he makes a peep in the next ten minutes."

"You did that?" Elaine said, her tone one of amusement rather than the cool appraisal Kelly had expected.

"Yeah," Kelly admitted. "Seemed like a good idea at the time, and I figured we were far enough back in the boonies that he wouldn't have to report it later to cover his own ass. Neither of us got anything in our jackets for that one, and he stopped tryin' to be a big hero like his old man—at least when he was in sight of me."

"This is the car," Elaine said. "We'll put your luggage behind the seats."

The car was a Porsche 944, new enough that the treads on both front and rear tires were almost unworn. It was painted a metallic green, the gloss overlaid by a light dusting of yellow grit from the parking lot.

"What," asked Kelly as Elaine unlocked the Porsche, "were you going to do if I showed up here with a steamer trunk?" An obvious answer struck him, and he looked around for a follow-car big enough to handle any possible load of baggage. Though he craned his neck and raised himself onto his toes, looking like a gigged frog because of his squat build, Kelly could see no likely vehicle nearby. "There isn't one, Tom," Elaine said dryly, flipping the driver's seat forward, "but don't worry"—she patted his left arm, whose muscles were rock solid with the weight of the suitcase they were supporting—"I'm packing."

" 'Yea, though I walk through the valley of the shadow of Death . . .'" quoted Kelly as he set the case into the car. It was a snug fit, but because the driver's seat was well forward there *was* a fit.

"And as for the rest," she went on when he straightened, "if you got off with more luggage than you'd boarded with in Frankfurt, we were going to have to hire a taxi for it—yes." She smiled.

The veteran held both hands out in front of him, palms down, and looked at them for a moment. Then he met Elaine's eyes and said, "Look, I know how I get. Don't—" He swallowed. "I've got real problems working close with people when it gets tense, I don't usually do that. I don't wanna, you know, somebody get hurt because I was pissed and there wasn't a whole lotta time."

Elaine touched his hands with hers, fingertips to

palms and her thumbs lying gently on his scarred knuckles. "You haven't had anyone you could trust before, Tom," she said. "You've got that now."

Kelly grinned and squeezed hands that felt so delicate that he could have crumpled them like cellophane. "Yeah, that's a change," he said, stepping around the back of the car to get to the passenger side. His fingers tapped idly on the black rubber spoiler as he passed it, wondering whether there would be any chance of putting the Porsche through its paces one of these days. He was going to need some relaxation. . . .

And he could've used somebody to trust as well, but he didn't have that on this operation either. You could trust the people beneath you, sometimes, if you'd trained them and worked with them before. But your superiors in a hierarchy could *never* by definition be expected to do exactly what you told them to—especially if the time were too short for what they thought was proper respect. People didn't get into positions of responsibility by abdicating responsibility.

Elaine Tuttle would be welcome any day as a member of a team Kelly put together, for her driving and her mind if nothing else. But right now she was, at a guess, a lieutenant colonel—and he was a master sergeant in the only scheme of things that a light colonel's mind could accept.

It would've been real nice to trust her, though.

Traffic on the long stretch of four-lane highway between the airport in Yesilköy and the city proper was heavy. Elaine, though she did not waste any time, wasn't pushing with the little car the way she had the first night on the Baltimore-Washington Turnpike.

"You haven't asked me," she said, "whether we'd gotten you the accommodations you'd asked for."

Kelly laughed. "Demanded, you mean," he said. At eye level out his side window were the rear axles of a fourteen-wheel semi, just like the ones immediately before and behind the Porsche. He had no doubt that the little car was as sturdy as anything its size could be, but the low seating position emphasized vulnerability to the trucks in a way that not even a motorcycle would have. "Look, I don't say you couldn't have failed, you know— maybe terrorists blew the place up this morning, that sorta thing, But you weren't going to fail and not tell me about it right off."

He turned to look at her profile, unexpectedly softer than any of the angles of the woman's frame—pleasant in itself, and much more pleasant than the angle-iron bumper with a Bulgarian license plate ten feet beyond the hood. "At worst, I'm going to decide you're a vicious bitch who's dangling me for whoever, the Russians, to bite. You won't *ever* convince me you're stupid."

It was the right thing to have said, because Elaine's reaction was wrong—to the speculation, not the flattery. The face compressed itself momentarily into the neutral expression that gave nothing away save the fact that something was hidden. She smiled so quickly that Kelly could have thought he had mistaken the reaction . . . except that long, bloody years had taught him when his instincts must be trusted and no human being could be.

"This is the route from Europe," she said, waving to

the truck ahead of them, "traffic from as far as Sweden and England, on the way across the Hindu Kush, some of it."

"Rather have your company than theirs," the veteran replied, his hand paralleling hers in a gesture toward the red airport bus ahead in the other lane. "Though mind you, the next time you pick me up, a fifty-passenger Mercedes like that one'd be a little more in keeping with the rest of the traffic than a two-seater Porsche."

Elaine laughed and made a pair of lane changes, cutting between bumpers more closely than she had previously that afternoon. The Porsche's exhaust blatted at the downshift followed by swift acceleration. "That make you feel better?" she asked, nodding toward the little Anadol—a license-built version of an English Ford—now just ahead of them. "You see, your wish is my command."

Istanbul was an exotic city with a history that went back long before the Roman conquest, much less that of the Ottoman Turks. Along the highway from Yesilköy, however, it resembled nothing so much as Cleveland, Ohio: another major industrial city decaying beside a major body of water.

It had ceased to be the capital in 1920, when the Allied powers had anchored warships in the Golden Horn—and had found that the only Turks they ruled were those literally within range of their guns. The Turks had been on the losing side during World War I, but their armies had defeated major attacks both at Gallipoli and in Mesopotamia. There was no longer an Ottoman Empire, but there was a new nation called Turkey. Other failed empires in the region—the Persians and the Greeks both came readily to mind—had their pride. The Turks had in addition an army ready to kick whoever's butt was closest. The planners in Washington who persisted in considering Turkey a client state of the US had no one but themselves to blame for the current anti-Americanism.

"What do you expect to do in Istanbul?" Elaine asked as they waited to cross the peripheral road surrounding the walls begun at least seven hundred years before Constantine renamed the city after himself.

"Talk to some people," Kelly said, shrugging. "Ahmed Ayyubi for one, Mohammed's brother. There had to be some reason Mohammed moved to Istanbul—or stayed here, if he was just catching his breath with his brother after Birdlike came apart. . . . Look, I'm playin' it by ear, that's as much data as I've got."

Elaine sent the car growling across the intersection and into the Old City proper. "We can help you locate people if you need that," she said with a nod—approval, or more likely reassurance. "As we did with Ahmed Ayyubi."

Kelly had asked her for a location on the dead Kurd's brother even though he would much sooner that his present employers not know of his interest. What can't be cured, though . . . Any damned fool would know that Kelly had to start with or near Ahmed Ayyubi; and though he could have gotten the man's address without official help, he could not—in Istanbul—have been sure that his interest would not have leaked back anyway.

Better to be up front about what you couldn't hide—it disarmed the brass hats who thought they owned your soul.

The Porsche turned left at Ataturk Boulevard, steeply uphill so that by twisting around Kelly got a good view of the Sea of Marmara. Though they had been driving parallel to the water for some time, the high corniche and the remains of ancient brick walls had hidden it from him.

Elaine, driving with the intention of making the best possible time, looked at her passenger in surprise. "Is somebody behind us?" she asked, and as she spoke her eyes flickered to the mirrors and the traffic around her.

I only get that paranoid in the boonies, thought Kelly, but that's probably because she's spent more time in cities than I've done. Aloud he said, "Oh, no problem. I just like to see something big and real now and again—to anchor me, you know?"

Elaine nodded acceptance rather than understanding and concentrated on her driving again. Though she hadn't any right to be pissed, Kelly knew that nobody likes to be frightened needlessly, even in innocence. Well, she could have let him take the bus and a taxi instead of picking him up at the airport.

The Old City of Istanbul was on a finger of land projecting into the Sea of Marmara, separated from the equally-steep ridge of the Pera District by the deep gash of the Golden Horn. All of the bodies of water—the Horn, the Sea of Marmara, and the Bosphorus, which connected the latter to the Black Sea—were the results of separate fault lines as the continental plates that were Europe and Asia clashed. The earthquakes that were a certain concomitant of those faults meant that all but the most massive structures were brought down on a regular basis or were devoured by the fires that resulted.

It was a city of apartments of concrete and yellowish brick, built in the late nineteenth century or the twentieth—not unattractive, many of them picked out by balconies or iron grillwork, but all the colors muted by the soft coal that had been the city's fuel for centuries. Only from above was there anything brighter, and that was the omnipresent red-orange of tiled roofs the shade of the rouge on a badly laid out corpse.

They crossed the Golden Horn on the Ataturk Bridge, early enough to miss the worst of the northbound traffic—tourists returning to the big luxury hotels in the Pera, and returning with them many of the personnel who had been catering to them among the ancient beauties of the Old City. Istanbul still had heavy industries, but there had been virtually no new development here since World War II. Only the tourists offered to preserve the city from sinking back into the state of somnolent ruin to which it had been reduced by the time the Ottoman Turks conquered it in 1453.

Elaine hadn't used the long drive to pump him, which was just as well since the Porsche was too small a box for the hostility that would have resulted. Such of his plans as she didn't know were things he hoped she wouldn't learn, and the reality of what he was to do faded as the time for execution approached. It was hard to believe that he was really back in Turkey; and the notion that he was here to track down aliens with too many bones and far too many teeth in their circular mouths was as absurd as it would have been the day before he saw the dead thing.

"Doesn't really matter if I believe any of it, does it?" Kelly said as Elaine swung the car around the rank of cabs waiting to load at the entrance of the Sheraton. "Just so long as I do my job."

He had spoken as much to himself as to Elaine, but the woman raised an eyebrow over her smile and replied, "Are you going to have difficulty working under those conditions?"

Before Kelly answered, she stopped the Porsche and handed the keys to the attendant, who had scurried in a failed attempt to open the door for her, "It might be as well," she said over her shoulder as Kelly too got out of the car, "if you carried the suitcase yourself. There'll be people waiting in the room."

"There's no difficulty," the veteran said as he tugged out the big case. "I spent years without thinking any of the people giving me orders knew what the hell they were doing. Doubting that *I* do's something of a pleasant change."

They took the elevators from the ground-floor service area. Kelly noted with amusement that Elaine waited a moment, watching him from the corner of her eye, before she touched the button for the seventh floor. Kelly grinned broadly at her, letting her wonder whether or not he knew which floor their rooms were on this time.

He didn't want to talk business with Elaine, and he didn't have anything but business—one way or the other—to talk with her. Unless—and he looked toward the ceiling of the elevator—he asked the question to which his mind kept returning, whether or not she ever wore a bra. His smile, carefully directed away from anything human, became innocence. A question like that struck him as a pretty good way to get his hand bitten off to the elbow, which would complicate his job a lot. . . .

"A penny for your thoughts," Elaine said, her voice more guarded than the words.

Kelly shrugged and faced her, the bulk of the suitcase on the floor between them. "Just thinking that maybe my first priority was to get my ashes hauled," he said, "so it doesn't get in the way."

She laughed as the elevator cage quivered to a halt. "Are you asking for a list of addresses," she said, "or would you just like the equipment delivered to your room?" She pointed down the hall, her arm a shadow within the puffy translucence of her sleeve. "Seven-twenty-five."

"Naw, no problem," the stocky man said. He wasn't embarrassed—cribs in the Anti-Lebanon had been ponchos pegged into three-sided windbreaks, which pretty well blasted the notion of sex being a private affair. It was useful to note that his case officer wasn't embarrassed either.

"Well, it wouldn't be a problem, you know," Elaine said cheerfully as she, a pace ahead of Kelly, stopped at a door and tapped on it. "All part of the unobtrusive luxury service you've been promised."

"Unobtrusive will do just fine," Kelly replied. Doug Blakeley opened the door with a frozen scowl on his face. There were two other men within the room carrying radio-detection equipment. One of them was smoking a cigarette.

"You've met Doug," Elaine said as she entered 725, moving Blakeley back away from the door by stepping unnecessarily close to him—giving Kelly and the suitcase room without need for the macho games of which both men were capable. "George"—she pointed to the fat, balding man with the tone generator—"and Christophe," she indicated the pale, almost tubercular smoker who wore headphones connected to the wide-band receiver slung from his right shoulder.

"Christophe, put the cigarette out in the toilet and flush it," Elaine continued. She kept her voice as neutral as if she were commenting on the view, being very careful not to raise the emotional temperature. "And where's Peter?"

"What's the matter with the cigarette?" demanded Christophe, taking the half-smoked cylinder out of his mouth to examine it rather than to obey. His English was accented, but it appeared to be German—Flemish?— rather than the French Kelly had expected.

"He's next door in your room," Doug was saying. "I thought we'd sweep his first, before we did yours."

The tone generator which George carried put out a known signal which would trip sound-activated bugs and cause them to broadcast. Christophe swept up and down as much of the electromagnetic spectrum as his receiver covered, unless and until he picked up the tone signal in his earphones. At that point, George could lower the intensity of the generator and move it around the room until the bug was physically located.

If the bugging device was combined directly with a tape recorder, then there was no signal to pick up on the receiver—but that sort of installation required that someone enter the room at regular intervals to change tapes, and it very considerably increased the bulk of the bugging unit. Similarly, a hardwired bug was possible but impractical in a hotel room like this because of the holes that had to be drilled through walls between the bug and the listening post. No sweep could be perfect, but this team appeared to know what it was doing—especially if the piece of hardware in a separate case by the door was the spectrum analyzer Kelly assumed it was.

"Christophe, when you get an order from me you *do* it," Elaine said in a deadly voice to the man at least a foot taller than she was.

Kelly walked over to the window, smiling, leaving behind him the suitcase and the incident developing in the room.

There was more to the woman's reaction than her authority, though there was that too. She'd picked up on the way Kelly felt about cigarette smoke—surely *that* wasn't in his psychiatric profile—and she had a not unreasonable concern that the veteran would use that as the excuse to void his grudging acquiescence to the wishes of a government he hated.

Hell, nobody'd twisted Kelly's arm; he was a big boy. He'd go through with the deal, whatever that meant and whatever roadblocks his superiors threw in his way.

But it didn't hurt to keep 'em nervous.

The window had a nice view of Taksim Square and the Monument of the Republic. The square served for major ceremonies and public gatherings because there was nothing of suitable size in the Old City. The Golden Horn, to the south, was invisible beyond the buildings of the Pera District, and the skyline was dominated by the twenty-story tower of a nearby hotel—the ETAP Marmar, the city's tallest building. Rooms on this side of the Sheraton were considerably cheaper than those with a view of the Bosphorus, but Kelly did find it pleasant to look out at the trees of Taksim Park—probably the only place in Istanbul that contained so much greenery.

Not that his choice of a room had anything to do with that aspect of the view.

Kelly turned. The exchange between Elaine and now both members of the sweep team had continued. Christophe's cigarette had burned almost to his fingers and scattered a lump of ash as he gestured with it.

"Goddammit, Christophe," Doug said sharply with his arms akimbo. "Put out the cigarette!"

The man with his headphones now loosely clasping his neck scurried to comply.

Kelly could afford to smile sardonically at Elaine's slim, tense back. And these were Europeans, not Arabs or even Moslems. Female officers must have a *really* great time working with locally-recruited teams. . . .

"Tell you what," said Kelly, "let's all just go next door, shall we?" He offered a clown's broad smile, keeping his lips tight. "That way the boys can do whatever they need to do there. And from now on, just for fun, let's not you or anybody you know come into 725, unless I invite him, huh?"

Doug started to bridle, but before he could reply Elaine said tiredly, "Yeah, that sounds like a good idea to me too." She looked at Christophe returning from the bathroom, and added, "And when they've swept my room, Doug, I don't want to see them again myself till you're told different."

Nobody moved for a moment. Then Doug snapped, "Well, why aren't you packing your gear, dammit?" George and Christophe eyed one another as they obeyed, but they obeyed the blond man without question.

There was no door through the partition wall between rooms 725 and 727, but neither was there anyone in the hall to watch the four men and the woman—forming almost as many subgroups as there were individuals—traipse from one room to the other. The gray fiberglass cases holding the debugging equipment were not standard luggage, but neither did they hint that they contained more than expensive cameras.

George tapped on the door of 727. As Peter opened it, Elaine said to Doug, "Give him his own room key now."

"Eh?"

Peter was black haired and heavily moustached, a very solid-looking man and younger than the sweep team. Kelly gave him a cautious once-over. There was no obvious reason why, but Kelly's gut wouldn't have let him keep Peter in a unit he commanded. Now he gave the man a friendly smile as they passed in the doorway.

"Give Tom the key to seven-two-five, I said," Elaine snapped.

Doug reached into the side pocket of his suitcoat, which sagged, Kelly had guessed, with the weight of a spare magazine. That guess had been wrong: the key which Doug handed him was attachéd to a brass bar rather than a tag or thin plate. Guests were intended to leave their room keys at the desk when they went out, and the management did what it could to make that easy to remember.

The sweep team was already unpacking its equipment, though Christophe paused to light another cigarette first. George got out what was indeed a spectrum analyzer and began walking around the room with it, staring at the peaks and valleys on its cathode ray tube display. His partner waited to rezero his own equipment because the oscillators in Christophe's wide-band receiver would themselves affect the electromagnetic spectrum within the room.

The view from Elaine's window was practically the same as that of Kelly's, something the veteran had counted on without being able to influence. So far, so good. Both rooms were of luxury hotel standards common across the portions of the world which served tourists. The spread of the double bed was a brocade of rich blue which clashed badly with the dress Elaine was wearing but matched the upholstery of the love seat facing the window.

Kelly sat down on the loveseat and spread his arms across the back, his big scarred hands dangling to either side. Peter watched him with a flat expression that Kelly recognized: the look that said the mind behind it was considering endgame in the most final and physical sense of the term, just to be ready when the time came.

"We have a car for you," Elaine said. The light through the window behind her silhouetted her body against a sky that otherwise held from Kelly's perspective only the upper stories of the ETAP Marmar.

"I don't need a car," the veteran said. "What I need is a cup of coffee, black; and I think it'd be real nice if you sent Peter down to get it"—he nodded toward the younger man, so nearly a physical double for Kelly himself—"instead of waiting for room service to bring it up."

The woman looked sharply at Kelly. Then she turned her head slightly in Peter's direction and said, "Yes, all right, get it. Get two. Anyone else?"

"Yeah, for God's sake, bring up six coffees and be done with it," said Doug to his subordinate. Then, proving that he had better judgment than Kelly would have credited him before, Doug added, "And don't argue about it, just do like you're paid to, take orders."

Peter frowned, but he left the room without the objection that would have really lit Elaine's fuse.

When the door closed she went on, "This is a Ford Anadol, like a million others in Turkey, Tom. You'll need transportation."

"I'll take taxis," he replied. He gestured to the door. "You know," he went on, "that one, your Peter, he could *really* get on my nerves in a hurry. I'm not gonna shout and scream about this, but if I see him again after he brings up the coffee, I go home. This time it's no shit."

Doug looked from Elaine to Kelly in genuine puzzlement. Elaine nodded and said, "All right, we'll see what we can do." She cleared her throat. "It's absurd for you to trust taxis to be where you need them. We can give you a driver, if you like."

It'd be absurd to accept a car with the array of tracking beacons that anything she'd provide would have, Kelly thought. Aloud he said, "I'm a tourist, I take cabs. When I change my mind, I'll let you know."

The sweep team had moved into the bathroom. The receiver in the spectrum analyzer was of lower sensitivity than the one Christophe used to listen for the tone they would generate in a few minutes. In order to pick up a hump on the display, which was the low-powered signal of a bug, the unit needed to be fairly close to the transmitter. "What's the bandwidth on that thing?" Kelly asked, nodding toward the bathroom.

"What?" said Doug. Elaine decided not to argue further

about the car. Both of them followed Kelly's nod toward the bathroom.

Kelly slipped the cavity resonator, a three-inch metal tube with a nine-inch antenna of flexible wire, between the back and the cushion of the loveseat. "I mean, what range in megahertz does the display cover? Eighty to three hundred? More?"

"I can't imagine, but you can look for yourself if you feel you must," the woman said in exasperation.

"That all we need to cover?" Kelly said, no more relaxed than he had been a moment before. "The car, I mean? Because if it—"

"There's money," Elaine said, lifting a Halliburton from the floor to the bed and opening it, "though you can always say you don't need *that* either."

"I don't," the veteran agreed, "but I'll take what's going." Hard to tell whether the asperity in Elaine's voice was fatigue, the difficulty in getting subordinates to take orders from a woman, or simply Kelly's own arrogance. Probably a combination of the three; and probably things weren't going to improve for the duration, because none of those factors were likely to change for the better.

Elaine tossed a fat, banded packet of Turkish lire onto Kelly's lap. They were used bills, bearing, as did all denominations of Turkish currency, the face of Kemal Ataturk, the republic's founder. "That's a hundred thousand," she said, closing the attaché case. Doug, literally and figuratively the odd man out, looked with his hands clasped from Elaine to the sweep team, which was beginning to make its circuit with the tone generator and receiver.

"It'd seem like a lot more," said Kelly as he stripped

off the banding, "if I hadn't checked the exchange rate in the terminal. Do I sign for it?"

"It's over a thousand dollars, Kelly," said the woman, "which ought to be handy—unless you plan to pay your bloody taxi fares with credit cards. There's more if you need it"—she spun the lock dials of her Halliburton with grim determination—"and if you need large sums, we'll talk.

"And the answer is no, *I* signed for it," she concluded with her eyes fierce.

Kelly wondered if she'd shoot him if he asked if she were on the rag just now. Probably not: she wasn't the type who ever really lost it, any more than Kelly himself did. "I appreciate the way you're covering for me," the veteran said calmly as he rose.

He slipped half the lire—pounds, from the Latin, just like the Italian equivalent and the British symbol for currency—into the breast pocket of his jacket, and the other half, folded, into the right side pocket of his slacks. "I suppose I get this way because I figure the best way to be left alone is to make you all"—he smiled around the room—"want to keep clear. But I do understand that you're keeping your side of the bargain. And that it can't be easy for somebody in your position."

He walked toward the door. Behind him, Doug called, "The coffee hasn't come yet."

"No," agreed Kelly as he stepped out into the hallway, "but Peter left, which was all I had in mind."

Room 725 had a pleasant feeling for Kelly as he shot the deadbolt lock behind him; not home, but a bunker. Bunkers were a lot more useful than homes.

A glance out the window at the sun told him that he had time to put his gear in order and still catch Ahmed Ayyubi at work. Before starting to unpack, he sat his little Sony radio up on the window ledge and scanned the FM band until he found a station—probably Greek, but that didn't matter one way or the other—playing music. There was a good deal of static, and the red diode that indicated tuning strength fluctuated feebly—which mattered even less to ears trained like Kelly's in the hard school of communications intercept.

He had not brought a great deal of clothing, and his choices emphasized variety rather than several versions of the same garb. He stripped off the sportcoat, hung it up with the slacks he had taken from the suitcase, and tossed the long-sleeved polyester shirt he was wearing on the bed. In its place he donned a checked wool shirt and a nylon windbreaker, both of them well-worn and of Turkish manufacture, as was the short-brimmed cloth cap he put on. He'd look a little strange to the lobby personnel at the Sheraton, but that was a cheap trade-off for avoiding comment when he talked to Ayyubi. The money in the sportcoat could stay there for the time being.

The last thing Kelly did before leaving his room was to walk over to the Sony receiver and poke number seven of the ten station preset buttons. The apparent effect was the same as if he had pushed the Off button: the sound clicked off, the LED went dark, and the liquid crystal display of the tuning readout went completely blank as if the power were off also.

What actually happened to the receiver, which a stateside acquaintance of Kelly's had hastily modified, was a good deal more complex. Preset seven tuned the unit to 88.35 megahertz, squarely in the midst of the upper side-lobe of Istanbul's sixty-kilowatt commercial FM station. The hump which a spectrum analyzer would show there was exactly what was to be expected, and a separate trans-mitter would have to be very powerful indeed to affect the appearance of the band on the display.

The Sony's output when operating on that preset was not to the speaker as an audible signal but rather through a shunt into the case intended for an external battery pack holding four C cells. It now contained a miniature tape recorder with a voice-activated switch. The false battery pack could be exposed by anyone who cared to open it; but Kelly had deliberately left an unmodified Sony and its accoutrements unattended at his apartment in Arlington during the week he was preparing for the mission, giving anyone who was curious ample opportunity to be reassured about its innocence.

It would be nice to learn that he didn't have to spy on the folks with whom he was working just now. But given Pierrard, he was going to be very surprised if Elaine and her friends were playing straight.

The breeze from the Bosphorus was cool enough to be bracing now. A few hours after sundown it was going to be damned cold, but that itself would be a help in returning Kelly's mind to operational status, like the process of scaling rust from armor plate. Working for Carlo Bianci, he had been able to stay warm enough all the time. That wasn't something you counted on in the field.

The lead taxi in the rank was a Fiat, older than the

driver, who cheerfully haggled in Turkish on a price to the Mosque of Sinan. It made a reasonable destination for Kelly, due east of the Sheraton and close to the Bosphorus—as well as being within two narrow, winding blocks of the agent's real destination, a neighborhood mosque in an alley off Maskular Street.

The neighborhood mosque was named for Sidi Iskender—Saint Alexander—and Kelly wondered fleetingly whether Alexander the Great himself might not have been sanctified in the myths of Turkish tribesmen riding westward through the land which the Macedonian had conquered centuries before. The west side of the courtyard looked as if it had sustained battle damage, but that was the result of ongoing refurbishment: the wall had been knocked down and was in early stages of replacement by a portico of four column-supported barrel vaults.

Precast concrete arches leaned against the side of the neighboring commercial building, but the stones of the square pillars were being fitted on-site from the pile of rough limestone ashlars delivered from the quarry. Two stonecutters and the half dozen short-haired boys kibitzing sat in a waste of rock-chips and yellow dust from the stone.

The older of the stonecutters stood straddling the column which he was forming into a hexagonal pilaster. His partner wore a cloth cap like Kelly's, a tan sweater pulled over a dark blue shirt, and baggy black trousers almost hidden by rock dust and the one-by-one-by-two-foot stone prism behind which he squatted with an adze. He was in his late thirties, clearly the elder Ayyubi brother, for his broad, dark face was a near double of that Kelly had last seen videotaped on a rainswept street in Diyarbakir.

Ahmed Ayyubi glanced up at the man approaching and struck the stone again with a blow deceptively light. Rock exploded, and the adze stopped half an inch beyond the point of impact.

"You," said Ahmed Ayyubi as he rose. The arm holding the adze fell to his side, but the tendons of the hand on the haft stood out with the fierceness of the Kurd's grip.

"We need to talk, Ahmed," Kelly said as he walked closer. He was trying to appear calm, but he stumbled on the rock chips—some of them the size of a clenched fist—covering the ground. Danger had made a tunnel of his viewpoint, and the peripheral vision that guides the feet had vanished under stress. The boys continued to chatter for a moment, but the other stonecutter paused with his own tool resting on the work face.

"Get out of here," Ayyubi said in Kurdish, and in a voice so guttural that Kelly could not have understood the words had they not been the ones he expected.

One more step put the American agent as close to the workplace as Ayyubi was, well within reach of the adze. "We *need* to talk," Kelly said. Tiny bits of stone floated in the sweat that sprang out suddenly from Ayyubi's brow. "Otherwise Mohammed's killing will be unavenged."

"*You're* responsible for his death, you know," the Kurd snarled.

Kelly reached out and touched the back of the stonecutter's right hand while he held eye contact. "Whatever responsibility I have for Mohammed's death, I will wash away in the blood of his killers. But you must help me find them."

And only when he felt Ayyubi's hand relax on the adze helve did Kelly realize that he had succeeded.

The stonecutter grimaced and set his tool on the work-piece. "Come," he said, gesturing beyond a pile of finished blocks toward the street. A couple of the boys jumped up to follow. "You go away!" Ayyubi said. "This is man's business." Though there was love in his gruffness, the hand he batted at the nearest lad would have flung the boy across the rubble if the blow had landed.

Traffic noise on Maskular and the adjoining streets was a white ambiance that may have been what Ayyubi was seeking. More probably the Kurd had needed time and the movement to clear his thoughts of limestone and his sudden fury at seeing Kelly again.

"I don't know what Mohammed was doing," Ayyubi said abruptly. Standing, he was three inches shorter than Kelly, but his neck and shoulders made even the stocky American look slight by contrast. "I wanted him to get into decent work, come in with me and Gulersoy"—his calloused thumb indicated the older stonecutter—"but he'd gotten the taste for being a hero, for getting rich without working. *You* did that to him."

"Yes, easy money," Kelly murmured. His right hand caressed the jacket over his left elbow. There was a four-inch scar there, where the skin had been laid open by the same bomb blast which had knocked him silly. Mohammed Ayyubi had carried him to safety a hundred and fifty feet up the sides of a ravine that a goat would have thought was sheer.

But soldier ants probably can't explain what they do to the workers in the colony, either. It was that sort of world, is all.

"This I know, and all I know is this," the stonecutter continued, prodding toward Kelly's chest with a thumb-thick finger. "He met a blond whore, a dancer, and let her get him into this. As you got him into the other."

"I didn't get Mohammed into anything I didn't get him out of," Kelly said softly, with his eyes on the middle distance and his mind on memories that had nothing to do with the business at hand. His body shuddered, and his eyes focused on Ayyubi again. "Tell me about the dancer. Is she a Turk?"

"No, a foreigner," the other man said. Something in Kelly's expression a moment before caused Ayyubi to frown, not in fear but with a different awareness of the situation and the man who questioned him. "I know nothing about her, only the name—Gee-soo-lah. A belly dancer, very expensive. Dances at the best clubs and parties of the very rich because she's blond, you see, and foreign."

"Right . . ." Kelly said. "Know where she's at just now?"

Ayyubi shook his head emphatically. "Sometimes here, sometimes she travels. Not with Mohammed, I think, but I know she was responsible." He paused and added, "Mohammed showed me a billboard once, but that was months ago. I never saw her, and I never let him talk to me about freeing Kurdistan and the big money he was making."

The stonecutter spat into the street. Some of the cars had their lights on by now. "Big money. It helped the family bury him."

"I'll let you know how things work out," Kelly said, wondering if anybody was watching him just now. Pierrard's people or others, not necessarily people. "Thank you, Ahmed."

"Wait," the Kurd said, touching Kelly's arm as the agent started to turn away. When their eyes met again in the dusk, Ayyubi said, "I thought it was friends of yours who killed him. Americans. They came to talk with me the week before Mohammed was shot, and I didn't know where he was to warn him. My *brother*."

Kelly clasped the other man's hand against him. "Ahmed," he said, "nobody who kills one of my people is a friend of mine." He squeezed the Kurd fiercely, then strode back toward the Mosque of Sinan and the hope of finding another taxi.

There was nothing particularly difficult about what came next, but the first three hours of it were simply preparation. He had to lose whoever might be tagging him on Pierrard's behalf or Elaine's—if there was a difference.

A properly trained team of at least a dozen agents could keep tabs on just about anybody in an urban environment, but that was a lot of personnel for anyone but the local security forces. Among US intelligence organizations in Istanbul, the Drug Enforcement Administration could probably put together such a team, and very possibly CIA could as well.

Pierrard, whoever he was and whatever funds he could disburse on special operations, had an insolubly different problem. You can't bring a tracking unit into a city where the street patterns and the language are both unfamiliar, not and expect the team to function. Money alone won't do it. And the most practical answer, to borrow trained personnel from friendly intelligence organizations, was also the least probable. There *were* no friendly intelligence services to people like Pierrard, least of all the other services employed by the US government.

Pierrard's attitude, of course, was fully supported by that of his CIA and DEA colleagues, who would have been delighted to get their fingers into a rival's turf.

For the moment, Kelly could be pretty sure that he could be being followed by only Doug and the three foreign nationals he had met at the Sheraton, perhaps with an equal number of Turkish drivers and the like. The Covered Bazaar—the Kapali Carsi in the center of the Old City—was the perfect place to dump any such tail.

There were eighteen entrances to the Bazaar and sixty-five separate streets within it, all covered by plastered brick arches with internal iron bracing. Kelly entered the three-acre maze of shops and pedestrians on Fuad Pasha Street across from the campus of the University of Istanbul. He ducked out again fifteen minutes later on Yeniceri Boulevard, spending no longer in the streetlights than he needed to hop into a brightly-painted Skoda taxi.

The trip back across the Golden Horn to the apartment on Carik Street in the Beyoglu District, not far from Taksim Square, was complicated by the fact that Kelly changed cabs twice more. The friend who was arranging this pickup owed Kelly less than he was risking by going up against Pierrard. The least Kelly intended to do was to prevent fallout in that direction.

The apartment was one of a series of six-to-ten-story

new constructions filling the block. The street level held a branch bank whose steel grating had been rolled down for the night, a jewelry store, and a rug shop with a silken Herike on display beneath concealed spotlights. There was a guard in the small elevator lobby, chatting with a policeman who probably found it worth his time to spend his entire shift right there.

Both men shifted to their feet with interest and hostile concern when Kelly stepped into the lobby. "I'm to pick up a case from Miss Ozel on the sixth floor," Kelly said in Turkish. "For Nureddin."

Mollified but still cautious, the civilian guard pressed buzzer six on the wall beneath the intercom grating while the policeman studied the taxi waiting outside.

"Yes?" a voice responded, its sex uncertain due to the distortion of the intercom.

"Lady, a man to pick up a package for Nureddin," the guard explained.

"Oh—thank you. Could you send him up yourself, as a favor to me?"

The guard nodded obsequiously to the speaker grating, causing the policeman to laugh and wink at Kelly.

"Of course, lady," the civilian said. He unlocked the elevator call button and gestured Kelly into the cage. Theoretically, someone from the apartment itself should have come down to accompany the visitor to the proper floor; but those who could pay for security like this could be expected to circumvent those aspects which caused inconvenience to themselves.

The sixth floor was a single suite. Its door was already ajar when the elevator stopped, and the woman waiting in the opening motioned Kelly within. "Robert—could not be here," she said in fair English. "He say—he say that this is what you look for."

What Kelly could see of the apartment was opulent with brassware and wall hangings, but a little overdone for his taste. The same could be said for the woman in a house-dress of multilayered red gauze over an opaque base. She had a fleshy Turkish beauty, with lustrous hair to her waist and breasts that would have been impressive on a much heavier woman . . . but there are no absolutes of taste, and only her smile was greatly to the taste of Tom Kelly.

"Thank you," the American said, stepping to the travel-trunk set in the entranceway to await him. "And more than thanks to Bob. It—it's just as well he's not here now, but—tell him I'll see him again. And I won't forget."

Kelly had met Bob's wife, a slim blond of aristocratic beauty whose ancestry went back several centuries in Virginia. Very cool, very intelligent, very nearly perfect . . . and thinking of that as he reached for the case, Kelly could understand Miss Ozel more easily.

"It's heavy," warned the woman. "I can get—"

"Thank you," Kelly repeated, lifting the trunk by the central strap as if it were an ordinary suitcase. Bob could be depended on to make sure the load was balanced.

Danny Pacheco, who had died below decks on the *White Plains*, had been a friend of his as of Kelly.

"I guess I need a key to get down, too," the American said apologetically. The weight of the case forced him into a counter lean as if he were thrusting against a gale.

The room beyond the entrance hall was furnished like

that of a wealthy Kurdish chieftain of the past century: the floor not carpeted but overlaid by runners a meter wide and five meters long. Little but the edge of any single carpet showed beyond the edge of the next above; and so on, across the room, while stacked pillows turned the juncture of floor and walls into a continuous couch.

Ozel glanced toward the inner room, then took an elevator key from a pocket hidden in her housedress. Unexpectedly she gripped Kelly's free arm and, staring fiercely into his eyes, said, "This won't hurt Robert. Will it?"

She shouldn't know there was anything different about this one than there was about anything Bob did for his employer, NSA. *He* certainly hadn't told her. Kelly blinked, reassessing the mind behind those cowlike eyes. She would have gotten physical signals from Bob, but she had to be able to think to process the data.

"No," Kelly said in Kurdish. "Not if I'm alive to keep it from hurting him." He squeezed her hand in reassurance and led her by it to the elevator switch.

Bob had done a rather better job the second time around, Kelly thought as the cage descended. Or maybe he really needed both women, needed the balance.

And what did Tom Kelly need? Nothing he'd found in forty years, that was sure. And not some of the things he'd never had; the love of a good woman, for a major instance.

Though the love of the right bad woman might be just the sort of stress a fellow like him needed to keep out of the really life-threatening forms of excitement.

Like the current one.

※　※　※

The ETAP Marmar was the tallest building in Istanbul, and from his sixteenth-floor room in that hotel, Kelly could easily look down on the room Elaine had booked for him in the Sheraton.

More to the point, his ETAP window looked down on Elaine's own room and permitted him to aim the microwave transmitter he had picked up from Ozel toward the cavity resonator he had earlier planted in the loveseat. The fact that the woman's rubber-backed drapes were drawn did not affect the microwaves with which Kelly now painted 727.

The trunk acted as both carrying case for the transmitter and the camouflage necessary for an unattended installation like this one in a room that would be entered for daily cleaning. Five sides of the Turkish-made trunk were standard sheet metal over light wood, with corner reinforcements, but the metal sheathing had been removed from one end and replaced by dull black paint. The change was noticeable but unremarkable and it was through that end that the parabolic antenna spewed a tight beam of microwaves.

Kelly rested his elbows on the ledge of the window and scanned the south face of the Sheraton with binoculars, a tiny pair of Zeiss roof-prism 10x20s. He had left his own drapes open in the Sheraton, and the Sony radio on the ledge there provided the certainty of location which he could not have achieved simply by counting windows. The window to the left of his own was the target. . . .

This room in the ETAP Marmar had been booked for Kelly by a woman who had left Bianci's staff a year before to join an Atlanta travel agency. The only question she had asked about the false name and the cash payment was how it affected Carlo. Kelly's word that it didn't had been good enough for her. A north-facing room high on the ETAP was certain to overlook a room in the Sheraton with a view of Taksim Square. While there had been no certainty that Elaine would book her own room beside the one Kelly had demanded, there had been a high probability of it.

And after all, there was no certainty in life.

The veteran gave final touches to the antenna alignment, switched on the power, and closed and locked the case sitting on the coffee table beside the window. The unit ran on wall current, so it was possible that a maid would unplug it despite the note in Turkish: Air Freshener Within—Please Do Not Unplug—left with a thousand lire bill atop the trunk. Its weight, primarily that of the transformers, made it unlikely that anyone would move it. Short of hiring someone to watch the room, there was no better way to set things up.

Whistling, Tom Kelly locked the door and the purring transmitter behind him. He figured he'd walk back to the Sheraton, but by the long way around the park.

He felt pretty good. He had his ass covered from his own side, more or less, and he could now get on with the job they had asked him to do.

Kelly expected somebody to be waiting for him in the lobby, but George was instead at the further end of the first-floor coffee shop where he was less obtrusive and had a full, if narrow, view of the front door. The American nodded to him cheerfully. No problem. He needed to get some information through Elaine, and he'd just as soon that she was expecting him.

With his own key in his pocket, Kelly tapped on the door of 727—"shave" with his index finger, "and a haircut" with the middle finger, he *was* feeling good—and the door opened before the veteran could rap "two bits" with both fingers together. Elaine, alone in the room as she gestured him inside, was wearing a beige dress that could have been silk-look polyester but probably was not.

"Glad to have you back, Tom," the woman said without emphasis. "Learn anything useful?"

"Learned I could get my watch wound with no help from the USG," Kelly replied with a chuckle, flopping down on the loveseat and spreading his arms as he had before when he set the cavity resonator. Somewhere up there beyond the curtains was a microwave transmitter aimed right at his breastbone, God willing.

Elaine grimaced involuntarily, but there was no sign that she wasn't taking the lie at face value. Not that it was a lie, exactly: Tom Kelly damned well *could* get laid without government assistance. The statement covered both the time he'd been gone and the new buoyance with which he returned. The hair on his chest tickled, but that was psychosomatic rather than a real effect of the microwaves. If, worst come to worst, his visit to Miss Ozel was traced, it explained that too.

"Perhaps we can get to business sometime soon," the woman said, with no more emotional loading than was necessary.

"Had dinner?" Kelly asked brightly. "We can call room service." The grimace, a momentary tic, was back.

Maybe she thought he was drunk too. He hadn't drunk alcohol since that boilermaker in the Madison. . . .

"Get me full poop on a blond belly dancer named— and this is phonetic, through Kurdish—Gee-soo-lah," Kelly said. "Claimed to be a foreign national, claimed to be a top act. Probably in somebody's files even if the computer doesn't kick her up for some other reason."

Elaine raised an eyebrow. "Excellent," she said, "but it'll take some time."

"Right," agreed Kelly as he stood with the smooth caution of a powerful man with too many scars to move unrestrained except at need. "And I don't guess you'll be burning off copies of the file yourself, will you?"

"I don't suppose so, no," the woman said guardedly.

"So why don't I," Kelly said with a grin as he walked past her to the door, "go take a shower while you make the arrangements? And then we'll go to dinner."

He paused with his hand on the knob. "For which you're rather overdressed, m'lady, but that's your business."

"Oh-kay," Elaine was saying as the door closed behind Kelly, her voice as quizzical as the expression on her face.

Istanbul had the nighttime beauty of any large city, its dirt and dilapidation cloaked by darkness and only shapes and the jewels of its illumination to be seen. The view from Kelly's window had the additional exoticism of an eastern city in which street lighting was too sparse to overwhelm the varicolored richness of neon shop-signs. The minarets of a large mosque in the distance were illuminated from within their parapets, so the shafts stood out around the dome like rockets being prepared for night lift-off.

Kelly sighed and walked into the bathroom to shower as he had said. He undressed carefully and set his trousers on the seat of the toilet. He would wear the same outfit for the rest of the evening . . . and that arrangement put the snubbie near his hand in the shower without displaying it to the unlikely possibility of optical surveillance devices planted within the hotel room. It was as easy to be careful, that was all.

When Elaine tapped on the door of 725 a few minutes after he had gotten dressed, Kelly had a twinge of concern that his comment regarding clothing would cause her to change into slacks. Istanbul was as cosmopolitan as London, in one sense, but the underlying culture was Sunni Muslim. Smart visitors to London didn't slaughter sheep in the street there, and women didn't go around in pants here without insulting a proportion of the people who saw them. That would be true even if she were a foreigner wearing some $200 Paris equivalent of blue jeans with a couturier's tag on the fly.

He needn't have worried. Elaine wore a high-throated black dress with a long-sleeved cotton jacket over it. Hell, she was smarter than he was and at least as well-traveled. Kelly nodded approvingly and joined her in the hall instead of inviting her into the room.

"Want to tell me what comes next?" Elaine asked as they strode toward the elevators, "or is the surprise an important part?"

"Well, you know . . ." Kelly said, poking the call button. Damn! but she seemed tiny when she stood beside him;

the full cheeks were so deceptive. . . . "You can get any kind of food in the world in Istanbul—though if you're big on pork, you're limited to places like this one."

He circled his hand in a gesture that indicated the Sheraton itself and its five-star equivalents on Taksim Square. "But I thought we'd be exotic and eat at a Turkish diner. You can find that too in the tourist hotels, with tables and the waitresses tricked out like they were on loan from the *Arabian Nights* . . . but I don't much feel like that."

The elevator arrived, empty. "Lead on, faithful guide," Elaine said as she stepped into the cage. When the door shut she added in a voice barely audible over the whine of the hydraulics, "The dancer is Gisela Romer, a Turkish citizen but part of an expatriate German community that settled here after World War II. There should be an extensive file in Ankara. I've put a first priority on it, so something ought to be delivered by courier as soon as it's printed out here."

"Nice work," said Kelly.

"I'm glad you're giving us a chance to help you, Tom," Elaine said seriously. "That's all that we're here for."

"I wonder if—" he started to say, timing the words carefully so that the elevator chugged to a stop at the lobby before he could complete the sentence. Elaine's face blanked, and she said nothing more until they had dropped off their keys and left the hotel.

Kelly did not see George or any other of her subordinates.

"I think we'll walk," he said, with a wave to the doorman and the leading cab of the rank beneath the hotel's bright facade. As they walked beyond the band of light, Kelly went on in a low voice, "You know, I wonder if you could find me a pistol if I needed one. I don't mean I do, I mean *if.*"

"I'd have thought you had sources of your own, Tom," Elaine said. Her smile asked more than the words themselves did.

"Yeah, needs must," agreed the veteran with false frustration. "I mean, it wasn't a turndown. But things're tight now, *real* tight, with Ecevit trying to get a grip on things. Somebody could take a *real* hard fall if, you know, something went wrong and the piece got traced back."

"What do you want?"

"I don't *want* anything," Kelly insisted, "but you know—if I do, something standard, a forty-five auto, a nine millimeter. And it'll just be a security blanket, if I turn out not to have enough guts to stay on an even keel without something to wrap my hand around."

"Doesn't sound like a problem," the woman said, nonchalance adding weight to the words. "Doesn't seem to me either that you need to feel you're going off the deep end if you choose to carry a personal sidearm under the—present circumstances."

They were walking down Independence Boulevard, which was flooded with traffic noise and the sound of music, mostly Turkish, from the open doors of many of the shops. A triple-tier Philips sign over an electronics store threw golden highlights over Elaine's short hair, Kelly bent closer to her to say, "I used to carry a piece all the time I was in uniform, a snubbie that wasn't good for a damn thing but to blow my brains out if things got too tough. Just as soon not get into that headset again, you know?"

Elaine nodded; and Kelly, his task of misinforming his case officer complete, focused on finding a place to eat.

A few doors down a sidestreet shone the internal lighting of a red and blue Pepsi-Cola sign with, lettered below, the name Doner California. "*There* we go," Kelly said, pointing with his offside arm to direct Elaine.

"Authentic Turkish, right," the woman said in mock scorn as she obeyed. "Do they have a quartet lip-synching the Beach Boys?"

"I'll eat every surfboard on the walls," Kelly promised as he pushed open the glass-paneled door and handed her within. "Watch the little step."

The floor of the diner was of ceramic tiles with a coarse brown glaze. There were half a dozen white-enameled tables, several of them occupied by men or groups of men dressed much as Kelly was. The sides and top of the counter were covered with green tile, similar to that of the floor in everything but color; but there was a decorative band just below the countertop, tiles mixing the brown and green glazes in an eight-pointed rosette against a white background.

Elaine was the only woman in the restaurant.

Though the evening was beginning to chill fog from air saturated by the Bosphorus, warmth puffed aggressively from the diner, heated as it was by a vertical gas grill behind the counter. A large piece of meat rotated on a spit before the mesh-fronted grill that glowed orange and blue as it hissed.

All eyes turned to the newcomers—particularly to Elaine—as they entered. The owner, behind the counter in an apron, made a guess at what variety of Europeans they were, and called, "Wilkommen!"

"God be with you," Kelly responded, in Turkish rather than German.

Elaine slid onto a stool at the counter instead of a hoop-backed chair at one of the empty tables. "If we're going to do this," she replied to the veteran's quizzical glance, "we may as well do it right. And you were right about the surfboards."

A ten-year-old boy with the owner's features and the skull-cap haircut universal among prepubescent Turkish males set out two glasses of water with a big smile.

"You hungry?" Kelly asked.

Elaine set her palm across the top of Kelly's glass and held his eyes. "The water's almost certainly okay," she said. "Worst case is you'll do anything *we* need you for before you're disabled by amoebiasis. Your choice." She slid the glass toward him and removed her hand.

Kelly hesitated. "Look," he said, "I've drunk—"

"And if you were in the field," Elaine interrupted calmly, "you might have to now. Your choice."

"Two Pepsis," Kelly said, smiling back at the boy. "And two dinners with double helpings of doner kebab, please," he added to the father.

"Turkish for shish kebab?" Elaine asked as the boy opened small bottles with the familiar logo.

"Shish kebab *is* Turkish," said Kelly, "and you can get it anywhere in the world. Doner's pretty localized by contrast, so I'm making you a better person by offering you a new experience. Not necessarily better than the familiar, but different."

The woman's body tensed into her "neutral" status while she attempted to follow the ramifications of what Kelly had just said. Her legs crossed instinctively, then uncrossed and anchored themselves firmly to the footrail of the stool when she realized what she was doing.

Kelly, grinning broadly, turned to watch the owner slice doner while his son readied the plates with cooked carrots, cooked greens, and ladlesful of rice.

The meat rotating before the gas flame was not the roast or boned leg of mutton it at first appeared. It was in fact a large loaf of ground mutton, recompressed into a slab in the ovine equivalent of hamburger, homogenous and broiling evenly on the vertical spit.

As the Americans watched, the man behind the counter swung out the spit and the integral driptray onto which juices spluttered with a sound that would have started Kelly's saliva flowing even if he had not gone most of a day without food. With a knife the length of his forearm, the Turk sliced away a strip of mutton so thin that it was translucent as it fell onto his cooking fork. The man pretended that he was not aware of the foreigners watching him, but his boy chortled with glee at the excellence of the job.

Rotating the spit with his fork—the motor drive shut off when the spit was removed from the fire—the owner stripped another portion of the loaf's surface.

"Aren't many useful things you can do with a knife sharp enough to shave with," said Kelly approvingly, "but this is sure one of them."

"You don't believe in sharp knives?" Elaine asked in surprise.

"I don't believe in—work knives," Kelly replied with a grin, "so sharp that the edge turns when you hit, let's say, a bone."

The meal was everything Kelly had hoped, hot and good and profoundly real in an existence that was increasingly removed from what he had known and done in the past. If incongruity were the essence of humor, then what Tom Kelly was doing with and to Pierrard's little playmates ought to be the laugh of a lifetime.

He sipped his Pepsi, put on a serious expression, and said, "I can never remember: should I have ordered lemon sodas instead with mutton?"

Elaine laughed, relaxed again. "We could ask the maitre d', I suppose," she said with a nod toward the owner beaming beside his grill.

"Who would tell us," Kelly said, slumping a little, "Efes Pilsen—like everybody else." His eyes swept the tables of other customers, crowded with the fat brown bottles of Pilsner beer. "And he'd be right, it's great stuff, but I don't suppose . . ."

Elaine touched the back of his fingers. "Tom," she said, "you've got more balls than anybody I ever met in my life. And it isn't because you act like you could tell the world to take a flying leap."

"Which it damned well can," Kelly grumbled. He was pleased nonetheless at the flattery, even though he knew that the woman was a professional and would have said the equivalent no matter what she really thought.

"I'm so very glad you're using me the way I'm here to

be used," Elaine continued without taking her hand away from Kelly's. "We both want the same thing."

Except that one of us would really like Tom Kelly to survive the next couple weeks, the veteran thought as he turned over his hand and briefly squeezed her fingers. And the other cares more about what the weather in Washington'll be like when she gets back. But nobody was holding a gun to his head just now.

"Let's go see," he said, rising with a broad smile for the owner and everyone else in the restaurant, "just how efficient a team we're all gonna be."

Elaine checked the clasp of her little purse as they approached the door of 727. Kelly caught the angry red wink of a light emitting diode and the woman stutter-stepped, not quite a stumble, before halting.

"Problems?" the veteran said, unaware of the growling catch in his voice as he stepped to the hinge side of the door.

"No, we were expecting a courier, weren't we?" Elaine mumbled back, but she tapped on the door panel instead of inserting her key.

Doug opened the door. The LED warning went off. "I've been *waiting* here with the file," the blond man said.

"Very tricky," said Kelly with an approving nod toward the intrusion indicator.

"Not in the goddam *hallway*," snapped Elaine, using the purse as a pointer to thrust her big subordinate back in the room.

Kelly closed the door behind them. "The light wouldn't come on if somebody hadn't opened the door?" he asked.

"Amber if the door hadn't been breached, no light at all if the transmitter had been tampered with," said Elaine absently. She kicked off her shoes. "Doug, thank you for bringing the file. You can leave us to it now."

She looked at Kelly. "Unless you want to be alone with this, Tom?" she asked, gesturing with the red-bordered folder Doug had just handed her from his Halliburton.

"We'll take a look together," the veteran said, seating himself at the desk. He felt momentarily dizzy and, squeezing his temples with both hands, brought the world he saw back into color and focus.

"Are you all right?" the woman asked. "Doug, wait a minute."

"No problem," said Kelly. "Haven't slept in, you know, the whole flight. And with food in my belly, the brain isn't getting all the blood supply it'd like to have. But no sweat, we'll run through this and get a jump on what we need."

"Blow?" Doug offered.

"You wouldn't like me on coke," Kelly said with a grin that widened like that of a wolf launching itself toward prey. "*I* wouldn't like me on coke."

He opened the folder and let his face smooth. "Quicker we get to work," he said, speaking into the frozen silence, "the quicker I get to sleep."

Elaine gestured Doug through the door, but he was already moving that way of his own accord.

"Well, what've we got here," Kelly murmured, not a question, as Elaine set a straight-backed chair against the doorknob to jam the panel if anyone tried to power through it from the hallway. She damned well *was* more paranoid than the agent she was running. . . .

What they had was a sheaf of gatefold paper, the sheets still articulated, printed on a teletype or something with an equally unattractive typeface. Each page was headed with an alphanumeric folio line, but beneath that the first page was headed: Romer, Gisela Marie Hroswith. Good enough.

Kelly began to read, tearing each sheet off when he finished with it and laying it facedown on the desk. The woman, sitting on the bed, leaned forward and took the pages as Kelly laid them down. Neither spoke.

Gisela Romer was thirty-one, an inch taller than Kelly, and weighed a hundred and forty pounds. At five-ten, that didn't make her willowy by Western standards, but it was as exotic a touch as her blond hair in a Turkish culture where a beautiful woman five feet tall would weigh as much. The telecopied newspaper photograph appended to the file was indistinct enough to have been Jackie Kennedy, but the high, prominent cheekbones came through.

As Elaine had said in the elevator, Gisela Romer was a Turkish citizen; but her father and mother were part of a sizable contingent of Germans who had surfaced in Turkey in the late forties, carrying South American and South African passports that might not have borne the most careful scrutiny. By that time, Berlin was under Soviet blockade and the Strategic Air Command was very interested in flight paths north from the Turkish bases they were constructing. Nobody was going to worry too much about, say, a Waffen-SS Oberfuehrer named Schneider who might now call himself Romer.

Information on Gisela was sparse through the mid-sixties—no place of residence and no record of schooling, though her father was reaching a level of prominence as a power in what was variously called the Service League or simply the Service—der Dienst.

"Is there an annex on the Dienst?" Kelly muttered when he got to the reference in Gisela Romer's bio.

"You've got the file," Elaine noted simply. "I can give you a bare bones now if there isn't. An import-export cooperative for certain expatriate families. Almost certainly drug involvement, probably arms as well in the other direction."

"There's an annex," Kelly said as he thumbed forward from the back of the clumsy document.

The printout on the Dienst was obviously a synopsis. The organization had been penetrated decades before, possibly from the very date of its inception. The file was less circumspect than Elaine had been about drug and arms trafficking. CIA used the Dienst as one of the conduits by which it increased its unreported operating budget through worldwide drug dealing. Drugs were not, by the agency's charter, its problem; and morality became a CIA problem only when one of its officers became moral and went public with the details of what he had been doing while on the agency payroll.

Clients for the Dienst's gunrunning were a more catholic gathering, though various facets of the US government were prominent among them. A brief notation brought to Kelly's mind the shipment of automatic rifles with Columbian proof markings which he had issued to his Kurds. It was useful—generally—to carry out policy through channels which permitted bureaucrats to deny government involvement. The Dienst was indeed a service organization, and not merely on behalf of the war criminals it had smuggled out of Germany.

"These guys are a bunch of Nazis," Kelly said wonderingly as he tossed the annex on the desk and returned to the main file.

"They appear to have no political ends, here or in Germany," his case officer replied. "There is—and it may not be here"—she tapped the paper with an index finger—"an involvement in espionage, with us and probably with the Russians. Perhaps just another way of buying safety by becoming useful to both sides."

"Which is where," Kelly said as he resumed reading, "Gisela Romer and her line of work come in, I presume."

Ahmed Ayyubi had called Romer "the blond whore," but there was nothing to suggest that the statement was literally true. The woman had been dancing professionally since she was fourteen. Her background and appearance would have gained her a following in any Moslem country, but her skill level was apparently equal to that of any competitor in Turkey. At over a hundred thousand lire per performance, her legitimate earnings approximated those of an international soccer star.

So the men she slept with were chosen for position rather than wealth: high police and military officials; bank presidents and airline officials, people who could facilitate movements of one sort or another; and members of the diplomatic community in both Istanbul and Ankara.

"Why the *hell* would she pick up Mohammed Ayyubi?" Kelly demanded as he flapped down the last page of the printout. "He's not in her *league*." He laughed. "Figuratively, I mean. Literally, hell, maybe he was."

"Does it say that there?" Elaine asked, picking up the sheet Kelly had just finished.

"Mohammed's brother says it," Kelly muttered, "more'r less. *God*, I'm tired. And what in *blazes* do either one of 'em have to do with that—thing in the freezer."

"Ayyubi isn't around to ask," the woman said dryly. "But if you want to meet Gisela Romer, that can be arranged."

Kelly stood up and stretched. Elaine waited tensely for her agent's face to take on an expression or for him to say something. The muscles of Kelly's shoulders bunched beneath his jacket and his eyes gave her the feeling that she was being watched over a gunsight.

"When. Where. How," the veteran said at last. The syllables were without tone, not even of interrogation.

"She'll be performing at a Turkish-American Friendship Society meeting tomorrow night. The file indicates her technique." Elaine fanned the sheaf of papers again. "If you attend with the US assistant military attaché here, she'll be interested."

The woman paused. Kelly gestured with one hand, palm upward. "Drop the other shoe."

"If we drop word of who you *really* are," Elaine continued calmly, "she'll hit on you for sure to learn what you're doing in Turkey again. And that could be the opening you need."

"Fucking *brilliant*," Kelly snorted. "And who else picks me up? I'm a bit of a target, don't you think, for what happened three years back?"

"That's not a problem with the Dienst," the woman said. "Quite the contrary. Nor with the Turkish government, which keeps the Israelis in line; you're not worth dynamiting the only diplomatic relations Israel has with an Islamic state. And we'll keep the USG off your back, now and from now on." She bent forward, though that meant she had to look up more steeply to meet the eyes of the standing man. "We're already doing that, Tom. That's the payment we're giving you that you couldn't buy with money."

"Convey my thanks to Pierrard and his budget officers," Kelly said with an ironic bow. They'd sell him to Shin Bet or for cats' meat—which might come to about the same thing—the moment it suited their purposes.

"All right," he continued, with a note of resignation, "she's the best handle I see just now." He held his fist out in front of him and stared at it as he raised his fingers one at a time. "I don't see very much, that's sure. What time's the party?"

"Seven-thirty," Elaine said, relaxing minusculely. "It's in the casino in the Hilton, five minutes walk, so that's not a problem. Probably better to have Commander Posner call for you here, though, so you arrive together."

"All right," said Kelly as he started for the door.

"What will you do till then?"

"Sleep," said the agent. "And probably nothin' else."

Which wasn't very much of a lie.

Kelly locked the door of 725 and turned on the shower.

He was taking a chance by deciding to review the tape as soon as he got back to his room, because the system could not record additional material while he was listening to what it had collected to date. A second tape recorder would have permitted both . . . but additional gear meant a greater chance of discovery, and anyway—he was Tom Kelly, no longer NSA, and there was only one of him.

So although there was a fair likelihood that Elaine was about to have a conversation Kelly would like to know about, he opened the false battery pack attachéd to the Sony and rewound the miniature metal tape. The shower was not to cover the sound of the tape—it played back through earphones attachéd to the radio—but rather as an explanation, if anyone were listening to the noises within his darkened room and wondering at the fact that he was not asleep.

The taping system worked. You never knew, when components had to be arranged separately and not tested until they were in place. And this installation had been trickier than most because the cavity resonator Kelly had planted in his case officer's room was nothing but a closed metal tube with a short antenna attachéd. One end of the tube was a thin diaphragm which vibrated with the speech of people in the room. There was no internal power source, no circuitry, nothing but the section of wave guide. The microwaves directed at it from the ETAP were modulated by the diaphragm, and the whole was rebroadcast on the FM band at a frequency determined by the resonance of the microwave signal, the wave guide, and the length of the antenna.

The recorder was voice-activated so the first syllable of any string was clipped, and there was the usual urban trash overlaying a weak signal. Kelly had been trained to gather content from as little as thirty percent of a vocal message, however, and he had no problem following the recording.

The first of it was the phone ringing followed by Elaine's voice, noncommittal but recognizable, saying, *"All right, good. Stay down there."* George reporting from the coffee shop that Kelly had returned to the Sheraton. That, and Kelly's own discussion with Elaine in her room, were of interest purely as a test of the system.

The next conversation was the case officer's side of an outbound telephone call which had to have been made while Kelly showered before they went out to dinner.

Click. "All right, he's eye-deed Gisela Romer and wants her file. We're going out to dinner, so have it waiting. I don't think it'll surprise him. He expects us to be efficient, and there isn't much time to fuck around."

Click. "He says he was getting laid. . . . Maybe, maybe. I can't tell with him, he's spooky. . . . What—?"

Click. "No, for God's sake run off a fresh copy. How are we going to explain photocopies of a dog-eared original? . . . I don't— . . . God damn it, Doug, get somebody there who can run the printer, even if it means dragging the Consul out of bed.

Click. "All right. Oh—and tell Romer we'll try to have Kelly at the dinner tomorrow night. She's to make contact with him there."

Click. "She's not paid to like it, she's paid to take orders. We've got to have a check on what Kelly's doing, and if it works out—he's perverse enough that he's just apt to trust her. At any rate, they can talk politics without getting into arguments. . . . Right."

The clunk of the handset returning to its cradle ended the conversation. There were several identifiable sounds—door opening and closing, someone muttering unintelligibly—probably Doug entering with the requested files. The discussion, the three of them and then the occasional muttered comments of Kelly and the woman as he read and she pretended to read the flimsies. Compression of the silences made the tape jar against Kelly's memory, but there was nothing really different about the conversation.

All but the auditory center of his brain was concerned with what he had just heard, anyway.

It wasn't quite as bad as he'd feared; they weren't setting him up for a long drop, not yet anyway. But they wanted to make sure they had him on a leash, even if that meant identifying him to a gang of Nazi criminals without his say-so.

. . . *they can talk politics without getting into arguments. Christ!* didn't anybody realize that ideology, religious or political, didn't matter a damn to Tom Kelly? The only things worth killing for—or dying for—were personal . . . and if Kelly had personally kicked the whole state of Israel in the balls, that didn't make him a Nazi. Given cause and opportunity, he would have done the same to Britain or any political group in the US of A.

And the other thing they didn't seem to realize is that you don't own ideologues just because they take your money. Intelligence operatives, effective ones, cannot make decisions on political bases any more than they can for personal reasons. They tend, as a result, to devalue both. Perhaps Gisela Romer was simply venal, in which case she would take anyone else's money as quickly as she did Pierrard's. The personality Kelly had gleaned from the file, however, was that of a woman who would take US money for the same reason that she gave head to the KGB resident in Istanbul: the Dienst, the Service, required it.

In neither case was she going to jump through a hoop simply because Elaine Tuttle told her to.

Kelly sighed. The tape wound through several seconds of silence after recording the door closing as he left 727 for his own room. He reached for the Rewind switch, planning to reset the unit to record. A clear voice where there should have been only blank tape said, *"Mr. Kelly, we must speak with you. You need fear no harm. We need you to save yourselves."*

There was no click or other recording artifact before or after the voice. Its volume level was higher than that of the recording previously, and there was no background of white noise as had clung to the sounds broadcast by the cavity resonator.

Kelly backed the tape and listened again. The end of his conversation with Elaine, the door closing, and nothing. Nothing again.

The voice he had heard was gone, except for what now stuck in his mind like a drug-induced nightmare.

He rerigged the camouflaged recorder by rote. Kelly's hands could do that or strip a firearm with almost no support from his conscious mind; and just now, there was very little support available in that quarter. As he let himself down on the bed, he remembered the shower was running. It took an effort of will to get him to his feet again to turn off the tap, and that only because he had spent too long in arid landscapes to let water waste itself down the sewers now.

Short men in dark overcoats lurked at the corners of

his eyes as he moved, but there was no one with him in the room and no light to have seen them by in any case.

Kelly dreamed while he slept, and his body flushed itself of the residues of tension and fatigue. There were no creatures with multijointed limbs, only men in tunics building and battling over a city on a river. Other rivers might have the sharp bank the swift-moving Tigris had cut through the soil of Mesopotamia, but there could be no doubt about the black basalt fortification: he was dreaming of Diyarbakir, or rather, of Amida—the city's name when it was part of the Roman and Byzantine Empires.

The wails rose and were ringed by Persian armies in glittering armor, a dream montage drawn from guidebook scraps Kelly had assimilated out of curiosity when he trained guerrillas nearby . . . but more than that as well, banners and equipment that he did not know, that very likely nobody knew at this distance from the event.

The besiegers raised a mound of earth and fascines, stripping the countryside of timber for miles. "No . . ." Kelly muttered in his sleep, because he knew what came next, and he had himself soldiered through in the wreck of other people's disastrously bad ideas. The wall of Amida rose regardless, propped and piled and jury-rigged to overmatch the encircling threat.

It was not a normal dream. It had the cohesiveness and inevitability not of nightmare, where fear makes its own reality for the duration of sleep, but rather of history. Kelly was an observer, and the frustration of watching rather than participating—even in a certain disaster—caused him to drench with sweat the bedspread on which he lay.

And the wall of Amida, thrown higher than reason to make the fortress impregnable, crashed of its own weight toward the Persian lines. The rubble of it lay in a broad entrance ramp, giving the besiegers a gentle slope up which they scrambled into the heart of the city, crying slaughter and the glory of their bloody monarch Shapur.

Kelly thought he would prefer anything to the rape and butchery his mind showed him in the same omniscient detail as it had the preliminaries. But what closed the dream at last was a nuclear fireball, expanding and devouring its way across not Amida but a thousand modern cities, each of them as clear in Kelly's brain as the screams of the first woman he had shot at close range.

He awoke standing, legs splayed and the snubbie in his right hand searching for a target in the dim light. He thought it must be dawn, but the digital clock in his little radio said that it was seven PM.

There was no one else in the room.

Kelly felt foolish as he put the revolver down, but coming alert with a gun ready had been a survival reflex for a lot of years. Hell, it probably was again. And if nothing was waiting for him in the room at the moment, then that certainly didn't mean that everything was normal.

He'd never had a dream like that in his life; and it seemed likely enough that whatever it was he'd just—imagined—it wasn't a dream.

The phone rang. Kelly jumped, cursed, and started to pick up the handset. His right palm and fingers tingled oddly, and not from his grip on the snubbie, that was too familiar a stress for him to notice its effect. Flexing his right hand, Kelly picked up the phone with his left and said, "Shoot."

"Thought I'd check in, Tom," Elaine said through a buzz of static more reasonable for a call from Lagos than from the next room over. "Commander Posner expects to meet you in the lobby in twenty minutes."

"No problem," said Kelly. "I was just getting dressed."

"Then I'll leave you to it. Good luck," the woman said and rang off.

She sounded cheerful enough, Kelly thought. Wonder if she'd be cheerful if she knew as much about the bug as the bug had told Kelly about her.

He should have been wrung out by the nightmare, but in fact he'd awakened feeling as good as he had in years. The length of time he'd slept didn't make sense, either. He'd *needed* eighteen hours of rest, but there was no way his mind should have let him get it. It didn't work that way when you were on edge. Catnaps maybe, but not uninterrupted sleep that genuinely refreshed you instead of just backing a notch or two off your tension.

The tingling in his right hand persisted for some minutes, finally wearing away at about the time he shrugged into the coat of his gray wool suit. It hadn't been anything serious, nothing that kept him from tying his shoes or would have kept him from putting all five rounds from the snubbie into a shirt pocket at fifteen yards.

But the feeling had been in the portions of his hand which had brushed the surface of the alien corpse in Maryland, and it could be that that meant something very serious indeed.

◼ ◼ ◼

"I don't *like* this," said Commander Posner for the third time, lighting a fresh cigarette from the butt of the one he had just smoked through. "Associating me with you and whatever you're doing is a public provocation to the host country, and it'll do a great deal of harm in the long run."

Posner was in civilian clothes tonight, a fact that surprised Kelly as did nothing else about the assistant military attaché. Military attachés—of all nations—have an advantage over other intelligence officers in that there is no dichotomy in what they are doing. They are, openly and by reciprocal treaty, spies in foreign countries. Not spies thinly masquerading as newsmen, AID officers, or vice-consuls, just spies. Their status makes it difficult for them to achieve results more remarkable than photographs of military parades, but it also permits them to believe that the world is as ordered a place as the bridge of an aircraft carrier in peacetime.

Posner's wife, a slim woman whose smile seemed no more likely to slip than that of the Mona Lisa, bent close to her husband's ear and whispered. He swore under his breath, glared at the cigarette, and ground it out in the clean ashtray with which a waiter had just replaced the overflowing one.

Mrs. Posner smiled at Kelly.

"I know," said Kelly with a nod of false condolence to the naval officer. "It's terrible to work for people as ruthless and *clumsy* as high military officers, ready to force the most ridiculous orders down the chain of command."

Commander Posner sat up sharply, blinking as if he thought he had misheard the statement.

As perhaps he had, because the noise in the big room was even greater than was to be expected by Western standards. A significant sample of the American official community was at the party, and, Kelly noticed, a high proportion of the Turkish nationals was not in fact ethnic Turks. Men—almost all the women in the room were the wives of Americans—of the Levantine, Kurdish, East European, and even Jewish communities in Istanbul predominated here. They were the folk who, rightly or wrongly, felt they might need outside protection in or from what was basically an Osmanli—Ottoman Turkish—nation state.

The US was unlikely to supply that help, should it ever come down to cases; but when you're nervous, a bad chance is better than no chance at all. Tom Kelly knew the feeling right enough.

There was a rattle of cymbals from the far doorway. A man in evening dress on the low podium in the center of the hall cried, his voice echoing through the ill-balanced sound system, "I give you Gisela!" in both English and Turkish.

Turkish music began at the far end of the hall. A man as tall as Doug Blakeley came in, carrying a large, chrome-glittering ghetto blaster, and stood by the doorway.

With a clash of finger cymbals, Gisela Romer appeared there. She was of a height with her assistant, though part of that was the pumps she wore.

Nothing in the file, photograph included, had prepared Kelly for the fact that the woman came as close to his ideal of beauty as anyone he had ever met in his life. Her shoulder-length hair was not the ash blond he had expected, but rather a richer color like that of polished brass or amber that has paled during long exposure to sunlight. Her choker, bra, and briefs were of those materials, brass and amber, and the gauze "skirt" depending from the briefs at her flanks and midline was silk dyed a yellow of low saturation.

The dancer moved down the hall toward the podium with a lithe grace and as much speed as comported with the need to make an entrance. Her arms reached above her head and twined at the wrists momentarily. Then, clashing the finger cymbals, she advanced, spinning with alternate hip jerks—each carrying her the length of a long leg closer to her goal. The man with the tape deck trailed her, accompanied by a shorter man playing what looked like a small acoustic guitar.

"I've never understood the attraction of Oriental dancing," said Mrs. Posner distantly, using the technical term not from concern for anyone's feelings but rather from a distaste for the word *belly*.

"Muscle control," Kelly said. He watched intently as the blond mounted the podium and went into a formal routine, rotating slowly around the semicircle of the audience. "I've never seen a dancer with muscle control that good. Well, once before."

Gisela's hips shimmied and threw the gauze draperies outward, drawing the eyes of most in the room. Kelly watched instead what the actual belly muscles were doing and was flabbergasted. The blond woman was taut-bodied and no more fleshy than the veteran himself was, so the horizontal folds which ascended one after another from briefs to rib cage were not accented into crevices by folds of subcutaneous fat. They were impressive nonetheless, and the precision with which they marched upward like the static arcs of a Jacob's ladder was nothing short of remarkable when combined with the flashier portions of the routine.

"Who was that?" someone asked.

Kelly glanced around him. Mrs. Posner waited, an eyebrow raised in interrogation, for the veteran's answer.

"Bev," said her husband with a grimace.

"A go-go dancer in Sydney," Kelly said, turning again toward Gisela as he spoke, "tucked six Ping-Pong balls up her snatch with the mouth of a beer bottle. While she danced"—from the corner of his eye he noted that Mrs. Posner's hand had lifted to cover her gaping mouth—"she spit 'em out into the audience again. I mean, she could really aim, and some of 'em landed in the third rank of tables."

The woman made a choking sound but did not say anything further. Kelly thought there was the least hint of a smile on Commander Posner's face.

The music thinned to a background of sharply-tapped drums, which Gisela counterpointed with her finger cymbals as she went into a long series of hip rolls, shifting position again with each thrust to make the whole audience part of the performance. Her face was not bored nor disfigured by slit-eyed, open-mouthed mimings of lust. Rather, she was alive and aware both of her audience and the fact that she was *very* damned good at what she was doing.

Gisela ran a full set on the podium before she began to work the room. Her stunning hair remained surprisingly still as her body, hidden from most angles in the narrow aisleways, shimmied and jerked.

Belly dancing was a form of gymnastics and, like other gymnastic routines, an acquired taste. The detailed muscle work, which distinguished this performance from that in a Sirkeci nightclub, was subtler than similar skill demonstrated on the parallel bars. As a result, the attention of most Westerners lapsed—even that of the men, who could see more flesh in cocktail bars in whatever city they called home.

But Christ! thought Tom Kelly, not flesh like that—unless they were dating gymnasts. And the Turkish citizens were noisily delighted, their enthusiasm making up for any lack of spirit among the foreigners present. Men at each table held up bills as the dancer swung close. In general Gisela smiled and shot a pelvis toward them, holding the pose long enough for them to tuck the money under the strap of her briefs.

The two music men accompanied her on her rounds, providing music—by Turkish definitions, rhythm by any—and a level not so much of protection as of presence, to keep matters from getting out of hand. Neither man was as young as Kelly, and the bigger one, for all that he looked fit, was closer to sixty than fifty. At intervals, as Gisela shifted her attention from table to table, the smaller fellow with the guitar plucked sweaty lire from the dancer's waistband and stuffed them into the side pockets of his jacket. Even granting that most of the bills would be hundreds—something over a US dollar—Gisela was making a respectable haul.

And there were exceptions. One table held a quartet

of fat, balding men with features similar enough to make them brothers. They had been drinking raki, Turkey's water-clear national liquor that clouded over ice. Its licorice flavor disguised its ability to lift the scalp of an incautious drinker. Though these four were not inexperienced, the volume of their intake tonight had loosened them considerably.

"Ho!" cried the nearest one as Gisela did a shoulder shimmy before him. He raised a bill over his head and flapped it. Kelly could not see what it was, but somebody at a nearby table hooted and clapped.

The blond woman responded with a belly roll that progressed to an amazing shimmy, a rattle of finger cymbals that overrode the drum taps from the boom box, and finally a forward thrust of her chest that brought her breasts within an inch of the man's face. A bangle, either a large topaz or tawny paste, joined the two bra cups. It was beneath that that the man thrust his bill. There was a cheer and general applause from the surrounding tables.

The brother to whom Gisela now directed herself already had a bank note ready, but instead of waving it he shouted, "Wait!" in Kurdish to the hip-swaying woman and fumbled again in his wallet. The two others at the table who had not yet joined the performance were doing the same, bumping empty glasses in their haste to get out more money.

The second target—"victim" would be a misstatement; he was paying for the honor of momentarily starring before an audience of his peers and powerful foreigners—came out with a second bill, raised one in either hand, and was rewarded with a hip thrust, front and center, and a kiss on the forehead which, not coincidentally, shot Gisela's crotch away from him as soon as he had inserted the money between the briefs and her pubic hair. You could get a lot more sex for a couple hundred dollars, but it would be hard to beat what Gisela had just provided the man in the way of thrills and public recognition.

When the dancer swayed from that table, her bra cups, pubic wedge, and the crack of her buttocks had all sprouted 10,000 lire bills. The engraved visage of Kemal Ataturk waved against the sweat-glistening flesh, and Kelly doubted that the hard-drinking old hero disapproved. Gisela left the crotch and tail pieces in place as encouragement for later tables as she continued her rounds.

The attendant with the recorder had swapped sides on his ninety-minute tape, and the blond dancer had been in motion from the time she entered the room. Kelly unconsciously caught a roll of flesh above his own beltline between thumb and forefinger. It wasn't flab, but it sure as hell wasn't muscle tone like that which Gisela was demonstrating. He hadn't been in shape like that when he was nineteen and humping nearly a hundred pounds of gear, rations, and ammo across a series of thirty-klick days. . . .

The woman swayed closer. The table Kelly shared with the Posners was, by chance or intent, almost the last on her circuit of the room. Commander Posner reached toward his breast pocket. His wife straightened with an expression of blank horror that would have suited her own impalement.

"Well, I don't know what the etiquette is," the naval officer muttered with a nervous smile. "This is the wrong sort of entertainment for a—for a diplomatic gathering, you see."

"Don't worry, sir," said Kelly dryly. "I'll sacrifice myself to uphold the honor of the flag."

He had two bank notes ready: thousands. The amount was a compromise between avoiding notoriety for a huge offering and the need to make reasonable the query on the scrap of paper between the two bills: *Later?* The three sheets were fanned slightly so that the note's white edge was visible between the engraved expanses of currency.

Gisela hip-jerked to the table, turning a full 360 degrees as she left the guests she had just milked and—by switching her pivot foot—striding six feet without appearing to have abandoned them. Those men would not feel plucked and foolish when they went home tonight. It was nice watching a pro work, thought Kelly; and it was not only the woman's dancing which was of professional quality.

She swung around, facing first toward Commander Posner, and did a slow belly roll with her arms twined above her. Posner clapped lightly in embarrassment but did not reach again for his wallet.

Close up, the two attendants looked as out of place as Kelly himself would have felt doing their jobs. There was quite a lot of similarity between what he saw behind their eyes and what he felt behind his own. . . . Both men could well be Germans, though the smaller one was as swarthy as Kelly and the taller one had certainly not been a "Nordic blond" before his hair went gray. They were armed—there were flat bulges beneath either's left armpit.

Gisela blew a kiss at Posner, tinkled her finger

cymbals toward Mrs. Posner (who winced) and switched
to Kelly.

She was tired, the veteran could see, and her midriff
glittered where sweat jeweled the tiny blond hairs which
would otherwise have been invisible. She began a hip
sway; and, as the taped music quickened to an accompaniment of chords clashed on the guitar, the sway sped into
a shimmy.

"My wife could have done that," Kelly said in
German, enunciating precisely so that he did not have to
shout to be understood. "But belly muscles like yours I
have never seen, fraulein."

The look on the woman's face had been one of
wariness masked by fatigue. Gisela tossed her heavy hair
in its blond net and, with a smile as real and wicked as
Kelly's own as he watched her, went into a belly roll that
speeded to the point that the movement but not the
individual folds were visible.

"Ha!" she shouted after what seemed to have been a
minute of frantic motion. She stamped her right foot and
shifted back into a gentle hip sway as if a control had been
thrown to a lower speed.

Gisela's pelvis was prominent above the line of her
spangled briefs. Kelly reached toward the point of her left
hip with the currency and question. Rather than thrusting
her flank toward him, Gisela bent and jerked her shoulders
back so that the tassels on her left bra-cup flicked out
against the bills.

"*There*," she directed in a Platt-Deutsch accent, "for
the thought. And I can do other things your wife never
thought of, too."

Her breast was warm; but then, so were Kelly's fingers and everything else in the big room.

There was a louder cheer than expected from local tables, because very few of the Americans had gotten into the spirit of the affair as Kelly seemed to have done. Gisela strode and swayed liquidly to the podium to finish her act there. Kelly had fanned the note briefly to show the dancer it was there, but as she moved away from him he noticed that her fingers brushed the three pieces of paper into a thin sheaf so that the query was not visible amid the currency.

They were both actors, going through motions choreographed by others; neither able to admit to the other what their real purposes and intentions were, or what they knew of the other party's. It was human society in microcosm, Kelly supposed.

Within moments of the time Gisela sprang from the room with a series of leggy bounds and double-handed kisses toward the guests to either side of her path, chairs and a speaker's stand were set up on the podium by members of the hotel staff.

"We really ought to stay for the speeches," Posner said apologetically in response to a whisper from his wife.

"They'll be in *Turkish*," Mrs. Posner replied, and in a tone that suggested she had been asked to go mud-wrestling.

Kelly looked at her, amazed. She seemed to think that after-dinner speeches at an affair like this were likely to be more boring in a language you didn't understand than they would be in one that you did.

A waiter approached, so soon after the dancer had left

that Kelly assumed he was changing the defense attaché's ashtray once again. Instead, the waiter offered a folded note to Kelly himself with a smirk. It was the paper he had slipped between the thousand lire bills, and beneath his own *Later?* was written in a loose, jerky hand, *Why don't we talk about it at the door to the parking lot?*

Well, that was fast. Kelly rose, setting his chair back with one hand while he balanced the weight of his torso over the table with the other. "Mrs. Posner," he said as he leaned toward the couple, "Commander, I appreciate your company, but I think I've found my own ride home." Or somewhere.

Mrs. Posner nodded distantly. Her husband, frowning, said, "Mr. Bradsheer—take care."

"Thank you, Commander." Kelly shook the naval officer's hand, then walked toward the exit.

The cooler, less smoky air of the hallway as he went to the elevators did not seem at first to clear Kelly's sinuses. Rather, motion and oxygen brought with them a pounding headache as smoke-constricted capillaries tried to adjust to the new demands.

The parking lot north of the big hotel was actually off the basement rather than on a level with the front entrance to the ground-floor lobby. A hotel here, where almost all the guests would arrive in and use taxis instead of their own cars, had less need for parking than a similar 450-room unit in Washington, but that meant there would probably be a great deal of congestion tonight. Kelly shrugged as he got off the elevator, loosening his coat and his muscles, trying to be prepared for anything at all.

Gisela Romer was, quite literally, waiting at the far end of the hall, beside the glazed outside door. The shorter of her two attendants was visible through the panel, glancing in through the door and out again toward the crowded parking lot with the wariness of a point man on patrol.

The woman wore a long cloth coat, belted and not buttoned. Kelly wondered momentarily whether she had simply thrown it on over her costume, but the beige frill of a blouse showed at the cuff when she waved at him. "Are you the sort of man a girl can trust in a wicked world, Mr. Monaghan?" she called. It was Kelly's war name from the time he trained Kurds rather than what was on his present ID as a Boeing Services employee.

"Well, you know," Kelly said as he strolled to her side. The man outside stared at him like a vicious dog which precisely knows the length of its chain. "If you drop a bowling ball, you can trust it to do certain things. You just have to know ahead of time if they're the things you want."

Gisela smiled, an expression that made the most of the width of her mouth. "I think I'll trust you to protect my life, Monaghan. As for my virtue, I'll decide later if that needs to be protected or not."

She made a quick, dismissing gesture toward the glass door without bothering to look around to see how it was received. Kelly saw the attendant's head go back in a nod of acceptance, but the motion might equally have followed a slap. The man strode away from the door, his back straight and his neck no longer swiveling. Christ, you'd think they'd be used to it, whatever the relationships were. . . .

"I'd like to talk, Mr. Monaghan," Gisela said as she touched the sleeve of his suitcoat and rubbed the fabric approvingly between thumb and forefinger. "I have a comfortable place, if you're inclined. . . . and we can take your car or mine."

"Does yours come with a couple kibitzers?" the American asked, feeling his face smile as his mind correlated the two operations: meeting a valuable source who was not trustworthy, and meeting a woman whom he intended at an instinctive level to fuck. The second part of the equation should have been too trivial for present consideration; but, because Tom Kelly was as human as the next guy, it was going to get at least equal billing until he did something about it.

"They'll go in the van," said the woman. She had exchanged her pumps for flats, and still only the thick Vibram heels on Kelly's shoes put his eyes on a level with hers. "I have my own car—and it has only two seats." Definitely a nice smile.

"Let's go," said Kelly, thrusting the door open for his companion, after whom he stepped into the night.

Mercury vapor lights on tall aluminum poles illuminated the Hilton lot well enough for Turkey, but the effect was very sparse by American standards. The lot was overparked tonight, as Kelly had expected. Close to the sidewalk was a British-style delivery truck, with roughly the wheelbase of a full-sized American car but a taller roofline than an American van. The sides were not painted with °GISELA° or a similar legend, but the attendant who had been watching over the dancer was walking toward the passenger side.

The second through tenth floors of the hotel overhung the ground floor and basement so that the glow from lighted guest rooms curtained the wall near the doorway with shadows deeper than they would otherwise have been. Nonetheless, the eyes of Gisela's attendant had been dark-adapted, and it was inconceivable that someone had been standing close to the door without being seen.

"Thomas Kelly," said a voice as clear and recognizable as what the agent thought he had heard on the tape in his room. He spun around.

"Do not be afraid because we must speak."

There were three short men in overcoats and hats with brims, shadows amid shadows against the concrete wall. One of them carried a transistor radio, from whose speaker the voice issued. The figures would not have been there unnoticed earlier, they could not have stepped through the concrete, and Kelly would have caught motion from the corner of his eye had they come running toward him alongside the building. But they were there now, ten feet away, their radio speaking as the attendant just getting into the van shrieked a warning.

Gisela cried out also. A purse dangled from her left wrist, but it was toward the side pocket of her coat instead that her free hand dived.

First things first. The shorter attendant and his companion, who stood up on the driver's side-step and looked over the van's cab, were both reaching for hardware. Kelly threw himself sideways, toward the line of yews fringing the thirty-foot walkway to the parking lot. His hundred and eighty pounds meat-axed the dancer ahead of him, out of the line of fire.

It occurred to him as the first shot banged from the cab of the van that he might be getting a personal demonstration of how Mohammed Ayyubi had died: in the wrong place at the wrong time.

Ricochets have a soul-freezing sound that rightly suggests the flattened bullet may rip a hole through you from any direction. This round cracked twice from the concrete, wall and overhang, before thrumming viciously into the night. Ten yards is spitting distance on a lighted pistol range, but shock and darkness made the gunman at the van as great a threat to the world at large as he was to his target.

As they crashed through the prickly branches of the shrubs, Kelly expected to hit the ground on top of the woman he was trying to save. He had not considered the fact that she was his superior as an athlete. She twisted in the air, using Kelly's own weight as a fulcrum, and hit the hard ground beyond him on braced fingers and toes. The weight of the gun in her right side pocket twisted the tail of the coat around behind her.

"Kelly—" the radio voice in back of him called. There was a snap as the American scrambled to his feet. The sound was not a gunshot like the volley blasting from around the van; it could have been the release of a bowstring.

"Your *car!*" Kelly cried to the woman beside him. Glass shattered from the building, and the man shooting from in front of the van splayed like an electrocuted squirrel as he fell backward.

Crouching, Kelly aware that the woman's light-colored coat made as good an aiming point as his own dark suit was a bad one, the couple broke for the asphalt lot at an angle which thankfully spread them further from the second attendant, who continued to shoot over the cab of the van. The three figures stood like sandbagged dummies, unaffected by the bullets. One round vanished in a violet flash that lighted the wall of the hotel instead of ricocheting away.

"This one!" Gisela shouted, motioning with her right arm toward a car parked at the edge of the asphalt. It was a Mercedes coupe with the slight rounding of lines that marked it as ten or fifteen years old rather than brand new. The mercury-vapor lamp was reflected as a rich blue pool from the bodywork of metallic silver, a German hallmark which Japanese automakers attempted to match with less success than they showed in matters of pure mechanics.

There was a second *snap!* and the remaining attendant catapulted from the van. Gisela, instead of dodging around the front bumper of the coupe, vaulted the hood which her dangling coattail struck with a clang. Kelly flattened himself on the ground, reaching up for the passenger-side door as he twisted his head back to see what weapons were being aimed. He had not attempted to clear the revolver attached to his waistband. All it was going to do under present circumstances was tie up his hand and make a target of him.

A better target.

Two of the figures, the men if they were men, ran toward him while the third's radio shouted, "Thomas Kelly, for your planet's sake—"

The long burst of submachine gun fire from a parked Audi sedan drowned the *cough-brap!* of the six-cylinder Mercedes engine catching.

Kelly expected the coupe's door to be locked. It was not. He threw it open and tossed himself into the passenger seat of the low car, wishing he were half as agile as the woman he was accompanying. The nearer of the two figures running toward the car toppled limply. The second froze and remained standing in a violet blaze as two or three automatic weapons ripped at it.

The Mercedes was accelerating before Kelly got his door closed. Gisela pulled a hard left turn, spinning the little vehicle in about its own length. The 280 SL had not been a dragster even when new, but its engine was in a sharp state of tune and snarled happily as the driver revved it through the powerband. Centrifugal force made the door in Kelly's hand a weight worthy of his strength as he drew it closed.

"Thomas Kelly!" the radio voice called over the roar of gunfire and exhaust. Shots raked the building in a cloud of pulverized concrete, lighted internally by spluttering arcs from the figure who stood in the midst of the bullets until he disappeared instead of falling.

As the coupe straightened in the aisle, heading in the direction opposite to the way it had been parked, Gisela's foot blipped the throttle so that the automatic clutch would let her upshift. There was a red and white glare from a second Audi, backing at speed across the head of the aisle to block them. The medley of tail and backup lights was as uncompromising as the muzzle flashes from the other German sedan.

The shriek of the Mercedes' brakes was louder than the angry whine of the Audi's gearbox being overrevved in reverse gear. The coupe's blunt nose slewed thirty degrees to the left as that front disk gripped minutely before its companion. Kelly's left hand was furiously searching the door panel for a way to roll down the window. Gisela had not switched on her lights, and the parking lot fixtures overhead did nothing to illuminate the car's interior to eyes dazzled by muzzle flashes and the electric coruscance which bullets had drawn from the three figures.

He poised the revolver in his hand, bumping the coupe's low roof with it as he readied to smash out the side window with the gun butt. Instead, Gisela flung his unbraced body against her as she downshifted again and cut the wheel right.

Inertia had carried the heavy sedan from its blocking position against the drag of its own brakes. As it lunged back against its springs when the tires got a firm grip, Gisela punched the coupe between the Audi and the rear bumper of the nearest parked car.

The sedan's bright headlights reflected explosively from the metallic side of the Mercedes squirming past it, accelerating. The Mercedes was too solidly built for competitive racing, but the little engine had enough torque to shoot them through a gap which neither Kelly nor the Audi's driver thought was present.

"Not yours?" Kelly shouted over the exhaust note reflected from the sides of parked cars. Lights scissored across the sky behind them as both sedans maneuvered in the parking lot.

"I don't know whose," Gisela shouted back, shifting into third up the short ramp to Mete Street. The headlights of a car parked illegally on the street flashed on. "What are you *doing*?" Her gearshift hand batted down at Kelly.

The car on Mete Street was a third Audi.

"You drive," said Kelly as he worked the gun from the woman's coat pocket. "I'll worry about the rest."

Gisela's hand touched the control standard on the left side of the steering column, throwing her headlights on and bright. That might have spooked the passenger in the third sedan into putting his burst of shots into the dirt and driveway curb instead of through the Mercedes' windshield. Alternatively, he might have been trying merely to disable the coupe by shooting out the left-side tires. Either way, the muzzle blasts and the ringing crash of a ricochet into one of the Mercedes' rocker panels confirmed a decision Kelly had more or less made already. The guy who shot at them had just clarified the rules.

Gisela had flinched as the bullet hit the car, but her hands were rock-steady now at the ten and two o'clock positions on the steering wheel. She crossed them right and straightened expertly to give the coupe room at the head of the drive if this Audi too attempted to drive across their path. The Mercedes lurched, brushing but not rebounding from the right-hand radius of the curb cut. Then they were in Mete Street, using the full considerable width of the pavement to hang a left turn while continuing to accelerate. There was more firing distantly behind them, but nothing passed close to the 280 SL.

The dancer's two attendants had carried pocket pistols, .32s by the sound of them: the highly-portable European answer to situations in which Americans tended to carry small revolvers. Both choices were guns you carried when you wanted to be armed but didn't expect to have to use your hardware.

The pistol Kelly hauled from Gisela's coat was something else again: a Walther P-38, old enough to have a steel frame and grooved wooden grips. It fired full-house 9mm Parabellum ammunition through a five-inch barrel, which, with the projecting hammer, safety, and front sight, made the weapon as bad a choice for pocket carry as could be imagined.

On the plus side, Kelly couldn't have asked for a better weapon to *use* if he had to be limited to pistols.

Behind them, the lights of a car bounced wildly as it plunged into Mete Street in pursuit. The Audi which had shot at them waited for its companion to clear the driveway before pulling a U-turn to follow. Kelly couldn't be sure through the rear window whether or not the third sedan was following also; but two, crewed by men with submachine guns, were certainly enough.

"*Goddam*," he muttered, then raised his voice enough to add, "See if you can lose 'em. They may not want us dead."

Men with submachineguns, and possibly a woman.

The Taksim District with its broad streets and low-density development—public buildings and luxury hotels landscaped like no other area of the city—was as good a place to drive fast as anywhere in Istanbul. That made it the least suitable place for them to lose pursuers in cars which, for all the coupe's sporting appearance, had the legs of them. Metallurgy and the technology of internal combustion engines had not stood still during the past fifteen years.

Gisela sent the Mercedes snarling past the Sport Palace—the enclosed soccer stadium—without shifting up from third gear, and entered what was supposed to be a controlled intersection at speed. As it chanced, the light was in their favor—but a '56 Chevy, for *Chrissake*, being driven with almost as much abandon as the coupe, was running it from Kadergalar, the merging street.

Kelly's feet were planted against the firewall and his shoulders compressed the springs of the seatback, anchoring him despite the violent accelerations of the car. Gisela yanked her wheel left, trusting the gap in oncoming traffic, as the driver of the Chevy slammed on brakes which grabbed on the right front and started his car spinning just before the moment of contact.

The result was something closer to elastic rebound than auto bodies collapsing within one another, though eight tires simultaneously losing their grip on the pavement sounded like a chorus of the damned.

The coupe's right headlight nacelle touched the left bumper of the taller American design, spraying glass and a cloud of tungsten which had sublimed in a green arc. The front ends counterrotated and the rear quarter-panel of the Chevy patted the Mercedes' back bumper with the control of a handball player's glove. Gisela, bracing herself on the wheel rim as her passenger did on the carpeted firewall, did not attempt input through the brakes or steering wheel until the tires regained enough traction to accept it.

The Chevy, its back end drifting to the right in response to the second impact, broadsided the end of the iron-tube barrier intended to separate cars and pedestrians at the intersection. The scattering of individuals waiting to cross the street at this hour leaped into recessed shop fronts or tried to climb the grated window of a branch bank as the car sawed itself in half with trunk and rear wheels on the sidewalk and the remainder sliding in the street.

Gisela's 280 SL swapped ends twice in a hundred yards of skidding while its tires shrieked without fatal overtones of metal dragging as well. The coupe's short wheelbase and tight suspension made the uncontrolled spin less physically punishing than it might have been in another vehicle, but the Chevy beside them separating in sparks both from friction and the sheared powerline feeding the traffic signal was a sight with heart-freezing elements of prophecy.

They missed an Anadol at the next intersection, marked as a taxi by its band of black and yellow checkerboard, because its driver had braked hard to watch the Chevy disintegrate. The Mercedes' left front brushed the little Ford just hard enough to give Gisela control again. She could not have managed the obtuse angle required to turn left onto Bayildim Street, but there was a cobblestone alley directly across the intersection. The Mercedes dropped into it like a bullet through the muzzle of a smoothbore.

The alley ran between the dun-stuccoed courtyard walls of multistory apartment blocks. The coupe's single remaining headlight filled the passageway, save for the black fingers of shadow flung ahead of the car by projections from the walls. Gisela's eyes and mouth were both wide open in an expression more masklike than fearful. The engine stuttered and boomed as she downshifted, but she did not lose the car's minimal traction except for the instant a driving wheel slipped on garbage and the coupe's right side streaked the plaster silver.

Kelly's left hand massaged his thigh where the hammer of the P-38 had bitten him while the car spun. His thumb touched the safety lever. Christ, it was on safe! The woman knew a lot more about cars than she did double-action pistols. When he had clicked the safety up to fire position, he also checked the little pin which projected above the hammer to show that a round was chambered.

Kelly didn't expect to need the gun now, given the likelihood that the collision would have screened their escape and possibly even blocked pursuit. The Chevy had not exploded as it well might have done—and he was glad it had not. Kelly lacked the willingness to ignore side effects displayed by certain of his superiors who would cheerfully have incinerated scores of Turkish civilians in a gasoline fire if it suited their purposes. The victims would be nonwhites, after all, wogs; and *certainly* non-Christians. Still, Kelly was not writing the Audis out; he unrolled his window as an unlighted lamp bracket beside a courtyard gate clacked against his door handle and Gisela braked hard. Only when she was sure of her clearance did she spin the wheel and the Mercedes hard right, up a slightly-wider alley leading back toward the Catholic church adjoining the grounds of the Technical School.

There was an echoing cry of metal behind them. The car plunging down the alley they were leaving had scraped twenty feet of stucco from the same wall the coupe had touched. The dazzle of headlights made the vehicle itself invisible, but the only reasonable question about its identity was *which* of the three Audis this one was.

"Pull right at the next street," Kelly ordered loudly in a voice as emotionless as the echoing exhaust of the twin pipes. "Drop me half a block down, and go like hell till I take care of the problem."

The woman glanced at her passenger. Kelly had reached across his body left-handed to unlatch his door and hold it ajar. He held the P-38 vertical beside his head, so that the muzzle was clear of his skull no matter what shocks the weapon received in the next moments.

"All right," she said, and the agent realized from her tone that she knew how sure she had better be that it *was* all right.

The Mercedes fishtailed onto Macka Street, losing just enough momentum in a downshift as it burst from the alley that it thrust a Fiat taxi out of the way, by presence rather than by collision, horns on both cars blaring. The taxi cut left, threatening oncoming traffic for a moment but giving the coupe what amounted to a third lane along the curb. Pedestrians and the shills in front of the few shops still open shouted more in enthusiasm than fear.

Gisela braked hard and the Mercedes slewed again, scraping the curb with the edge and sidewall of the front tire as the Fiat that had continued to race them for the slot in traffic shot ahead in a Dopplered howl of alarm. Three more subcompact sedans swerved outward from the coupe's blazing brake lights, honking and cursing but without real animus. Gisela's present maneuvering was not greatly out of the ordinary for the streets of the densely-built old city.

Kelly let the inertia of the door swing it open against the coupe's braking effort, and stepped out onto the sidewalk. He immediately tumbled, balling his head and

limbs against his torso to save himself serious injury from
the unintended somersaults. Only to the agent's speeded-
up senses had the car stopped. It and he were still moving
at about ten miles an hour when his foot hit the concrete,
and the small contact patch provided by his right heel
could not possibly bring to a halt his hundred-and-eighty-
pound mass as he intended.

The 280 SL accelerated away, surely enough to save
the door's hinges though not to latch it firmly again. Kelly
skidded to a stop on his back, the suit coat bunched
beneath his shoulders. He rolled to his feet and stood,
looking back toward the alley they had left.

Men in sweaters or baggy suits who had run to help
him up scattered when they saw the big pistol in Kelly's
hand. There was holster wear at the muzzle and the
squared-off edges of the slide, and the external bar that
was part of the trigger mechanism had polished a patch of
bluing from the frame. That only meant that the P-38 had
been used, however, and guns were meant to be used.

Horns and tires competed in cacophony behind Kelly,
with the insistent note of rubber skidding on concrete
probably the winner of the contest. He spun, bracing his
left palm against the blistered paint of a light pole. He had
expected the Audi which was their immediate pursuit to
exit the alley momentarily; headlights already blazed from
its mouth across the intersecting street.

But another of the German sedans had expertly
circled the whole warren of alleys on Sport Street—named
because of the stadium—and had been speeding north on
Macka Street past the Technical School when the driver
caught sight of Gisela heading in the other direction.

The way the Audi changed front and scrubbed off velocity in an all-wheel drift was testimony both to the driver's skill and the fact that the sedan had four-wheel drive. Otherwise, the weight shift during braking would have unloaded the rear wheels and thrown the vehicle into an uncontrollable spin as the driver tried to change direction.

Gisela had made room for herself in the southbound lane by bluff and audacity. The Audi sedan was a 5000, heavy and as close to a full-sized car as anything made in Europe save for six-door limousines. It simply brushed aside a Skoda pickup which crashed to a halt against the barred front of an apothecary's shop twenty feet south of the agent.

A man Kelly did not recognize from behind was hanging out of the passenger-side window as the Audi regained forward momentum in its new direction. The P-38's thin front sightblade and its U-notch rear were almost useless in the bad lighting, but the Walther pointed like his own finger as Kelly squeezed the trigger through its first long double-action pull. The muzzle blast of the 9-mm, even from a relatively long barrel, was a deafening crash more painful than that of larger and more powerful cartridges operating at lower levels of pressure.

Handgun recoil was always more a matter of perception than physical punishment, and the P-38's was mild by reasonable standards in any case. The barrel had a right-hand twist, giving the gun a torque opposite to what a shooter expected as it recoiled and returned to battery, but neither that nor the lift of the light barrel kept Kelly from putting out a second aimed shot within a fraction of a second of the first. Ears ringing and his retinas flooded by purple afterimages of the huge flashes from the muzzle of his weapon, Kelly rotated back to the Audi which he had intended for his initial target when he jumped from the coupe.

Kelly had aimed not at the passenger, though the man presumably had a submachine gun, but rather at the side window behind him. Reflection from the smooth glass made the empty rectangle a good aiming point, and Kelly's quartering angle on the sedan meant that the bullets would snap across the tonneau and the space most likely to be occupied by the driver's head.

The Audi spun broadside as the driver's hands flung the wheel away and his foot came off the gas before he had quite compensated for the momentum of the vehicle's drift. An oncoming bus smashed into the right side of the Audi just as an Anadol hit the sedan from what would have been behind a fraction of a second earlier. The man leaning from the right-hand window rebounded twice between the door and window posts before sprawling, as limp as an official explanation, against the door.

It hadn't mattered to Kelly—and probably not to the driver bouncing inside the crumpling sedan— whether or not he actually hit the man at the wheel. The 9-mm bullets were supersonic. Their ballistic crack within inches at most of the driver's ears and the way the windshield exploded into webbed opacity as they exited were enough to throw the best wheelman in the world into a disastrous error in this traffic.

The people in the second Audi had seen enough of what happened to target Kelly even as he turned back to face them. The passenger opened up with an automatic weapon as the sedan, its side streaked surreally by the battering it had taken in the alley, pulled halfway up on the curb with a snarl of low-end power as it came toward Kelly.

God himself couldn't count on hitting anything from a moving car. That was why Kelly had jumped from the Mercedes when it became obvious that they were not going to shake the pursuit. The Audi gunner's long burst lifted the muzzle so that bullets spalled concrete from the sidewalk halfway between weapon and target, riddled the neon tobacconist's sign above Kelly's head, and sparked from a rooftop flagpole halfway down the block.

One ricochet gouged ten inches of fabric from the left tail of Kelly's coat unnoticed, and the spray of hot glass from above made him flinch and send an unintended third shot after the two he aimed at the Audi's windshield, at the place where the gunner's torso should be if his head was behind the blinding muzzle flashes of the submachinegun.

If the windshield was bulletproof, Kelly was shit outa luck—but surely no one could drive at night with the skill these men had shown if there was a thick plate of Lexan between their eyes and the road.

The submachine gun fell, banging off one more round as it hit the concrete and skittered. The gunner slumped back, his right forearm flopping against the outside of the door. The two bullets through the windshield had crazed most of it into a milky smear.

Kelly had stepped away from the light pole when he switched targets. The halogen headlights of the sedan bearing down on him flamed the plate glass of shop windows into dazzling facets and threw shadows like curtains over the door alcoves the lights did not penetrate.

The quartz-iodide lights did not blind Kelly as he shifted his left foot a half step to swing his gun and rigid arm. He fired pistols one-handed, not because he thought it was better than modern two-hand grips but because it was the way he had first learned—and thus was better for him. The car, twenty feet away and jouncing closer, was too near for the lights to interfere with his sight line toward the driver.

The Audi slammed to a stop so abrupt that the nose dipped and the undamaged portion of the windshield reflected flashes of advertising signs like a heliograph. The car lurched into reverse and, with its right front wheel still on the sidewalk, crunched again to a halt against some unfortunate econobox in the traffic lane.

Kelly held his fire, shielding his eyes now with his free left hand. The sedan was cocked upward, lights on and motor racing as the driver leaped out.

"No!" he screamed to Kelly, throwing his own hands out before him in unintended mimicry. It was the first time Kelly had actually seen one of the men from the Audis.

It was George, the balding member of Elaine's team, who apparently handled driving chores as well as sweeping for bugs. Christ on a crutch.

Kelly fired, aiming between the Audi's headlights, the clanging of his high-velocity bullet against metal an instant counterpoint to the muzzle blast. George leaped as though he had been hit and ran across the street, regardless of the cars trying to extricate themselves from the chaos of multiple collisions.

Maybe the ricochet or flecks of metal ripped from the bullet and the car *had* hit him. More likely it had been pure terror, an emotion Kelly could well appreciate. His own thighs were wet with something, probably sweat or blood and lymph where the fall from the car had scraped him. But he could've shit himself; it happened more often'n anybody who hadn't been there'd believe.

And "there" was a place Tom Kelly was back to this night for sure.

The right 9-mm loads had penetration up the ass, so it was possible that the bullet had holed the aluminum engine block. The steam that gushed from the sedan's grill proved that Kelly had taken out at least the radiator, which made the car undrivable even if somebody shut off the motor before it melted itself down. There was still one car not accounted for, but Kelly intended to limit further pursuit as completely as he could.

Without killing additional friendlies. More or less friendly.

Gunfire had cleared the sidewalks almost as thoroughly as if all the pedestrians had been shot. Cars still moved or tried to, and the windows of apartments on upper floors were thrown open by curious occupants.

Kelly was trying to look down the street, shielding his eyes from the Audi's halogen glare with his left forearm, when what had been the shadowed side of the pilastered wall before him brightened with light from a new direction. He spun.

The indicator pin told him there was still a cartridge

in the chamber; but he couldn't remember how many shots he had fired, nor did he know whether the piece had originally been loaded to its full nine-round capacity. The snubbie was still where Kelly had dropped it on clearing the Walther, in the side pocket of his coat—and thank the dear Lord that he hadn't found time to refix it at the base of his spine before skidding down the sidewalk on his back. The short-barreled revolver was as bad a choice for shooting at vehicles as the P-38 was a good one.

A car was driving up the sidewalk toward him, opposite to the flow of traffic which the nearer lane would have had if George's Audi had not blocked it. A net bag full of soccer balls, dropped by some shopper or peddler to the sidewalk, burst and spewed its contents in all directions as the car neared at twenty miles an hour.

The car had only one headlight, the left one. Gisela had come back to fetch him, despite the tangle and the bloody violence that anybody with sense would've driven like hell to avoid. One thing about having the shit hit the fan: it taught you who you wanted to keep among the people you knew.

Kelly stepped off the curb to let the Mercedes by and flung open the door of the coupe that squealed to a halt beside him.

"There's another one out there," Kelly said, meaning the Audi and too wired to wonder whether or not he was understood. He flopped onto the low seat and pulled the door closed after him. "Hope to God it doesn't find us."

The dancer pulled around the tangled Audi and the car it had backed into, then cramped her wheel hard and bumped off the curb again with a clang from the low undercarriage. The vehicle immediately behind the cars paired by the collision had begun to back clear to skirt the obstacle. Gisela accelerated through the momentary gap, ignoring both the screamed curses and the clack as she smashed off her outside mirror against the fender of the higher car.

"I'm taking you to the pickup point," she said in German. They had spoken in English before, but stress had thrown the dancer back to her birth language. Kelly was fluent enough in German that the change didn't matter to him, but the fact of it was a datum to file. "We—we've needed somebody like you, for the people you know. This has proven how little time there is."

Kelly started to say, "Wait," although waiting was the last thing he really wanted to do in this confusion with its chance of fire and explosion and its certainty of heavily-armed patrols descending at any moment. Instead, as Gisela negotiated the acute turn onto Tesfikige Street, bumping over the curb again to clear the van stalled in the intersection, Kelly said, "Gisela, run me back to the Sheraton. There's something I need in my room there."

"Are you sick in the *head*?" she demanded, sparing him a glance.

"Didn't say it was a great idea," the American said as he met her eyes. "But I've never volunteered for a suicide mission, and that's what tonight'll have been if I don't have some way to cover my ass." He grimaced and looked away. "Yeah, and get a change of clothes, too. These"—he felt the back of his coat with his free left hand— "haven't come through the night much better than I have."

"But you'll come," the woman said. She was driving

normally. The traffic now was Istanbul's normal dense
matrix, and there was no reason to call attention to
themselves by attempting to break out of it. There was
no particularly good way to get from one place to another
in the ancient streets laid out by donkey-drivers, so their
present course was not a bad one from Kelly's stand-
point.

"I'm with you as soon as we're outa my hotel," the
agent agreed, sliding forward in his seat so that he could
replace the little revolver at the back of his waistband. He
didn't want it to clank against the Walther he intended to
carry in his trouser pocket, screened by the coattail, when
he got out of the car. "I go up to the room, grab my stuff
like I'm just changing clothes to party some more, and I
think anybody listening's going to leave me alone until
they've got a better notion of what's going on tonight.
Better'n *I* do, anyway."

Why in the *hell* had they shot at him, George and
whoever had been with George or at least issuing his
orders? Confusion rather than deliberate purpose, perhaps,
but you don't issue somebody a gun in a civilized venue
unless you trust him not to shoot first and ask questions
later.

Except that to Doug and his ilk in their English suits
and Italian shoes, Turkey *wasn't* civilized; it was part of
the great brown mass of Wog-land, where a white man
could do anything he pleased if he had money and the US
government behind him.

So they might have thought there were—use the
word—aliens in the Mercedes, and they might have
thought it was Kelly about to pull something unstructured

on his own. Either way, somebody had made the decision to stop the car at any cost.

They just hadn't realized who would be paying most of that cost.

"Got another magazine for this?" Kelly asked, tapping the slide of the P-38. His eyes searched traffic for anything his trigger reflexes needed to know.

"No," said Gisela. She had switched back to English, but the shake of her head was a bit too abrupt to have been without emotional undertones. "It was . . . it was my father's before they killed him. The *crabs*. They took even his body away."

"It'll do," said Kelly, unwilling to remove the magazine and check the load on the off chance that he'd need the weapon fully functional during those few seconds. "Why did they murder your father?"

Nothing in the files Elaine had showed him said anything about direct contact between the aliens and the Dienst. More important, nothing in the conversation Kelly had bugged suggested that his case officer and her chief subordinate had any inkling of the connection. Maybe there was more in Kelly's meeting with Gisela Romer than a way of gaming his employers. . . .

"I don't know," she said miserably, reacting to the concern in her passenger's voice. It was genuine enough, concern that a human being had been killed by monsters; but Kelly displayed his feeling because it was politic to do so, the way it would have been politic to display affection if he were trying to get into the woman's pants . . . which might come yet, the aftermath of the adrenaline rush of the firefight accentuating his lust.

"We've known about them for three years," Gisela went on. She forced her way in a blare of horns onto Besiktas Street, through a light that had already changed. None of her memories were keeping her from being as aggressive a driver as Istanbul traffic required. "Ever since the—they made the Plan—my father and the other Old Fighters—the crabs, the aliens, have been attacking us one by one, all over Earth."

"Which plan was that?" asked Kelly mildly, to give the impression that he was just making conversation.

"You'll have to learn," said Gisela. A sudden distance in her tone implied the question had not been delicate enough. "But not from me, it is not my place."

Three truckloads of Paramilitary Police passed at speed with their two-note hooters blasting as Gisela turned past the open-air stadium on the Bosphorus side of the huge Taksim Park. Kelly kept his left hand over the pistol in his lap, knowing that the blue-bereted policemen hanging off the sides of their trucks might catch a glimpse into the interior of the low coupe. On a terrorist alert like this, a burst of automatic rifle fire through the Mercedes was a very possible response.

Perhaps because of a similar thought, the woman glanced at Kelly and said, "You saved my life, didn't you? Was it your job to do that?"

Wonder what Elaine's answer would be, Kelly thought, but he didn't wonder at all. Aloud he said, "Look, dammit, maybe I needed a driver."

It bothered him to be thanked for what he thought of as acts of simple humanity, getting somebody out of the line of fire, getting somebody to a dust-off bird. . . . It meant that either Kelly's vision of humanity was skewed, or that other people's perceptions of Kelly himself were very different from his own.

Two taxis and a BMW sedan were picking up passengers under the marquee of the Sheraton. Gisela pulled ahead of them and as far up onto the sidewalk as permitted by the posts set to prevent that behavior. "I'll be quick," Kelly said as he got out.

The driver's door thumped closed an instant before Kelly's own did, Gisela was already striding toward the hotel's uniformed attendant. The agent caught up with her just as she handed the Turk a bank note folded at a slant so that the numerical 1000 on two corners was clearly visible. "No trouble if we run in for a few minutes, is there?" she asked cheerfully in Turkish, smiling down at the attendant from her six-inch height advantage.

"Well . . ." the door man temporized, but his fingers had closed over the bill and were refolding it apparently of their own volition.

"Another one for you when we return," Gisela promised, taking Kelly's left arm with her own right hand and beginning to stride toward the entrance.

The doorman looked at the thousand-lire note, then toward the back of the leggy beauty who had given it to him. Kelly himself got only a bemused glance, though from the rear his coat and trousers were in worse shape than the coupe's battered right side.

"Listen, this may get hot," Kelly hissed in angry German as he pushed open a door for them. He had not spoken earlier because he did not know of any language he had in common with Gisela which the doorman did not share. "Having you along makes it worse." He was trying to read her expression at the same time that he searched the lobby and alcoves for an observer or even an ambush.

"It makes it *better,* darling," Gisela purred as her hand moved up to stroke his shoulder blades as they walked toward the elevator. "You want to convince them there's nothing wrong, it's all innocent—we'll convince them." She giggled—was the woman really *that* relaxed?—and added, "All *not* innocent, not so?"

Christ, thought Kelly as he stepped onto the elevator. She was probably right, but if the shit hit the fan again . . . The P-38 would be even harder to clear from his pants pocket than it had been from Gisela's coat, and the snubbie was positioned for concealment rather than instant use.

But maybe nothing like that would be necessary. Maybe he'd waltz into his room, change clothes—pick up the radio and tape recorder—and waltz out again. By now, Elaine or whoever had survived the mess in the parking lot and afterwards would know that something had blown wide open . . . but in the darkness, with at least four sets of participants involved, nobody might be absolutely sure of Kelly's own role in the business. Not even George, who, at best, saw not Kelly but a dark suit and a pistol aiming at him. They'd want to talk to him, but to brace Kelly now— with his target, if they recognized Gisela, or with an innocent bystander if they didn't—would be breaking too many rules.

Unless they knew already what their agent had done to the teams in the Audis.

There was no one in the seventh-floor hallway.

"Well, I tell you, honey," Kelly said as he slipped his left hand around Gisela's waist, "you give me a few minutes to change, and then you can show *me* how to show *you* the best time in Istanbul." He shifted Gisela to his other side and drew the Walther from his pocket, using the bulk of both their bodies to shield it from sight of anything but the door of 725.

Left-handed, he inserted the room key, which he had cut from its brass tag to make more portable. Kelly had not *expected* to reenter the Sheraton looking like something the cat dragged in, but he had considered the possibility that he would.

There was no sound from 727, the next door down, and there was no tense aura of someone waiting within Kelly's room. Electronics weren't the most trustworthy indicators available to a trained human.

He closed the door and bolted it before turning and taking a deep breath with his palms flat against the panel. That was as close to collapse as Kelly could permit himself to come for a good long time yet.

Moving again with deliberate speed, Kelly strode to the window and closed the mechanical slide-switch of the Sony 2002, shutting off the recorder hidden in the battery pack as well. He telescoped the antenna and locked it in place, then put the units, still linked so that no one would open the pack simply because of ignorance as to its outward purpose, in his limp attaché case.

"Say, honey," he called over his shoulder as he straightened, shrugging off his abraded jacket and turning instinctively so that the butt of the snubbie would remain concealed from his companion, "you wanna use the john, go ahead, it's—" Kelly's tongue missed a syllable, two syllables, as he looked at the woman for the first time since they entered the room, "just like America," he concluded.

The light between the twin beds had gone on when Kelly flicked the switch in the short hallway. Its shade was the color of old parchment and the wallpaper was cream. Between them they enriched the sheen of Gisela's hair, of her beige knit dress, and of the breast which she had lifted above the scooped-out neck of that dress.

"I want a good time right now," she said.

Kelly scowled angrily. He would ignore her, dammit! He started to bend to unlace his shoes since their thick soles would catch in his trouser legs if he tried to change pants without taking the shoes off first. The P-38 jabbed his thigh with its front sight and safety lever, it was a *terrible* gun to carry unholstered, and he drew it from his pocket to toss it on the bed next to the dancer's overcoat.

The Walther wasn't perfect but it did its job; so what was he bitching about?

"Come on, honey, that's right," the woman said, leaning her shoulders against the wall where the hallway broadened into the room proper and thrusting her hips out toward Kelly. There was a smile in her voice, but her face was as neutral as Kelly's own and the laugh with which she followed the words was brittle. She was tight, the American realized, tight as a cocked mainspring, but she was too accomplished a professional to let that show to the audience on the other end of the possible listening devices.

She seemed to know exactly how she wanted the show to proceed.

"Well, I don't know," said Kelly, fumbling at his shoelaces so badly that he had to look down to see what he was doing. *Dammit!* "I've got reservations. . . ."

The lie was an unintended pun, and in any case his *body* had no reservations at all. His erection was so obvious when he stood again that it brought a really cheerful giggle from the dancer's lips. "*That's* right," she said again.

Kelly stepped closer to Gisela as he tried to unbutton his shirt. It, like the coat, was torn in back and probably bloodied as well. Since his fingers didn't goddam work at the moment, and he needed *some* sort of release under the circumstances, Kelly gripped his shirttails and ripped it open.

Buttons rather than fabric gave, popping and pattering around the laughing dancer like the leading edge of a sleet storm. The cuffs still held him, and he hooked his fingers in the left one as he bent closer to Gisela. "How the *hell* long do you think we've got?" he whispered. "Later!" He jerked his hand downward and, after the sleeve button popped off, the whole cuff tore away in his hand.

"How long did you think it was going to take?" Gisela murmured back. There was nothing wrong with *her* fine motor control as she unbuckled Kelly's belt. Kelly's trousers dropped around his ankles abruptly, pulled by the hidden snubbie, leaving him bare though he scarcely noticed it.

Gisela's whole body was taut as a guitar string, and like a string it vibrated as he met her lips. He was thinking with his dick, which was about as good a way to get killed as he knew of; and right now, nothing he knew mattered except the way that his left hand cupped her bare breast and lightly pinched the already-erect nipple. She began to lift her dress with one hand while the other gripped Kelly's member firmly to the soft fabric still covering her groin.

"I was going to fuck you tonight, not so?" she whispered in German as she laid her cheek against Kelly's, eyes closed. She tongued the lobe of his ear. "Why should I not because you save my life and make me *want* you?"

Who the hell expects anything to make sense, thought Kelly. His free hand fondled her buttock, bare now that she had raised the hem of her dress high enough. There could be somebody in the room after all, waiting for the right moment to deck him from behind, or a team in the hallway poised to smash through the door as soon as Gisela shouted the code word. She could have a dozen diseases, ranging from loathsome to incurable. God *knew* who'd dipped his wick in her over the years—

And none of it fucking mattered, because just now fucking was the *only* thing that mattered.

Gisela wore a slip, but no hose or underwear, which helped explain the speed with which she had changed from her costume to street dress in the Hilton. Her hip muscles were ripplingly powerful, but the layer of sub-cutaneous fat common to all women, whatever their level of exercise, was like plush beneath Kelly's palm.

Gisela's pubic hair was darker than that of her head or the fine down covering her body, but like the mane of a lion its bronze highlights made it more than simply brown. Kelly's shirt still dangled from the agent's right wrist; now he stepped on the tail and pulled off everything except the cuff itself.

The dancer rose onto her toes to increase her height

advantage and, gripping Kelly's member firmly, rubbed the head of it against the lips of her sex. She was dry and tightly closed, her body in this event rebelling against her will. She was murmuring something, but Kelly could not tell whether actual words were intended.

He bent to the nipple of the breast he held awkwardly from the dress, aware that the pair of them must look ridiculous. He was more concerned at some level of his mind about that than he was over the fact that he had just killed a number of people and that he might die himself before the night was out. He chuckled mentally at himself and, though he did not lose his erection, fully regained intellectual control over what he was doing.

Kelly shifted his weight and cupped her groin from the front with his right hand. The knit dress spilled down and both of them made simultaneous left-handed clutches for the garment. "'Good," Gisela muttered in German with her eyes still closed as Kelly inserted a finger. "Good. Good."

The one-syllable approval was delivered in a technical tone, but the dancer's muscles were in full operation, clamping with a rhythmic pulse which drew him more deeply within her.

Gisela's eyes opened and the corners of her mouth spread widely in a smile of beatific happiness. Like Kelly himself, she expected her equipment to work when and as required, and that included the hardware she had been issued at birth.

She turned away, still gripping the shaft of his member with her own right hand. "What . . . ?" Kelly said as her hips brushed his groin and he was nestled momentarily between her buttocks while she pulled the hem of the dress up to her waist.

"Now," Gisela said firmly as she planted her left palm and forearm on the wall and rested her forehead against them. She inserted the head of his member into her vulva where his thrust and her eagerness drew it home at once.

It also drew Kelly into a climax more sudden than anything he had experienced since being rotated to base after sixty-three days in an outpost with no female company save a ewe with a smile that had begun to look flirtatious.

Gisela's simultaneous gasp passed unnoticed, but her cry a moment later as her hips pumped was loud enough to be heard in the next room with no need for bugging devices.

No partner of Kelly's had ever come as quickly as that, and certainly the dancer was as well able to fake a climax as anyone he'd met. Still, the vaginal spasms as he continued to thrust *seemed* uncontrolled; and the Lord knew, they'd both been ready for this or it wouldn't have had even the chance to happen. The whole business had taken approximately a minute and a half; and hell, he'd needed to undress anyway.

"Oh," Gisela said in a fairly normal tone. She chuckled as she straightened up with a friendly twitch of her buttocks against the man. "Yes, a very good time. Very good."

Kelly leaned over and scooped the tatters of his shirt from the floor. He held it to their paired groins before he withdrew from her and began to wipe himself dry with the tail. "Wonder if you can buy terry cloth shirts," he murmured as Gisela mopped at herself with a sleeve. "Might lay in a stock before the next time you'n me get together."

Gisela turned, dropping the damp shirt sleeve and letting her dress fall normally. She kissed him lightly on the tip of the nose, knelt, and, brushing away Kelly's hand and the shirt, engulfed very nearly the full length of his still-erect member with a momentary pause for adjustment at the halfway mark.

She released Kelly, rising again and flashing him the smile which had already become his identification point for memories of Gisela Romer. "Another time, we will take *more* time, not so? When we come back tonight, I think. But now you must dress."

Perfectly, Teutonically, correct, Kelly thought as he shuffled to the closet and chose another pair of slacks. He palmed the snubbie as he stepped out of his ankle-lapping trousers, uncertain as to whether the woman had already caught sight of the gun or not. The point of a real hideout gun is the surprise it offers the user, not primarily its function as a weapon. If people already know you're armed, then you may as well go for something that'll really do the job—like an automatic rifle.

Not that the P-38 he also stuck into the side pocket of the clean pants would be a surprise to anybody likely to be interested in the fact. You did what you could. . . .

"If it's okay to ask where we're going," Kelly said as Gisela drove east on Ciragan Street, away from the hotel and beyond it the Old City, "then I'd kinda like to know."

He kept his eyes on the fender before him, bent up at

a sharp angle like a foresight where it should have been curved smoothly over the headlight. If he looked at her while he spoke, it would imply that he was pressing for the information. He *did* want to know, but pushing her was a damned bad way to learn anything.

She looked at him, the planes of her face a pattern of reflections moving at the corner of his eye. When she did not speak for a moment further, he went on, "Look, this car's going to be pretty conspicuous. I've got an address'r two where we might find something a little less so." He turned squarely toward her and smiled. "Isn't going to be as nice, but maybe for a couple days . . . ?"

"First, we're going to Asia, Tommy," Gisela said, beginning to smile herself as her eyes returned to the traffic.

"For Chrissake, don't call me that," Kelly protested with a laugh. Fine, it was a friendly conversation and not an interrogation session. "Call me Tom—hell, call me muledick if you want . . . but not Tommy, huh?"

"Pun," the woman said, a plosive sound rather than an attempt at words. Her smile toward the bumper of the leading car, a late forties Mercury, of all things, broadened. "We go to Asia, Tom, where you will meet people with whom you will discuss, not so? And if we choose to proceed, as I think we will, then this car will remain at the place of meeting, yes."

Asia. Well, he'd known they were headed toward either the Bosphorus Bridge or the Black Sea, and the latter was a hell of a long way north. Kelly wasn't in control, hadn't *been* in control since the moment he agreed to meet Gisela Romer. His alternative had been to disappear, to hunt up acquaintances in Diyarbakir and hope that they'd lead him closer to the aliens.

Which might have worked. But gathering information was a lot like deer hunting: people who stomp around making noise are less likely to nail what they're after than are the folks who settle themselves in a suitable location and let targets step into range.

"It . . ." Gisela looked over at her passenger again before continuing. "The crabs may appear again and you will be ready." She was speaking in the didactic certainty of a teacher coaxing a student into proper behavior. "But usually they do not twice so soon between. And you *must* not threaten my colleagues. That would be worse for you and for your country than you imagine."

"No problem," said Kelly. "I don't generally threaten people anyhow."

He'd pulled the Walther from his pocket as they drove away from the Sheraton and lowered it between his seat and the door panel, where he held it now.

Pierrard's gang had given Kelly credentials with the Dienst so solid that, it crossed the agent's mind, perhaps it had all been part of the plan. That seemed unlikely, upon reflection. Even if they had been willing to write off six figures worth of cars and every operative within gunshot of Tom Kelly, both of those possible decisions by the Suits, there was simply no way to be sure that Kelly and the dancer wouldn't be added to the butcher's bill. That had been live ammo being fired from the Audis.

Perhaps they didn't know the extent to which these German exiles were involved with the aliens. But there was no reason to have Kelly penetrate the group. They already had adequate access to it through Gisela. Who seemed to have played her American "employers" for right fools, feeding them information on illegal activities they would wink at—and hiding the very fact of the aliens, and of the Plan . . . which wasn't Kelly's job tonight either.

"We'll need the toll," Gisela said. "do you—? My purse is in the back."

Kelly nodded and took a five hundred-lire bill from his breast pocket, left-handed. Gisela had tossed her purse behind the seat, into the coupe's luggage compartment, with a thump almost as solid as that which the Sony radio in Kelly's attaché case had made. He assumed she had another gun there, the standard place for a woman to carry her hardware, though it was a lousy choice unless she walked around with one hand under the flap the way Elaine Tuttle had done the night Kelly met her.

But why had Gisela tried to draw the awkward P-38 from her coat when the aliens appeared, rather than going for whatever she had in her purse? Well, people didn't always do what you expected them to in a crisis. Kelly would trade a bad decision on pistols for the way she brought the car back for him any day.

The Bosphorus Bridge was lighted into a display unique in Turkey as the Mercedes slowed and eased into one of the multiple approach lanes to the toll plaza. The bridge was a mile long; and while there might have been more impressive engineering feats elsewhere in the world, this one joined two continents. The nearer of the five-hundred-foot-high suspension towers was in Europe, and the second was, as Gisela had said, in Asia. The span and its approaches curling uphill from either end were illuminated by closely-spaced light standards, and sidescatter from the floodlit towers picked out the higher portions of the suspension cables as well.

Gisela paid, then accelerated through the mass of other vehicles merging into the three eastbound lanes. There was no need for special haste, but the challenge had brought out the competitiveness never far beneath the surface of the dancer's mind. She flicked her passenger a glance, saw him facing forward, smiling and as relaxed as a sensible man ever is with his hand on a gun butt, and downshifted again to surge into a slot in the traffic.

"You don't like the way I drive," Gisela said flatly as they settled into a steady pace.

"I love it," said Kelly, patting her thigh with his left hand. "When I drive, I push when I don't need to and get all tied up in knots." He grinned.

"Yes, well," she said as her hand squeezed Kelly a little closer to her, "someone must lead and someone must follow, that is so. That it should be *we* who follow—the minutes do not matter, but *that* does matter, perhaps."

Kelly should have felt nakedly open on the bridge, with a two-hundred-foot drop to the water beneath them and a major sea to either side of the long channel over which they passed. There were people looking for him, and there were things that weren't people—he didn't need Gisela's warning to tell him that. They wanted something from him, but the Dienst might be able to tell him what that was. Maybe not the best way to learn, asking somebody's enemy what the first party intended, but it had the advantage of involving fewer unknowns than the direct approach.

There were some *real* unknowns in this one.

The lighting created a box around the huge bridge and the vehicles on it, separating them from sea, sky, and the feeling of openness. The illumination curtained even the city behind them, much less anyone searching the bridge with binoculars from the surrounding high ground. Someone could be following them, since there was no need of a close tail on a vehicle forced to a single direction and speed. Nonetheless, Kelly felt better for the blanket of light that hid his enemies from him. To the extent there was a justification for that emotional response, it was that when there was really nothing you could do, you might as well relax.

The contrast of the highway to Kisikli and Ankara beyond, lighted only by the heavy traffic, brought the American again to full wariness, though his left hand continued to rest on Gisela's thigh. Camlica and the heights which gave a panorama of the whole city, its blemishes cloaked by darkness, led off on a branching road.

Just beyond that, but before they reached the clover-leaf that merged the Istanbul Bypass with the major routes through Anatolia, Gisela turned off. After a hundred yards on a frontage road serving a number of repair shops, closed and grated, the Mercedes turned again past the side of the last cinder-block structure in the row.

The roar of traffic dissipated behind them as the coupe proceeded, fast for rutted gravel and a single head-light, down a road marked by Turkish No Trespassing signs. There was brush and scrub pine, but no hardwoods and very little grass along the route. The one-lane road itself seemed to have been bulldozed from the side of the hill to the right and the rushes to the other side suggested at least a temporary watercourse. The possibility that a car was following the Mercedes had disappeared at the moment they turned to the frontage road.

"How far—" Kelly started to say as the coupe twisted again with the road and a ten-foot chain link fence webbed the road in the beam of their headlight. The red-lettered sign on the vehicle gate was again in Turkish, stating that this was the Palace Gravel Quarry, with no admittance to unauthorized personnel. There was a gatehouse within, unlighted, and no response at all to Gisela's blip on the horn.

Kelly got out, closing the door quickly behind him to shut off the courtesy light. He walked a few steps sideways, knowing that the galvanized fencing still reflected well enough to make him a target in silhouette to a marksman behind him. Dust from the road drifted around him, swirling before the car as it settled, and the only sound in the night was a fast idle of the 280 SL's warm engine.

"It's chained," he said loudly enough to be heard within the car, through the window he had left open. He held the P-38 muzzle-down along his pants leg, as inconspicuous and nonthreatening as it could be and still remain instantly available.

Gisela switched off the headlights and called, "There should be someone. Take this key and be very careful."

Her hand was white and warm when Kelly took the circular-warded key from her. A high overcast hid the stars and the lights of a jet making an internal hop to Ankara, but the sound of its turbines rumbled down regardless. If there was a gun in Gisela's purse, she had left it there.

At the loop-chained gate, Kelly loosed the heavy padlock and swung inward the well-balanced portal. There was still no sound but that of the car and of the plane diminishing with distance and altitude. He walked into a graveled courtyard, sidling to the right enough to take him out of the path of the coupe. He waved Gisela in with his free hand, the one which was not gripping the big Walther.

Subconsciously, Kelly had thought that the grunt of the Mercedes' engine and the crunch of stones beneath its tires would cause *something* to happen. Gisela circled the car in a broad sweep in front of the building which the fence enclosed, a metal prefab painted beige where it was not washed with rusty speckles from rivet heads and the eaves. The headlight and the willing little motor shut off when Gisela faced the car out the open gateway again, and the night returned to its own sounds.

Gisela's door closing and her footsteps were muted, not so much cautious as precise applications of muscular effort by a woman whose physical self-control was as nearly complete as was possible for a human being.

"Who are we looking for?" Kelly asked softly as the woman paused at arm's length.

"I'll try the building," she responded, with enough tremor in her voice to indicate that she was as taut and puzzled as the American—which, perversely, was a comfort to him.

They walked toward the warehouse door, Kelly a pace behind and to the side. The weight of the pistol aligned with his pants leg made him feel silly, but he was willing neither to point the weapon without a real target nor to pocket it when the next moment might bring instant need. It would have been nice if he had known what the hell was happening, but as usual he didn't—it wasn't a line of work in which you could expect to understand "the big picture."

Unless you wore a suit, in which case you probably didn't understand anything, whatever you might think.

The warehouse had a vehicular door, made to slide sideways on top and bottom rails, and next to it a door for people. There was also a four-panel window, covered on the outside by a steel grating and on the inside by something that blacked out the interior.

Kelly expected the warehouse to be pitch dark. He stepped close to the hinge side of the door as Gisela opened it, so that he would not be silhouetted against the sky glow to anyone waiting within.

The big square interior was as well-illuminated as the courtyard, and as open to sky; what appeared from the ground to be a flat-roofed warehouse was four walls with no roof, only bracing posts along the hundred-foot sides. It held a vehicle backed against one corner of the structure, a van like the one which Gisela's attendants had been entering when the shooting started. Apart from that, the interior seemed as empty as the courtyard.

"Come," snapped Gisela, motioning Kelly peremptorily within and closing the door behind him, a precaution the American could not understand until the woman switched on a flashlight she had taken from a hook on the wall.

"What—" began Kelly, unable to see anything worth the exercise in the flickering beam of the light.

"'Nothing, nothing, *nothing*!" the dancer said, her inflection rising into spluttering fury. She strode fiercely toward the van, the tight beam of the flashlight bobbling up and down on the windshield like the laser sighting dot of a moving tank. "They could've left a *note,* surely?"

The floor of the warehouse was gravel, marked in unexpected ways. There were the usual lines and blotches of motor oil and other vehicular fluids inevitable in any parking space. The drips, however, were absent from the center of the enclosed structure, so far as Kelly could tell. Why wall so large an area if only the edges were to be used?

Gisela jerked open the van's door. The courtesy light went on but had to compete with the beam of the flashlight which the dancer had angrily twisted to wide aperture. "Nothing," she repeated in a voice like Kelly's the day they told him what had happened to Pacheco and another hundred of the *White Plains'* complement.

"This is the one your—" the American began, touching the side panel of the van.

"Yes, Franz and Dietrich," Gisela snapped as she straightened to slam the door of the vehicle closed. "They must have come back from the hotel, told them I'd been"—her hands writhed in a gesture that aimed the light skyward until she thumbed it off, plunging them back into darkness—"whatever, killed, captured. And they went off and *left* me!"

"They could get a job with some of *my* former employers," the American said, briefly thinking of his own Kurdish guerrillas. "But look," he added with a frown, "I saw your people go down. There was a flash and they went over when the whatevers were trading shots with 'em."

"That doesn't mean they were dead," the dancer said

bitterly as she walked back toward the door through which they had entered. She couldn't see any better than Kelly could, but she knew there was nothing in the way. "We've had it happen before, people they've shot but not taken away as they usually do, the crabs. They'll come around again, in half an hour or so, and have headaches for a week—but live."

"It doesn't sound like your crabs," Kelly said, frowning, as the woman opened the door and stepped out, "are quite as hard-nosed about what they're doing as maybe I'd—"

"*Tom*," the woman said.

It was too late to matter because Kelly was half through the doorway already and the hand-held spotlight that switched on was as blinding to him as it was suitable for sighting whatever guns were arrayed behind it. For a moment he thought of the P-38, but a voice from behind the screen of light said, "Try it, fucker."

It was Doug Blakeley's voice, and Kelly was in no doubt as to what would happen in a fraction of a second if his pistol didn't drop on the gravel.

As the Walther slipped from Kelly's fingers, an automobile engine spun to life with a whine and a rumble. There was nothing sinister in the noise—but every unexpected sound was a blast of gunshots to Kelly's imagination, and he almost dived after the pistol in an instinctive desire to die with his teeth in a throat.

"Assume the position, Tommy-boy," called Doug in a hectoring voice. Rectangular headlights replaced the spotlight even more dazzlingly. Doug and whoever he'd brought along had driven through the open gate and poised there, waiting for their quarry to exit. Now they were using the car's lights for illumination, the way somebody in Diyarbakir had lighted Mustapha and the alien the night they were gunned down.

Kelly turned to the "warehouse" wall and gingerly permitted it to take some of his weight through his arms. The structure was less stable than it appeared—a roof contributed more to strength than any amount of bracing in the plane of the walls could do. To judge from the amount of weathering, however, this construct had survived at least a decade of wind and storms, and the wall only creaked when the veteran leaned against it.

Chances were that Doug Blakeley had gotten everything he knew about body searches from cop shows or watching other people do the work. Kelly took a minor chance, spreading his legs and angling his body—but not so much that he could not spin upright by thrusting himself off with his hands. The P-38 lay at his right foot, throwing its own flat shadow across the gravel to the base of the wall.

How many were there behind the lights? If Doug were alone, this was going to end *real* quick no matter where Gisela decided to stand in the business.

Which was an open question in Kelly's mind right now, because the woman had sidled a few steps from his and was shielding her eyes with an uplifted forearm. She looked disconcerted, but not nearly as shocked by this as she had been by the fact that her friends had gone off and left her.

The situation made reasonable sense to Kelly, waiting for a frisk or a gunshot, if Doug Blakeley was one of the dancer's friends.

The asthmatic wheeze of a turbocharged engine at low rpms masked but did not hide the sound of footsteps. Kelly's eyes were adjusting to the glare. Without shifting the position of his limbs or body, he turned his head and squinted over his shoulder.

There were two of them approaching, one from either side, their shadows distorted by the corrugations of the metal wall. The man to Kelly's left said, "Peter here told me I should shoot you right off, Tom-lad. Blink wrong and we do just that." It was Doug.

Kelly snapped his head around to center it between the lines of his shoulder blades. Peter has good sense, motherfucker, he thought, but not so good that he doesn't take orders from you.

Gisela moved unexpectedly closer to the American. "I hadn't thought you would arrive like this," she said pleasantly, in English.

Peter, the bull-necked professional to the right, knelt and picked up the Walther without removing his gaze or the muzzle of his weapon from Kelly's chest. He and Doug both carried compact submachineguns—Beretta Model 12s whose wire stocks were folded along the receivers. Beretta 12s were easily distinguished from similar weapons by the fact that they had handgrips both before and behind the magazine well. Given his choice of wraparound bolt submachine guns, Kelly would have picked an Uzi or an Ingram, where the magazine in the handgrip facilitated reloading in a tight spot.

But given his choice, Kelly would have held the gun instead of being at the muzzle-end of two goons who were at least *willing* to blow him away.

Peter handed the P-38 to Doug, the shadow of the transfer warping itself across the beige metal wall. Both men carried their submachineguns in what was to Kelly the outside hand: he could probably grab either of his captors, but not both, and he could not grab either of the guns.

The engine of the car suddenly speeded up. It was an automatic response triggered either by the headlights' load on the alternator or the block's need for greater cooling than the fan could provide at a low idle. Peter snarled something in Bulgarian toward the vehicle, however, indicating both that he was jumpy—as Kelly would have been, forced to hold a gun on Peter—and that there was at least a third member of Doug's present team.

Elaine might possibly speak Bulgarian, but it wouldn't be the gunman's choice of a language in which to address her, even at the present tense moment.

"He didn't have a gun," said Doug, "and then he's got this to use on us. How do you suppose that happened?"

Kelly was so focused on himself and his own problems that he did not realize he was the subject of the sentence, not the question, until Gisela said, "He took—" and Doug slapped her alongside the jaw with the butt of the pistol.

Had the weapon fired, it would have punched a nine-millimeter hole down through Doug's belly, pelvis, and buttocks, a good start on what the fellow needed. . . . But Walthers, save for those churned out with bad steel and no care in the last days of the Nazis, were about as safe as handguns could be. The wooden grips cracked loudly on Gisela's jawbone, and the wall rang as the blow threw her head against it.

The veteran turned a few degrees to the left, enough to give him a direct view of what was happening without providing an excuse for Peter who had backed a step away.

Doug flung the P-38 toward the darkness. The fencing, thirty yards away, rattled angrily when the pistol struck it. "Oh, 'I just made a mistake'?" shouted the blond American as he hit the woman again with his open hand. The blow had a solid, meaty sound to it, and this time Gisela collapsed as her legs splayed. The black gloves which Doug was wearing probably had pockets of lead shot sewn into the palm and knuckles, giving his hand the inertia of a blackjack.

"Did you expect to get *away* with that shit?" he screamed to the woman who toppled onto her face, away from the wall, when her hips struck the ground.

Facing the wall squarely so that nothing in his stance would spark anger, Kelly said, "Look, Mr. Blakeley, maybe we all oughta sit down with Elaine and see about—"

Doug hit him, and the question of whether the blow was backhand or with clenched fist was beyond the veteran's calculation. The blond American wasn't just big—he had real muscle under that fine tailoring, and he put plenty of it into the blow.

The roar to which Kelly awakened was real, not his blood; Peter was shouting something in anger to his employer. Kelly knelt on the gravel, his palms and forehead against the painted steel wall. All his senses were covered by a screen that trembled through white and red, attenuating the sights and sounds of the world. His skin was hot, sticky hot, with the exception of his left cheek and jaw where something cold had gnawed all the flesh away.

Kelly had blacked out for only a fraction of a second, but for moments longer he had no idea of where he was or what was happening. "Don't *point* that thing at me!" Doug shouted over Kelly's head. "You *hold* him like I tell you!"

"I—" Kelly found as he tried to look up at Doug that his neck hurt and his tongue was thick and fiery. A hand gripped his left shoulder from behind, grabbed a handful of fabric and lifted. Doug punched him in the ribs.

Kelly's breath sprayed out with blood from the tongue and cheek, cut against his teeth by the previous blow. The veteran sagged back, his knees brushing the ground, but Peter's strength was enough to hold him.

"Higher," ordered Doug, breathing heavily himself.

Kelly didn't think his ribs had cracked that time, but his whole chest felt as if it were swelling, bursting. He knew where he was now, being beaten by a hotshot American who had finally found a way to assert his authority—while a Third World thug waited to blow holes in him if he didn't sit and take it.

Stand and take it. Peter dragged Kelly fully upright and Doug punched him again.

He aimed at the veteran's face, but the lead-burdened fist moved slowly enough that Kelly was able to duck so that Doug hit the point of his forehead instead of the nose. Even though the blond man was wearing a sap glove, the result was more likely to break knuckles than to do Kelly serious injury.

The veteran blinked against the jumbled dazzle of

light caused by his brain bouncing within the bone. He went limp again, at least partly by volition, and his weight forced Peter back a step.

The Beretta was short for an automatic weapon but still, at seventeen inches, much longer than an ordinary handgun. In order to point the weapon at Kelly without letting the muzzle touch him, Peter had to hold the veteran out at arm's length with his left hand. The gunman was strong, but Kelly's solid weight was an impossible load under those conditions.

"Get Tomashek!" Peter growled in English.

"Big, bad man who thinks he can shoot my people," Doug said as he panted. He had been trying to keep his Beretta muzzle-up as he swung at Kelly with his right hand alone, but the eight-pound submachine gun pulled itself down toward the gravel as the blond man tried to catch his breath.

Peter swore bitterly.

The cold patch on Kelly's forehead was probably blood cooling, but it felt as if the blow had lifted off a patch of skin. Flashes of light moved across his vision like the rotary shutter of a movie camera, but through them he could see Gisela still slumped where she had fallen. Kelly couldn't be sure, but he thought one of the dancer's legs flexed minutely when the blond man's shoe brushed it.

"Straighten him up," Doug ordered, wiping his forehead with the back of his gloved hand.

"Look, I said get Tomashek," Peter said. "I'm not—"

"*Listen,* you bastard!" the blond American roared. "You want to spend the rest of your life in a cell in Buca, you just give me lip once more. *Lift him!*"

Peter grunted in a combination of anger and effort as he obeyed. He bent his left arm at the elbow and half knelt, then used his leg muscles to jerk the veteran into place for another punch.

Kelly hurt in more places than the glove had touched him directly, signals scrambled when his brain jounced, but the inexpert beating had not thus far made him non-functional. He'd been in worse shape after a night drop into steppe country once—and that hadn't kept him from blowing up hardware that somebody else shouldn't have left behind and trekking out again himself.

He wasn't a boxer, but neither was Doug, and the fist the blond man aimed at Kelly's face was slow and clumsy. The veteran jerked his head to the side instinctively, even though part of his mind knew that it might be better to accept the punch than to piss off Doug further by dodging it. The fist touched the lobe of Kelly's left ear before momentum carried it into Peter's shoulder.

Peter blurted a curse, again in Bulgarian. Doug screamed incoherently and swung the Beretta at Kelly's head.

The looping sideways blow was beyond Kelly's ability to dodge, but Peter's own flinching reaction gave the veteran enough slack to avoid the worst of it.

The submachine gun's stock glanced off Kelly's skull, just above his right temple, and the shock jarred the gun's heavy bolt off the sear. The bolt clanged forward and fired the top round in the magazine.

The muzzle blast of the nine-millimeter round was deafening to all three men; gas and unburned powder bloomed simultaneously from the muzzle in a yellow-orange flash, stinging Peter's cheek as the bullet itself gouged a long slot through the wall. Sparks flew, and the howl of the unstabilized bullet cut through the echoing crash of the sheet metal.

"You have pig shit for brains!" Peter shouted as he grabbed Doug's weapon by the magazine and twisted until the muzzle was safely skyward. Kelly, sprawled on his back, tangled the feet of the two men who had been beating him a moment before. "Either you're going to get more help here or you're going to do it *alone*, I swear to you!"

Kelly reached under himself as his heels and shoulders lifted the small of his back from the ground.

The Beretta's wire stock had flexed enough on impact to keep the veteran's skull from cracking, but there was still a four-inch pressure cut in his scalp, and blood had begun to mat the black hair before his body hit the ground. It felt as though he had been struck by an ax, laying his brain open to the chill night air, and a part of him was quite sure that he was dying.

"*Watch*—" one of the men above him shouted as Kelly lifted the aluminum snubbie and shot twice, close enough to Peter's belly that the shirt caught fire.

Kelly's vision was sharp, though he had no color sense at the moment. Both submachine guns were still pointed up, but Peter had started to lower his to cover the man on the ground when the bullets hit him like punches in the solar plexus. The gunman doubled up, clamping both elbows to his wounds. The muzzle blasts had jerked the front of his shirt out of his pants, to smolder over the oval entrance holes just beneath his rib cage.

The cup-pointed bullets had perforated the diaphragm and meandered upward through the gunman's right kidney and lung. Neither nicked his heart, but the blood vessels they destroyed before they lodged under the skin of Peter's upper chest were sufficient to pour his life into his body cavity in a matter of seconds.

Hunched over and mincing because his knees were bent, Peter tried to run along the front of the warehouse to escape the glare of the car's headlights. Doug had stumbled back a pace when his employee released the Beretta. The blond man's mouth was open in a snarl of disapproval. Kelly, still on his back, aimed for the center of Doug's mass and fired twice more.

The muzzle flashes were red to the victim, bright gray to the shooter, and black swirls on the wall where the halogen beams were distorted into shadow by the balls of powder gases.

Doug's wire-slim belt buckle pinged as a bullet scalloped a section through its upper rim, and there was a black hole marring the mauve-gray-and-white striping of his left shirt pocket. Minusculely later, blood spurted to distort the clean outline the wadcutter had punched in the shirt fabric.

The blond American started both to turn away and to lower the submachine gun. Gisela scissored her legs, catching Doug at the ankles, and sent the big man down in a sprawl.

The gasp of the car's intake manifold trying to increase flow coincided with a sideways shift of the head-lights, throwing shadows along the wall in an exaggerated reciprocal of the car's motion. Doug scrabbled on all fours toward the vehicle, splashing dark blood on the gravel every time his damaged heart pulsed. When his arms failed him, his legs continued for several seconds to thrash and hump his buttocks.

As the car started to move, Kelly sat up and tried for the first time to aim his revolver. The short radius and tenth-inch blade sight would have made real accuracy impossible, even if the veteran himself had been up to it. He fired at the broadside of the vehicle as it turned. There was no clang or smack of glass to indicate that he had hit anything. About all Kelly gained by the shot, his last, was to learn from the flash that he was seeing in color again.

"Here," said the dancer. She handed Kelly the sub-machine gun she had wrestled from Doug during the moment that she and the wounded American had threshed together on the ground.

The car was turning so sharply that the power steering belts rubbed and screamed. It was by European standards a large sedan, very probably another Audi 5000 Quattro, now in silhouette against the chain link fencing which its own lights illuminated. Kelly aimed, wishing that he had enough leisure to unlatch the stock and butt the weapon firmly against his shoulder.

There were two push-through selectors at the top of the rear handgrip. One of them was presumably the safety, while the other selected single shots or automatic fire. Kelly had no idea what combination would permit him to fire the bursts he wanted; but the best way to tell was to align the rear notch with the hooded front blade and squeeze the trigger.

Which gave him a three-round burst and a new

respect for the Beretta because the front grip and the comfortably slow rate of fire made the weapon perfectly controllable at its rock-and-roll setting.

There were no tracers in the magazine, but Kelly caught the spark of one bullet beyond the muzzle flashes, snapping through the air a foot above the sedan's roofline. He had been sighting instinctively on the fence, against which he could see the post and notch, for the car merged with the gunsights in a uniformly dark mass. As the Audi fish-tailed to center itself with the gate opening, Kelly lowered the muzzle a fraction of an inch and squeezed off again. He was smiling.

Glass flew up like early snowflakes, winking in the powder flashes and reflected headlights. The car, which had begun to straighten, went into a four-wheel drift to the left instead. Kelly gave the broadside fifty feet away a long burst. At least half the bullets appeared as red flecks on the door panels as friction heated both lead and sheet metal when the nine-millimeter rounds punched their way through the car body.

These muzzle blasts were less shocking than the first had been. In part, that was a matter of psychology, but the earlier shots had been literally deafening, and Kelly's back was now to the warehouse wall that had acted as a sounding board initially.

The headlights swung across Kelly and the dancer once more; then the Audi came to a stop with the driver's door to them. The engine had died, but bits of metal cooling at differential rates hissed and pinged.

Kelly walked a final burst across both front and rear doors, aiming six inches above the rocker panels to catch anyone cowering on the floor. Then for a moment, nothing moved at all.

Gisela dusted herself briskly with her palms, started for her Mercedes, and stumbled.

"Wait," said Kelly, and he began to walk toward the Audi, whose headlights seemed already to be yellowing as they drained the battery, though that might have been an illusion. He couldn't hear properly. There was a high-pitched ringing in his right ear, and cocoons of white noise blurred the edges of all the ordinary sounds, his voice or the scrunch of feet on the gravel.

Because of the pain, each step the veteran took threatened to topple him onto the ground. It wasn't the blow to his chest, though sharp prickles warned that at best the muscles there were cramping, while at worst they were being savaged by the edges of broken ribs. The battering his head had taken, from the leaded glove and the steel tube of the receiver, was a different order of problem. The brain has no pain receptors of its own, but it has ways of making its displeasure known. Kelly's stomach and throat contracted with transferred discomfort every time his heel touched the ground.

Holding the Beretta by the back grip as if it were a pistol, Kelly tried to open the driver's door. It resisted; though the door was unlocked, one of its edges had been riveted into the frame by a bullet. There was a sharp whiff of gasoline near the car which cut the sweetish, nauseating odor of nitro powders and the chemicals which coated them.

Nothing gurgled from a punctured tank, and the smell of gas was vagrant enough to result from the way the car had stalled rather even than a clipped fuel line. Whatever the cause, thank the *Lord* that the Audi hadn't ignited. They were too far from the highway for the shots to have been noticed, but twenty gallons of gasoline flaring up would arouse interest for sure.

The courtesy light shone directly on the face of a man Kelly had never seen before. His feet were tangled with the gas and brake pedals, but his upper body lay on the floor of the passenger side. The bullet hole above his left eye could have been either an entrance or an exit wound. Its greenish edges had puckered back over the puncture. No one else was in the tonneau of the car. Kelly turned and closed the door. Gisela stood ten feet away, rubbing her jaw and waiting.

The waiting was over for Doug Blakeley, who lay belly-down on the gravel with his limbs splayed into a broad X, The huddle beside the sheet-metal wall, twenty feet from the place shooting had started, was Peter. That one was too dangerous to have been safely forgotten, but there'd been, no time to worry about him when the worries would have been justified.

And the poor anonymous bastard in the car, who might have reported to somebody if a jacketed bullet hadn't churned his brain to jelly. . . .

The veteran knelt down. Being hit on the head was making him feel nauseated.

Bits of safety glass which had shattered into irregular prisms now glittered at Kelly amid the crushed granite. Then his stomach heaved and splashed most of its contents onto the ground. A second spasm followed, with just enough of an interval for Kelly to move the submachine gun he still held a little farther away from his stomach's target area.

He couldn't say that he felt good as he panted on all fours, trying to catch his breath; but he felt a lot better.

Gisela Romer was standing beside the Mercedes. She had taken her purse from the coupe and was rummaging in it. Kelly heard sounds from her and thought for a moment that the woman might also be vomiting. It sounded more like sobs, however. Kelly rose, spat, and wiped his mouth with the back of his left hand as he walked over to the dancer. He could feel his individual injuries separately now, even the dimples left on his knees by the rough stones while he lost his dinner. The long list of pains, however, was a lot better than the total malaise which had preceded it, and his skin was no longer swollen with what had seemed to be three degrees of fever.

Gisela lifted something from her purse and cracked it down on the fender of the Mercedes.

That was the side that had crumpled in the alley. The action shocked Kelly however, since the coupe was too well cared for not to be loved by its owner. "What . . . ?" the veteran said as his free hand closed over Gisela's when she lifted it for another blow.

The woman surrendered the object to Kelly's grip without struggling. He'd been right about the sobs.

"He told me it was to call for help," she said as Kelly examined the object. "He said I should be careful, that you were very dangerous. If I needed help, I should throw that switch."

The object was a prism, three inches by two and about

half an inch deep. The casing was dark resin, featureless except for a thumb slide on one of the narrow faces.

Kelly reached into the car, twisting the ignition key to the auxiliary position and then walking the radio up and down the dial. There was a loud squeal at the bottom of the FM band, near 85 megahertz. Sliding the switch back and forth did not affect the signal.

"Just a beacon," the veteran said as he dropped the little signal generator on the ground. "The slide's a dummy. Doesn't look like they trusted you."

He brought his heel down on the center of the case. He couldn't feel anything give, but the squealing on the coupe's radio vanished in an angry crackle of static.

"Wouldn't help a lot in town," Kelly added in an emotionless voice, "but once we got out on the road where the signal doesn't get lost with all the buildings, it'd home 'em right in." He turned off the radio and the ignition.

Gisela still said nothing.

"Do you know where your friends've gone?" Kelly asked, pointing at the empty, roofless structure. "Unless Doug and his boys were who you were looking for?"

"No!" the woman snapped. She shook her hair out, her visage relaxing slightly now that she had been able to let some of her anger loose. She went on, "There should be someone in Diyarbakir. But it will take us days . . . ."

Kelly shrugged, "Not if we fly," he said. "And I figure that's a lot better idea than sticking around here."

He closed his eyes and pressed the palm of his free hand against the bruise in the center of his forehead. "They deserved it, more'r less," he said very softly. His stomach threatened him briefly when a breeze brought him a reminder of Doug Blakeley, whose sphincter muscles had relaxed to empty his bladder and bowels as he died.

"Might not've made any difference," Kelly continued, speaking to something more shadowy than the blond woman beginning to frown at him. "Wasn't going to be a clean way out, maybe. But maybe if they hadn't knocked me half silly, I'd have tried harder. I can run on reflex, but it ain't real pretty."

He opened his eyes to meet Gisela's. "Is it?" he added, putting a period to words he already regretted saying.

Gisela looked around her, at the bodies and the silent sky, before she faced Kelly again. "All right," she said. "What do *I* need to do?"

"Drive us to Yesilköy Airport," the American replied as he gathered his attaché case from the Mercedes, "and I learn whether my authorization codes are much use there at the military terminal. If you've got the keys to that van"—he waved toward the vehicular door in the wall— "then it might be politic to take it. Can't guarantee we've cleared up all the—road hazards—with these."

"All right," the dancer repeated.

Gisela had a key to the sliding vehicular door. As she manipulated it, Kelly searched the shadows for his aluminum Smith and Wesson. It seemed none the worse for having been fired and dropped without ceremony, though it would get a proper cleaning if Kelly had the opportunity. He had no .38 Special ammunition, so the gun was useless for the moment, as well as a dangerous link to the killings here. Peter and the driver weren't going to be a problem: very likely they weren't Turkish citizens, and they *certainly* weren't Amcits. But Doug was another matter, one that could land Tom Kelly in shit to his hair line—on the slim chance that he survived long enough for that to matter.

He velcroed the snubbie back in place on his waist-band anyway. It'd been a friend when he needed one; and people who ditched their friends at the conclusion of present need wound up real quick with no friends.

The door rolled back with the rumble of well-oiled trunnions.

"The only thing I can't figure," said the veteran easily as he followed Gisela to the van, "is you working so close with the Jews and not figuring what they'd do if they got ahold of me."

The woman froze stock-still, then turned. "What?" she said sharply. "I do not understand."

Kelly blinked in false puzzlement. They were standing close; he could see her face was set like a death mask. "Well, you know about me, don't you?" he said. "About the *White Plains* and—an' all?"

"What do you mean about the *Jews*?" Gisela demanded. She had reverted to German, and her tongue flicked unin-tentional spittle when she said "die Juden."

"Well, who the hell did you think Doug worked for?" Kelly responded, adding an undertone of anger, equally false, at the woman's obtuseness. "*Surely* you knew."

Gisela was swaying. "The American Central Intelligence Agency," she said in a distant voice, a mother begging the surgeon for the answer his face had already told her was a vain hope.

"*Christ,* I thought you people were professionals,"

Kelly snapped. "He's Shin Bet, the section of Israeli intelligence that reports to their Ministry of Defense. They really *did* play you for suckers, didn't they."

And then he caught the blond woman as she stumbled forward into his arms.

"*Easy*," the veteran said as he patted her back, pretended concern in his voice and unholy joy in his heart for having won one, having manipulated a subject into total submission. In this case, on the spur of the moment and without any significant amount of preparation. . . . "Easy," he repeated gently. "Are you all right to drive? I just thought you knew."

Gisela straightened as if bracing herself to attention—shoulders back, chin out, arms stiff at her sides. "Yes," she said, and drew a shudderingly deep breath. "Yes, of course. I'll have to report this to the . . ."

She turned around abruptly, perhaps to hide her expression or a tear, but she reached back for Kelly to show that she was not trying to cut herself off from him. "Come," she said, "we must get first to the airport." She was speaking English again and her tone, if urgent, was not panicked.

"Right you are," murmured Kelly.

The doors of the van were not locked, nor did the vehicle have a lockable ignition. Gisela turned the switch on the steering column and stepped firmly on the clutch so that the back of the clutch pedal engaged the starter button beneath it on the firewall. The engine spun easily and caught at once. The woman turned on the headlights and cautiously engaged what turned out to be a sticky clutch.

"You must understand," she said, her face set, as she reversed to face the vehicle toward the door, "that I acted in accordance with my orders."

She braked, shifted gears, and went on, "We worked with the ones we thought were CIA, but it was always to further the Plan, to gain time until the day came. Not for—their purposes, though we did not know they were the Jews."

They drove out into the courtyard, past the parked coupe and the bullet-shattered Audi. "Soon it will not matter, but—whatever I can do to make it up to you, Thomas Monaghan, I will do."

"What you're doing already is all I could ask for," said Kelly, meeting the woman's eyes in the dash lights. "I need friends real bad. Take me to your top folks and, if they'll help me, I'll do everything I can about the crabs with them. With you all." He paused before adding, "And my real last name's Kelly, but Tom's just fine."

There was one thing more the veteran needed to do before he tried to talk his way—bluff his way, in a manner of speaking, but he was doing *precisely* the job he'd been tasked to do—onto a military flight at the airport. Kelly unzipped one pocket of his attaché case to remove his radio, the concealed tape deck, and the headphones. Working by the greenish light of the gas and temperature gauges, Kelly rewound the tape and set it to play back whatever it had heard in Elaine's hotel room.

The lengthy hash with which the tape began was, Kelly realized after a minute or two, neither jamming nor a malfunction: the maid had entered 727 and was vacuuming it. He advanced the tape and, as he was preparing to blip forward a third time, heard the wheezing vacuum replaced by a click of static and the recorded ring of a telephone.

Click. "Go ahead," said the voice of Elaine Tuttle, who picked up the handset before the completion of the first ring.

Click. "Having sex, he says. It's, I don't know. Could be true, certainly could be."

Click. "Doug, lis—"

Click. "No, just listen to me. He doesn't have a gun right now, but he could get one very easily. We don't want to push him, that's not what we're—"

Click. "Of course we don't trust him. I'm saying we've got to give him the room to do what he's tasked to do, or there was no point in—"

Click. "Except that wasn't your decision or even mine," Elaine's voice said, each word as distinct as a blade of obsidian set in a wooden warclub. *"If you want to take that up with those who made the assignment, then I'll give you liberty right now to get on the next plane."*

It was noticeable that though she had not raised her voice, this time she was able to finish her sentence without being cut off by the person on the other end of the line.

Click. "All right, I'm not neglecting the long-term. Trace them, it'll be good to cross-check Kelly as well as adding to our database on those Nazis. But don't crowd him; he's still as good a chance as we've got of coming up with the link between the Dienst, the Kurds, and the aliens."

Click. "All right. But be careful, sweetheart, he's dangerous even if he doesn't have a gun."

There was nothing more of interest on the tape, not even the slam of the door as Elaine went out. Twice, the toilet flushed loudly enough to trip the recorder, but there were no phone calls and no face-to-face conversations after Elaine had signed off with a warning that Doug Blakeley had chosen to ignore. She had waited in her room, ready to relay information or orders, and neither had come.

Doug should have reported on the shooting in the Hilton parking lot. Either he'd been afraid because he was sure that his career had ended in the melee; or, more likely, he was afraid that the orders he would get would clearly debar him from the revenge he intended to take on one Tom Kelly, the working-class slob who was the cause of all the trouble . . . because there *had* to be a single cause for Doug's mind to grip. Otherwise there was nothing at all to keep him from slipping into a universe with no certainties at all.

Kelly took off his headphones and touched the Rewind switch of the recorder. Wonder if there's anybody left to give'er a phone call, he thought, or if she's going to read about it all in the papers. Maybe George has the number to call.

"What?" asked Gisela Romer, over the rattle of the van's body panels in the wind of their passage.

If he was going to start thinking out loud, then he was an even bigger damned fool than he'd realized. "I was thinking," Kelly said truthfully, "that if people had been less interested in fucking with me, then I'm not the only one who'd have been better off."

The woman looked at her passenger's frowning profile. "You won't regret the help you have given me—given us," she said. "There has never been greater need for men like you, men willing to act resolutely."

Guess even Doug'd give me high marks for that, Kelly thought. Especially Doug.

"He's dead, so I guess he deserved to die," the veteran said aloud. "That's the only way there is to figure, just let hindsight do it."

"Pardon?" said the woman. "I don't understand."

"Me neither," said Tom Kelly. He squeezed her right thigh firmly to assure himself that it was real and the world was real. "But we'll do what we can anyway."

Kelly was almost glad for the way his head hurt because when everything started to slip away it slipped toward the crevasse that seemed to have been banged in his skull.

That focused him and brought him back to awareness of the heavily-guarded terminal building.

It still hurt like hell.

The airmen could be distinguished from the National Police because the former wore khaki and carried automatic rifles while the police were in green with submachine guns. There were six in each party, pausing in their banter to track Kelly and the woman from the little-used portion of the parking lot to the military terminal.

Some airports pretended to be cities of the future, with ramps and glass and cantilevered buildings. Yesilköy was by contrast an aging factory district, where the pavement was cracked and the structures had been built for function, defined by an earlier generation, rather than ambiance.

Tom Kelly wasn't feeling much like a man of the future himself.

Gisela Romer did not exactly stiffen, but her stride became minutely more controlled. The veteran could almost feel her determining which persona she would don for the guards—haughty or sexy or mysterious. Most of these Turks were moonfaced and nineteen—and the same stock as those who stormed through naval gunfire at Gallipoli to drive the Anzacs back into the sea at bayonet point.

"Keep a low profile, love," Kelly said, risking a friendly pat on the woman's shoulder. He winked at the troops, one GI approaching some others, and all of them on fuckin' government business. "This is exactly the sorta thing they expect if I'm doing my job, and I've got authorizations up the ass."

It just feels funny because the people I just blew away were supposed to be my support, he added silently. And of course, the general fucked-upness of trying to do anything through channels wasn't to be overlooked as a factor.

"No sweat," he said jauntily.

Kelly figured he could spot the head of the National Police contingent, but the Air Force section was under a senior lieutenant with pips and a bolstered pistol to make identification certain.

"Sir," said Kelly in Turkish, taking out a billfold bulging with the documentation his case officer had given him, "we have urgent business with the flight controller's office."

The Turkish officer looked carefully at both sides of

the card he was proffered, feeling the points of the seal impressed through the attachéd bunny-in-the-headlights photograph of Tom Kelly. The back was signed by a Turkish brigadier general from the Adana District, in his NATO capacity.

After a pause that wouldn't have been nerve-racking except for the fact that Kelly had put so many bodies to cool in the recent past, the Turk saluted and said, "An honor to meet you, Colonel. Do you know where you're going, or would you like a guide?"

Christ, he hadn't noticed the rank she'd given him for this one. Tom Kelly couldn't remember ever meeting a colonel with whom he'd have willingly shared a meal.

"Is there, ah," the veteran said aloud, "an American duty section?"

"Of course," said the lieutenant; and, if his tone was a trifle cooler, then Kelly was still speaking Turkish.

Too many of the Americans who entered the terminal took the attitude that anybody understood English if you raised your voice enough, and that Turks had about enough brains to be busboys. There were no American bases in Turkey; there were many Turkish installations dedicated to NATO and manned by Americans . . . and if more Americans kept that distinction clear, a demagogue like Ecevit would have found it harder to divert attention from the corruptness of his government with anti-American rhetoric.

"Corporal," said the officer to one of the men with worn-looking G-3 rifles, "take Colonel O'Neill to the NATO office."

Kelly gestured the dancer ahead before he himself

followed the sturdy-looking noncom through the terminal doors. Neither he nor the Turk had referred to Gisela, who was not specifically covered by the authorization. On the other hand, she was only a woman and as such under the colonel's control. Much had changed since the Revolution of 1919, but the Turks were still the people who had given the word *seraglio* to the rest of the world.

What was now the military terminal had presumably been built in past years for civilian uses, long outgrown. It had the feel inside of a train station, with wainscots and plaster moldings, now dingy but painted in complementary pastels. The lobby, at present empty, was equipped with backless wooden benches.

"Are you expecting a flight any time soon?" Kelly asked, mostly to put their guide at ease.

The corporal turned and flashed a smile that was unwilling to become involved, the look of a well-dressed pedestrian faced with a man-in-the-street reporter.

Kelly shrugged.

As he and Gisela followed their guide down a side hallway they saw a portly figure in khakis coming the other way and calling over his shoulder, "Well for *Chrissake*, Larry, get it off when you can, okay?" The fellow spoke English with a Midwestern twang and wore USAF sleeve insignia—master sergeant's, Kelly thought, but it was always hard to tell with the multiplicity of winged rockers the Air Force affected to be different.

The Turkish corporal gestured toward the sergeant, said "Sir," to Kelly, and whisked himself back toward his unit with a slight rattle of his weapon's internal parts.

"Yes, can I help you, sir?" asked the sergeant as he

paused in the doorway of an office which was lighted much better than the hall which served it.

Kelly stepped close to the sergeant to use the light in finding the right document this time. The blue nametape over the man's breast pocket read Atwater. His moustache was neat and pencil-slim, and despite carrying an extra forty pounds, he had the dignified presence called "military bearing" when coupled with a uniform.

"Yes, sergeant," said Kelly, handing over a layered plastic card with an inset hologram of the Great Seal and another bad photo of Kelly. "My companion and I need to get to Diyarbakir soonest, and we don't have time to wait for the Turkey Trot."

"Ummm," said Atwater, frowning with concern at the card as he led the others into his office. "That could be a bit of a problem, sir. . . ."

The phone on his desk began to ring. He lifted the handset and poked the hold button without answering the call. The light began to pulse angrily. "You see," he continued, "there's some kinda flap on, and . . ." His voice trailed off again as he shifted the card between his thumbs and forefingers to move the seal in and out of focus.

Atwater was not giving them a runaround; he was genuinely concentrating as he stared at the card. Kelly, though his face did not change, was chilling down inside, and it was at the last moment before the veteran exploded that Atwater stood up.

"Look," he said, "I'll see what I can do. I don't have any equipment on hand and the Turkey Trot—there's not another for two days anyway." He raised his hand. "Besides you don't want to run that way, I know, sir."

Kelly nodded guardedly. Every week, a C-130 transport made a circuit of the major US-manned installations in Turkey like an aerial bus route. The delay would be a problem, but the questions and whispers of the military types and their dependents sharing the flight made that option even worse.

"I'm going to check with the indigs, see if I can pull a favor or two," the sergeant continued. "If it was just you, sir"—he spread his hands—"maybe we could stick you in the rear seat of something. Two of you, that's a bit of a problem—not anything to do with *you*, you understand, ma'am."

Kelly had been sitting on the arm of one of the office chairs along the wall. Now he stood up but faced the plastic relief map of Anatolia instead of the sergeant to avoid making a threat by his posture. "Ah, look, Sergeant Atwater," he said, getting his voice back under control after the first few syllables, "that card really means what it says, *absolute* priority. If that means stranding the ambassador in Kars, that's what it means."

He turned carefully, thrusting his hands in his hip pockets and looking at the desk before he added, "And if there's a Logistics Support aircraft handy, it means that too."

Gisela had judged the conversation perfectly. She sat as still as the chair beneath her, examining her nails. Because she so perfectly mimicked a piece of furniture, the two Americans were able to hold the necessary discussion for which she should not have been present.

"Yessir, I sorta figured that," said Sergeant Atwater with a grimace. He rubbed his forehead and thinning hair with his palm, then returned the card to Kelly. "There's a bird here, you bet; only, you see, I don't dispatch 'em, exactly."

The hefty noncom spread his hands again. "It's not Logistics Support, it's Communications Service. For this week at least. But I won't BS you, it's just the situation that's the problem."

"Well, you've got the codes, haven't you?" the veteran asked in amazement. "I know it's got to be authorized stateside, but it *has* been. Just punch it in and the confirmation'll be along soonest. This signature"—he raised the card so that the back was to Atwater— "ain't a facsimile, friend."

"Right, Colonel, didn't think it was," the sergeant said.

He was sweating profusely, though his manner was one of angry frustration rather than fear. Atwater was within a year of retirement and he knew that if he did his job by the rules, his ass was covered no matter *how* hacked off anybody got about it. But that wasn't the way to do a job right; and, like most members of most bureaucracies, the sergeant really liked to do his job right.

"Look, the way it is, I can't *get* stateside on a protected line to check those codes," he said, gesturing with a crooked finger at the card Kelly held. "I can't even get Rome, which'd be good enough. All the secure lines're locked up with priority traffic. Somebody's really dumped manure in the blender"—he nodded to the silent Gisela and a drop of perspiration wobbled off his nose—"if you'll pardon me, ma'am. It don't seem to be Double-you Double-you Three from anything BBC or Armed Forces radio say, they're talking progress in Geneva . . . but it's a flap and no mistake."

"I think," said Tom Kelly, looking at the woman who was as still as a blond caryatid, "we'd better get to Diyarbakir."

Gisela raised her head and nodded. "Right," said Atwater, sucking his lips inward so that his moustache twitched. "We'll go talk to the man, and if he'll fly you, I'll log it as authorized pending confirmation." The sergeant led the way down the hall. The next room had a Dutch door, both halves closed, with the legend Messages on the top portion and a counter built out from the lower one. Kelly's face stiffened as he strode past and he felt the weight of the tape recorder in his attaché case. "Hang on," he said, though part of him knew he ought to wait until he was wheels-up from Istanbul. He rapped on the door.

The upper panel was opened at once by an American airman. Behind him a partition baffled the remainder of the room from the hallway. "Look, Don," he said, looking past Kelly to Sergeant Atwater, "it'll go when it goes. What can I say?" There was a muted clatter of static and machinery from behind him.

"I've got something to go out in clear," Kelly said, pulling the top sheet from the memo pad on the counter before he started to write on it with one of the stub pencils there for the purpose.

"Sir?" said the airman, raising an eyebrow.

"He's got authorization, Larry," said the sergeant, before Kelly, having finished with the cable address, could take out his card case again.

"I gather there's some problem with encrypted material," the veteran said, shuttling the code clerk's eyes back to him as he set the miniature tape deck on the counter. He opened the case to display the workings of the recorder within. "I don't want encryption anyway. For all I care, you can put this on the twenty-meter amateur band and beam it right off the tape."

He paused before locking his eyes with those of the young airman. "You *can* get it out in clear, can't you, despite the tie-up?"

"Yessir," said the airman. He blinked to break eye contact so that he could look at the camouflaged recorder.

"Output's through what would be the battery jack," Kelly said. "You people can handle that, I'm sure."

"Oh, yes sir," the airman agreed, turning the memo slip to face him. He blinked again and said, "Jesus."

The veteran smiled as their eyes met again over the counter. "No sweat, buddy," he said. "It'll give you something to play with while the priority channels're busy with other people's worries."

"Check, sir," agreed the airman. He managed a smile of his own. "It's just that—I thought NSA Headquarters got even requests for furniture polish encrypted."

"Not this time, my friend," said Kelly as he waved to chop the conversation, then turned away. "This time the idea's for a whole lotta people to know what went down. The medium damn well *is* the message."

The door leaf swung closed behind him. "That's that, sergeant," the veteran said to Atwater's expressionless face. "Let's see about transportation."

The hall ended in a metal door that gave out onto the airfield itself. They reached it just as a Turkish Airlines 727 was lunging skyward beyond the wire-reinforced window. As Atwater knocked on the unmarked door to the right of the metal one, the roar of the commercial jet's engines shook the building like a terrier on a rat.

"Shine!" the sergeant called through the lessening rumble. "I got a proposition for you."

"Is she—" said a voice as the door opened. The speaker was a black man, five-five or-six, wearing a one-piece gray flight suit. His hair was cropped so close that he could have passed for a Marine in boot camp.

When his brown, opaque eyes flickered past Atwater's shoulder, the pilot paused with his mouth already shaped to speak the next word. "Well, Jesus and his saints," he said instead, "it's Monaghan, isn't it, or have I died and gone to hell?"

"We've been to hell, Shine," said Kelly with a sudden recollection of tracer bullets crisscrossing the makeshift flare path and the high-wing aircraft setting down. "It didn't kill us, did it?"

He gave the pilot a lopsided smile. "Ready for another little jaunt? A real piece a' cake, just a ferry run to Diyarbakir."

Shine cocked his head and looked at the sergeant. "He got his clearances?"

"We've got that problem with the message traffic, like you know," Atwater replied, looking at a corner of the Ready Room. A magazine lay open on the rumpled bunk from which the pilot had risen. "We'll get through when through, but . . . Colonel here seems to think there's a bit of a crunch."

"Colonel, are we?" said the pilot. "Hadn't heard you were on quite those terms, Tommy. Guess you figure I owe you one for not going in for the rest of your team when they pulled the plug on Birdlike?"

Kelly shrugged. "I'd walked away from that one before you did, Shine. We all do what we do."

The black grinned and traced a line across the side of his skull, miming the track of blood matting Kelly's hair. "So-o-o," Shine said, "a milk run, no flak a'tall. Till I come back and try to explain why I flew you, m'friend. There's gonna be a *lot* of flak then."

"Look, Shine—" began Sergeant Atwater with a puzzled frown.

Kelly touched the sergeant's arm to silence him and said with his eyes meeting the pilot's, "I'm not going to tell you you're wrong, man."

"Shit, let's fly," the pilot said, lifting a zip-lock folder and his flight helmet from the shelf beside the door. "*I* figure I owe you one. Or I owe somebody and you're closest."

The aircraft being rolled from a hangar to meet them, a Pilatus Turbo-Porter, was, like the pilot, on twenty-four hour standby with its preflight check already completed. Its straight wing, exceptionally long and broad for an aircraft of the size, was fitted with slotted flaps to lower the stall speed even further.

The Porter's undersurfaces were painted a dark blue-gray that better approximated the shade of the night sky than black would. The upper surfaces were whorls of black over brown and maroon almost as dark to keep the aircraft from having an identifiable outline from above.

Kelly knew where the Logistics Support unit in Istanbul had been flying three years before. Now that the political situation in Greece had stabilized—or reverted, depending on your bias—he was mildly surprised that an agent-transporting aircraft was still based here. Some things had their own inertia, especially when the secrecy of the operation kept it out of normal budgetary examinations. Score one for inefficiency.

Shine—his last name was Jacobs, Kelly thought, or at least it had been when he had been on the eastern border of Turkey supporting Kurdish operations—ducked through the port-side entry doors, springing off the step attachéd to the fuselage. The Porter was awkward to board because its fixed landing gear was mounted on long struts to take the impact of landings that closely approached vertical. Even the tail wheel was lifted by a shock absorber.

Kelly started to hand the woman up the high step, an action as reflexive for him as was her look of scorn as she entered the cabin unaided. Hell, the veteran thought, he was the one who needed help. Walking to the hangar had brought him double vision, and the two steps to enter the aircraft rang like hammers in his skull.

He'd been hurt worse before, plenty times; but he'd never been this *old* before, any more than he'd ever be this young again. If he didn't start using common sense about the things he let his body in for, the aging problem was going to take care of itself real quick.

A ground crewman closed the cabin door while the starter cart whirled the Porter's turbine engine into wailing life. Shine was forward in the cockpit, and Gisela eyed the sparse furnishings of the cabin. There was a fold-down bench of aluminum tubing and canvas on the starboard bulkhead across from the doors, and individual jumpseats of similar construction to port.

Kelly unlatched a seat, then the bench, as Shine ran the five-hundred-horse turbine up to speed. With his mouth close to Gisela's ears, the veteran said, "You got any problem if I rack out on the bench?" He pointed. "I'm not . . . I mean, I think I could use a couple hours, it that's okay."

Gisela smiled grimly at what both of them recognized as an admission of weakness—and an apology for treating her like a girl moments earlier. "Fine," she said, and nodded toward the cockpit. "Do you think your friend will mind if I sit next to him?"

Kelly glanced forward toward the back of Shine's helmet, just visible over his seat back. The right-hand cockpit seat was empty. "Not unless he's changed a hell of a lot since I last knew him," the veteran said with a chuckle. "He'd screw a snake if somebody held it down. Of course, it'd have to be a *girl* snake."

The woman laughed also and patted Kelly's shoulder as she slid her way into the empty forward seat. He could not hear the brief exchange between Gisela and the pilot a moment before the Porter began to taxi, but the dancer's laugh trilled again above the turbine whine.

Kelly seated himself and belted in as the aircraft waited for clearance. The belt wasn't going to do a hell of a lot of good with a side-facing seat bolted onto the frame of a light aircraft; but it was the way he'd been trained, and his brain was running on autopilot. Christ, it felt as if each revolution of the spinning prop was shaving a little deeper through his skull.

He'd be better for sleep. If he could sleep.

The runway could accommodate 747s, but Shine took off within the first hundred and twenty yards of the pavement. The Porter lifted at a one-to-one ratio, gaining a foot of altitude for every foot of forward flight. In a straight-sided gulley or a clearing literally blasted in triple-canopy jungle, such a takeoff might have been necessary. Here, it was necessary only because Shine needed to prove that he and the plane could do it every time— because next time it might not be a matter of choice.

They climbed at over a thousand feet per minute toward whatever Shine chose to call cruising altitude for this flight. It had been possible that he'd fly the entire seven hundred miles on the deck to prove his capabilities in the most bruising way possible. Probably he wanted enough height to engage the autopilot safely—and leave his hands free, since Gisela had decided to sit forward.

Even before the Porter leveled off, Kelly had unbuckled his seat belt and stretched out on the narrow bench. A severe bank to port would fling him across the cabin lengthwise like a log to the flume, but Shine wouldn't do that except at need. The bench, trembling with the thrust of the prop and the shudder of air past the skin of the aircraft, made a poor bed . . . but better than some, and, in the event, good enough.

He dreamed again of ancient Amida, its black basalt walls shrugging off attack by the Romans who had raised them initially. And he dreamed of the Fortress; but in the way of dreams and nightmares, the two merged into a single, stark threat, in space arid on the empty plains of Mesopotamia.

It was still dark when he awakened to the gentle pressure of Gisela's hands on his shoulder blades. Shine was making his final approach to the airbase at Diyarbakir, headquarters of the Turkish Third Tactical Air Force.

And perhaps the headquarters of the Dienst and its Plan, as well as whatever the aliens had been doing when one was shot with Mohammed. Rise and shine, Tom Kelly, there's no rest for the wicked in this life.

The airfield at Diyarbakir had been paved for fully-laden fighter bombers, but, as on takeoff, the pilot had his own notions of proper utilization. Kelly was scarcely buckled in across from the woman who had awakened him when the Turbo-Porter hit the ground at an angle nearly as steep as that at which they had lifted off.

The cabin bucked and hammered in sudden turbulence as Shine reversed the blade pitch and brought the aircraft to a halt against the full snarling power of the Garrett turbine. The engine braked them to a stop within seventy feet of the point they first touched down.

Shine throttled back. Over the keening of the turbine as it settled to forty percent power through a medley of harmonics, he shouted, "You got ground transport laid on?"

"Ought to," Kelly answered, nodding and finding that the motion did not hurt him nearly as much as he had expected. The nightmares he had seen and joined had wrung him out mentally, but his physical state was surprisingly close to normal. He unbuckled himself and stood up, rocking as Shine changed blade pitch to taxi and tapped on the left brake to swing the nose.

Through the windscreen Kelly could see a control tower of dun-colored brick, with corrugated-metal additions turned a similar shade by the blowing dust. At the edge of the building was parked a Dodge pickup truck painted Air Force blue. While the pilot centered the Porter's prop spinner on the vehicle, its door opened and the driver got out.

Shine braked and feathered the prop again, only ten feet from the bumper of the pickup. "Door-to-door service a specialty," he shouted.

Kelly gestured Gisela toward the cabin door but stepped forward himself so that he could be heard, and heard privately. "Appreciate it, man," the veteran said, shaking the pilot's hand between the two seatbacks. "You done a good thing."

Shine laughed without much humor. "Yeah, well, Tommy," he said, "you meet up with any of the types who got back anyway, the ragheads—you tell 'em I'm sorry. There was orders, sure, but . . . you know, the longer I live, the less I regret the times I violated orders, and the less I like to remember some of the ones I obeyed. You know?"

"Don't feel like the Lone Ranger," Kelly said, squeezing the pilot's hand again before he turned to follow Gisela.

Moments after the two passengers had stepped onto the concrete and dogged the hatch closed, the Porter rotated and lifted again—a brief hop to the fueling point a quarter mile farther down the runway—instead of taxiing properly.

"Not exactly the least conspicuous vehicle," Kelly muttered as he and the dancer stepped toward the truck.

"But I didn't think we'd do better through Atwater, even if I kicked and screamed for something civilian. The folks who were supposed to arrange that sorta thing for me are either dead or wish I was."

The man standing beside the truck was in his mid-twenties, wearing a moustache and sideburns which were within, though barely, the loose parameters of the US Air Force. "Colonel Monaghan?" he asked without saluting; neither he nor Kelly were in uniform, and there was a look in the man's eyes that suggested he didn't volunteer salutes anyway.

"Yessir," said Kelly, nodding courteously. The other man's eyes had drifted to the dancer. "I much appreciate this. I know it's not the sort of thing you're here for."

There were only a few US liaison officers at the airbase here in Diyarbakir. This man and the vehicle had to have been requisitioned from the NSA listening post at Pirinclik, fifteen miles west of the city, where the midflight telemetry of tests from the Russian missile proving ground at Tyuratam was monitored. Pirinclik was staffed by the US Air Force; but nonetheless, Sergeant Atwater must have called in personal chips to arrange for a vehicle over a general phone line.

"Here's the key, sir," the younger man said with a modicum of respect in his voice. "There's a chain to run from the steering wheel to the foot-feed. No ignition lock, you know?"

Kelly nodded. "Much appreciated," he repeated as he opened the driver's side door and handed Gisela behind the wheel. She knew where they were going, Lord willing. "Hope you've got a way back?" he added, suddenly struck by the fact that the airman looked very much alone against the empty background of runways on an alluvial plain. "We're in more of a time crunch than . . ."

"So I hear," the younger man agreed with a tight smile. At a base like Pirinclik, there were more sources of information than the official channels. It struck Kelly that this fellow might know a lot more than he and Gisela themselves did, but there really *wasn't* time to explore that possibility. "I'll call and they'll send a jeep. Just didn't want to tie up two vehicles on so loose an ETA." He nodded toward the Turbo-Porter, shrunken into a dark huddle at the distant service point.

Gisela cranked the engine, which caught on the second attempt, just before the airman called, "Pump once and—"

"The gate's off to the left," Kelly said as he closed his own door, wondering how often he'd flown in or out of the Third TAP base. More times than he could remember, literally, because once he'd been delirious, controllable only because he was just as weak as he was crazy. . . .

They paused for the gate, chain link on a sturdy frame, to be swung open by Turks from the sandbagged bunkers to either side. There was no identification check for people leaving in an American vehicle, though the guards showed some surprise that the driver was a blond woman. Gisela turned left on the narrow blacktop highway and accelerated jerkily while she determined the throw and engagement of the pickup's clutch.

"You've been here before," Kelly said, noting that the woman turned without hesitation.

She glanced aside, then back to the road. "Not here," she said in a cool voice, aware that the American was fishing for information—and willing to give it to him even though he had not, by habit, done her the courtesy of asking directly. "Not the airfield. But of course, I've spent a great deal of time at our base in the city."

The landscape through which they drove as fast as the truck's front-end shimmy permitted was as flat as any place Kelly had ever been. It appeared to be rolling countryside, but the scale of distance was so great that it gave shape to what would otherwise have been considered dead-level ground.

But the plains were neither smooth nor green—at least this early in the year; Kelly knew from experience that by early summer the oats and barley planted in some of the unfenced fields would have grown high enough to hide the rocks.

The soil of Mesopotamia had been cultivated for millennia, for virtually as long as any area of the Earth's surface. Every time a plow bit, it sent a puff of yellow-gray dust off on the constant wind and diminished the soil by that much. The rocks, from pebbles to blocks the size of a man's torso, remained . . . and from a slight distance, from a road, those rocks were *all* that remained of what had been the most fertile lands on Earth. One could still cultivate with care and hardship, however, and pasture sheep.

"We—concentrated here in Diyarbakir, when the Plan was developed," Gisela said deliberately, "in part for recruitment's sake—the Kurds." She looked over to make sure her student was following. Kelly nodded obediently.

"But more because it is, you see, not developed," the woman continued, "but still there are the airbase and the

tracking station. Competing jurisdictions, do you see?"
The tutor looked over again.

"So that if things should be seen that neither under-
stands, your NSA or Turk Hava Kuvvertli"—Gisela used
the indigenous words for Turkish Air Force within the
English of her lecture—"both blame the other . . . but not
blame, because of security."

She smiled toward the windshield as, downshifting
the long-throw gearbox, she passed a horse-drawn wagon
in a flapping roar. Communication among friendly forces was
a more necessary ingredient of success than was intelligence
of the enemy, but it was notable that whenever military
bureaucracies set priorities, information flow came in a bad
second to security. Perhaps that was a case of making a virtue
of necessity, since it was almost impossible to pass data
through a military bureaucracy anyway.

"So each thinks the other responsible and says nothing,
so as not to embarrass an ally and to poke into what is not
their own business," Gisela concluded. "Bad practice of
security."

The road off to the right, past a small orchard of
pistachio trees, could have been a goat track save that it
meandered in double rather than single file. Gisela found
the brakes were spongy and downshifted sharply to let the
engine compression help slow the truck. They made the
turn comfortably, though the pickup swayed on springs
abused by too many rutted roads like this.

"Reach into my right coat pocket," the woman directed.
She had crossed right arm over left to take the turnoff,
and even in the moment it took her to reposition her
hands afterwards, the steering wheel jibbed viciously.

Kelly obeyed, expecting to find sunglasses or something similar. Instead there was a round-nosed cylinder that could have been a lipstick, save that it was clicking against three others like it—and a fifth, buried deeply in a corner of the lining.

He drew out the handful of .38 Special cartridges, a full load for the cylinder of the snubbie now nestled empty against his spine. "Well, I'll be a sonofabitch," said the veteran softly as he drew the weapon to load it.

The rounds were US Government issue, bearing Lake City Arsenal headstamps and 130-grain bullets with full metal jackets. They were really intended for 9-mm autoloaders and would literally rattle down the bore of most .38 Special revolvers. When fired, however, they upset enough to take the rifling.

They weren't a perfect load for the aluminum snubbie, but they were a hell of an improvement over an empty cylinder . . . and the fact that Gisela had procured them for him, just before he was to be introduced to her associates, was a sign more valuable than any real protection that the weapon gave him.

"I got them from the pilot," Gisela said needlessly. "I thought you wouldn't ask, to call attention. So I asked, and it won't be reported."

Kelly hunched forward to replace the little revolver. He'd carried it a lot of years and never used it before the previous night, but that didn't mean he wouldn't need it again soon. Lightning was liable to keep striking the same place so long as the storm raged and the tree still stood in its path.

The ground became broken to either side of the road,

lifting in outcrops of dense rock shaded by brush instead of sere grass. Gisela downshifted again into compound low. A moment later, the hood of the truck dipped as the ruts led into a gorge notched through the plain in two stages.

They drove down the upper, broader level; then Gisela cramped the wheels hard left to follow the track across a single-arched bridge of stone, vaulting the narrow center of the gully. There was enough water in the rivulet below to flash in the sun before the truck began climbing from the declivity with a shiver of wheelspin.

"How old was that bridge?" asked Kelly, craning his neck to look out the back window, an effort made vain by the coating of dust over the glass.

"Seljuk at least," answered the woman, with a shrug which merged into a shoulder thrust as the steering fought her when they rattled out of the gully. "Maybe Byzantine, maybe Roman, maybe—who knows? There's probably been a bridge there as long as men have lived here and farmed . . . and that is a very long time."

"And now you're here," Kelly said quietly. "The Service."

"Here." Gisela's smile was more arrogant than pleased. "And soon, everywhere. To the world's benefit."

The ground dropped a few feet on the left side of the road. Gisela swung to the right around a basalt rock face and then pulled left toward the recently refurbished gate of a han, a caravanserai, ruined by time.

The walls of basalt blocks weathered gray gleamed in the sunlight, but the shadowed gaps in the dome of the mosque which formed one corner of the enclosure were as black as a colonel's soul. The dome was crumbling; but, though the ages had scalloped the upper edge of the wall around the courtyard, it was still solid and at no point less than eight feet high.

The original gateway had been built between the mosque and a gatehouse, but part of the latter had been demolished when the new gate was constructed. This was steel, double-leafed and wide enough to pass a semi-trailer. The posts to which the leaves were hinged were themselves steel, eight inches in diameter and concrete-filled if they were not solid billets.

In the far corner of the facing wall there were arrow slits, in the walls and the blockhouse. It struck Kelly that the stone edifice was proof to any modern weapons up through tank cannon, and that the embrasures could shower machinegun fire on trespassers as effectively as the arrows for which they had been intended.

Gisela pulled up to the gate and honked imperiously. The dust cloud they had raised in their passage continued to drift forward, settling on Kelly's right sleeve and the ledge of his open window. The back of his neck began to tingle. He shifted in his seat, unwilling to draw his revolver but certain that a premonition of danger was causing his hair to bristle.

The woman honked again and said, "If somebody's asleep at *this* time, they'll—"

"Jesus *Christ*!" shouted Kelly. He unlatched his door so hastily that his feet tangled as he got out of the cab. He did not draw his gun, any more than he would have thought to do so if he found himself in the path of a diesel locomotive.

At first it was more like watching time-lapse photography of a building under construction, for the object was huge and silent and rising vertically in a nimbus of brilliant light. Hairs that had been prickling all over Kelly's body now stood straight out, and when he reached for the car door to steady himself a static spark snapped six inches from the metal to numb his hand.

It wasn't a cylinder rising on jacks from the han courtyard: it was a disk fifty feet in diameter with a bluntly-rounded circumference and a central depth of about twelve feet.

It was a fucking flying saucer.

Gisela was out of the truck also, shouting and waving her clenched fist in obvious fury. The underside of the saucer was clearly visible, so it could scarcely be called an unidentified flying object. The veil of light surrounding the vehicle as it rose was pastel and of uncertain color, shifting like the aurora but bright enough to be visible now in broad daylight.

The skin of the flying saucer was formed of riveted plates. The junctions of the plates and the individual rivet heads stood out despite the nimbus because the portion of the field emanating from those surface irregularities was of a shade which contrasted with that of the plates themselves.

The whole aura shifted across the spectrum and, as the saucer continued to rise, faded. The craft climbed vertically. A bright line appeared from the rim to the central axis, as if the nimbus had been pleated there and trebled in thickness. The line rotated across the circular undersurface faster than the second hand on a watch dial, hissing and crackling with violent electrical discharges. The rate of the saucer's rise accelerated with the sweep of the line, so that there was only a speck of dazzling corona by the time the full surface area should have been swept. Then there was nothing at all.

"It was Dora," said Gisela brokenly. She touched the truck's fender with a hand for balance, looking as staggered as she had been the moment Doug had slapped her with a shot-loaded hand.

"Have the aliens come and taken your friend?" Kelly demanded harshly in order to be understood through the woman's dismay.

"No, not the crabs," Gisela said petulantly, turning so that both her palms were braced against the vehicle.

The breeze that was too constant to be noticed made enough noise in the background that she was hard to hear, since the truck separated her from Kelly. He stepped around the front of the vehicle to join her, though he was nervous that his appearance of haste would silence her. By focusing on the details of gathering information, Tom Kelly was able to avoid boggling inertly as a result of what he had just seen.

Whatever he had just seen.

Gisela met his eyes and straightened. "That was Dora," she said in a firm, emotionless voice. "The first of the Special Applications craft, the prototype which escaped to the Antarctic base from the Bavarian Alps in 1945. She must have been sent to make the final pickup. And we have missed her."

The blond woman's face was as cool as that of a marble virgin, but tears had begun to well from the inner corners of her blue eyes. "We may as well go back into the city, Thomas Kelly. We'll be able to communicate from the office there, but I'm sure no one will have time for us until everything has been accomplished.

"They have begun to execute the Plan already, and I am not a part of it."

Tom Kelly took the woman's hands in support, but only a small portion of his mind was on Gisela anymore. He was far more concerned with the fact that not all of the UFOs being sighted were under the control of aliens whose motives were at least uncertain.

Some of the spacecraft were in the hands of Nazis whose motives were not doubtful in the slightest.

Kelly started back to Diyarbakir with Gisela slumped as his passenger against the other door. He drove with the caution demanded by the loose steering and his own unfamiliarity with the roads.

Besides, there was no longer any reason for haste.

"I didn't think they'd leave before dark," Gisela said.

A front wheel bucked in a rut, jolting her hard against the doorframe and recalling her to her dignity. She straightened in the seat and gave a body-length quiver like the motion of a snake casting its skin. "But of course, now it doesn't matter—secrecy. No need for it, no chance for it either. And they left me behind."

The sky had darkened abruptly, as if the flying saucer had punched a hole in the stratosphere and let the storm rush in. That was what had happened, near enough in the larger sense, Kelly supposed. Not asking the question wouldn't make the situation go away, though.

"Exactly what *is* the Plan?" the veteran asked, while his hands and eyes drove the truck and left his intellect free for things he would have preferred not to think about.

"To control the world by using your Fortress," the dancer said, destroying with her flat voice any possibility that Kelly's imagination might have run away with him.

"At first we had the base in Antarctica," Gisela continued. "My father was commander of the detachment guarding the salt mines at Kertl, in Bavaria. When British troops were within five kilometers and they could hear Russian guns in the east, so near were they, a motorcycle arrived with orders that they should leave at once for Thule Base in the Antarctic, taking all flyable Special Applications craft."

The woman was speaking in German, and her voice had the sing-song texture of a tale which had been repeated so many times.

"Only Dora, the fourth prototype, could be flown," said Gisela. "Some of those at Kertl wished to wait still further for the aircraft from Berlin Tempelhof they had been hoping would arrive. Others would have fled to the British in order to escape the Bolsheviks, but they feared to entrust themselves to a journey of twenty thousand kilometers in a craft which had thus far been the subject only of static testing.

"But my father understood that orders must be obeyed, not questioned; and he understood that there was sometimes no path but that of ruthlessness to the accomplishment of a soldier's duty."

Kelly's hands gripped the steering wheel more fiercely than the road itself—the highway to Diyarbakir, now—demanded. The American agent had seen enough things in his own lifetime to be able to imagine that scene in the foothills of the Alps close to the time he was being born. Electrostatic charges from Dora, the prototype built so solidly that she still flew like nothing else on Earth, must have lighted up the salt mine in which the laboratory hid from Allied bombers. It would have been like living in the heart of a neon lamp while the powerplant was run up to takeoff level.

But the machinery was only part of the drama. The rest was that of the men and women wearing laboratory smocks or laborers' coveralls, the personnel who had decided to ignore the order from Berlin and stay behind. As Dora readied to attempt her final mission, those who were not aboard her would have begun to understand exactly what decision they had *really* made.

The guard detachment of Waffen SS would have been in spatter-camouflage uniforms and carrying the revolutionary MP-44 assault rifles which could not win the war for Germany but which armed a generation of liberation movements after the Russians lightly modified the design into the AK-47. Even the pick of Germany's fighting strength there at the end would have been a far cry from the triumphant legions of the Blitzkrieg: boys, taller and blonder, perhaps, than their classmates, but still fifteen years old; and a leavening of veterans whose eyes were too empty now to show weariness, much less mercy.

Tom Kelly had been a man like that for too many years not to know what it would have been to have stood with those guardsmen; and how little he would have felt when Colonel Schneider gave the order to fire and the bellow of a score of automatic rifles echoed itself into thunder in the walls of the tunnel.

"Thule Base was safe, unapproachable," said Gisela. In her voice was a memory of ice and snow and a constant wind, with even bare rock so deep ice had to be excavated to reach it. "But it was useless save as a place to hide while we reorganized and gathered the wealth required for the task. Three U-boats of the Type XXI rendezvoused with the refugees from Dora, and there was the original complement of Thule Base . . . but still very few, you must understand."

A few oversized drops of rain splattered down, followed by a downpour snaking across the highway in a distinct line. The dust on the hood and windshield turned immediately to mud which the desiccated wiper blades pushed across the glass in streaks when Kelly found their switch. "Others provided aid, supplied us with connections and part of the money required," the woman said, raising her voice over the drumbeat of raindrops as though addressing a hall of awestruck, upturned faces which hung on her words. "But there were two secrets which the Service kept: those original strugglers at Thule Base and their descendants like myself. We kept the secret of Dora. And we kept the secret of the last flight from Tempelhof, a special Arado Blitzbomber as planned—but north, to one of the Swedish islands, where those who flew in it transferred to a U-boat which would proceed to Antarctica to meet us."

They were getting close to the incorporated area of the city. Diyarbakir had spread to the north and west of ancient Amida. The city walls to the south loomed on an escarpment, free of modern buildings, and the eastern boundary was the steep gorge of the Tigris—now and as it had been for millennia.

In the heavy traffic they were entering, bad brakes and the universal-tread pattern of the pickup's tires made Kelly concentrate more on his driving than he wanted to. The rhythm of outside sounds and the greasy divorcement of the rain-slick highway were releasing Gisela's tongue, however. They were in a microcosm of their own, she and Kelly; not the universe that others inhabited and one which had secrets that one must never tell.

"We could buy equipment easily," the woman said. "Through sympathizers, sometimes, but easily also through those who wanted drugs or wanted arms that we could supply. However, there was no place on Earth where we could safely produce what we needed for the day we knew would come, when the Service would provide thousands of craft like Dora for the legions of New Germany to sweep away Bolshevism and materialism together."

Brake lights turned the road ahead of them into a strand of rubies, twinkling on their windshield and on the rain spattering toward the street. A major factory, one of the few in a city almost wholly dependent on agriculture, was letting the workers out to choke the road with motor-cycles, private cars, and dolmuses—minivans that followed fixed routes like buses, but on no particular schedule and with an even higher degree of overloading than was the norm for Turkish buses.

"Turn here," Gisela said with a note of disapproval. "You should have turned at the last cross street. We enter the Old City best by the Urfa Gate."

Kelly nodded obsequiously. Colonel Schneider's— Romer's—daughter was telling him things now, in a state divorced from reason, which she had not told even when she was convinced that he had saved her and her Plan from Israeli secret agents. Then she had been willing to take him to those whose business the explanations were— but not to overstep her own duties. Irrational snappishness when he missed the turn to a location unknown to him was a small price for the background he was hearing.

Gisela cleared her throat with a touch of embarrass- ment as she ran her comment back. "I apologize," she said in English. "Our office is to the right on the inner circum- ferential, facing the walls."

"No problem," the veteran answered in German. He inched forward, thankful for the rain-swept traffic that kept them from what might be the terminus of their conversation. "How did you get over the problem with fabrication, then?"

"By putting the assembly plant on the Moon," said Gisela calmly.

Kelly, shifting from first into neutral, lost the selector in the sloppy linkages of third and fourth when his arm twitched forward. "Okay," he said when he thought his voice would be calm. "I guess I thought maybe you had a satellite of your own. Like Fortress."

"It was easier to armor against vacuum than it was the winds and convection cooling at Thule Base," said the woman. "And the Moon had what neither Antarctica nor an orbiting platform could provide: ores. Raw material to be formed into aluminum for the skin and girders of the fleet. Dora had been built of impervium, chromium-vanadium alloy; but that was not necessary, the scientists who escaped with my father decided.

"The instruments and the drive units, the great electromagnetic engines that draw their power from the auras surrounding the Earth and Sun, had to be constructed here; but that was easy to arrange, since the pieces divulged little of their purpose. They are shipped as freight to our warehouse at Iskenderun and there loaded on a motorship which the Service owns through a Greek holding company. It sails with only our own personnel in the crew and, hundreds of miles from the coast, the cargo is transferred to Dora or one of her newer sisters."

Traffic surged forward like a clot releasing in a blood vessel. The wall above the Urfa Gate was whole and fifty feet high, with semicircular towers flanking the treble entrances and rising even higher. Only the arched central gateway, tall enough and wide enough to pass the heaviest military equipment of Byzantine times, was used for vehicular traffic. It constricted the modern two-lane road; Kelly swore under his breath as he watched the cars ahead of them slither on the pavement, threatening traffic in the other lane and stone walls that had survived at least fifteen centuries of collisions.

"And then you Americans started to build your nuclear Fortress, and we knew that fate was on our side, despite the disasters of the war and the hardships that we underwent while the Service huddled in Antarctica and—and after."

There was a tendency, in Kelly as surely as in other people, to assume that what somebody did in the course of his job—or her job—was what he liked to do. It made him mad every time somebody read his file and looked at him with face muscles stiffening as if that would armor the person against the monster calling itself Tom Kelly.

But he did the same thing, even knowing better; even knowing that there were worse things in the life of Gisela Romer than years spent on the Antarctic ice, but you did what had to be done. . . .

There had been a pitiable attempt to landscape the approach to the Urfa Gate with trees. Those which still survived at twenty-meter intervals along the boulevard were trees like those found throughout the inhabited Middle East: stunted, the major branches a yard or so long from the point they forked, and a burst of first-year twigs splaying from the cut ends like the hair of a drowned woman. Firewood was at a premium, and each year these trees would be pruned back secretly by those whose only choice was to freeze.

And sometimes the long-term choices people made for themselves and for mankind weren't a whole lot prettier; that was all.

Pedestrians hurried along the sidewalk within the circumferential, bent and squinting as though they could shut themselves off from the battering rain. The hooped iron barrier which separated them from the vehicular way gleamed silver in the lights of cars turning into the Old City, providing a touch of fairyland for a scene otherwise harsh and squalid. The girdered tower holding a transformer substation just within the walls could as well have been the guard post of a concentration camp. Life is not exotic while it is being lived. The walls which made Diyarbakir an archeological treasure were proof of a past reality as cruel as anything that put Fortress in orbit above the Earth today.

Kelly knew now why he had been dreaming about ancient Amida and her walls, past which he now drove a pickup truck, turned against their builders. He had a pretty good idea of who—of what—had caused him to have those dreams.

But he was damned if he knew what he'd been supposed to do about the situation.

"What was the message you sent out from Istanbul?" Gisela asked unexpectedly. She had talked her way through her shock at being left behind at the crucial juncture. She had reason to ask the question, and Kelly had no reason at all to lie in his answer.

"I was set up last night," he said, leaning forward for a better angle through the windshield. At least it had been raining hard enough to wash the dust from the glass. Presumably he would get further directions when it was time for them.

"*We* were set up," Kelly went on, amending his initial words. "I got a tape of it, back at my room. What we picked up before heading for the airport, too late for it to do *us* any good right then."

The woman grinned as the same memory struck both of them simultaneously. She ran her fingertips up Kelly's right thigh, then cupped his groin firmly. "There will be more of that, you and I," she promised with a wink.

Kelly laughed. "There isn't a bad time to think about sex," he said. But there were more important things to think about which were very bad indeed.

"Set up by my own people," the American continued because Gisela expected him to. "I—" He paused, then went on, "Assuming I get through this in one piece, I'm going to be deep in shit for blowing away the people I did."

The woman nodded. "Yes," she said seriously, "we know how closely your country works with the Jews. That is why it was so, of so much importance to us to find someone like you who had access to your intelligence community but who could be trusted not to be a puppet of the Jews."

Yep, thought Kelly, that's exactly why they handed me to you, Elaine and her bosses. Tom Kelly's a fuckin' Nazi, he'll get along just fine with these other Nazis, and maybe we'll learn what kinda games the Service's been playin' with the funny-looking gray guys in the flying saucers.

The hell of it was, things had worked out just about the way Pierrard would've wanted them to—except maybe in detail, though Suits didn't like being bothered with details about who'd been killed and where and how many. The thing Pierrard really wouldn't like was the fact that he'd been so slow off the mark that the information was probably getting to him through the evening news.

Knowing the type, the delay was going to turn out to be the fault of some subordinate—very possibly the fault of Tom Kelly. Officers called that "delegation of responsibility."

"So," the veteran continued, "I figured that the tape of that conversation sent clear text so there's no way in *hell* they could be sure who'd heard it, all over the world— that'd give 'em another bone to gnaw instead of me."

His tongue touched his lips again. "Besides," he added so softly that his passenger could not have been sure of the words, "they gotta learn: If they stick it to me, I stick it right back. Whoever they are."

"We can either park here," Gisela said, "or you can go left at Gazi Boulevard and left again at once in the alley, unless somebody's blocking it."

She had the same trick he did, Kelly noticed, of giving directions without raising her voice unless they were very goddam important. Him driving around in the rain because he was too dumb to listen to a normal voice wouldn't have been that important; and he *wasn't* too dumb to listen.

"Here" was an area within an angle of the walls, set off from the occupied portion of the city by law and the circumferential road. The big circular tower at the apex of the angle was a famous one, the Married Tower, though Kelly couldn't remember the reason for that name if he ever had known. The clear area would have been a park if it were landscaped. At the moment, it was a wasteland whose dust had been wetted to mud by the rain—too unusual a circumstance for grass to have secured a foothold.

There were bushes planted at the edge of the circumferential, but the hard conditions had opened several gaps in the attempted hedge through which the truck could drive without doing further damage. The truck with US Air Force plates could sit undisturbed there, and, in this downpour, more or less unnoticed. The buildings across the circumferential were raised on common walls, and the alley behind them would have been laid out when donkeys were the sole form of transportation.

Kelly shifted down into the granny gear, standing on the brake pedal as he did so to warn the driver behind him. He pulled hard right, and the truck bumped over the curb with less commotion than it had negotiated the road to the han where Dora hid.

The shock of recognition which Kelly felt was real enough to send a tingle up his arm from the finger which was switching off the headlights. He swore softly as the rain-streaked glow faded in his memory.

Not that it should have been a surprise.

"This is where Mohammed Ayyubi bought it," Kelly said, gesturing with his chin toward the walls thirty feet away. The rain paused, then sent a fierce lash of droplets across the hood and windshield. The stark battlements were hidden beyond the rain and glass, but Kelly's mind superimposed the videotaped scene in Congressman Bianci's office on the image his headlights had just shown: the same wall, the same dripping illumination. . . . Bodies only in what the camera had recorded; at least so far.

"Yes, Mohammed made the initial approach and screening for the Kurds we recruited for the Field Force," Gisela agreed. "We couldn't recruit in Europe, not safely. And besides, Europeans—even the Aryans—have grown soft."

The woman shrugged; the act gave her the look of a person rising from catastrophe. "He was coming to meet me at the office here. There were the shots and many vehicles. We scattered, of course, though there was no attempt to make arrests . . . and afterwards, who can say? The crabs, we thought once, but they do not use guns— though one was killed there. A colonel of police was full of tales of the *thing* that the Americans had bundled away from the site."

Her eyes had been on the inner curve of the wind-shield, on her reflection or her memory. Now she turned to the American agent and said, "He spoke of you often, you know, Tom Kelly. I think now perhaps it was the Jews who killed him."

"Something like that," said Kelly as he opened his door and felt water drip on the bare skin of his wrist. "Could well be."

There was no street lighting, and the lights of the traffic hid rather than illuminated Kelly's surroundings by levering shadows through the sparse hedge in a counterfeit of nearby motion. The courtesy light in the cab winked as Gisela got out on her side. The vehicle neatly plugged the gap through which Kelly had driven. He stepped around the front of the pickup, toward the woman and another opening in the hedge.

"Thomas Kelly," said a voice that he recognized, "we must speak with you. It may be that there still is time to save your world."

There were three of them again, one on either side of the pickup and the third facing the vehicle's hood and the two humans. The pair on the flanks were utterly motionless, but white noise surrounded them in a palpable cloak. The words were coming from the little radio in Kelly's attaché case, though its power was turned off. The rain that fell with fitful intensity was disintegrating away from the standing figures, without the fiery enthusiasm of bullets the night before but with an accompaniment of sound.

Gisela, arm's length from the American, made a grab for the gun beneath his waistband.

She was lithe and very strong; but not so strong as
Kelly, nor as quick. He caught her right wrist in his right
hand and, with the other, tried to grip her about the waist.
"Wait!" he cried.

One of the frozen-seeming pair of strangers changed
appearance. He—it—remained motionless, but the
frosting and sizzle of rain that did not quite touch the form
now wetted it normally. *"Wait!"* Kelly screamed again,
this time to the figures who stood like wooden carvings of
humanity.

Kelly was not willing to hurt the dancer, and she was
willing to do whatever was necessary to escape. During
the preceding day he had twice saved her life—so *she*
thought at any rate—and gained such intellectual trust as
a person like Gisela Romer had to offer. But her fear and
hatred of the aliens were matters ingrained for years and
redoubled by the fate of her father.

Her muscles flexed against Kelly's grip by habit, sure
from experience that she could tear herself free from
any man before he realized her strength. Kelly held her
like a band of iron. The point of her shoulder jarred his
forehead hard enough for pain to explode in sheets of
light across his optic nerves. Even then the veteran's grip
did not loosen, but his eyes missed the motion of her free
hand.

He knew what she'd done surely enough when her
knuckles slammed him in the groin.

On a conscious level Kelly thought he was still winning,
still in control. He could block the pain while he reached
for Gisela's left hand also and his lips ordered her to—

His lips passed only a rattle like that of a strangled

rabbit. His belly muscles had drawn up so tightly that he could not breathe, much less speak. And the will was there, but the strength had poured from his muscles like blood from the throat of a stuck pig. Gisela lunged back and away from him. Kelly still did not feel the pain he knew must be wracking him, but he could not feel anything at all between his knees and his shoulders.

Christ, that woman could break rocks with her bare hands.

He toppled as she twisted aside and froze, a splendid Valkyrie, in a dazzle of light as sharp and sudden as a static spark. Neither of the man-looking figures Kelly could see as his shoulder hit the ground had moved, though the one to the truck's side began to hiss and shimmer again at the touch of raindrops. One or both must have shot the woman, but Kelly could only deduce that from the result. He reached back toward the Smith and Wesson he had refused to draw a moment before.

"*Please*, Mr. Kelly," begged the radio voice. "She is not harmed. Please, we *must* speak with you while there may be time."

"Christ," muttered Tom Kelly as mottlings of shadow and light from the roadway quivered across the fully-human face of one of the strangers. The rain on his own face and forehead felt good because it both cooled and dampened skin which felt as though it had been parching in an oven. He had feeling throughout his body again, an ache radiating from his groin in steady pulses with random flashes of pain to add piquancy.

Gisela'd done her usual professional job. If this trio didn't want to shoot him the way they had her, they'd have plenty of time to stomp Kelly down into the muddy gravel before he, in his present state, could clear the snubbie.

Hell, he'd needed to talk with 'em anyway. And if Gisela was as dead as her boneless sprawl implied—there'd be a time to fix that, the only way a man like Tom Kelly knew to fix things. . . .

"The neuroreceptors of her brain are blocked," said the voice of the stranger, who/which might either be reading Kelly's mind in good truth or making a shrewd estimate on the basis of file data. They must have files, or they wouldn't have found reason to track him across Anatolia; though the Lord knew what those reasons might be.

"She will be well in half an hour," the central stranger continued as Kelly rose carefully to his feet. The other two figures in dark overcoats, darkening further as the rain wet them, minced in slowly from either side. "You must believe me, Thomas Kelly, that we will not kill even to save a world. Even to save your world from itself."

"Keep away from her," Kelly grunted to the silent figures as they began to kneel beside Gisela. He stepped to her, steady enough, though the muscles in his thighs trembled as if with extreme fatigue.

The stranger across from him paused, looking up at the veteran with a bland face that almost certainly emanated from the medallion on the figure's chest. Kelly shouldered the other one aside. He could feel the give of bones and joints that were as inhuman as the corpse in the freezer back on Fort Meade.

"Alive, is she?" Kelly said as he, himself, knelt, and touched the woman's throat. The carotid pulse was as strong and steady as Kelly's own.

"Oh, boy," the veteran said. He rocked back on his haunches and exhaled the breath which he had not realized he was holding. Gisela's throat felt warm, not hot, and that reminded him that his own bare skin was chilled by the rain. The woman needed to be under shelter, or her final state would be the same as if the—hell, the aliens—had used .45s.

"Look—" Kelly began.

The two silent aliens knelt again, reaching for the woman, and the radio's speaker said, "We will carry her within the office of her organization." The central alien pointed with his whole arm past the hedge and road to the two- and three-story building facing the walls.

"There is no one there now," the alien voice continued as the figure refolded his arm against his chest with a motion which was grossly wrong for what he appeared to be. "But she will be warm and dry and recover quickly."

Kelly frowned, but he stepped back to allow the other pair to lift Gisela. They were lighter than men and Kelly had assumed they were frail, but they handled the dancer's solid form as easily as two humans of the veteran's own build could have done.

"Another time," the alien voice said as his companions walked the woman through a gap in the hedge like men with a friend who had drunk herself insensible, "we would have held her as we hold others of her organization, so that they could not execute their Plan. But we did not hold enough of them. Now it is too late for prevention, Thomas Kelly, and the cure is something that we cannot do for you.

"We cannot kill, even to save a world."

Tom Kelly stretched his arms out stiffly behind him and bent forward, then back, from the waist. His head spun in slow circles when he lowered it, and the throb radiating from his groin picked up its tempo when the motion of his torso thrust his hips out. For all that, he felt better for the exercise; felt human at any rate, and that was an improvement over the way he'd felt since Gisela punched him in the balls.

Since he thought he saw her killed. No point in kidding himself about what the worst part of the shock had been.

Kelly stepped to the open door of the truck and picked up the radio, shielding it from the continuing drizzle with the flap of his coat.

"Somebody told you I was the right guy to contract out killing to, did they?" said Kelly. He was relieved enough that she was alive and he was alive—and for Chrissake, that somebody saw a way clear of a world disaster that was real clear even without the details—that the implications that he had just made overt didn't bother him the way they usually did.

Not that it wasn't true. The Lord knew he'd painted his reputation in the blood of more men than Doug and his buddies . . . and women too, bombs weren't real fussy, and he'd used bombs when they seemed the choice.

The two of them were alone now, Kelly and the alien who talked. The other pair were jaywalking Gisela across the boulevard; safer, perhaps, than it looked because the traffic was crawling despite being bumper to bumper— but he'd let 'em go ahead for lack of a better idea, and he wasn't going to second-guess matters now. "Do you have a name?" he demanded, wishing that it wasn't raining, wishing a lot of things.

"Call me Wun, Mr. Kelly," said the alien through the speaker beneath Kelly's coat, and the face smiled as a fragment of headlight beam trolled across it. The "skin" surface reflected normally, even showing streaks of rain, but Kelly knew from the corpse and the videotape that the perceived features were wholly immaterial.

"One. as in *bir*, digit?" Kelly asked, translating the word he understood into Turkish and raising a single index finger.

"No, Mr. Kelly, more like the Spanish Juan," said the other. "But just Wun. Are you not comfortable here?" He raised his arm toward the sky. "Should we go inside your vehicle?"

Kelly chopped his hand like a blade in the direction of the ancient walls. He didn't feel like putting himself in a metal box, no, but the basalt ramparts were shelter of a sort against both rain and the breeze. He wondered if Mohammed Ayyubi had thought the same thing the night those stones had backstopped the bullets which killed him.

"Come on," he said aloud. "Dunno that I'm ever going to be comfortable, but we can get outa some of the rain."

"The Dienst has taken over your Fortress," Wun said as they walked together, man and not-man, toward walls that were a stone patchwork of more than a thousand years. "They think to rule the Earth, at least to their satisfaction, because they are invulnerable and have the power to destroy whatever targets they may choose."

No sign of bullet pocks on the hard stone, no certain sign in this light at any rate: The rubble and concrete foundations were Roman; the sections of large ashlars which sprawled across the fabric like birthmarks were probably Byzantine repairs; and the Turks, both Seljuk and Osmanli, had rebuilt the upper levels, perhaps many times, with squared stones of smaller and less regular size. The presence of the massive edifice gave Kelly a feeling of protection which he knew was specious, but anything to calm his subconscious was worthwhile so long as it let his intellect get on with what it needed to do.

"All right, then," the veteran said, focusing his mind by planting his right palm against the wet stone, "it's government level now and I'm tactical. So hell, it's in somebody else's court, and I don't know that Gisela and *her* buddies are much crazier than some of the folk who've had their fingers on the button officially."

"It *is* your business, Mr. Kelly," said Wun. His dark-coated body was almost invisible, close to the basalt and farther from the light flickering from the circumferential. Kelly thought the alien was shivering, however.

"Don't *tell* me my business," the American snapped. "Look, I walked into this, and if I'd been in time I'd've done something about it, sure. I don't need to be tasked before I'll blow my nose. But it's *gone*, fucked—and that's *not* my problem."

"The Soviets will not believe the space station has changed hands, Mr. Kelly," Wun said with inhumanly-precise enunciation. "They are convinced that the events of the past hours, including the nuclear destruction of the shuttle launching facilities at Luke and Kennedy Space

Command bases, are all part of American policy. When the Dienst presses its demands on Russia by attacking major cities in addition to the space launching facilities which have already been destroyed, the Soviets will react against those they believe to be the true aggressors. Your world will survive the result, Mr. Kelly; but your civilization will not, and your race may not."

Kelly's mouth opened to repeat that there was nothing he could do about it. Before he spoke the words, he heard them in his mind, being spoken by everyone he'd heard say them in the past, every cowardly shit who wouldn't act and wouldn't let Tom Kelly act when something really had to be done.

"Christ," said the veteran, and he took a deep breath. "All right, what is it that I can do?"

"You must enter Fortress and destroy it," replied Wun as calmly as if he had not considered that Kelly might make any other answer. "We can bring you from orbit to the structure, but we cannot enter a solid object, and we will not help you further in a work of death."

"*Christ,* you're sweethearts!" Kelly said. "You oughta run for Congress, you'd fit right fuckin' in with the clean-hands crowd."

"We do not have to ask you to understand principles, Mr. Kelly," the alien said. "You have principles yourself. They differ from ours; and yours will permit you to save your world from consequences which could never occur to our race. We *will* not kill."

"Yeah, sorry," the American said, turning his eyes toward the stone, tracing the irregular courses upward till they blended with the sky and the rain washed the embarrassment from his face. They might be crazy, Wun and his buddies, but they were crazy in a better way than most anybody else Kelly knew. You had to draw lines, and no damn body else in the world had a right to complain about lines *you* drew and chose to live by.

"'Fortress' isn't a public relations gag," he said aloud. "If those Nazis've really taken it over, then its going to be a bitch to get close without getting blown into dust clouds."

"We can get you to the satellite unnoticed, Thomas Kelly," said Wun. "We can do no more."

"Guess that oughta be enough," said Kelly, stretching his arms overhead and pulling the wet fingers of one hand against those of the other. He *had* to think that way; he'd have gone off in a shivering funk *years* ago if he hadn't believed at bottom that he could do any job he was willing to undertake.

The movement of Kelly's body worked the slick metal of the revolver against the base of his spine. "Why me?" he demanded flatly, fixing the alien with his eyes as firmly as he could in the half-light. Now that he'd made his decision, he had to have the background information that anyone with good sense would've demanded earlier.

"Because of the physical contact," the alien said. His hand mimed a face-rubbing gesture, and Kelly recalled the way he had touched the corpse of the alien that night on Fort Meade. He'd done that to prove to the Suits that he wasn't afraid—and to himself, that he could do whatever he had to do, even if he *was* scared shitless. . . .

"We could find you then, Mr. Kelly," Wun was saying, "and even before we found you, we could begin to speak to you, through your mind. You felt us, surely? We are not expert on your race's psychology. Though we have observed you for a century, it is only in the past three years, since you achieved stardrive, that we have been permitted to interact with you. We still have much to learn."

"*Stardrive*," the American repeated, filing the remainder of the statement to be considered at some other time.

"Wun, space travel's something I'm paid to know about. We're still talking chemical rockets here, unless you mean the monocle ferry—and that's a low-orbit system, pure and simple."

"The researchers at Cambridge University who are responsible for the discovery," Wun replied, "still think they are working with time travel. We know better, however, and that is sufficient for those to whom we must report on the progress of our oversight. Without that, Mr. Kelly, we could not have attempted to immobilize the members of the Service; and I could not now be talking to you."

"Okay," said Kelly, pressing his hands firmly against his face, fingertips to forehead. The tight skin over his nose and cheekbones crinkled and lost some of the numbness that the tension and cool rain had brought. His coat was soaked across the back. "Okay. But you'll have to get me there, all the way. I doubt I can get outa Diyarbakir the way things are. There'd be too many people to convince. Christ, there's like as not a scratch order out on me right now. And my chances of even getting a message out, much less listened to, when I'm in West Bumfuck and there's been nukes going off in ConUS—zip, zed, zero."

He pointed toward the dark sky. "If you need me, Wun, you carry me all the way in your ship."

"Our ships are not on Earth. We cannot carry you to them as we are carried, because you—were not there already, Thomas Kelly," the alien said.

Wun *was* shivering, though his seeming face and bare hands were motionless. Wun's arms and torso quaked beneath the dark overcoat, however. "Whatever message you need to pass, we can pass for you—to anyone, anywhere. For now, you must move yourself on your own world and from it."

"You *did* leave a message on my tape," Kelly said "Told me you had to see me or like that. It wasn't in my head; I was really hearing it through the earphones?"

Wun nodded. "Yes," he said, "of course. We dared not leave a longer message for you then until you had seen us in person."

Kelly laughed. "You know," he said, "I was thinking there was no way you'd be able to get into the Tank . . . and maybe there isn't. But if you can punch my message through to the heart of the Pentagon, then it's going to save a whole lot of time. Because even if they don't believe me—which they won't, not after some of what's gone down lately—they'll damn well hop to meet whoever can play games that way with their codes.

"Come on," he added, striding back toward the truck. "You may not need this written out, but I need paper to compose it. There'll be a destination sheet and a clipboard in the pickup, and we'll just use the back of that."

The funny thing was, Kelly thought, that he felt pretty good. Oh, he'd been in better physical shape than he was now—but hell, he was functional, and that was a long sight better than he'd felt in the recent past. Hurt didn't matter; he'd been hurt before.

And he was in the middle of something that was either going to work or it wasn't—but it wouldn't fry its circuits just because the folks he depended on for support made a policy decision to do something else. He trusted Wun in a way that he had never trusted a human in a suit or an officer's uniform. Partly, that was crazy; and a gut reaction was, by definition, irrational.

But he *could* find reason to justify the way he felt. They'd come a very long way to lie to Tom Kelly, if they were lying, and what Wun had just told him about Fortress was exactly what the veteran had extrapolated from Gisela's words.

The aliens didn't have to be altruists—they could want Earth for themselves, for any damn reason you cared to name. If they managed to save the place from a bunch of Nazis with H-bombs, then what else they wanted could be dealt with in its own good time.

And if Tom Kelly could do something to help with the problem, then it was about the first time in twenty years he'd been tasked to do something he really believed in.

It occurred to Kelly that he might simply get lost in the sprawling airbase.

Third TAF was one of the two combat divisions of the Turkish Air Force, and the bureaucracy at its Diyarbakir headquarters was both extensive and unfamiliar to the American. If all went well, someone in Washington would shortly be sending a message about Tom Kelly to someone in Diyarbakir Air Division. Who the recipient was going to be, and through what combination of Turkish, NATO, and American channels the message would be delivered, were both questions at whose answer Kelly could not even guess; and that meant that he hadn't the faintest notion as to where on the base he ought to be waiting to be noticed when the time came.

The veteran smiled as he approached the main gate of the airbase again, visualizing the end of the world in nuclear cataclysm while Turks sped through the halls and grounds of the great airbase, too intent on what they understood were their own duties to pay any attention to the American screaming himself hoarse,

Like a lot of things, it didn't cost any more to laugh.

In the hours since Kelly had driven the borrowed pickup out the main gate, there had been some subtle changes. Instead of a squad on duty to check IDs, there was a platoon—and the earlier relaxed atmosphere was gone. A barrier of concertina wire on a tube-steel frame had been swung across the road, and behind it waited an open-topped Cadillac-Gage armored car with an airman ready at the pair of pintle-mounted machineguns.

The guards must have recognized the truck's markings, and a few of them probably recalled Kelly himself driving away in the vehicle. Whatever word was out regarding the world situation—nothing on local civilian radio, Kelly knew from sweeping the shortwave and AM band with his portable—it had sure convinced Third TAF to raise its state of readiness.

Three airmen and a lieutenant with automatic rifles

were waiting outside the barrier. They ran to the truck from both sides as soon as Kelly stopped, and the way their guns pointed caused him to get out and remove his card case with slow, nonthreatening motions.

It made his decision as to where to wait relatively easy, however.

While two airmen peered at the—empty—bed of the pickup to make sure that it was not packed with explosives and acetylene tanks, Kelly handed his Turkish ID to the lieutenant.

"Sir," the American said in the officer's own language, "sometime in the next—I don't know, it might be a day"— it might be never, but there was no point in thinking that—"there are going to be orders sent regarding me. Then things will have to move very fast. For now, I think it's best that I remain here at the gate, outside if you prefer. But it is absolutely critical that the Officer of the Day and the head of base security both be informed immediately that I *am* here, and that I'll stay right here until sent for."

He paused, but before the Turk could frame a reply, Kelly added, "In addition to the name on this card, they may come looking for Thomas Kelly."

Elaine would very likely have been furious had she known Kelly was carrying his own North Carolina driver's license with him, but there were times you simply had to have real ID. The Lord only knew which of Kelly's various cover names the Pentagon would reference him under— assuming the message had gotten through—but at bottom, they would probably include the real name.

Kelly gave the driver's license to the officer; if it saved

only five minutes in the course of the next twenty-four hours, then five minutes could be real important.

"One moment, please," the lieutenant said. His lips pursed and he frowned as he looked at the cards, practicing the unfamiliar names under his breath. Then he walked back to the regular guard post, stepping through the narrow gap left between the gate post and the barbed wire barricade.

"Any notion of what's going on?" Kelly said to the airmen, primarily to make conversation; people don't let their guns point at folks with whom they're holding a friendly conversation.

"It's a full alert, sir," one of the Turks responded. "They're fueling and arming everything that'll fly."

The lieutenant, watching Kelly through the glass of the guardpost, hung up the phone and barked an unheard order. Six airmen trotted past the officer as he strode toward Kelly. They grabbed crossbars extending from the concertina wire and began to drag the barricade to one side.

"You may come in, sir," the lieutenant said, a little less dourly hostile than he had seemed before. Perhaps he had just been afraid of being chewed out by his superiors for reporting something nonstandard. Now he handed back the two identification cards. "Your pass permits that, and for the rest—it will be as God wills. The Officer of the Day says he will report your presence to General Tergut, as you requested."

"Thank you, Lieutenant," the American said as he got back into the truck. The rain had stopped by the time he made it out of the walled city, but the vehicle's heater had

not even begun to dry his soaked clothing. He sneezed as
he put the pickup in gear, wondering whether after everything he had gone through he wasn't going to wind up a
casualty from pneumonia. Inshallah—as God wills it.

That was about as good a philosophy for a soldier as
any Kelly had heard. And right now, it might be as much
as you could say for the world itself.

Kelly saw the lights at the same time the phone rang
in the guard post beside which he was parked. There
were two vehicles speeding toward the gate from the
heart of the installation, both of them flashing blue
lights and crying out the hearts of their European-style
warning hooters. The road was asphalt-surfaced, but the
vehicles raised plumes of surface dust to reflect the
headlights of the follow-car and the rotating blue party
hats of both.

It hadn't been a long wait, but Kelly found as he
stepped out of the truck that his muscles had stiffened.
The Turkish lieutenant ran to him, leaving his rifle behind
this time. "Sir!" he shouted to Kelly, "they're sending a car
for you!"

"Thank you, Lieutenant," the veteran said as he
twisted some of the rigidity out of his torso, "I thought
that"—he nodded toward the oncoming flashers—"might
be me being paged."

Wun was on top of things for sure, Kelly thought as
the vehicles—a van followed by a gun jeep, both of them
blue and marked HP for Air Police—skidded to a halt
with their hooters still blaring.

Of course, it was just conceivable that this was a result

of the shootings in Istanbul and hadn't a damn thing to do with Fortress.

Kelly jogged to the passenger side of the van even before the doors unlatched. There was an empty seat in the jeep, but he had no intention of being carried any distance in it if there were an alternative. A short wheelbase and four-wheel independent suspension made jeeps marvelously handy; but that also made them flip and kill hell outa everybody on board when the driver turned sharply at speed. There was nothing about the way the Hava Polis driver had approached the guard post to make Kelly trust his judgment.

The man who jumped from the van was heavyset and wore a US Air Force uniform with rosettes on the epaulets. In the colored light of the flashers, Kelly could not be certain whether the rank insignia were the gold of a major or a lieutenant-colonel's silver.

"Thomas Kelly?" the Air Force Officer shouted through the chest-cramping racket of the hooters. He thumbed toward the doors at the back of the van being opened by a Turkish airman. "Hop in, we've got a flight for you to Incirlik."

"*Colonel* Kelly," said the veteran. "And *you* can ride in back if you need to come along, Major Snipes." The name tag over the officer's pocket was clearly visible, and he obeyed Kelly without objection.

"Yes?" said the Turkish driver when Kelly slid in beside him. The back door banged and latched.

"Take me where we're going," Kelly replied in Turkish, giving the airman a lopsided smile.

Grinning back, the Turk hauled the van around in a

tight, accelerating turn that must have spilled the occupants of the side benches in the back onto the floor and into one another's arms. Kelly, bracing his right palm against the dashboard, smiled broadly.

To the veteran's surprise, the two-vehicle entourage did not halt at one of the administration buildings. Instead they sped along access roads to the flight line, passing fuel tankers and firefighting vehicles. Men bustled over each of the aircraft in open-topped revetments which would be of limited protection against parafrags or cluster bombs sown by low-flying attackers.

Or, of course, the nukes that Nazis in orbit could unload here in the event they decided it was a good idea.

But that made him think about Gisela, and the blond dancer was one of the last things Tom Kelly wanted on his mind right now.

The van's right brakes grabbed as the driver stepped on them hard, making the vehicle shimmy against the simultaneous twist on the steering wheel to swing them into a revetment. There was already a car there, a Plymouth, and the men waiting included some in Turkish and American dress uniforms besides those in coveralls servicing a razor-winged TF-104G.

"This one's Kelly!" called Major Snipes, throwing open the back of the van before Kelly himself was sure that they had come to a final stop.

He opened his own door and got out. Two Turkish airmen, followed by a captain, ran up to him with a helmet and a pressure suit, the latter looking too large by half. "Who gave us the size?" the captain demanded. "Come on, we'll take him back and outfit him properly."

"Wait a minute," an American bird colonel said as he grabbed Major Snipes by the coat sleeve, "how do we *know* this is the right guy?"

"Look I'll pull it on over my clothes," said Kelly, taking the suit from the now-hesitant airman. "So long as the helmet's not too small, we're golden."

"Well, he had ID—"

"No, the suit's no good if it doesn't fit," insisted the Turkish captain.

"*Any* body could have ID—"

"What the *fuck* do you expect me to do, Colonel?" Kelly roared as he thrust his right leg into the pressure suit, rotating a half step on the other foot to forestall the captain, who seemed willing to snatch the garment away from him. "Sit around for a fingerprint check? How the hell would I know to pretend to be me if I wasn't?"

"He is not the man you wish?" asked a Turk with a huge moustache and what Kelly thought were general's insignia. His English was labored rather than hesitant, suggestive of bricklaying with words.

"Robbie," said Snipes to the colonel, "it's all copacetic. The fat's in the fire now, and the last thing we need is for a review board to decide it was all the fault of US liaison at Diyarbakir."

"Colonel," Kelly put in more calmly as he checked for torso fasteners, "I'm the man they're looking for. It's not the usual sort of deal"—he tried on the helmet which, for a wonder, fitted perfectly—"but it's the deal we've been handed this time."

He started walking toward the plane that had obviously been readied for him, hopeful that the colonel wouldn't decide to shoot him in the back. Sometimes Kelly found it useful to remember that during the disasters of Ishandhlwana and of Pearl Harbor, armorers had refused to issue ammunition to the troops because the proper chits had not been signed. The military collected a lot of people to whom order was more important than anything else on Earth. Trouble was, the times you really *needed* the military, the only thing you could bank on was disorder.

No bullets. No shouts, in fact, though squabbling in Turkish and English continued behind him as he strode away.

The TF-104G was a thing of beauty, the two-seat conversion trainer modification of the aircraft which had seduced the top fighter jocks of the fifties and sixties and had killed literally hundreds of their less-skilled brethren. The F-104 was fast, quick, and maneuverable. It also had the glide angle of a brick and offered its crew no desirable options when the single J-79 turbojet failed on takeoff.

But this was also a situation in which a fast ride was preferable to a safe one. For that matter, the Turks—one of the last major users of the F-104 in several variants— hadn't had nearly the problem with crashes that others, particularly the Luftwaffe, had experienced. West German maintenance was notoriously slipshod, and the F-104 simply didn't tolerate mistakes.

That wasn't an attitude Kelly could object to, even in a piece of hardware; and anyway, like he'd told the colonel behind him, it was the deal he'd been handed this time.

Turkish ground crewmen helped Kelly up the narrow steps to the rear seat in the cockpit. They grinned and gestured to point out the warning arrows setting off the jet intake. The rushing whine of air to the turbine would have overwhelmed human speech.

Kelly dumped himself into the seat behind the pilot. He flew enough that he sometimes thought he'd spent five years of his life in airplanes; but he was strictly a passenger, with neither knowledge nor interest in the sort of thing that happened in the cockpit. That included, he began to realize, matters like where to put his feet, and how to buckle himself into the ejection seat, which he supposed included a parachute.

The pilot—Turkish or American?—didn't care any more about Kelly's problems than Kelly would have had their positions been reversed. As soon as the passenger dropped into the cockpit, the TF-I04G's brakes released with a jerk and the aircraft slid out of its revetment on the narrow undercarriage splaying from its fuselage. The wings were too thin to conceal a tire.

The cockpit canopy closed smoothly, bringing blessed relief from the howl of the jet being reflected from the berm. Kelly found the oxygen mask and fitted it while the right brake and the delicate, steerable nosewheel aligned the aircraft with the runway. There had been a minimum of rollout; this was a combat installation, not a commercial operation handcuffed by the need to serve thousands of passengers.

There was probably a connection for the radio leads dangling from his helmet, the veteran thought while the turbojet shrieked and shuddered as the pilot wound it out. Then acceleration punched him back into a seat which seemed remarkably uncomfortable.

The hell with the radio, Kelly thought as the needle

nose lifted and the Earth fell away so sharply that he had nothing with which to compare the sight.

It occurred to him, however, that this was only a fore-taste of what awaited him in El Paso if things worked out the way he had planned.

He also found himself thinking that the F-104, even at its worst, had never approached the hundred-percent failure rate that the monocle ferry held to date.

Knowing that he was still in Turkey, Kelly could have told from the air that they were over Incirlik Airbase by the planes deployed on the ground; C-141 Starlifters and a flight of F-15's. Incirlik had no home squadron of its own, but it was American-staffed and trained, in rotation, all the US tactical wings based in Europe. Turkey herself could afford neither the big cargo aircraft nor state-of-the-art fighters like the F-15. Despite that, the performance of Kelly's pilot and his aging F-104, without notice and on a nontasked mission, suggested that the Turkish Air Force would hold up its end just fine if it came to a crunch.

They touched down firmly, jarring off knots, and the thump and shock that lifted their nose again startled Kelly until he realized that a drag chute was deploying behind them. The F-104 slowed abruptly. Presumably in response to instructions from the tower, the pilot braked to a near stop and turned onto a taxiway.

As the cockpit canopies began to rise again, the veteran looked to the side and saw that a car was driving parallel with them, a midsize American station wagon. Well, he couldn't complain that he wasn't getting the full treatment. Not red carpet, of course, but he didn't *want* red carpet, he wanted functional. If they decided to parachute him out over Fort Bliss instead of landing, he couldn't rightly complain.

Though as long as it'd been since he last jumped, he'd probably wind up cratering the mesquite.

The TF-104 halted in the middle of the taxiway. An American, carefully donning his saucer hat as he stepped out of the back door of the car, waved to Kelly and shouted something not quite audible. The man's upturned face looked anxious in the aircraft's clearance lights,

Kelly started to get out and was pulled up short by the feed of his oxygen mask. He unhooked it and swung himself out of the cockpit. He felt as if someone had conducted a search and destroy mission in his sinuses. He could not find the last of the miniature toeholds in the aircraft's polished skin. Grimacing, the veteran let himself drop. The officer who had just gotten out of the car gave a squawk when Kelly sprawled at his feet, but there was no harm done.

"Mr. Kelly," said the officer, gripping the veteran by both forearms and lifting, "we have a flight waiting for you. They've just been cleared."

Kelly wasn't in any shape to object to the manhandling. He ended it the quickest, simplest way by entering the car as if it were a burrow and he a fox going to ground. The greeting officer, another captain, hesitated a moment before he ran around to the far door. The driver, watching them in the mirror, had the car rolling even before the door closed.

"Where am I cleared to this time?" Kelly asked, enunciating carefully. He straightened himself in the seat as precisely as if he were a diplomat arriving at a major conference. He wasn't so wrecked that he couldn't act for a few minutes like the VIP these people had been led to expect. He didn't know of any reason why he *had* to put on a front, but it was cheaper to do so than to learn later that he should have.

"Sir, I really don't have that information," the captain replied. "From, ah—from rumor, I'm not sure that the flight crew does. This flight was originally headed for Rome, but that's maybe been changed along with the—the cargo."

They were speeding toward one of the C-141s, whose white-painted upper surfaces drew a palette of colors from the rising sun and made the gray lower curves almost disappear. The wings, mounted high so that the main spar did not cut the cabin in half, now drooped under the weight of four big turbofans, but in flight they would flex upward as they lifted the huge mass of the aircraft and cargo.

Kelly was thoroughly familiar with C-141s, the logistics workhorse of the Lebanon Involvement. They were aluminum cylinders which hauled cargo very well and very efficiently, so this one was of particular interest to him only because he was apparently making the next stage of his journey on it.

The scene on the pad was a great deal more unusual.

Separated from the aircraft by thirty yards and what looked like a platoon of Air Police was a huge clot of civilians, women and children. The driver had to swing wide around them in order to approach the plane's lowered tail ramp. As he did so, a number of civilians darted from the larger group and blocked the vehicle's path.

The driver swore softly and slammed the transmission into reverse.

A woman struggled up to Kelly's window. Her rage-distorted face might have been cute under other circumstances, and the amazing puffiness of her torso was surely because she was wearing at least six outfits on top of one another. A child of perhaps three, similarly over-dressed, tugged at the tail of the long cloth coat on top; and because she held an infant in her left arm, she had to drop her suitcase in order to hammer on the window while she screamed, "You bastard! You've got to let Dawn and Jeffie aboard! What kind of—"

An airman wearing a helmet instead of a cap caught the woman from behind by wrist and shoulder, dragging her back as the car reversed in a quick arc. More grim-faced police spread themselves in a loose barricade against the would-be refugees while the driver accelerated toward the ramp.

"My God," said the captain, "I've never seen anything *like* that."

"Goddam," said Kelly, trying to mop his forehead and finding that he still wore the flight helmet.

There were no additional officers waiting for Kelly at the ramp of the C-141. The captain who had greeted him at the TF-104 now shepherded him onto the ramp alone. "Good luck, sir," he said, and offered his hand.

Offhand, Kelly couldn't remember anybody saying that—and sounding like he meant it—since this business began.

"I appreciate that," the veteran said as they shook hands. "And—folks pretty high up"—which described the aliens as well as anything could—"tell me it'll all be fine if I do my job. Which I do."

"Door's lifting," said the loadmaster at the cargo bay's rear control panel, but his hand did not actually hit the lifter switch until the captain had sprung back down the ramp. As the ramp started to rise, the loadmaster called a terse report on his commo helmet, glanced at Kelly, and then looked down the nearly empty cargo bay.

The benches were folded down and locked in place along both windowless sides of the fuselage. During the Starlifter's usual "passenger" operation as a troop transport, the broad central aisleway would have been loaded with munitions and heavy equipment. It was empty now. Beneath one of the benches, however, was a child's suitcase of pink vinyl.

The loadmaster strode over to the piece of miniature luggage, jerked it from its partial concealment, and hurled it underhand toward the tail. The suitcase bounced from the ramp and out the narrowing gap to the concrete.

The C-141 was already moving, rotating outward in a manner disconcerting because nothing outside the cargo bay was visible. Kelly took off the helmet; he would not need it on this flight. The curving sides and roofline gave him the feeling of being trapped in a subway tunnel which echoed to the roar of an oncoming train.

"Well, that kid'll need it more'n we will, won't she?" the loadmaster demanded loudly as he walked over to the veteran. He was a burly man, unaffected by the motion of the aircraft through long familiarity.

"Got a problem, friend?" asked Kelly as he sat down on the bench. If anything *did* start, the bulkhead anchoring him would be better than a fair trade-off for the height advantage that he surrendered.

"You really rate, doncha?" the crewman continued. "Had 'em all aboard, over two hundred dependents. Another three minutes and we'd have been wheels-up for Rome. Then, bingo! Off-load everybody and prepare to take on a special passenger. Not, 'a special passenger *and* the dependents.' Oh, no. And the ones who don't *move* quick enough, there's nightsticks to move 'em along. So my wife and kids are out there on the fuckin' *pad,* and you've got the plane to yourself, buddy."

"Think Rome's going to be a great place if they nuke it?" Kelly asked in a tone of cool curiosity. His right hand gripped the strap of the helmet, ready to use it as a club if things worked out that way,

"I'd be with them, at least," the loadmaster said harshly.

"There's people who think if I get back to the World quick enough, there won't be any more nukes," Kelly snapped in a voice that could have been heard over gunfire. He stood, dropping the helmet because it wasn't going to be needed. "Who the *fuck* do you think I am, Sergeant? Some politician running home from a junket? Don't you *want* this shit to stop?"

The loadmaster blinked and backed a step. "Oh," he said. "Ah . . ."

"Christ, I'm sorry, buddy," Kelly said, looking down as if he were embarrassed. "Look, I'm really tight. I left some people behind too, and—" He raised his eyes and met the crewman's in false candor. "—Wasn't a great place, you know? Even if this other crap quiets down."

"Ah. . . ." said the crewman. "Aw, hell, we're all jumpy. You know how it is." He tried out a rather careful smile. "Want to go forward before we lift?"

"Lemme strip this suit off," the veteran answered with an equally abashed smile, textured for the use. "After we get the wheels up, I'll go say 'hi' . . . but this is the part of the plane I'm used to."

He grinned, this time genuinely—not that the difference was noticeable. "Only thing is, it's a *lot* bigger'n the ones I've had to jump out."

"You bet your ass," the crewman agreed proudly, then reported on his commo helmet as he settled himself in a seat by the tail ramp.

The flight was uneventful. It would have seemed uneventful even if Kelly had not spent much of the air time asleep. The crew had a job to do, and they were cruising at twenty knots above normal speed; even with the agreed need for haste, there was no reasonable way to wring more out of a big bird optimized to move cargo.

The cockpit windows showed the clouds below or, through the clouds, the Mediterranean. The wall of gauges and displays in front of each flight engineer had more potential interest, at least—the possibility that boards would suddenly glow red and the sea would take on a reality beyond that of a backdrop for the hole the C-141 was punching through the sky.

But sleep was useful, once the demands of socializing had been met. The new routing was to Torrejon, just outside Madrid. That could change at any moment; since this Starlifter was a B model with air refueling capability in addition to a lengthened fuselage, their final touch-down could be El Paso—if the Powers That Be decided.

Kelly dreamed of Fortress, but not as he had seen it in photographs and artists' renderings. Now there was a trio of saucers tethered near the docking area. Their design prevented them from using the airlocks in normal fashion, but a saucer was still connected to Fortress by a thick umbilicus configured at its nether end to mate with the station in the same manner as the nose of a Space Command transporter.

Fortress showed no sign of the struggle in which it had been captured. The outer doughnut of raw bauxite and ilmenite from the Moon, the same material that was refined and extruded in the solar furnaces with which Fortress built itself, was beginning to weather into greater uniformity under the impact of micrometeorites and hard radiation. It was not scarred by anything more major, the high-explosive or even nuclear warheads against which it gave reasonable protection.

The close-in defense arrays visible from the north pole of the space station were empty, the spidery launching frames catching sunlight and shadowing one another at unexpected angles. Two of the launchers were missing, sheared down to their bases when their rockets gang-fired.

The space station itself was a dumbbell rotating within the hoop of shielding material. Each lobe of the station was a short length of cylinder connected by a spoke to the spherical hub. Now the dream-viewpoint shifted, angling across the center of the doughnut toward the windows, through which mirrors deflected sunlight into the living quarters of Fortress. Polished slats repeatedly re-reflected light while filtering the radiation which would otherwise have entered through the windows as well.

As Kelly's mind watched, the trailing end of one of the lobes flew outward in slow motion. The aluminum panels twisted under stress but kept their general shape and even clung in part to the girders on which they had been hung. Glass-honeycomb insulation disintegrated, providing a spinning cloud which mimicked the bloom of white-hot gases to be expected from a normal explosion.

The real blast had been only a small one—strip charges laid along the inner frame of the panel. The difference in pressure between hard vacuum and the part of the space station which had just been opened to that vacuum was sufficient to void most of the chamber's contents, however. Flimsy furniture, sheets of paper, and over a hundred living men spewed into space along with the metal and shredded glass.

Some of the men flapped their arms vigorously, as if they were trying to swim to the hub or the brightly-sunlit saucers docked there. In the event, when a few of them did collide with bracing wires, they spun slowly away; they had lost the ability to comprehend what might seem a hope of safety, though they still were not legally dead.

The viewpoint narrowed on the opened chamber itself, though with none of the mechanical feeling of a camera being dollied. When a gun fires, some residues of the reaction remain aswirl in the breech. Similarly, there was a single human figure still drifting in the chamber from which his fellows had been voided. At one point he had been trying to grasp the screw latch of the airlock to one of the adjoining compartments. His grip had lost definition, though it had not wholly relaxed, and now he floated with his fingers hooked into vain claws.

The victim had been a stocky man of medium height. His beard, moustache, and white tunic had been sprayed a brilliant red with blood when air within his body cavity expanded to ram his empty lungs out his mouth and nostrils. Kelly did not recognize the rank insignia on the tunic sleeves, but the SS runes on the collar were unmistakable.

Kelly knew the victim, and that knowledge was not the false assurance of a dream. He could not recall the fellow's full name, but he was known as ben Majlis, and he had been leader of a squad of Kurds while Operation Birdlike was up and running.

The body twitched harshly, mindlessly, not quite close enough to a bulkhead or the floor for the movement to thrust against something solid. The corneas of ben Majlis's eyes were red with ruptured capillaries, and ice crystals were already beginning to glitter on them.

One of the hands flopped toward Kelly's point of view, driven by the Kurd's dying convulsions. As it did so, something touched the veteran's shoulder in good truth. He leaped up with a cry and a look of horror that drove back the loadmaster who had just awakened Kelly to tell him that the C-141 was making its final approach to Torrejeon.

The Starlifter's crew greased her in, the instant of touchdown unnoticed until the thrust reversers on the big turbo-fans grabbed hold of the air and tried to pull the aircraft backwards. Skill in a fighter meant quickness; skill in a transport was a matter of being smooth, and sliding a hundred and some tons onto a concrete slab without evident shock was skill indeed.

"What's the drill from here?" Kelly asked the load-master, who now had his helmet's long cord plugged into a console near one of the forward doors. Neither of the men in the echoing cargo bay could see anything save the aluminum walls around them, but the crewman was in touch with the flight deck through his intercom.

The loadmaster spoke an acknowledgment into the straw-slim microphone wand and stepped closer to Kelly in order to explain without shouting, "We're going to taxi to N-2. There's a bird waiting there for you already."

He paused, then touched the intercom key of his helmet to say, "Gotcha." To Kelly he then went on, smiling, "Seems like you're stepping up in the world, Colonel Kelly."

"It used to be 'sergeant,' and right now it's 'civilian'— whatever I tell people that have more use'n I do for brass," the veteran said with a smile of his own. "I gonna need the flight suit?" He had surprisingly little stiffness or specific pain from the battering he'd taken in the past few days, but he found when he shrugged that his whole body felt as if there were an inch of fuzz growing on it.

"On an Airborne Command Post?" the loadmaster said. "Nossir, I don't guess you will."

The big crewman paused again, this time in response to memory rather than a voice in his earphones. "Look sir, you were serious about putting a lid on this? Word is . . . word is, they've already pooped a nuke. If they did . . ."

"Thing is"—Kelly frowned, as he chose words that could explain things simply—and hopefully—" 'they' aren't the Reds, not yet. They're a bunch of terrorists. And I can't do a damn thing for what's gone down already; but yeah, I can put a lid on it."

He grinned a shark's grin. The loadmaster remembered the fight he had tried to pick when his passenger came aboard. "I can put some people," Kelly said, "where they won't be a problem till Judgment Day."

One of the three men waiting in civilian clothes atop the truck-mounted boarding steps was General Redstone. That was good because the other two had the look and the size of folks who'd be sent to take Kelly out of play.

If they'd wanted to do that, of course—especially after what had happened at the landing site near Istanbul—there were going to be more than two guys sent.

"Christ, that's *beautiful*," Kelly blurted as he stepped from the Starlifter onto the landing of the boarding stairs.

"Hang on," directed Redstone, and the two—call them attendants—each grabbed Kelly firmly with one hand while anchoring themselves to the railing with the other. "Somebody thought this'd—"

The truck backed away from the C-141 in an arc, then braked sharply enough that Kelly gripped one of the attendants and the closest portion of the railing himself. The big men's touch had shocked him, but they had not tried to immobilize his hands. The truck accelerated forward, toward the open hatch of the plane that had drawn Kelly's exclamation.

The aircraft was a Boeing 747 which had few external modifications beyond the slight excrescence on the nose for accepting a refueling drogue, and the radome which recapitulated in miniature the bulge of the flight deck on which it rested.

Kelly's vision of the Strategic Air Command had been molded by the tired B-52Ds which had flown to Lebanon out of Akrotiri, painted in camouflage colors and carrying tens of tons of high-explosive bombs under the wings. But an Airborne Command Post was as close to being a showpiece as SAC had available; and in these days, when budget cutters reasonably suggested the nuclear strike mission be left wholly to Space Command and Fortress, the manned-bomber boys weren't going to miss any opportunity for show.

The big aircraft was painted dazzling white, with a blue accent stripe down the line of windows from nose to tail. Above the stripe, in Times Roman letters that must have been five feet high, were the words *United States of America*. The forward entrance hatch was swung inward, awaiting the motorized boarding stairs.

"Geez," Kelly muttered, "do they paint 'em like that to make 'em easier to target on?"

"Maybe somebody told 'em white'd make the damn thing more survivable in a near nuke," responded Redstone with a grimace of his own. Red hadn't been the smartest fellow Kelly had met in the service, but his instincts were good and he'd been willing to go to the wall for his men. How he'd made general was a wonder and a half. "Of course," Redstone continued, "that flag on the tail's going to burn seven red stripes right through the control surfaces."

"Purty, though," Kelly observed. He was squinting.

Twenty miles an hour seemed plenty fast enough when you hung onto a railing fifteen feet in the air.

Grit was blowing across the field, along with fumes from the big turbofans of the aircraft they approached. The odor left no question but that the bird was burning JP-4 rather than kerosene-based JP-1. The gasoline propellant could be expected both to significantly increase speed and range, and to turn the aircraft into a huge bomb if it had to make a belly landing.

Well, Kelly's taste had always been for performance over survivability. His plans for Fortress didn't strike him as particularly survivable, even if everything worked up to specs.

The truck slowed. An attendant in the doorway of the 747 was talking the driver in. A flat-topped yellow fuel tanker pulled away from the other side of the aircraft which it had been topping off. Kelly wondered how long the Airborne Command Post had been idling here, ready to take off as soon as the Starlifter from Incirlik landed its cargo.

"Something you might keep in mind, Kelly," said General Redstone as the truck began to nestle the stairs' padded bumpers against the 747, "is that a lot of 'em don't like you, and I don't guess anybody believes *everything* you put in that cable—me included. But nobody knows what the fuck's going on, either. If you keep your temper— that's *always* been the problem, Kelly—and you keep saying what you say you know . . . then I guess you might get what you say you want."

The boarding stairs butted gently against the .aircraft. Kelly rocked slightly and the two attendants released him.

"'I say,'" he quoted with a grin. " 'I *say*.' You know me, Red. I say what I mean." He took the precedence the general offered with a hand and strode aboard the Airborne Command Post.

"This way, please," said a female attendant whose dark skirt and blazer looked like a uniform, though they had no insignia—military or civilian. Kelly followed her, keeping the figure centered in a hallway which seemed extremely dim after the sunblasted concrete of the Spanish airport outside. The corridor was enclosed by bulkheads to either side, so that none of the light from the extensive windows reached it.

There was a muted sound from the outer hatch as it closed and sealed behind them, and all the noises external to the aircraft disappeared.

Offhand, Kelly couldn't think of any group of people with whom he less cared to share a miniature universe than the ones he expected to see in a moment.

"They're here," said the female attendant to the pair of men outside the first open door to the right. The guards could have passed for brothers to those who had received Kelly on the boarding stairs and who now tramped down the hall behind him. The aircraft was already beginning to trundle forward,

One of the guards turned his head into the room and murmured something. The other shifted his body slightly to block the doorway, but he focused his eyes well above Kelly's head so that the action did not become an overt challenge.

"Yes, of course!" snapped a male voice from within, and the guards sprang aside with the suddenness of the

Symplegades parting to trap another ship. Kelly gave the one who had blocked him a wry smile as he passed. Working for folks who got off by jumping on the hired help wasn't his idea of a real good time. By now, at least, they must realize that Tom Kelly wasn't part of the hired help.

The plaque of layered plastic on the door said Briefing Room, and within were thirty upholstered seats facing aft in an arc toward an offset lectern. "*Good* morning, Pierrard," the veteran said to the miasma of pipe smoke which was identifiable before the man himself was, one of a score of faces turned to watch over their shoulders and seatbacks as the newcomers arrived.

"Sit down and strap in, Kelly," directed the white-haired man in the second of the five rows of seats. "We're about to take off." He pointed to the trio of jump seats now folded against the bulkhead behind the lectern.

Kelly slid into the empty seat nearest the door instead. The upholstery and carpet were royal blue, a shade that reminded the veteran of Congressman Bianci's office. For a moment he felt—not homesick, but nonetheless nostalgic; he didn't really belong in that world, but it had been a good place to be.

Redstone, whose seat the agent had probably taken, grimaced and found another one by stepping over a naval officer with enough stripes on his sleeves to be at least a captain. "It's no sweat, Red," Kelly called over the rumble of the four turbofans booting the 747 down the runway on full enriched thrust. "I'm cool, I just like these chairs better."

Everyone waited until the pilot had lifted them without wasting time, though with nothing like the abrupt intent of the Starfighter at Diyarbakir some hours before. It was still a big enough world that traveling across it took finite blocks of time. Within the atmosphere, at any rate; the orbital period of Fortress was ninety-five minutes, plus or minus a few depending on how recently the engines had been fired to correct for atmospheric friction.

That was the maximum amount of time before any particular point on Earth became a potential target for a thermonuclear warhead on an unstoppable trajectory.

After less than two minutes, despite what it felt like to all those in the briefing room, the big aircraft's upward lunge reached the point at which cabin attendants on commercial flights would have begun their spiel about complimentary beverages. Kelly turned his eyes from the windows, past which rags of low cloud were tearing, and took a deep breath. He might or might not switch planes again. Either way, this room and these men—they were all men—were the last stage of the preliminaries.

"Will somebody tell him to get up there where he belongs?" demanded someone in a peevish voice.

"Bates," said Pierrard in a voice whose volume and clarity suggested the anger behind it, "we'll proceed more smoothly if only those with business choose to speak."

The room paused. Kelly nodded approvingly to the white-haired man, who then continued into the silence he had wrought. "How *did* you manage to insert your report that way, Mr. Kelly?"

The veteran laughed. Everyone else in the room was twisted in the bolted-down chairs to see him, save for those in the last row—behind him—who had a direct view of the back of his head. He would've gone to the lectern as directed except that he *had* been directed; and besides, it would feel a little too much like being a duck in a shooting gallery.

"Oh, that wasn't me," Kelly said, looking down. "NSA's good, but we're not *that* good. That was the aliens you sent me to find." It had been disconcertingly natural for him to verbally put on a uniform again the way he just had.

There was a ripple of talk, more of it directed at neighbors than at the veteran. Pierrard was giving himself time by lifting his pipe to his lips, though smoke continued to trickle from the bowl in indication that he was not drawing on it.

Kelly rose, resting his buttocks on the seat back and curling his right foot directly beneath his hip to lock him there. "Look," he repeated, "I *couldn't* have gotten through any way I know about, not from Diyarbakir, not if I were the *President*."

The veteran's eyes were adjusting to the light and his mind was locking down into the gears suitable for the present situation. He nodded to a man he recognized from the office of the National Security Advisor—not the Advisor himself, a political opportunist whose pronouncements always sounded as though he were still a Marine battalion commander.

"Anyway," Kelly continued, finding that his new perch was less stable than he had thought—the 747 was still climbing—"the important thing is dealing with the situation. I can do that with a little cooperation. A lot less cooperation than it took to put all you people together in one room, believe me."

Kelly's mind was cataloguing the faces turned awkwardly over their seats toward him, and he found that he recognized a surprising number of them from his years on Capitol Hill. They were not the men who discussed crises on-camera. They—like Kelly—were the ones who did the groundwork, or the dirty work, required to solve the real problems.

"What *is* the situation, in your view, Mr. Kelly?" asked a Space Command colonel named Stoddard. Kelly had been on a "Tom and Jim" basis with him for over a year, ever since Stoddard became the Command's liaison— lobbyist—with Congress. Kelly couldn't blame him for not making a big thing about their association just now, when the veteran's status was at best in doubt.

"A small group of Nazis," Kelly said, projecting his voice and his gaze at the men around him with consciousness of the power which knowledge gave him, "and I don't mean Neo-Nazis; these're the real thing, holdouts and their kids. Anyway, they've taken over Fortress, using trained Kurds as shock troops. I assume all the station personnel are dead. I *know* the Kurds have been eliminated now that their job's done, so there's no possibility of outsiders within Fortress being turned, even if you had a way to contact them."

He paused, but added through the first syllables of response, "*I'm* your way to contact Fortress, and I've told you how."

"We don't know they're actually Germans because they say they are," said the shorthaired, red-faced man, whom Kelly now recognized as Bates. "Maybe they're Russkies, maybe they're these aliens you claim you're right about."

"Maybe if you had a brain in your *head,* Bates," Kelly snapped, "you'd have some business here." Almost in the same breath, he said, bending toward General Redstone, "I'm sorry, Red, I didn't mean to do that. S'okay now."

"Bates, *for God's* sake, keep your mouth shut," Pierrard said angrily. He followed it with a spasm of coughing from which spurted pipe smoke that he had not exhaled properly before speaking.

"Yeah, they're for real, the Nazis," Kelly said quietly, making amends for his outburst. "They call 'emselves the Service, the Dienst, and I guess everybody here's data bank's got a megabyte of background on 'em."

He smiled and shook his head ruefully. "You know, they'd be just as harmless as they look, except they got outa Germany in '45 with a flying saucer"—he spread his hands toward his audience, recognizing the incredulity they must be feeling—"and engineers to build more of the damn things."

"I suggest," said Pierrard, touching the wave of his white hair with the fingers of his left hand, "that for the present we ignore the question of responsibility and move on to a discussion of Mr. Kelly's proposal for action."

One of the men Kelly remembered from the orderly room at Fort Meade slipped out of the Briefing Room in response to a signal the veteran had not seen Pierrard give. Checking on the Dienst, no doubt, through the Airborne Command Post's shielded data links with every computer bank in the federal government. The question the old man said he would ignore was obviously one that had already been answered to his satisfaction.

Pierrard was a bastard, but Kelly had never assumed

he was a stupid bastard. The fact that the veteran had been met by this particular aircraft and the men aboard it suggested more clearly than Redstone had that a sufficient "they" were willing to go along with, if not trust, Tom Kelly.

"I was told," Kelly said carefully, "that the ferry pads on both coasts, and the Russian equivalent at Tyuratam, have all been nuked."

"*Who* told you?" demanded a man who'd been a GS-16 in Defense when Kelly last talked with him. "*No* information on that subject has been released."

"They'd know at Pirinclik!" someone else suggested excitedly. "Has he been allowed into the compound at Pirinclik?"

"*Look*," Kelly shouted, exasperated by men who were stuck with their own functional areas instead of focusing their minds on the real problem. "It was the fucking aliens, I *told* you, the little guys like the one in the freezer at Meade—and it doesn't *matter.* All it means is, unless you've got another way to lift me to orbit, I go up on the monocle ferry at Bliss. You got a better way, let's hear it, because I'm just counting on enough of the bugs to be worked out that it does like it's supposed to one time."

"Yes, well," said Pierrard, meeting the veteran's eyes while his right hand played with his meerschaum pipe, "there's also the question of who goes up in the ferry if we do choose that option. There are—"

"That's not a question," said Kelly. "I go."

"There are younger men with better training both in—" Pierrard began.

"God *damn* it," said the veteran, stepping forward

from his perch and leaning toward Pierrard across the intervening seats and startled men. "Just one time in my life there's going to be something I did that I point to and say *I* did it; good, bad or indifferent. You *chose* me. I'm *going!*"

"We didn't choose you for this, Kelly," said General Redstone, the only man in the room willing to argue calmly in the face of the veteran's obvious fury.

Kelly took a deep breath. "Sure you did, Red," he replied in a husky, low-pitched voice as he rubbed his eyes and forehead with both hands. "Sure you did, even if you didn't know it just then."

"I—" Pierrard said as the stocky agent paused.

"Look," Kelly continued, loudly enough to interrupt but without the anger of a moment before. "Used to be something'd come up and I'd be told, 'Right, but that's not in your area any more. It's in the hands of the people who take care of that.' This is what you made my area, folks." He looked grimly around the room. "This is what I've done for you for twenty years. Killing people."

"Not for *me*, buddy," someone unseen rumbled.

Kelly turned in that direction and smiled. No one else spoke for several seconds.

"The aliens won't take orders from you, Mr. Kelly," said Pierrard, using the word *aliens* with none of the incredulous hesitancy that had plagued others when they found they had no alternative.

"Won't they, Pierrard?" replied Kelly, continuing to smile as he reached overhead and stretched his legs up on tiptoes besides. His fingers couldn't touch the ceiling. This was a hell of a big plane, and as steady as a train through the skies besides. "How do you know? You can't even speak with them."

"Do you—" someone began.

"One moment," snapped Pierrard, his eyes meeting Kelly's as the veteran lowered his hands and stood arms akimbo, relaxed in the way a poker player relaxes when he has laid down a straight flush to the king.

Pierrard got his moment, got several, while smoke from his pipe wreathed him and the hand with which he stroked his hair seemed as rigid as a claw. "Mr. Kelly," he said at last, "there are quarters provided for you, and there's a lounge. If you'd care to—"

"My room have a shower?" the veteran interrupted.

"Yes." The syllable Pierrard spoke held no emotion, but there was rage in his eyes to equal that of Kelly a few minutes before.

"You've got my address," Kelly said with a brittle smile.

When Kelly opened the hall door, the two guards snapped to alertness. "Take this gentleman to room sixteen," called Pierrard from behind Kelly, just before the veteran closed the door again.

One of the guards touched the key of his throat mike. "Bev, report to the Briefing Room," came from his lips and was syncopated by the same order whispering down the corridor from a speaker forward.

"Christ, people, I can find a room number myself," the agent said with a grimace. He had done so and was opening the door when the earnest-looking female attendant scurried past. High levels of government were the wrong places to look for women's liberation. Generals and their civilian equivalents liked perks to remind them of their power, and chirpy girls in menial positions were high on their list of requirements.

The room wasn't huge, though it had two windows with a nice view of clouds a hell of a long way down. The fittings were more than comfortable—chair, writing desk, and a bed which seemed a trifle longer than standard. VIPs tended to be men of above-average height, and the Strategic Air Command certainly had its share of officers who could not be comfortably fitted into fighter cockpits:

There was the promised shower, not an enormous luxury so far as space went . . . but the weight of the water to feed it and the other similar facilities was something else again. No wonder the bird in this configuration had an all-up weight of four hundred tons.

The water felt good, as it always did. Soap, dust, body oils, and dried blood curled down the drain as a gray slurry. By adjusting the taps as hot as he could stand it, Kelly was able to knead with his fingertips the injury that seemed most bothersome: the welt across his right temple where Doug had slapped him with the submachine gun. The general pain of the hot water provided cover for him to work loose the scabs and get normal circulation flowing.

The pain had another benefit. It made Kelly think of Doug as a figure beating him . . . displacing, for the moment, at least, memory of Doug as something recently human, huddled now and forever in a pool of blood and feces because Tom Kelly had made him that way.

Kelly hadn't locked the door, hadn't even looked to see if there *was* a lock.

It was no surprise to hear the door open, and a relief

but no surprise that the intruder—water sprayed toward the bed when Kelly swung open the stall's frosted glass door without first closing the faucets—was General Redstone, rather than six or eight of the husky attendants.

"Hey, Red," said the veteran, shutting off the water, "good to see you." Which was true on a number of levels.

"I thought you'd, you know, hold it against me I didn't come with you when you left," Redstone said, settling himself in the swivel chair bolted down in front of the desk. Light gleamed from his bald scalp, and the older man had gained at least twenty pounds since he had last toured the training camp outside Diyarbakir in a set of khaki desert fatigues.

"Hell, I'd rather have a friend in court than somebody to hold my hand," said the agent.

He hadn't left Redstone behind as a friend, exactly. Red was the sort of guy who would sacrifice his firstborn if God in the guise of the US government demanded it. Not that he wouldn't argue about the decision.

But Kelly also knew that Redstone wasn't going to let one of his boys be fucked over just because that seemed like a good policy to somebody in a suit. He would spend Kelly or spend himself; but, like Kelly, only if that were required to accomplish the task.

"Well, what they going to go with, Red?" the agent asked as he spilled the cartridges onto the bunk and began to clean the revolver. "Me or nothing?"

"We've got a preliminary report from Istanbul," Redstone said, looking toward the windows instead of the nude, scarred body of the man who had once served under him. "About Blakeley."

"That mean I'm out, then?" Kelly asked in a bantering tone. His hands concentrated on feeding a corner of the towel into each of the chambers. He hadn't had a chance to clean the weapon properly since he'd used it on Doug. . . .

"Funny world," said Redstone idly. He looked at Kelly. "Convinced some folks you meant what you said. God knows *I'd* tried. Means you're on, on your terms. Nobody had a better plan that didn't include you, and nobody seemed to think you were going to mellow out any time soon."

"Jesus," said Kelly. He sat down on the bed, still holding the towel-wrapped gun but without pretending any longer that it had his attention. The cartridges rolled down the bedspread and against his right thigh. "Well, at least they got that'n right."

"Now," said the older man, leaning forward with his hands clasped above his knees, "are you going off and do it your way, or are you willing to listen to reason on the hardware?"

Kelly pursed his lips. "I'm willing," he said slowly, "to talk things over with somebody who knows which end of a gun the bang comes out of . . . which"—he grinned—"is you and nobody else within about seven vertical miles."

"Then take an Ultimax 100 instead," the general said earnestly. "Twelve and a half pounds with the hundred-round drum, rate of fire low enough to be controllable even in light gravity, and absolutely reliable in or out of an atmosphere."

"Sure, nice gun, Red," said Kelly, the individual words agreeable but the implication a refusal. He resumed the task of cleaning the Smith and Wesson while the air and bedspread got on with the business of drying his body. "But all thumbs'd be mild for the way I'll be, rigged out in a space suit. A machinegun won't cut it."

"Well, there's been some talk about that . . ." said Redstone. Both men were relaxing now that the conversation had lapsed into routine and minutiae. The general locked his fingers behind his neck and stretched out his legs, demonstrating in the process that the chair back reclined. "If you blow each segment as you go through, then everybody's on the same footing. You say they terminated the Kurds, right?"

"Sure." Kelly held the revolver with the cylinder open so that light was reflected from the recoil plate through the barrel to his eye. "I'm probably on better'n even terms with each one of the maybe twenty Germans. Not great odds, buddy, and I can't watch both directions at once. I need something that'll take 'em out section by section— fast, because it's *me* that's gotta move to get to the control room. If I wait to blow doors instead of just opening them, they'll sure as shit get around behind and scrag me."

"You'll be awkward as a hog on ice, lugging all that gear, baby." Redstone grimaced, though his relaxed posture did not change.

"I'll be awkward as hell in a space suit anyway," Kelly agreed with a shrug. "Red, you got anything thin enough to feed through this bore or do I tear off a bit of the sheet?"

Redstone fished in his top pocket for a handkerchief. "We can probably hunt you up a proper cleaning kit," he grumbled. "Carry a backup, hey? Those things fuck up more ways than a seventeen-year-old kid."

"Thought maybe a shotgun," the veteran agreed, keeping his eyes on the gun. "Look, Red. You find a way to put a platoon in orbit *fast*, then we'll do it that way. Otherwise, this is the choice, and I don't need any shit about it. I'm *right*." He glared fiercely at the older man.

"Never said you weren't," Redstone agreed with a shrug. Businesslike again, he went on, "I'll call in, have 'em cut down a Model 1100 and put a pistol grip on it."

Kelly cocked his head. "Figured a pump gun from stores," he said. "Why an autoloader?"

"You figure to have both hands free, Kelly?" the general replied with a grin. "Besides, it'll function better, especially with you in a suit and likely to shortstroke the slide." He raised his hand. "*Don't* tell me it wouldn't happen to you. It *won't* happen if you let a gas valve do all the thinking the times that you've got other things on your plate."

"Yeah, okay," Kelly said. He began reloading the cylinder of his snubbie. "Suppose anybody thought to bring me a change of clothes? *I* didn't think of it."

"We'll rustle something up," the general said, evaluating the veteran's body with a practiced eye. "You're in pretty good shape, Kelly. Be nice if you were nineteen and still had your experience, but I guess the experience's the choice." He nodded toward the door, then started to get up. "There's people waiting to brief you on layout and the control sequence as soon as you're ready to hear about that."

"Right," said Kelly. "Find me a pair of slacks at least and send 'em with the briefing team."

"Right," Redstone agreed, but big hands stayed on

the back of the chair, which he swiveled in a pair of short, nervous arcs.

"Spit it *out,* Red," the veteran said sharply, his eyes narrowing. "Hard to tell when you'll get a better chance."

"Why'd you blow her that way, Kelly?" Redstone said, each word chipped from stone. "Elaine, I mean. Why'd you fuck her over?"

"Goddam," Kelly said in surprise. "Red, I didn't know you knew the lady."

"Answer the goddam question," the general whispered.

"Roger," said Kelly coolly. "Because she lied to me, and because she set me up. Any more questions?"

"Goddammit, she *didn't* set you up!" Redstone burst out. "I heard the fucking tape! You were supposed to get the kid gloves treatment, and except for that shithead Blakeley you'd have gotten it!"

He turned toward the wall, and for a moment Kelly thought the older man was going to break a hand trying to punch a hole in the bulkhead. He sagged instead, bracing himself with his hands flattened on either side of the doorframe.

"I'm sorry, Red," Kelly said as calmly as he could. "If I'd known a little more, maybe some things I'd have done another way. But I'm not psychic, man."

"Shit, Kelly, shit," General Redstone muttered to the door. He faced the agent again. Moments before he had been flushed, but now he looked sallow and very old. "We all lie," he said. "Sometimes it's hard to draw the line, I guess." Redstone shook his head violently from side to side, as if to clear it of something clinging. "Sorry," he muttered. "Sorry."

"Red." Kelly waited until the other man met his eyes. "Somebody greased Mohammed Ayyubi in order to get me into this whole thing. I told his brother I'd even the score." He took a deep breath. "I'm going to, Red. Someday I'll learn who gave the scratch order, and then I'll handle it. If that's something you need to pass on, then that's how it is."

"Oh, Christ, Kelly," the general said with an operational smile that relaxed the veteran as no words could have done, "you already took care of that one. It was Blakeley, and—and it got cleared afterwards because of the other, the funny gray guy. But that was when they decided that somebody ought to be brought in over Blakeley to ride herd."

Redstone nodded a period to his thought. Then, in a voice that could have been Tom Kelly's in a similar case, he added, "And if you hadn't nailed him, soldier, I would've done it myself after the bucket he put—a whole lotta people in."

He turned quickly, mumbling as he opened the door, "I'll see to your pants."

"Damn, it's bright out there," said Tom Kelly as Redstone slid closed the door of the van. The latch stuck and the panting general had to bang the door again to jar loose metal covered with El Paso's omnipresent yellow-gray grit. "I ought to eat more carrots."

"It's an old wives' tale that carrots improve vision," said the passenger who had arrived with the van. They were idling beside the low terminal building until the rest of the entourage had mounted up. The cavalcade of locally available transportation included a pair of canvas-topped Army three-quarter-tons. At least they'd put Kelly in something air-conditioned, though that was probably because he was riding with Pierrard. "Are you having trouble with your eyes?"

"You're a doctor?" Kelly asked, squinting. The thirtyish man had short hair and a short-sleeved shirt with a tie.

The car radio sputtered. The driver with a plug earphone turned and said "Sir?" to Pierrard.

"Drive on," ordered the white-haired man, scowling.

"I'm an MD, if that's what you mean," the passenger said. "Also a Ph.D. Name's Suggs." He offered Kelly his hand.

The veteran shook it, saying, "Then you ought to know that carotene helps the eye adapt to rapid changes in light level—which is the only eye problem I've got."

Dr. Suggs jumped as though Kelly had hit him with a joy buzzer.

"Kelly, calm down," said General Redstone. "Doctor, you're here to do a quick physical, not to talk. Why don't you get on with it?"

The landscape beginning to slide past the van's windows was not dissimilar to that in the vicinity of Diyarbakir, though the mountains in the distance here seemed neither as extensive nor as high.

"Will you roll up your sleeve, please?" said the doctor distantly as he took a sphygmomanometer from his case.

"How tight's the timing?" Kelly asked Redstone. The van rocked more violently than the condition of the road seemed to require. The vehicle was loaded well below its normal capacity of nine persons and luggage, so the springing seemed unduly harsh.

"This isn't the time to discuss the situation," Pierrard said in a flat voice.

"It's the goddam time we got," Kelly snapped back as Suggs started to fit the rubber cuff on him. "Look"—Kelly waved and the doctor sucked in his lips with a hiss of anger, poising as if to capture the arm when next it came to rest—"you've got a lieutenant colonel *driving*, for Chrissake. If you'll go that far for a secure environment, then *use* it. Even if you don't like me, okay?"

The uniformed driver's eyes flickered back in the rearview mirror, though he neither spoke nor turned his head.

Pierrard had taken his unlighted pipe from a side pocket of his suit. Unexpectedly, he dropped it back and said, "I don't like very many people, Mr. Kelly, and that has not in general affected my performance."

He smiled, and though the expression itself was forced, the attempt was significant. "I think it may be that you don't cringe enough."

"Naw," said the veteran. "When I'm scared, I fly hot. And you scare the crap outa me, buddy, that I'll tell you."

Redstone, seated behind Pierrard and kitty-corner across the van's narrow aisle from Kelly, looked from man to man and squeezed unconsciously against his own seat-back.

"The gun in your pocket," said Pierrard, nodding toward the borrowed trousers over which Kelly let the tail of the borrowed shirt hang. "That's the one that killed Blakeley?"

"That's the one," Kelly agreed. He kept his hands plainly in sight on the back of his seat and the one in front of him. Suggs, on the other half of the double seat, tried again to fit the cuff.

"I assumed so," Pierrard said. "I think I can say that at least we share common emotions, Mr. Kelly, when we're forced to deal with one another."

The old man paused, then went on. "We—the proper parties—are in negotiation with the parties who claim to have captured Fortress."

"Claim?" repeated Kelly, glancing over at Redstone.

"I misspoke, Mr. Kelly," Pierrard said. "Litotes when bluntness would have been appropriate. They have accurately targeted and released a number of the nuclear weapons from Fortress, so common sense indicates that they are fully in control as they claim."

Pierrard's hand began to play with the hidden meerschaum. "They did not," he continued, "expect that news of a nuclear attack could be obfuscated; I cannot claim that it was totally concealed for over a day in both the countries which were victimized. There has been a considerable outcry at 'launching disasters' with attendant loss of life . . . but the, the 'Aryan Legion,' as they choose to style themselves now, has received no publicity. As you can imagine, the capabilities designed into Fortress do not include general broadcast equipment." He permitted himself a tight smile.

"So you figure they're going to up the stakes with something you can't cover up," Kelly suggested.

"Moscow and Washington, we feared," agreed Pierrard. "Perhaps only Moscow, if they are what you tell us, Nazi holdouts . . . but the result will be the same, since the Soviets can be expected to respond against the presumed perpetrators, the West."

"Yeah, I've heard that estimate already," the veteran agreed, remembering the rain-swept walls of Diyarbakir and the thing, Wun, that spoke to him there. "Shit." He made sure he held the older man's eyes as he added, "How did the X-ray lasers work?"

Something else he hadn't any business knowing, Kelly thought and Pierrard knew quite well. *That* one wasn't going to be decoyed into answering a question whose premises went beyond anything Kelly was cleared for.

"Perfectly," Pierrard said coolly. "The Soviets attacked with three flights of twenty missiles apiece. Each salvo was destroyed by a single unit of the defensive constellation, operating presumably in an automatic mode. We do not know that the"—he coughed— "Aryan Legion can launch additional defensive satellites as the normal complement would have done . . . but since on the next pass both the silo farms from which the Soviets launched received multiple bombs from Fortress, neither superpower is likely to proceed further in that direction."

"Yeah, well," Kelly said. He turned to look out the window, although without seeing much of the scenery— one-story buildings, mesquite bushes, and dust. "Yeah. Well, I'll be glad to get it over with myself."

"You can't see out the cockpit windows," said Tom Kelly cautiously. "*I* can't see through the windows."

"Ummm," agreed Desmond, the project scientist who had been the bright spot in Kelly's previous visit to the

Biggs Field installation. "You're going to have enough problems, Mr. Kelly, without being cooked by the beams that raise the ferry. They're very precisely directed, but both the distances and velocities involved are considerable and will magnify slight misalignments."

"Check," said Kelly, nodding ruefully. "And we're talking the same wavelengths as the warming racks at the local hamburger joint. Sorry, should've thought."

The suit—the space suit, though it shocked Kelly to think of it that way—was bulky and constricting because of its weight and stiffness, though it did not feel tight. His mind was treating the garment as protective armor rather than a burden. That was good in a way, but the suit really was both—and the fact that his subconscious was more concerned about the threat to him than the object he had to achieve was more than a little bothersome.

"You won't be able to do anything with the controls anyway." The scientist seemed to think he was offering reassurance. "So it doesn't matter whether or not you can see."

"Great."

The makeshift crew vehicle pulled up at the ferry pad.

Well, it wasn't really any different from a night insertion by helicopter; you couldn't see a damned thing, you couldn't change a thing either, and you had to trust not only the hardware but the skills of the man in control of it. On the plus side, nobody'd be shooting at him on this leg of the operation; lift-off would occur while Earth eclipsed Fortress from El Paso. The battle station was not a reconnaissance satellite, but there was no point in risking disclosure because some Nazi glanced at southwest Texas and wondered what the bright flash was.

Desmond opened the door of the van. This one had been modified by the removal of the three seats across the middle to provide more room for a man wrapped in the bulk of a space suit with breathing apparatus in place. "I'm sorry," said the physicist, "you'll have to walk the remainder of the way. We don't have proper equipment for this."

Kelly ducked to look out the door at the monocle ferry, over which waited a castered framework meant for the maintenance crews. There *were* no crew accommodations here; all the testing was ground controlled, as this flight would be as well. "Guess I can make twenty yards," he said, and, when Desmond did not precede him, he stepped past the physicist onto the ground.

The pad was hexagonal, for no particular reason, and four feet above the surrounding soil, higher than most of the dust stinging along on the constant wind. A tank truck preceded by dust and steaming with the blow-off of its remaining load of liquid hydrogen drove away, downwind.

Kelly led the scientist to the pad's steps, realizing as he walked that his center of balance was farther back than he was used to. Desmond, who carried the helmet, was simply making sure that he was in position to support the veteran if he stumbled backward. The ferry looked larger at each of the six upward steps. That was reassuring. Though Kelly had been close to the Frisbee-shaped vehicle before, his mental image throughout the planning was of a tiny disk beneath his seat in the helicopter, preparing to disintegrate as an even tinier speck above him.

"How will you arrange for transfer?" Desmond asked

as Kelly reached the top of the pad. Several men in coveralls stood beside the ferry, but they were service crew rather than a send-off committee. The brass was all in the control bunker; there were no choppers orbiting today.

Kelly tried to glance over his shoulder, but the suit got in the way and his balance wasn't that good anyway. "Honest to God, I don't know," he called against the force of the breeze. He had no idea of how much the physicist had been told. From the fact that Desmond had scrupulously avoided comment on the attempt, whose risks he knew and for whose failure he would feel responsible, Kelly assumed that the man must know a great deal.

"Right up here, sir," said a technician, steadying the tube and steel mesh service bridge with one hand and gesturing toward the nearer flight of steps with the other. "Please don't touch the mirrored surfaces when you step into the cockpit."

The bridge was two flights of metal steps supporting an angle-iron walkway that skimmed the upper surface of the cockpit, either closed or clam-shelled open as now. The railing appeared to be one-inch ID waterpipe, and the whole ensemble had clearly been built in a base workshop. It was sturdy, functional, and almost certainly superior to anything General Dynamics would have achieved with a $350,000 sole-source Space Command contract to the same end. There were advantages to being the poor relation.

The upper surfaces of the ferry were dazzling, the structural members even more so than the sapphire hexagons that accepted the laser beams. Kelly had expected the windows to be bluish, but the segments had only the color of what they chanced to be reflecting—the bridge, the pale sky, or the sun like the point of a blazing dagger.

"We'd better lock this down," Desmond said, offering the helmet to Kelly.

The agent bowed slightly so that Desmond could fit the helmet instead of just handing it over. "There's a certain amount of dust on the surface anyway," he said without inflection.

"Yes, the raised platform was only to lessen the accumulation," the physicist agreed as he lowered the helmet, "not to eliminate it." His voice becoming muffled as the padded thermoplastic slid down over Kelly's ears, he continued, "It burns off cleanly in the laser flux. We've retrieved enough of the earlier test units to be sure that wasn't the cause of failure."

The locking cogs began to snap into place around the base of the helmet. Very softly, the veteran heard Desmond conclude, "Enough pieces."

There was a crackle in Kelly's ears as the project scientist connected the earphones to the power pack. "Do we have a link?" demanded a compressed voice. "*Dancer One*, do you read me? Over."

"Yes," Kelly said as he mounted the steps, bending forward at the waist because the base of the helmet cut off his normal downward peripheral vision. The pure oxygen he was now breathing flooded his sinuses like a seepage of ice water. "Now get off the air. Please."

"*Dancer One*, are you having difficulties with the boarding bridge? Should we get you some personnel to help? Over."

Kelly paused, found the power connection with his

gloved hand, and unplugged the radio. Then he resumed trudging to the middle of the walkway where the railing had been cut away. He lowered himself carefully, one leg at a time, into the cramped cockpit. Where they thought there'd be room for anybody to lend a hand with the process was beyond him. Maybe a gantry, but there weren't any available on-site.

His position in the saucer was roughly that of an F-16 pilot or a Russian tank driver: flat on his back with his head raised less than would've been comfortable for reading in bed. In the contemplated operational use, there would have been a condenser screen in front of the pilot and a projector between his knees to throw instrument data onto that screen.

For this run, the heads-up display had been removed so that the fuel and pressure tanks of Kelly's additional gear could fill the space. More than fill it, as a matter of fact; what would have been a tight fit now nearly required a shoehorn. The boarding bridge clattered as a technician and Dr. Desmond climbed on from opposite ends.

"I'm all right, dammit!" Kelly snapped, his scowl evident through the face shield, though his words must have been unintelligible.

The physicist nodded approvingly, reached down for the throat of the fuel tank, and lifted it the fraction of an inch that permitted Kelly's legs to clear to either side. The veteran sank back thankfully onto the seat, aware of his previous tension once he had released it.

The technician began to close half the cockpit cover. His hands were gloved; a handprint in body oils on the reflective surface would dangerously concentrate the initial laser pulse. Desmond stopped the man, pointed at Kelly's helmet, and then mimed on his own neck the process of reconnecting the veteran's radio. It would be next to impossible for Kelly to mate the plugs himself in the strait cockpit.

Kelly smiled but shook his head, and the doors above shut him into blackness.

Then there was nothing to do save wait; but Tom Kelly, like a leopard, was very good at waiting for a kill.

Kelly's mind had drifted so that when the monocle ferry took off, its passenger flashed that he was again riding an armored personnel carrier which had just rolled over a mine.

That—the feeling at least—was an apt analogy for the event. The ferry lifted off without the buildup of power inevitable in any fuel-burning system. The laser flux converted the air trapped between the pad and the mirrored concavity of the ferry's underside into plasma expanding with a suddenness greater than the propagation rate of high explosive. Kelly left the ground as if shot from a gun.

The roaring acceleration was so fierce that it trapped the hand which reflex tried to thrust down to the shotgun bolstered alongside Kelly's right calf. The ferry shifted to pulsejet mode as soon as the initial blast lifted it from the pad. The low-frequency hammering of the chambers firing in quick succession, blasting out as plasma air that they had earlier sucked in, so nearly resembled the vibration of a piston engine about to drop a valve that anticipation kept the veteran rigid for long seconds after g-forces had decreased to a level against which he could have moved had he continued to try.

The rim of the ferry with the firing chambers spun at high speed around the cockpit at the hub. Kelly had expected to be aware of that gyroscopic motion, to feel or hear the contact of the bearing surfaces surrounding him. There was no such vibration, and it was only as he found himself straining to hear the nonexistent that the veteran realized he had not been blown to fragments above the Texas desert the way the test units had gone.

Worrying about minutiae was probably the best way available to avoid funking in the face of real danger.

There was a pause. Thrust was replaced by real gravity: lower than surface-normal, but genuine enough that Kelly felt himself and the couch on which he lay begin to fall backward.

Instinct then told him falsely that there had been a total propulsion failure. His mind flashed him images of air crashes he had seen, craters rimmed with flesh and metal shredded together like colored tinsel, all lighted by the flare of burning fuel—

Fuel. And the slamming acceleration resumed. The chambers began valving the internal hydrogen as reaction mass in place of the atmosphere which had become too thin to sustain the laser-powered ferry's upward momentum.

This was *worse* than insertion by parachute—at least Kelly'd done that before. If the Nazis didn't scare him any worse than the manner of the reaching them was doing, he was still going to wind up the mission with white hair.

Though that, unlike carrots for the eyes, *was* wholly myth.

Because operation of the monocle ferry was new to Kelly, the occurrence of something that would have amazed Dr. Desmond did not cause the veteran to wonder what was happening. The reaction chambers continued to blast in rapid succession, but the feeling of acceleration faded into apparent weightlessness. Only then did the vibration stop, leaving Kelly to think about when and how Wun and his fellows would reach the ferry.

Whether they would reach the ferry.

And then the cockpit opened, the two halves moving apart as smoothly as if they were driven by hydraulic jacks instead of the arms of gray, naked monsters like the creature dead at Fort Meade.

Kelly's first thought was that the pair of aliens stood in hard vacuum, having somehow walked to the rising ferry without a ship of their own. He began to lift himself against the cockpit coaming, gripping the metal firmly with his thick gloves for fear of drifting away. There was, to the veteran's surprise—weren't they in orbit?—gravity after all; a slight fraction of what he was used to, perhaps a tenth, but enough to orient and anchor Kelly while he untangled his suited legs.

The monocle ferry floated against light-absorbent blackness that held it as solidly as had Earth gravity and the concrete pad. The aliens who had undogged the cockpit had firm footing also, on something invisible a hand's breadth above the mirrored surface.

Kelly could see the monocle ferry, his own suited limbs, and the aliens clearly, though without the depth that shadows would have given. There was, however, no apparent source of light nor any sign of stars, of the Sun, or of the Earth, whose sunlit surface should have filled much of the spherical horizon at this low altitude.

The veteran was still supporting himself on the lip of the cockpit. Grimacing, he took his hand away and found that he did not fall back onto the seat. He reached down into the cockpit for the equipment he had brought with him, noticing that he moved without resistance but that, apart from volitional actions, his body stayed exactly where he had last put it.

"Very well done, Mr. Kelly," said Wun's voice through the helmet earphones that Kelly had not reconnected. "How much time do you need before we place you at your Fortress?"

"Wun, can you hear me?" Kelly asked, turning and wondering whether he should open his face shield. The two visible aliens, stepping back on nothing now, wore no clothing, protective or otherwise.

Wun stood a few yards behind the veteran. Unlike his fellows, he wore a business suit and a human face which was at the moment smiling. "Yes," he said, his lips in synch with the voice in Kelly's earphones, "very well. And please do not open your helmet. It will not be necessary."

"Yeah, right," said Kelly. He pursed his lips. "Wun, where the *hell* are we?"

"It does what a ship does," said the alien. "Therefore I described it as a ship. We will be able to return you to Earth whenever you please now that you have reached here."

"Yeah, that's great," said Kelly, checking his equipment. Looked okay; and if it wasn't, he'd use the shotgun that weighted his right leg. Hell, he'd tear throats out with his teeth if that was what it took to get the job done.

Or he'd die trying . . . but that would mean he failed, and failure wasn't acceptable.

"How quick can you get me to Fortress?" the veteran asked, returning to Wun's initial question but not answering it until he had further data.

"Momentarily, Thomas Kelly," said the alien, bobbing his head in what was either an Oriental gesture or something indigenous to his own inhuman species.

"Okay," Kelly said, a place holder while he thought. He met the alien's eyes, or what passed for eyes in the human simulacrum. "You showed me—the dream, I mean—the balance half of the dumbbell was blown open. If that's still the case, can you land me at that opening instead of the docking hub?"

"Yes," Wun said simply, bobbing again.

"You know—" Kelly began and caught himself. Of *course* the aliens knew that the lobes were spinning around their common center. If Wun said they could land him there, that meant they would match velocities and land him there.

Now that he was within the alien "ship," he could understand Wun's confidence at being able to avoid the radars and X-ray lasers guarding the space station. Previously, he had taken the alien's word for that simply because there wasn't a damn thing to be done if Wun was talking through his hat.

The Nazis had probably achieved surprise by approaching in a wholly-unexpected trajectory, claiming to be from the American lunar base when they were finally challenged—and having only a minimal German crew with the Kurdish shock troops aboard the leading saucers, the ones that would take the salvos of Fortress's close-in defenses. Even so, the highest leaders of the Dienst would have waited well apart from the attack, in Antarctica or on the Moon, until the issue was decided.

"Okay," said Kelly again, hefting his gear. "Gimme a hand with this. It's been modified to strap on me, but the suit doesn't bend so well I can even get the straps over my shoulders myself."

He was starting to breathe fast. Hell, he'd hyperventilate on oxygen if he didn't watch out. "And then," the veteran concluded, "you set me aboard Fortress. And keep your fingers crossed."

Between the air supply on his back and the weapons pack slung across his chest, Tom Kelly looked like a truckload of bottles mounted on legs. The bulk felt friendly, though, even without the weight that should have accompanied it.

The thing that nobody who directed war movies understood—and why should they? It would have come as news to rear echelons in all the various armies as well—was that the guys at the sharp end carried it all on their backs.

The irreducible minimum for life in a combat zone was water, arms and munitions, and food. In most environments, heavy clothing or shelter had to be factored in as well; exposure in a hilltop trench would kill you just as dead as a bullet.

Helicopters were fine, but they weren't going to land while you lay baking on a bare hillside traversed by enemy guns; so you carried water in gallons, not quarts, and it was life itself. If you ran out of ammo, they'd cut you apart with split bamboo if that was what they had . . . so you carried extra bandoliers and extra grenades, and a pistol of your own because the rifle you were issued was going to jam at the worst possible time, no matter who designed it or how hard you tried to keep it clean.

Besides that, you carried a belt of ammo for one of the overburdened machinegunners or a trio of shells for the poor bastard with the mortar tube on his back. You were all in it together; and besides, when the shit hit the fan you were going to need heavy-weapons support.

And the chances were that, if you were really trying to get the jump on the elusive other side, you had a case of rations to hump with you as well. Every time a resupply bird whop-whopped to you across hostile terrain, it fingered you for the enemy and guaranteed that engagement would be on the enemy's terms.

So you didn't move very fast, but you moved, and you did your job of kicking butt while folks in strack uniforms crayoned little boxes and arrows on acetate-covered maps, learnedly discussing your location. That was the way the world worked; and that was why Tom Kelly felt subconsciously better for the equipment slung on his body as he shuffled into combat.

"All right," Kelly said with his shotgun drawn in his right hand and his left extended to grasp the first hold chance offered. Recoil from the charge of buckshot would accelerate the veteran right out of business if he hadn't anchored himself before he fired. Not that there was supposed to be anybody in this half of Fortress.

"Just walk forward, Mr. Kelly," said Wun's voice, "as if it were a beaded curtain."

There wasn't supposed to be a gang of Nazis in control of Fortress, period—if you were going to get hung up on supposed-to-bes.

"Right," said Tom Kelly, shifting his weight and stepping through a wall that was nothing, not even color, into Fortress.

The alien ship—the *place*, if even that did not imply too much—from which Kelly stepped could be seen only as an absence of the things which should have been visible behind it, and even that only in a seven-foot disk without discernible thickness. The disk, which could only be the point of impingement between the universe which Kelly knew and wherever the hell the aliens were, rotated at the same speed as the space station, so that the veteran had not expected to notice motion as he stepped aboard Fortress.

He had forgotten the shielding doughnut of lunar slag within which the two lobes of the dumbbell spun at a relative velocity of almost two hundred miles an hour. The gap between the portal and the space station was only a few inches wide, but that was enough to give Kelly the impression that he was watching a gravel road through the rusted-out floorboards of a speeding car. This job was assuredly finding unique ways to give him the willies.

The first thing he noticed when his feet hit the bare aluminum planking of the dumbbell's floor was that he had weight again, real weight, although not quite the load that he would have been carrying in full Earth gravity. Fortress spun at a rate which gave it approximately .8 g's at the floor level of either dumbbell. The arms revolved at nearly two revolutions per minute, fast enough to displace a dropping object several inches from where it would have fallen under the pull of gravity instead of centrifugal force. It would play hell with marksmanship also, but Kelly with his gloves and helmet hadn't the least chance of target accuracy anyway.

The corpse in the SS uniform lay exactly where it had in Kelly's dream.

The chamber was brightly illuminated by sunlight reflected through the solar panels above. Where it fell on the dead Kurd, his skin appeared shrunken and darker than it had been during life—a shade close to that of waxed mahogany. One outflung hand was shaded by a structural member, however, and it gleamed with a tracery of hoarfrost. Ice was crystallizing from the corpse's body fluids and from there subliming into vacuum, leaving behind the rind of a man that would not age or spoil if it lay here until the heat death of the universe.

Perhaps houris were ministering to ben Majlis's soul in Paradise. Ben Majlis deserved that as much as any soldier did; and as little.

The next part was tricky. Kelly stepped past ben Majlis's body to reach the door the Kurd had tried to open. The doors of Fortress did not lock, but it was possible that the Nazis had welded this one shut before blowing their Kurdish cannon fodder into the void at the end of their perceived usefulness. If the door *was* welded, Kelly would have to punch his entrance with explosives, and that was almost certain to warn those who had taken over the station.

Awkward because of his glove and the fact he was

using only his left hand on a mechanism meant for two, Kelly rotated the large aluminum wheel that latched the door between this compartment and the remainder of Fortress. The dogs freed with no more than the hesitation to be expected when plates of aluminum are left in contact long enough for their oxide coatings to creep together.

The agent pulled. Nothing gave. His lips curled to rip out a curse; and as he reached back for the self-adhesive strip charge hanging in a roll from his left hip, he noticed that the panel was beveled to open away from him instead of toward him as the plans and instructor on the Airborne Command Post had assured him. Somebody had misread the specs, or else the construction crew had reasonably decided that it didn't matter a hoot in hell which way they hung the doors so long as the seal was good.

Kelly hit the panel with a shoulder backed with all his mass and that of the equipment he carried. The seal popped enough to spray air from around half the circumference. Then the door opened fully, and the veteran lurched inside behind his shotgun.

The air that escaped around Kelly scattered and softened the light which until then had lain flat on the panel of aluminum/ceramic fiber sandwich. It ruffled the sleeve of ben Majlis's uniform as it surged past, but it lacked the force and volume that would have been required to eject the corpse from the open chamber.

As soon as he was inside the undamaged compartment, Kelly thrust the door shut and fell to his knees with the ill-controlled effort. Despite the air that had puffed into the void, the residual pressure within the compartment slammed the door firmly against the seals.

This compartment was about as empty as the one whose wall had been blown away. It had attachment points up and down both long walls, but nothing was slung from them and there were no bodies on the floor. The vertical lighting did display a line of oval punctures stitched at chest height across one wall: bullet holes punched at an angle through the metal facing but swallowed harmlessly by the glass core—all save one which was covered by a piece of Speedtape. Somebody from the original complement of Fortress had made it this far; and then, no doubt, made it into vacuum as just another body, shortly to be followed by the Kurds who had gunned him down.

And now it was the turn of the Nazis.

The atmosphere-exchange vents which had swung closed when air surged through the open door had reopened when the pressure drop ceased, bringing the chamber back in balance with the remainder of the space station. Kelly turned the inner door wheel to lock the dogs home, keeping his eyes and gun on the door at the far end of the chamber.

The quantity of air lost when Kelly entered the space station had probably registered somewhere; but since the "leak" had shut off immediately, the new owners of Fortress would probably not notice anything amiss. The pointed shotgun was cheap insurance, however . . . and by the time Kelly had finished latching the door, he was sure that the chamber's oxygen level had returned what was normal for Fortress, a partial pressure equal to that of Earth at sea level, although the quantity of nitrogen in the atmosphere was only half that of Earth by unit volume.

With the atmosphere back to normal, Kelly could

unlimber the flamethrower he had brought as his primary weapon.

The two cross-connected napalm tanks and the smaller air bottle which pressurized them weighed almost fifty pounds here, even though all were constructed of aluminum. The flame gun itself had a pistol grip with a bar trigger for the fuel valve, easily grasped and used despite Kelly's protective clothing. The ignition lever just behind the nozzle was of similar handy size.

The veteran went to the far end of the compartment and twisted the latch wheel of the door which would be, according to the plans, the central one of the five in this lobe of the dumbbell. Then, with his hands on both controls of the flame gun, he kicked the panel open.

The third compartment was stacked with crated supplies, primarily foodstuffs, and one cage of the dual elevators waited beside the helical staircase which also led toward the hub. There was nothing alive to see Kelly burst through the doorway.

Each of the elevator shafts was fifteen feet in diameter, large enough to handle any cargo which could be ferried to orbit on existing hardware. The elevators' size had determined the thickness of the spokes connecting the lobes of the dumbbell to the hub, since strength requirements could have been met by spokes thinner than the thirty-five feet or so of the present structure.

The elevators were intended to move simultaneously and in opposite directions, one cage rising as the other fell, though in an emergency the pair could be decoupled. As a further preparation for emergency, stairs were built into part of the spoke diameter left over when the elevator shafts were laid out, and it was this staircase by which Kelly had intended to cross to the hub.

Using the elevator that gaped like a holding cell would be crazy, Kelly thought as he shuffled to the stairs. With one hand on the railing to keep from overbalancing, he bent backwards to look up the helical staircase. Dabs of light blurred like beads on a string on the steps and the closed elevator shafts beside which the steps proceeded upward. From the bottom they seemed an interminable escalade.

Hell, he'd take the elevator. If he weren't crazy, he'd have stayed home.

Kelly hadn't been briefed on the elevators, but the controls could scarcely have been simpler. The door was a section of the cage's cylindrical wall. It slid around on rollered tracks at top and bottom when Kelly pulled at its staple-shaped handle. The door did not latch, nor did there appear to be any interlock between it and the elevator control.

After considering the situation for a moment, Kelly slid the door open again, faced it, and prodded the single palm-sized button on the cage wall with the muzzle of the flame gun. Nothing happened for long enough that the veteran reached for the door handle again, convinced that he must have been wrong about the interlock. The cage staggered into upward motion before his arm completed its motion. There was simply a delay built into its operation, probably tied to a warning signal in the other elevator, which would start at the same time.

That might or might not be important. Holding the flame gun in a two-handed grip, Kelly grinned toward the elevator shaft that slid past his open door.

He did not see the metal sheathing, however. His mind was trying to imagine the face of the next person it would direct the veteran's hands to kill. Over the years, he had come surprisingly close a number of times. . . .

The elevator shaft was almost nine hundred feet high—or long, in a manner of speaking, because the cage ceased to go "up" as it neared the hub and the effect of centrifugal force lessened. The drive was hydraulic and very smooth after the initial jerk as the pumps cut in. As the impellers pressurized the column to raise the cage in which Kelly rode, they drew a partial vacuum in the other column to drag the cage down from hub level. Ordinary cable operation would not work in the absence of true gravity, and a cogged-rail system like that of some mountain railways would have put unbalanced stresses on the spokes, whose thickness and mass would have had to be greatly increased to avoid warping.

The portion of the design that was critical at the moment was the fact that the pumps were in the lobe, not at the hub, and that the elevator's operation was therefore effectively silent at the inner end. It didn't mean that the approaching cage would not be noticed; but at least there would be no squalling take-up spool to rivet the attention of all those in the hub on the elevator shaft.

Kelly's hands were clammy, though his gloves would keep them from slipping on the triggers of the flame gun. This wasn't like Istanbul, where he was in too deep too quickly to think. Three hundred yards, three football fields end to end, with the cage moving at the speed of a man walking fast. Plenty of time to review the faces of the men you'd already killed—only the ones you'd really *seen*, not the lumps sprawled like piles of laundry on the ground you'd raked. . . .

Some people had nightmares about the times they'd almost bought the farm themselves. Kelly saw instead faces distorted by pain or rage or the shock waves of the bullet already splashing flesh to the side. He was as likely to awaken screaming as those who feared their own death; and he was surely as likely to slug his brain with alcohol to blur the memories he knew it could not erase.

But it was the only thing Tom Kelly did that his gut knew he could win at, and he was only really alive during those rare moments that he was winning.

The edge of the spherical hub began to rotate past the open door of the cage. A gray-haired woman in a skirt and bemedaled jacket glanced over her shoulder toward the cage. Kelly squeezed the valve lever in the pistol grip and, as the nozzle began to buck, fired an ignition cartridge with the lever under his left hand.

Recoil from Kelly's shot, a five-pound stream of napalm, thrust him back against the wall of the elevator cage, but that was of no significance to the effect of the short burst. The veteran had only a momentary glimpse past the uniformed woman before his flame obliterated the scene, but there were at least two dozen figures in the center of the hub. They all wore formal uniforms and were attempting to stand braced in formation, despite the tendency to float in the absence of gravity.

Kelly's flame devoured them. The effect of his weapon under these conditions was beyond anything he had seen or dreamed of on Earth.

The compressed air tank could send the jet of fuel fifty yards, even with gravity to pull it down. Here it easily splashed the thickened gasoline off the far side of the hub, barely a hundred feet from the weapon. The lowered air pressure, half that of Earth, combined with the high relative oxygen level to turn what would have been a narrow jet of flame into a fireball which exploded across the open area like the flame-front filling the cylinder of a gasoline engine on the power stroke.

The gush of orange blinded Kelly and kicked him back against the wall from which he had begun to recoil from the thrust of the napalm itself. The suit he wore was designed to protect its wearer against the unshielded power of the Sun and insulate him against the cold of objects which had radiated all their heat into the insatiable black maw of vacuum. Its design parameters were sufficient to shield him here against the second of ravenous flame he had released. Blinking and wishing he had flipped down the sunshield over his faceplate before he fired, Kelly thrust himself off the wall of the stationary elevator and into the hub proper.

The great domed room was filled with violent motion. Smoke and occasional beads of napalm still afire swirled in the shock waves rebounding from the curved walls.

The men and women who had shared the room with the fireball cavorted now like gobbets spewed from a Roman candle. Their hair and uniforms blazed, fanned by the screaming, frantic efforts of the victims to extinguish them. Nazis, blinded as their eyeballs bubbled, collided with one another and sailed off across the dome on random courses, pinwheeling slowly.

Slender poles were set every twenty feet or so in the floor and walls of the room to give purchase to those who, like Kelly at present, were drifting without adequate control. The veteran snagged one of the wands in the crook of his left arm. He locked his body against it to kill the spin he had been given by the elevator cage which rotated with the spoke. When he had anchored himself, he was able to survey the room and the possible threats it held.

The bodies, some corpses and some still in the process of dying, which drifted like lazy blowflies over carrion, were no danger to anyone. A touch on the back of Kelly's leg caused him to twist in panic, cursing the way the helmet limited his peripheral vision. Something smoldering had brushed him, surrounded by a mist of blood from lungs which had hemorrhaged when they sucked in flame.

Here in the hub there was a walkway seven feet wide at the point the spokes mated with it and the elevators debouched.

The plane of the walkway was continued by solid flooring across the hub, so that the sphere was separated into slightly unequal volumes. The larger one was the open, northern portion which served for zero-gravity transport between the lobes and from them through the docking module to the rest of the universe. Beneath the flooring, the other moiety of the hub was given over to the controls which ruled both the defensive array and the three thousand fusion warheads waiting for the command that would trip their retro rockets to set them on the path to reentry.

The elevators to the other lobe of the dumbbell were not moving, and the circular doorway to the control section was closed and flush with the floor across which Kelly's boots floated. The portal to the docking module above him, however, at the north pole, was sphinctering open. Keeping the pole within the circle of his arms, Kelly leaned backward and aimed the flame gun toward the opening portal.

The recoil of two gallons of thickened gasoline shoved him down against the floor this time, but the pole anchored him well enough to send most of the three-second burst into the docking module. Ammunition carried by some of the men inside blew up with a violence that sprayed bits of metal, plastic, and bodies down into the dome.

Only after the explosion did it occur to Kelly to wonder whose arrival had caused the personnel who had conquered Fortress to draw themselves up for inspection. Well, it didn't matter now.

The second jet of flame, though of longer duration than the first, had a more limited effect because the chamber's oxygen had been depleted faster than the ventilation system could replenish it. Napalm spluttered, each drop wrapped in a cloud of black smoke as it drifted lazily back toward Kelly.

It was time to move anyway. He dropped the flame gun and let it trail behind him from its hose as he thrust himself toward the control room door.

The doorway was surrounded by a waist-high trio of inverted U's made of aluminum girder. There was room for a man, even suited and laden as Tom Kelly was, to walk between each adjacent pair, but the U's provided not only handholds the way the wands did but also protection for the doorway in the event that any high-inertia object sailed down from the docking module.

Kelly braked himself left-handed, tensing his muscles fiercely to halt his considerable mass without using his gun hand as well. The trigger guard of his shotgun had been cut away so that he could use the weapon with gloves. He was by no means certain that his motor control in his present garb was fine enough that he could count on not putting a charge of shot god knew where. He might well need all five of the rounds in the gun. The door handle was a flat semicircle that the veteran had to flip up before he could turn it. The men who briefed him on the Airborne Command Post assured him there was no locking mechanism, but that didn't mean the Nazis hadn't welded a bolt in place after they took over. There was the explosive tape if they had, but—

The handle turned. Kelly swung the door up, gripping a stanchion between his booted feet so that he could point the shotgun muzzle down the opening with his right hand. If the job Kelly set himself had been to clear Fortress of the Nazis who had captured it, he would have squirted his remaining gallon of napalm into the control room before he went in himself with the shotgun. Some of the men arguing on the Airborne Command Post had considered that at least the most desirable option.

The trouble was that the Soviets, driven to the wall by the fact of Fortress, had almost certainly been pushed beyond that point when the weapon was actually used against them. If something very final did not convince

Moscow of America's good faith, the Soviets would themselves precipitate the holocaust they assumed was certain in any event.

And a final, unequivocal act of good faith meant that the controls had to be intact.

Kelly went through the doorway, swinging the panel closed behind him against the rain of napalm—though most of the droplets had sputtered to expanding globes of soot by now. He expected someone to meet him in the enclosed hallway—a squad of aroused gunmen at worst, at best a trembling technician left on watch while the ceremony went on above. But there was no one in the hall, and no one in the computer rooms past which the veteran drifted, their cryonic circuitry made practicable by radiation through heat exchangers on the shaded surface of the station.

Even the control room itself, at Fortress's south pole, was empty, though the defensive array was live and programmed, according to its warning lights, for automatic engagement.

He couldn't possibly have been the one who had been arriving? Christ, he'd have been almost a century old. Though in a low-gravity environment like the Moon . . .

It didn't matter. There was a job to do.

The control room of Fortress was designed to have three officers on duty at all times. Under full War Emergency Orders any two of the consoles could be slaved to the third—with an appropriate accompaniment of lights and sirens. The arrangement was a concession to the paired facts that nobody in his right mind wanted a single individual to have the end of the world under his fingertip—and that if Fortress really had to be *used*, there wasn't going to be time to screw around with authorization and confirmation codes.

The Nazis had, as expected, linked the consoles already. Kelly unstrapped the flamethrower and settled himself into the seat at the master unit, drawing himself down by chair arms deliberately set wide enough to fit a man in a space suit. There was a palm latch that would have permitted Kelly to move the back cushion to clear his life-support package. Rather than fool with nonessentials, he scrunched forward, aimed the waiting light pen at the screen, and began to press the large buttons.

Kelly was not trained to operate the console, to understand the steps of what he was doing. There had been neither time nor need for that aboard the Airborne Command Post. This was rote memory, the same sort of learning that permitted his fingers to strip and reassemble a fifty-caliber machinegun in the dark.

There were twelve weapons in the first rota which the Nazis had punched up on the screen. Their targets were given as twelve-digit numbers, not names—zip codes to hell. Warhead data appeared on the line beneath each target designator. The first target was selected for a 1.1 megaton warhead. Rather than change those parameters, Kelly flashed his light pen to target two, already set for a 5 megaton weapon, and engaged the launch sequence with the button whose cage was already unlocked.

When the launch button was pressed the first time, the printing on the screen switched from green-on-white to black-on-yellow. All data for the other weapons in the rota shrank down into a sidebar in the left corner, while ten additional data lines for the selected target appeared in large print. A black-on-red engagement clock began to run down from 432 in the upper left corner.

Kelly drew the light pen down the screen to the seventh data line, time delay, and pressed the cancel button. The number 971 blinked to yellow-on-black. Kelly keyed in the digit one, bending awkwardly to see the alphanumeric pad through the curve of his faceplate. He palmed the Execute key.

A gong went off loudly enough that Kelly heard and felt it through his suit. The top two inches of the screen pulsed Invalid Command in blue and yellow. The engagement clock continued to run down, but the top half of its digits changed from red to blue. Kelly hit the Execute button again. The data line changed from 791 to 1, and the visual and aural alarms ceased.

The veteran's hand reached for the Launch button to confirm. He was warned that something was happening behind him, not by the sound but rather because when the door to the north section of the hub opened it reflected a shimmer of light across the console at which Kelly was working.

Reflex sent his hand to his gun instead of completing the motion it had started; instinct wrapped his gloved fingers around the butt of the weapon he had laid across his lap, though he could neither see nor feel it, garbed as he was. He twisted in the seat.

Three men, all of them wearing what looked more like aircraft pressure suits than anything intended for hard vacuum, were groping hand over hand down the passageway, past the computer rooms. Kelly fired before he could see whether or not the newcomers were armed. He had to aim overhead, and, even though gravity was not a factor, the awkwardness of the position made the fact that his buckshot missed almost inevitable.

The newcomers were in straggling echelon across the width of the passage, so one pellet glancing from the wall paneling gouged its way across the flank of the rearmost man—without drawing blood. The cut-down shotgun recoiled viciously from the heavy charge, making the veteran's right palm tingle through the glove. Kelly clamped his left hand on the fore-end before triggering a second round.

If the trio of newcomers had startled Kelly, then the clumsiness with which they started to unsling the submachine guns they did in fact carry suggested that they had not recognized him as an enemy until that moment. The veteran could not tell whether they came from the other lobe of the dumbbell, from the docking module and the vessels positioned there, or even from some other location. All that mattered was that the chest of the nearest surrounded the front sight of the shotgun as Kelly squeezed off.

Recoil thrust the veteran against the seat cushion as he swung the muzzle toward the next man; the buckshot punched a dozen ragged holes through the first target's chest in a pattern the size of a dinner plate. Kinetic energy chopped the victim backward, into his fellows, with his limbs windmilling and a spray of blood swirling from the pellet holes.

The third of the newcomers fired wildly as the dead man tangled with him, the muzzle blasts cracking sharply despite Kelly's muffling helmet. The veteran switched his aim to the man who had his gun clear. He fired, shattering the face shield and hitting the target's own weapon with several pellets which drove it off on a course separate from that of the man who had used it.

The German in the middle of the group still had not managed to unsling his gun when Kelly's buckshot slammed his lower abdomen and spun him back up the aisle. The center of the passageway was now a fog of blood.

Kelly paused a fraction of a second to be sure that the trio's movements were the disconnected thrashing of dying men. Then he turned his head down to the console and the screen on which the engagement clock had run down to 221 seconds. Enough time. He thumped the Launch button again, setting the new parameters which would detonate the 5 megaton warhead one second after Fortress released the reentry vehicle.

There wasn't a prayer of getting out the way he had entered the space station, but the docking module was a relatively short path to vacuum. There was at least a chance that Wun would be waiting wherever Kelly exited Fortress. Might as well hope that, because otherwise Kelly didn't have a snowball's chance in hell of surviving.

He launched himself up the passageway, suddenly terrified by knowledge that in a little over three minutes, Fortress was going to reach the orbital position from which it would automatically release the weapon he had cued.

Thrust in weightlessness had its own rules. The veteran moved in a surprisingly straight line, but his body tumbled slowly end over end, so that he had to catch himself with his free hand on the jamb of a computer-room doorway at the midpoint of the aisle. One of the men Kelly had just killed floated in the same doorway. The German looked to have been about Kelly's age when he died . . . and there was a radio with a loaded whip antenna set into the right side of his helmet.

The veteran, poised to jump the rest of the way to the door, had an instant to wonder what his victims might have reported. The burst of fire from the doorway answered the question even as it was being formed.

Lighting in the passageway was dimmer than that in the domed room above, and the gunman was sighting past the bodies of his fellows besides; his target was not Kelly, lost among the corpses, but rather the motion down by the control console. The burst of submachine gun fire rang on the flamethrower twisting gently in the air currents, rupturing the pressure tank with a bang louder than that of Kelly returning the shots from his doorway.

The last charge of buckshot lifted the German, now faceless, up in a slow arc toward the top of the dome.

The flamethrower air bottle was still pressurized to several hundred atmospheres when it burst, so bits of it gouged deep holes in the aluminum panels nearby. The control consoles had been protected from the blast by the napalm tanks, so the engagement clock continued to count down, unimpaired.

Kelly snatched the submachine gun, a Walther, from the unresisting fingers of the body beside him. The three-shot burst he fired emptied the doorway of the figures already poking guns over the circular lintel . . . but there was no way the veteran was going to escape in that direction.

He pushed himself fiercely back toward the control consoles. No one had briefed him on the way to abort a launch sequence, and the clock was down to 97 seconds. A shot through the console or bursts into each of the incredibly complex computers up the hall would probably shut down the operation—but that would not save Kelly, only delay his end until hostile manpower overwhelmed him, and it would pretty well guarantee the failure of his mission. Fortress contained too many warheads for their release onto Earth, even unguided, to be an empty threat.

Tom Kelly was a fox with hounds waiting to rend him at the mouth of his burrow. Well then, he'd dig out the back—and if it didn't work, it was still a long step up from resigning himself to his fate.

The south pole of the hub, like the north with its docking module, was clear of the doughnut of shielding which surrounded the lobes of the dumbbell. Kelly flattened himself against the curve of the control-room floor which corresponded to the roof of the dome at the other axis. Locking his boots around the chair bolted in front of a console, the veteran reeled off a strip of his blasting tape. He was duck soup for any gunman who came through the door just now—but if the survivors weren't more cautious than their fellows had been, they were bloody suicidal.

The adhesive was only on one side of the thick tape, so when Kelly folded the strip at an angle to make a corner, the second length did not stick to the bulkhead against which it lay. Fucking bad design, but he should have checked it on the ground himself, and anyway it'd have to do. . . .

Kelly stuck down the third side of the square he was taping as a long burst of automatic fire squirted from the north side of the sphere. The muzzle blasts were blurred by the helmet and the shots' confusion, with their own multiple echoes, but the ringing of bullets which hit the bulkhead near Kelly was clear enough. Dust puffed, and the tip of his left little finger, extending the final length of tape, flicked away from a hole in the aluminum.

The veteran had been wounded in worse ways, but nothing had *hurt* him like this since an ant buried its mandibles in the joint of his big toe. Kelly screamed and crimped the igniter lever in the end of the roll an instant sooner than he had intended. Five seconds—and at least the pain of his missing fingertip as he lunged away gave him something to think about besides the blast radius and the question of whether the gunman was aiming shots or just spraying them down the passageway.

There was movement in the direction of the door, the floating bodies twisting under the impact of bullets and fresh men plunging down the passage to finish the job. The submachine gun Kelly had appropriated had vanished, drifted off unnoticed while the veteran worked with the blasting tape. He looked desperately for the gun, wondering if the Nazi bullets had already shattered the launch control mechanism. The attackers were acting with a furious disregard for the equipment on whose capture they had invested so much effort. Maybe they—

The outline of PETN explosive blew a square out of the bulkhead so sharply that a green haze quivered along Kelly's optic nerves. He dived forward blindly, over the console that had shielded him from his own blast and into the stream of air rushing out the opening. Vacuum would not affect the suited Germans, but neither should it harm the control-room hardware. The shock of the blast might or might not cause an abort. It'd be okay if the designers had done a proper job of isolating the computer banks from the structure of Fortress, and it was too late to worry about that anyway.

Kelly's head and the hands he had thrown up to protect his faceshield were sucked neatly through the opening, but his thighs slammed the edge. He hadn't realized just how fierce was the outrush until that blow; it felt as though a horse had kicked him with both hind legs. Kelly spun head over heels from the space station, like a diver in an event which would continue throughout eternity for anything he could do to change it.

The tip of his left little finger stung. The veteran reached for it instinctively with the other hand and squeezed the glove instead against the portion of finger above the second joint—the part that remained. The tears that burned worse than the blood freezing on the stump were not shed for pain but rather for loss. A part of Tom Kelly's body was gone as surely as his youth and his innocence.

The plume of air from the hub was dazzling where the reflection of the north polar mirror caught it. Closer to the hull from which it spewed, the venting atmosphere was a gray translucence lighted only by rays scattered higher in the plume.

The array of nuclear weapons through which Kelly tumbled was as black and brutal as a railroad marshaling yard at midnight.

The weapons that were Fortress's reason for being were anchored to the south hub by a tracery of girders, balancing the docking module and lighting mirror at the other pole of the axis. In schematic, the framework suggested precise randomness like that of a black widow spider's web, each crossing of strands supporting a nodule of thermonuclear warheads. The blunt curves of individual reentry vehicles were encased in aluminum pallets which supported clusters of small solid-fuel rockets.

The rocket motors simply counteracted the orbital momentum which each bomb shared as part of the space station. The pallet dropped away from the reentry vehicle after no more than thirty seconds of burn. For the remainder of its course, the warhead followed a ballistic trajectory governed by the same principles which had controlled the projectile fired by a fourteenth century bombard.

It was only after the reentry vehicle reached its target that advanced technology took over again, and the warhead detonated with more force than all of the explosives used in all the wars until that time.

There was no sign of the aliens who Kelly had prayed would meet him.

He had come out of the hub at an angle, but the nest of warheads was spread widely. Kelly saw that at each of his own slow rotations, an outlying node of bombs—six of them attachéd like petals to a common center—was growing in silhouette against the blue-white splendor of Earth. Distance was hard to judge in the absence of scale and atmosphere, but it looked as if the array were going to be close enough to touch.

The bomb should have gone off by now; he had drifted

for what seemed at least five minutes. His strip charge or the flying bullets must have aborted the sequence. Kelly twisted, trying to follow the framework as it floated behind his head. He could not move even his body for lack of a fulcrum, but if he could catch hold of some solid object he could halt himself. Then he could wait for the aliens. Or for the Germans to locate and riddle him. Or for the moment he emptied the air pack from which he had been breathing since the monocle ferry was sealed.

The bombs were coming into sight again, past Kelly's toes. He *was* going to collide with them; the retro rockets of the nearest were within two yards and growing as the—

The rockets fired.

There was a puff of exhaust that clouded the metal from the ablative coating of the reentry vehicle itself. Then the cold vapors became three glowing blossoms while the bomb broke away from the cluster, the equivalent of five million tons of TNT fused to detonate one second after release.

With a horrified scream in his throat, Tom Kelly drifted through an invisible portal that left him collapsed at the feet of Wun, who still looked like a swarthy businessman, in his human suit and face.

When Kelly wanted to watch the destruction of Fortress a third time, the aliens looped the final twenty seconds of the event and played it over and over while they worked on the human's finger.

"Does that hurt, Mr. Kelly?" Wun asked through the speakers of the helmet now resting beside Kelly.

"Just a little," said the veteran, though his wince a moment before had been diagnostic. "Look, it's okay."

Three aliens with no concession to human design or accoutrement bent over Kelly's outstretched left hand. Beyond them and seemingly as much a part of present reality as the five figures—theirs and Kelly's and Wun's— hung a vision of Fortress from about a kilometer away. The doughnut was viewed at a flat angle from the south pole, so that the four saucers at the docking module were partly visible over the curve of shielding material. Dora had joined her three dull-finished aluminum sisters and was linked to Fortress by an umbilicus.

The webbing holding the nuclear weapons was illuminated by a flash so intense that aluminum became translucent and only the warheads themselves remained momentarily black.

Most or all of the weapons which absorbed the sleet of radiation from the first 5 megaton warhead also detonated a microsecond later. Fortress—the space station, the saucers which had brought the Nazis to it, and the kilotons of shielding material—became vapor and a retinal memory in a blast that devoured the entire field of view . . . and faded back to the start of the explosion.

"Mr. Kelly," said Wun peevishly, "the question is not whether you can *stand* the pain but rather if we can eliminate it. Which we can do unless you pretend stoical indifference."

Another of the aliens poked toward (though not *to*) the stump of Kelly's finger with an instrument that looked like a miniature orange flyswatter. "Does *that* hurt?"

"There's a dull ache on the—the lower side," said the

veteran, pointing with his right index finger. He hated to look at the amputation, though the aliens had closed the wound neatly with something pink the texture of fresh skin. He'd get used to the loss, as he'd gotten used to other things.

The orange instrument twisted. The ache disappeared. Fortress vaporized again in the ambiance beyond.

"Where will you have us place you when your injury is repaired, Mr. Kelly?" asked Wun, his eyes on Kelly while his voice came disconcertingly from the helmet at an angle to the figure.

"You're going to get in touch with governments now?" Kelly said. Lord knew what that blast would do to communications on the planet below, but there'd be auroras to tell the grandkids about. There'd *be* grandkids for those who wanted them, and that made it worthwhile. "Formal contact, I mean?"

Hell, it'd have been worthwhile if Tom Kelly had become part of the ball of glowing plasma he'd created with the help of Wun and a lot of luck. And whatever.

"We can return you to the base from which you were launched into orbit, for instance," said Wun. The other three aliens stepped back as if to admire the repair work they had completed on the human's finger. It was as perfect as it could be without the portion the bullet had excised.

The loop of destruction flared again. Cheap at the price.

"I've been told in worse ways I oughta mind my own business," said Kelly, grinning at Wun. "And no, I don't want to go back to El Paso any time soon."

The stocky human stood up and stretched. It felt good to move without the bulk of the suit, good to breathe air that smelled like Earth's on a spring day. It felt very good to win one unequivocally.

It would have felt even better to have forgotten the scene in the dome as he left it, the drifting, smoking bodies. At the time, that part had seemed like a win also. . . .

"No," he said, "there's a couple people I owe . . . I dunno, maybe an explanation. Maybe just a chance to take a shot at me."

Kelly's face softened as he thought about his past, recent and farther back, as far as he could remember. "If I had good sense, I'd just walk away from that," he said. "But I never did have much use for people who walked away from things."

The three evident nonhumans had vanished. "You wish to be returned to the neighborhood of the woman Tuttle or the woman Romer?" said Wun, who either was psychic or understood how Kelly's mind worked better than anybody born on Earth seemed to have done.

"You can do that?" the veteran demanded.

"Either one," responded the alien. "Which would you prefer?"

"I—" began Tom Kelly. He laughed without humor, a sound as sharp as the warheads outlined against the first microsecond of the destruction of Fortress.

Then he reached into his trousers pocket to see if there were a coin he could flip.

The Following is an excerpt from:

MONSTER HUNTER LEGION

LARRY CORREIA

Available from Baen Books
September 2012
hardcover

⊰Chapter 1⊱

Most of the things Las Vegas has to offer to its hordes of tourists don't hold much appeal for me. Having been an accountant, I am way too good at math to enjoy gambling. As a former bouncer, I'm not big on the party scene. Strip clubs? Happily married to a total babe who could kill me from a mile away with her sniper rifle, so no thanks. Sure, there were plenty of other things to do in Vegas, like over-priced shows, taking your picture with Elvis, and that sort of thing, but as a professional Monster Hunter, I'm pretty jaded when it comes to what constitutes *excitement*.

However, there is one thing in Las Vegas' extensive, sparkling arsenal of tourist-from-their-dollars-separating weapons that I'm absolutely powerless to resist, and that is a kick ass buffet.

The flight in had taken forever and I was starving. So first thing upon arrival at our hotel, I had called up every other hungry member of Monster Hunter International that I could find and we'd set out to conquer the unsuspecting hotel buffet.

This was a business trip. Normally *business* for us meant that there was some horrible supernatural thing in dire need of a good killing, but not this time. Las Vegas was the site of the first annual *International Conference of Monster Hunting Professionals*.

The conference was a big deal. Sponsored by a wealthy organizer, the ultra-secret ICMHP 1 had been billed as an opportunity to network with other informed individuals, check out the latest gear and equipment, and listen to experts. There had never been an event like this before. Every member of MHI that could get away from work had come, and though we were the biggest company in the business, we were still outnumbered five to one by representatives of every other rival Monster Hunting company in the world. In addition there were representatives from all of the legitimate supernaturally-attuned organization and government agencies, all come together here to learn from each other. Despite just oozing with all of that professionalism, we had all taken to calling it *ick-mip* for short.

The conference started tomorrow morning, which for most of the Hunters meant a chance to party or gamble the night away, but for me, it was buffet time. As a very large, high-intensity lifestyle kind of guy, I burn a lot of calories. I may lose at the gambling table, but I never lose at the dinner table. Plus the food at the upscale establishments tended to be above average, and since Hunters made good money, my days of eating at the dumpy places were over. Besides, all of the ICMHP guests were staying at the new, ultra-swanky, not even totally open to the public yet, Last Dragon hotel. The Last

Dragon's buffet had actual master chefs from around the world, and was supposed to be one of the best new places to eat in town. The internet had said so, and who was I to argue with the Zagat survey?

My team had just gotten back from a grueling mission and most had simply wanted to crash. I'd only been able to coerce Trip Jones and Holly Newcastle into coming, though Holly had complained about watching her figure and said that she was going to *take it easy*. When it came to food I had no concept of easy. Despite his aversion to being around humans, Edward had been tempted by my wild tales of hundreds of yards of glorious meats, none of which needed to be chased down and stabbed to death first. However, his older brother and chieftain, Skippy, had forbidden it. Turns out that it is really difficult to eat in public with a face mask on. It is tough being an orc.

There had been an incoming flight due shortly with a couple of Newbies onboard, and Milo Anderson had volunteered to stay and be their ride to the hotel. Earl Harbinger had said these particular recruits were especially talented, so they'd earned the field trip. Lucky them. My Newbie field trip had been storming the *Antoine-Henri* and fighting wights.

Last but not least for my team, my lovely wife Julie had said she was tired, encouraged me not to hurt myself at dinner—she knows how I can sometimes be over-enthusiastic for things that come in serving sizes larger than my head—and then went to bed early. She had been feeling a little under the weather during the trip.

After ditching our luggage, which mostly consisted of

armor and guns, we'd snagged a few of the other Hunters staying on our floor. Most of the floors of the Last Dragon hotel was still in the finishing stages of construction so the place hadn't even had its grand opening yet. Officially, the hotel wasn't ready yet, but since ICMHP was supposed to be secret anyway, it was a perfect place for several hundred Hunters to stay, and the ICMHP organizers had even gotten us a killer discount. ICMHP would be the first ever event for its conference center, but luckily, the casino, shops, and—most important—restaurants were already open to the public.

"Wow . . ." Trip whistled as he looked down the endless food trays of the top-rated all-you-can-eat place on Earth. "That's one impressive spread." It really was. Lots of everything, cuisine from every culture, all of it beautiful, and the smells . . . They were absolutely mouth watering, and that wasn't just because I'd spent most of the day squeezed into a helicopter smelling avgas fumes and gun smoke, this place was awesome. "This is how Vikings eat in Viking heaven."

"Valhalla," Holly pointed out. "Viking heaven is called Valhalla."

"I know that," Trip answered. "Surprised you do though." It was a lame attempt at teasing her, since everyone present knew that Holly just worked the dumb blonde angle to manipulate people who didn't know her well enough to know that she was an encyclopedia of crafty monster eradication.

"Sure I do. I had this really sexy valkyrie costume one Halloween," Holly answered, completely deadpan. "The chainmail bikini was *so* hot . . . Though it did chafe." And then she started to describe it in graphic detail. Watching the always gentlemanly and borderline prudish Trip get too embarrassed to respond coherently was always fun for the whole team, but luckily for him the hostess called for Owen Pitt and party of ten, and seated us before it got too bad.

I'd managed to gather several other Hunters who hadn't been too distracted by the pretty flashing lights and promises of loose slots to forget dinner. The Haight brothers were from Team Haven out of Colorado, and though Sam was dead and Priest had been promoted to be their leader, they would always be called Team Haven. Cooper and my brother-in-law, Nate Shackleford, were from Paxton's team out of Seattle. Gregorius was from Atlanta and since the last time I'd seen him he'd decided to ditch his old military grooming standards and I had to compliment him on the quality of his lumberjack beard. My old buddy Albert Lee was stationed at headquarters in Alabama and he was always fun to hang out with. VanZant was a team lead out of California and Green was one of his guys. I'd worked with all of them at one point or another, either from Newbie training, battling Lord Machado's minions at DeSoya caverns, or fighting under the alien insect branches of the Arbmunep.

The Last Dragon's buffet was in a large, circular, glass enclosure inside the casino's shopping mall. The whole place slowly rotated so that the view out the windows was constantly changing murals, gardens, and fountains. The diners got to watch as one story below us hundreds of consumers blew all their money on overpriced merchandise. It was kind of neat if you liked people-watching as much as I did. Inside the restaurant there were even ice sculptures and five different kinds of chocolate fountains.

After heaping food on our plates we took our seats. It had been a while since I'd seen most of these particular coworkers, and in short order my arm had been twisted into talking about the case we had wrapped up just that morning. In fact, my team hadn't even thought we'd be able to attend ICMHP at all, because we'd spent two fruitless weeks trolling the crappiest parts of Jackson, Mississippi looking for our monster. It was January, and we'd gotten rained on the whole time. Bagging that aswang at the last minute had been a stroke of luck, giving us an excuse to pack right up and hightail it to Las Vegas where we could be much warmer and dry for a bit. I like telling stories, but whenever I started exaggerating to make the monster even more disgusting Trip would correct me. He always was good at keeping me honest. Besides, since the damned thing had been an imported mutant Filipino vampire with a *proboscis*, you didn't need much hyperbole to make it gross. This was not the sort of dinner conversation that you would have with polite company.

MHI tended to be a noisy, boisterous, fun-loving bunch, and as you filled them with good food and drinks they just got louder. Soon, everyone else was cracking jokes and telling stories too, interrupted only by the constant trips back for more food. Green was skinny, and VanZant's nickname was "the hobbit" because he was maybe a stocky five foot four, but even our small Hunters had appetites, not to mention that Gregorius was about my size, so we were putting a hurting on the place.

However, as Nate pointed out, at seventy bucks a head, we were darn well going to get our money's worth. Luckily, they had seated us far enough to the side that we weren't bugging the other, more normal, patrons.

They had stuck together a few tables into a long rectangle for us. I was sitting at one end across from Green and next to VanZant. Green was bald, hyperactive, and had been a San Diego police officer before MHI had recruited him. I'd accidentally broken his collarbone back in Newbie training, but he'd never seemed to hold a grudge about it. Green was a scrapper, one of those men that wasn't scared of anything, so getting severely injured in training was no biggie. I'd lost count of how many beers he had drunk, and apparently he'd already hit the mini bar in his room before coming down. The waitress just kept the refills coming, because since we had to walk past slot machines to get out of this place, the management probably wanted their guests as incapable of making good decisions as possible. His boss, VanZant, just frowned as Green got into a noisy argument with bomb expert Cooper over the proper use of hand grenades.

VanZant was a courteous man, so he waited until there were several different conversations going on before leaning in to ask me quietly, "So how's Julie doing?"

The question was understandable. VanZant had been with Julie when she'd been injured during Hood's attack on our compound. He was one of the few who knew something about how she had survived, her lacerations sealed by the lingering magic of the Guardian, leaving only black lines where there had once been mortal wounds. "Pretty good. Mostly we don't think about it." Which wasn't true at all. The thought that she had been physically changed by magic from the Old Ones was always there, gnawing away at our peace of mind, but there wasn't much we could do about it.

VanZant's concern was evident. "Has there been any… change?"

He meant to the supernatural marks on my wife's neck and abdomen, reminders of things that should have killed her. "Still the same as before." The marks had saved Julie's life three times, from Koriniha's knife, a flying undead's claws, and even the fangs of her vampire mother, but there was no such thing as *gifts* when the Old Ones were concerned. Everything from them came with a price. We just didn't know what that price was going to be yet. "We've been trying to find more information about the Guardian, who he was, where the magic comes from, maybe even how to get rid of it, but no luck yet."

One of the Haights was telling a story about parking his truck on a blood fiend when the hostess led another big group into our section of the restaurant. There was a dozen of them, they were all male and all dressed the same, in matching tan cargo pants and tight black polo shirts that showed off that they all really liked to lift weights. Every last one of the newcomers was casually scanning the room for threats. It was obvious that the half of them that couldn't sit with their backs to the wall were made slightly uncomfortable by that fact.

They were Monster Hunters. A Hunter gives off a certain vibe, and these men had it. Wary, cocky, and tough, they were Hunters all right, they just weren't as *cool* as we were. VanZant scowled at the gold *PT Consulting* embroidered on the breast of every polo shirt. "Oh no…" he muttered. "Not these assholes."

"Friends of yours?" I whispered as the hostess seated them a few feet away. I noticed that most of them were studying us the same way we were studying them. Apparently my table gave off that Hunter vibe too. There was a little bit of professional curiosity and sizing up going on from both sides.

VanZant wasn't happy to see them. "They're a startup company headquartered in L.A. They've been around about a year. Loads of money, all the newest toys. They're professional, but…"

From the look on Green's face, he didn't like PT Consulting much either. He spoke a little louder than he probably should have. "Their boss is a real prick and they've been weaseling in on some of our contracts. They'll swipe your PUFF right out from under your nose if you aren't careful."

A few of them seemed to have overheard that, and there was some hushed conversation from the other table as they placed their drink orders. "Easy, Green," VanZant cautioned his hotheaded friend before turning back to me. "PT Consulting is prickly. They've got this *modern bushido*, code of the warrior culture going on. They take themselves real seriously. Their owner is a retired colonel who got rich doing contract security in Iraq. When he learned the real money was in PUFF, his company switched industries, lured away a bunch of MCB with better pay, and set up shop in my backyard."

"You don't sound like a fan…"

"He gives mercenaries a bad name, and MHI is mercenary and proud. I'd call him a pirate, but that's an insult to pirates."

"Prick works," Green supplied again. "Thieving pricks, the bunch of them."

I noticed a couple of angry scowls in our direction. They recognized us too. It probably didn't help that I was wearing a t-shirt with a big MHI Happy Face on it. *Oh well, not my problem.* I just wanted to enjoy my second plate of steak, sushi, and six species of shrimp.

The oldest of the PT men got up and approached my end of the table. He was probably in his early fifties, but built like a marathoner, sporting a blond buzz cut, and suntan lines from wearing shades. His mouth smiled, but his eyes didn't. "Well, if it isn't Monster Hunter International. What an unexpected pleasure to run into you gentlemen here. Evening, John."

VanZant nodded politely. "Armstrong."

Armstrong scanned down our table, sizing us up. Unlike his company, my guys were dressed randomly and casual, except for Cooper and Nate being dressed fancy so that the single young guys could try to pick up girls later, and the Haights looking like they were on their way to a rodeo. Armstrong saw Gregorius sitting toward the middle and gave a curt nod. "Hey, I know you from Bragg . . . Sergeant Gregorius, right? I didn't know you'd joined this bunch."

We had recruited Gregorius after the battle for DeSoya Caverns, where he'd been attached to the National Guard unit manning the roadblock. Apparently he knew Armstrong in a different professional capacity, but judging from the uncomfortable expression on Gregorius' face, he shared VanZant's opinion of the man. "Evening, Colonel . . . Wife didn't want me sitting around the house retired and bored. This sounded like fun."

Armstrong's chuckle was completely patronizing. "I didn't recognize you with that beard. You look like Barry White. Staying busy I hope," he said as he scanned over the rest of us. He paused when he got to me. I was pretty sure I'd never met him before, but I am rather distinctive looking and had developed a bit of a reputation in professional Monster Hunting circles, some of which was even factual. So it wasn't surprising to be recognized. "You're Owen Zastava Pitt, aren't you?"

"In the flesh."

"I'm Rick Armstrong." He said that like it should mean something. *Rick Armstrong.* Now that was a proper super hero secret identity name. "I'm CEO of PT Consulting." I stared at him blankly. I looked to Trip, but my friend shrugged. "PT Consulting..."

"Potato Tasting?" I guessed helpfully.

"No. It's—"

"Platypus Trampoline?"

"Paranormal Tactical," he corrected before I could come up with another.

"Nope." I shrugged. Armstrong seemed let down, but tried not to let it show. What did he expect? I was too busy battling the forces of evil to pay attention to every new competitor on the block. Julie took care of the marketing, I was the accountant. "Doesn't ring any bells."

"Oh, it will." He smiled that fake little smile again. "I'm sure we'll have some teaming opportunities in the future."

I didn't know this Armstrong character, but something about him simply rubbed me the wrong way. Plus, VanZant's opinion was trusted, and if one of our team leads said that they were assholes, that was good enough for me. "You should leave me your card, you know, in case we're too busy doing something big and important and a little case pops up that we don't have time to pay attention to." I can be a fairly rude person when I just don't give a crap.

"Well, MHI is *established* . . ." Armstrong said, meaning *old*. So that was how it was going to be. "But we're the fastest growing Hunting company in the world. We've got experienced men, a solid business plan, financial backing, the best equipment, and top leadership."

"Nifty. I should buy some stock."

"Speaking of leadership, there's a rumor going around about MHI's." The way he said that sounded particularly snide.

"Oh?" I raised a single eyebrow. This conversation was cutting into my precious shrimp time. "What about our leadership?"

"Word is that Earl Harbinger's been off his game lately. I heard he disappeared for a few months, came back depressed and missing a finger. Rumor is that he had something to do with that incident up in Michigan. You know, that *mine fire*," he made quote marks with his fingers, "that killed half a town in their sleep, or so the MCB said. I'd hate to think that was one of his cases that went bad."

Sure, Earl hadn't been the same since Copper Lake, but that was none of Armstrong's business. I didn't know all the details about what had happened in Michigan, but I knew enough to know that Earl wasn't *off his game*, he was *angry*. A government agency that he didn't want to name had put his girlfriend into indentured servitude.

"Maybe Harbinger's thinking about hanging it up? That would be *such* a shame. A real loss for our whole industry."

"I'll be sure to pass along your concern. Because, wow, if Earl Harbinger were to retire, who would men like you look to for inspiration?" I gave him a polite nod that I intended to say *shove off dirt bag.* "See you at the conference."

"Tomorrow then. Looking forward to it. I've got work to do. You boys have a nice supper." He went back to his table to say goodbye to his men. I swear half of them had to resist the urge to salute.

"I *hate* him so much," Gregorius said softly, but didn't elaborate further.

"Well, you do sorta look like Barry White," Cooper told him. He flinched when Gregorius thumped him in the arm.

Soon enough our conversations had picked back up, and if anything, were even louder than before. Milo called my cell to tell me that he would be here soon, and that he and some of the Newbies he'd picked up at the airport would be joining us for dinner. I'd met the crazy elf girl, Tanya, when she'd impersonated an elven tracker to tag along on one of our jobs. She and Edward had saved some kids that had blundered into a pocket dimension filled with telepathic fey monsters. She was the first elf MHI had ever hired, which I still wasn't convinced was entirely a smart move, but Milo assured me that she would easily be able to pass for human in public. The other Newbie was named Jason Lacoco, a name I recognized as the Briarwood Hunter Earl had recruited during the Copper Lake incident, but who I hadn't met yet. I told Milo I'd have the hostess pull up another table.

By the time I put my phone away, Green was telling a very animated and inappropriate story, and using a cream puff for special effects purposes. Most of my group was laughing loudly at him. The PT men were all stoically chewing, glaring his way occasionally. Apparently the modern warrior code meant you weren't supposed to carry on in such a manner in public.

I was filling plate number three with nachos, potstickers, and mozzarella sticks when Nate came up beside me. He had been sitting at the far end of the table, so had missed my chat with the PT leader. "Hey, Z. I need your help with the black shirt dudes."

"What do you mean?"

"They keep eyeballing us."

"It's because we're so damned handsome, Nate. They just can't help themselves."

"You say so, but they seem *angry*."

I looked over as Green downed another beer, belched loudly, and then wiped his mouth with the back of his hand. I couldn't hear what he was saying, but Trip seemed distressed and everyone else was amused. Trip, ever the voice of reason, seemed to be trying to get Green to quiet down. VanZant's seat was empty. He'd probably gone to the bathroom and left our drunken vice cop momentarily unsupervised. A few of the PT consultants were looking fairly belligerent at this point. "Is Green trying to pick a fight?"

Nate sighed. "He's still mad about a job his team did all the dangerous work for, but PT swooped in and claimed the PUFF at the last minute. Green was personally out twenty grand and one of their team almost got drowned by a giant squid in the process."

"So you don't need my help with Pontoon Tactical, or whatever their name is, you need help controlling some of our men. Look, why don't you go tell Green to chill out? You are a Shackleford. This is your family's company." I know Earl was expecting a lot from Nate, as he was the one expected to carry on the Shackleford family name. That was a lot of pressure, especially since his big sister pretty much ran the nuts and bolts of the operation already. Nate was tough and enthusiastic, but still trying to figure out his place in the company. The tall young man looked sheepishly at his shoes. "But you won't . . . Because you don't want to come off as the boss's grandson and annoying wet blanket on everyone's good time . . ."

"Reverse nepotism is a hell of a thing. I'm still low man on the totem pole. I say anything and I'll just come off as a whiner trying to throw Julie's weight around."

"If you imply Julie is heavy, she will shoot you." I knew that wasn't what he meant. Besides, Julie was in great shape. My wife was a 5'11" Amazon warrior southern belle art-chick sniper. "And you know she doesn't miss much."

"You know what I mean," Nate pleaded.

"Ask Holly. Nobody will mess with her."

"Are you kidding? I think she finds the whole thing

amusing. Please, Z, I don't know all these guys very well, but they respect you."

"I'm no team leader." Some of us had headquarters' duties above and beyond being on Hunter teams, but as far as the actual MHI org chart went, I was only the finance manager. Which put me at about the same level as our receptionist, only Dorcas had been around longer and was scarier.

"You're also the God Slayer."

Valid point. Travelling to another dimension and blowing up a Great Old One did earn you some cool points with this bunch. "Leadership sucks sometimes, Nate. You're going to have to get used to it." His older sister would have simply kicked everyone into line, but the youngest Shackleford hadn't found his groove yet. He'd been a Hunter longer than I had, but it was tough to grow up in the shadow of legends. "Alright, fine. Just let me grab some more fish sticks."

By the time I'd plopped back down in my seat, I could tell that Green had clearly egged the two nearest PT Hunters on to the point that they were itching for a confrontation. The man certainly had a gift. I could sense there was ugly in the air. Normally that wouldn't bother me too much, but we were supposed to be professionals, we were outnumbered, and I was pretty sure that I recognized one of the PT men from watching Ultimate Fighting on TV.

"Z, that one dude keeps looking at me!" Green exclaimed, voice slurred. "He must think I'm sexy!" Then he looked over at the Ultimate Fighter and licked a cream puff suggestively.

The Ultimate Fighter got up quickly, and Green, being stupidly fearless at this point, did too. Trip intercepted Green and one of the PT Hunters grabbed the Ultimate Fighter's arm. Me and my tray of goodies stepped between the two sides as I tried to play peacemaker. "Whoa! Easy, man." He bumped me and I got Thai peanut sauce on my shirt and most of my food landed on the floor. It says something about how much I've matured over the last couple of years that I didn't knock him the hell out for wasting such precious cargo. About half of the PT Hunters got up quickly. On my side the Haights and Gregorius jumped up, looking eager, while the rest of my side had that inevitable resignation look of *I'd better help my idiot friends* on their faces. Say what you will about Hunters, they always have your back. "Everybody, relax. No harm meant. My friend's just had a few too many."

Trip dragged the sputtering Green back into his chair. Luckily, Trip was the stronger of the two.

I tried to defuse the situation. "I've seen you on TV, right? Light heavyweight. You were great. I love that stuff—"

"Keep your idiot on a leash," Ultimate Fighter snarled as he was guided to his seat. "Uncivilized Alabama rednecks."

I thought that Green was a Californian, but saying so probably wouldn't have helped matters. In fact, I think Nate was the only native Alabaman at the table and he was well spoken and wearing a tie. I sat down. "Green, you dumbass. Chill the hell out already or I swear I'll break *another* one of your bones."

"Sorry, Z. It isn't my fault they're such jackasses. I was

just telling everybody about how PT is a bunch of no-good, backstabbing, lying, cheats, and Armstrong is a thieving sack of—"

"Dude, use your *inside* voice," Trip suggested as he studied the table of muscle and testosterone growling at us. "I don't want to get beat up."

Green giggled. "I'm not worried. We got Z. Just hide behind him. That was my plan. He's *huge*."

"Thanks," I muttered. "I'll remember that when I'm getting my teeth kicked in."

A server came by, and I quickly apologized for the mess and slipped her a twenty. Luckily nobody had called security, and it looked like everything was going to be cool. VanZant got back, saw that some of the staff was cleaning up my spillage and everyone looked tense, and asked what he'd missed. I jerked a thumb at Green. "I think he needs to sleep it off."

VanZant shook his head sadly. "He gets spun up some-times. I've got him. Come on, man. Why don't you go splash some water on your face or something." He dragged Green up by his collar.

"But, I didn't finish my creampuffs!"

"My apologies, Z. He is a really good Hunter when he's sober."

Crisis averted, I went back for replacement food as VanZant led our most inebriated Hunter away. I caught sight of a small man with a gigantic red beard waving at me from the entrance, and so I pointed Milo in the direction of our table. The last of the MHI dinner party had arrived.

Plate partially reloaded, I was preoccupied with using

tongs to pick up some crab legs when somebody bumped into my arm. Another solid fellow had been reaching under the sneeze guard at the same time. "Pardon me," he said politely.

"Sorry about that," I answered as I moved a bit to the side. "Didn't see you. Easily distracted by crab legs, you know."

"Thanks." He scooped up several pounds of crustacean and dumped them onto his plate. Crouched, he still barely fit under the sneeze guard. He straightened his back and towered over me. I'm 6'5", was wearing thick-soled combat boots, and he still had me beat by a few inches.

"If you've seen that show about how hard these are to catch, that just makes them taste even better . . ." I trailed off. The man seemed strangely familiar. Probably thirty, he was thickset, with biceps like hams stuffed under his black t-shirt. His enormous head was stubbly with short dark hair, and there was a crease running down the middle where he'd had a severe skull injury or maybe brain surgery. Beady eyes narrowed as he got a better look at me. One of his eyes wasn't pointing in quite the same direction as the other one. A look of confusion crossed his wide, flat face.

Where did I know this man from?

Of course I hadn't recognized him at first. He'd aged. After all, it had been several years, and he hadn't had that scar on his head nor the bad eye. Plus the last time I'd seen him I'd been kneeling on his chest and dropping elbows against his bloody and unconscious face until his eye had popped out and his skull had broken in half.

"*You!*" we exclaimed at the same time.

His tray hit the floor with a clatter. The other patrons around the seafood area were suddenly quiet. The giant's mouth turned into a snarl and his hands curled into a fist. "Son of a bitch!"

The final illegal, underground, money fight I'd ever participated in had been against this monster. All I'd known going in was that he was a killer, a prison hardened, brutal machine of a fighter, and then he'd beaten the living hell out of me until I'd finally taken him down, lost control, and nearly beaten him to death. I'd never even known his name.

I took a step back. He was right to be mad. I'd lost it. It was the worst thing I'd ever done. "It was an ac—"

"Accident?" Veins were popping out in his neck. "I was out, and you didn't stop hitting me until they dragged you off! You put out my eye!"

"Sorry." *Man, that sounded pathetic.*

"You ruined my life!" And with a roar, the giant charged.

I lifted the metal serving tray like a shield just in time for his fist to bend it in half. The tray went flying and a waitress screamed. Dodging back, I thumped hard into the table with the ice swan. An instinctive duck kept my head attached to my body as the giant threw a massive left hook that decapitated the swan. Then he lowered his shoulder and rammed into me, taking us both onto the table. The ice swan toppled, hit the floor, and exploded, sending bits everywhere. The table collapsed beneath us and we went rolling off in separate directions.

There were a few seconds of shocked silence and then fight or flight kicked in for everyone in the buffet. For the regular people, it was flight from the two very large men crashing about. Sadly, flight wasn't the normal first reaction for a Hunter. There was a battle cry from near the exit. "That PT guy hit Z!" Green shouted as he shoved his way through the people . *The man that had attacked me was wearing a black shirt* . . . Green sprinted across the restaurant yelling, "Fight! Fight!" Then he dove and tackled a random PT employee who was getting a piece of pie from the desert bar.

"No! It's not them." I got up, but the giant was already coming my way again, and then I was too busy protecting my vital organs from his sledge hammer fists to communicate.

The occupants of the MHI table had all stood up to see what was going on, and so had the Paranormal Tactical crew. The two sides looked at each for just a moment . . . and then it was *on*. The last thing I saw was one of the Haight brothers clubbing a PT Hunter in the jaw, because then I had to concentrate on my own problems.

The giant was coming my way, hands up and loose, protecting his face. Even enraged, he was moving like a pro. The last time we'd squared off had been a close one. This was the toughest human being I'd ever fought, at least now that I knew Franks didn't count as human.

"I don't want to fight you," I warned.

"Should'a thought of that before you tried to murder me."

He came in quick, but this wasn't a ring, and I wasn't fighting fair. I kicked a chunk of ice and he instinctively flinched aside as it zipped past him. I yanked a cloth off a table and threw it over his head like a net. I'd like to say that I did it dramatically and all the plates and pitchers stayed in place, but they didn't and most of them shattered on the ground. Temporarily entangled in the tablecloth, he couldn't defend himself very well, so I charged in swinging. I slugged him twice in the stomach, and when his hands went down, I reached up and tagged him with a shot to the mouth.

But then he threw the tablecloth back over me, and I think it was an elbow that got me in the side of the head. I was seeing stars when he slung me around and put me into the meat area. Ham broke my fall. The meat-slicing buffet employees ran for their lives. Getting up, I hurled a pot roast at the giant and he smacked it across the room.

We clashed. There wasn't any finesse at all; it was just a slug fest. We went back and forth, trading blows. Too busy trying to protect my face, I got hit in the ribs, which sucked, and then he nailed me in the stomach, which really sucked, and suddenly I was regretting the several pounds of food I'd just consumed. His shoe landed on a piece of ice, and as he slid off balance, I snap kicked him hard in the thigh of his grounded leg.

He went to his hands and knees. "Stay down!" I ordered.

The restaurant patrons were evacuating. Green had someone in a choke hold and another PT man on his back. I'd forgotten that VanZant had used to be a champion welter-weight, and he was knocking the snot out of a PT man twice his size. The Haights seemed to be having a jolly time, until one of them got hit with a chair. Gregorius was wrestling a PT Hunter next to the soda machines. Ultimate Fighter had Cooper in an arm bar. Albert, despite the cane and leg brace, was a shockingly tenacious fighter, and he was facing two PT Hunters at once, which apparently Trip didn't think was very sporting, because he slammed one of them *through* a corner booth. Even Holly had gotten into it. A PT man hesitated, not wanting to strike a girl, until she groin kicked him like she was punting a football.

Turning back to the giant, I didn't see that my opponent's hands had landed on another serving tray, which he promptly swung and clipped me in the temple. That one rocked my world. I landed flat on my back. The giant came over to stomp me, but Nate body checked him into the soft serve ice cream machine. Too bad the Shacklefords were from Alabama, because the kid showed a lot of promise as a hockey player.

The vanilla spigot had broken off and soft serve came spooling out. "Got no problem with you," the giant said through gritted teeth. "Just him. Get out of my way."

"You mess with MHI, you mess with all of us!"

The giant cocked his misshapen head to one side. "What? *MHI?*"

Nate tried to punch him, and though he was fast and relatively skilled, the giant was simply out of his league. He effortlessly slapped Nate's hands aside, grabbed my brother in law's tie to hold him in place, then slugged him. One, two, three solid hits before Nate's brain had even recorded the first impact. Nate went down, out cold.

That really pissed me off, and I came off the floor, ready to kick some ass.

Hotel security guards were pushing their way inside. Since the restaurant rotated on a platform, the whole place was shaking badly under the stampede. The other ice sculpture fell and broke, and somehow somebody had managed to throw something hard enough to break one of the chandeliers. There was some screaming as Green got pepper sprayed and more screaming as Lee shoved a rival Hunter into the chocolate fountain.

One of the PT men got in my way and I dismantled him. I didn't have time to dick around with these chumps when there was a real enemy to fight. I stepped into the clumsy swing and drove my forearm and all my mass into him so hard that he went spiraling over a table. Another of the black polo-shirted Hunters had gotten between us, so the giant simply picked him up and tossed him over the sushi bar, not even bothering to slow his pace. We met in the middle and proceeded to beat the crap out of each other.

He was fast for a big man, and so was I, but he had a reach advantage, so I had to keep moving to stay ahead of him. I wasn't used to being the smaller and lighter fighter. We locked up on each other as we hit the far end of the buffet, both of us throwing knees and elbows. Between the two of us we probably weighed close to seven hundred pounds, and the furniture broke around us like someone had turned loose a herd of enraged wildebeests. I didn't realize we'd gone too far until my shoulder hit the cold glass of the restaurant's bubble. The glass cracked.

I caught my boot against the railing, heaved the giant back, and managed to hit him with a staggering overhand right. That slowed him down.

"Lacoco! Stop! Z! Owen! What the heck? Quit hitting that Newbie!" Milo was running our way, just ahead of a bunch of casino security and a Las Vegas police officer. "You're on the same team!"

The giant must not have heard Milo's words, because he bellowed, launched himself into me, caught me around the waist, and we hit the interior window. The glass shattered around us and then we were falling, *briefly*. We hit water, but it wasn't particularly deep, because right after the water came tile. And the tile was *very* hard.

Groaning, I lay there, flat on my back in half a foot of water, covered in sparkling shards, the wind knocked out of me, staring up at the hole in the buffet's glass wall one story above, as cold water from a dragon headed fountain spit on us. The giant was on his side next to me. He had a few nasty cuts on his face and arms from the glass. I probably didn't look much better. I realized then that his not-quite-in-the-same-direction eye was fake, because it had popped out and was sitting at the bottom of the pool between us.

A huge crowd of gamblers and shoppers were standing there, gaping at us. Many of them started taking pictures.

At least the fall had finally knocked the fight out of him. The giant looked over at the MHI Happy Face on my tattered shirt with his good eye and groaned.

"Jason Lacoco?" I gasped.

"Uh huh…"

"Owen Zastava Pitt." I coughed. "Nice to meet you. Welcome to Monster Hunter International."

Then several police officers converged on the fountain to arrest us.

The Hero with Michael Z. Williamson
(pb) 1-4165-0914-3 • $7.99

■ ■ ■

Citizens ed. by John Ringo & Brian M. Thomsen
(trade pb) 978-1-4391-3347-7 • $16.00
(pb) 978-1-4391-3460-3 • $7.99

Master of Epic SF
The Council War Series
There Will Be Dragons
(pb) 0-7434-8859-8 • $7.99

Emerald Sea
(pb) 1-4165-0920-8 • $7.99

Against the Tide
(pb) 1-4165-2057-0 • $7.99

East of the Sun, West of the Moon
(pb) 1-4165-5518-87 • $7.99

Master of Real SF
The Troy Rising Series
Live Free or Die
(hc) 1-4391-3332-8 • $26.00
(pb) 978-1-4391-3397-2 • $7.99

Citadel
(hc) 978-1-4391-3400-9 • $26.00
(pb) 978-1-4516-3757-1 • $7.99

The Hot Gate
(hc) 978-1-4391-3432-0 • $26.00

■ ■ ■

Von Neumann's War with Travis S. Taylor
(pb) 1-4165-5530-8 • $7.99

The Looking Glass Series
Into the Looking Glass
(pb) 1-4165-2105-4 • $7.99

Vorpal Blade with Travis S. Taylor
(hc) 1-4165-2129-1 • $25.00
(pb) 1-4165-5586-2 • $7.99

Manxome Foe with Travis S. Taylor
(pb) 1-4165-9165-6 • $7.99

Claws That Catch with Travis S. Taylor
(hc) 1-4165-5587-0 • $25.00
(pb) 978-1-4391-3313-2 • $7.99

Master of Hard-Core Thrillers
The Last Centurion
(hc) 1-4165-5553-6 • $25.00
(pb) 978-1-4391-3291-3 • $7.99

■ ■ ■

The Kildar Saga
Ghost
(pb) 1-4165-2087-2 • $7.99

Kildar
(pb) 1-4165-2133-X • $7.99

Choosers of the Slain
(hc) 1-4165-2070-8 • $25.00
(pb) 1-4165-7384-4 • $7.99

Unto the Breach
(hc) 1-4165-0940-2 • $26.00
(pb) 1-4165-5535-8 • $7.99

A Deeper Blue
(hc) 1-4165-2128-3 • $26.00